· BARBARA ALDRICH · STEPHEN VINCENT BENET
LOUIS BROMFIELD · GLADYS HASTY CARROLL
· MARIAN B. COCKRELL · WHITFIELD COOK
ELIZABETH DUNN · PAUL ERNST · SUSAN ERTZ
· ROBERT FONTAINE · ROSE FRANKEN · ZONA GALE
VALERIA WINKLER GRIFFITH · F. HUGH HERBERT
· IAN HAY · KATHARINE HAVILAND-TAYLOR
WALLACE IRWIN · LOUISE ANDREWS KENT
· GRAEME AND SARAH LORIMER · RUTH McKENNEY
LOUISE DICKINSON RICH · MARY ROBERTS RINEHART
· RUTH BURR SANBORN · MARION STURGES-JONES
CORNELIA OTIS SKINNER & EMILY KIMBROUGH
· DOROTHY THOMAS · MABEL HERBERT URNER
GLADYS TABER · ALEXANDER WOOLLCOTT

THE
Family
READER

COMPILED BY

MARJORIE BARROWS

PEOPLES

BOOK CLUB

EDITION

CONSOLIDATED BOOK PUBLISHERS
CHICAGO

PRINTED IN THE UNITED STATES OF AMERICA

Table of Contents

iii

CONTENTS

Publisher's Foreword

THE FAMILY READER is a book for your lighter moments, for those times when you want to relax and lose yourself in a good short story. In its collection of delightful short stories by universally loved writers, you will meet again some of your old friends, make the acquaintance of many new ones.

Remember Clarence Day's famous father? Rose Franken's Claudia? Booth Tarkington's Penrod? James Hilton's Mr. Chips? They are all here, together with characters created by authors like Faith Baldwin, Zona Gale, Mary Roberts Rinehart, Susan Ertz, Stephen Vincent Benét, and Alexander Woollcott.

The book represents months of patient search by the editors, for "friendly" stories—stories that would share with the reader the warmth and gaiety of human experience. There is plenty of romance and young love. Some of the stories are highly amusing. Others will hold you spellbound with suspense, or carry you along with swiftly moving action. All of them are about people such as those you know—the newlyweds down the street, teen-agers like your own youngsters, neighbors like those next door.

The Family Reader is planned for your enjoyment and that of your family and friends. We know that it will furnish many hours of fine entertainment. We hope that it will become one of your favorite books.

You'll Hear from Hallie Thane

BARBARA ALDRICH

Won't you lunch with Hallie Thane and her two famous college chums and see if the college prophecy worked out after twenty years?

MRS. ADAMS stood in the kitchen studying a recipe for chiffon white cake with mocha frosting. New recipes fascinated Mrs. Adams. Tomorrow she'd have to try it. Jim, her husband, loved desserts. It was too late now—almost time for his bus.

And then the telephone rang. "Hello, Hallie, is it really you?" a woman's voice said. "Darling, it's been simply years! Where have you been? What have you been doing? Stop hiding your light under that bushel and come on out."

"Camilla," said Hallie, "Cam, where in the world—"

"So you're still buried in the same place, Cuckoo! I just took a chance on finding you. Are you all right? Are you still married to Jim? 'What's become of Hallie Thane?' everybody's saying. What has happened to you?"

"Nothing at all," said Hallie. "I'm fine." (*"What's become of Hallie Thane* sounds like a cheap play," she thought.) "Of course I still live here. It's my home. Of course I'm still married to Jim."

"Come in to town this minute. We've got a table in the Persian Room, and I've got a man who'll adore you. Wake up that husband of yours. I'll bet he's snoozing this minute."

"Oh, Cam, I'd love to, but we couldn't possibly. Cam, where have you been?"

"All around, sweetie. I came up from Palm Beach yesterday. Got put out of France. You should have seen me. I'm a refugee. Have you changed, Cuckoo? I'm a complete hag." Cam's voice was right in the room now. It seemed to stir up the house. "Could you meet me tomorrow? Joseph's at one. You can't escape me." (*"The food's still unbelievable, I suppose," Hallie thought.) Cam's voice rippled on.

I

"Lunched there today with Bunty. Remember Bunty? He's just back from the Far East, and the stories he can tell! He's plastered with medals and divinely handsome."

That would be Cam—Joseph's chocolate whip with brandy, and a hero thrown in.

"This is for dear old Westerly, darling. Gale's coming, too. I caught her right after her show. Her pictures are certainly strewn around the city. Wait till we get her alone. We knew her when."

"Not Gale, really," said Hallie faintly. "I'm sorry, but I'm afraid I can't make it, Cammie. You see—" ("I've nothing to wear, nothing to talk about. There's Joan's dress to finish and the Children's Aid meeting and the house to clean before Pete gets here, and it's my day at the Exchange.") "There's something else I have to do."

"If you don't, I'll come out and spend the winter. Do you still wear the same kind of hats? I was crazy about your hats. Are you still the same funny Cuckoo?"

"Listen," said Hallie, "I'm Chairman of the Church Guild. I'm Vice-President of the P.T.A. Nobody's called me Cuckoo in years." She could hear Cam laugh. "I guess I'd better wear a red carnation."

"Then you *will* come. That's wonderful. Good-bye, angel. I've got to run. They're waiting for me. Joseph's at one—or else!" The receiver clicked.

Mrs. Adams turned back to her recipe: two cups of sugar, the well-beaten whites of four eggs. Suddenly the words from the Westerly Hall Yearbook dangled before her eyes. "You'll hear from Hallie Thane."

Hallie looked out the window and saw Jim coming up the path through the snow. She'd shoveled that path and was proud of it. Jim would say when he came in that there was a lot of snow for this time of year, and she'd answer, yes, wasn't there? She was glad he'd worn his old suit today. That would save the blue one. Clothes don't grow on trees. And then she thought, "Why, that's what Aunt Lizzie used to say." Aunt Lizzie was an old woman when she said it.

Chris, her younger son, came pounding down the stairs with his air gun and tin hat. "Jack Norman's mother's going to Seattle tomorrow. She's always going somewhere. Why don't you go someplace, Toots?"

"Don't call me 'Toots,'" she said, but actually it pleased her. No one else called her that. "And, darling, don't tell one of those long

2

stories at supper tonight, and don't let the cat upstairs. You know how your father is when he first gets home."

"WELL, what kind of day did you have?" asked Hallie while they were having dinner. Tonight it seemed to her that she sounded like a well-worn phonograph record. "Don't you want a drink, Jim?"

Jim shook his head. "Keeps me awake lately. I'm dead tired. I'll finish dinner and go to bed."

They ate in the kitchen nowadays, for the dining room was cold and with no maid it was simpler. It was a nice kitchen, though.

She'd wait a minute to tell Jim about Cam. Maybe she wouldn't tell him at all. Instead, she said: "The Guilds want us for dinner Saturday—gin rummy. I've got to let them know right away."

Jim said: "Can't tell yet. I've got a heavy schedule at the plant. McDermott isn't working out. I don't know whether I can make it."

"I saw Ruth Arnold at the market today. I do feel so sorry for her, Jim, with Ted leaving her and everything. How do you think she feels?"

"Listen," said Jim, "if you'd think about yourself now and then, you'd be better off. Did the phone bill come?"

"It's on the mantel," said Hallie.

"Any more news about Pete's leave?"

She shook her head. "But he might turn up any day. They're shipping them over so fast now." Her voice was very calm. She started to tell him about the Town Hall speech Mrs. Smith had asked her to make and how pleased she'd been; but, somehow, after Cam's call— "Guess who called me today, of all people! Camilla. After all these years. Remember Cam?"

Jim Adams looked up from his plate. Suddenly he didn't look so tired. "Sure, I remember Cam."

"What do you suppose she's like now? She was so attractive. Men were just crazy about Cam, weren't they?"

"Oh, I don't know," said Jim. "She always talked too much."

"She wants me to have lunch with her tomorrow. Gale Leslie's coming, too."

"Those two glamour girls! Are you going? That will be something."

"I should say not," said Hallie. "I hate warmed-over meetings. There'd be nothing to talk about, nothing really to say. They're just sentimental. They're—they're corny. That's what Joan would call it."

Hallie was getting the coffee now, and she turned to look at Jim. He was looking at her almost as though she'd been away. A queer, creepy feeling came over her. "Maybe I've changed and he's just noticing it now," she thought.

When supper was over and Hallie had finished the dishes, it was only eight thirty—but Jim was sound asleep in his chair. You couldn't blame him. He'd had a long day. Breakfast at six, two hours each way to the plant.

Hallie walked to the window and looked out at the snow. She didn't feel like reading or sewing or listening to the radio. The moon was enormous and cold and terribly bright, and there was no one in sight. She turned away. She didn't like the moon tonight.

Jim roused. "I think I'll turn in," he said. "I've got quite a day tomorrow." He patted her shoulder.

Funny how you never do the things you plan to do. She'd never wanted a husband who went to sleep right after dinner. That's what her father used to do. She'd never dreamed she'd live in the suburbs in a Victorian house. She'd wanted to be right in town, in the middle of things.

AT BREAKFAST Jim didn't talk much. Maybe it would be different if she had a new dressing gown. You got so you didn't pay attention to things like that.

"Why did you scramble me three eggs?" Jim complained.

"I didn't," she said, feeling unaccountably like crying.

"Are you going to town to lunch?" Jim asked. "If you do, give my best to Cam. And will you tell the laundryman if he doesn't sew those buttons on my shirt I'll get rid of him?"

Hallie didn't answer.

"Oh, have a little courage and run along and have lunch. Find out the score," said Jim. He finished his breakfast hurriedly, put on his coat, and left.

Courage! Mrs. Adams suddenly got angry. She had had courage, all right. What had that to do with this? She went upstairs and looked through her closet. She hadn't thought much about clothes for ages. These days you didn't bother about clothes—you'd be ashamed to worry about such trivialities. But this morning. . . . She wasn't going, but if she did go, black was the thing. The black suit would do, although the skirt was too full.

4

Chris was still reading in bed. "Chris," she cried, "get right straight up and get ready for school. Your breakfast's ready. I may be going to town, and you're to stay with Daisy this afternoon. If you go to the movies, one show only."

"I'll take care of everything, Toots. Run along and have yourself a time. Do you good."

Sometimes it seemed as though Chris knew more than Hallie did.

After Chris left, the house was very still. It might do her good to get out, go to town. She didn't have to meet Cam. She could get her hair done, see the dentist about Chris' teeth, get his Boy Scout knife, look for a spring coat for Joanie.

Hallie just caught the bus, and the bus just made the train. Elmsdale looked drab and bare, and she tried to think just why they had moved there. Oh, yes, of course. The best schools anywhere around. The old house someone had left Jim. And, after all, the elms.

For a long time she hadn't thought much about Gale and Camilla. When people in Elmsdale said of Gale: "Isn't she marvelous? We had to stand in line for hours! . . . The critics gave her rave notices! . . . She looks about twenty," Hallie never said: "I used to know her. I went to school with her." She didn't like to think about her. But she liked to remember Cam, who always was doing things that didn't seem like her: kneeling and saying her prayers, whipping up a wonderful dress out of a remnant, washing and setting her own hair—even after she married Ross and his money. If Cam liked you, she'd give you the shirt off her back.

The trip to town usually seemed too long, but today it seemed too short. When Hallie got to Fifth Avenue, the sun was shining. She stopped at a window before a big photograph of a man. The face was powerful and rugged and strong, as though the man could take care of everything. Senator Breckenridge. Joe Breckenridge.

When Jim found fault or when Joan said, "Mum, that hat is all wrong!" even when Peter said, "Mum, don't be a sissy," she thought of Joe Breckenridge.

Once when she saw him in a newsreel, she said to Jim, "If it hadn't been for you, darling—why, he used to eat out of my hand!" Someday he'd be President, people said. Hallie Thane, who might have been Hallie Breckenridge—First Lady.

At twenty-one he'd been big and awkward, and his clothes were all wrong when he went to the Junior Prom. Once Jim asked, "Why

5

didn't you marry the guy?" And she answered, "You wore better-looking clothes." But that wasn't the reason.

One night when they were riding on an old open street car, Joe Breckenridge asked Hallie Thane to marry him. "I get scared, Hallie. I need you. You know things. Things are going to happen to you. Things are going to happen to me, too. Just wait and see." She hadn't waited, but now she saw.

In the next block Hallie stopped again, for there was a picture of Gale Leslie. She was wearing a plain white blouse, and her hair was like a golden halo. Gale was being sweet in this picture. Gale was always being something.

"Old Home Week," Hallie thought as she walked along.

Now she was at 52nd Street and there was Joseph's. For a moment she looked at the grilled iron door of the restaurant, and then she remembered Jim's saying: "Have a little courage. . . . Find out the score." The stubborn Thane line came around her mouth, the one that was there when she married Jim, and she went into the restaurant.

The captain looked at her as though she were a worm. "Who're you waiting for?" he asked rudely. And she couldn't remember Cam's new name—she'd had so many. "Miss Gale Leslie," she said, and his face changed.

The lobby was jammed, and people were talking fast, as if there were many things to say and no time for them all. Hallie sat motionless on a pale-green, velvet chair. She felt like a child whose feet don't quite touch the floor.

"You're Hallie Thane, aren't you?" a voice said. Hallie didn't recognize the woman. "I'm Ann Bridgeman." The name came back like a ghost. "I remember you—you and Gale Leslie. I thought of you two as inseparable. Tell me, what is she like now?"

"I don't really know," said Hallie slowly. "I'm seeing her today."

"It was you I always thought of as being—" the woman hesitated —"well, as being the actress. You were so wonderful in the senior play. I remember how everybody raved."

Then someone put hands over Hallie's eyes and said, "Guess who?" Hallie smelled the same perfume, which no one could get these days. A whiff made her homesick.

6

"Cuckoo!" cried Camilla. "It's not you who need the red carnation. You haven't changed a bit, darling."

"Neither have you," said Hallie. "You look just the same. Marvelous." For a minute she forgot that any time had passed. Cam's hair was still as black and soft and shiny, and her skin as white, and her legs were just the same. You always looked at Cam's legs. She was wearing a violet suit that made Hallie's rose one look dull. Hallie had decided against wearing her black suit, after all.

They edged their way through the crowded room, where the tables were filled and people kept stopping Cam, and then they were at the best table of all.

"'Tell me everything quick, darling," said Cam. "Tell me about Jim. Is he just as sweet?"

"Why, Jim—he—" She couldn't think of anything at all to tell about him.

Sweet? You couldn't exactly call him sweet these days. Maybe he missed Petey as much as she did. Now he went duck shooting alone. Never invited her along. He really wasn't very understanding, either; got mad if she asked him questions. Got cross at Chris, too. But he was so tired at night. Never read the things she did. And the fights they'd had! No one would believe it, really. The James Adamses—substantial, salt of the earth. When company came, he was very nice. The women often said, "If I had a husband like Jim—" But after they left— She'd learned pretty well how to get along with him, though, all the angles and quirks.

Nothing spectacular, nothing much to tell. Jim had learned his business from the ground up. Now he was treasurer of the company. As high as he could get, some of the Elmsdale men said; but the business was growing, and you never could tell. They'd always got along all right, saved money for the children's education, an automobile, a cottage at the beach, a trip now and then, insurance. But really there wasn't anything to tell Cam about Jim.

So Hallie said: "It's about you I want to hear, Cammie. I really don't know any news."

"I guess I've lived almost everywhere, Hallie, everywhere I ever wanted to. I always seemed to marry men who could travel. You'd have loved my house in Versailles, with white violets and white roses all around. The living room was white, too. You always were going to have a white room, remember?"

7

It was true. Once Hallie had wanted a white room, but she'd forgotten about it. She visualized the Elmsdale house. It looked shabby these days. With Petey and Joan away, wear and living showed up; but when all the children were home, you didn't notice. Hallie thought of the chair in which the spaniel slept, Chris' white mice and the parrot cluttering up the sun porch, her great-grandmother's bureau Pete had hammered and been spanked for, the divan they'd got instead of a trip to Florida, the refrigerator that was Jim's overcoat, the terrace that was the loveliest gray evening dress she'd ever seen. Nothing really went together in the house, though somehow everything seemed to fit. Yet she'd meant to have a white room.

"Still in love with Jim? Jim with you?" Cam asked.

"I suppose so," Hallie said slowly. It was so safe in Elmsdale. Perhaps it would have been better if there'd been something, or someone, to fight for or against, to be jealous of. Everything had been on such an even plane.

General Somebody was bending over Cam now, and Hallie heard the words *India, Russia, Cairo, camel sandwiches,* and *bombing London.* "How lucky you were, my dear," said the General. "But it was quite a show." And Cam said, "I wouldn't have missed it for anything."

Mrs. Adams sat eating her chicken, and felt awkard and stiff and older than she should—or much younger, as though she hadn't lived at all. She felt oddly guilty, too. She had lived quietly in Elmsdale for twenty years, while empires rose and fell, and an old world died and a new world was being born.

In Elmsdale there weren't any generals. There was really nobody much, just the Drakes and the Smiths and the Winslows and the Bennetts, and you got to know them all too well. She thought of the picnics they used to have. They'd make a fire and broil steaks, and she'd bring her famous brownies, and Peg Arnold would bring that wonderful ham, and all the children would swarm around. You'd get mad at the children, but they had such a fine time. Petey loved Elmsdale and the old house. "I'm always going to live in this town, Mum," he'd say. And she'd say, "Oh, pooh, I don't believe you."

Now Hallie heard a laugh she knew—that soft, husky, throaty laugh that reached you even in the balcony's last row. And there was

Gale across the room—Gale, who could twist a million people around her little finger.

Hallie thought of the room she and Gale had lived in that first summer in New York, while they were looking for jobs on the stage. A terrible room, and it was ninety in the shade; but they didn't care. Hallie could almost smell the front hall, stale and dank and musty. She could see the chocolate peppermints in Gale's bureau drawer and the black velvet hat with the pink lining they both wore. She could see the mail on the yellow-oak dresser by the street door of the boardinghouse.

It was she, Hallie, who'd been going places then. "Hallie, when you're famous, will you speak to me? You'd better," Gale told her. It was Hallie, not Gale, who was to be the great actress, the comet, the star. It was Hallie who had driven Gale.

Jim's firm had sent him West for a year. Jim wouldn't wait forever, and forever was one day more. If it hadn't been for Jim—

She remembered Joan's saying, "Mummie, you never told me you went to school with Gale Leslie."

"We'll go see her next week, backstage," Hallie had answered, more briskly than she'd felt.

At the theatre Joan had sat starry-eyed. After the play they'd gone backstage. "Oh, I'm an old friend," Hallie had said. "She'll see me." When she'd seen Gale close, with her make-up on and her hair so light and her pale-pink robe tied tightly around her, Gale hadn't looked real at all. "But that's just make-up," Hallie had thought. "Why, we're old friends. Our paths just went different ways."

"Darling," Gale had said, "how divine of you, ducky," and had flung her arms around her.

"This is Joan," Hallie had said.

"You look like your mother." But Joan didn't at all.

There hadn't been a chance for Joan to say, "You're so wonderful," for all at once people had crowded between them, and Hallie and Joan were out in the cold, dark alley. Gale had been real, all right, then. It was almost as if she had pushed them out.

"Why, the old meanie," Hallie had thought, "the old meanie," and something had crept into her mind that Gale had said years before: "You won't like me after you know me a while. No one ever does."

"But I always will," Hallie had told her.

Joan hadn't said a word on the train.

9

When they'd got home, Jim had asked, "Do you think she's pretty, Joan?"

Joan just had shaken her head, and then she had thrown her arms around her mother's neck. "Mummie, you were too wonderful last year in the Christmas pageant. Really you were!"

GALE was walking toward them now, in that eager, friendly way, as if her arms were full of presents. "Darlings," she said. "Cam, Hallie, it isn't really you!" Then she was hugging Hallie, and Gale felt light and soft and lovely.

Hallie looked at the black dress with the heart-shaped neck, the pearls, Gale's hair. It was ash blonde now, and Hallie thought of all the ways it had been—brown at school and done in a funny loop. She'd been fat then—Tubby Leslie—and she'd worn a Peter Thompson and had freckles and couldn't do her math.

"I'm sorry, darlings," said Gale. "Just coffee and then I've got to run. I've a full afternoon ahead."

"Relax, Tubby," said Cam. "Don't be so purposeful. Give. We want to know all about royalty and what the King said to you and what it's like to be famous and every little thing."

"You'll never change, ducky, will you?" said Gale.

Hallie thought of all the flowers that had been sent to Gale. Why, they'd stretch from here to California. She loved flowers. There's nothing like getting a box of flowers, but Jim—well, when Jim wanted to be nice, he cut off the best part of his steak and put it on your plate.

"A call for you, Miss Leslie," the waiter said. "Will you take it here?"

Gale stretched out her hand, and her voice was honeyed and low as she answered. Then her voice changed. "Oh, it's you, Hickson. You can't reach him? Of course you can. Try Philadelphia or Baltimore." Her voice rose a bit. "Don't be stupid, Hickson, speak up. I can't hear." She wanted something she couldn't get. Hallie knew that voice. Gale stood up. "I can't hear a thing. Forgive me." And the room watched as she swept out.

Cam gave Hallie a poke. "Heart trouble. She can't hold her men. Darling, I feel terrible today." She fumbled in her great alligator bag and took out her gold compact and lipstick. She hadn't changed much, but there were little lines around her eyes. Still, she had been up late the night before.

Hallie hadn't seen Cam since that summer in New York when Joan was born. Cam, fresh from Reno, brought her flowers and bed jackets and pale-pink blanket covers and caviar and books. And Cam had the loveliest clothes.

Hallie would lie in her hospital bed and watch Cam. And when Jim arrived, Hallie would say: "Have dinner with Jim. He must be lonesome." But Jim never would say anything to Cam.

Sometimes Hallie would think, "I guess he doesn't approve of her." Finally she said, "Be nice to Cam, please, Jim."

"She doesn't need anyone to be nice to her," said Jim.

But that night he and Cam went to dinner, and after that they seemed to get along better. Then suddenly Cam went to Paris and married Vin.

Now Cam said: "You haven't told me a thing about Jim. What's going on? Are you holding out on me?"

"Jim's just the same. He's got the same job. Listen, Cam, you're the one that things have happened to. I haven't seen you since you left Ross, that summer Joan was born."

"Ross was all right," said Cam. "I never loved him, though. You must know that. Ross was crazy about you. You could have had him by quirking your little finger. But there was Jim, of course."

"Goodness," said Hallie, "that's news."

"I should have married that boy from Denver."

"Why didn't you?" said Hallie. "I never knew that."

"Sweetie," said Cam sharply, "wake up. Why do you think the family sent me to that high-hat school? Little Cam Oakes from Grand Junction, Colorado. Why, to meet people like you. Family, social register, coming-out party. To meet Hallie Thane. I did. I wanted to be like you. That's why I married Ross."

"*You* wanted to be like me?" said Hallie weakly.

"Then Vin came along." Cam was talking very fast. "You don't understand, do you? Didn't you ever want anyone else? Didn't you ever want to get away from Jim?"

"Maybe I've missed a lot," thought Hallie. "Maybe I don't know a thing."

"Hallie, you get tired of playing around. I felt rotten, and Ross was so decent. I was always meeting Vin. It was such a bore, lying. I couldn't help it, Hallie. I was crazy about Vin. Vin and I got married and had a fine time for a while and went everywhere. Vin drank a lot, and I had to keep up with him. Then I ran into Don Burns."

"The writer," said Hallie. "What was he like, Cam? It must have been romantic, knowing Don Burns." There'd been nothing especially romantic about Jim, not even when he married her. "I never even had an engagement ring," Hallie thought and looked at the rings on Camilla's hands. And then she thought of the night Peter left for the Army camp in Texas and Jim found her crying in the barn. He led her into the house and gave her a drink and said: "Come eat your dinner. What happens to you, happens to me, and vice versa, kid." Yes, that was something.

Cam shrugged. "Don was all right, but I got tired of him. I'm in his next book. Just wait till it comes out. I don't remember quite what happened, anyway. But then I met Tim Atherton and married him. Tim's in England now—Intelligence. Oh, everything's all right between Tim and me. Only he's away. I'm rather at loose ends, I guess." She sounded tired.

"Whom did you like the best?" said Hallie, like a child. She studied Cam's profile. She could see how Cam had looked when she was very young and how she would look when she was old. Her face looked sharper, tighter, more searching, as if she knew what was ahead. You can't always go on finding someone new.

Cam was studying Hallie, too. "I don't know whether you've grown up or not, Hallie, or whether you've been wrapped in tissue paper. You seem to have everything in the palm of your hand."

"Me?" said Hallie.

"Do you happen to know a man named Jim? Remember Jim?"

"Jim," said Hallie. "Jim who?"

"Jim Adams, sweetie pie. Your husband."

"But Jim!" Hallie laughed. "Why, Cammie—"

"But Jim! Lord knows why I'm telling you, but that summer you were in the hospital—remember, Hallie? I had two weeks to get him. Exactly two weeks. I'd rather have had Jim Adams than anything else in the world, Hallie. I'd have taken him, too, even though I love you. That's the way I am, Hallie."

Hallie's mind went into dives and tail-spins. Cam and Jim! "Be nice to Cam, please, Jim." Cam wanting Jim. Jim wanting Cam— for even one single second. Jim, who went to sleep in his chair every night.

12

CAM was saying: "Take it easy, Cuckoo. I shouldn't have told you. It's all dead and buried. Forget it, Hallie. You always get the best of everything. I couldn't budge that donkey, Jim. You got him back as good as new. . . . I've got to fly, darling," she said. "Tonight I'm going out with Duke Rogers. He's a lamb, but just a baby. Where is that devil Gale? Oh, here she is now."

"Sorry," said Gale. "It couldn't be helped. I've got to leave for Washington tomorrow. Pin something on the President, you know." Gale was looking at Hallie. "Those wings you're wearing, ducky. New beau?"

"They're Peter's," said Hallie.

"Peter? Oh, your son Peter. He's not old enough, Hallie?" said Cam. "Not really! I'd love to see him, Hallie."

"He's eighteen, and he got his wings last week," said Hallie. "He's awfully good-looking," she said. "He's six feet three, just like his father."

There was a queer, flat silence, and Cam stopped talking, and Gale had that baffled look in her eyes. Then the waiter brought the check and they paid and left the table. Cam, after brief farewells, hurried away.

Gale caught Hallie's hand. "Don't be mad at me, Hallie. Come home with me for just a minute. Please."

Hallie didn't want to go, but she did. Gale Leslie always got her audience.

When they reached Gale's apartment, Hickson opened the door. She looked scared. "I haven't reached him yet, Miss Gale. They think he's left for the Coast, but I'll try again."

"You mean he didn't call? He left no word? He won't be here for dinner?" Gale's voice rose. Hallie could hear her again saying, years ago, that no one really liked her after knowing her a while.

"Hickson, call again." Gale was almost screaming.

The apartment was full of flowers, too full. When Hickson came back, her voice was calm; but underneath you could hear it shake. "He's gone, Miss Gale. He left at one today for the Coast."

There was an awful silence, and no one spoke. Then Gale said very politely, "You'll have dinner with me, won't you, Hallie?"

"Gale," said Hallie, "I'm sorry."

"It's my birthday," said Gale.

"Birthday," cried Hallie. "Gale, I didn't know."

"It's my birthday, all right," said Gale. "And you know how old I am. There's no performance tonight—that's the way I celebrate. Try Miss Bradford, Hickson." She was walking up and down the room.

Hickson left, then returned. "Miss Bradford is out for the evening," she said. "Anyone else, Miss Gale?"

Gale shook her head.

Hickson hesitated. "Is it all right for me to go now?"

"Go? Go where?"

"We agreed about tonight, you know. You seemed to prefer it. And I made my plans. But if—"

"Oh, get out, Hickson. Get out, both of you. Run along, ducky," she said to Hallie. "You, too. Get your old train." Gale went to the mirror and studied her face.

"Let your face alone. It's all right," said Hallie, and it was like school again.

"I remember a dress you let me have, Hallie, when you gave me your part in the play," said Gale. "If you hadn't married Jim, I'd never have got that part. Hallie, I swear you don't look any different. How do you do it?"

"Nonsense," said Hallie. "Neither do you."

They talked for a long time. Hallie thought of the years when she'd have been thrilled to have dinner with Gale. "I had dinner with Gale Leslie—Tubby to me—an old school friend." But now she wanted to go home. She wanted her husband. She wanted Jim Adams.

A bell rang, and Hickson came in. "It's a Miss Camilla," she said, "and she's on her way up."

Then Camilla stood in the doorway. She was dressed for dinner, and she looked lovely. She had a white camellia in her hair. She began to laugh. "I just took a chance, Gale. Never dreamed I'd find you in. I got the brush-off. My new beau stood me up."

"You're not the only one," said Gale.

Hallie stared at them as though she couldn't believe her eyes. "I've got to telephone, Gale," she said. She hoped Jim hadn't left the plant, and when she heard his voice, she sighed. "Oh, Jim," she said, "I'm so glad I got you. I went to that luncheon after all. I'm still at Gale's, and Cam's here, too, and listen, darling, they haven't changed at all."

"*You listen*," said Jim. "Guess who's here! Wait till you see him!"

"Pete!" she cried. "Oh, Petey!"

"What about picking you up in town?" said Jim. "Pete wants to cele-brate, and so do I. We'll meet you anywhere. What do you say?"

"Why, Jim—" She hesitated, then she said quickly: "How about Joseph's? The food is unbelievable, that chocolate whip with brandy. You'd better get a table for five, darling, if you don't mind." And then, hoping her voice didn't sound smug and too happy and too sure, she added: "There are two glamour gals who are sort of lonely I might bring along. And listen, tonight when we get home, I'll tell you the score."

Susan's Dinner Party

DOROTHY ALDIS

Dorothy Aldis' story of how Susan's pesky young brother puts a spark and a bang in her first grown-up party will make you chuckle every time you read this.

It was ben wade. Susan could see him taking off his hat in the hall. Wouldn't you know it?—right away she'd have some introducing to do. She wished she'd asked Rosy to come early! It was too horrible being the only girl! What's more, her mother wasn't even ready yet. But just as Ben came into the room Mrs. Brown started running downstairs. Couldn't she at least *walk* like other mothers?

"Mummy, this is Ben Wade."

"Hello, Ben, so glad to see you."

"How do you do, Mrs. Brown. Hello, Susan," Ben said, making Susan realize she hadn't spoken to him herself which was simply too ghastly. So she held out her hand but Ben didn't see it, and by the time he had and was holding out his both of Susan's were clamped so tightly around her red and silver striped evening bag that her knuckles showed up white and shiney. They all sat down then, and Susan's mother said she imagined Ben liked dancing school now but how in the world had his mother managed to get him going at *first*, and did he think Richard could ever be persuaded—just as though

Ben had ever even heard of Richard—and Ben, who was terribly shy, said, well, his father had bribed him. Fortunately, before this could be gone into any further the doorbell rang again and Susan sat hoping and praying it would be a girl, but it wasn't—it was Buzzy Butterfield and Jimmy Rowe. Buzzy was at least wearing different pants from the ones he'd had on That Horrible Night. These hadn't been let down either though. And Jimmy at least wasn't wearing that loud checked coat. When Susan introduced Jimmy to her mother he said, "Good evening, Mrs. Brown," instead of just how do you do or hello as Ben and Buzzy had. And when she asked him some absolutely dopey question he not only answered it but went right on talking in a way that made the other boys laugh in a relieved sort of way. Yes, horrible though Jimmy was, you at least had to hand it to him for being sort of like Rosemary, Susan thought; for making things seem not as bad as they were somehow—for, anyway, opening his *mouth*, while Buzzy, who was generally such a complete and absolute scream, had nothing to say for himself at all.

The bell again!

The extra maid had kept right on standing there by the front door so Susan didn't have long to wait to know her next guests were Rosy and Ann, thank goodness—and Mary Lou and Kathy, too! Heavens, they'd all come together! The extra maid told them where to go to leave their coats and junk upstairs and Susan thought they would absolutely never come down! She could hear them shrieking and laughing together up there. *And why didn't Chrystine bring in the tomato juice?*

"Well, looks like you're throwing a stag party, Suse," Buzzy suddenly said, which was something, at least, and just then the girls began clunking downstairs in the high heels they weren't at all used to, except for Rosemary, of course. Great swishings and rustlings and gigglings, but the giggles stopped abruptly as they came through the living room door with wide, embarrassed smiles on their faces. Although there were only four of them, in their long sticking-out skirts they seemed practically to fill the room. Mrs. Brown jumped up so pleased to see them, too pleased, Susan thought: after all, she didn't have to put on a perfect *act*, did she? After the girls had said how do you do, they all sat down close together on one side of the room, Rosemary, too, while Susan was still left stuck off with Ben and Jimmy and Buzzy and her mother. Nobody talked but her mother, who told a story which wasn't funny in the least but naturally everybody had to laugh. At the end of it Rosemary said:

"Oh, how simply killing, Mrs. Brown. Buzzy, have you started inter-school football games yet?"

"Next week we do. Say, where's our big star, anyway?"

The four girls on the sofa looked at one another and giggled. Ann said: "He couldn't find his dancing pumps, wouldn't you know it?" This made everybody really laugh, so when Ted Means came into the room it seemed as though everyone were laughing at *him*—at least he looked as though he thought they were and his hand went up to his tie to be sure it was there. It certainly *was*, Susan thought: my gosh, what a tie! Mrs. Brown knew Ted Means's mother so Susan didn't have to introduce him, at least, and now Chrystine came in and started passing the tomato juice, which gave them something to do at least. But wouldn't you know it, Susan's mother had to jump up and pass the little thingamajiggies herself! She walked around from person to person making terrible jokes with her stomach sticking out, and once Susan caught Jimmy Rowe absolutely staring at it! If she'd realized, though, what her mother was thinking while circulating among the guests, then Susan would have absolutely died. Looking up, Mrs. Brown fancied it was as though she were lifting her eyes to a tangle of friendly giraffe heads waving and bobbing above her, the boys' necks were so long, their Adam's apples so prominent, their actual heads so much too small for their nobbly long bodies. She wished she could pat their cheeks, she was thinking. She wished they would laugh and talk some more so she could hear their hoarse, uncertain voices. At night, she thought, they must lie in bed and grow so hard that they pushed the feet and head boards farther and farther apart—

"Won't you let me, Mrs. Brown?"

"Oh, how nice of you, Jimmy, thanks."

When Jimmy took over the passing of the peanut butter and bacon thingamajiggies, Susan had another simply too ghastly thought: Just supposing, in spite of all their indebtedness to her, the brats should suddenly take it into their heads to come down and steal Eastfay.

The doorbell again, and a second later Shorty West walked in.

"Hello," Susan said. "Mummy, this is—Mummy, this is—"

"Why, hello," said Mrs. Brown quickly. "So glad to see you. Why, but you're not one bit late." Everyone had noticed though. Susan absolutely knew everyone had seen her standing there with her mouth wide open *forgetting Shorty West's name.*

"Where did you finally find your shoes, lug?" his sister asked him.

"In the fireplace," grinned Shorty. (He had a slow way of grinning and speaking.) On the shout that followed this Chrystine came in to announce dinner and they all moved out to the dining room and found their places at table. Mrs. Brown smiled and waved and said, Well, she'd be seeing them later.

From then on things got rapidly worse.

Most of the time you could hear a pin drop it was so quiet, and then there would be little eruptions and spurts which only made the silences afterward worse. Even Rosy didn't talk much. Oh, she tried, and Jimmy and Shorty would sort of grin and croak back, but they never really answered her at all. Furtively watching Shorty, Susan thought that being the manager of the school debating team ought at least to make him be able to say one whole sentence. Perhaps not to Mary Lou but certainly to Rosy! After all, if you're supposed to be so absolutely crazy about a girl!

Right in the middle of a silence Susan heard poor Kathy, who was sitting on the other side of Ted Means, ask him what his tie was supposed to *represent,* for gosh sakes, but Ted didn't hear her or something. Anyway, he didn't pay any attention; instead he asked Ben Wade a question about the Green Bay Packers, which started them off on football, which was certainly all wrong for a Boy-Girl party—a hostess sitting completely and absolutely ignored while football was talked across her! Well, at least she certainly wasn't acting crazy about either of them, Susan thought, to try and comfort herself. At least everyone was eating an awful lot. Already the helping maid had refilled the little pink-frilled nut container things three times. Chrystine, breathing hard the way she always did, was passing the chicken now for seconds—thank goodness, the pieces weren't too dinky—and as she raised her arms to maneuver a platter above Tom's head, Susan realized that up to now she'd been blissfully happy and carefree: Chrystine was perspiring freely! There were dark half-moon circles under each arm!

Susan lived through a perfect haze of horror till dessert. Everything had been as bad as it could possibly be. She knew that never in all her whole entire life would she suffer as much again. Ted Means and Ben were still jabbering football across her, and over the roses—

six white and six pink—Susan watched Shorty pick up his spoon, but before he'd finished loading it with chocolate ice cream and marshmallow sauce he dropped it, and Rosemary burst out laughing at the clatter it made hitting his plate.

"Score one for West," said Shorty in his slow grinning way, which made several more people laugh at that end of the table, but they couldn't keep on laughing forever, and when they did stop the silence was the worst one yet.

Bang!

All over the table a shower of little white pebbles! All in the ice cream. All over the place. The boys were standing up, were climbing on their chairs. Shorty was excitedly testing the table to see if it would be okay to stand on when Mrs. Brown came running in with Nosey barking at her heels.

"Say, Mrs. Brown, do you suppose we could have a ladder? They came from inside that light fixture. Gee."

But Chrystine and the maid who'd come in to help were already pulling the ladder through the pantry door. Everyone got up from the table now. Half of them pushed, half pulled it over to one side of the room. Everyone was talking. The ladder was set up. His curly head bumping the ceiling, Shorty slowly made his report.

"My gosh, quite a thing. Firecrackers attached to the ends of candles. The candles must have been lit two or three hours ago. When they burned down of course the fuses caught. Say, the explosion just about shot out all the pebbles. See—these are all that are left." He showed them, looking pleased.

All the boys, Susan noticed, were looking terribly pleased. All the girls were chattering and squealing. "How thimply *too* thenthational!" cried Mary Lou. And even after they were sitting down in their chairs again and finishing their ice cream, they kept right on talking. All together now. Boys *and* girls. Why, screaming, really! And when Ted Means of all people actually threw a cake across the table then Susan absolutely knew the party was a wow.

After dinner one of the boys found the little red ball that Bud had told Susan to take back to Poop as a present from him, and they started right in playing catch while Nosey rushed around absolutely wild with excitement. Pretty soon Susan's father and Richard came home. Her father looked really awfully nice, and Richard, for an absolute wonder, was clean. But even if he hadn't been Susan realized it

19

wouldn't have mattered much because everyone was so terribly interested to know how he'd managed his trick. As they crowded around him Richard just stood there and answered their questions and didn't say anything awful at all. He even gave some of the credit to Butch, which was awfully nice of him, Susan thought. It was the dopiest thing but just for a minute there she felt—well, proud!

Love Me, Love My Sailor

FAITH BALDWIN

Barnacle Bill really is a sea dog, a terrier with a penchant for chasing sailors. He breaks up a love affair for Pam but introduces her to Terry, who seems like the real thing. Nautical but nice.

THE KITCHEN was small and lively. It wore yellow petticoats on the windows, and the earthenware was yellow and blue. The walls were yellow and the shelves were blue. The girl who ate her dinner on the kitchen table was also small and lively. Her yellow hair matched her kitchen.

She had a chop, a baked potato, and a salad. She had a big, round orange for dessert. She was not undernourished; she was beautifully equipped.

Her name was Pamela Martin and she lived alone and liked it very much. She had a job, which she also liked. She had friends and she had beaux. Why, then, was she eating this solitary dinner on a fine spring evening?

The answer was, uniforms.

Most girls love uniforms. Any uniform. Walk down Fifth Avenue and see the uniforms go by: Army, Navy, Marine, Coast Guard, R.C.A.F., R.A.F.—the boys in blue with wings and the names of strange, far countries on their sleeves—Australia, New Zealand, Norway, Poland perhaps, and a lot more. Watch the feminine heads turn, young heads and old. There is an aura about women who look at uniforms, an aura like a sigh. "Ah—h—h!" they say.

Not Pam. Pam hated uniforms.

Most of her beaux were in uniform. They were in camps scattered all over the country; they were at navy bases; they were in the air and on the sea and marching over deserts; they were in Guadalcanal. Every day brought her letters, with *Free* written where the stamp might have been, or little letters which had been photographed. Now and then a uniform Pam knew came to town and asked her, "Will you have dinner and go dancing? I have just three days' leave." Or, "How's about getting married? I have two whole weeks."

No.

Now she had a civilian beau. He was forty. He was a lawyer, and Pam was his secretary. A nice man, a widower. A little on the pudgy side physically, but there was nothing wrong with his brain, which was, so to speak, lean and muscular. He earned a fair income and had prospects. His late wife had not produced children. His name was Robert Innis and he wanted a new wife, a young wife, who would settle right down and have a family.

ROBERT could have worn a uniform. He could have been something or other, with considerable rank, in the Judge Advocate's office. But, he said, if he got in, it had to be action. He might as well sit home and try cases as try 'em somewhere else, in uniform. Besides, he had a little war job. Intelligence. Pam didn't know just what. He never told her, he was far too intelligent for that!

Consuming the chop, a rare viand which the butcher had saved for her because he liked her, Pam reflected that she was being silly. Why couldn't she make up her mind to marry Robert?

She could love Robert, safely. He wouldn't be off somewhere on the high seas, with torpedoes spinning around and planes diving; he wouldn't be creeping through jungles; he wouldn't be flying over the clouds, with pursuit planes after him or antiaircraft guns hunting for him. He wouldn't be marching across a desert filled with booby traps.

The trouble was, she was fond of Robert, but she didn't love him. Not yet, anyway. She picked up the chop by its fragile bone and did a little unemilypostish gnawing.

Perhaps that wasn't any trouble at all. For if you loved anything terribly, you lost it. She'd loved a dog once, and a white kitten, and a yellow canary which was like sunshine with a voice. She had lost them all. She had loved her parents with a single and violent devotion, and a train had crashed through a trestle, and she had no parents.

Better just be fond of someone, particularly of someone not in uniform.

Katie's husband was missing in the Solomons, and Rosalie's fiancé had fallen like a star from the clouds over the Channel. The younger of Betsey's two boys was fathoms undersea with the bones of his ship.

Every day Pam read in the papers about girls she knew and girls she did not know, and saw their pictures. They were marrying corporals and sergeants, lieutenants and captains, privates and seamen. They were marrying . . . what? Uniforms, glamour, excitement. They were wedding danger; they were pledged to fear; they were love in bloom, with the blossom forced by the glasshouse tension of the times.

Not Pam. She would help the war effort any way she could; she was an air-raid warden and a nurse's aide; she sold bonds and collected scrap. But she would marry Robert. She would have her home and her babies, and she would whistle at shadows. . . .

Her doorbell rang.

Pam rose. She was wearing a house coat in which she looked something like a forget-me-not. She went to the door.

On the threshold stood a uniform. A navy uniform. There were stripes which added up to lieutenant commander. The uniform stretched tall, and under the cap a brown face peered down—a nice brown face, with good gray eyes. There was the beginning of a smile.

Attached to the uniform there was a leash, and on the leash was a dog. The dog was an Irish terrier. He wiggled, a little.

"Miss Martin?" asked the uniform.

"Yes," said Pam, "but—"

He said, "I've brought you your pup."

She had a sensation of complete insanity. She said, "Mine?" with a slight quaver. "But I didn't order one."

Said the uniform, "I'm Terry Johnson. May I come in?"

Pam stood aside, as there was little else she could do. She was aware of her hair, slightly disheveled. Her hands were probably dripping with chop and sticky with orange. The terrier barked, briefly. He must have smelled the chop.

The living-room was small, and very pleasant. Like Pam.

She motioned to a large chair, and Terry sat down. The terrier looked at him inquiringly, sighed, and lay at his feet.

22

Pam said, "I'm afraid I don't understand."

"Jimmy Harkens sent him to you," said Terry, "from Ireland. We were shipmates."

Pam started. Jimmy was the uniform who had said, "Marry me. I have two whole weeks." But that was a long time ago, and since then . . .

Terry read her thoughts. He said, "Yes, I know. Jimmy married a navy nurse and was transferred, but I didn't know that until I'd brought Bill here. Barnacle Bill. Jim said, 'Next time you have a chance, get a pup and take it to Pam Martin. She likes pups.' "

Pam said uncertainly, "Jim and I lived next door to each other in San Diego when we were youngsters. I had a dog then. He remembered."

"Sure," said Terry. His eyes were smiling at her. "I've heard a lot about you. We were classmates, Jim and I. He often said, 'I want you to meet Pam.' But San Diego was a long way off, then. And now—"

Pam leaned down and touched Bill's rough head. He was quite still under her hand. He wasn't friendly, he wasn't unfriendly, he was just indifferent.

Terry said apologetically, "He isn't used to women. It was quite a while before I had a chance to get him. Then we were a long time at sea. He's a sailor. He spent a lot of his time on the bridge. The entire outfit was nuts about him. You should see him climb ladders. We ran into some very nasty weather, but Bill didn't care. He wasn't even seasick. More than I can say for myself."

She said weakly, "It's very kind of you . . . and good of Jim . . . but what in the world can I do with a dog?"

Bill put his cold nose in Terry's hand. And Terry said, smiling, "What does anyone do with a dog? Love him, feed him, give him a home and someone to live for—that's all dogs ask. That, and a bit of brisk discipline."

He rose. He said, "He's yours."

"But—"

"We're shoving off very soon," said Terry. "I'm going home, to South Carolina, for what's left of a short leave, but I'll be back some time. Mind if I stop around and see how Bill makes out? It won't be easy for him once he realizes he's swallowed the anchor."

23

Somehow, she was on her feet looking up; somehow, she was at the door and he was looking down. Her hand was engulfed by his hand. He was saying, "Look after Bill, will you? And I'll be seein' you."

THE door closed, and Bill scratched at it and barked. Also, he wept, in a manly dog fashion. He was very unhappy.

Well, thought Pam wildly, *I've got to feed him something and find him a place to sleep.*

But what could she do with a dog? She was gone all day. That meant bribing the elevator boy to do a spot of dog-walking. It meant having proper food and water. It meant taking Bill to a vet for shots and things. She bet the crew of a battleship or a destroyer or a cruiser or whatever it was hadn't thought of that. It meant taking a walk nights, herself.

It meant that Robert would be very much displeased, because Robert didn't like dogs, except bird dogs, good ones, which were never treated as pets.

"Oh, heck!" said Pam, very close to tears, while Bill, looking at her, howled dismally. . . .

You adopt a dog because you don't know what else to do with him, and your entire life changes, Pam soon found out. She tried, very guiltily, to give Bill away, but nobody wanted him.

It wasn't as though Bill had come to her seeking affection and protection. Far from it. He was amiable toward her, but aloof. He seemed to know that since she was all he had, he must make the best of her. She provided the bed, the board, and the touring along the horrible city streets, which were gray, like decks. But the resemblance stopped there. Decks tilted and were continuously in movement. They were wet and they were salt. You braced yourself, with the wind in your whiskers. Streets were another matter. They were dirty. They were filled with inferior dogs and with people. There were too many skirts on streets. Bill didn't like skirts.

Said the elevator boy one late afternoon when Pam came home, "That Bill's a terror! He chased a sailor darn' near two blocks and all but yanked me off my feet. He went plain crazy."

"Chased a sailor!" repeated Pam, horrified.

"Yes, Miss Martin. A sailor."

She didn't take Bill out herself, except at night, until the first Sunday rolled around. She was lunching at the Plaza with Robert, and had the mistaken idea that it would be nice to take Bill walking in the Park. She could check him during luncheon in the cloakroom.

The Park was green with spring, and sweet. Pam and Bill went walking by a lake. Error number one. Bill took one look at the water. He tugged and he hauled. He huffed and he puffed. He wasn't such a big dog, but there was a lot of pull in him. Pam was a very small girl. She found herself at the water's edge. "Bill!" she called. "Bill," she pleaded, "come back. Oh, darn you!" cried Pam, whose feet were wet.

Bill's, too. This was water, if not the right kind of water. It was flat, sissy water, without an atom of salt in it. Still, it was water.

And out on the lake, just as in the comics and the cartoons, were boats with sailors in them. Real sailors in blue; with their caps a little slanted. Having a busman's holiday, rowing in Central Park.

"Bill!"

Bill was barking, deciding to take a swim. People, passing by, stopped and regarded the scene with interest. Bill made up his mind, gave a mighty tug—and Pam fell flat upon her pretty little face.

When she rose, her very chic suit—navy faille it was, with a pale pink blouse—was covered with mud. Upon her yellow head there had been a small article of navy blue straw with a pale pink rose. It wasn't on her head now.

A cop sauntered by. Here was one uniform you could trust. He, too, regarded the scene. He asked, "What's the matter, miss? Is that a seagoing dog?"

"Apparently," said Pam bitterly.

If it hadn't been for the sailor, walking with his girl, even the Law could not have restrained Bill. But the sailor stopped, grinned, and whistled. Maybe he was whistling because of Pam. But Bill was a vain pup, and here was one of his own. He left the water and cast himself upon the sailor.

There wasn't time, when things eventually subsided, to go home and change. Robert disliked being kept waiting. A punctual man, Robert. So Pam staggered over to the Plaza, made herself as presentable as possible, and procured paper towels with which to rub down Bill. When she finally checked him and went to meet Robert, she was thirteen and a half minutes late.

Pam thought, *I'll make a good story of it.* And she did, a charming little story full of seagoing dogs and sailors rowing on a lake, and Robert didn't think it funny at all. He said, "You'll have to get rid of that dog."

Funny thing about Pam. She didn't like dictators. A few minutes ago she had wished with all her heart that she could get rid of Bill, in a nice way, of course, so that if Terry Johnson ever turned up again she could tell him, "It wasn't possible for me to keep him, but he has a wonderful home." But now her spine stiffened. She said, coolly, "I don't wish to get rid of him, Robert."

They had a little quarrel.

ROBERT had planned for them to spend the afternoon with his irascible uncle. Pam was to be eased into the family that way. Uncle Bolivar had a prejudice against marriage. The only woman he had ever wanted to marry had laughed herself into hysterics, forty years ago, and married a penniless nobody with more chin and less nose than Uncle Bolivar. He had never forgiven her nor any member of her sex. During Robert's brief, boyish marriage Uncle Bolivar had cut him out of his will. Robert didn't want that to happen again.

For months now he had been endeavoring to break the news of a possible Pam to his uncle. Today being a Sunday in spring, he had planned to bring her to tea.

Fine thing, quarreling over a dog.

Robert decided to make the best of it. They would uncheck Bill and take him back to the apartment. Pam could change her frock. He would wait. They would go to Uncle Bolivar's.

Pam had two runs in her best pair of stockings. She had also a scraped knee. The faille suit needed attention. She had had mud in her eye. She was madder than all get-out at Bill, and so she was just as mad at Robert.

She wouldn't go to his darned old uncle's. She said so.

She went home with Bill, wondering why she had fought with her boss—her almost fiancé.

Bill, plagued by unhappy memories, trotted along beside her, soberly. Until along came a sailor.

This sailor was alone and he was very young. He looked no more than seventeen. He was idling along, his cap slanted and his eyes wistful, when Bill hurled himself at him, also hurling Pam, who was

26

on the other end of the leash. It wa
extricate herself and Bill. She felt she

She said breathlessly, "He—he was
a friend in the Navy. He got used to
forms, navy uniforms."

"He's a swell pup," said the boy in bl

And that's how she found herself as
than a thousand miles from home, with a
know anyone in New York. His shipma
Apparently he didn't make dates easily, and

Pam remembered the canteen where h
There would be girls there, and things to eat
all that. She could direct him, and she did.

He thanked her and started off, with Bill
any stopping Bill, so Pam had to go along.

That's how she went to the canteen, and fou
The sailor lad was taken care of and Bill was
place was full of sailors.

It was a wonderful afternoon, in a way. The
and there was music, and the boys played cards a
were coffee and cakes and doughnuts, and dishes

Funny, how soon it was evening. Odder still t
But it was the first time she had ever seen Bill rea

IT WAS, of course, because of Bill that she went ba
She simply couldn't stand having him whine and cr
the door, and then come over and implore her with hi
and whiskers. It was a lot easier to go to the canteen re
at least, Bill could find his fill of sailors. On the evenin
the hospital she left Bill at the canteen, and called for hi
home.

This routine very naturally upset her life. It also upset
couldn't or wouldn't understand. She had, after the Plaza
him by appointment at Uncle Bolivar's, on the following Su
noon. But she made the mistake of taking Bill with her.

If there was one member of the animal kingdom whi
Bolivar hated more than a woman, it was a dog. It appeared
girl who had been clear-sighted enough to refuse his offer of r
had possessed a pup. The pup had bitten him.

So the
butler in
of superb
Pam
Robert s
He said
her faul
that he
templa
Pam
He
she w
Pam
would
Th
self a
muc
staff
B
way
gre
tim
ga
ph
th
a

arrival of a pretty girl plus an Irish terrier threw the spectral
o a snit, Robert into a tizzy, and Uncle Bolivar into a rage
proportions.

eparted, without tea. She was glad to go, and so was Bill.
ed after her presently, and they had words in her apartment.
that Uncle Bolivar had nearly had a stroke; he said it was all
. Uncle Bolivar, said he in hollow accents, had informed him
would, on the morrow, send for his lawyer. If Robert con-
ed marrying again, he'd better think twice about it.

asked, "Well, are you thinking about it?"
had been, he admitted. Perhaps if she got rid of Bill? Perhaps if
nt around to Uncle Bolivar's and apologized?
n asked quietly what had given him the impression that she
l care to marry into a family of lunatics.
e upshot of all this unpleasantness was that Miss Martin got her-
nother job, with another lawyer. She also got herself a uniform,
n to her astonishment, and found herself, with Bill, on the canteen

eing in uniform, somehow, made a difference. It was, in a curious
, a protection against masculine uniforms. She grew to know a
at many boys well for a little while; boys you saw once, twice, three
es, and never again, perhaps; boys who told her about their farms,
stations, drugstores; about their homes. Boys who showed her
otographs of girls who were going to wait. That was the important
ing with all of them.

And then, after six months, Terry Johnson telephoned her. He
sked, "Remember me? How's Bill?"

It was a Sunday. Terry came to the apartment and they took Bill
walking in the Park. Bill was very nearly out of his Irish-terrier mind.
He ate Terry up, he looked at him with such love and longing that
Pam laughed, and then found out that it would have been just as easy
to cry. And, walking along the lake, Bill behaved himself like a
gentleman. He didn't have to chase the Navy now; he had the Navy
with him.

They had lunch at a restaurant on the Avenue, and then went back
to the apartment and Terry talked. He talked to Bill mostly. He said,
"Remember how it was, old-timer?" He said, "Remember how you
used to tear up and down the ladder?" He said, "We miss you."

When he said that, he looked at Pam.

Pam had a cup of tea, Terry had a whisky and soda, and Bill had a dog biscuit. That was cozy, the three of them having an afternoon snack.

"I wanted to write you," said Terry. "You see, I knew you pretty well. Jim had pictures, back in our plebe days. I envied him."

She asked, looking at Bill, who winked at her, "Why didn't you?"

"What?"

"Write."

"I was scared."

She said, "You must write to lots of girls."

Terry grinned. He said, "Not me. I had a girl once, a long time ago. She married someone else. It was just as well. She didn't like the Navy. . . . By the way, do you?"

Pam nodded her daffodil head. She said, "Bill converted me."

"Why 'converted'?"

"Uniforms," she said. "You'll think it silly, but I was scared. Of them; and of myself. Of getting caught up in a sort of rosy cloud and then . . . no parachute. I knew too many girls who—" Her voice trailed away. She said fiercely, "I didn't want any part of it. I was afraid of getting hurt."

"I see. And Bill made you change your mind."

"Well . . . you see, he made me work at a canteen," said Pam. "It was either that, or be dragged all over town following sailors."

He looked at her for a long time. He said, "I'll be back. You believe that, don't you, Pam?"

She said, "Yes," in a small voice. She had suddenly become aware that if she wanted to live she had to believe it. Yet it wasn't living to go on feeling safe and smug.

He said, "We'll have dinner together tonight. I'll take up all the time you can give me while I'm here. It won't be for long, Pam. But when I shove off again, I'll write. And you'll write me, won't you? And tell me about Bill?"

Pam nodded. Bill looked at her and barked. Bill was perfectly happy. After six months he was used to Pam. She wasn't bad, for a landlubber and a skirt. *And if I stick to her*, thought Bill, in his own fashion, *I'll see the tall man in the blue uniform again. Often.*

29

"Pam," said Terry.

"Yes?"

"If a guy knew that he had a girl and a dog—waiting?"

SHE smiled. It was too soon, but there'd be this leave, and perhaps another some time. There'd be mail. There would be memories. There would be fear and despair and frantic, voiceless prayers. But that was part of it. She looked at the brown face and the gray eyes which had seen so much that was unknown to her and terrifying, and she thought, *Well, at least I didn't fall in love with a uniform. I fell in love in spite of it.*

Bill barked. He felt neglected. No one had looked at him or spoken to him for a long time. He yawned, and went to sleep, dreaming himself back on a wet and tilting deck. He was, in his way, a philosopher.

Barnacle Bill, the sailor.

The Sobbin' Women

STEPHEN VINCENT BENÉT

What happened when the courtin' Pontipee boys brought home the sobbin' women ahead of the posse? A tall tale of the Tennessee Valley by one of America's great writers.

THEY CAME OVER the Pass one day in one big wagon—all ten of them—man and woman and hired girl and seven big boy children, from the nine-year-old who walked by the team to the baby in arms. Or so the story runs—it was in the early days of settlement and the town had never heard of the Sobbin' Women then. But it opened its eyes one day, and there were the Pontipees.

They were there but they didn't stay long—just time enough to buy meal and get a new shoe for the lead horse. You couldn't call them unsociable, exactly—they seemed to be sociable enough among themselves. But you could tell, somehow, from the look of them, that they weren't going to settle on ground other people had cleared. They

30

were all high-colored and dark-haired—handsome with a wilderness handsomeness—and when you got them all together, they looked more like a tribe or a nation than an ordinary family. I don't know how they gave folks that feeling, but they did. Yes, even the baby, when the town women tried to handle him. He was a fine, healthy baby, but they said it was like trying to pet a young raccoon.

Well, that was all there was to it, at the start. They paid for what they bought in good money and drove on up into Sobbin' Women Valley—only it wasn't called Sobbin' Women Valley then. And pretty soon, there was smoke from a chimney there that hadn't been there before. But you know what town gossip is when it gets started. The Pontipees were willing enough to let other folks alone—in fact, that was what they wanted. But, because it was what they wanted, the town couldn't see why they wanted it. Towns get that way, sometimes.

So, it was mostly cross questions and crooked answers when the Pontipees came into town, to trade off their pelts and such and buy at the store. There wasn't much actual trouble—not after two loafers at the tavern made fun of Pa Pontipee's fur cap and Pa Pontipee stretched them both before you could say "Jack Robinson." But there wasn't a neighborly feeling—yes, you could say that. The women would tell their children about the terrible Pontipees and the men would wag their heads. And when they came in to church—which they did once a year—there'd be a sort of rustle in the congregation, though they always took a back pew and listened perfectly respectful. But the minister never seemed to be able to preach as good a sermon as usual that Sunday—and naturally, he blamed the Pontipees for that. Till, finally, they got to be a sort of legend in the community—the wild folks who lived up the valley like bears in the woods—and, indeed, some said they turned into bears in the winter time, which just shows you what people will say. And, though the boys were well set up, they might as well have been deaf-mutes for all the notice the town-girls took of them—except to squeak and run to the other side of the road when the Pontipees came marching along.

While, as for the Pontipees—nobody knew what they made of it all, for they weren't much on talking. If one of them said "It's a fine day" and another admitted it was, that was conversation that would last them a long while. Besides, they had work enough and to spare, in their own valley, to keep them busy; and, if Ma Pontipee would have liked more society, she never let on. She did her duty by the

31

boys and tried to give them some manners, in spite of their backwoods raising; and that was enough for any woman to do.

But things never stand still in this world, and soon enough, the boys weren't boys any more, they were men. And when the fall of a tree took Pa Pontipee, his wife didn't linger long after him. There was a terrible fuss about the funerals too—for the Pontipee boys got the minister, but they wouldn't let the burials take place in town. They said Pa and Ma wouldn't feel comfortable, all crowded up among strangers in the churchyard, so they laid them to rest in the Valley where they'd lived, and the town found that queerer than ever. But there's worse places to lie than looking out over the fields you've cleared.

After that, though, the town thought some of the boys, at least, would move in from the Valley and get more sociable. They figured they'd have to—they figured with their Pa and Ma gone, the boys would fight amongst themselves—they figured a dozen things. But none of the things they figured happened at all. The Pontipee boys stayed out in the Valley, and when they came to the town, they walked through it as proud as Lucifer, and when they came to the church, they put just the same money in the collection-plate they had when Ma and Pa Pontipee were alive. Some thought it was because they were too stupid to count, but I don't think it was that.

They went on just the same, as I say, but things didn't go quite the same for them. For one thing, the hired girl couldn't keep the place the way Ma Pontipee kept it. And besides, she was getting old herself. Well, pretty soon, she up and died. They gave her as good a funeral as they knew how—she'd always been part of the family. But, after that, though the farm went ahead as well as ever, things in the house began to go from bad to worse.

Menlike, they didn't notice what was wrong at first, except there was a lot of dust around and things didn't get put away. But, after each one of them had tried a week of cooking for the others and all the others had cursed out the one who was cooking something proper, they decided something had to be done about it. It took them a long time to decide that—they were slow thinkers as well as slow talkers, the Pontipees. But, when they decided about a thing, it got done.

"The flapjacks are greasy again," said Harry Pontipee, one evening —Harry was the oldest. "You know what we've got to get, brothers? We've got to get a woman to take care of this place. I can lay a tree within two inches of where I want it to fall. I can shoot the eye out of a grey squirrel in a treetop. I can do all a man should do. But I can't cook and make it taste human."

"You're right, brother," said Hob Pontipee—Hob was the youngest. "I can tan deerskin better than an Injun squaw. I can wrestle under-holt and overholt and throw any man in this county. I can play on a boxwood fiddle—but I can't sweep dust so it stays swept. It takes a woman to do that, for there seems to be a trick about it. We've got to get a woman."

Then they all joined in saying what they could do—and it was plenty—but they couldn't cook and they couldn't dust and they couldn't make a house comfortable because that was woman's business, and there seemed to be a trick about it. So they had to get a woman to keep house for them. But where were they going to get her?

"We could get a hired girl, maybe," said Hosea Pontipee—the mid-dle one—but, even as he spoke, there wasn't much hope in his voice.

"That hired girl we had was the last one left in the East," said Harry Pontipee. "Some may have growed up, since her time, but I don't want to go back across the Pass on the chance of an out-and-out miracle."

"Well then," said Hob Pontipee, practical, "there's just one thing to do. One of us has to get married. And I think it ought to be Harry —he's the eldest."

Well, that remark nearly caused a break-up in the family. Harry kicked like a cow in fly-time at the bare idea of getting married, and tried to put it on to Halbert, who was next in line. And Halbert passed it on to Harvey, but Harvey said women was snares and de-lusions, or so he'd heard, and he wouldn't have a strange woman around him for a brand-new plow.

So it went on down to Hob and he wouldn't hear of it—and it wasn't till a couple of chairs had been broken and Hob had a black eye that the ruckus quieted at all. But, gradually, they came to see that one of 'em would have to get married, as a matter of family duty, or they'd all be eating spoiled flapjacks for the rest of their lives. Only then the question came up as to who it was to be, and that started a bigger disturbance than ever.

Finally, they agreed that the only fair way was drawing straws. So Hob held the straws and they drew—and, sure enough, Harry got the long one. Sick enough he looked about it—but there it was. The others started congratulating him and making jokes—especially Hob.

"You'll have to slick up, tomorrow," said Hob, glad it wasn't him. "You'll have to cut your hair and brush your clothes and act pretty, if you're going to be a bridegroom!"

Next morning they got him down and cut his hair and put bear's grease on it and dressed him up in the best clothes they had and sent him into town to look for a wife.

It was all right when he started out from the Valley. He even took a look at himself in a spring and was kind of surprised at the young man who looked back at him. But the nearer he got to town, the queerer and tremblier he felt, and the less able to go about doing what he'd promised.

He tried to remember how it had been when his Pa and Ma had been courting. But, naturally, as he hadn't been born then, he didn't know. Then he tried to think of various girls in the village, but the more he thought of them, the more they mixed in his mind—till, finally, all he could think of was a high, wild bank of rhododendron flowers that mixed and shimmered and laughed at you the closer you came to it.

"Oh, Lordy! It's a heavy responsibility to lay on a man!" he said and mopped his forehead with his sleeve.

Finally, however, he made up his mind. "I'll ask the first woman I see, pretty or ugly!" he said to himself, with the perspiration fairly rolling down his face, though it was a cold March day. And he gave his horse a lick.

But, when he got into town, the first woman he saw was the store-keeper's wife. The second he saw was a little girl in a pinafore—and the third was the minister's daughter. He was all set up to speak to her—but she squeaked and ran to the other side of the street as soon as she saw him and left him standing there with his hat in his hand. That sort of took the courage out of him.

"By the whiskers of Moses!" he said to himself, "this marryin' job is a harder job than I bargained for. I guess I'll go over to the tavern and get me a drink—maybe that will put some ideas in my head."

It was there he saw her—feeding the chickens out in the poultry-yard. Her name was Milly and she was a bound girl, as they had in those days. Next door to a slave she was, for all she'd come of good stock and had some education. She was young and thin, with a sharp little thoughtful face and ragged clothes, but she walked as straight as an Indian as she went about the yard. Harry Pontipee couldn't have said if she were pretty or plain, but, as he watched her through the window, feeding the chickens, something seemed to tell him that he might have better luck with her than he'd had with the others.

Well, he drank his drink and went out.

"Hello, girl," he said, in one of those big voices men use when they're pretending not to be embarrassed.

She looked up at him straight. "Hello, backwoodsman!" she said, friendly enough. She didn't look a bit scared of him and that put him off.

"It's a nice morning," said Harry, louder, trying to lead up to his point.

"It is for some," said the girl, perfectly polite but going on feeding the chickens.

Harry swallowed hard at that. "It'd be a nice morning to get married, they tell me," he said, with the perspiration breaking out all over him again. He'd meant to say something else, but when it came to the point, he couldn't.

Well, she didn't say anything to that so he had to start all over again.

"My name's Harry Pontipee," he said. "I've got a good farm up the Valley."

"Have you?" said the girl.

"Yes," he said. "It's a right good farm. And some folks seem to think I'd make a good husband."

"Do they?" said the girl. I guess she was smiling by now but Harry couldn't see it—she had her head turned.

"Yes they do," said Harry, kind of desperate, his voice getting louder and louder. "What do you think about it?"

"I couldn't tell on such short acquaintance," said the girl.

"Will you marry me and find out?" said Harry, in a perfect bellow, shaking all over.

"Yes, I will, if you don't ask me quite so loud," she said, very prim —and even Harry could see she was smiling now.

Well, they made a queer pair when they went up to the minister —the girl still in her chicken-feed clothes, for she didn't have any others, and Harry in his backwoods finery. He'd had to buy out her

35

time from the innkeeper for twelve beaver pelts and a hunting knife.

But when the wedding service was over, "Well, we're married," said Harry, with great relief. "And now we'll be going home."

"Oh, no we won't," said she. "We're going to the store first and buy me some cloth for a decent dress—for landless I may be and dowryless I may be, but I'm a married woman now, and what's fit for a chicken-girl isn't fit for a married woman."

In a sort of daze, he saw her lay out the price of twelve more beaver pelts in cloth and woman's fixings, and beat down the storekeeper on the price, too.

He only asked her a question about one thing—a little pair of slippers she bought. They were fancy slippers, with embroidery on them. "I thought you had a pair of shoes," he said. She turned to him, with a cocky sort of look on her face. "Silly," she said. "How could anyone tell your wife had pretty feet in the shoes I had?"

Well, he thought that over, and, after a while, something in the way she said it and the cocky look on her face made him feel pleased, and he began to laugh. He wasn't used to laughing in front of a girl, but he could see it might have its points.

Then they rode back to the Valley, her riding pillion, with her bundles in the saddlebags. And all the way back, she was trying him and testing him and trying to find out, by one little remark or another, just what kind of a man he was. She was a spunky little girl, and she had more education than she let on. And long ago, she'd made up her mind to get out of being a bound girl the first way that offered. But, all the same, marrying Harry Pontipee was a leap in the dark.

But the more she tried and tested Harry, the better bargain she seemed to think she'd made. And that took courage to admit—for the way was a wild one and a lonesome, and, naturally, she'd heard stories of Pontipee Valley. She couldn't quite believe they lived with bears, up there, but she didn't know.

And finally, they came to the house, and there were dark things moving outside it. "Bears!" thought Milly, kind of hopeless, and her heart went into her throat, but she didn't let on.

"W-what's that, Harry dear?" she said, holding on tight.

"Oh, that's just my brothers," said Harry, kind of careless, and with that those six hungry six-footers moved into the light.

"Oh!" said Milly, "you didn't tell me you had six brothers." But her voice wasn't reproachful, just sort of soft and quiet.

"I guess it was the wedding kind of knocked it out of my mind," said Harry. "But, there—you'll see enough of 'em anyhow, because we all live together."

"Oh," said Milly again, kind of soft. "I see." And the brothers came up, one by one, and shook hands. They'd intended to cut quite a few jokes on Harry if he did come home with a wife, but, somehow, when they looked at Milly, they forgot about that.

Well, they brought her into the house. It was a handsome house, for the times, with genuine windowglass. But Milly rubbed her finger along a window sill and saw it come off black and then she wrote her name in the dust on the mantelpiece.

"What a lovely big house!" she said, coughing a little with the dust she'd raised.

"It's mebbe a little dusty now," said Harry. "But now you're here—"

"Yes," said Milly and passed on to the kitchen. Well, the kitchen was certainly a sight. But Milly didn't seem to notice.

Presently, "What a great big jar of flapjack batter!" she said. "And what a big tub of salt pork!"

"That's for tonight," said Harry. "Me and my brothers is hearty eaters. We haven't been eating so well since we had to cook for ourselves, but now you're here—"

"Yes," said Milly and passed on to the laundry. The laundry was half full of huckaback shirts and such that needed washing—piles and piles of them.

"What a lot of wash!" said Milly.

"That's so," said Harry, kind of pleased. "Me and my brothers is kind of hard on our clothes—all seven of us—so there's lots of washing and mending, but now you're here—"

"Yes," said Milly, swallowing a little. "And now all you men clear out of my kitchen while I get supper. Clear out!" she said, smiling at them, though she didn't feel much like smiling.

I don't know what she said to herself when they'd left her alone. I know what a man would have said and I guess she said that, too. I know she thought at least once of the money in her stocking and how far it was back to town. And then her eye happened to fall on that great big jar of flapjack batter—and, all of a sudden the whole thing struck her as funny, and she laughed till she cried.

But then she found a clean handkerchief and blew her nose and straightened her hair and set about her work.

Those boys hadn't had a supper like that in months and they treated it respectful. And Milly didn't say a word to them about manners then, though, later on, she said plenty. She just sat and watched them, with a curious light in her eyes.

When it was over finally, and they were stuffed, "Mrs. Harry," said Howard. "You're a wonder, Mrs. Harry!" and "You're sure a wonder, Mrs. Harry!" chorused all the rest of them, down to Hob. She could see they meant it, too.

"Thanks," she said, very polite and gracious. "Thank you, Howard, and you, Hosea, and all my brothers."

At the end of three months, there wasn't one of those boys that wouldn't have laid down his life for Milly, and, as for Harry, he just worshipped the ground she walked on. With all that work to do, naturally, she got thinner and thinner and peakeder and peakeder, but she didn't complain. She knew what she wanted and how she was going to get it—and she waited her chance.

Finally Harry noticed how thin she was getting and he spoke to her about it.

"Can't you ever sit down and rest, Milly?" he said one day, watching her fly around the kitchen, doing six things at once.

But she just laughed at him and said, "I'm cooking for you and your six brothers, and that makes work, you know."

Well, he thought that over, inside him, but he didn't say anything, then. But he came up to her in the laundry another time, and when she was dusting the house another time—she was looking peakeder each day—and asked her if she couldn't rest a spell. The last time, he brought his fist down on the table with a bang.

"This has got to stop!" he said. "Me and my six brothers is wearing you to skin and bone with our victuals and our shirts and the dust we track in the house, and I won't have it no more! It's got to stop!"

"Well, Harry," she said, sort of quiet, "if it's got to stop, it's got to—and pretty soon, Harry. Because, I'm expecting, and a woman that's expecting can't work like a woman in her usual health."

Well, after he got his sense back, after hearing that, he called the whole family into consultation that evening and put it to them plain. They'd do anything for Milly by then.

She led the conversation where she wanted it to go, though she didn't seem to, and finally they decided it was up to Halbert, the second oldest, to get married, so his wife could take some of the work off Milly's hands. So next day, Halbert spruced up and went to town to look for a wife. But when he came home, he was alone and all dejected.

"They won't have me," he said, very mournful. "They won't none of 'em have me—and I asked fourteen of 'em."

"Why, what's the matter?" said Milly.

"Well," said Halbert, "it seems they've heard about the seven of us and the lot of victuals we eat and the wash and all—and they say only a fool would marry into a family like that and they don't see how you stand it, Milly."

"Oh, that's what they say, is it?" said Milly, with her eyes as bright as candles. "Well, your turn next, Harvey."

So Harvey tried it and Hosea tried it and all of them tried it. But none of them had any luck. And then, finally, Milly let loose at them, good and proper.

"You great big lumps of men!" she said, with the cocky look on her face. "There's more ways of killing a cat than choking it with cream. If they won't marry you after you've asked 'em—why don't you marry 'em first and ask 'em afterwards?"

"But how can we do that?" said Harvey, who was the stupidest.

"Well," said Milly—and here's where her education came in that I've made such a point of—"I read in a history book once about a bunch of people called Romans who were just in your fix." And she went on to tell them about the Romans—how they were settled in a country that was unfriendly to them, just like the Pontipees, and how they all needed wives, just like the Pontipees, and how, when they couldn't get them in the ordinary way from the other people of the country who were called the Sobbin's or the Sabbin's or some such name, they raided the Sobbin' town one night and carried off a lot of the Sobbin' women and married them.

"And, if you can't do as well for yourselves as a lot of old dead Romans," she ended, "you're no brothers of mine and you can cook your own suppers the rest of your lives."

They all sat around dumbfounded for a while. Finally Hob spoke up.

"That sounds all right, in history," he said, "but this is different. Supposing these women just cry and pine away when we've carried them off—supposing that?"

"Listen to me," said Milly. "I know what I'm talking about. Every one of those girls is crazy to get married—and there's not half enough men in town to go round. They think a lot of you boys, too, for I've heard them talk about you; but they're scared of your being backwoodsmen, and scared of the work, and each one is scared of being the first to leave the others. I'll answer for them, once you've married them. Is there anybody around here who can marry people, except the regular minister?"

"There's a sort of hedge-parson just come to town," said Hob. "I reckon he can tie a knot as tight as any preacher in the county."

"All right," said Milly. "That settles it."

It was the evening of the big sociable that it happened. They held it once a year, around Thanksgiving time, and those who had rifles and weapons left them at the door. The Pontipee boys had never attended before—so there was a good deal of stir when they marched in, all seven of them, with Milly in the middle. The brothers were shaved and clean and dressed up spick and span and Milly never looked better, in a dress she'd made out of store cloth and her embroidered slippers.

There was quite a bit of giggling from the town girls, as the Pontipees entered, and a buzz around the hall, but then the fiddler struck up and people began to dance and play games and enjoy themselves, and pretty soon they forgot the Pontipees were there at all, except that the Pontipee boys acted very polite to everybody—Milly'd taught 'em that—and, I guess, before the evening was over, some of the town girls were wondering why they'd turned down boys like that just because they lived in the backwoods.

But they didn't get much chance to think about it, at that. Because, just as they were all going to sit down to supper—"Ready, boys?" called Milly, in a voice that cut through all the talk and commotion. Everybody turned to look at her. And then there was a gasp and a cry, for "Ready!" chorused the six bachelor Pontipees; and suddenly, each one had one hand on a rifle and the other holding a girl, while Harry and Milly trained a couple more rifles on the rest of the community to keep them quiet. It happened so sudden, half the folks didn't even know it was happening—till the Pontipee boys had their girls outside in the street, and the big doors locked and bolted behind them.

Then there was Cain to raise for fair in the meeting-hall, and people started to beat and kick at the doors—but they built solid, in those days. There wasn't any use in trying to shoot the locks off, because the Pontipee boys had tied up the guard over the weapons and dumped him and them outside in a shed.

It wasn't till pretty near dawn that the doors gave way—and when they did, the townspeople took one look outside and groaned. For it was snowing, lickety split, till you couldn't see your hand before your face—and when it snows, in our part of the country, it certainly snows. The blizzard didn't let up for four days, either, and by that time, the pass through the hills to Pontipee Valley was blocked solid, and nothing to do but wait for Spring and the thaw.

And, meanwhile, Milly had her work cut out for her. It wasn't an easy job, convoying three sleigh-loads full of hysterics all that long, cold ride. But she let them hysteric away, and by the time they got to the Pontipee house, the stolen brides were so tuckered out that they'd quieted down a good deal.

Still, at first, they swore they wouldn't take bite or sup till they were restored to their grieving families. But Milly had some tea ready for them, in a jiffy—and a woman will usually take tea, no matter how mad she is. Well, Milly let them get warm and a little cozy, and then, when they were on their second cups, she made her little speech.

"Ladies," she said, "this affair makes me mighty sad—to see fine girls like you stole away by a lot of uncouth backwoodsmen. And I'd never have lent a hand to it if I'd known the truth of the matter. But, you and me, we'll turn the tables on them yet. You can't get back to your families till the blizzard lets up, but, while you've got to stay here, I'll see you're treated respectful. And just to prove that"—and she took a bunch of keys from her pocket—"I'll lock this house up tight, with us inside it; and, as for those backwoods Pontipees, they can sleep and eat in the stable with the livestock. That'll teach them they can't fool us!"

Well, that little speech—and the tea—cheered the girls up quite a bit. And by the time Milly showed them to their rooms—nice-looking rooms, too—and let them bolt themselves in, they were pretty well convinced that Milly was their friend.

So a week or so went by like that—the girls keeping house for themselves and never seeing hide nor hair of a Pontipee.

At first, it was a regular picnic for the girls. They allowed as how they'd always wanted to live without any men around, and, now they were, it was even better than they'd thought. And Milly agreed with them as hard as she could agree. She made them little speeches about the worthlessness of men in general and husbands in particular that would have raised the hair off any man's head. And, at first, the other girls listened to her and chimed in, and then they listened, but you could see they were being polite. And, by the end of the week, it was awful hard for her to get a real audience.

So, when she began to catch them looking out of windows when they should have been dusting, and peeking from behind curtains to try and get a sight of the terrible Pontipees, she knew it was time for the next step. For things got duller and duller in the house and little spats and quarrels began to break out among the girls. So, one afternoon, she suggested, tactfully, just to break the monotony, that they all go up and rummage in the garret.

They rummaged around and had quite a bit of fun, until finally the minister's daughter opened a long box and gave a little squeal of joy.

"What a lovely wedding-dress—whose was it?" she said, and pulled out the long white veil and the dress itself, while the rest stood round and admired.

"Oh, shucks, that's just an old wedding-dress those backwoodsmen made me make when they thought you were going to marry 'em," said Milly, in a very disgusted voice. "Put it back!" But the girls weren't paying attention.

"Will it fit me, I wonder?" said the minister's daughter.

"It's bad luck, trying on wedding-dresses, if you're not going to have a wedding!" said Milly. "Let's go downstairs and have tea." But the minister's daughter was stepping out of her regular clothes already. The other girls helped fix her up—and then they oh-ed and ah-ed, for, I must say, she made a handsome-looking bride.

"That Pontipee boy named Hob's got curly hair," said the minister's daughter, trailing out her veil. "I always did have a liking for curly hair."

"Hob's not nearly as good-looking as Halbert," said the lawyer's niece, quite violent, and another one said, "Handsome is as handsome does—the one they call Harvey isn't so handsome, maybe, but he certainly has nice eyes."

"There's something about a man around the house that brisks things up remarkable," said a fourth one. "Not that I want to get married, but Howard's a nice name, even if Pontipee is hitched to it and—"

"Girls, girls—are you crazy, girls?" said Milly, shocked and horrified.

42

But the minute she started to reprove them, they all turned on her, most ungratefully, and there was a regular revolt. So, at last, she had to give in and admit that there were five more wedding-dresses in the garret—and that if anybody was thinking of getting married, there just happened to be a hedge-parson, spending the winter with the Pontipees. But one thing she was firm about.

"Get married if you like," she said. "I can't stop you. But I'm responsible for you to your families—and, after the ceremony's ended, your husbands go back to the stable and stay there, till I know your families approve of them." She looked very fierce about it, and she made them promise. The hedge-parson married them all—all six in their wedding-dresses—and then the boys went back to the stable. And, at dinner that night, the minister's daughter burst out crying.

"I hate men just as much as ever!" she wailed. "But it's terrible to be lawful married to a man you can't even see, except now and then out of a window!"

So Milly saw she had to make some new rules and she did. Three afternoons a week, the boys were allowed to call on their new wives, and once in a while, for a great treat, they could stay to supper. But, always with Milly to chaperon.

Well, at first, the husbands and wives were mighty stiff and formal with each other, but, gradually, they got better and better acquainted. Till, pretty soon, the minister's daughter was letting Hob hold her hand, when she thought Milly wasn't looking, and the lawyer's niece was asking permission to sew a button on Halbert's coat—and there was a general atmosphere of courting around the Pontipee place that'd make an old bachelor sick.

Milly took it all in but she never stopped chaperoning.

Well, finally, it was one day along in January. Milly woke up in the morning—and she knew she was near her time. But, first thing in the morning, as always, she reached underneath her pillow for her keys—and then she smiled. For somebody must have stolen them while she was sleeping—and when she got up, and went to the window in her wrapper, the door of the house was wide open. And there was Hob and his wife, helping each other shovel snow from the doorstep, and Halbert and his wife were throwing snowballs at Harvey and his, and Howard was kissing the doctor's eldest behind the kitchen door. "Praise be!" said Milly. "I can have my baby in peace"—and she went down to congratulate them all.

Only then, there were the families and the relatives still to fix. But Milly had a plan for that—she had plans for everything. When they stole the girls away, they left a letter she drew up, signed by all the boys and expressing all the honorable intentions you could put a name to. But she was afraid that wouldn't cool down the townspeople much, even when they thought it over, and it didn't.

One day when the first thaws had come and Milly's baby was about six weeks old, Hob came running in from his lookout post.

"They're coming, Milly!" he said. "The whole dum town! They've got rifles and scythes and ropes and they look mighty wild and bloodthirsty! What'll we do?"

"Do?" said Milly, perfectly calm. "You get the boys together and keep out of sight—and tell the girls to come here. For it's women's work, now, that'll save us, if anything will."

When she got the girls together, she gave them their orders. I guess they were a bit white-faced, but they obeyed. Then she looked out of the window—and there was the town, marching up the road, slow and steady. She'd have liked it better if they'd shouted or cried, but they didn't shout nor cry. The minister was in the lead, with his lips shut, and a six-foot rifle in his hand, and his face like an iron mask.

She saw them come up to the gate of the Pontipee place. The gate was wide open and nobody there to hinder. She could see them take that in—and the little waver in the crowd. Because that made them feel queer.

Then they caught themselves and came tramping along toward the house, the minister still in the lead. Milly caught her breath, for they still looked awful mad. She knew what they'd expect when they got near the house—every window barred and every door bolted and red-hot bullets spitting through the loop-holes in the walls.

But the windows were open—you could see white curtains in them; there were plants on some of the sills. The door of the house stood ajar and Milly's cat was asleep on the doorstone, there in the sun.

They stood outside that door for quite a little bit, just milling around and staring. It was very quiet; they could hear their own breath breathe and their own hearts knock. Finally the minister brushed his face, as if he were brushing a cobweb away from it, and he gripped his gun and went up on the porch and knocked at the open door. He'd intended to stomp up those steps like a charge of cavalry, but he walked soft, instead. He couldn't have told you why.

44

He knocked once and he knocked again—and then Milly was standing in the door, with her baby in her arms.

Somebody at the back of the crowd dropped the scythe he was carrying, and another one coughed in his hand.

"You're just in time to christen my child, your reverence," said Milly. "Have you brought that rifle to help you christen my child?"

The minister's eyes dropped, after a minute, and he lowered his rifle but he still held it in the crook of his arm.

"Your child?" he said, and his voice was as low as Milly's, but there was a fierceness in it. "What about my child?"

"Listen!" said Milly, raising her hand, and the whole crowd fell dead still. Then from somewhere in the house came the hum of a spinning-wheel, low and steady, and a woman's voice, humming with the wheel.

"That's your child you hear, your reverence," said Milly. "Does she sound hurt, your reverence, or does she sound content?"

The minister hesitated for a moment and the crowd fell dead still again. Then they all heard the hum of the wheel and the hum of the woman's voice, humming back and forth to each other, as they did their work in the world.

"She sounds content—heaven help me!" said the minister, and a twist went over his face. But then there was a sudden outburst of cries and questions from the others. "My child, what about my child?" "Where's Mary?" "Is Susy safe?"

"Listen!" said Milly again, and they all fell silent once more. And, from somewhere, there came the splash of a churn and the voice of a woman talking to the butter to make it come; and the rattling of pans in a kitchen and a woman singing at her work; and the slap of clothes on a laundry board and the little clatter a woman makes setting table.

"There's your children," said Milly. "Hear 'em? Don't they sound all right? And—dinner will be ready in about half an hour—and you're all staying, I hope."

Then the daughters came out and their folks rushed to them; and, after all the crying and conniptions were over, Milly introduced the parents to their sons-in-law.

My Ninety Acres

LOUIS BROMFIELD

This selection from Pleasant Valley, *told with great tenderness and simplicity, reveals the great love of a man for his wife and his land. A story of faith-keeping which made Walter Oakes' farm the best in the valley.*

I HAVE A FRIEND, a little old man, who lives just over the hill in Possum Run Valley in a small neat white house on a farm which is generally known as "My Ninety Acres." It has never actually been given that name as other farms are named "Long View" or "Shady Grove." The name is not painted on the red barn or on a fancy sign. Nevertheless, throughout the valley everybody always refers to Walter Oakes' farm as "My Ninety Acres." At first, years ago when Walter was still a young and vigorous man, they used to speak of "My Ninety Acres" with a half-mocking, half-affectionate smile, especially the big farmers who owned a lot of land, because Walter always talked about that ninety acres as if it were a ranch of many thousand acres like the vast King Ranch in Texas or a whole empire, as if he were Augustus Caesar or Napoleon referring to "My Empire." Some of the old farmers, I think, believed Walter a bumptious and pretentious young man.

But as time passed, and Walter turned into a solid middle-aged farmer and later into an old man, the smiles and mild sense of mockery went out, and My Ninety Acres became simply the name of the place the way a farm was known as the Ferguson Place or Shady Lawn Farm. Nobody in the valley any longer finds anything confusing or absurd about the name. I think this is so partly because in places like the valley, people come to accept the name that is natural to a place, and partly because as the years passed old Walter earned the right to say, "My Ninety Acres," as Augustus Caesar might say "My Empire."

He had a right to speak of it with pride. It wasn't the conventional

46

Currier and Ives farm one expects from the long tradition of American farming—a bright, new place, with new wire fences, and cattle standing like statues in a pasture that was more like a lawn than a pasture. There was, indeed, a certain shagginess about it, a certain wild and beautiful look with that kind of ordered romantic beauty which was achieved by the landscape artists of the eighteenth century who fell under the influence of Jean Jacques Rousseau's romantic ideas regarding nature. The white house was small, but always well-painted and prosperous in appearance, and there was no finer barn than Walter's with its red paint, its big straw shed and its ornate shutters and cupolas painted white, and there were no finer cattle in the whole county than those which stood behind the white-painted wooden fences of the barnyard staring at you, fat and sleek and contented, as you drove past My Ninety Acres.

The romantic shagginess appeared too in the garden around the small white house with its green shutters that stood beneath two ancient Norway spruces. The patches of lawn were kept neatly mowed, but surrounding them grew a jungle of old-fashioned flowers and shrubs—lilacs, standing honeysuckle, syringa, bleeding heart, iris, peonies, tiger lilies, day lilies, old-fashioned roses like the Seven Sisters and the Piebald and the Baltimore Belle. At the back, the little vegetable garden was neat enough with its rows of vegetables and its peach and pear and quince trees in a row inside the white picket fence.

But beyond the borders of the garden the shagginess continued. There weren't any bright, new, clean wire fences. The wire along the fencerows was hidden beneath sassafras and elderberry and wild black raspberry, and the woodlot on the hill above the creek was not a clear place with the grass eaten short by cattle; the cattle had been fenced out and the trees, from seedlings to great oaks, grew rankly.

But despite the farm's shagginess, no fields in the valley produced such big crops or pastured such fine cattle and hogs as My Ninety Acres. The shagginess didn't exist, the neighbors came to understand, because Walter was lazy or a bad farmer—there was no more hardworking man in the whole valley. They were that way because Walter wanted them like that—Walter and Nellie.

I never saw Nellie Oakes—she died before I was born—but my father told me about her. In his time she had been the prettiest girl in the valley, and she taught at the Zion High School until when she was twenty-two she married Walter Oakes. People wondered why she chose him when she might have married Homer Drake, whose father owned four hundred and fifty acres of the best land in the county, or Jim Neilson, whose family owned the bank and the feed mill in Darlington. She could have had her choice of any of the catches of the valley and she chose Walter Oakes, who had no more than ninety acres of poor hill land he had just bought because he didn't have money enough for anything better.

In the parlor of the little white house on My Ninety Acres there hangs an enlarged photograph of Walter and Nellie taken at the time of their marriage. It is hand-colored and the bride and bridegroom are standing like statues, each with a clamp obviously fastened at the back of the head in order to "hold the pose," but even the stiffness and artificial coloring cannot alter or subdue the look of youth and health and courage that is in both of them.

Walter, the thin, bent old man who was my neighbor and friend, stands there in the photograph, stalwart and handsome and full of courage, one big muscular hand on Nellie's shoulder. He was blond with blue eyes and the gentle look which big, strong men often have because there is no need for them to be pugnacious or aggressive.

On a chair, beside and a little in front of him, sits Nellie in a white dress with leg-of-mutton sleeves and a full-flounced skirt—dark, more beautiful than pretty, with big dark eyes, holding in her small hands a lace handkerchief and a bunch of lilacs. I think Nellie was beautiful rather than pretty because of the look of intelligence. Even today, you sometimes hear old people in the valley say, "Nellie Oakes was a mighty smart girl—the only woman I ever knew who was as smart as she was pretty."

Nellie, so far as I can discover, never told anybody why she chose to marry Walter instead of one of the catches of the valley, but I know from all the long story that it was because she was in love with him. As it has turned out, she was right because the big four-hundred-and-fifty-acre Drake place which Homer inherited had gone downhill ever since Homer took possession of it, and today, with its wornout fields and decaying buildings, it wouldn't bring as much as My Ninety Acres. And Jim Neilson died long ago, a drunkard, having lost both the bank and the feed mill. But My Ninety Acres is the richest, prettiest farm in all the county, although Nellie isn't there to enjoy its beauty and prosperity. I say she isn't there because she died a long time ago, but sometimes when I walked about My Ninety Acres with

48

old Walter, I wasn't at all sure she wasn't there, enjoying its beauty and richness as much as Walter himself.

I am forty-eight years old, and Nellie died before I was born when she gave birth to her second son, Robert.

My father was a gentle man. He tried a great many ways of making a living for his family and none of them succeeded very well, I think because his heart was never in them. His heart was always in the land, in the trees and the wild birds, in streams and fields of corn, and in people. He loved people and talk and friendliness, and among his good friends was Walter Oakes. My father never went through the valley without stopping at My Ninety Acres; usually I was with him, for there was between us, even when I was very small, the knowledge that we both loved the country.

Sometimes when we stopped at My Ninety Acres for a meal or for the night, I stayed and played about the barn with Robert Oakes, who was two years older than I, and his brother John, who was two years older than Robert. Sometimes, if it was a Sunday, we went fishing or swimming. Sometimes I simply trudged behind my father and Walter Oakes and his two sheepdogs as they walked about My Ninety Acres. I did not know then that among men who were as close to each other as my father and Walter Oakes, conversation wasn't necessary.

I was always surprised at how often Walter would say, "Nellie wanted me to put this field into permanent pasture, but we couldn't afford not to use it for row crops." Or: "It's funny how many good ideas a woman can have about farming. Now, Nellie always said . . ." Sometimes I'd return to the house believing I would find there the Nellie whom I had never seen, waiting for us with a good supper on the table.

But Nellie was never there. There was only an elderly widow-woman named Mrs. Ince, a distant cousin of Walter's who came to keep house and look after him and the boys after Nellie Oakes died. She was a queer old woman, very thin and very active, who was always asking Walter how Nellie had molded the butter or pickled the beets, because she wanted everything to be the way he liked it. She could not have been more than fifty, but to a small boy like myself, she seemed immensely old.

She was, as I remember her, plain and kind and dull, with the meekness which often characterized indigent widows of her generation who were grateful for a roof over their heads, something to eat and a little spending money. When she came to My Ninety Acres some of the old women in the valley talked of the impropriety of her living there in the same house with Walter. I know now that anyone who had ever known Nellie must have been mad to think Walter Oakes ever had any thoughts about poor, drab Mrs. Ince. She was someone to do the housekeeping for a vigorous man and two wild, vigorous boys.

People in the valley couldn't see why Walter Oakes didn't get married again. And a good many widows and spinsters certainly set their caps for him.

But Walter never showed any signs of marrying again. He was always polite, and his blue eyes sometimes twinkled when he saw what the good ladies were up to. He didn't leave My Ninety Acres save to go to town to buy or sell something or to go to the valley church on Sunday with Mrs. Ince and the boys. He'd come home, change his clothes and spend the rest of the day walking round the place. Sometimes, to the scandal of the old ladies of the valley, he'd make hay with the boys on a Sunday afternoon.

I remember him saying to my father, "They talk about my working on Sunday or plowing, but when the ground is ready or hay has to be taken in, it has to be taken care of. The good Lord wouldn't like to see His beasts eating poor hay all winter because some old woman said it was wrong to work on Sunday. Nellie always said, 'The better the day, the better the deed,' and quoted that bit of the Bible about the ox falling by the way."

The two boys were nice kids, and smart like Nellie. John, the older one, looked like her, with dark eyes and dark hair. Robert, the younger, looked like Walter. The father wanted both of them to go to college and get a good education.

WITH ALL my family, I went away from the county and the country when I was fourteen, and I was gone for thirty years. At first my father heard from Walter, brief, unsatisfactory letters written on lined paper torn out of a copybook; but neither Walter nor my father was a very good letter writer. They were the kind of men who could not communicate without the warmth that came of physical presence. Letters didn't mean much. When they met again, even after years, the relationship would be exactly the same.

I know very little of the details of what happened during those years, only a fact or two, and what little I picked up from Walter as an old man. The war came, and in it John, the older son, whom Walter secretly loved best because he looked so much like Nellie, was killed at St. Mihiel. He was twenty-one and just finished with agricultural college. Walter had counted on his returning to the farm, marrying and producing grandchildren to carry it on. Robert did not stay on the farm. He was smart, like Nellie, but he didn't want to be a farmer.

Robert had ambitions. He had had them even as a small boy. Sometimes when the three of us as kids sat naked among the wild mint by the swimming hole, we talked about what we were going to do in life, and Robert always said, "I'm going to be a great man and get rich and have an automobile with a man to drive it."

In the thirty years I was away from the valley Robert had achieved exactly what he had planned. By the time I returned to the valley Robert was president of the Consolidated Metals Corporation, and he had made many millions. I think he must have had both Nellie's "smartness" and Walter's steadfastness.

At the end of thirty years I came back to my county to live for the rest of my life, and I bought a farm in the valley over the hill from My Ninety Acres. In the first weeks I never thought about my father's friend, Walter Oakes. Indeed, I had very nearly forgotten his existence. And then one day I heard Wayne, one of the boys on the farm, say something about My Ninety Acres, and I asked, "Is Walter Oakes still alive?"

"Alive!" said Wayne. "I'll say he's alive! The livest old man in the county. You ought to see that place. Brother, that's the kind of farm I'd like to own! He raises as much on it as most fellows raise on five times that much land."

Wayne, of course, was only twenty. He couldn't remember how once people had laughed when Walter Oakes spoke proudly of My Ninety Acres. Clearly, they didn't laugh any more. Clearly, Walter was the best farmer in all the county.

The next Sunday I walked over the hills to My Ninety Acres. As I came down the long hill above the farm I saw that it hadn't changed much. The house still looked well-painted and neat with its white walls and green shutters, and the barn was a bright new prosperous red. But the shrubs and flowers had grown so high they almost hid the house. It was a day in June, and as I walked down the long hill the

51

herd of fat, white-faced cattle stood knee-deep in blue grass watching me. I hadn't taken the dogs because Walter always kept a couple of sheepdogs, and I didn't want a fight.

As I walked down the hill I thought: This is the most beautiful farm in America; the most beautiful, rich farm in the world—My Ninety Acres. The corn stood waist-high and vigorous and green, the oats thick and strong, the wheat already turning a golden-yellow. In the meadow the bumblebees were working on clover that rose almost as high as a man's thighs. In all that plenty there was something almost extravagant and voluptuous. The rich fields were like one of the opulent women painted by Rubens; like a woman well-loved whose beauty thrives and increases by love-making.

I pushed open the little gate and walked into the dooryard with the neatly mown grass bordered by lilacs and peonies and day lilies. The door stood open but no one answered my knock, and thinking the old man might be having a Sunday nap, I stepped into the house and called out, "Walter! Walter Oakes!" But no one answered me.

I hadn't been in the house for thirty years, and I didn't remember my way about it, so when I opened the door which I thought led into the long room that had once been used both for eating and living, I found that I was mistaken. I had stepped into the parlor, instead.

It had that musty smell of country parlors and the shutters were closed, but there was enough light for me to see the enlarged hand-colored portrait of Walter Oakes and his bride Nellie above the fireplace. Out of the stiff old picture they looked at me, young, vigorous, filled with courage and hope and love. It struck me again how pretty Nellie was.

I stood for a little time looking at it and then turned and closed the door behind me. I went out through the living room and the kitchen, where everything was clean and neat, and I thought: He must have a woman to look after him.

By now, I remembered that I should find old Walter somewhere in the fields. Sunday afternoon he always spent walking over the place.

So I went down toward the creek, and as I turned the corner by the barnyard I saw him down below moving along a fencerow. Two sheepdogs were with him, the great-great-great-grandchildren of the pair I had known as a boy. They were running in and out of the hedgerow yapping joyously. The fencerow bordered a meadow of deep thick hay, and below among feathery willows wound the clear spring stream where I had often gone swimming with Walter's boys—John, who had been everything Walter had hoped for in a son, and Robert, who had gone away to become rich and powerful. There was something lonely about the figure of the old man, and I felt a lump come into my throat.

Then I noticed that there was something erratic in his progress. He would walk a little way and then stop and, parting the bushes, peer into the tangled fencerow. Once he got down on his knees and disappeared completely in the clover.

Finally, as he started back, I set off down the slope toward him. It was the barking of the dogs as they came toward me that attracted his attention. He stopped and peered in my direction, shading his eyes with his big hands. He was still tall and strong, although he was well over seventy. He stood thus until I was quite near him, and then I saw a twinkle come into the bright blue eyes.

"I know," he said, holding out his hand. "You're Charlie Downes' boy. I heard you'd come back." I said I'd been trying to get over to see him, and then he asked, "And your father? How's he?" I told him my father was dead. "I'm sorry," he said casually, as if the fact of death was nothing. "I hadn't heard. I don't get around much." I explained that my father had been ill a long time and that death had come as a release.

"He was a good man," he said. "A fine man. We sort of dropped out of writing each other a good many years ago." He sighed. "But after all, writing don't mean much." The implication of the speech was, clearly enough, that friends communicated without writing, no matter how great the distance between them.

Then suddenly he seemed to realize that I must have seen him ducking in and out of the fencerow. A faint tinge of color came into his face, and he said shyly, "I was just snoopin' around my ninety acres. I like to see what goes on here, and I don't get time during the week." He looked down at his big hands and noticed, as I did, that some of the black damp loam of the fencerow still clung to them. He brushed them awkwardly together. "I was just digging into the fencerow to see what was going on there underground. A fellow can learn a lot by watching his own land and what goes on in it and on it. My son John—you remember, the one that was killed in the war—he went to agricultural school, but I don't think he learned more there than I've learned just out of studying my own ninety acres. Nellie always said a farm could teach you more than you could teach it, if you just kept your eyes open. Nellie . . . that was my wife."

"Of course," I said, "I remember."

Then he said, "Come with me, and I'll show you something." I followed him, and presently he knelt and parted the bushes. I knelt beside him, and he pointed. "Look!" he said, and his voice grew warm. "Look at the little devils."

I looked and could see nothing but dried brown leaves with a few delicate fern fronds thrusting through them. Old Walter chuckled and said, "Can't see 'em, can you? Look, over there by that hole in the stump." I looked, and then slowly I saw what he was pointing at. They sat in a little circle in a tiny nest, none of them much bigger than the end of one of old Walter's big thumbs—seven tiny quail. They sat very still, not moving a feather, lost among the dry brown leaves. I might not have seen them at all but for the brightness of their little eyes.

"Smart!" he said, with the same note of tenderness in his voice. "They know! They don't move!" Then a cry of "Bob White!" came from the thick, fragrant clover behind us, and Walter said, "The old man's somewhere around." The whistle was repeated, again and then again.

Old Walter stood up and said, "They used to laugh at me for letting the bushes grow up in my fencerows, but they don't any more. When the chinch bugs come along all ready to eat up my corn, these little fellows will take care of 'em." He chuckled. "There's nothing a quail likes as much as a chinch bug. Last year Henry Talbot, next to me, lost ten acres of corn, all taken by the bugs. Henry's a nut for clear fencerows. He doesn't leave enough cover along 'em for a grasshopper. He thinks that's good farming, the old fool!"

WE WERE walking now up the slope from the creek toward the house, and he went on talking. "That fencerow beside you," he said, "is full of birds—quail and song sparrows and thrushes—the farmer's best protection. It was Nellie that had that idea about lettin' fencerows grow up. I didn't believe her at first. I was just as dumb as most other farmers. She said bushes in fencerows was natural, and it was wrong to upset the balance of nature. Nellie was hardly ever wrong . . . I guess never."

As we reached the house, old Walter said, "Funny how I knew you. I'd have known you anywhere. You're so like your father. I've missed him all these years, especially when anything happened he would have liked," he chuckled, "like these baby quail today. Come in and we'll have a glass of buttermilk."

I went with him into the springhouse. It was built of stone with great troughs inside cut out of big blocks of sandstone, and the water ran icy-cold out of a tile that came through the wall. Cream, milk, butter and buttermilk stood in crocks in the icy water, each covered by a lid held in place by an ancient brick with velvety moss growing on its surface.

He picked up a pitcher with buttermilk in it, and I asked, "Who does your churning for you?"

He grinned. "I do it myself of an evening. I kinda like it."

We went and sat in the living room, and he brought glasses and two white napkins. It was buttermilk such as I had not tasted in thirty years—creamy, icy-cold with little flakes of butter in it.

I said, "What became of Mrs. Ince?"

He said, "Oh, she got old and sick and went back to live with her sister. I just didn't get anybody to take her place."

"You mean you're living here alone?"

"Yes." I started to say something and then held my tongue, but old Walter divined what I meant to ask and said, "No. It ain't lonely. I've always got the dogs. Jed Hulbert comes down and helps me with jobs I can't do alone, and his wife takes care of my laundry and cleans up once a week. Jed and his wife like the money, and they're nice people."

He smiled. "It doesn't seem to me like a farm is a lonely place. There's too much goin' on. Nellie used to say she didn't understand the talk of those women who said they got lonely. Nellie said there was always calves and horses and dogs and lambs and pigs, and that their company was about as good as most of them women who talked that way. And she always had her posy garden. Did you notice it coming in? It's mighty pretty now. Nellie planted everything in it, just the way they are today."

He was about to say something else, but checked himself and looked at me strangely. A secretive, almost sly look came into his eyes, and he turned away.

After an awkward pause I said, "Well, Robert did all right by himself. He always said he wanted a big automobile and a driver and a lot of money."

Then old Walter grinned at me. "Yes, I guess he got just about what he wanted. He's a good boy, but he's got some funny ideas." The old man chuckled. "He's been trying for years to get me to retire and live in the city where I could take it easy, or go down and live in Florida. I wouldn't know what to do with myself in a place like that. And what would become of my ninety acres? Or he's always wantin' to buy me a bigger place with a house full of gadgets or to buy me a lot of machinery. What would I want with a bigger place? Ninety acres is enough for any man if he takes care of it right, like he should. And anyway, it wouldn't be the same as my ninety acres. And I don't want machinery bought with his money. My ninety acres ought to buy its own machinery, and it does." A fierce note of pride came into his voice. "All the machinery it needs. Robert wants me to hire a couple to live here and do the work for me, but I wouldn't like that. Robert doesn't understand how I feel. I guess he thinks I'm a little crazy."

It was getting late and I rose, but the old man went on talking. "It's a pity about Robert not having any children. I guess his wife is all right. I don't see much of her. We don't have much in common. But it's a pity Robert never found a woman he could love."

That was the first and last time I ever heard him speak of his daughter-in-law, but out of the meager speech and the look in his eyes and the sound of his voice, I divined what she must be like.

"Robert comes to see me about once a year and stays for a day or two, but he's a pretty busy man with all the big affairs he has to manage."

"Tell him to drive over to see me the next time he comes," I said, "and you come over too."

He opened the screen door for me. "I'm afraid I don't get off my ninety acres very often any more. The place takes a lot of time when you're working it alone."

It wasn't the last time I saw old Walter. Before long, the Sunday-afternoon visits to My Ninety Acres became a habit. And I found gradually that old Walter knew more of the fundamentals of soil, of crops, of live stock than any man I have ever known. Some of them he had read in books and in farm papers, but he didn't trust the things he read until he tried them out, and many of them he didn't even

56

attempt to try out. Instinctively he rejected things which ran counter to the laws of Nature.

"Nellie," he would say, "always said that Nature and the land itself was the best answer to all these questions. If it wasn't natural it wasn't right, Nellie would say, and I've never found that she was wrong. She used to say there were two kinds of farms—the 'live' farms and the 'dead' ones, and you could tell the difference by looking at them. A 'live' farm was the most beautiful place in the world, and a 'dead' farm was the saddest. It depended on the men who worked them—whether a fellow loved the place or just went on pushing implements through the ground to make money. Nellie was awful smart about a lot of things."

A Man's Mother

GLADYS HASTY CARROLL

The old lady in the club car had said quietly, "The only reason a woman wants children is to do for them. When she can't do that. . . ." Read how Mother escaped her "understanding" family!

ALMOST BEFORE his train had pulled out of South Station, Carl P. Webster had taken a chair in the club car, was comfortably filling his pipe with a rich, spicy tobacco, and glancing up, with great good humor, at each fellow traveler who pushed open the door and cast an inquiring glance inside.

Carl was a big, ruddy-faced man. Insurance was his business. He wore a well-cut, gray tweed suit, blue shirt and tie, highly polished, intricately perforated brown shoes. And he was feeling fine.

He certainly was feeling fine, and when Carl felt that way, he liked to talk about it. Not a bad habit either. Too many seem to carry around a mouthful of trouble and worry, especially for strangers, especially lately. Carl was not like that. Not a bit. But who was he to criticize the rest? A man is made as he is. And as for a woman—

He chuckled, half aloud. Women, now. You couldn't get along without them, you certainly couldn't. As far as they went, they were fine. But times always came—and came pretty often—when nothing would do but a man.

Dorothy had certainly felt the need of one when she wrote that letter. Of course she had her husband, Ed, but apparently he was not much use. There are differences even in men. Ed Woodward was the kind to just keep quiet, let things run their course and handle themselves. Well, sometimes that works, but oftener it doesn't, and it's likely to come hard on womenfolks.

Dorothy sounded pretty desperate in that letter. It still wasn't clear to Carl why. Didn't she know he would come if she sent for him? Or did she have an idea he couldn't accomplish what he set out to, once he had set out? Maybe she had kind of forgotten what her brother was like, through these last twenty-five years that he had been getting back into Northern Maine only for a day or two in the summer now and then.

He shuffled through the papers in his bulging breast pocket and extracted, with discriminating thumb and forefinger, a cheap, thin envelope addressed in Dorothy's small hand. Studying this, he sighed, shook his head, and drew from it the letter within.

Dear Carl: I don't suppose you could plan so as to get up this way before long? I hate to bother you, but I've put it off as long as I dare to. I'm at my wit's end about Mother. She insists she is going back to the farm just as soon as it is warm enough. She won't even listen to anything I say about it. She just goes right ahead getting ready. She wrote up to Morris Bascom to fix the roof, and had Maud Bascom go in and clean, and she has ordered her stove wood. Isn't that awful?

It worries me for fear you'll think we haven't treated her well this winter, but if you could talk with her, I know she would tell you we've waited on her by inches. Both the young ones and I; yes, and Ed, too. You certainly have paid us well for her board, Carl, but honestly, I don't believe she could have got as much anywhere else for twice the money. I've cooked for her, every meal, just exactly what she wanted, whenever she would say. Mary-Sue has carried in her tea and crackers the first minute Mother stirred every morning. We put all the most comfortable furniture in her room, and still, of course, she'd had the run of the house. Ed hitched up her radio. Well, there, nothing has been too much, and she says so herself.

But still we can't do one thing with her when she gets contrary. She wants her own way, and she will have it. It's been so all winter. And now what she is set on is going back up there to the farm. I warn her how strange it will seem to her without Evie, and ask her what in the world she would do if she should fall, all alone so, and how she would feel in time of thundershowers. And I remind her how nice and careful you planned everything, as soon as Evie died, how you got help in to paint and paper my guest room, and bought that nice bed. I've even told her I know you wouldn't put up with her being there, if you knew of it—and of course you would have to know! But as I say, she will not listen to one word from me. Ed says I'm only blowing my breath against the wind. And I'm just about sick over it.

If you can't plan any way to get up here, do try to write to her as soon as you can. Though I must say I don't know if she would read the letter if she saw you were starting in about her not going back up home. She is simply bound and determined!   . . .

Smilingly shaking his head, Carl folded the paper into its creases, put it back into the envelope, and returned it to his pocket. He would show it to Minna, when he got back home, now that everything was settled.

It would not have done to let her see it before. A man can't expect his wife to feel the same about his mother as he does himself. It wouldn't be natural. Minna had kind of opposed him—in a nice way, of course—when he told her, at the time of his sister Evelyn's funeral last fall, how he had arranged for his mother to go right to Dorothy's house in the village, to stay.

"Does she want to, Carl?" Minna had asked.

"Want to? My dear, she's so upset right now that she don't know what she wants. But it's obvious she can't stay here alone, on this old rock heap. A woman 'most seventy-four years old? Don't be foolish. Why, Evie's told me, summers past, that she's all but had to breathe for Mother ever since—why, ever since Father died! She never got over the shock of that, Evie thought. Now, of course, losing Evie—well, she'll just have to learn to lean on Dorothy, that's all. And she will. They'll be good to her down there. They'll make her happy."

But all Minna would say was, "I know Dorothy will try."

It had been kind of aggravating to Carl, with all he had on his mind just then, to feel Minna hanging back. But all he could do, of course, was act as if he didn't notice. You can't blame a woman if her husband's family seem pretty much strangers to her. She can't be expected, for instance, to know how he feels about his mother . . . thinks of how she used to tuck him up when he was little, sing to him, and wait on him; and how he likes to feel, after he's got his growth, that one way or another he is making it up to her.

Big, ruddy-faced man that he was, Carl pulled out his handkerchief and blew his nose. He had to make quite a business of it, and when he finished, he found he had a neighbor at last; a stout, bright-eyed little old lady with a lapful of knitting. She glanced at him briefly and cheerfully, across her flying needles, and Carl felt instantly that they would understand each other.

Fifteen years ago his mother had looked rather like this. That was before his father died; about the time Dorothy married and went away; just before Evelyn, who was so much older than the others, gave up her teaching and came home. This little woman was somebody's mother, too, he thought.

"What you knitting?" he asked gently.

"Socks," she said. "Refugees'. About everybody, seems as though, is making sweaters, so I said to myself, I guess times call for anybody that can turn a heel to be turning 'em. I could knit a sock smooth as a smelt before I was eight years old, and even if I have let my hand get out these late lazy years, there's nothing to prevent its getting in again. It's going to be a cold winter in Europe."

"Well, now," Carl told her, "that's an idea for my mother! I don't know when she ever did any knitting, but no doubt she could. Yes, sir, I'm going to have my wife box up some yarn and send it to Mother as soon as I get home. That's an idea!"

"Maybe you'd better wait and talk it over with your mother. Maybe she'd have a better one. As I say, some knit sweaters and some socks; other ones get along faster on baby clothes. Or tacking comforters. It depends on where you're handiest."

Carl said largely, making a smoke ring, "Well, you see, I probably won't be talking with my mother again right away. Just been up there. Away up in the far corner of the coast of Maine. Can't get that distance from my office very often. Not more than once a year, generally. But I was up last fall. And now I've just been up again, getting her settled. She's had kind of a hard adjustment to make. Last fall she lost the daughter she'd been living with for years, and now she's making her home with another one. Yes, it's been hard for Mother, but she and I've had a nice little visit together, and we understand each other pretty well; always have. She's all straightened out now. She does need something to take up her time, though. And seems to me knitting would be just the thing. But I'll mention the sewing materials to her, too, and if she wants them, Minna can send them up."

The old lady only nodded, did not speak. Carl did not feel she had lost interest in him. It seemed that she was thinking busily about what he had said, perhaps trying to picture him and his mother together.

His own thoughts, too, went back over that visit with pride and a kind of wistful pleasure. He was glad, of course, that he had grown to such stature, in body and mind, that he could take a man's place with his mother when she needed one; glad that she had such a son to lean on in the weakness of age. Still, he felt a little sorry for himself that there was no one left now, no one at all, who thought of him as a boy; and sorry, too, for her—who had once been as sturdy and upstanding, crisp-talking and bright-eyed as this one beside him, independent and full of advice to others—that she must revert to child's estate, meekly lean on his arm, accept his guidance, yield to his authority. Such shifts are not made without a wrench; but made, of course, they must be.

He had been disappointed, he realized now for the first time, when his mother did not meet him at the village station. It had been a good many years since he had gone home by train, but in the old days—when he came from college, or from waiting on tables at a summer hotel—it had always been his mother who trotted down the platform beside his coach, a brisk little figure in wrinkled, rusty black coat and a navy-blue hat bent into an astonishing shape, not only by wind and rain but by lying forgotten in a back corner of some crowded closet shelf. She would swing her handbag gaily—always an old one, cracked, with the handle about to split, no matter what he had given her last Christmas—and as soon as she met him, would seize his elbow in her strong fingers and steer him swiftly around the corner of the station to where she had her horse and buggy hitched.

She had been a quick-moving person in those days, and favored a good, lively horse. How straight she used to sit on her buggy seat, driving him out to the farm, telling him from the corner of her mouth about the chickens and the apple crop, with her reins in one hand and trim little whip in the other.

But yesterday there had been only Dorothy and her towheaded boy waiting for him, and Ed Woodward's grubby old coupe to ride in to the Woodwards' brown-shingled bungalow. The boy had sat with the bags in the back, his legs dangling and the steel cover jacked up over his head like the sharp shadow of doom; and Dorothy had taken anxious pains, it seemed, to drive well over on the left side of the street, talking constantly, in her light, thin voice, of how hard she tried all the time, but how little success she had.

"Don't you worry," he kept telling her in a big, confident voice. "Don't you worry. Just leave this all to me, Dollie!"

"There, Carl, I'm only too glad to. But I honestly don't believe you know what you're letting yourself in for. And I don't myself. I wish I did. Whether she'll take it calm while you're talking, and then simply rebel, or whether she'll go to pieces and have hysterics, or something—I worry about her heart! Of course at her age it can't be what it was—but there, she's an awful strong-minded woman, Carl! I never realized it any more than I have this winter! Why, if her body was up with her spirit—"

"Now, don't you worry," Carl kept saying. "Mother and I understand each other pretty well. Always have. There won't be any trouble. Don't you worry."

But it had been another shock—he realized now—that when the car turned into the Woodwards' yard, his mother was not on the porch, or even at the window, looking for him. He had to get into the house and through the living room, kiss Dorothy's thin, towheaded daughter, and be led by her into a bedroom which opened off the living room, before he saw his mother at all. She was sitting in a big Cogswell chair, with her feet on the hassock and a bright new afghan in parrot colors spread across her knees, and she had on a white dress with big, full sleeves, and lace gathered up around her neck, and a lavender scarf across her shoulders, and her hair crinkled up fuzzy across her forehead and around her ears. Her face seemed so much the least of her.

"Well, hell-o, Mother! How's the girl?"

"Why, I'm all right, I guess, Carl."

She had always been a hard one to kiss. The best way used to be to pick her up in your arms, swing her right off the floor and hold her there until she squealed and dropped her head in confusion. Then you could find her cheek, surprisingly soft and warm, never cold and tissue-papery, like some old ladies'. But now, of course, she could be handled only very gently, and Carl stood over her, big, burly, awkward as a bear.

"Sit down, Carl. How did you leave Minna? Why didn't she come too?"

"Well, I'll tell you, Mother. You see, I made up my mind kind of sudden, and she had a lot of meetings scheduled— she's into war work, head over heels. Besides, where I was coming by train—"

"Something new for you, ain't it—getting about by train? Anything happen to your car?"

"Oh, no. No, Mother. But I thought I'd save time traveling by night. It's a pretty busy season at the office right now, so I'm kind of in a rush. This way, you see, I get here in good season in the morning and have my daylight hours for visiting with you!"

He smiled at her broadly, pushing his cheeks back.

"You going again tonight, then?" she wanted to know.

"Oh, no. No, Mother. Not by any means. Not until an eleven-o'clock train tomorrow forenoon. That'll get me to the office Thursday morning, soon as it opens, and hardly anybody will have had time to notice I was gone!" He insisted, "So we've got the whole of today, and this evening as long as you feel like sitting up, and the best part of tomorrow for our visit. Pretty good, don't you think?"

"Why, there," she said. "Of course it's better than nothing. Still, I should rather waited until you could stop long enough to get a little change yourself. You look to me as if you stayed shut in too much. Reminds me how your father said when you went off to college, 'There, he's going—going to shut himself up to learn how to live shut up!' What you need, Carl, is a couple of weeks anyway to roam the fields, just the way you used to, and go off fishing down the brook with some meat and biscuits in a paper bag in your pocket. Remember how good your little pickerels used to taste when I fried 'em up in pork fat and corn meal for supper, soon as you got home?"

"Good!", Carl exclaimed. "Well, I guess they tasted good! Why, I've told people who got excited about broiled brook trout in fancy New York places that they didn't have an idea what fish could taste like! My mother, I've told them—"

Right then her feet had given a jerk, as if of their own accord, and dropped to the floor. The afghan slid off and lay in a lurid swirl. When he bent to pick it up, she kicked it away.

"Don't bother," she said. "It's got my legs now so they feel as if they was in a oven. I let Mary-Sue lay it there because she wanted you to be sure to see it. She's been working on it all winter. An awful waste of time, it seemed to me, but I managed not to say so. Poor young one."

She looked discontentedly around the room with its new bed and paint and paper, all Dorothy's most comfortable chairs, the electric lamps, the flowered art square.

"As I am here," she said, "I don't ever have a chance to cook a fish or anything else. I can't even boil a pot of coffee, and I do think Dorothy makes the worst coffee I ever put my mouth to. Thick and rank—it's terrible! I don't know what she can do to coffee to make it taste the way hers does; I'm sure I don't."

"Well, now, Mother," Carl told her soothingly, "I don't see any reason why you shouldn't have a place fixed somewhere to plug in a coffeepot and maybe a toaster, so you can fix your own breakfast anyway, if you wanted to. I know a lot of people—"

"Well, there is plenty of reasons," his mother snapped, "even if you don't see 'em. One is that Dorothy would be so hurt she'd have her never-get-over-it. Tears come to her just as easy, Carl, as they ever did!"

They both laughed, but he noticed that his mother grudged herself this levity. She had serious matters on her mind and did not wish to be distracted from them.

"Another reason," she said, "is that meals have to be cleaned up after, and I haven't got anything to clean up with and Dorothy wouldn't let me use it if I had. She'd be in here wiping and brushing and clattering around 'til noontime every day, while I tried to keep out from underfoot!

"But the best reason is that I don't like your electrical contraptions! I always made my coffee on a stove! And I don't like toast, either! I always had warmed-up potatoes and a piece of meat or an egg and some good, fresh bread and doughnuts for my breakfast, and you know it! I always said I never was myself 'til I got a good, hearty breakfast into me, and now I never get one! I ain't had one for six months!"

Carl hoped that Dorothy and her towheaded children had principles which kept them from eavesdropping. He did not want them to hear this plain speaking, and wanted even less for them to know that he could think of no answer to make to it, at the instant, beyond an unconvincing chuckle.

Then, sitting up as straight as ever she had on a buggy seat, but now with her hands clasped in her lap, his mother demanded shrewdly, "What set you out to make this rush visit anyway, Carl? I know something did. It never just happened. You ain't that kind, to go off halfcocked, any more than I ever was. What are you here for? Let's not beat around the bush any longer."

So there had been nothing for it but to begin, and that was what he did. He pulled his rocker a little closer to the Cogswell chair, put his big hand over his mother's little clasped ones, and began to talk, telling her what Dorothy worried about, and what she had written him; how of course it was all Dorothy's imagination; that he knew beyond a doubt his mother was too sensible by far to have any such idea in her head; why, he could remember his father saying a thousand times that she had just as good judgment as any man!

He talked about how far the home place was from neighbors, and all the bedrooms were upstairs, and how she would remember that sometimes when the telephone went out, it didn't get repaired for days. But here in the village with Dollie, it was different; if she wanted anything in the night, she had only to speak, and the doctor was just two doors away. If there was anything she wanted changed—anything at all—any time, she had only to let Carl know. Confidentially, he was thinking that maybe she was feeling a little cramped in such close quarters, and if that was so, he would do what he could to help Ed into a bigger house before another winter. Everything was going to be all right—he had made up his mind to that—just right for his mother; to keep her safe, and well, and happy.

She listened closely, without interrupting and without taking her eyes from his face.

Some way, to keep on talking to her while she just sat like that, was one of the hardest things Carl ever did.

But when he finished, she only caught her breath in a short, soft sigh, and said, "I see what you mean. You needn't have come so far to tell it over. You could have wrote it just as well. It ain't right you should be bothered this way. I never meant to be a bother to you; never, Carl. You've been a good boy. You've been a good son and a good brother all your life, and I want you to remember, as long as you live, that I said so. When the time comes that—that you don't have me to tend out on, I want you to remember I said you thought of every-thing—and done everything—and I was a lucky woman to have you, always so generous—and thoughtful. You plan everything just as you see fit, Carl. I shan't make you any trouble."

In the club car, beside the little old lady with the steel needles fly-ing among gray yarn, Carl had to take out his handkerchief and blow his nose again. He was not at all ashamed. He smiled around at her with his eyes still wet.

"I keep thinking," he said, "what a time my mother and I've just had. I wouldn't have believed it could happen. I tell you, it was like that poem, 'Backward, turn backward—' you know? 'And make me a boy—' You see, my mother's a real old lady. Seventy-four years old, and been delicate for a long time. But yesterday morning, seemed as if seeing me kind of brightened her right up, and she told me there was just one thing she wanted with all her heart, and that was for the two of us to have one more night alone together on the old place. Well, it was a nice, warm day—hot, really, for the season—so I told her, I said, 'By George, we will!' And we did. She packed up what she thought she'd need; I got her into my brother-in-law's car; I bought what she told me to at the store where she always traded; and we drove off up into the hills. . . ."

A smoother road than it used to be, but with, for the most part, the same curves. The same dark, clean, brave-sounding brook running alongside. The same old houses peeling paint, sitting in their small, rocky fields and peering out like old faces from the woods, or like Barred Rock hens burrowing in sand and ruffling their dusty feathers. At one place a man was plowing with a single horse. At another, two children, barefoot, dropped cut potatoes along open rows. Carl re-membered how he had done this, too, laying his potatoes on marks which his father had made with the corner of a hoe, that the hills should be just so far apart and no farther. There was always this smell of white lilacs slowly opening, in planting time, and wild pear blossoms; it hung on the air and was folded into the ground with the potatoes.

"Luckily, the house was clean as a whistle. Mother had had a neighbor see to it when she was harboring some notion she might go up there to stay a while this summer. Of course that was foolish. She couldn't do that alone, at her age, and of course there is nobody free to go with her. It wouldn't be safe anyway, so far from town—doctors, you know, and so on. But we had our one night, anyway. As I say, the house was clean, and the shed full of wood. So I made her sit on the porch in the sun, out of the wind, while I built up big, roaring fires in both stoves. Then we left them to dry out the place, and mother and I walked over just about every foot of that farm. I wouldn't have believed she could do it. Why, she wouldn't even let me give her a hand in the rough spots. Just went skipping along, like a girl, almost, until I had to sprint to keep up with her. Seems it frets Mother that the land has been neglected so, since Father died, and trees that have died out in the orchard haven't been replaced. Says they always wanted that place to be a shelter and haven for their children, if the time ever came that they needed it. Says the way things are looking now, a farm is a pretty good piece of property to have!"

Carl chuckled.

"Why," he said, "the president of a big corporation never had more on his mind to check up on than my mother had yesterday!"

But then when they did get back to the house, and he let her go inside, she was all woman again on the instant. Maud Bascom was a pretty good hand to clean, she said, but whiffle-minded, and always had been; dishes never went back into cupboards in the order that she took them out, and there was almost always at least one place she missed—like this closet under the stairs! She made Carl take the wood-box to the door and sweep it out before he filled it, and she scrubbed the water pails before she sent him to the spring.

She wouldn't let him touch the beds, but told him to go see how the cellar had got through the winter, and when he came back, the beds were all made with sheets and blankets they had brought from Dorothy's, and she had towels out which smelled of spice, the way hers always had. She let him set the table, but scolded him because he forgot napkins and put the tumblers—thick ones, which dried beef had once come in—on the wrong side of the plates.

"Won't you never learn?" she scolded. "There's a right way and a wrong way, as the feller says, but seems as though the wrong way always comes first. . . . Now, I don't just like the looks of that water. Here's a pair of your father's overalls. You see if that spring don't need cleaning out! What we've brought along will do us for this noontime, but before I leave here, I want my fill of some decent-tasting water. How folks live with all these chemicals they swallow nowadays—"

The spring bubbled up between the sprawling, naked roots of an old oak tree, and at the far end of the little pool it made, ferns grew. The sand in the bottom was white as the best Maine beach. A branch from the oak had fallen into it, but Carl took that out, scooped up the floating bits of bark, and now there was nothing at all the matter with it. It was just as it had always been. He sat beside it a long time, drawing the lace of a stalk of fern between his fingers, and remembered the potato hole his father had once dug into the sidehill there, to hold a bigger crop than he had room for in the cellar. That had been a great fall, when Stephen Webster could fill his cellar with potatoes, sell enough to buy a barrel of flour, a barrel of sugar, and still have potatoes left to stow away in the "tater hole" on the sidehill, just above where water bubbled out of the earth as inevitable as breath from a man's mouth, and more so.

"Carl! Your dinner's ready! Come along in and eat it while it's hot!"

She had always wanted them to eat while the food was hot. Carl smiled, remembering, and went more quickly than his father often had.

He washed his face at the sink, slopping water over his hair. There were still combs in the steel case—pieces of combs, anyway—and the same cracked mirror in a gilded frame.

"There," his mother told him. "Don't bother slickin' it back so. It won't stay. That kink's grown right into it. Your Uncle Orrin's was just the same."

They had a blue-and-white-checked cotton cloth with darns in the center and frayed corners, the heavy red bowl with a spoon thrust deep into the sugar, green pepper-sauce bottle, molasses jug with yellow spots like thumb prints, and big aluminum salt and pepper shakers. There was fish hash in a white oval dish, and hot biscuits, and chopped pickles, and tea.

"I wish we had reddishes up," she said, a little plaintively.

"And peas, Mother?" he asked, laughing. "And cucumbers?"

"There," she told him. "I know it. I'm always impatient for green stuff to grow, almost before it's planted!"

"Won't be long now," he said, and looking past her, it almost seemed he saw brown earth lying rich and loose just across the road. He looked again, and exclaimed, "Why, Morris has planted right over here this year, hasn't he? Seems as though it won't be very handy—so far from his house."

"I know it," his mother said. "I thought of that myself. But I guess

68

he don't mean to let any of his land run down the way ours has. Morris is one that tends to things pretty close."

When they finished, with pieces of warm apple pie and more tea, she said, "There, now, Carl, I want you to see if you can't catch a fish. Your old bamboo pole's right where you always kep' it, on the shed door there, and I don't doubt there's worms out beyond the clothes yard, where there always was. You go along. I've got my mouth all fixed for a mess of pickerel!"

So, still in overalls, he had gone out to dig his worms. He might have felt foolish, but there was no one to see.

There was a good feeling about driving a fork deep into spongy ground by the slow pressure of one foot, and turning up the blind, white roots, the long, live, pinkish worms. He whistled, digging. He found a rusty, blue-banded pail, thinking it must be the same one he had once used to carry berries in. He went down through the orchard, out into the sun of the pasture, on again into the shade of alders which covered both banks of the brook. Here there were dragonflies, skimming. . . . A bobolink . . . Two . . . His line sang through the air and settled. . . . Silent . . . When he took a step, the whole woods listened. . . . But only woods, and birds, and darting insects . . .

"We had our pickerels all right," Carl told the old lady in the club car. "I got four. Small ones, but enough for the two of us for supper. Mother fried them to a turn, rolled in cornmeal, with saltpork fat. And, if you'll believe it, with all the rest, she had dug up, and cleaned, and cooked—dandelion greens! The way she does, she boils her potatoes right in with the greens. They sure taste good. Boy, what a meal we had!"

He shook his head, chuckling.

"I helped her wash up the dishes, took the milk and butter down cellar, and got in more wood. Then we sat down beside the sitting-room stove—one of these—you know?—they used to call chunk stoves —and we talked until almost twelve o'clock. You'd have thought she really wanted to hear all about how my business is running, and how conditions might affect it the next few years; and, I don't know, I guess I was just in the mood to tell it over.

"Why, if she took in half of what I said last night, she knows twice as much about my affairs right now as my own wife does, and that's a fact. You see, some way, ever since I knew Minna I've always taken

69

all responsibility for the business; seems to me, that's only fair; she has her own problems—social and community service, and all that. But sitting there by the stove with Mother last night, and a kerosene lamp on the table, and a curled-up old almanac hanging by a string from the mantelpiece, just carried me right back to other nights when she used to help me plan how I could get into college, and after I got there, how I could stay there! And even though, in those days, I knew I was a lot smarter than anybody else in my family, I did grant Mother that she had managed to bring us up on just about nothing, so she ought to know as well as anybody how I could make a little money where none was! Anyway it used to be a help then just to have somebody listen to me think out loud, and, I don't mind telling you, it was again last night. I kind of think it did her good, too. Pleased her, anyway. And after that—why, I don't know when I ever had such a night's sleep!"

The same bed under the eaves, with a patchwork quilt and a rag rug, and a sliding screen to put in under the window when he opened it. There was the picture of a boy making a snowball, with a slate hung by a strap from his shoulder; and, when the lamp went out, the same stout smell of the oily wick cooling off, giving out its scent with its warmth, and then only the turned-up ground, the seed in the ground, the white lilacs, the wild pear, and the sound of the brook, of the frog song, of wind coming drowsily down from the hills and falling asleep in the valleys. . . .

"I guess she slept fine, too," Carl chuckled tenderly. "This morning she was up, chipper as a lark, calling me just like she always did, brisk and strong: 'Carl? Breakfast! Come right along down! Coffee's on!' She always knew that about the coffee would bring me. I don't like it after it's set any better than she does. So we had our last breakfast there—just the kind she likes—and we washed up the dishes, and packed our stuff and sat out on the porch. She did have one more notion. She wanted to ride over the old road once more behind a horse. And I knew just how she felt. She wanted to see every inch of it, you know, every stone and clover leaf and blade of grass and trickle of water. You can't do that from a car.

"So I got a neighbor to come over with his horse and an old democrat wagon. His boy went ahead with my brother-in-law's car, but Mother and I rode out of the yard just the way we always used to—except that we were on the back seat instead of the front, and she wasn't driving. She used to be a great one for a horse. She thought of that too. She said as she was climbing in, 'Yes, Morris. I've got so I have to take a back seat now!' But she was very cheerful. I was surprised. I don't know but what she felt more cheerful than I did. She never looked back once, and when she noticed I did, she said, 'There, don't you worry about it, Carl. It's all right. It's got a good tight roof. It'll be right there if you ever need it, just like your father and I always said!' "

Carl stopped for a minute and cleared his throat.

"It isn't much of a place, of course," he said. "Just a little white house with an ell, like the rest of them. A coat of paint would do it good, but still it will stand a good while even if none ever touches it again. The barn is like new. Father built that not long before he died, right after the other one was struck by lightning."

"How old is your mother?" the knitting woman asked. "Did you say?"

"Seventy-four," Carl answered. "Would you have believed she could do all this? And when she left me at the station she was just as chipper. I wouldn't let her get down out of the wagon because I was afraid Morris wouldn't be careful enough of her, getting her back in. Of course when they got over to Woodwards', my sister would be there to help. So when my train pulled out, I stood on the platform of the last car to wave to her, and there she was sitting up as straight as I ever saw her, scrubbing the tears out of her eyes, and smiling away, and waving her handbag, and I noticed then for the first time that she had the craziest-looking old hat on! Must have been one she found up home! I don't know what my sister said when she saw that riding in!"

"Maybe," the old lady said quietly, "it didn't look any worse to your sister than some your sister wears look to anybody your mother's age—and mine! I don't suppose you'll take my word for it, young man, but I'm going to tell you, anyway—seventy-four is nowhere near so old as it seems to somebody who is forty! Or I can put it like this—is forty as old as eighteen thinks it is? I'm seventy-five!"

"Now, now," Carl said incredulously, "you don't expect me to believe that?"

"You might as well," the old lady said coldly. "I'm seventy-five years old, and I'm beginning to think that if I don't look and act it, it's because I haven't got any children to coddle me and boss me and interfere with me! If I know anything about it, never having been a mother, the only reason a woman wants children is to do for them. When she can't do that, she's willing to die. And when they turn around and start doing for her what they think she ought to have done for her, she *wants* to die, because she's heartsick, because she's somehow on the wrong end, and everything is unnatural—and shameful!"

She snatched up her knitting.

"I know this is harsh talk," she said, "but somebody ought to talk it. Mothers can't, very well. You and your sisters aren't to blame for what you've done. You thought it was right, of course. But you've kept her shut up for fifteen years; just like putting a plant in the cellar. All you did yesterday was take her out once more and let her see the sun. Now you've put her back again. Hasn't she got a right to live —and hasn't she got a right to die—where she wants to? Just because she is your mother, hasn't she any rights?"

The woman went away.

The other passengers went on talking, reading, smoking.

Carl refilled his pipe and lit it, but it did not taste good. He thought of the spring at home with the white sand in the bottom and the ferns around the edge. He went back to his section, and lay and thought of the brook, but he did not sleep.

Finally, he began to figure, but all the figures came out wrong. It was a long night. He told himself that a second night on a train is always a hard one. The first you don't notice, and by the third you are used to it. But the second—

In the gray fog of Grand Central in the morning, he was pointing out his bags to a redcap when Minna came up and rubbed her nose against his shoulder. He was surprised and pleased. He did not know when he had ever been so pleased to see her.

She was a very trim little person in a gray suit with some violets pinned on her lapel. Her hair was tucked up under her small, tilted white hat, but a few curls got away from it and bobbed on her forehead, and they were a bright chestnut, almost red. Sometimes he called her Redhead. Her eyes were the color of the flowers, and big, steady, and—for New York—astonishingly aware and kind.

Carl made the redcap wait while he kissed her right there in the morning light.

"What does this mean, gamin?" he asked. "Been in town all night?"

She shook her head.

"I just drove up. Had an urge. Can't explain it. Thought we might have breakfast together. If you have breakfast still to eat—"

"I certainly have. And with you it's got to be at the Brevoort. Swell idea. Come along. . . . Taxi entrance, boy."

They were hardly off when he felt her hand slip under his arm. He pressed it against his side, and smiled down at her.

He was feeling better all the time. He was certainly feeling better. It is strange how the second night on a train—

"Didn't miss me?" he asked Minna.

"A little," she admitted. "So did the dogs. Soapy howled most of both nights. And I heard Cook telling Pauline yesterday, 'I hate a house without a man in it; it don't eat!'"

"Humph!" Carl chuckled. "It's only city women who don't eat. You ought to see what my mother can tuck away! For anybody seventy-four years old—"

Now, riding down the Avenue, he could think of his mother again with scarcely a qualm. By daylight it came clear that the old lady on the train had been the kind that likes a scene. These women! He squeezed Minna's hand again. You couldn't do without them, though; you certainly couldn't.

"You're marvelous, Carl," Minna said. "You certainly are."

He scowled at her in surprise. She was never very free with words like that.

"What do you mean?" he asked. "Marvelous?"

"I know your secret, you see," she told him, laughing. "I've found out what you had up your sleeve when you went sneaking away, so noncommittal. This letter came in late last night and I opened it, thinking it might be something I should wire you about, to the train!"

He looked down at it.

Another cheap, thin envelope addressed in Dorothy's hand. Sent air mail. Air—

"What's it say?" he asked quickly. "What's the matter?"

Had they let his mother fall, getting out of that wagon? Had she collapsed as the strain of her undertaking let up?

"Nothing at all," laughed Minna. "Less than nothing. Read it."

He managed to get the sheet of paper out. This time another was folded inside it, a big, old-fashioned sheet with blue lines.

He read Dorothy's first. It was shorter.

73

Dear Carl: I don't know of anything to do but just write you that Mother never came back! She never came back to my house at all! After they left you, Mr. Bascom took her right up to the farm. I was here, still watching and waiting for her, when the grocery boy brought me this note. I simply don't know what to think.

The thick sheet was his mother's. She must have torn it from a block she found in a bureau drawer or on the mantelpiece up home.

Dear daughter: I want to tell you, as I have told Carl, that I appreciate all the both of you have done for me, and all you wanted to do, but now I've got my own home all comfortable, I am going to stay in it.

He cleaned out the spring for me, and we have got everything nice and dry up here, and Morris has planted right in his field across the road, so I could arrange to pick my own green stuff and get it cheap and fresh too. Morris's boy will come down every day to get in the wood and water. Morris has got a kitten he wants to get rid of, and I will have a telephone put in when I can. Now, that's all I need, and all I want, and you just forget me and tend to your own family.

Of course, I want you all to come up to see me. But not for a couple of weeks. I want a chance to get everything righted around. Evie never thought just as I did about how things ought to be placed. Besides, I need a little while to clear my head. But I'll let you know. You must come up for a Sunday dinner, before strawberries go, and I will treat you to a real shortcake. It is a good deal different from a few berries and a daub of whipped cream on a slice of sponge cake, and I bet Ed will say so.

Later on, I will take Mary-Sue for a couple of weeks and try to teach her something about bed making and dough mixing. She can see how I can my pears too. It looks to me as if a time was coming when girls would need to know how to do useful work, just like they used to.

If Carl sends me what he has been sending you for my board—as I don't doubt he will—I am going to put it, along with what I have got, right into this place. It is dreadful the way the land has been let to go back, and the orchard, and I'm bound to get it where it will be worth something to leave to you young ones when I am through with it. I hope you will not have to sell it, because it seems to me families that rent need to know that there is a roof somewhere that will not charge for keeping rain off their heads, and ground where they can raise something to eat. Anyway, Carl ought to be here for his vacations. Why, just a little while here took years off him—

Well, the sly—Carl thought. *The—the sly little fox!*
He glanced down at Minna, saw that she was laughing, and began to laugh too. With the laughter, a weight which he had not realized was on his chest lifted and dissolved. Now it was out of his hands. His mother was out of his hands, out of all their hands. They had done what they could. Perhaps it had been wrong, though they had never doubted for an instant that they were right. But anyway, she had escaped them—Carl's patronage, Dorothy's fretful care, the children's tea and afghans and curling irons, the Cogswell chair, the silly, ballooning white dresses, and the doctor only two doors away! Why, this very minute she was sitting, straight as a ramrod and proud of herself, at her table with that blue-and-white-checked cloth, red sugar bowl and spotted molasses jug, eating warmed-up potatoes, eggs, biscuits, doughnuts, and her own brew of coffee!
There, she was thinking, *with a good hearty breakfast into me, I feel like myself again.*
"It was so clever of you both," Minna was laughing. "And so marvelous of you, darling, as I say, to aid and abet. I really feel much better about you than I have for a long time. Of course, this is a little hard on Dorothy, but then something always is hard on people with no sense of humor. It was the only way, of course—simply to slip her out from under—"
"Oh, well," Carl said largely, standing tall and ruddy beside Minna under the blue-and-white canopy of the Brevoort just where it cut the morning sun. "I understand Mother pretty well. It's generally true, I guess. A man generally understands his mother pretty well. . . . How much does that read, driver?"

The Man Who Was Born in Grand Central

ROBERT CENEDELLA

What could a letter say that would cause a man to lose his memory, solve his domestic problem, and find himself again?

"JERRY," Frank Barringer asked me, "how well do you know me?"

I decided to hold my tongue no longer. "Well enough to have trusted you for years," I said, "until today."

"I've been behaving badly?"

"Very." I thought that would bring him to himself. I expected he would apologize.

Instead, he said, "Jerry, have you met my wife?"

"Oh, my Lord," I said. "You know I haven't."

Consider the situation. Frank was my broker, and for six years we had lunched together every Thursday at Francesconi's. Today when I had walked past his secretary and into his office at the usual time, he had just stared at me until I'd said: "Well? How about lunch?" Then he'd murmured: "You're Jerry."

He'd said nothing else until we'd reached the street, and then he'd started in the wrong direction. When I finally had led him to Francesconi's, I had tried to talk business; but he had been worse than vague; he had asked me three times what stocks I owned. And now over the coffee he wanted to know if I had met his wife!

"You know I haven't," I said. "You know that we've been business friends and that's really all."

"I see." He lifted his cup halfway to his mouth and then forgot it while he stared with blank eyes across the restaurant. "Jerry," he said, "what's your last name? On the calendar pad it said, 'Lunch with Jerry.' Jerry what?" He was not joking. His eyes meeting mine were troubled, but something in my expression caused him to smile suddenly. "Melodramatic, huh? The fact is—" his mouth was humorous —"I was born last Monday."

"You mean that's as far back as you can remember?"

"Yes."

"But—look, you were at your office."

"Yes."

"But if you really had amnesia—"

"I found my office," he said. "I'm unusual, I guess, for a man who's lost his memory. I'm pretty sure a psychiatrist would call me unusual."

"Psychiatrist. Have you seen one?"

"No."

"You ought to. Right away."

"Yes, I ought to. And still, you know—" He broke off abruptly. "Listen, Jerry," he said, "have you got time—"

"I'll make time," I said. "I want to hear about it."

I WAS BORN Monday (Frank Barringer said) in Grand Central Station. It felt like coming out of a sleep, except that I was walking. Walking and yawning. Yawning great, shuddering yawns. But I had no sense of identity, nor any sense of loss. Not at first, anyhow. I just yawned and walked with dragging feet while people all around me hurried and took no notice.

Then I looked at the clock over the information booth, and as my mind registered that it was half past four, quite suddenly I was awake. I was alert. I was born.

This was Grand Central Station. These people moving so quickly all around me were commuters and soldiers and redcaps and travelers. All these concepts I recognized in a rush. I knew what that clock was for and where the trains were and that over to the right was the newsreel theatre. I knew there was a war going on and where the subway was and—

But I didn't know who I was.

Ever been in a panic, Jerry? I was then. I stood there lost and lonely and scared. I took an indecisive step or two and then stopped. I wanted to run, but I was scared to. It was awful.

I did run, finally. I cut through the station to the right, crossed Lexington Avenue without looking at the traffic lights, and went into a restaurant. I don't know why.

The hostess gave me a table near the window, and I sat catching my breath and watching the activity on the street without really seeing it. I was reviewing what I knew about amnesia. God knows where, but I had heard that no one lost his memory unless he wanted to—that is, unless his subconscious mind wanted to. Something was so terribly unpleasant, something made you so miserable, that your mind played a trick on itself by just forgetting.

That meant there was some situation I wanted to forget, I couldn't face.

A waitress came, and I ordered a pot of tea, but as she left, it came to me that I might not have any money. My hand went automatically to the right pocket and felt a wallet and a letter. I found bills in the wallet and then laid it on the table. It frightened me.

You see why? The wallet must hold identification. It must hold something that would tell me my name, something that might make me remember. And I didn't dare think about it.

Besides, there was that letter in my pocket. The wallet probably wouldn't say to me: See here, you are a murderer or a foreign agent or—well, just a supremely unhappy man. But the letter—

I didn't want to think about the letter. I concentrated on the wallet. With the napkin I wiped sweat from my palms and picked it up.

I must be a neat man. There were none of the little scraps of paper that most men put into their wallets and then forget. There were just an automobile registration, a commuter's train ticket, a notice of draft classification, a driver's license, an A book for gasoline, and a business card. I spread them out on the table.

I examined the draft classification first. I was Frank Barringer. My lips formed the name fearfully: Frank Barringer. It meant nothing to me. I was 4-F. I wondered about that. I still wonder. You don't know why I'm 4-F, do you?

Well. Anyhow. I looked at the other things. I lived in Pelham. Pelham. That was in Westchester. New Haven Railroad. That seemed familiar, though I couldn't have said what Pelham looked like. And here was my commuter's ticket, half used. And my business card. I was a broker. Frank Barringer, broker, of Pelham.

Suddenly I gathered up all these things, left that restaurant without waiting for my tea or paying my check, and went across to Grand Central. I got on a train for Pelham.

Jerry, do you know why? Yes, I know it was the reasonable thing

So the arrival of a pretty girl plus an Irish terrier threw the spectral butler into a snit, Robert into a tizzy, and Uncle Bolivar into a rage of superb proportions.

Pam departed, without tea. She was glad to go, and so was Bill. Robert sped after her presently, and they had words in her apartment. He said that Uncle Bolivar had nearly had a stroke; he said it was all her fault. Uncle Bolivar, said he in hollow accents, had informed him that he would, on the morrow, send for his lawyer. If Robert contemplated marrying again, he'd better think twice about it.

Pam asked, "Well, are you thinking about it?"

He had been, he admitted. Perhaps if she got rid of Bill? Perhaps if she went around to Uncle Bolivar's and apologized?

Pam asked quietly what had given him the impression that she would care to marry into a family of lunatics.

The upshot of all this unpleasantness was that Miss Martin got herself another job, with another lawyer. She also got herself a uniform, much to her astonishment, and found herself, with Bill, on the canteen staff.

Being in uniform, somehow, made a difference. It was, in a curious way, a protection against masculine uniforms. She grew to know a great many boys well for a little while; boys you saw once, twice, three times, and never again, perhaps; boys who told her about their farms, gas stations, drugstores; about their homes. Boys who showed her photographs of girls who were going to wait. That was the important thing with all of them.

And then, after six months, Terry Johnson telephoned her. He asked, "Remember me? How's Bill?"

It was a Sunday. Terry came to the apartment and they took Bill walking in the Park. Bill was very nearly out of his Irish-terrier mind. He ate Terry up, he looked at him with such love and longing that Pam laughed, and then found out that it would have been just as easy to cry. And, walking along the lake, Bill behaved himself like a gentleman. He didn't have to chase the Navy now; he had the Navy with him.

They had lunch at a restaurant on the Avenue, and then went back to the apartment and Terry talked. He talked to Bill mostly. He said, "Remember how it was, old-timer?" He said, "Remember how you used to tear up and down the ladder?" He said, "We miss you."

on the other end of the leash. It was all very distressing. Pam had to extricate herself and Bill. She felt she had to explain.

She said breathlessly, "He—he was brought to me from Ireland, by a friend in the Navy. He got used to the ship. He's crazy about uniforms, navy uniforms."

"He's a swell pup," said the boy in blue.

And that's how she found herself asking questions. A boy, more than a thousand miles from home, with a little time to kill. He didn't know anyone in New York. His shipmates had dates. He blushed. Apparently he didn't make dates easily, and didn't want to.

Pam remembered the canteen where her friend Evelyn worked. There would be girls there, and things to eat and tickets for movies and all that. She could direct him, and she did.

He thanked her and started off, with Bill after him. There wasn't any stopping Bill, so Pam had to go along.

That's how she went to the canteen, and found them short-handed. The sailor lad was taken care of and Bill was perfectly happy. The place was full of sailors.

It was a wonderful afternoon, in a way. The rooms were crowded, and there was music, and the boys played cards and dominoes. There were coffee and cakes and doughnuts, and dishes to be washed.

Funny, how soon it was evening. Odder still that she stayed on. But it was the first time she had ever seen Bill really happy. . . .

IT WAS, of course, because of Bill that she went back to the canteen. She simply couldn't stand having him whine and cry and scratch at the door, and then come over and implore her with his eyes and paws and whiskers. It was a lot easier to go to the canteen regularly. There, at least, Bill could find his fill of sailors. On the evenings she went to the hospital she left Bill at the canteen, and called for him on the way home.

This routine very naturally upset her life. It also upset Robert's. He couldn't or wouldn't understand. She had, after the Plaza episode, met him by appointment at Uncle Bolivar's, on the following Sunday afternoon. But she made the mistake of taking Bill with her.

If there was one member of the animal kingdom which Uncle Bolivar hated more than a woman, it was a dog. It appeared that the girl who had been clear-sighted enough to refuse his offer of marriage, had possessed a pup. The pup had bitten him.

to do, but that wasn't it. I was going to Pelham because it seemed to me that if I didn't, I would have to take that letter from my pocket and read it. And that, somehow, would be terrible.

It's NOT a long ride to Pelham—half an hour or so. When I got off the train in the twilight, I looked curiously around me, but recognized nothing.

I got out the wallet and looked up the license number of my car. And then I went to where the other commuters were climbing into cars and snapping on the lights and backing out. I walked along, looking at license numbers. And then I found my own, and my heart pounded.

There was a woman behind the steering wheel!

I turned and started to walk away. The blood had rushed to my head, making it heavy and dull. Somewhere behind me a woman was calling: "Frank! Frank!" I hurried on.

"Frank! Frank!"

I stopped with the realization that this was my name. Frank. Frank Barringer. She'd seen me. There was nothing to do but turn and go slowly back to that car.

When the woman saw me coming, she slid over, leaving the driver's seat for me. I walked directly to the car and opened the door.

The woman was about thirty-five years old. The dashboard lights were on, so I stood looking at her and she sat looking at me. She had on a mink coat, and her legs were slim and very nice. Her fingernails were scarlet. She wore no hat, and her hair, recently waved, just missed being blonde. A very nice-looking woman, except for her expression. Her face was nice-looking, but it was a little thin. It had a drawn look.

"Well, why weren't you on the earlier train?" she said.

"Oh. Oh. Well, I had some work to do."

"No," she said. "I called the office and Miss Gleason said you left early."

"I had a business appointment," I said.

"I'll just bet," she said scornfully.

I stood there awkwardly.

"Well," she said. "Get in. Get in. Let's get home."

I started to obey, and then I realized I didn't know where home was. "Look," I said. "You drive. I'm tired tonight."

"I bet," she said. "I'll just bet you're tired."

79

But she took the driver's seat, and I circled the car and got in on the other side.

THIS woman must be my wife. She didn't like me, apparently. She was intent now on her driving, so she did not speak to me. But after the way she had been speaking, I was just as glad.

Of course, she might not be my wife. After all, maybe I wasn't even married. Maybe—

We turned in at a concrete driveway beside a brick house on a street full of brick houses. We pulled into a two-car garage in the back, and the woman got out of the car and walked without a word or a backward glance into the yard. I hastened to follow. She went up three steps to a door and into the house. She closed the door behind her.

That's when it came to me that possibly this woman's dislike of me was justified. I thought about the few sentences she had spoken to me, and it seemed to me that there was in them a suspiciousness, a feeling that I was a pretty rotten sort of person. Well, was I? I didn't know.

Anyhow, what lay before me in that house was not pleasant, and I stood in that dark back yard wondering whether I should go in. But something forced me slowly across the yard and up those few steps—something somehow connected with the letter in my pocket.

There was a small entryway, then another door, which I pushed open.

I was in a large, fine, modern kitchen, well lighted and filled with the smell of roasting chicken. I realized only then that I was hungry.

A large, red-faced, middle-aged woman looked around from the sink as I shut the door behind me. "Good-evenin', Mr. Barringer," she said. She was smiling affectionately. "You're late."

I smiled back. "I'm sorry," I said.

At that she laughed. "Sorry! Well, you don't have to be. *I'm* not going to scold you."

I smiled again and walked across the kitchen, but I had not missed her implication that although she wasn't going to scold me, somebody certainly was.

I pushed through a swinging door and entered a large and beautifully furnished living room. A tremendous Oriental rug covered the floor. There was a big stone fireplace on the far side. There were pictures. The chairs and the two divans looked deep and inviting. I thought there was no one there, and I had advanced to the center of the room when I was stopped by a young girl's voice.

"Hello, Daddy."

She was on a window seat and apparently had been looking out into the night. She was perhaps thirteen years old, leggy and thin, wearing a green sweater too large for her. Her hair, like that of the woman who had met me at the station, just missed being blonde.

"Hello, Daddy," she said again and came toward me, smiling.

She was awkward when she walked, as thirteen-year-old girls are —with the awkwardness that is more throat-catching than a ballet dancer's grace. Her hands went to my shoulders, and she stood on tiptoe to kiss my cheek. I patted her arm and turned away toward one of the deep chairs, because the tears had started in my eyes. I didn't know why.

She sat on the arm of the chair. "Mother's upstairs," she said.

"I see."

"She said she wouldn't be down until dinner. She said—" The girl hesitated. "She said she wouldn't be down until dinner," she repeated lamely.

"That wasn't all she said, was it?"

"Well, she was angry with you."

"I see. Well, I took a late train." I picked my words so that they might have meaning whether or not the woman who had met me was "Mother."

The child and I were silent then for a long time, and the silence was a deep and restful thing that belonged to both of us. She sat, as I said, on the arm of my chair, but she did not touch me; yet there was communication between us because there was sympathy. She had walked across the room, awkward because she was thirteen, yet graceful because it was I she was going to, and she had said little; but already I knew I loved this child and she loved me. I did not know her name, I could not remember her face or what she had been like this morning or yesterday or last year; but something in me knew what it was to have a child like this, and I realized that she was part of whatever had brought me to this house tonight.

"You're tired, Daddy," she said.

"I'm all right," I told her.

THEN the light went on beyond an archway opposite us. It was a dining room, with the table set. The woman I had met in the kitchen was there.

"Dinner's ready," she said.

My daughter jumped up. "I'll get Mother," she said and ran upstairs.

I waited until she returned, followed by the woman who had met me at the station. There was no doubt, then, that this was my wife. There really never had been. There had been only a hope.

I went into the dining room with them. By following their lead, by simulating absent-mindedness, by saying practically nothing, I got through that meal without giving myself away. The woman I had met in the kitchen—perhaps I'd better call her the cook, it's easier—served us, and I was glad she had carved the chicken into individual helpings. If I had had to carve, I might have been expected to know who liked dark meat and who liked white. As it was, I was able to sit back and learn what I could about my wife and daughter. And I did learn something from that meal.

For one thing, I learned to like my wife better.

She talked mostly to my daughter—for which, of course, I was grateful. It seemed she was teaching the child dressmaking. "You sew well, Paula," she said, "but there's more to it than that, you know."

"Paula," I said.

"What, Daddy?"

"What? Oh, nothing. I—I was just saying your name. I like it."

She flashed a quick and lovely smile toward me, but turned back to her mother. "You didn't like the style of the blouse?" she asked.

"It's all shoulders, Paula," said her mother.

"I see."

"I know what you were trying for. Style. Form. But it's overaccentuated. Now—" She explained how Paula should have made the blouse.

I DIDN'T understand much of it, but I did understand the important thing—this mother and daughter had found a bond that made them sympathetic to each other. That it was dressmaking was due to their sex, but that the bond existed at all was due to something fine in both of them. They were relaxed, easy, and interested as they talked. That is not common, I think, between mother and daughter, and I felt relieved.

I felt relieved because when Paula had kissed me and talked to me in the living room, I had wondered if perhaps she was not taking sides in some quarrel between her mother and me. Now I knew that she was the daughter of both of us, in spirit as well as in fact, and I could build on that.

Hear what I said? "I could build on that." That shows how far I had gone in an hour or so. Something was wrong between my wife and me. At the railroad station I had not cared, but since I had met Paula I had known that for her sake it must be set right.

Paula finished outlining her ideas for a dress.

"You'll be a dressmaker yet, Paula," said her mother, smiling.

The child flushed and smiled. "Gosh," she said, "I hope so."

When dinner was over, we went into the living room while the cook, whose name seemed to be Grace, cleared the table.

"Paula will help you when you're ready, Grace," said my wife.

"Oh, Mother!"

"This is your night, Paula. I don't complain on my nights, do I?"

"Okay," said Paula.

We were settling into chairs in the living room, and by this time I was positively admiring my wife. She was not only sympathetic toward Paula, but she reared her well. Her face was softer than it had been at the station.

"I talked with Doris Gregory today," she told me.

I tried to look intelligent.

"She says Tom is better."

"Oh. Good." That seemed safe.

She went on with what Doris had told her about Tom—something about an operation. It made no sense to me, of course, but the fact that it was the sort of placid talk that goes on normally between husband and wife puzzled me. I had made up my mind that my wife did not like me, and while that might be true, certainly she could not hate me as she had seemed to at the station. I had felt that she could not be civil to me, and now she was more than civil, she was pleasant.

I wondered if Paula's presence had something to do with it, if my wife was pretending for the child's sake. But when Paula left to help in the kitchen, there was no change in tone. A silence fell between us, finally, but a comfortable silence.

I sighed. "This is a nice house," I said.

"I hate it," said my wife.

That shocked me. We had been so peaceful. I looked at her. Her face had gone hard again. I hesitated. Maybe I should know why she hated our home, but— I took a chance. "Why?" I asked.

She flushed then and squirmed in her chair. "I don't know," she said. "I don't know why I said that, Frank."

Which told me nothing, of course, but which made me think. She was restless, certainly. Could she be having an affair? That might explain her changing moods, her shifting attitudes toward me. She might like me well enough, but love somebody else.

Suddenly I felt a surge of jealousy, and just as suddenly it was over, because I saw the absurdity of it in the circumstances. I laughed. She looked inquiringly at me, and her face was soft again.

"Nothing," I said. "I thought of something, that's all."

Or could I be having an affair that she knew about or suspected? That could account for everything she had said, and it could fit with my amnesia.

Then quite suddenly I wanted to cry. "Excuse me," I said, and went upstairs.

The strain I had been under had been too much. I had been holding myself in rigid control for too long. Upstairs I found light switches, found a bathroom, locked myself in, and cried like a baby.

After that I was exhausted, and I found a bedroom that, from the belongings in the closets and from the fact that it had twin beds, must surely be ours. I undressed, put on the pajamas that hung in the closet, and stretched out on the nearer bed without removing the coverlet. I was just all in.

AFTER a while my wife came into the room. "Switching beds?" she asked.

It took a minute for me to understand. "Oh—no," I said. "I just flopped. I'm tired. I worked hard today."

"I bet," she said. "Oh, I bet you worked hard."

I said nothing.

"Well," she said, "I'm going to read a while."

I got up from the bed and kissed her on the cheek. I was the lonesomest man in the world.

She pulled away and looked sidewise at me. "Don't you do that again," she said.

She left the room, and I sat down on her bed again. I felt forsaken and lonely—a man with no memory and no friend.

Then quite suddenly she came back into the room. She stood, not looking at me, her expression sullen, as though she were about to do something difficult.

And you know, Jerry, I found myself thinking about her, not about myself and my loneliness at all. She was just a grown-up child standing there. I knew why she had come back. I laughed. "Well?" I said with mock sternness.

"I'm sorry," she said. Her face was still sullen. "It was nice of you to kiss me, and—I'm sorry."

Again I got up, smiling now, and again I kissed her cheek; but this time she patted it and looked at me with all the sullenness gone. She wore a curious little smile.

"Nice," she said. "Good-night."

I got into my own bed and stared at the ceiling. Apparently a kiss was an event in this house. I didn't know much about my wife, but I knew this much: she didn't understand her own reactions any better than I did. And I would have to learn to understand them. I'd just have to.

I wanted to wait for her to come upstairs, but I fell asleep with the light on.

I was awakened by an alarm clock. It had been turned off before I rolled over and saw my wife leaving the room in her nightgown. I was bewildered at first, as I had been in Grand Central the day before, but gradually I remembered everything that had happened since. I lay trying to make my memory go back beyond yesterday until my wife returned, fully dressed.

"Get up," she said, "if you're going to work." And she left.

I dressed and went downstairs, to find that Grace had breakfast for me in the kitchen. My wife was just finishing, and Paula was just starting. It seemed that Paula went to school. Naturally, but I had not thought before of her having a whole big life of her own.

"Well," said my wife sharply, "if you're going, you'll have to hurry."

I smiled at her. It was an effort, because her face was hard again, but I wanted to try to recapture last night's soft mood. "Maybe I'll stay home," I said. "Maybe I won't work."

"I'll bet," she said with scorn. "I'll just bet." Apparently it was an expression she always used when she was in this mood.

She drove me to the station, recklessly and grimly and silently. I made another attempt at conciliation before I left the car, leaning over to kiss her good-bye, but she turned her head and said, "Don't *do* that!"

When I reached the city, I did not go straight to my office. I had to plan my conduct there, so I sat in a cafeteria with a second cup of coffee and did some thinking. All I knew about my business life was the address of my office, which I had on my business card, and the name of my secretary, which my wife had mentioned the night before. Miss Gleason, my wife had called her. It was little enough to go on.

For one thing, there might be other employes. And I might have a dozen appointments this morning with people I should know. There would be phone calls. There would be—well, there would be my lack of familiarity with the physical layout of the office.

Of course, I could telephone, say I was ill, and stay away. But I'd have to go to the office sooner or later, and I was anxious to. There I might learn something about myself that would give me a clue to my trouble.

I went there, finally. I had to find out from the list of tenants in the lobby what floor I was on. Then I went up.

You know my office, Jerry, probably a good deal better than I do. You can imagine how relieved I was when I opened the door and found the outer office so small, with only one door leading from it to an inner office.

Miss Gleason—I supposed it was Miss Gleason, and I was right, of course—was typing when I went in. "Good-morning, Mr. Barringer," she said and stopped typing. "Are you feeling better?"

"Much better." I smiled and started to walk past her.

"Mr. Barringer." She swung around in her chair to face me. "Mr. Drohan called, and he was very anxious for your decision. Couldn't we call him back and tell him—"

I looked down at her. She was nearly thirty, neat, brisk, sensible. Probably not the understanding and sympathetic person I had wished for, but obviously a good and efficient business girl—which meant that she would be loyal.

I made a decision. "Never mind that now," I told her. "Please lock the outside door and come in here with me."

"Lock the outside door?"

"Yes. For now, anyhow. I don't want to be interrupted."

I went into my office. While I was looking at my desk—too neat, too unrevealing—I could hear her moving to obey me. After a moment or two she came and sat down beside my desk with her stenographer's pad on her knee and her pencil poised over it. It was plainly a protection against any personal relationship.

"Miss gleason," I said, and watched her to see that she *was* Miss Gleason, "what was the matter with me yesterday?"

"I don't know," she said. "You didn't feel well, but—"

"You're sure you don't know?"

"No, Mr. Barringer."

"You wouldn't think, for example, that any of the—the business we did yesterday would upset me?"

"Of course not."

"Of course not." I took the cue from her and spoke as though my question had been foolish. "It was just another day, wasn't it?" She nodded, and I smiled. "You know, I wasn't sick, Miss Gleason. I was upset. I was troubled."

She said nothing.

"What would you say troubled me yesterday, Miss Gleason?"

"That's not for me to say, Mr. Barringer."

"You have a theory?"

"It's none of my business, Mr. Barringer."

"I see." I got up and walked to the window to look out on a dreary succession of roofs. I spoke without looking around at her. "How long have you been with me, Miss Gleason?"

"Nearly five years, isn't it?" she said.

"Yes. Yes." I turned then. "And after five years you won't venture to say what caused me to be upset?"

"Well—" her eyes were down now—"I suppose it was that letter. The—the letter marked personal that—well, you were waiting for it, and you wouldn't let me open it, and after you had read it—" She faltered for a moment and then stood up suddenly. "Mr. Barringer, I don't like this," she said and walked out quickly.

Jerry, I was sick. I moved to my chair like a man in fever and lowered myself into it like a man with arthritis. The letter I had been afraid to look at yesterday—that was what Miss Gleason was talking about, almost certainly. It was still in my pocket. It was a thin letter—probably just one folded sheet inside the envelope—but it seemed to me right then that I could feel it against my chest. I reached into my inside pocket and felt the letter, and then my hand came out, empty and trembling.

I went into the outer office. "How much do you know of my personal life, Miss Gleason?" I asked.

"Really, Mr. Barringer, I don't want—"

"Would you say I am happily married?"

"I'm sure I don't know."

"Can't you guess?"

She was silent then, biting her lip and avoiding my eyes. I stood motionless, watching her, waiting for her answer.

Finally she spoke, slowly, not looking at me. "Mr. Barringer," she said, "this is none of my business. I'm your secretary, that's all. But—well, when you come in from home upset or when you get upset after you call your wife or she calls you—well, it's none of my business, Mr. Barringer, but—" She bit her lip again.

"But what?"

"Well—" She looked straight into my eyes and blurted it out. "Why can't you be strong and—and masterful at home, the way you are in business? Why do you let your wife upset you?"

We looked at each other. She looked defiant, as though she had said something that had been on her mind for a long time.

"You figure I let my wife run me?"

"I don't know anything about it," she said. "I'm sorry I spoke that way, Mr. Barringer. Only you—you *asked* me, and I can't help knowing how Mrs. Barringer affects you, and—I'm sorry," she said.

"Don't be," I told her. "You're very helpful, Miss Gleason." I hesitated. "Look," I said finally, "I'm leaving. I won't be back again until tomorrow morning. Tell people I'm sick, will you?"

I went back to Grand Central and took the train to Pelham.

It was my home life.

Nothing in the way of business had upset me yesterday. I had almost hoped that I was going bankrupt or had embezzled money. I had hoped to find something wrong at the office—anything, so long as it would mean that my home was reasonably happy. But it was my home life. There was no question about it now.

And I had to find out what was the matter. I had to find out, and I had to set it right.

Maybe you wonder, Jerry, why I felt that way. After all, if I had no remembrance beyond yesterday, what did I care about my home life? I can answer only that I did care, and wonder with you why that should be so. Perhaps it was Paula. A little child had come across a room and kissed me, had looked at me with a look that meant I was the most fabulous man in the world, and somewhere within me there had stirred some half-remembered feeling, some choking sense of beauty, some intimation of a purpose and a meaning in life.

Or perhaps it was my wife. I sat in the train throughout the ride and pondered that, and I gradually came to feel that my wife was not whole—not as I had seen her. She was unfulfilled. She was a fine person who somehow had been turned from some purpose or mission of her own. I thought of how she had talked to me in the living room last night, and thought for a long time of how she had acted in the bedroom, first turning from me, then apologizing sullenly, then rubbing her cheek where I had kissed it and looking so curiously pleased. "There is something wrong between us, but nothing," I thought, "that cannot be made right."

But first I had to find out what was wrong.

Yes, Jerry, I guess I could have found out by reading that letter, but I had resolved that it would be bad for me to read it. The letter might make me as I had been in the unremembered past—however that was —and in the past I had not solved my problem.

I took a taxi home, and for the first time in my new life, I used my front door.

My wife was in the living room, carpet-sweeping. She was a picture of arrested motion as I went in, one arm outstretched on the handle of the sweeper, one foot barely touching the rug, just ready to be lifted, and her eyes surprised.

"Hello," I said.

She straightened. "What are you doing home, Frank?" she asked. There was only questioning in her tone—no bitterness, no hardness.

"Look," I said, "will you sit down with me? I think we ought to do some talking." I wished that I knew her name. You can put tenderness into a name.

89

She stood the carpet sweeper against the wall and followed me to one of the divans. We sat down side by side.

"Has something happened, Frank?"

"Yes," I said. "Something's happened to us."

"Oh," she said.

"And I want to know what it is."

"I don't know," she said. "Frank, I don't know."

"You know what I'm talking about?"

"Yes, Frank."

"Look," I said, "do you remember how it was when we got married?"

She smiled wistfully. "I remember," she said.

"WELL, how was it? I mean, from your point of view."

"It was—well, what's the use talking about it? It was a long time ago, Frank." She suddenly laughed. "Remember when you used to work for Graham's and didn't have to be in town until ten?"

"Yes," I said, remembering nothing.

"And yet you used to get up and go in early with me—just so I wouldn't be lonesome riding to work?"

"Is that the trouble now?" I said. "Are you lonesome here at home?"

"No," she said. "No. Not lonesome. I have the housework, and Paula, and—no, I'm not lonesome."

"How much of the housework does Grace do?"

"Frank, I've told you a dozen times. She does the kitchen and the bedmaking. And the cooking, of course. I do the cleaning."

"Why don't you hire someone for that?"

"Frank, I've told you I don't want to. Good heavens, I've got to do *something!*"

A long silence fell between us then. There we sat, a husband with no memory and his wife with memories that made her smile a tender smile at the thought of them. There we sat in a house that more than the proverbial third of a nation would have envied, and my wife said she had to do *something.*

"I've told you so many times, Frank, I don't need anyone to help me. Why, everything's done before the middle of the day as it is."

"I see," I said. "I just thought—"

"Well, don't think," she said sharply. "And if that's all you came home to say—"

I held up my hand to stop her. "That isn't all I came home to say," I told her. "I—look, do you know you have very nasty moods?"

"Well, what if I—" There was truculence in the way she started, but she checked herself. "Yes, Frank," she said finally. "Yes, I know I do."

"Do you realize *when* you have them?"

"When? No."

"Well," I said, "take yesterday. You were nasty to me at the station, when you met me."

"Well, you were late. You—" She checked herself again. "I see what you mean," she said. "I'm always nasty when I meet you at the station."

"You were nasty this morning when you drove me to the station," I said.

"Yes, Frank. Yes. I'm sorry."

I got up and walked to the fireplace. There was a package of cigarettes on the mantel, and I lighted one. I turned. "I think you ought to get someone to do the housework," I said slowly, and lifted my hand to stop her protests. "And I think you ought to go back to work."

And do you know, Jerry, my wife looked at me for a long, long moment, and then her hands went up to her face and she was crying.

Frank barringer smiled at me.

"I don't get it," I said.

"She was crying because she was happy," he said.

"I still don't get it."

He shrugged. "When she came to meet me at the train, she was bitter," he said. "When I talked about business, she was bitter. Don't you see? She envied me, Jerry. I had work to do. And there she was, a woman who had worked before she was married and even for a while afterward, a woman of energy who finished her housework before the middle of the day and then had nothing to do. She didn't know it, Jerry, but she envied me. She wanted to work as hard as I did, but my success made it something not even to be thought of."

"You were able to figure all that out?"

"Well," he said, "I didn't have a lot of memories to clutter my mind and lead me down false trails. It was simple, really. I stayed home again yesterday, and we planned the whole thing. She's going to open a dress shop, and Paula's going to help her."

"Does she know about—"

"No," said Frank Barringer. "I haven't told her that I've lost my memory, because I still don't know *why* I lost it."

"Wasn't it your domestic situation?"

"How could it have been that? That was so trivial. That was so easy to straighten out. No, it—" He hunched forward and regarded me earnestly across the table. "Look, Jerry," he said, "the answer is in that letter. I'm sure of it. And I haven't dared open that letter. I wanted to wait until I had someone with me who knew, who—" He made an effort to smile. "Someone who's just a business friend and no more," he said.

I said slowly, "You're afraid it might shock you too much?"

"I don't know. I don't know, but—" He took the letter from his pocket but did not look at it. "Will you read it to me, Jerry?" he asked.

I took it from him. It had been opened before. It was on the stationery of a hotel in Palm Springs.

"Read it out loud," said Frank.

"It's signed *Joe Weatherly*," I said. "Does that mean anything to you?"

"No. No. Read it," he said. He played with a button on his jacket while I read.

Dear Frank:

I can imagine how agitated you were to have written to me while I was on vacation. Maybe I have all the understanding and intelligence you credit me with, because I know just what caused you to write. I know that your wife has been hostile in her attitude, that she has shut you out of her secret thoughts, that she's made cryptic and nasty cracks, and that you feel you don't deserve any of it. But that wasn't why you wrote. You wrote because you want sympathy, but I'm afraid I can't give it. You say you're in a torment. Well, Frank, what can I do? Whenever you've cried on my shoulder before, I've told you that you were partly at fault, that you probably rather liked being an injured party. I've told you you ought to forget yourself and your injuries and try to understand your wife for a change. But you ran away from that solution. It was too easy, but at the same time it was too hard. It left you with the necessity of exercising understanding when what you wanted was to brood.

Well, should I offer the same advice now? I think not. I know this

92

*is going to shock you, because I think you love your wife and I know
how much you and your wife both love little Paula. But if you cannot
forget yourself for a change and help your wife out of whatever
causes her despondency, then even if it means giving up Paula, I'd
recommend divorce.*

Sincerely,
Joe Weatherly

I looked up. Frank had stopped fiddling with his button. His eyes
staring into mine were large and glassy. He swallowed once, hard.

"Frank," I said, "does this letter—"

He stopped me with an upraised hand. "Go away," he said. "Go
away. Just leave me alone."

"But—"

"I'll be all right. Just leave me alone."

I got up quietly, leaving the letter on the table. I went to the bar
and paid the check. When I looked back, Frank was still sitting with
his hand upraised, as though he did not realize yet that I was gone.

WELL, that was yesterday. I called him twice yesterday afternoon,
but he never went back to his office.

I could see what had happened. He never had wanted a divorce,
he never even had thought of a divorce. And when that letter had
brought him face to face with the possibility, it had been too much,
and amnesia was the result. But something deep below his consciousness had remembered the alternatives: either an intelligent solution or
divorce. He was too attached to his family for divorce, so even in his
sick state he had made himself resolve the difficulties in his home life.

But now what? I was worried.

And then this morning he called me. His voice was cheerful. "My
memory started coming back while you were reading that letter," he
told me. "I'm all right now. I'm much more all right than I've ever
been. And, oh, I've told my wife the whole story, and we both agree
it's about time a good customer like you came to our home. What
about next Wednesday?"

I said next Wednesday would be fine.

"Oh, and by the way—" Frank was laughing—"my wife's name is
Paula. Just like my daughter's."

93

Big Operator

MARIAN B. COCKRELL

When a boy dates his best pal's sister and trans-
forms her from a Plain Jane into a kissable girl
there can be only one result. It's love in a breezy,
delightful adolescent style.

IT WAS THE FIRST high-school-fraternity dance of
the school year, and Duncan Brewster sauntered along the edge of the
floor, looking things over appraisingly. The familiar scene—the
pounding swing band, the big room with its windows through which
the agile and lucky could slip in without a bid, girls' shoulders in all
stages of tan, the smell of perfume and cigarettes, with an occasional
whiff of liquor from a passing male—was the same as last year, but it
was no longer a part of Duncan's life. In two weeks he would leave
for college; already he felt apart, a little alien.

Gin Mill Martin, also headed for college, came along, and Duncan
hailed him. "Whatcha sayin' there, bwa?"

"Ah ain't sayin', brother, Ah ain't sayin'. I see you got on yo' fawmal,
bwa." Gin Mill referred to Duncan's new Tuxedo, which he was taking to college with him.

"Yeah, brother, I'm a big operator. Got some big deals on."

"You stag?" Gin Mill inquired, and Duncan nodded firmly. "You
said it, bwa." This was because Corinna Mayfield had another date;
in fact, Duncan was now morally certain Corinna was subtly shifting
him to second place, leaving Calahan Miller, who would still be in
town and available, as head man.

The lovely Corinna floated by just then in the arms of a college
sophomore.

"Hello, hag," Duncan said sourly.

"Ank, ank," Corinna responded amiably as she went by.

Duncan felt hostile toward the sophomore for being experienced
in something he had yet to learn, and gazed after him with rancor.
Gin Mill, beside him, wore a like expression.

They stood silent, swaying in time to the rhythm, fending off couples who came too close, the imminence of change rendering them indecisive and vague. In two weeks things were going to happen, but just now all this activity they were no longer a part of whirled about them faster and faster, leaving them becalmed in an aimless in-betweenness.

"This town is dead," Gin Mill observed glumly.

"Man, you said it."

Gray Mare Gibson came trucking over and leaned on Duncan's shoulder. "Hi, big shot. You standing in for a corpse?"

Dunc and Gin Mill immediately became animated. "Just looking over the field, dude, just looking over the field," Dunc said. "Who's that homely tomato over there?" He gestured disparagingly with his head toward a girl sitting in a chair against the wall where Charlie Yokum had left her some minutes ago.

Gray Mare looked. "Confidanchully, that there's the Duchess of Bustlebritches, bwa!"

"Here's Harry the Horror," Gin Mill said. "Ask him. . . . Hey, Harry!"

Duncan surveyed Harry with distaste and noted that he was already wearing his prep-school uniform. "Hello, pretty," Dunc said insultingly. "You know all the women, dream man. Who's that homely tomato over there? Your date?"

Harry glanced at the girl by the wall and his face got grim. "That," he said belligerently, "is my sister," and took a step toward Duncan.

"Gulp!" said Gray Mare loudly.

Duncan could see that he had to think fast. "Boy!" he said quickly. "She sure can dance!"

Harry hesitated, and then came on threateningly. So, with a casual wave of his hand, Duncan turned his back and strolled toward the girl.

Harry the Horror was in the habit of socking people, and it was only by chance that their mutual dislike hadn't ended in battle before this. Any other time Dunc would have been glad to oblige, but tonight he had on his new Tux. It had taken only a breath for the important fact to slide through his mind that he could take off the coat, but he couldn't take off the pants.

Therefore he yielded to discretion; Gin Mill and Gray Mare stepped between his retreating form and the bewildered Harry; and there he was in front of the homely tomato, asking her to dance.

She looked up at him incredulously, her big brown eyes wide behind the shell-rimmed glasses. She wore a sick smile, and her front teeth stuck out a little. She had long, dark, straight hair which was wound on her head in braids, giving her a top-heavy look. Her dress was obviously the one evening dress of a girl who never needed a new one.

"Why, thanks, Duncan; I'd love to," she said, and stood up eagerly. She was eager all over—horribly so—and her face was strained with the effort of covering misery with unconcern.

The music stopped, and she sat down again, but Duncan pulled her up. "Let's mingle," he said, conscious of their conspicuousness. He steered her into the crowd, where he found frequent necessity to speak to people, and that's all the conversation they had. The girl— he remembered her name now: Gwendolyn—ugh!—said nothing.

"Soon be back at school," he said desperately.

"Yes," she said, and sighed.

"What's the matter? Don't you want to?"

"Oh, I guess so. But Miss Newsome's is so—so dumb."

"Oh," he said. Harry's sister would go to Miss Newsome's. No wonder he had forgotten who she was—hadn't seen her since grammar school. Everybody went to Russell, the public high school, except girls who flunked out there, or were so unnoticed they couldn't stand the loneliness, or so boy-crazy their parents wanted to hold them down.

The music started, and Duncan grasped her determinedly. She was stiff as a window dummy. Gin Mill, passing, winked at him over her shoulder, put his hand to his forehead as if he felt faint, and staggered away. Duncan gathered that Gin Mill was not going to cut in. Rosemary Brice danced by, and her eyes and mouth opened as she saw his partner.

"Hello, Gwendolyn!" she called sweetly. Duncan began to get mad —at these dopes who made cracks and faces at him, at himself for getting into this, but mostly at this twerp for being such a twerp.

"Ree-lax!" he said impatiently. "You're not Pinocchio!"

"Oh-h," she gasped softly. "I'm trying, Duncan." Her hand trembled on his shoulder and he felt a quick pity for her. But her glasses slipped down on her nose, and as she raised her hand to put them back, his patience departed.

"Give me those things," he said, pulling them off and putting them in his pocket.

"Oh, give them back! Duncan, the doctor said I was to wear them all the time!"

"Gnats. You can see enough. Where's the case?"

"I won't give it to you! You haven't any right—" She was getting huffy, and that annoyed him too. He reached into the bag on her wrist and took out the case, put the glasses in it and slipped them back in his pocket.

"Your purse is open," he said helpfully.

Gwendolyn stopped and stamped her foot, and feeling that everyone in the room was watching, he grabbed her roughly and danced off. But she stubbornly stopped again, and he had to stop too, or drag her.

He was afraid she was going to cry.

"Aw, Gwendolyn, I didn't mean to get you sore. But honest, you look swell without them."

Cajolingly, he put his arm around her and she came along, looking mutinous and bewildered. The music stopped just as something began to dawn on Duncan.

"Say! Gwendolyn, when you were mad and not paying any attention, you danced swell! Look how we've been cuttin' it these last few minutes!"

Gwendolyn raised her large brown and nearsighted eyes in amazement, and he realized that he hadn't been too far wrong when he said she looked swell without her glasses.

"Why," she said, "I did, didn't I?"

"Yeah." Gwendolyn was saying something about how she could always dance all right with the girls at Miss Newsome's, but he didn't get it all, because he saw Gin Mill pointing him out to Calahan Miller and snickering. The rats.

"I got a new step," he said suddenly. "Let's duck in a corner and try it." If the dame could just dance, he could pretend to be having such a good time they'd get tired following him around. But he didn't have much hope, as he hadn't been able to teach it to Corinna or Denny Lassiter, the best dancers he knew.

"Look," he said when they arrived at a clear space. It was a little

97

nifty he had dreamed up—a good deal of footwork in and out, with a touch of trucking in the middle, and all on the offbeat.

"Again," she said. She did it slowly with him, started over, tried it again, and had it. They did it over and over, absorbed, in the groove. It wasn't a conspicuous step, no finger waving or swinging far apart —just dignified and complicated.

They passed Gray Mare. "Hey!" Duncan called. "She's got it!"

"She's got it?" Gray Mare stood and watched. "Cripes, she has! Say, lemme break a minute." Gray Mare also was fond of complicated steps, and most tomatoes felt that dancing with him was a good deal like being tripped up all the time.

Duncan stood there a moment, and then walked off, realizing that he wasn't stuck any more. He saw Corinna, and snagged her.

"Get stuck?" she asked sweetly.

Dunc gazed into her mocking blue eyes, and thought about Calahan Miller, and how he didn't mind so much being given the runaround as he did her thinking she was getting away with it. "Not for long, babe," he said, smiling at her tenderly. "She can do that step you couldn't learn."

Corinna elevated her nose slightly. "How nice for you," she said, "to have something to do all that time."

Duncan was trying to think of a comeback when somebody broke, and he wandered away, still thinking. Unconsciously, he drifted back to the vicinity where he had left Gwendolyn, and saw that Gray Mare had handed her back to Charley Yokum. She had that strained look on her face again. Duncan cut in.

"Stop looking like that," he ordered, but she already had. She was looking into his face with a glad smile.

"Like what?" she said.

"Like you wished somebody would break," he said brutally, and got a perverse satisfaction out of the wounded look on her face.

"I know," she said, lowering her head so that all he could see were the heavy dark braids. He leaned closer to hear what she was saying and her hair smelled good. "It's just—I hate to dance with Charley, because I know he doesn't want to."

"Well, what'd you come with him for?"

"Because Blanche Crawford is visiting me, and she wouldn't come unless her date got a date for me, but I'd lots rather she'd just left me, and Charley hates—"

"Sure. I get it. Well—" The music stopped; there was a roll of drums, and the leader announced the fourth no-break. This was the one—the one no-break Corinna had found it convenient to save him.

It was obvious from her face that Gwendolyn didn't have it taken. "How 'bout giving me this one?" he said. Boys began looking anxiously for the no-break partners of the girls they were with, as they weren't free to find their own dates until these girls were taken care of. Girls who didn't have the no-break taken nevertheless looked earnestly about as if searching for someone.

When the music began, some boys slid up at the last moment, claiming their girls and releasing other boys, who dashed madly off in search of other girls.

"I bet you had it," Gwendolyn was saying.

"Nah. Swear I didn't." Corinna hated to be stood up on no-breaks. He tried to think of some way to let her know he was standing her up intentionally, and wasn't just stuck.

After the no-break he decided to teach Gwendolyn his other good step, and they bumped into Gin Mill. "Outa my way, bwa!" Dunc said, shoving him. This had the direct effect of making Gin Mill cut in.

"Break," he said, and whirled her away. Duncan grinned, and thought how it would fix old Gin Mill if he got stuck. Then he thought of that look on Gwendolyn's face, and hoped he wouldn't.

He edged out to the side line where the dancers were sparse, and heard Charley Yokum talking to another boy. "I'll get rid of her at intermission," Charley was saying, "and we can—"

Duncan stepped up close to him and gritted his teeth. "You're rid of her already," he said. "I'm taking her on right now."

He walked away before he got madder, because, after all, he still had on his new Tux. *Now I've done it,* he thought glumly.

After that he had to keep an eye on her and see she didn't get stuck, but when his guardianship was noted, other fellows came and danced with her—they weren't risking anything—and she did pretty well. Dunc forgot to dance with Corinna any more.

THE next morning Duncan woke up at a conservative eleven-thirty, and lay there letting pictures run through his mind. He strolled the campus at the university, people yelled at him frequently, he went in and out of buildings—no classrooms were included in these visions—

and walked with a couple of coeds. Prettier than Corinna. Thinking of Corinna brought to mind the evening before.

He had taken Gwendolyn—what a name!—to Dewey's after the dance, and bought sodas and kidded the curb boy, and changed parking places two or three times to visit with different cars and see what was going on. She had loved it.

He could still see her face as she told him she had never had so much fun. *I bet,* he thought, and felt a little uneasy at the memory of her adoring gaze.

He didn't try to analyze his reaction, but the fact was that she shouldn't look like that, either. No matter how a girl went for somebody, she shouldn't let it shine out that way. It gave him a feeling of responsibility and irritated him.

He dressed, and the cook came down from doing the upstairs and plied him with eggs and toast and milk. Then he fidgeted around and decided he might as well see what everybody was doing.

On the way out he stopped suddenly at the phone. He had to look up the number. A girl answered.

"Gwendolyn?"

"Yes"—hesitantly.

"That little black-headed gal with all the hair?"

"Oh," she said. "Me?"

"Is yo' name Gwen-do-line, honey?"

"Oh. Y-yes. Is—this you, Duncan?"

"Ol' Blitzkrieg Brewster himself. Got your car?"

"Yes. I—guess so."

"Well, meet me at Dewey's. Pronto."

"You mean—now?"

"Naw. Pronto means next week."

Gwendolyn giggled. "Oh. Well, all right, Duncan."

"Make it snappy," he said, and hung up. "What do I think I am, a social worker?" he asked himself. To prove he wasn't, he circled past a few selected houses, blowing his horn violently, and then he happened to think how she'd feel down there by herself, and sped toward Dewey's at risk of his and other people's lives and cars.

At Dewey's, where you saw everybody and made dates and didn't speak to people you had broken up with, there wasn't a vacant parking place beside Harry the Horror's open convertible, in which Gwendolyn was sitting, talking to Gin Mill, who leaned against the door. Dunc parked down the line and walked over.

"Where to, gargoyle?" he said to Gin Mill, shoving him away. . . . "Hi, dream toots."

"Hi," Gwendolyn said shyly.

Dunc walked around the car to get in the front seat, but Bird Dog Bullings slid in ahead of him.

"Hey!" Dunc protested.

"I'm sitting in Harry's half," Bird Dog said.

"The hell!" Duncan said. He got in the back seat and suddenly zooped over and landed between them.

"What a pal!" Bird Dog said disgustedly.

"Have a coke," Dunc said to Gwendolyn.

"I don't—think I can. I've had two," she said. "Chester—"

"Arrgh!" said Gin Mill.

"That is, Gin Mill bought me one"—Duncan didn't like the way she smiled at Gin Mill—"and Bird Dog."

"Oh, well," Duncan said, "have a malted."

"Well, thanks," Gwendolyn said.

"Hey, bwa! Two chocolate malteds, and don't wait for them to walk over here by themselves!"

The curb boy looked cross-eyed and gave him the bird, which meant that the order would be along in time.

The car beside Gwendolyn's backed out and Corinna's car slid into the vacant space. She had Harry with her.

"There she is, Harry," she said. "With Blitzkrieg Brewster, the jitterbug's joy."

"Gimme the car," Harry said abruptly.

Gwendolyn looked at him a moment. "No," she said politely but firmly. "It's half mine. Just because I don't use it much—"

"Look." Harry took a more conciliatory tone in the face of her refusal. "I'll take you home."

"No," said Gwendolyn. She looked unhappy, but determined.

"Give it to him. I'll take you home," Duncan said. "Any hurry?" he asked Harry.

"Any time, any time," Harry said, mollified by this unexpected civility from Duncan.

"Hold your nose and drink this," Dunc said, as the curb boy appeared with the tray. "I think Zombie must have mixed it himself, by the taste."

"I'll be glad to mix you a drink any time, droopsnoot," the boy replied with meaning.

"I was sorry you couldn't get there for our no-break," Corinna said. He could tell she was sore.

"Oh, Duncan!" Gwendolyn said, mortified. "You said you didn't have it!"

"Shut up," he whispered. "Only way I could get you to break the one you had," he said aloud. "Sorry, Corinna, but I didn't think it would make any difference to you."

Corinna's eyes narrowed as she said, "How much difference do you think it did make?"

"I'll come over sometime and find out," Duncan said. Gosh, she was pretty! All that yellow hair. What was he doing getting her sore— and legitimately, too—on account of this dumb little cluck?

"I can tell you enough over the phone," Corinna said.

Duncan dug into his pocket and brought out some change. "Think I'll tip the Zombie. Give him a shock."

"A *pourboire* for the poor bwa," Gwendolyn said.

Dunc stared at her. "Say! Did you hear what she said? That's good. . . . Hey, Gin Mill, she said, 'a *pourboire* for the poor bwa'!"

"Haw-haw!" Gin Mill yelled from three cars over. "Say, listen to what Gwendolyn said!"

"Let's go, hag," Duncan said, pulling her out of the car. Her face lighted up at the epithet. He was beginning to like her face. *Too many dead pans around here,* he thought.

As they got in his car, Duncan said, "Look, I'm going to call you Lynn. Lynn Archer, that's not bad. Gwendolyn smells."

"Why, that's—I like it. Dunc, do you think anybody else will ever call me that?"

"Sure, sure," he said. "Make Harry. Say you'll demand your rights on the car if he doesn't. And look—" He was staring at her intently. If she'd only do it— "Lynn," he said solemnly, "have you got five dollars?"

Lynn looked at him in surprise. "Five dollars? Why, yes."

"You can get it with no questions asked?"

"Uh-huh." She was staring at him wonderingly.

"Well. We're—" Dunc swallowed. He didn't know how this was going over. "Lynn, we're going to cut off your hair!"

Lynn drew back, her eyes widening. "Oh, no, Duncan! I—I'd better not!"

"You got to," he said. There was apprehension in her face, and fear of consequences, but no denial of his decision. "Come on," he said inexorably. "We'll drive by your house and get the dough."

"This afternoon—now?"

"Certainly. You want to be a knockout, don't you?"

"Yes, but—Dunc, do you think I will be?"

"I said so, didn't I?" This was fine stuff. He had been under Corinna's thumb lo these many months, and now his own thumb was getting in some long-overdue exercise. . . .

They parked in front of the Lakeside Beauty Shop, which was next door to Dewey's, deserted now for the brief lunchtime lull. They slipped in fast.

Miss Adeline, who knew all the kids, looked up in surprise. Gwendolyn had never needed her services. Neither had Duncan.

"Hello, big shot," she greeted him. "Your mother want an appointment?"

"Nah. We—uh—Lynn wants her hair cut."

"What? . . . Honey, does your mother know about this?"

"No," said Lynn honestly.

"Come on, take it down," Dunc said, and began extracting hairpins wherever he could find them. Two long dark braids fell almost to her waist.

"Now listen, you kids. I can't go cutting Gwendolyn's hair—"

"Her name's Lynn," Dunc put in.

"—without her mother says so."

"I'm sixteen," Lynn said uneasily. "I ought to have some say. I—"

Miss Adeline looked adamant. "But maybe I'd better ask her."

"You've asked her before," Dunc reminded her.

Lynn nodded sadly.

"Can't do it," Miss Adeline said regretfully. "It would look better, but I can't ruin my business."

Gwendolyn got up slowly, regret and relief mingled in her face.

"Oh, no, you don't!" Duncan said. He wasn't going to stop now. He seized a large pair of scissors, and off came about a foot of soft plaited hair. Amid the shrieks of the two women, he got the other braid off before they got into action.

"You little devil!" Miss Adeline said.

Gwendolyn burst into tears.

Duncan, unnerved and sailing along on pure bravado, talked fast to keep from folding up. "Listen," he said. "All she wants is an end curl, not one of these frizzy jobs like you gave that Bascom girl. See?"

"I know my business!" she said, looking at him grimly, but with a touch of admiration in her eyes.

"And you," Duncan said, gripping Lynn's shoulders. "Shut up, babe. Hear? You're going to be a knockout."

She raised woeful, tear-wet eyes, and he turned away, a bit shaken. "I'll be back in an hour or so," he said in a hard voice. He picked up the two severed braids. "I'll keep these," he said, "and if it doesn't turn out all right I can hang myself."

He heard Lynn giggle as he walked off, his hand clutching a fistful of soft hair. It was sort of a pity—her hair was pretty. But she could let it grow again when she got older.

An hour and a half later, on his third trip, Miss Adeline informed him that Lynn was being combed out, and in a moment she appeared fearfully for his inspection.

Duncan looked, and made a sliding gesture with his hand. "O.K., Adeline. So I don't strangle you. Can you stand to be seen with me, glamourpuss?"

Lynn was starry-eyed to the point of a fixed stare. She was in a daze, as he led her outside, where girls shrieked congratulations and boys were tersely but unanimously approving. They hadn't had any lunch, so Duncan bought sandwiches and malteds. He certainly was laying out dough on this tomato.

"And another thing," he said as he bit into a ham-and-cheese: "You got to go to Russell. Miss Newsome's smells, Lynn."

Lynn lifted her head, which felt strangely light, shook the soft curled ends of hair about her face. "I am," she said with determination. "I'll—I'll do it. I've only got a year left. I ought to have that much."

By the end of a week Lynn had had two dates besides the ones with Duncan, and he was proud of his handiwork. Her mother hadn't minded the hair so much, but her father had hit the ceiling, and still glared at Duncan whenever he met him, which was as seldom as Duncan could manage. But he and Harry now met in polite and sheepish friendliness, their rancor having disappeared back into its mysterious source. Perhaps its origin had had something to do with Corinna.

As for Corinna, things were shaping up there too. She was coming as near running after him as Corinna ever permitted herself. At first she had made sarcastic cracks about Pygmalion, but now she was just trying to hold onto what she had. Duncan guessed he'd invite her to the Christmas dances at the university. She sure was good-looking. So was Lynn, for that matter.

Every time he thought of Corinna he thought of Lynn along with her. Lynn wasn't good-looking in the same way as Corinna, who was like something out of Vogue. But he kept seeing Lynn's big brown eyes that shone so when he was around, and her full soft lips, and her beautiful teeth that stuck out just a little, not much. Hell, Deanna Durbin's did, too, and she was feeling no pain!

"This is my last week, you know. Did you save me a date?" he asked Lynn. He was lying on the floor by the telephone table, with his feet up the stairs.

"I—didn't make any," Lynn's voice came back. "Bird Dog asked me; and you know who? Charley Yokum! But I said I couldn't tell until later."

"And why did you say that?" he asked with deliberate obtuseness.

"Why—oh, Duncan, I just wanted—oh, well, it doesn't matter."

"Yes, it does," he said cruelly. "I have to know."

"You already know!" Lynn flared up. "I just—just waited so you could have whatever time you wanted and they—they could have the rest!"

And they could have the rest! That was what he liked to hear. Was he a big operator?

And immediately on the heels of his gratification came the feeling that she shouldn't do that. It was rotten technique.

"Don't ever tell a guy anything like that," he admonished her severely. "Not unless you're engaged to him or something. You sound too easy."

"I—I'm sorry," she said faintly on the other end of the line. She sounded horribly embarrassed.

"I didn't mean me," he said hastily. "I meant other people. I meant it's just the principle of the thing."

"Oh," said Lynn tonelessly.

"Well how about Monday, Wednesday and Friday?" he asked. "I have to be there Saturday to register."

"Fine," she said. "If you're sure you want them, Duncan."

"Certainly I'm sure," he said irritably. He hadn't meant to have three dates with her his last week. But she sounded so hurt he didn't want her to think he thought—that he didn't want—oh, hell, he didn't know why he had asked for three.

THAT left Tuesday and Thursday for Corinna, and made a full week, with his mother dragging him downtown to shop as soon as she could get him up every day.

Lynn, Corinna, Lynn, Corinna, and finally, Friday night, Lynn again. Everything had been satisfactory with Corinna—that is, she had been much nicer than usual, and he had been noncommittal. As for Lynn—

They were sitting in Duncan's car in front of her house. It was eleven-thirty, and she had to go in at twelve. There was just enough moonlight to see a little bit.

Duncan felt tense and unnerved, and he knew she did too. In half an hour they were going to say good-by. He looked down at her just as she raised her eyes to his, and they were so full of complete and utter adoration that he was gone, absolutely lost, and he knew he was in love.

He put his arm around her and she ducked her head against his shoulder and he pulled her against him. "Lynn," he said. He could hardly hear himself. "Lynn, I—love you."

She pressed her head harder against his shoulder and said something in a whisper.

"What?" he said softly. "Honey, I couldn't hear you."

She sat up and clasped her hands in her lap and stared at them. "I do too," she said distinctly, but she couldn't seem to raise her head.

Duncan was fumbling at his vest. He got it loose, and said, "I want you to wear this, Lynn. Lynn!"

She looked at it and said, "Oh, Duncan!"

Clumsily he pinned it on her.

"Shall I—do you want me to wear it all the time?"

"Of course," he said.

Lynn raised her head with a little toss of resolution. "I will," she said, looking at him with love. "I'll wear it all the time." Her face was as transparent as ever, and he knew immediately what she was thinking. Rather, what had passed through her mind and been dismissed. If she wore his pin all the time she'd be sewed up, tied to one man; guys would take her out, but it wouldn't be the same.

A girl who'd never had any fun ought not to have a tag on her.

"You know what it'll mean if you wear it all the time?" Duncan asked.

"Yes," she said, and the briefest wistfulness passed across her face for the barely tasted joys of popularity. "But—oh, Duncan, I don't care!"

"Hell," he said. "I was just kidding. Don't tell anybody, but just keep it. You hear?"

"I'd like to wear it!" she insisted.

"Well, you don't, see? Give it back; I don't trust you."

He snatched at it and she clutched it quickly. "I won't, Duncan. Really."

"You can wear it when you come to the Christmas dances at the university," he told her. All right, so he was a sucker.

"Duncan!" she said, her eyes shining.

She was looking up at him again, and he leaned toward her. She didn't draw away or seem reluctant, but kissed him back as he put his lips to hers, with all the naturalness and fervor of her devotion.

Duncan raised his head and pressed his cheek against hers. He was shaken and stunned by the violence of his feeling. He could feel her trembling. "Oh, my darling!" he said.

He hadn't meant to. He had never spoken so solemnly to a girl in his life. Even his most serious feelings had been cloaked in levity.

In reaction he pulled away a little and his mouth drew up into his habitual slightly jeering smile. "Tell me," he said, "how many other guys you kissed?" He already knew the answer, though.

"Not any," she said in a low voice. It was the first time he had believed that, and the first time he had ever been the first to kiss a girl. It made him feel funny.

He kissed her again. "I got to go," he said.

He went around and opened the door and helped her out, and they walked silently up the walk to the steps. "You write," he said, and she said, "Yes."

"And listen, babe." He had been acting screwy all week, so he wasn't much surprised any more to hear himself cutting his own throat. "About this kissing—if you want to, you can, see? If you want to, not them. Even a girl has to get a little experience. Just act as if—as if we—well, you know—"

"As if I didn't love you?" She brought it out in plain words, and Duncan backed up and said, "Yeah, yeah," in a hard voice.

"You mean, you wouldn't be jealous?"

"Maybe I would," he said to her harshly. "Maybe I've lost my mind. But you don't know anything. You ought to have some fun your last year. You—"

"I won't ever want to," she said fervently. "But I do think—I think you're—"

Duncan couldn't stand this, so he stopped it by kissing her again, and then shoved her toward the door, where she stood bursting with the bliss of having been kissed three times in one evening by the man she was in love with, watching Duncan stride down the walk.

He started his car, cursing. He was in love. He had given a girl his pin and told her not to wear it. He had kissed her and told her to kiss other people if she felt like it. He had asked her to the Christmas dances, where she would be twice as much trouble as Corinna, and would have to be taken care of, and so forth.

"I'm losing my wheels," he muttered. "Absolutely off my nut." He raised his head and stuck out his jaw, his eyebrows climbed a half inch, and his nostrils widened. He felt so noble and magnanimous he was fairly bursting. "Am I a sucker!" he snarled.

Romeo and Violet

WHITFIELD COOK

When Violet, the unpredictable brat, played the part of Juliet, she put into her role her heart and soul and a few lines that would have surprised even Shakespeare. Her audience loved it. You will, too!

VIOLET AND AUNT ESTHER sat in the hushed theater audience watching Laura Lamson play the final scene of *Antony and Cleopatra*. Violet sat spellbound. It was the second time she had ever been to a play. She clutched her program in hot hands and breathed down the neck of the woman who sat in front of her. Her eyes never left Laura Lamson's face; and she found herself acting, too. She and Laura Lamson and Cleopatra were all dying together. Miss Lamson moved her big, glamorous eyes, and Violet moved her little bespectacled ones. Miss Lamson drew her sensitive mouth into a bitter smile, and Violet did likewise. When Violet saw the handmaiden with the asp, she felt her heart begin to thump painfully. She knew *exactly* what it felt like to be the queen of Egypt, bravely killing herself in the most dramatic way possible. She twisted one pigtail with excitement, knowing that in a moment the life would pass from her beautiful body and she would join her beloved Antony in the Elysian Fields.

"Stop blowing on that woman," hissed Aunt Esther, tapping Violet's arm.

Violet paid no attention.

Laura Lamson's throaty voice was crying out:

"Give me my robe, put on my crown; I have
Immortal longings in me: now no more
The juice of Egypt's grape shall moist this lip—"

Violet felt her eyes swimming with emotion. She straightened her little backbone regally as Laura Lamson stood with queenlike dignity and took the asp into her hand.

"Oh, dear, I *don't* like snakes," whispered Aunt Esther.

"*Ssssshh!*" said Violet, outraged at these interruptions.

And then the asp was doing its deadly work. And Violet and Cleopatra and Laura Lamson died, stretched out on the royal divan.

When the play was over, the matinee ladies clapped politely, and Violet sank back into her seat with exhaustion. But it had been glorious. Cleopatra was a woman after her own heart. She *did* wish her school was doing *Antony and Cleopatra* instead of *Romeo and Juliet*. Juliet seemed a little pallid after Cleopatra.

She pulled herself together and looked at Aunt Esther. "Now we're going backstage, huh?"

Aunt Esther, who had known Laura Lamson slightly years ago, had promised Violet they'd go around and speak to her after the performance.

They picked their way around scenery and over cables in the dusty dimness of backstage.

"Now, Violet," said Aunt Esther, "*do* be polite to Miss Lamson."

"Of course, I'll be polite. I think she's a *very* good actress. . . . Did you say she'd been married twice or three times?"

"And *don't* talk about her private life!" moaned Aunt Esther.

"But that's what's interesting about an actress!" said Violet.

A colored maid ushered them into Laura Lamson's dressing room, and Miss Lamson, free of the queenly garb of Cleopatra, received them in a worn black kimona.

"Why, Esther Granden!" she said. "It's wonderful to see you."

"This is my niece Violet," said Aunt Esther.

"How do you do?" said Laura Lamson, smiling her very red lips at Violet.

"I'm a little limp now, thank you," said Violet. "Your performance drained me emotionally."

"Did you like it?" asked Miss Lamson.

"Oh, very much," said Violet. "You play Cleopatra just about as I would. Though of course I really haven't the figure for it—yet."

Miss Lamson raised her eyebrows.

"Violet thinks she wants to act," said Aunt Esther hurriedly.

"I'm going to have a stab at it," said Violet. "Miss Kilbridge's School for Girls is going to do the balcony scene from *Romeo and Juliet*. It's a contest among several schools for the most original production of Shakespeare. I'm going to play Juliet."

"How nice," said Miss Lamson, looking with some alarm at Violet's determined little face and her big glasses.

"As you can see," continued Violet frankly, "I'm not exactly the type for Juliet. I wanted to do Cleopatra or Lady Macbeth or Ophelia. But the school wouldn't hear of it. They're *awfully* conservative. I can scare the wits out of the girls by just *reading* Macbeth. I have a flair for horror." She stared at Miss Lamson thoughtfully. "I suppose one reason you're such a good actress," she continued, "is that you've *lived* so much."

Miss Lamson laughed. "You mean I've *suffered?*" she said with exaggeration.

"Uummmm," said Violet. "Marriages and divorces and all that. That's what worries me about *my* performance, I'm afraid maybe it'll be shallow. Because, after all, I haven't really suffered very much. And I'm not even *sure* I've ever been in love. I ought to have been in love at least *once* in order to play Juliet, don't you think?"

"Such talk!" said Aunt Esther.

Laura Lamson smiled knowingly at Esther. "Oh, now, you must have been pretty fond of *some* little boy at one time or other."

Violet tried solemnly to remember. "No, I really don't think so. Of course there was Horace Smith. But I don't think that was love; I think it was just that he had a pony."

Laura Lamson laughed. "Violet," she said," I have a feeling that your performance of Juliet will be something unique."

Violet wasn't sure how to take that.

Violet was spending this week end at home in the apartment on West Twelfth Street. It was an unusually quiet week end. Her brothers and sisters were all away, and in the apartment there were only Pete, Lily, and Aunt Esther.

After dinner they sat around immersed in their own individual problems. Aunt Esther, an enormous sewing bag by her side, was making a ten-year-old child's shirt over for an eight-year-old. Aunt Esther was always altering clothes. And sometimes she forgot which of the six children she was doing it for. Pete had spread a number of his canvases and water colors around the room and was staring gloomily at them and sucking absentmindedly on his pipe. Lily was seated at the desk writing letters. Violet was lying on her stomach on the floor idly looking at a pulp magazine which she had picked up on the bus, mainly because Aunt Esther had said it was "trashy." That word was always a challenge to Violet.

"I think," said Violet sadly, "that I've been leading too protected a life."

Nobody thought it worth while to encourage that line of thought. When Violet started talking that way, it might lead to anything.

"I don't think I've really *lived* yet. What I need is a B.E.E.—a Big Emotional Experience."

Still nobody paid any attention.

"Look at these things!" said Pete, indicating his pictures. "Will somebody please tell me why the hell they don't sell? They're *good!* They ought to be making me some money. I *know* they're good."

Nobody answered that, either. They'd heard Pete carrying on that way before. Aunt Esther just smiled a sort of vague Girl Scout smile at him and threaded a needle. The clock struck eight.

Lily looked up from her letter-writing. "Pete, my lovely," she said, "would you mind if Bea Voorhees, you know, that Boston friend of mine, stayed with us for a couple of days next week?"

"Will there be room?" said Pete.

"Well, when do the children come back?"

"Ask Esther."

Aunt Esther put down her sewing. "Wait till I get my files," she said. She picked up a card index from the desk and referred to it.

"Well, I don't know," she said, frowning. "Arthur is due back from his mother in ten days. But we cheated a few days when we sent him to her, so she *may* send him back to us earlier. In that case he'd arrive next week. Then Bruce is at his grandmother's, but she's about to go to Wisconsin. And when she does, he has to come to us. Oh, and my goodness, here's a note I stuck in here months ago. As a special favor, will we take Evelyn the first week in April so she can be in New York to hear *Parsifal*. Oh, really, I'd forgotten that. Then there's a complication about Susie. . . ."

Lily was looking very frigid. "I'm sure there is," she said icily. "Let's just forget the whole thing."

Aunt Esther tried to be soothing. "Of course, if the children *don't* arrive next week. . . ."

"They'll arrive," said Lily. "They always do." She glared at Pete. "The Granden Home for Transient Tots." She turned back to her letter. "I'll just tell Bea Voorhees she better come twenty years from now. By that time the children will be grown up."

Violet rested her chin on her cupped hand. "Listen, Lily," she said, "if you wanted to live a Full Life, how would you set about it?"

"Ask your father," said Lily acidly. "He's lived a full life, all right." Pete stared at her morosely.

"What's he ever done but have children?" said Violet with exasperation.

"That's what I want to know!" answered Lily with considerable feeling.

"Picking on me again, huh?" growled Pete, lighting his pipe.

"What would *you* do, Aunt Esther?" persisted Violet.

"What's that, dear?"

"If you wanted to live a Full Life?"

"My life is full enough, thank you, Miss," said Aunt Esther.

Violet pooh-poohed that. "Have you ever had a B.E.E.—a Big Emotional Experience?" she challenged.

Aunt Esther looked right at her. "Violet, you sound moody. Have you been taking your iron every day?"

"*Don't* keep treating me like a child!" said Violet indignantly.

"You are a child, aren't you, dear?" said Aunt Esther, quite unruffled.

"Technically, maybe," said Violet with considerable firmness. "But puberty is just around the corner. I heard Dr. Melvin say so. And, anyway, I'm an old soul. And I always have been. And you know it."

"Such talk!" said Aunt Esther.

Violet went back to her magazine and turned the pages with annoyance. Then suddenly she seemed to find something that interested her. When Pete, a few minutes later, grinned down at her and said, "So you want to know how to live a full life, do you?" Violet didn't even look up. "Never mind," she said, swinging her feet in the air, "I think I've found out how."

Shortly after that she went to her room, and behind a firmly closed door, she flopped down on her bed and turned to the back of the magazine she had been reading. She had found something which delighted her. It was a lonely hearts department called "The Friendship Mart." And underneath that heading it said, "Somebody Wants You for a Friend." Then there was a whole series of published letters from both men and women who wanted to meet people. The idea was that if you wanted to correspond with any of the writers of those letters you wrote them care of The Friendship Mart, and your letter was forwarded. It all sounded *very* intriguing, and glamorous! What's more, she had found a letter which she considered pretty romantic, and she intended to answer it. Here was her chance for adventure and perhaps a B.E.E.

She read the letter over a third time.

DEAR FRIENDSHIP MART:

Well, hello, all you readers between twenty and thirty. I am a boy of twenty-three, and I would very much like to exchange letters with some of you boys and girls of the above ages. I am five feet nine and have light hair and gray eyes. And I am a little inclined to be serious, I guess. Anyway, I have always gone with people older than I am. That does not mean I do not like a good time, however, as I can laugh as well as anybody else when I hear a good joke. I have studied the cornet, though I do not play it much now. But I have always kept up my hobby of collecting cigar bands. Do you have any? I work in the office of a paper bag company. I like movies, particularly James Cagney and Veronica Lake. I have traveled quite a bit, once even living in Texas! I like girls who dance well, though they must have something in the upper story too as I like serious discussions as well as the lighter side of life.

Would anybody like to exchange letters?

"JEEPERS"

Violet felt herself getting quite excited. She went to her desk and took out her very best writing paper, which had the fish swimming across the top. She took her fountain pen in her hand and prayed it wouldn't leak as it sometimes did. Then she started writing:

DEAR "JEEPERS":

Well, yes, I would like to write letters to you. I think your letter is very interesting specially since I am the serious type, too. I definitely have something in the upper story, Jeepers. So you do not have to worry about that. And I was glad to read your letter, because I think there is a awful lot of silliness in the world today, and I think when two people who have serious thoughts get together, they are lucky. To get together, I mean. I lead a pretty busy and interesting life. But lately I am beginning to think it is not full enough. I think maybe it is not so hot emotionally. Lately, Jeepers, I think I may be stagnating. I need new horizons. Cleopatra said "I have immortal longings in me." Only she was talking about dying but I am talking about living so I guess mine are "mortal longings." You don't mind if I quote Cleopatra, do you? She was a very interesting queen. I am glad you have studied to play the cornet and I think you should play it. It is nice in symphony orchestras. Do you like Bach? He is the BEST composer. That is just my opinion. And if you think differently you have a right to your opinion. I am not ever narrow about things like that. Do you like the theatre? I am an actress and right now I am getting ready to act Juliet in Wm. Shakespeare's "Romeo and Juliet." I have blue eyes and brown hair and nobody has ever said I looked like Veronica Lake. But I have just been thinking I almost could. In a way. In certain lights. Anyway I think we have a lot in common, Jeepers, don't you? And so I hope you answer this letter. And then I will answer yours. And so on.

Very sincerely, your friend,
"AMARYLIS"

P.S.—I haven't any cigar bands. But I will keep on the look-out for them from now on.

When she read it over, Violet thought it was a beautiful letter. She sighed and put it in an envelope and addressed it to "The Friendship Mart." In the morning she would mail it, and then *anything* could happen.

ON MONDAY she went back to school and left firm instructions with Aunt Esther to be *sure* to forward her mail.

"I'm expecting something *very* important," she said.

Monday morning she had a rehearsal of *Romeo and Juliet* at which things didn't progress very well. Miss Russell of the English Department was directing the play. Her practical knowledge of the theater was derived from the experience she had received playing The Fifth Deadly Sin in a pageant at Bryn Mawr. She considered herself an authority on acting. Violet did not. Violet felt she knew a great deal more about it than Miss Russell. Consequently, Miss Russell was often jamming her hairpins into place with annoyance. When Miss Russell grew annoyed, she lost hairpins.

Violet was in a critical mood. "You know, Miss Russell," she said, "this is supposed to be done in an original way. What's original about the way we're doing it?"

"I have not asked for criticism," said Miss Russell sharply.

"I think this old balcony scene is too *short*," continued Violet. "Why couldn't we add some of Juliet's other speeches onto it?"

Miss Russell was horrified. "I wouldn't even *think* of tampering with Shakespeare!"

"I would," said Violet frankly.

Miss Russell turned to speak to another member of the cast; and Violet frowned unhappily, still wishing she were playing Cleopatra.

Miss Russell tapped a chair. "Now, let's try this scene again. And, Violet, please let yourself go more. Let us *hear* the ache in your heart."

They started the scene.

"I think it would help," said Violet, "if I took off my glasses."

"By all means," said Miss Russell.

Violet struck an attitude and looked sad. She tried frantically to make tears come into her eyes. When she couldn't, it made her pretty mad.

"It's too flat," said Miss Russell. "More lovelorn. More desperate."

"Listen, Miss Russell," said Violet, putting her hands defiantly on her hips. "I don't know how to feel lovelorn. But just give me time. Don't rush me. By this time next week, I *may* be so lovelorn you can hardly stand it."

Miss Russell kept her temper with difficulty.

Two days later, Violet received a letter from Jeepers. She hurriedly locked herself in a bathroom and sat down to read in private.

DEAR "AMARYLIS":

Well, I certainly was tickled to get your letter. It was a dandy, and it made me feel I certainly would like you for a friend. I think our letters should be very interesting to each other. Like you say, two people who have serious thoughts are lucky to discover each other. It is weird, kind of, isn't it? Like fate or something. And I have never known an actress before. What a fascinating life you must lead. I was interested in your quoting Cleopatra who must be a very intriguing historical personality. I do not know much about her. But she was "hot stuff" I guess. You ask me if I like Bach. Well, I don't know his stuff very well, though I believe he is very good as you say, because Benny Goodman plays something of his. Like me, Benny Goodman has his more serious moments. Please do not think that Veronica Lake is absolutely my dream type. I like other types, too. So don't think I would be for one moment influenced by whether you looked like her or not. We all have to look like ourselves, I guess. That is human nature. Well, I could go on a lot more about human nature, but I want to get this off and besides I am at the end of a page. Now I am going to tell you my name and address. And I hope you will tell me yours.

Your devoted friend,

ERNEST CLAPHEE

790 Washart Street

Jersey City, New Jersey

P.S.—Do not worry about the cigar bands. My interest in them is really not so much. I have already made eleven ashtrays out of them. I don't believe I'll

make any more. I also collect cigar coupons. Have you any? It is wonderful
what you can get with them. Like my Aunt Vera, who got an Egyptian
incense burner. She had 1833 coupons.

Violet was in seventh heaven over this letter. Now she actually
knew who she was in love with. Ernest Claphee! What an interesting
name! She'd never known anybody named Ernest. Nor had she ever
been to Jersey City. But it sounded fascinating. Here she was carrying on a secret correspondence with a sort of a blind date in Jersey
City! What could be more adventurous?

She decided to write him at once. She had twenty minutes before
her next class. She sat down at her desk and twisted her legs intensely
around the legs of the chair.

DEAR ERNEST:

Since you came right out and told me your name, I guess it is all right
for me to call you "dear Ernest." I feel we are getting to know each other
better and better. And there is no telling where this may end. That's what I
hope, anyway. Wouldn't it be funny if you were just the person I'd been looking for to widen my horizons? Wouldn't it be funny if you were going to be the
one to make me live a Full Life and Suffer? An actress has to, you know. And
lately I've been in sort of a rut, I guess. And for that reason I am delighted to
make the acquaintance of someone in another state like New Jersey. Jersey City
is not far from New York, is it? *I hope not.* Do not worry about not knowing
much about Bach. I will teach you a lot, and you can play fugues on your
cornet. I am sorry to say, dear Ernest, that I have no cigar coupons. But I will
try to get some. That's how much I think of you. Do not think I am being
brazen in this letter, please. I am just the sort of woman who believes in speaking her mind. And anyway, why waste time? *Tempus fugit,* you know.

Longing to hear from you soon, I remain. . . .

Violet hesitated with her pen in mid-air. There was something so
awfully final about signing her name to that letter. Suppose Ernest
in a moment of eager passion, feeling he could stand the separation
no longer, suddenly appeared one day at her family's apartment? He
would ask for Violet Granden and be told at once that she was at
school. Then he'd learn she was only twelve. It was a thought which
made Violet's heart sink into her toes. That would be *too* revolting.

She sat wondering what to do; and then it occurred to her that
Aunt Esther was going to go away for a while. It might be safer to
use *her* name. Then if Ernest appeared and inquired for Esther

Granden, he'd simply be told she wasn't there. Yes, that seemed best. She finished the letter:

> Longing to hear from you soon, I remain
> ESTHER GRANDEN
> 32 West 12th Street
> New York City

P.S.—Please address me as Miss E. Violet Granden. Though I'm usually called Esther.

P.P.S.—I'll explain to you about Cleopatra sometime when I know you better.

That afternoon Violet was marvelous at the rehearsal of *Romeo and Juliet*. At any rate she felt marvelous. And Miss Russell had to admit she was giving the part a new fervor. "You're almost giving it too much," said Miss Russell. "Don't overdo it now."

Violet was indignant at that. "What you'll get in my performance of Juliet, Miss Russell, is a reflection of life."

Miss Russell wished earnestly that she had given the role of Juliet to some meek little girl. She was beginning to think that personality in a child was not at all to be desired, after all.

ON FRIDAY what Violet had feared might happen happened. But Aunt Esther had not gone away, which made things very complicated, indeed.

Aunt Esther answered the doorbell when it rang, and there stood a smiling young man who was quite definitely fat. He had round smiling cheeks and rather boyish blond hair. He carried a little black case and looked shy.

"Miss Esther Granden?" he said.

"Yes."

"I'm Ernest Claphee."

Poor Esther never could remember names. And she didn't think she had ever seen this fat young man before. But she might have. And it seemed she must have met him, since he knew her. Oh, dear, she thought, why wasn't her memory better!

"Oh . . . yes," she said, smiling politely and racking her brain.

"I thought I'd just call. If you don't mind. I thought I'd like to get together."

Aunt Esther looked even vaguer. "Oh . . . yes. Uh . . . won't you come in?"

Ernest came in and sat down shyly in the living room, still smiling broadly and holding nervously onto his hat. Esther sat down and smiled back at him.

"What can I do for you?" she said.

"Well, I just thought . . . we ought to say hello to each other, sort of get better acquainted, you know. After all, we have a lot in common . . ."

Aunt Esther looked completely lost. Her nice eyes grew wider, and she put a hand to her chin thoughtfully. "Oh, dear . . ." she said hopelessly, and she blushed. "You know I'm just terrible at remembering things. And . . . and I just can't place you. I *know* I've seen you somewhere, but I just *can't* remember . . ."

"No, you've never seen me. I only described myself in my letters. Remember?" Ernest was looking worried himself now. "You . . . you said I was going to widen your horizons, don't you remember? I thought that was a pretty nice thing to say." He smiled pleasantly at her.

Esther's head was spinning. There must be something awfully wrong *somewhere*. "Now let's get this straight," she said. "*When* did I say that . . . that about the horizons?"

"Why in your last letter," said Ernest.

"But I've never written you any letters!"

"Well, I've got them right here in my pocket. You . . . answered my letter in The Friendship Mart. You *are* Esther Granden, aren't you?"

Ernest had taken Violet's letters from his pocket and held them out to Esther. She took them and read them. As soon as she came to the references to Bach she began to see light. Violet was always talking about Bach.

"Oh, dear," said Esther, "I'm *afraid,* Mr. Claphee, that you have fallen into the clutches of my niece."

"Your niece?" said Ernest, not understanding.

"She's a vixen of twelve years, and it is obviously she who has been wanting what she calls a Big Emotional Experience . . ."

Ernest grew red and looked very uncomfortable. "*Twelve years old?*" he said.

"Yes," nodded Esther consolingly. "That's why she used my name."

"Then . . . then," spluttered Ernest, "it was all sort of a joke!"

"Well, it wouldn't be a joke to Violet. She considers herself very grown up."

Ernest just sat still for a moment, brooding. Then he said, "Hell!"

"I'm *so* sorry," said Esther, who saw that Ernest was really very much disappointed.

Ernest looked at the black case by his feet. "And I brought my cornet and everything."

Aunt Esther thought for a moment he was going to cry. She felt he was *such* a nice young man. So polite and all.

"Were—were you going to play something?"

"Yes. She was going to introduce me to Bach."

Esther looked sympathetically at him. "There's some music over on the piano," she said.

"I had to get my cornet out of hock, too," said Ernest, still feeling sorry for himself.

"Oh, what a shame!" said Esther, who by this time was feeling definitely responsible for Ernest Claphee. "Well, why don't you try a little of her music. She wouldn't mind. And maybe it'll make you feel better."

Ernest just sat for another few seconds. Then suddenly he took his cornet out of its case and cleaned it a bit. Then he walked over to the piano, where he gloomily thumbed over some of the sheet music.

"Little girls have no right to do things like that," he said angrily.

"I quite agree with you," said Aunt Esther. "Now *do* play something."

Ernest raised the cornet to his lips and played. He had very strong lungs.

That's how it happened that when Pete and Lily returned to the house, the living room was filled with something which hardly resembled bird song. It was considerably louder; and it made things vibrate. They stood in the living room door, completely baffled by the sight of one fat young man blowing his heart out on an old cornet.

Pete frowned angrily and stamped out toward the kitchen, where he hoped to find Esther.

Esther was busy, a little smile on her face.

"Who," demanded Pete explosively, "is that fat Gabriel in the living room?"

Esther looked perfectly blank. "Who, dear?"

"That strange, fat young man who's making those awful sounds!" He gestured wildly toward the front of the apartment.

"Oh, him!" said Esther, suddenly remembering. "I'd forgotten all about him. He's a young man who plays the cornet."

"*That,*" snapped Pete, "is fairly obvious. Or at least he *thinks* he plays it. But who is he?"

Esther frowned. "Oh, dear, I've forgotten his name."

Pete tried to be patient. "I don't ask much around here," he said, "but when I come home and find people making a deafening racket in my own apartment, I *do* like to have some idea who they are."

"He's not 'people,'" said Esther. "He's just one young man; and he's rather sweet."

"But he *is* making a deafening racket. You can't deny that."

A blaring crescendo of shrill notes shook the apartment at that moment, so Esther couldn't deny it.

"He's rather lonesome, I guess," said Esther, "and I said he could play some of Violet's music. You see, it was Violet who wrote him the letters."

"Ah," said Pete bitterly, "enter the menace. Of course, Violet *would* be in it. . . . *What* letters?"

Esther did her best to explain.

At that moment, Violet entered the front door, having come home for the week end. She paused, amazed, in the living room door. She frowned at the sounds Ernest Claphee was making. It never occurred to her who he might be, since she had never suspected that her beloved Emotional Experience might be fat. She beat it down the hall and into the kitchen.

"Who," she demanded," is that fat man who's murdering Bach?"

Pete glared at her with a look that was far from paternal.

"Violet," he said, "I'm at the end of my rope. I cannot have this sort of thing. My home is my castle. You *cannot* make it ludicrous! I won't have it!"

"Keep your wig on," said Violet. She turned to Aunt Esther. "Who *is* he?"

"He's a man who says you wrote him letters."

Violet for once in her life was almost speechless with shock.

Pete waggled a finger in her face. "You signed your Aunt Esther's name and sent it through the mails. That's forgery. It's fraud!"

Violet didn't hear him. She just stared at Aunt Esther. "*That fat man is Ernest Claphee?*" she gasped.

"That's right."

Violet closed her eyes with horror. "Oh, my gosh!" she said.

Pete decided to be stern. He flung down his hat. "Why did you do it?" he demanded.

Violet looked very dignified. "I was trying to enrich my emotional life," she said succinctly.

"Oh, good Lord!" said Pete.

"To improve my acting," continued Violet.

"Oh, so it's your acting that started all this nonsense, is it? Well, then, young lady, you'll just have to do without your acting."

"Now, Pete," said Esther, trying to smooth things over.

"This time I'm going to be firm," said Pete. "Violet *has* to be taught to behave properly . . . Listen, little Miss Thrill-Seeker, I'm not going to allow you to be in this play. Do you understand? *That's* going to be your punishment! Maybe that'll teach you a lesson!"

Violet looked stonily at her father and swung her hat defensively. "They couldn't *possibly* do without me. I'm Juliet."

"Not any more, you're not! I'm going to call Miss Kilbridge right now."

Violet didn't think he really would; but he did. He went firmly into the living room and asked Ernest Claphee to leave and take his cornet with him. He said he was sorry for what his daughter had done.

Ernest still looked morose. He glared at Pete. "She said she was an actress," he muttered. "Gee, I was all excited. I got my cornet out of hock and everything."

"Too bad," said Pete.

"People shouldn't bring children like her into the world," said Ernest, shifting the blame to Pete.

"There's no use locking the barn door after the horse is gone," said Pete tersely.

Then Ernest Claphee left. And Pete phoned Miss Kilbridge and said firmly that Violet could definitely not play Juliet. They would have to get somebody else.

Violet ran into her room and slammed the door. The tears were coming into her eyes, and she hated to have anyone see her cry. She flung herself across the bed and wailed. It was all too much. The discovery that Ernest Claphee was so fat in itself was enough of a blow.

But having the part of Juliet taken away from her was worse. She guessed she had never felt so miserable. Her sobs made her shake all over. And then suddenly she became quiet. She had a fascinating thought. She had wanted to suffer. And she was. She was *really suffering!* She was so pleased with the idea she found it hard to cry anymore. She rushed to the mirror in order to see her tears before they dried completely away.

By Monday Violet had already begun her campaign to get back the part of Juliet. It involved money, of course. Why was it, she thought sadly, that she always had to pay for what she got!

At school, she discovered that the part had been given to a girl named Nancy Vickley, who was an athlete and didn't give a hoot about acting. That made Violet even more angry. She got Nancy up into her room.

"Look here, palsy-walsy," she said, "you don't really want to play Juliet, do you?"

Nancy was caught off guard for a moment. "No," she said. But then she caught a look in Violet's eye, and her shrewdness came to the fore. "Yes," she said.

"No, you *don't* want to play it. You don't care about acting at all. All you care about is basketball. Now I'm *determined* to play that part. I'm a born actress. I don't have blood in my veins, I have grease paint."

"Hooey," said Nancy sweetly.

"Besides," said Violet confidentially, "I have an idea how to make Juliet particularly original. Now, look, Nancy, why don't you just get sick a day or two before the performance. Then they'll have to let me play it. And you won't have to go through all that dreadful stage fright."

Nancy looked very businesslike. "What's in it for me?" she said, straightening her socks.

"Why should there be anything *in* it for you?"

"I might do it. For cash," said dear little Nancy.

"What kind of a friend are you, anyway?" said Violet, hurt.

"I never said I was your friend. Look, Stoop, I'll promise to get sick two days before the performance *only* if you pay me ten dollars. And it has to be in my hand before that date."

"I bet your father's name is Shylock," said Violet.

Nancy prepared to go. "Those are my terms. Take it or leave it."

Violet sat and brooded. She counted up the days. She had twelve days in which to raise ten dollars. And she had at the moment seventy-nine cents to her name. It was an awful predicament. She would, of course, investigate as many pay phone booths and candy machines as possible. Out of the return slots she *might* garner about twenty-five cents. And she could pawn the little gold watch which Great-aunt Jessie had given her for Christmas. (It had been a disappointment, anyway, since she had *asked* for an encyclopedia.) She could probably sell her Mexican hat to Lydia, her roommate, who had often observed it covetously. Maybe she could get a dollar fifty for it. And she would sell Bruce the privilege of using her chemical set for a percentage of his allowance. Still, all that would not bring her in enough. She must think of something else.

The next day she discovered the *Daily Mirror* was having a "Charming Child Contest"; and she promptly entered a photograph of herself, confident that she would win one of the weekly prizes of ten dollars. When she told Nancy about this, however, Nancy refused to consider the deal clinched. She expressed actual doubt about Violet's ability to win a "Charming Child Contest" or even to place, for that matter. She would still wait for the cash in hand.

Violet retained her somewhat haughty dignity but decided she'd better keep trying to raise other money. That was when the idea involving her father's pictures came to her. It was a simple plan. The next week end she simply took a lot of her father's small canvases and rented them out like books from a rental library. She went from door to door all over the neighborhood offering a canvas for twenty-five cents a week. A renter could enjoy it for that long and then return it.

The idea amused people, and Pete's canvases were pretty good; and Violet found she had collected five dollars and seventy-five cents in rentals. That was enough, with her other sums of money, to buy off Nancy.

Violet went quickly back to school before her father discovered what had happened to his masterpieces. She somehow thought it best not to be around at that fatal moment.

Two days before the performance of *Romeo and Juliet*, Nancy, according to agreement, developed a mysterious ailment. Naturally Miss Russell was frantic, and all she could do was to ask Violet to play Juliet. She was the only one who knew the lines.

Violet said she would be glad to help out in a pinch, even though it meant disobeying her father's orders, a thing which she didn't think any little girl should do. Miss Russell agreed but promised to make it all right with Mr. Granden.

At last Violet was actually going to make her debut as an actress. After all her trials and tribulations, the great day dawned. And it was to be a day no one would forget, least of all poor Miss Russell! She hoped she would never again have to live through anything as nerve-wracking as that performance.

Just before the program began, things looked pretty rosy. The two other schools which were competing were doing scenes from *Midsummer Night's Dream* and *As You Like It*, neither of which Miss Russell considered nearly as good as the balcony scene. *Her* pupils, she felt quite sure, were going to seem much more professional.

Their scene was last on the program, and during the intermission preceding it Miss Russell was rushing around in an ecstasy of excitement seeing that the prop benches and the balcony were placed correctly. Violet climbed up a ladder and stood waiting just behind the balcony window.

"Now, Violet," hissed Miss Russell, "give it all you've got."

"Miss Russell," said Violet with confidence, "you'll be amazed at what I'm going to give it."

"Good luck," finished Miss Russell.

"Happy landing," said Violet, adjusting her costume.

And then the auditorium lights were lowered, and the curtain went up. And in the wings, Miss Russell, with a dazed smile on her face, stood tensely by the side of the prompter.

Romeo, a staunch lad of fourteen, who had big brown eyes, a cowlick, and fine buck teeth, leaped into the garden, and his friends and relatives applauded loyally. Then Violet moved dreamily onto the balcony. Out in the audience Pete and Esther and Lily applauded. Violet draped herself romantically against the railing and sighed.

Romeo finished his speech.

> "Oh, that I were a glove upon that hand,
> That I might touch that cheek!"

That was Violet's cue. She was supposed to say "Ah, me!" And then Romeo would continue. She said it all right, but before Romeo could launch into his next speech, Violet had continued right on into something else. Something which the startled Romeo had certainly never heard at rehearsal:

> "O that I might see
> But such another man!"

Violet was saying.

> "His face was as the heavens; and therein stuck
> A sun and moon, which kept their course, and lighted
> The little O, the earth . . ."

Miss Russell thought her heart had stopped beating. She grabbed the shoulder of the poor little promptress. "Good heavens," she gasped. "What's she saying. Oh, good heavens! What ails the child!"

The promptress, completely lost, looked frantically at her script. That certainly was not *Romeo and Juliet*. On stage, Romeo just stared at Juliet with wide-open mouth, an expression of sick horror on his face.

Violet was going magnificently on:

> "Where think'st thou he is now? Stands he or sits he?
> Or does he walk? Or is he on his horse?
> Oh, happy horse to bear the weight of Romeo!
> Give me some music—music, moody food
> Of us that trade in love."

Miss Russell gasped. "It's out of *Antony and Cleopatra*," she said. "They're Cleopatra's lines! She's put Romeo's name in place of Antony! What *is* that child thinking of!"

The promptress was excited, too. "But they sort of fit in all right!" she said to Miss Russell.

Violet finished the speech and said, "Ah, me!" again very pointedly, so Romeo would know it was his cue.

Romeo picked up the scene again, swallowing hard.

Then for several speeches everything went smoothly. Violet stuck to her regular lines. Miss Russell, in agony, peered out at the audience through a peekhole. They seemed very attentive.

Then suddenly the distraught teacher heard Violet's voice soaring off beautifully into another unrehearsed speech:

> "Let me not to the marriage of true minds
> Admit impediments. Love is not love
> Which alters when it alteration finds . . ."

Miss Russell nearly collapsed. "It's one of the sonnets," she gurgled, almost choking. "*Why* is she saying one of the sonnets!"

The promptress didn't even bother to follow her script. She listened wide-eyed, to Violet. "But, listen, Miss Russell," she whispered with awe, "it fits. It fits right into the scene."

Violet finished the sonnet and picked up her speech in order to give Romeo his correct cue. Romeo was by this time sweating profusely. But the audience for the most part seemed interested and unsuspecting. Most of them apparently knew the lines were Shakespeare's and so supposed they belonged in *Romeo and Juliet*. And Violet was reading them very well.

But when Romeo said:

> "Look thou but sweet,
> And I am proof against their enmity."

and Violet took it as a cue to go into:

> "The quality of mercy is not strained;
> It droppeth as a gentle rain from heaven . . ."

Miss Russell practically fainted dead away.

In the audience, Lily whispered to Pete. "Isn't it strange, I would have *sworn* that speech was in *The Merchant of Venice*."

"If you ask me," whispered Pete, "something's rotten in the state of Denmark and I *suspect* it's Violet!"

Violet finished Portia's well-known speech and returned to Juliet, dutifully giving Romeo his proper cue. For a while the scene progressed quite normally. But Romeo was feeling his legs shake. Violet, on the other hand, had never been in better form. She felt triumphant! There was nothing like improving Shakespeare with Shakespeare!

Then when Romeo said:

> "O, wilt thou leave me so unsatisfied?"

Violet was off again. Back to Cleopatra this time.

"Cold-hearted? Me? Ah, dear, if I be so,
From my cold heart let heaven engender hail,
And poison it in the source; and the first stone
Drop in my neck . . ."

Before she finished the scene she had also managed to get in a speech of Ophelia's from *Hamlet*. Miss Russell was nearly prostrate. And the little boy who was playing Romeo was glassy-eyed with the strain of it all.

The curtain came down to a shower of genuinely appreciative applause.

"That must be the uncut version of the balcony scene," someone was heard to say.

Miss Russell and Miss Kilbridge rushed out onto the stage and confronted Violet.

"You *dreadful* child," wailed Miss Russell, "*why* did you do it? You've ruined everything!"

"That balcony scene needed a little pepping up," said Violet, in a glow of happiness. "Besides my part was too short. I made it a little longer. Now I can say I've played Juliet *and* Cleopatra *and* Portia *and* Ophelia."

"I'm afraid you've made the whole school seem rather ridiculous," said Miss Kilbridge, frowning fiercely.

"Nonsense," said Violet. "The audience loved it."

And then an aged railroad magnate, who was one of the judges, was stepping before the curtain.

He beamed at the audience. "I have the honor to announce," he said smiling shyly, "that in the opinion of the judges the most original performance of Shakespeare was given by Miss Kilbridge's School for Girls in their—uh—potpourri version of *Romeo and Juliet*."

Great applause from the audience.

Miss Kilbridge and Miss Russell stared dumfounded at Violet, who smiled sweetly, forgivingly at them.

Then the two teachers looked at each other.

"Apparently, Miss Russell," said Miss Kilbridge, "it doesn't really matter *who* wrote Shakespeare's plays—Shakespeare, or Bacon, or Violet!"

Father Hires a Cook

CLARENCE DAY

Clarence Day's immortal Father, that lovable tyrant, is at his best (or is it worst?) in this delightful Cook's tour de force. Uninhibited is the word for Father.

ONE LATE AFTERNOON when Father came up from downtown, he found his home much upset. Our cook had walked out and left us. I was a child of four, George was two, and there was a new baby besides. Mother was ill. She hadn't been able to leave us to go to an agency. And as she was no hand at cooking herself, the outlook for dinner was poor.

This state of affairs was unprecedented in all Father's experience. In his father's home, they never changed their servants suddenly; they seldom changed them at all; and as his mother was a past mistress of cooking, he had always been doubly protected. Since his marriage, he had had to live a much bumpier life. But this was the worst yet.

He asked Mother, who was lying in bed, what she was going to do about it. There were no telephones then, and she couldn't do anything at all, at the moment; but she said she would try to go to an agency in the morning and see what she could find. "In the morning? Good God!" Father said. "Where is the place, anyhow?" And he clapped on his hat and strode out again, over toward Sixth Avenue.

As I heard the story years afterward, it was late when he got there, and he bounded up the front stoop two or three steps at a time, and went quickly into the little office, where the gaslights were burning. He had never been in such a place before, and to his surprise it was empty, except for a severe-looking woman who sat at a desk at one side. "Where do you keep 'em?" he urgently demanded, his mind on the question of dinner.

She looked at him, got out her pen, and opened a large book deliberately. "I will take your name and address," she informed him, "and then, if you please, you may give me the details as to what **kind** of person you require and when you would wish her to call."

But Father had no time, he told her, for any damned fol-de-rol. "Where do you keep 'em?" he said again. She was standing in the way of his dinner. I can imagine how his face must have reddened and how his eyes must have blazed at her. "I am asking you where you keep them!" he roared.

"Why, the girls are in there," the lady explained, to calm him, "but clients are not allowed in that room. If you will tell me the kind of position you wish me to fill for you, I will have one come out."

Before she'd half finished, Father had thrown open the door and gone in. There sat a crowd of the girls, young and old, sickly and brawny, of all shapes and sizes; some ugly, some pretty and trim and stylish, some awkward; nurses, ladies' maids, waitresses, washer-women, and cooks.

The manager was by now at Father's elbow, trying to make him get out, and insisting that he tell her the position he wished her to fill. But Father was swiftly glancing around at the crowd, and he paid no attention. He noticed a little woman in the corner, with honest gray eyes, who sat there, shrewd-looking and quiet. He pointed his cane over at her and said, "I'll take that one."

The manager was flustered, but still she kept trying to enforce her authority. She protested she didn't yet know the position. . . .

"Cook," Father said, "cook."

"But Margaret doesn't wish to be a cook, she wants—"

"You can cook, can't you?" Father demanded.

Margaret's plain little face was still pink with excitement and pleasure at being chosen above all that roomful by such a masterful gentleman. Father had probably smiled at her, too, for they liked each other at once. Well, she said, she had cooked for one family.

"Of course she can cook," Father said.

He said afterward, when describing the incident, "I knew at once she could cook."

The manager didn't like this at all. The discipline of the office was spoiled. "If you are going to take her anyhow," she said acidly, "what day would you wish her to come, and will you please give me your name?"

"Yes, yes," Father said, without giving it. "Come on, Margaret." And he planked down the fee and walked out.

Margaret followed him through the door and trotted over to our home at his heels. He sent her down to the kitchen immediately, while he went upstairs to dress.

"I don't know why you make such a fuss about engaging new servants. It's simple enough," he said comfortably to Mother that evening, after Margaret's first dinner.

It was the first of a long series, for she stayed with us twenty-six years.

Woman's Work

ELIZABETH DUNN

Let's take a peek at gay, irrepressible Candy who couldn't do mathematics, but who could add one Pan and one George to equal one couple. Didn't this multiply her problems!

IT WAS ALMOST the end of a long afternoon of bandage rolling. Candy added her last two-by-two square to the pile in front of her, and stretched. She thought hazily that she must remember to get David more zwieback tomorrow and that she liked the smell of Hope Morgan's house—a curious combination of floor wax, daffodils and dogs.

Hope poked her in the spine. "Wait till they've gone. I've got something to tell you."

It was after five when at last Hope dropped on the sofa. She was a big-boned, handsome woman, who loved dogs and a few people—particularly her husband, Lobby Morgan, a large, kind, silent man whom everyone liked and nobody thought about. Amy Bunnell had once said that Lobby was just like one of Hope's Airedales. "You know," Amy had elaborated, "energetic, loyal and illiterate."

The Morgans' purebred butler brought in a silver-laden tray, and Hope gave Candy some tea. As Ashburn left, she said, "Baby, I have sinned."

Candy said, "Hope, darling, I have exactly twenty minutes before

131

I have to go home and feed David his supper. If you have anything sordid to say, you'd better hurry."

"You and your David," Hope grumbled. "How old is he now—six months? Why doesn't he feed himself? You're ruining that child."

Candy giggled. "Oh, we're giving him a terribly sheltered life. Go on. What have you done?"

"I have no idea," Hope said gloomily. "But I must have sinned, because I am being visited by Pan. Next week."

"Make sense," Candy urged.

"I am. Pandora. Pan Peters. The dear friend of my girlhood whose talented neck I would gladly wring. She's coming here for a month, she and her horrid little airplane."

"Why, I didn't even know you knew Pan Peters." Candy was enchanted. "You mean the war correspondent? The one who wrote *Pegasus Is a Lady?*"

Hope nodded. "She's been to Teheran and Russia and goodness knows where, and now she's coming here to get over it."

"But she must be perfectly fascinating."

"She's fascinating, all right," Hope agreed darkly. "Even **Lobby** is slightly in love with her. But it's my brother George who's causing the trouble. My brother George has been in love with Pan Peters ever since I brought her home from Miss March's for spring vacation in 1930."

"Why doesn't he marry her?" Candy asked reasonably.

"Because she won't. She's had millions of beaus, but she won't get married. You see, she doesn't want a home—at least she doesn't want to *make* one—and George is as domestic as a bedroom slipper."

"Your brother George is domestic?" Candy was politely skeptical.

"I know, I know. The glamour boy of journalism—owner and publisher of *Meridian,* that unique newspaper as modern as tomorrow —the Boy with a By-line. But he *is* domestic—probably as a reaction from growing up with me. He wants his little wife to stay home, picking oakum and dipping her own candles."

"And Miss Peters won't. But doesn't that settle it?"

"Settle it! When Pan gets here," Hope prophesied grimly, "George will come out every week end and mope around like a disillusioned setter till about Sunday noon, when he and Pan will have a fight that'll make the clocks strike out of sheer nervousness. And then he'll flounce off in a rage and come back the next week end for an encore."

"I don't see why," Candy said mildly, "George should have everything *his* way."

Hope looked shocked. "But George is—well, I mean, he's *George*," she explained.

"Oh," said Candy.

"And you," Hope went on, "are going to put a stop to this nonsense."

"Me?"

"Listen." Hope swung her feet off the sofa. "George has almost got to the place where he'll take Pan on any terms, even her own—and that mustn't happen. I'm very fond of Pan, but I adore George, and Pan would break his heart and ruin his life and make a hash of his career. Now you and Bill make domesticity look as attractive as illicit love. I mean you sort of *enjoy* your house and your baby and everything."

"Sort of!" Candy snorted.

"Well, that's what I mean—and you do it so well, Candy. I want George to see it. I want to show him what a happy married life is like—what a real wife is."

"Well, of all the ridiculous— I suppose I'm to whip up a little five-course dinner, in a tulle evening dress and a straw hat with ribbons, meanwhile singing the Bell Song from Lakmé, and giving the cradle a brisk kick in passing?"

"You get things so quickly, dear," Hope said acidly.

"And shall I tell George that I make all my husband's clothes out of skins?" Candy inquired.

"Now listen, are you going to help me or are you not?"

"I'll help," Candy assured her. "Not that it will do the slightest good."

"Why not?" Hope was truculent. She didn't like Candy's attitude.

"Well, I mean, things don't work that way. For instance, I only got domestic *after* I got married, and I've noticed that most men don't seem to like girls who are just terribly domestic *before* they get married. If you see what I mean. . . . Never mind, never mind. Will you bring Miss Peters and your brother George to lunch next Sunday?"

"I will," said Hope. "And you'd better make it good, see?"

CANDY twisted her back hair with her left hand and groaned aloud. Bill shot his neck around the wing chair. "Gosh—what's the matter, darling?"

Candy raised tragic eyes to his. "Bill, I've made a terrible discovery."

He was bending over her in an instant. "What, darling?"

Candy buried her head in her arms and her voice was thin with despair. "I can't add."

Bill blew out his breath explosively. "Heavens, I thought you had an incurable disease, or something."

She lifted her head. "Bill, isn't the bank ever wrong?"

"Never. People who work in banks run by machinery. You can't win."

Candy stared at the checkbook inimically. "There's not enough."

"Enough what?" Bill was patient.

"Money."

"Why, two weeks ago we had what I should have described as a rude plenty. What's happened to it?"

"I haven't spent a cent of it," Candy said. "Honestly, Bill. The bank takes it or something."

"You've made a mistake," Bill said smugly. "You'll find it." He started toward his chair, and Candy seized his coattails.

"LISTEN, Bill," she said desperately. "In this house we run things as a partnership, don't we? You do certain things—I do certain things. I paint furniture, talk on the telephone, answer all letters from your family and plant flower seeds. Right?"

"Right," said Bill.

"And you fix the fire, take care of the car and get anything I happen to want after I've turned out the light and opened the window."

"Right," said Bill, with feeling.

"From now on," said Candy, "you also do the bills."

"Think so?" Bill inquired cautiously.

Candy pounded the desk with passionate conviction. "There are certain things that are not women's work, and this is one of them. I'll do anything else you want, Bill. I'll weave and churn and vote intelligently—like you—but I will not—I will *not*—do the checkbook any more!"

"Get away," Bill said indulgently. "I'll do it. You can get out on the roof and mend that shingle that blew off in January."

"Some women could even do that. Some women can—oh, that reminds me! Darling, who do you think is coming to visit the Morgans?"

Bill plucked at his hair. "And five is twenty-three. . . . Santa Claus. The stork. Monty Woolley. Who? And let's not guess."

"Pandora Peters."

"Oh, really?"

"But aren't you excited?"

"Sure. . . . Carry two."

"The Morgans are bringing her here for lunch on Sunday."

Bill's pencil stopped and he glanced up at his wife. "Really? Well, it'll be fun to see Pan again."

"*Again?* Do you know her?"

"Certainly I know her. I've known her for years."

"You never told me," Candy said accusingly.

Bill returned to the checkbook. "You never asked."

"Do you know Winston Churchill?"

"No."

"General Eisenhower?"

"Nope."

"Mary Martin?"

"No!"

"Well, don't say I never asked you," Candy warned him. "When did you meet Pan Peters?"

"Five or six years ago."

"Oh. Before you knew me."

"Yep."

"Attractive?"

"Very."

"Did you—did you see much of her?"

"Listen," said Bill, "I find that I can't add, either."

"But did you?"

"If you mean did I fall for her, no, I did not. I saw something of her. So did about forty other men."

"Do you know Hope's brother, George Deming?"

"Fifteen, twenty, twenty-seven. . . . Everybody knows George Deming."

"He wants to marry her."

"Fine. Congratulations, George. Hope you'll be very happy. Fifty-four, sixty-three, sixty-eight, seventy."

"But Hope doesn't want him to. She thinks he'd be very unhappy. Because you see, Bill, he's very domestic and Hope says Pan isn't a bit home-loving. In fact—"

"Be still, woman!" Bill roared suddenly, and Candy jumped. "All this prattle about sex—my mind is going! Go away and let me add in peace."

SUNDAY morning dawned sapphire and gold—the sort of day when to stay indoors is a crime against Nature. A disproportionate part of Candy's morning was spent in convincing Bill that the garden furniture needed washing. After that she got a very special lunch, with the help of Irish Ellen, pressed David's yellow sun suit and finally retired to her room, to make herself the picture of cool, competent serenity. Just as she was finishing her hair, Bill came in and collapsed on her bed.

"What do you want me to do now?" he inquired weakly. "Build a wing on the house? There's just time before lunch."

"I never saw anyone so feeble," Candy told him sternly. "Why, I do three times as much in a day—"

"Women have more endurance. It's been proved. What's for lunch —ham?"

"Ham!" Candy shrieked. "My good yokel, we're having avocado pears and chicken à la bonne femme and that thin corn bread and strawberries for dessert. It's going to be heavenly—just like one of those French picnics that Renoir painted. Now go and get dressed, darling. It's late."

"What do I wear?" Bill asked in a tone of resignation. "A boating costume?"

Candy held out a mass of flowered chintz. "Darling, before you go, just help me into this, will you?"

Bill recoiled. "What is it—a slip cover?"

"It's an apron. It seemed sort of appropriate. Aunt Essie sent it to me for Christmas and I don't know exactly how to get into it, but it said on the card 'For a busy little bride,' so it must be very practical."

Bill examined Aunt Essie's garment. "Any little bride," he said at last, "who gets in and out of this is bound to be busy. Turn around."

After some minutes he asked feverishly, "Wouldn't it be simpler if I just tied you hand and foot and locked you in a steel box and lowered you into the East River? If I get you into this, you'll never get out again. And I can't see why you suddenly want to wear an apron to lunch anyway."

"Hurry!" Candy implored. "I hear a car stopping."

She fled out to the apple tree; there was just time for one last glance at the round garden table, set demurely with white milk china on a pink cotton cloth. Then Hope's voice rang across the lawn, and Candy turned as four people came toward her.

She had been prepared to be either awed or irritated by George Deming, but she had not been prepared for his charm. He was a slight, well-built man, quite unlike his sister except for his coloring. He smoked continually, with quick, nervous gestures, and his dark eyes looked tired and sardonic and alive. *He's nice!* Candy thought at once, and smiled on him warmly.

"Candy, this is Pandora Peters," Hope's voice broke in.

Candy turned. She heard herself sounding like a hostess and other people sounding like guests; but she was quite unaware of the words that were spoken, so intense was her concentration on Pandora Peters —on her straight blond hair that fell so casually in exactly the right places, her enormous, intelligent dark blue eyes, her exquisite complexion and fragile, perfect little figure. She was wearing impeccably cut slacks of black gabardine, her jacket hung on one shoulder.

What, Candy thought, *is the matter with George, anyway? Does he want all this and a hausfrau too?* "I read your book, *Pegasus.* I loved it," she said.

"Thank you," Pan Peters said, almost with surprise. "That's nice of you."

They smiled at each other; and the side door slammed. Bill came toward them across the lawn, and Candy felt a little flame of pride leap up inside her: dear Bill. He looked so nice in his gray flannels, with his hair brushed.

"Why, Bill Stewart, I don't believe it!" Pan Peters cried. "How absolutely wonderful! I didn't know—"

They were shaking hands, and everyone was talking: "Do you remember that little place in the Village?" . . . "Of course during Prohibition—"   "Those were the days when—"

CANDY looked down at Aunt Essie's apron; she felt suddenly bunchy and fluffy and unbearably ruffled. Bows, curls, chintz—and those slim black slacks, that heavy white silk shirt.

"Bill!" she said sharply. "Open the ginger ale, will you, please?"

She was instantly conscious of Pan Peters' glance. *Now why did I have to sound like that—all bossy and bad-tempered?*

"What a delightful spot this is, Mrs. Stewart," said George Deming. "Look at us! We look just like one of Renoir's picnics in modern dress. Except you. You're right off the canvas."

Candy smiled at him again, with affection. *Hope is right; George is George, and he mustn't be allowed to ruin his life—he'd be miserable with that kind of girl.* For a fleeting second there was a sequel to the thought: *What kind of girl?*

Pan's giggle mingled with a shout from Bill. "And then, do you remember, Bill, we all got in the taxi, the whole eight of us—"

"Candy only has a maid three times a week," Hope told George with possessive pride. "I simply couldn't do it—I can't boil an egg. Can I, Lobby?"

Lobby smiled at his wife and said, "Don't have to."

"This chicken thing is wonderful!" George said. "I love to cook. How do you make it? Will you tell?"

"Of course I'll tell," Candy said. "You begin with six little white onions, and when they're fried brown you—"

"Well, of course they kept the press miles away from the palace," Pan's voice said clearly. "But one of the guards—well, he told me to be at the west gate at eleven that evening—"

Candy looked at her guests. Every eye was on Pan's vivid face—even the perfidious Hope's. *So I'm left holding six little white onions while everybody else gets smuggled into a palace. What palace? Where?* She listened, and found herself spellbound. Pan Peters might not be able to clean house, but she could tell a story; and the things that had happened to her made good telling. The sun made a pattern of green and gold lace on the innocent pink cloth and the red country strawberries.

"So he laughed and said—in French, because he didn't speak any English—'Well, I don't know how you got here, young woman, but here you are, so what do you want to know?' Of course I asked him right off whether it was true—"

Hope suddenly awoke. "George!" she barked, and everyone jumped. "Don't you want to hear how to make this chicken thing?"

In the sunny silence, Candy heard the sparrows insulting one another on the garage roof, and met Bill's eyes, filled with startled incredulity. "But I don't—he doesn't—" she babbled, and halted miserably.

"Shall we hear the end of Pan's story first?" Bill suggested mildly, and Candy blushed to the roots of her hair.

"My sister Hope," said George in her ear, "whom I love very dearly, is a half-wit. Although I do want to know how to make this chicken thing."

Candy smiled unhappily at him. *Sometimes I hate tact.*

They had finished lunch and were lying on the grass when Ellen brought David across the lawn.

"Isn't he beautiful?" Hope cried. "Hold him, Candy."

Candy took her fat son. *We will now give George the Madonna business. He is to be spared nothing.*

"George loves babies, don't you, George?" said Hope blandly.

"I like this one," said George. "Hi, fella," and he offered a finger to David, who accepted it cordially.

"Don't you adore babies, Pan?" Hope pursued.

Pan said, laughing, "I'm scared to death of them, and they know it. I think they're all mind readers and it unnerves me."

"Know too much. Always thought so," said Lobby.

Bill got up. "Come and look at my tampala. It's about six inches high. Delicious too."

"Like to see that," said Lobby. "Artichokes, sort of."

Pan got smoothly to her feet. "I say it's spinach, Chinese version. I'm sure I had it once when we were dining with the Chiangs. It's funny stuff."

They wandered off toward the garden.

George stretched out. "I'd forgotten that places like this still exist, Mrs. Stewart."

"Oh, call her Candy," Hope said.

George smiled. "May I? I'd even forgotten there were girls like you left in the world: simple and uncomplicated; your husband's very lucky."

Certainly he's very lucky. He's in the garden with Pan Peters. "I often wear slacks myself," she said. George looked startled.

"George," said Hope firmly, "why don't you go and look at the tampala?"

George went.

"This," said Candy to Hope, "is a lot of nonsense. It's not proving a thing."

"Darling, don't stop now," Hope implored. "It's just beginning to take effect. Can't you see how George is basking? It's exactly the life he wants for himself."

"I don't believe it," Candy said flatly, digging grass out of David's mouth. "George wants things to happen. He doesn't want his women simple and uncomplicated—not for a minute."

"Sooner or later," said Hope impressively, "George is bound to realize that Pan's sort of life is nervous and high-strung and geared to such a speed that it has no time for the—er—for the simple essentials."

"When did you make up that speech?" Candy inquired politely.

HOPE grinned. "It's just something I jotted down on the back of an old envelope. No, but honestly, Candy, it's true. Please don't let me down."

"It's the silliest plan I ever heard of, and I don't know why I ever lent myself to it." Candy picked up David. "But since I've started, I'll finish. Only, I warn you"—her eyes slid away to the vegetable garden, where the three men stood around Pan—"if anything happens—"

"What can happen?" Hope demanded. "Don't be ridiculous!"

CANDY suspended her hairbrush and looked over her shoulder at Bill, who was rooting in his bottom bureau drawer. "What are you looking for?"

"Snapshots," said Bill. "I've got some somewhere of a picnic we went on."

"Which picnic do you mean?"

BILL cleared his throat. "I mean one Pan and I went on. I thought she'd be amused by it."

Something sliced at Candy's heart. *A picnic "we" went on.* . . . "Pandora is a funny sort of name, isn't it?" she observed. She sounded just the way she meant to sound: impersonal, mildly interested.

"Romantic mother, I suppose," said Bill.

"But don't you think it's odd to name a child after the girl who opened the box and let all the trouble into the world?" Bill grunted noncommittally, and Candy looked at herself in the mirror. "I wonder why she doesn't marry George."

Bill began taking off his shoes. "Why should she?"

"Well, Hope says he's been in love with her for years."

"Funny way of being in love," Bill remarked. "Always trying to reform a girl. What's the matter with her the way she is? Everybody else likes it."

"Oh," said Candy. "Yes."

"George," said Bill, "makes me tired. The Great Deming." And he got into bed.

In the darkness, Bill seemed very far away, very—somehow—separate. Suppose there were no Bill at all—Candy snuggled under the covers.

I'm a young widow and I have lots of money and a wonderful nurse for David (but he still loves me best) and I travel all over—doing what? Not writing books—taking pictures, that's what. I'm a famous photographer and I have marvelous clothes and I'm much better looking than I am now—really almost beautiful. When I walk into the Stork Club, half the people say, "Don't look now, but there's Candy Stewart," and the other half say, "Oh, do you know her?" And the first half say, "I wonder why she never married again—she could have anyone she wants." Candy darling, when are you going to settle down? Heavens, dear, I don't know, why should I settle down? This life is perfect, absolute freedom all sealed up in a green glass bottle like a little ship. I must be going to sleep with my hair all waved like a lawyer's wig. . . .

CANDY was always to look back upon the next few weeks as the blackest patch in her life; blacker, perhaps, because she had no confidante. Indeed, there was nothing to confide. Nothing but a formless, growing fear; and when you are not even sure of what you are afraid, how can you put your fear into words, even to yourself?

Pan insisted that she was resting, and she would see no one, go to no parties, in no way celebrate her return. But a few days after their Sunday lunch, Bill remarked at dinner that she had rung him up at the office.

"She's writing an article on airplanes after the war. She seems to think I can help her."

That, Candy told herself, was perfectly reasonable. After all, airplanes were Bill's business. And it turned out that Bill had lots of ideas that Pan could use. He took her to lunch with other men who had ideas. He introduced her to his boss, Mr. Denstone, who was president of International Airways and who fell an instant victim. In fact, Pan was right: Bill could help her.

The article she was writing was for *Meridian,* and it had been George Deming's idea in the first place.

"Oh, very smart," Hope said sourly. "Now they can part forever on Sunday and George can come back on Friday night with a straight face—on business. I wish I'd never tried to help him. I'm a bundle of nerves."

"*You're* a bundle of nerves," Candy said coldly. "What do you think *I* am? I have to bind up George's wounds every Sunday evening. That nesting act you got me into—"

Hope grinned. "That's no act, darling. Not for you. George thinks you're the most wonderful woman he ever met. He says going from our house to yours is like going from a monkey house to a mountain lake. But he still looks at Pan—well, you know the way he looks at her."

Candy nodded soberly; she knew the way men looked at Pan. They looked interested and admiring and sort of specially wide-awake. That was what was so frightening, really. Because if Pan had been the sort of girl to drug a man into a fatuous coma, there might have been some hope for his eventual awakening.

Three weeks went by. Candy and Bill played tennis and went swimming in the Lorings' lake. They went to two parties and several movies and bought another War Bond. David stood up in his play pen.

Then one evening at about six, Candy heard the screen door slam. It had been the hottest day of the year and David had chosen it to cut his first tooth. Candy had had an argument with the laundress and had been unfairly defeated; and she hadn't had time to wash her hair. She burst out of the kitchen in shirt and shorts, roaring:

"Bill, you've got to fix the garbage pail! I'm going mad!" Then, pursuing her course through the dining room, she continued unabated: "I can't get the top on tight and every dog for ten miles around has been here all day and besides it isn't san— Oh."

FOR there in the front hall stood Pan Peters in a sleeveless black linen dress and a huge hat. She wore a diamond starfish on one shoulder and her blond hair shone. She looked like a mermaid in mourning.

"How do you do," Candy said idiotically. "Won't you come in?"

"She is in," Bill pointed out. "Go and sit down while I get us something to drink."

Candy sat on her own sofa with her hair in hot wisps and pretended that she was unaware that there was a large aluminum spoon in her right hand. "Where do you keep your plane?" she asked politely.

"At LaGuardia Field," said Pan with her ravishing smile.

"That's right near Bill's office, isn't it?"

"Yes, quite near. . . . How is your baby?"

"Very well, thank you. He's getting a tooth."

"Really? How exciting."

"Yes, isn't it?" *This conversation sounds like something out of Swedish in Six Easy Lessons. It's because she thinks my only subjects of conversation are babies' teeth and little white onions.* As soon as she could, she left Pan with Bill and went back to the kitchen.

After Pan had left, Bill appeared, looking vaguely embarrassed. "What came over you, baby, shooting off like that? It wasn't very polite."

Candy was busy slicing tomatoes. "I'm sorry," she said shortly.

"I don't know what Pan must have thought."

"Does it matter?"

"Of course it matters. You like her, don't you? She likes you. She said she wished she knew you better."

"She's very clever," Candy said distantly.

"Clever and yet sort of pathetic, too, poor kid. She can do too many things, that's her trouble."

She certainly can. If she'd just stick to flying her airplane around the world and driving George Deming crazy— "I fail to see anything in the least pathetic about her."

BILL put one hand gently on her shoulder. " 'Smatter, angel? Dave been pretty tough today?"

Ignominious tears burned her eyes. *I'm expected to cook and sew and clean and fight my weight in laundresses and be a delightful hostess when my hair's dirty. Well, I can't compete with sirens and I won't.* She longed to throw herself into Bill's arms and be told how valuable she was, how efficient, how utterly indispensable; so she shrugged away his hand and said shortly:

143

"No, nothing's too tough. Supper's ready."

She saw his lips tighten to a controlled line. *So he's married to a shrew. Well, he can always get Pan Peters to appreciate him.*

It was impossible to swallow the tomatoes.

PAN's visit came at last to its inevitable end, and with it the Morgans' farewell dinner. It was a small party: besides George Deming and the Stewarts, Hope had invited only Mr. Denstone, Bill's boss and Pan's fondest admirer, and Pan's two closest friends, Raymond Pond and Serena Perry. Every family in America who owned a radio had heard the news from Raymond Pond, and those of America who had never seen Serena behind footlights had certainly seen her on celluloid.

Then, three days before the party, Hope dropped in in a state of nerves. "It's that weevilly butler of mine. If he'd only come right out and complain, instead of glooming around like a frozen asset. And Hilda's just as bad. I'm so afraid—"

"But what's the matter with them?" Candy asked.

"The matter with them is Pan," Hope said savagely. "That girl— I adore her, but honestly, she ought to establish a permanent residence in a club car. Never on time to a single meal; ginger ale at all hours; cigarette ashes all over the house, and she never puts one out either— she's driving me mad, and Ashburn and Hilda too. She never puts anything away—phonograph records, books, pages of manuscript that mustn't be touched, sweaters, bags, fountain pens, compacts—even her shoes! I suppose I'm a cat to mention it, but it's beyond belief. Somebody ought to hit her." And she stamped away, looking grim.

The morning of the party was hot and heavy, with an ominous haze near the horizon. Bill seemed very silent at breakfast; but then, he had been silent for days.

Candy looked at his back as he moved to the door, and the words seemed to hang in her mind like thick black smoke: *Bill, I'm jealous.* If she said them aloud, would he laugh at her and kiss her and tell her she was silly? Or would she see disgust, impatience, even quick contempt in his black eyes? Would the words, spoken aloud, perhaps even crystallize his feeling for Pan? *But men don't just change their minds about their wives—like that,* she told herself fiercely. *Not men like Bill. He loves me—and David. Not Pan Peters, not anyone else.*

She got up briskly and began to clear the table; everything was all right again. Of course it was all right—but the words still hung in her mind as oily and choking as real smoke. They settled down on every other thought, they obscured her vision and the day itself. *I'm jealous. I'm jealous and I hate it. I hate it.* But she didn't say it aloud, because it wasn't something you said aloud. It was something you hid in darkness, a bitter taste on your tongue that you tried to swallow and couldn't. There was no getting rid of it. It grew and grew, and at last you had to face it: after all, this happened to other people. There was no reason in the world why Candace Stewart should be exempt. Pan Peters was a fascinating woman. Bill was a most attractive man.

It was almost a relief when the thunderstorms came. It was late in the afternoon, and there were three of them, splitting the inky sky with terrifying violence and followed by sheets of rain; when the last one rumbled off to the south, it was long after six.

Candy tried to call Bill at his office, and discovered that the telephone was dead. It was still dead at seven, when she had to leave for the Morgans' party, and still Bill had failed to appear.

Candy shut her mind up in a small, tight box, along with her emotions. *Don't think, don't feel at all. Just go and pretend you're that young Mrs. Stewart who's so happily married. People will say Pan and Bill have been delayed by the storm—just those two, no one else. And you'll agree: "Yes, it must have been the storm. Of course it was the storm."*

Voices came from Hope's terrace, and George Deming met her at the door. "Candy, my dear, you look beautiful. How are you?"

She smiled brilliantly at him. *I'm fine, Mr. Deming, just dying slowly—nothing serious.* . . . "It's most becoming, Mrs. Stewart." . . . "Thank you, Mr. Deming."

"Things," said George lightly, "seem to have blown up in our faces, don't they? My best girl and your husband have eloped. Ha-ha. And of course, on the home front—"

Hope strode into the hall, her black eyes glittering with rage. "Have you heard? Did he tell you? Those two blackhearted—"

"Steady, my girl," George advised. "Remember the Deming blood pressure."

"—fiends!" Hope stormed. "And when I think what I paid them— to have them walk out on me, two hours before dinner and not a soul available in this whole town on a Saturday—"

"What are you talking about?" Candy asked steadily.

"My dear—Ashburn and Hilda! I've telephoned every cleaning woman I know. And then to have Pan late on top of it—and keeping Bill with her—I knew I shouldn't give this party—something told me—"

"What are you having for dinner?" Candy asked quickly.

HOPE ground her teeth. "Squabs and broccoli and *vichysoise* and an iced thing that takes hours—"

"Hilda must have made that this morning, then," Candy interrupted. "Squabs are easy."

"Not for me," Hope pointed out acidly. "The only thing I know about squabs is how to eat them. And Lobby can only cook hamburgers. There's nothing to do but go to Ye Olde Englishe Tea Room, and the very thought sickens me."

"Don't be silly," Candy said briskly. "Where's an apron?"

Hope's face was a mixture of horror and delight. "Candy, darling, you don't mean—oh, I can't let you!"

"Certainly you can let her," George stated firmly. "That's the kind of girl she is. And I will help. I have a very light hand with burned toast."

Through the kitchen window Candy could hear snatches of talk from the terrace: "Candy's going to . . . doesn't want us to help . . . perfectly marvelous . . . now if those two would turn up . . . I told her this morning . . ." And then Mr. Denstone's deep voice: "I wonder what's delayed Stewart?" And somebody laughing: "I guess our Pan has delayed Stewart!"

Quite suddenly, the box that had held her emotions so neatly flew apart, and Candy was blindly and flamingly angry. It wasn't enough that Bill should put her in this humiliating position—he had to make his superior officer a witness to it. Mr. Denstone was a conventional gentleman of enormous integrity, a brilliant executive and a power in the company. He liked Bill and gave him opportunities; it was not too much to say that a good deal of Bill's success had been due to Mr. Denstone. *And now Bill calmly stays away from a dinner party because of a little blonde who can't empty her own ash trays.* Her hands were shaking so that she had to put down the butter dish.

"George," she said loudly, "where do you suppose those two are?"

George glanced up and grinned. He was getting rolls out of a paper bag and he looked absurdly handsome in a long white apron. "How would I know? Pan probably decided to fly to Mexico and took Bill along. You never can tell about her."

"Well, you've always been able to tell about Bill—always up to now. Personally, I think this is all your fault. . . . Put those rolls in a pie plate. I want to heat them."

George stared. "*My* fault!"

"If you had any sense," Candy said fiercely, "you'd have married Pan years ago and taken care of her."

"Haven't I been trying to?" George was still too astonished to be more than aggrieved.

Candy turned on him. "And why haven't you succeeded? Because you have some idiotic notion about the way she *ought* to be! You want everything your way, George Deming, and then you can't understand why a girl like Pan won't marry you! . . . Here, put this in the icebox."

George took the butter dish automatically and said, "Listen, all I ask is a home—the kind of home you have yourself."

"Why should you make all the conditions, anyway? Suppose Pan said she wouldn't marry you unless you were good at putting up shelves? Why, I bet you can't even hang a picture, George Deming!"

George stood in the middle of the kitchen, clutching the butter dish and looking rather as though a high wind had passed over him. He swallowed. "I bet I can," he said feebly.

Candy's rage vanished as swiftly as it had come. She turned away. "Get those soup plates, will you? . . . I haven't got a home myself any more. The master seems to have departed."

"Departed?" George sounded stunned.

"With Pan," said Candy calmly. "So pooh to your beautiful domesticity."

"But," said George simply, "he'll be back. You're married to him."

"What kind of a marriage do you think it is when he—when—" She choked.

George looked at her hard. Then he said quietly, "No kind at all, Candy. No kind at all." He paused, then asked, "Has Bill ever let you down before?"

"No. That's what—"

"So the very first time he fails to appear, you decide he's not to be trusted. He's off with a pretty girl—therefore he's no husband of yours. When **are you** going to divorce him?"

"**Why**"—Candy whirled on him in terror—"how can you—of course **I'm** not—you don't understand—"

"Sure I do." George, in his scorn, sounded almost good-natured. "You're just one of those girls who want everything their own way. You're jealous—for no reason. You're a baby."

There was a long pause. Then Candy said icily, "Put the soup in the dishes, will you, please?"

"There's no sense in getting mad at me," George pointed out. "You just stay mad at Bill."

Candy felt as though her mind were filled with bits of resentment, as sharp and hurting as tiny pieces of jagged broken glass; and the enthusiastic gratitude of Hope's guests was no balm. She scarcely heard Serena's lovely voice, saying charming things to her, nor Mr. Denstone praising the squab. It tasted like cardboard, and nothing else had any taste at all.

"Pan doesn't know what she's missing," said Raymond Pond.

And the telephone rang.

Mr. Pond was nearest it; and at his first words, all conversation stopped. "Good heavens—where? . . . Killed? . . . O.K.—I'll be there in half an hour. Get Earl in Baltimore. . . . Yes, hook it up." He dropped the receiver and turned to them. "Plane crashed north of Baltimore," he said quietly. "Sorry, Hope, I've got to go. They want it broadcast on the nine-o'clock news."

Candy stared at him, and found that he was invisible because there was nothing in the room but a gigantic whiteness filled with a terrible pounding. *You wanted it to happen. You even said, "I'm a young widow." You pretended there wasn't any Bill. But without Bill—I can't—*

GEORGE's voice, sharp and urgent, cut through the white cloud. "Here, drink this, quick. It's not them, my dear. It's the American Eagle—the big one. Twenty passengers."

Like the opening of a door, voices came back. Mr. Denstone's, heavy with shock and speaking more quickly than she had ever heard him: "No one in my house. Mrs. Denstone's away. They must have tried to get hold of me. May I go with you, Mr. Pond?"

No one had noticed Candy. She turned to George, and found that he was halfway to the door. "Me, too, Ray! I've got to be on the spot for the papers. Lobby, come on and help."

Then they were all in the hall, and the telephone screamed again. Candy, who was beside it, put out her hand instinctively, and Hope nodded.

"Baltimore calling," said a tiny official voice. "Ready with your call, Baltimore."

"Hello," said another voice, tiny, too, and faraway.

"Pan!" Candy cried. "Where are you? Are you all right?"

"Yes. Listen, Candy, Bill is out at the accident and he said to—"

"Where?" said Candy.

"There's been a plane crash. The Eagle, and a lot of people killed. It's bad. Listen, Candy, this is important: he wants you to find Mr. Denstone. The office can't reach him."

"Mr. Denstone is right here," said Candy, suddenly in command of her wits.

"Then listen. Tell him Bill tried and tried to get him when the news of the crash came, but he couldn't. And the two other big shots were on vacation; I forget their names—you know. And the planes at the field were grounded, and Bill was frantic because he knew somebody ought to be here, so we came in the Gnat—"

"What's she saying?" Mr. Denstone demanded testily.

"She flew Bill down," Candy told him. "He couldn't find you."

"And he says"—Pan's voice waned and almost disappeared—"he says to ask Mr. Denstone if he wants him to come back and send someone else down here."

"Do you want to send someone else?" Candy asked swiftly.

"Good heavens, no! Tell him to keep in touch with me. I'll be in my office all night. Tell him good work—"

"He's to keep in touch," Candy shouted. "Mr. Denstone says good work. That's your doing, Pan."

For a moment, she thought Pan had gone completely. Then her voice came again, clear and strong. "Is George there? Tell George to come. Tell him to get a plane."

"George," Candy said over the mouthpiece, "she says to come."

"Tell her I'm halfway there," George said. "Tell her she's got a breakfast date with me in Elkton, Maryland."

Candy laughed helplessly at the telephone's crackling response. "She says no, George—she has a run in both stockings."

"And anyway, I want white satin!" Pan screamed. "Tell that so-and-so I won't be married without a piece of heirloom lace if I have to make it myself. Tell him to hurry up. So long, Candy."

"Give Bill my love," said Candy, and the voice answered:

"We'll be home for breakfast."

BILL sat at the kitchen table, wolfing muffins. He was haggard and his trousers were mud to the knees, but he looked happy. The morning sun fell on his shoulders. He was talking through a muffin.

"All the way down she kept saying how she wished we could have reached George, so he could have come along and done an eyewitness account for *Meridian,* and finally I said, 'I thought you didn't care so much about George,' and she just stared at me. 'Care about George?' she said. 'Why, I'm crazy about him! I thought you knew that.' I said, 'Why don't you marry him, then, for heaven's sake?' and she said, 'Because George keeps wanting to remodel me into a chattel and it makes me mad.' And I said, 'Listen, Pan, why don't you marry him and remodel George?' She stared at me again and then she began to laugh. She kept laughing and laughing and saying, 'Why didn't I ever think of it? Everybody always seems to think George is the ulti-mate product of civilization.' And about then we ran into the storm."

"What storm?" Candy asked, her eyes fixed on his face.

"Well, it was somewhere north of Baltimore. Honestly, I didn't think she could make it. If she wasn't half bird, we wouldn't have. I thought, 'This is it.' And you know what?"

"What, Bill?" Candy asked in a small voice.

"I was so scared I couldn't think. I felt as though my mind were all glued up with fear. It was horrible. There was only one thought way in the middle of my mind, and you know what it was?"

"What?" asked Candy weakly.

"I thought, 'If I die now, I won't see Candy grow old. I've just *got* to see Candy grow old.' It's bad to be that scared. . . . Is there any more coffee?"

Candy stood at the stove with her back to him. "I'm glad you thought that. I mean specially glad, because I thought you were getting a little tired of me."

She poured his coffee and Bill looked up at her. "Is that why you've been acting funny? I put it down to hot weather. Tired of you!" He pulled her down and kissed her.

Candy leaned her nose on his and gazed at him dotingly. "I thought maybe," she said, "you liked the glamorous Miss Peters better."

Bill exploded with pleasure. "Get away, girl, you make me cross-eyed."

"Well, she's so much smarter," Candy said defensively, "and she's beautiful too."

"Sure, I know," he told her. "You're dumb and ugly; but if I deserted you your father would be irritated, and I'm scared of your father. You know what? I am prepared to admit now—but privately, Candace, privately—that *all* women are smarter than *all* men."

"Oh, no!" Candy said, shocked.

"They do just as much work," said Bill, "and they look prettier. You look awfully pretty." He got up and put his arms around her, and Candy wished passionately that she could do something for him—something difficult and unpleasant—to show him how she felt.

"Darling," she said into his unshaven cheek, "would you like me to do the check-book again?"

Bill looked at her tenderly. "No, angel. You have sons and marry people off, but I will add and subtract."

Candy sighed with happiness.

Didn't I Tell You?

PAUL ERNST

Ever read about a seemingly drab and dusty town transformed suddenly into a vibrant place, welcoming home its Willy with his Congressional Medal of Honor? Ever get a lump in your throat? Read this heroic story and then answer the question, "Didn't I tell you?"

IT HAPPENED in a hot August, which would not be worth mentioning save that perhaps the heat and lack of rain had something to do with the shaping of events. Certainly they helped shape Bart Kinney's mood as he stared out the train window.

Bart was a big man of thirty-two, dark of hair and eyes, and while he was used to heat it was not this kind of heat and he'd been dressed differently for it. He scowled at the sign ahead: "We regret that wartime emergency forces us to use this nonair-conditioned car."

It was a new word, nonair-conditioned, and Bart Kinney didn't like it. He didn't like the way the torrid car was jammed, either, and he almost didn't like the girl who entered the car at that moment and threaded the aisle with light steps, giving to the movement of the train in an unconscious little dance.

She was a small girl in a tan linen suit with a frilly white blouse that still gave an air of crispness. She had amber eyes and sun-colored hair. She looked about nineteen and rather helpless; and Bart scowled again, knowing that she was twenty-seven and one of the best photographers, male or female, in the land.

She said, "Hello there, Kinney," with her eyes half mocking as always. Bart was a fairly well known reporter, with a column of his own while he was in the Pacific and with a byline here at home. But Ruth Harrison knew bigger fish than Bart, though she knew no bigger fall guys, he reflected, remembering that while he did not want to marry this girl, or any girl, he still could not delete her from his mind.

He said abruptly, "The William Detweiler story?"

She nodded. "Typical small-town American boy, poor, no military background—and now he's a one-man army with the Congressional Medal of Honor. The magazine wants a feature on him."

"I MIGHT have known you'd be assigned." Ruth Harrison smiled, showing excellent teeth. She had no right to look so nice, Bart thought. "I'd have expected you too, only I hadn't heard you were back from New Guinea," she added.

"Just got in, to take a few weeks' rest. But our Sunday supplement wants a feature too, so this is the rest I get." Bart stared around at the hot packed coach.

"Where you going now?" asked Bart.

"I was going back to the club car," said Ruth.

"You and two hundred others . . ." Bart stopped as he saw the camera in Ruth's small white hand. Little, she looked? Helpless? He said, "Ring me in on it too. I'll tag along and not make any trouble."

The line for the club car extended through the car ahead, ending in solid humanity against the door. Ruth Harrison lifted her camera high and started through the mass.

"Pardon me. I'm sorry. Just a moment, please . . ."

She looked official with the flash reflector brilliant over her head. People drew in upon themselves to make a path, and smiled experimentally. Maybe there'd be pitchers took.

"Why not?" said Ruth. At the end of the car she lifted the camera and a flash puffed out. She smiled a little at the people and then she and Bart jimmied their way into the club car. She took three pictures in there. "For Candid Magazine," she told the steward. He was impressed. Places appeared for her and Bart.

"O fragile little flower," said Bart sardonically.

Her face, quite petal-textured, was calm as she stared up at him. "You sentimentalist. You really want a fragile flower, don't you?"

"I want no kind of flower," said Bart. "In a world like this? A wife and kiddies?" He ordered a drink.

Her eyes were amused and just a little sad. But all she said was, "Intoxicants in this heat!" She ordered a large orange juice and put her camera into its case with deft fingers that Bart had sometimes sheepishly imagined busy at domestic tasks around an apartment near her magazine and his paper.

She said, "You know William Detweiler, don't you?"

"Yes. That's why the office cut my vacation to send me for his story. I saw a lot of him in New Guinea. They called him Walloo Willy."

"Don't tell me, let me guess." Ruth concentrated hard. "I know! Because he came from Walloo."

"Wrong, funnyface. Because he was always talking about Walloo. All the guys out there talk at least a little about their home towns, but Walloo Willy never stopped. That was why I saw him so much—I used him as a kind of symbol of all our homesick kids. Exaggerated, as all symbols are. And I like him too." Bart lighted a cigarette. "According to him there never was another town like Walloo. It's the most beautiful charming spot on earth, filled with the finest most gracious people."

"He sounds all right."

"He is. But it got so that every time Walloo Willy would come up to somebody, they'd start in: 'Population sixteen hundred. Biggest public park of any town its size in the state. Bandstand concerts every Wednesday and Sunday night. Situated on beautiful Walloo River. Finest climate east of the Rockies, huh, Willy?'"

"Oh, the poor kid," said Ruth.

"He didn't mind. He'd just grin and say, 'That's right, bud. Nobody else's home town is as good as my home town. You ought to see the Walloo River with the moonlight on it, with the band playing in the park and the girls and fellas listening.' Lord, that kid loved home."

"Was he really a hero?"

Bart nodded. "You wouldn't believe how many Japs he killed. Of course some of it's luck. You're in the right place at the right time with a heavy machine gun, or you're not. But the man enters in too, and believe me, Willy entered in!"

"And now he's coming home." Ruth's eyes were soft. "Is Walloo so beautiful, Bart?"

"Never saw it," Bart said. "It can't be so perfect as Willy remembers, but it must be pretty fair, at that. Willy was no dope."

"A little town on a little river, with its proud park and its bandstand," said Ruth. "Just easygoing and nice, but the finest spot on earth to its sons across the seas."

"Oh, stop talking in captions," said Bart. "Where are your things? It's about time to get off."

"We're near Walloo?"

"Not too," said Bart. "We change at the next stop for a local south. And I mean local."

BART helped her with her things, trying to avert his eyes from her—this girl always exceeded your remembrance of her.

The local was composed of an engine out of the Smithsonian, two cars that must once have had chimneys, and a boxcar.

"The boxcar would be coolest," Ruth said wistfully. She took a picture of the train. They sat beside an open window and their journey Walloo-ward continued over flat country.

"You know," said Ruth, "these boys with their nostalgia for little towns may have something, Bart. Small towns can be pretty nice."

"Now don't go Willy on me," snapped Bart. " 'You ought to see the moon on Walloo River, and hear the band . . .' "

"After this trip I can use an hour loafing on a bench in that park beside the river with a nice cool breeze and under a nice cool tree."

"A shower for me. Wonder how the hotel is."

"Didn't Willy say?"

"He said the Walloo House was swell. He said salesmen went half a day off their route to stay there. 'And the girls that walk past along Main Street! Whee-ew!' "

"Bless his heart!" said Ruth. "I hope he won't be too let down. Has he a girl?"

"Has he! Her name is Margaret Sorenson. Most Walloo girls are pretty but Margaret tops them all."

"What is his family like?"

"There's just his mother. She lives on the second floor of some place along proud Main Street. She, by the way, is something special in the way of parents. You haven't eaten pie if you haven't tasted Ma Detweiler's."

"Stop! You make him sound like an idiot, Bart."

"I don't mean to." For once Bart's tone lacked its sharpness. "He's just an extra-young youngster, franker than most about his home-sickness. He was born into a nice little frame and never got out of it until the draft. Now he's built it up until heaven wouldn't do. He's going to be disappointed, of course."

"Maybe not. There's something about slow-paced villages with trees arching over Main Street and a bridge across the river where the boys and girls meet at dusk . . ."

"Walloo," called the conductor morosely.

"Where?" said Bart.

And then the train stopped and Ruth and Bart got out and Bart said, "Oh, Lord!"

They stared around at Walloo and then they stared, appalled, at each other.

There was the gingerbread depot with its loading platform warping in the heat. There were the bright hot rails, straight and level over a level treeless plain. There was Main Street, stretched along the tracks so that it had only one side. The buildings were all of old clapboard, which does not sag gracefully, or of new red brick shimmering like red-hot stove lids. Like fretful children various smaller streets hung back from Main, lined with boxlike houses.

"The park," said Ruth, voice muffled.

The space behind the station was of course bigger than two handker-chiefs, but it didn't seem so. In the center, not quite large enough to hold one fat tuba player, was the bandstand. It was white with old green showing through in patches. The weeds in the park were knee-high, brown with drought.

"The river," Ruth said weakly.

Along one end of the park was a ragged arroyo with walls of pale cracked brown. In the bottom was a discouraged brown fluid like coffee spilled on a beige tablecloth. Two smallish trees stood lonesomely on the bank.

" 'The moon on Walloo River,' " Ruth said. "The poor lamb."

"The poor fool," contradicted Bart harshly. "He's a mental case—or will be when he sees what he's been vaporing about for twenty-six months. Two years! How could you get so far from reality in two centuries?"

Ruth picked up one of her cases. Bart picked up the other and his own. They crossed Main Street with little wisps of fine white dust rising at each step and went into Walloo House. It would be kindest to draw a veil over that two-story tin-roofed structure. The proprietor, a Mr. Fuller, suggested rooms with washstands. "It's kind of warm."

"Kind of?" Bart blinked. "It's like this often here?"

Mr. Fuller, preceding them to the second floor, looked as if he hadn't thought of it before. "Guess it's a *little* warmer'n some summers. And it's real dry. We need rain."

"Make mine snow," said Ruth disappearing into her room.

THEY dined at one of five tables in an oven churned to torment by a noisy fan. Mr. Fuller served.

"Can't get help," he said sadly and left them with the coffee, which reminded Bart of Walloo River.

Bart was silent through the coffee, frowning now and then, snapping his fingers. Ruth watched him with the half-amused half-sad look.

Bart said, "We ought to do something."

"About what, and for why?" said Ruth.

"You know what we're both thinking. An earnest but mush-headed kid is heading back for heaven, and will find—Walloo. The least that could be done for a Congressional Medal of Honor man would be to gild this pesthole up a little."

"Such as?"

"They could at least mow their silly park, couldn't they?"

The two got up and went to the lobby. There Mr. Fuller leaned against the desk, mopping his cheeks absently.

"Mr. Fuller," said Bart, striving for geniality, "we have a problem here. You know I met Willy Detweiler in the Pacific?"

Mr. Fuller indicated indifferently that he hadn't known.

"Well, I did," said Bart. "And I talked to him enough to know what kept him going. It was Walloo. Memories of home. You know? All he could think of was Walloo and when he could get back to it. His home town was the finest any man ever had . . . that sort of stuff."

Mr. Fuller nodded. He looked as if anything as substanceless as a memory would not be in his book.

"Now, Mr. Fuller, your town is very nice indeed, don't get me wrong. But there are a few small things that could be sort of slicked up without much trouble. I mean, here's your Medal of Honor boy coming home, remembering how beautiful the town was when he left it—"

"Same now as when he left," said Mr. Fuller.

"Yes, yes, of course. But a man builds things up in his mind. He's away from his wife—she's the finest woman in the world. He's away from his town—it's a corner of paradise. You may think that's silly—"

"Nope," said Mr. Fuller. "I went away from here too and come back. Last war."

"Fine." Bart rubbed his hands together. "Then we're talking the same language."

"Yep. But I don't see what can be done. Not with a place like Walloo."

RED touched Bart's neck. Ruth stepped forward before his anger broke into words. She tried a different tack.

"In a few weeks millions of people all over the country will see pictures of Walloo," she said. "I know you'll all want them to see the town in its best light. If just a few things could be done? The park grass cut? The bandstand given a quick coat of paint? A little bunting along the station eaves? Will there be a band, Mr. Fuller?"

"Nope. Only one man left who can play." Mr. Fuller mopped his cheeks. He said to Ruth patiently, "More men have left Walloo than you might think. The park grass, now. Have to be tractored, then raked, then mowed. There ain't a man around has time for that. And painting the bandstand. There are two painters here. They used to be six. There just ain't men for frills, miss."

"But for heroes?" Ruth said softly.

"We're wasting time," said Bart. "Does Walloo have a mayor? We'll talk to the mayor."

"You are," said Mr. Fuller. "I'm him." He mopped his face. "There'll be some friends to meet Willy. I'm contributin' some ice cream. I don't know what else we can do."

Ruth took Bart away before the heat and His Honor's indifference led to an explosion. "We've planted a seed, anyway," she said. "Maybe it will sprout. And there's all day tomorrow for it to grow in."

"You'd think a guy like Willy came home every day," fumed Bart. "Won't even mow their park." This seemed to stick. "If they would sickle it, or whatever, I'd mow it myself."

Ruth laughed at the thought of Bart Kinney, newspaper columnist, pushing a mower in that heat. "You big tough two-minute egg," she said.

He glared at her. "Are you going after background stuff, or aren't you? Let's call on Mrs. Detweiler."

MRS. DETWEILER lived in the top half of a Main Street building that was not at all proud. She lived over the Walloo Bazaar, which stocked magazines, newspapers, games, notions and other miscellaneous items. She worked there days, helping the owner. When Bart and Ruth rang she was sitting upstairs in the dark. She snapped the light on and let them in.

Willy's mother was a small lean sixty with dark gray hair and patient gray eyes. When she moved her arms the cords and lean muscles ridged the skin. She went back to her chair by the open window and to her palm-leaf fan. The fan was needed; it must have been nearly a hundred up there.

Ruth introduced herself and Kinney, and Mrs. Detweiler just nodded. It seemed that everyone in Walloo was lacking in excess words.

In answer to their questions she said, yes, she was very glad about William coming home. She said she hadn't heard from him much, he was no hand at writing letters. She said yes, she'd been worried about him. She said William had always been a good boy. And she fanned her thin face and throat with hands well used to work, while Bart made sparse notes and Ruth took pictures and both steadily melted in the heat.

"Like living in a frying pan," said Bart, loosening his collar when they reached the street. "Background stuff! The story of Walloo Willy!

I've seen ten million mothers of sons who look just like Mrs. Detweiler. Only most of them talk more."

"You're a stuffy old shirt, aren't you?" said Ruth wearily. "I'm for
bed. I think if I roll around enough I can baste evenly. More about
Willy can wait until tomorrow."

"And maybe," said Bart hopefully, "His Honor will get Walloo
policed up just a bit."

But by noon next day there was no sign of this. A few dozen cars
were parked untidily along Main; a few people moved listlessly over
the sun-baked walk from time to time. Aside from this Walloo was
dead. Inside the buildings, however, there was activity, as Ruth and
Bart found out.

They went to the garage where Willy had worked. The owner was
a man named Kluff; when they entered he didn't even look at them.
He was lifting the motor out of an old, old farm truck with a chain
hoist and he was sweating. Not having time to wipe his face, he just
blew upward periodically.

He said yes, Willy had worked for him—would again, he hoped.
He said Willy was fair with a motor, though a little weak on ignition.
He said Willy was a good boy. He said, "Look, I have four trucks to get
out before Sunday and it's Wednesday, and I'm alone here." As he
talked the chain hoist clinked steadily.

They went to see Willy's girl, the incomparable Margaret Sorenson.
She lived in a big house two blocks back of Main, a boarding-house,
as was advertised by sound and aroma. Margaret came from the
kitchen with a blue kerchief around her head and little wisps astraggle
from its edges. She was rather tall, too thin, with dark eyes much too
large for her thin serious face. She said yes, she and Willy had gone
together for a long time. She said yes, it was wonderful that he was
coming home. She said Willy was a good boy. . . . And all at once
she burst into tears.

"Now, now," said Bart, distressed and helpless and annoyed. But
Ruth put her arm around the thin shoulders and made appropriate
clucking sounds.

"I'm sorry." Margaret dabbed at her eyes with her apron. "I'm
awfully, awfully sorry. I guess it's because it's so hot back there in the
kitchen."

In mercy, they went away. There could be pictures of the greeting when Willy's train arrived at eight. But anger welled up in Bart's throat.

"She might have gushed at least once," he snapped. "Isn't there anybody in this town who cares if Willy is alive? This kid is big stuff. Don't they know that?"

"It is hot, Bart. . . . What did you expect?"

"At least a spark of interest," growled Bart. "It isn't bad enough to find what sort of place it really is that Willy has longed his heart out for; now we have to find that the people in it are just as drab and dusty."

"There are still a few hours," said Ruth. "We've just about time to see the uncle. Maybe when we get back we'll find a flag or two around the depot."

WILLY's Uncle George lived twelve miles out. There was one car for hire in Walloo and with great effort Ruth and Bart pried its owner from his filling station and were driven over the flat, flat land. The driver was taciturn. Yes, it was nice Willy was coming home. Why did they call him Willy instead of Bill? He wouldn't know. Was there an official reception committee? He hadn't heard of none. Just look at that corn! The drought . . .

The corn was browning at the bottom, though the tops were green and fair. It was evidently serious; at least Willy's Uncle George took it seriously. A heavy black-jowled man, he kept staring past the barnyard at his corn while Ruth and Bart talked.

Yes, Willy had worked there vacations. He was fair, had to watch over him Saturdays or he'd quit early. No, as far as he knew Willy'd never hunted much or had much to do with guns. He was a good boy. If we don't get rain soon . . .

Ruth and Bart were deposited back on Main Street at seven o'clock. The background stuff they'd collected could be put in the left eye. And there were no flags around the depot. Nothing.

"All right," rasped Bart. "A boy comes back in glory up to here. He is a big hand in San Francisco. He beats off reporters and bum photographers like you way across the country. He stays three days in Chicago as the city's guest. And at his own lousy little home town he steps off the train to be met by a roaring committee of two— his mother and his girl. And maybe he sees someone on the street and he says, 'Why hello, Willy, have you been away?' All right! So why should I worry about it?"

"Why should you?" agreed Ruth. But she put her hand on his arm, a thing she hadn't done before, and kept it there while they went into Walloo House to attack temper and temperature with applications of cold water.

WILLY's train was due at eight-ten, and Ruth and Bart had meant to stay away from the depressingly empty depot platform till just about that time; but at quarter of eight they found themselves heading gloomily for the door. Ruth said hopefully that she thought there were more cars strewn along Main Street than there had been earlier.

"Fine," sneered Bart. "With luck there may be a couple of dozen curiosity mongers hanging around at train time. I would like to be here when they read what I write about Walloo and its reception of its favorite son!"

"I've never seen you so roiled up."

"Well," Bart said lamely, "this Willy—he's not bad. I saw him a lot. I told you why . . . not that it really matters to me," he added crisply.

Ruth put her hand on his arm again and they walked across the street with dust spurts kicking from their heels. The sun was half under the horizon but seemed hotter than at midday. Across the tracks the tired splotched bandstand leaned in its weedy little park.

"Five of eight," said Bart when Ruth finally asked the time. And down the street there was a siren sound.

"Fire?" said Ruth lifting her sleek head. "Wasn't that a fire siren, Bart?"

"Relax," Bart said. "It's nowhere around here or you could see the smoke."

He stared irritably at Main Street, at the store where Mrs. Detweiler worked until she had that exhausted look, at the drugstore where neon lights of a particularly violent green had just come on, at the small streets leading into Main.

"Look," he said awkwardly, "this Willy is really likable when you get to know him. Why couldn't we sort of fix up a jaunt for him between us—ask him to the city and high-spot him around? I'll bet Candid and the paper would go for that."

"You imbecile," said Ruth. "You nice dope." But when some cars of a vintage best left untold began to drift from the flat country onto Main Street, and when a few people began appearing from the side streets, she was as relieved as he. "There'll be quite a few on hand, Bart, I do believe."

ACROSS the street, the drugstore lights went on inside, and in a little while a knot of people came from the store. Among them was Margaret Sorenson, talking to half a dozen other girls, and none of them looked better than she did. She wore no kerchief or grayish apron now; she looked all right. Plain, but all right. And down the street a bit later the siren sounded again and the big red fire wagon came out of its stall onto Main Street. It turned toward the station, and the roar was not all from its motor. It was covered with riders and they were singing The Little Marine.

Along the track sounded the whistle of the evening train and Ruth began looking to her cameras and Bart to his book, but they looked at each other oftenest. Because more and more people were appearing from practically nowhere. And in one group, talking and laughing with an animation you'd hardly have believed had you seen her the night before, was Mrs. Detweiler in a good blue dress.

It was all about what might have been expected, but Ruth and Bart, who had had every reason to expect nothing whatever, found themselves grinning at each other like a couple of fools. Why, there'd be several hundred at the station.

The fire engine came to a quick brave stop at the platform and the gang piled off and straggled to the tiny park and after them came others, so that as the train whistled again down the track, there were heads everywhere you looked; and still the people came. You wondered where they'd all been hiding from the sun. And onto Main Street rolled cars from both directions with more people, hastily slicked up from the day's work.

The train came up the track, clanging, slow like a presidential special, and Ruth's fingers clutched Bart's arm hard because it was all so much better than they'd feared. The town itself was still a sun-baked graceless place, but there would be a welcome after all.

"Oh, a nice welcome!" called Ruth pitching her voice to carry to Bart's ear a foot away. "Gracious! There must be a thousand people here."

Bart looked around and nodded, grinning. At least a thousand. It was impossible, but there they were, crowding up on each side—from the park and from Main Street—as the train, clanging beautifully, wheezed and stopped.

From his high cab the engineer beamed down on them. He waved his hand at them. On the step between the two coaches the conductor appeared, beaming too.

"Okay folks," he yelled. "Here he is. Willy Detweiler. Give your Walloo boy a hand."

The roar that went up seemed to curl the station eaves. It filled the town, the night. It ran off over the flat land all around and filled that too. And over the conductor's shoulder appeared a boyish grinning face.

"Willy!" yelled the crowd. "Yay, Willy!"

He climbed down, a startlingly small fellow, not more than five feet six. He put an arm around his mother and the other around his girl and his cap fell off and somebody retrieved it and put it back upon his head. A blonde head. A towhead.

Someone lifted Willy onto a baggage truck. The ribbons twinkled on his chest. "Speech. Speech. Come on, kid, speech!"

"Well, say," said Willy. His voice was high but carrying. "I didn't think there'd be anything like this. About all I can say is—I'm glad I'm home."

"We're glad too, Willy," some girl cried and the crowd boomed its approval. They loved Willy. You could see that. They always had. A good boy, Willy.

Then Willy saw Bart Kinney and his eyes widened and warmed some more. He jumped down from the truck and people parted for him. "Bart," said Willy, mother on one arm, girl on the other. "I didn't expect to see you here. A big shot like you."

Bart tried to say something about Willy being the big shot, but of course he couldn't make himself heard. He couldn't even introduce Ruth Harrison, busy with her flashlight bulbs in all directions but oftenest in Willy's direction.

Willy caught Bart's arm. "Didn't I tell you how swell my town was, Bart?" he shouted. "Didn't I keep telling you?" He looked around at all the people. "It's sure wonderful to be home."

There wasn't time for more. They got him to the fire truck, behind the wheel, with Mrs. Detweiler and Margaret Sorenson. "Drive it, Willy. The way you used to, boy."

"Our house," came Margaret's voice, clear above the noise. There was nothing plain about her face. Her eyes were luminous. "All who can get in—our house."

"I'll fetch the ice cream," came Mr. Fuller's voice from somewhere in the pandemonium. "Need some men to help . . ."

THE little depot, the small park with its weeds now trampled flat, were very still when all that crowd had drained away behind the shrieking fire engine. You could still hear crowd sounds up two blocks around the Sorenson boarding-house. Here and there in the dusk house lights went on.

Bart turned to Ruth. "Hel*lo!*" he said. "You little tough two-minute egg."

"Oh go s-soak your head," said Ruth wiping her eyes. She packed her camera case. She became brisk, all business. "Shall we amble to the Sorensons'?"

"Later," Bart said. He put her hand back on his arm and walked her, not in any hurry, to the river. There was a piece of moon above and hanged if it didn't find enough fluid to glint on down in there.

Bart said, "We've known each other quite a while, haven't we, funnyface?"

"Why . . . yes," said Ruth, "we have."

"We're in the same crazy business. We get along." Bart cleared his throat. "I've always sort of come back to you when I've been away places. Never admitted it. And you're always better than I remembered . . . if you know what I . . . that is, I don't see any reason why we couldn't get . . . you know."

"Yes, I know," said Ruth not quite steadily. "I've known for years. But Bart—a wife and kiddies? In a world like this?"

"You must admit," said Bart, "that what it smells like isn't violets. . . ." He stopped. For him there'd been no smell of violets in Walloo, either. But there had been for Willy.

Maybe, he admitted grudgingly, to some slight extent what you saw in a world was what was already in your pretty blue eyes. He thought of remarking on this, but could see no urgent reason for more words. The trampled weeds cushioned the fall of Ruth's camera case, which was generous of them when you come to think of it, after all the unkind thoughts they had received that day.

164

Big Frogs and Little Frogs

SUSAN ERTZ

*Here's a story for all of us who suddenly become
tongue-tied when seated next to fame. It is tender
and sympathetic and humorous!*

WHEN SHE HAD PUBLISHED her second novel—
which repeated the discreet success of her first—Eunice Maud Raikes
joined the New Argosy Club. She asked several people's advice about
it first and, on being told that it could do her no harm, presently
found herself a member of one of the largest and best-known literary
societies in London.

Being extremely diffident, however, she attended none of its dinners.
Regularly notices were sent out to her: "The next dinner of the New
Argosy Club will take place on such-and-such a date. 7.45 for 8."
Regularly she said to herself: "This time I really must go," but as
regularly her shyness conquered her. The thought of appearing like
a nervous, anonymous little ghost in that blaze of greater and lesser
luminaries alarmed her too much, and though it was her privilege to
invite a guest, there was no one she cared to take with her to be a
witness to her ordeal.

Then, quite suddenly, and to the surprise of her friends, she married
a simple, admiring business man named Corry Brewster, who never
noticed that she possessed no social gifts, and having read few novels
but hers, thought her a genius. With him to uphold and defend her,
she resolved to make her first appearance at the next meeting.

It happened that on this occasion one of the great, iron-clad literary
figures of the day was acting as Chairman and, whether by accident
or design or merely to show the democratic nature of the New Argosy
Club, Eunice Maud Raikes, upon arrival at the place of assembly,
was shocked to find that she was to be seated on his left hand at
dinner.

When the plan of the tables was shown to her, her knee-joints seemed to loosen and melt, and the roar of talk all about her went far away and then surged back again, trebled in volume. She looked wildly at Corry, only to see on his face a faintly pleased and gratified smile. "Well, why not?" he said. "Very nice for him. Now who do you suppose they'll put me next to? I hope it'll be somebody human." Corry liked people to be human above all things. It was very nearly all he asked of his fellow-beings. When he heard someone he knew condemned or criticized, he would say: "Oh, I don't know; he's human." Further study of the plan now revealed that he was placed between a Miss Haro Naguchi—the New Argosy was nothing if not international—and a lady called, rather cryptically, Mae Moss.

"At least they're not famous, so far as I know," said Eunice, "so you're in luck."

"I'm not afraid of any of them," said Corry. "Besides, I didn't come here for my own pleasure. You're the one that matters."

"I wish I could change with you," she said, trying to keep her teeth from chattering. "I do wish I could. I'd give anything to be sitting next to someone decently obscure."

"Why, what's the matter? I thought you'd always wanted to meet What's-his-name. I thought he was one of your heroes."

"I'd like just to be introduced to him," said Eunice. "It's quite another thing to be put down next to him for two whole hours at dinner."

"All the better, I should think."

"I'd much rather have been sitting next to you," she said, loving with a heightened love that safe, comfortable presence. "I wish I'd asked to be. I didn't know. Lots of husbands and wives do seem to be sitting together."

The crowd, surging and craning and chattering about the board displaying the big plan of the tables, swelled from minute to minute, and as it swelled it pushed the Brewsters into a corner, from which they stood silently watching the scene. All about them friends were greeting friends and introductions were being made. "Oh, are you really the man who wrote *Hypocrite's Holiday*? I simply adored it." Or, "I hope you're coming to the first night of my new play next Thursday." Stout women and thin ones, plain women and a few pretty ones laughed and chattered and pushed as politely as they could through the crowd, while among the coloured scarves and flounces and silks and velvets, the male members of the New Argosy Club looked insignificant and a little apologetic.

"Looks to me," said Corry, "as if writing was a woman's job."

But Eunice didn't answer. She could think of nothing but what so unaccountably awaited her, the heavy honour that had been so strangely laid upon her. What would the Great Man be like? What would he wish to talk about? Would he know who she was or would she have to tell him? Not that it would mean anything to him when she did. She felt sick with nervousness, her heart thudded unevenly under her best white satin. The palms of her hands were moist, her lips dry.

She was, if a wit at all, a bedtime wit. She thought of the things she would like to have said when she was brushing her hair or her teeth, hours after the moment to say them had passed. She missed her opportunities with a regularity that astonished and abashed her. When she met Interesting People she was tongue-tied, or said those things she ought not to have said, and instead of doing herself justice, longed to melt away out of sight and hearing; to disappear, like hoarfrost before the noonday sun. Only Corry's serene faith in her put stiffness into her spine and kept her legs from folding at the knees. How, oh, how was she to hope to interest the Great Man? She hated silly women and had a dread of being thought one. She was afraid of being betrayed by her own timid and unreliable tongue into seeming precisely the sort of woman she most despised.

At last the crowd surged towards the dining-room. All about her was the din of talkers trying to make themselves heard through the talk of others. Even the men's voices sounded strident.

"Scene is laid in Tibet, I believe. . . . Always thought her writing would fall off if she ever left him. . . . Quite the best of the Swedish novelists. . . . Hope I shan't have to sit next to a foreigner. . . . Who's that monolith in pale green lace? . . . Asked me if I'd mind saying a few words about the present trend of Soviet literature, but I told them I . . . Well, anyway, he ought to have got the Nobel Prize for it. . . . Hush, my dear, she's just behind you. I hope she didn't hear. . . . To meet two of the younger German dramatists on Sunday. . . . I simply can't read his poetry. I know I ought to and I've tried, but I just can't. . . ."

A sea of white or grey heads; black and brown and blond ones among them, but not so many; a little Chinaman in black silk and blue silk almost lost and smothered in the crowd but smiling politely upwards as he was carried along; a young Irish Republican with a jutting jaw, his straw-coloured hair falling into his eyes; a pretty, eager girl in blue velvet craning her long white neck for a glimpse of some celebrity; a tall Belgian writer with a marble-pale face half hidden in a spreading brown beard; the Great Man courteously inclining his head to hear the eager twittering of a small, white-haired woman beside him—("I do wish I knew what she's talking to him about," thought Eunice)—all were borne along in the dinnerward tide of chattering humanity.

Eunice clung nervously to Corry's arm, her small pale face looking strained and frightened.

"I can't bear you to leave me, darling, I can't bear it, I can't bear it."

"You silly girl! What's it all about? You're all nerves to-night. This is no more exciting than a City dinner, and heaven knows they're dull enough."

"Oh, Corry, I wish . . . why didn't I. . . ?"

"Here's my table, number eight. Here's where we part. You'd better follow the Great Man as you're sitting next to him. Off you go, darling. Let go of my arm. Enjoy yourself."

She was swept on, and as the distance between them widened she thought how easy it was to write a book sitting by oneself in a quiet little room. That was nothing. Then it got published, and sooner or later this sort of thing followed. One was sucked into a whirlpool of strange human beings, and confused and deafened and dizzied and made to talk and to produce a personality that was acceptable to others.

She followed the Great Man, fixing her eyes on him as a doomed person fixes his eyes on his doom. He had reached his table now. He had found his place, facing the whole length of the room. She saw him pick up her place-card, glance at it, and put it down again. On his right was a tall, generously planned woman in blue at whom Eunice had caught herself staring more than once. So that was the famous Mrs. Breed; Constance Breed, the foremost woman novelist of the day. A real personality. So real, indeed, was the personality that emanated from her, so solid, that one felt one could see it and touch it. Whatever happened, Eunice thought, in whatever situation she might find herself, that great, warm, gentle, pervasive, and perfectly reliable personality would always be steadily functioning. In bed it wouldn't alter, in church it would be just the same; on a lecture platform, in a bus, anywhere.

"What wouldn't I give," Eunice thought, "to be the owner of a personality like that? It's impregnable. It would make its owner invulnerable. People could come and take little bits of it away for souvenirs, and there would always be plenty more."

And then Mrs. Breed leaned forward and, inclining a gracious bust, smiled and bowed to Eunice across the Great Man's shirtfront, and Eunice, easily captured by that carelessly thrown net, returned the bow with warmth. Mrs. Breed's gesture, like the slow bending of a proud vessel to meet some wide green valley of the seas, had seemed to say: "I don't know who you are, strange little woman in white, but you are here, and it is proper and expedient that we should signal to each other in a friendly way, thus establishing a cordial, pleasant atmosphere about us."

The Great Man, after a courteous good evening to Eunice, was now studying the menu with frowning concentration. Eunice turned to look at the person on her left who had just fitted himself into his seat and saw that it was a stout old gentleman who looked like an admiral. And glancing down at his card she saw that he was one, and recalled —for she read all the reviews—that he had written a book on the Battle of Jutland. He had small, agreeable blue eyes and a large, humorous nose. When addressed he placed a big square hand behind his ear and leaned nearer to catch what was said. After he and Eunice had exchanged embarrassingly loud confidences, he admitting that he had not dined away from his home for three years, and Eunice that it was her first big literary dinner, there seemed little else to say. She turned her head and looked cautiously at the Great Man's profile. It was a profile that photographed well and was worth looking at; strong, a little bleak, but in its way handsome. The lips were cold and precise, the chin immensely firm, the fine, domelike forehead noble and forbidding. Opposite her sat the little Chinaman, smiling happily and shyly, and while waiting for his soup he kept his hands tucked inside his wide blue sleeves. Eunice thought he looked very nice, and forced herself to speak.

"Do you write books?" she asked, leaning forward.

His smile broadened at once, baring prominent teeth.

"No, thank you. Poetry. I write poetry. Not good poetry, I think. Read only in China. Not good enough for Europe. Thank you very much."

"Oh," she said, "how interesting."

"Thank you," he said again and smiled at her lovingly.

"I once tried to write poetry," she faltered, "when I was younger."

"Oh, yes," he said, smiling affectionately. "Very interesting."

And then it struck Eunice that this wasn't very brilliant, and that the Great Man probably couldn't avoid hearing. So she smiled at the little Chinaman and broke off. Presently the Great Man turned to her.

"Turtle soup," he said, "seems to be inevitably requested and as inevitably granted wherever two or three hundred are gathered together in one place."

"Oh," said Eunice, with a nervous little laugh, "is it? I suppose it is. I don't often go to big dinners."

He looked tolerantly at her and turned to Mrs. Breed.

"My dear Constance, I assure you the Lapponicum Flavidum likes the sun. All the Lapponicums like the sun. You were right to put your Sarcococca in the shade, and your Thomsoni will do best in half-shade, but don't, don't deny the sun to your Lapponicum. Take my word for it, you'll regret it if you do."

"Well, but my dearest Henry," Mrs. Breed said, "I was talking to Brixon only yesterday, and he warned me that, as my rock-garden faced full south, the Lapponicums might get more sun than was good for them. He agrees with you entirely about the Thomsoni and the Sarcococca, however."

Eunice lost the rest of the conversation in the din about her. Everyone was talking, talking. Everyone had a great deal to say. She tried to catch a glimpse of Corry, but he was hidden from her by the black bulk of the lady she supposed was Mae Moss. She thought about the Great Man and Mrs. Breed. Henry . . . Constance . . . they'd probably known each other for years. A great literary friendship. Lovers once perhaps. She peeped at Mrs. Breed's benign, large-featured face, and thought, yes, quite likely, when she was younger. She looked rather like George Eliot now, or would have looked like her had she worn her hair that way.

The Great Man would probably turn back to her in a moment and then what could she possibly find to talk to him about? Lapponicums? She didn't know what they were. His last book? What would she dare to say about it except that she loved it, and how banal and school-girlish that would sound?

The Admiral had ordered hock, and, turning to her, he gallantly proffered the bottle.

"Now young lady, a little of this will do you good. A nice, dry hock. Wouldn't harm a baby. My wife won't touch it; the doctors have frightened her, poor dear, but you and I don't listen to doctors."

"I'm afraid I don't drink wine," said Eunice, raising her voice.

"Dear me, dear me, what are young people coming to? Try a little; it will do you good."

"Well," said Eunice, "just a little then. I'm afraid it's wasted on me."

He filled her glass and then turned to his wife who was trying to attract his attention.

"What's that, my dear? Kitty Dalgetty? Can't be. What'd she be be doing in this rogue's gallery? Somebody's guest? Well, maybe, maybe. I'll just put on my glasses and have a look. 'Pon my soul, I believe it is. And my dear, I'll swear that's the same purple dress she used to wear when we were in Malta."

Eunice sat sipping her wine. She wanted to make it last as long as possible. Just a tiny sip, and then presently, another. It gave her something to do, she found, between the courses. She thought of speaking to the little Chinaman again, but could think of nothing to say to him. Then suddenly the Great Man turned to her once more.

"If all the novelists writing to-day were placed end to end," he said, "how far do you suppose they'd reach?"

Feeling a little like Alice Through the Looking Glass, Eunice faltered and said: "Is it a riddle? Is there an answer?"

"There must be an answer," he said, "though I don't happen to know it. But it would be a pleasing sight."

She laughed politely, and tried to think of a suitable reply, but such was the effect of his Greatness upon her that her mind was empty of a single thought. "Yes," she replied, "it would, wouldn't it?"

He looked down at her card.

"You'd be one of the endless chain yourself, I suspect. Eunice Maud Raikes. An oddly discreet name. Tell me what you've written."

"Only two books," she stammered. "Just novels. I'm afraid they're not very good."

"Still," he said magnanimously, "only two. I think you might be discharged with a caution."

She laughed again and had almost thought of a possible retort when he turned away.

"It's all very well for you, Constance," she heard him say, "to insist on the importance of the chilli peppers, but your Mrs. Gorme knows how to use them. When I ask Martha to suggest to Mrs. Crawley that a slight flavour of chillies would improve the sauce, she puts in enough to set the Houses of Parliament on fire. The woman has absolutely no idea of moderation. Time and time again I've told her so myself, but I might as well talk to the kitchen wall."

"What an odd conversation," thought Eunice, and it seemed to her that these famous people were unaccountable and mysterious. She saw that the little Chinaman was smiling at her with a smile that seemed to embrace her and all the world. "Poor little man," she thought, "no one's talking to him either." And she had just decided to ask him how he liked England when the lady on his right, an earnest-looking young woman in red, addressed a remark to him, and he turned, beaming, to answer her. For some time Eunice busied herself with roast saddle of lamb, then the Great Man spoke to her again with unnerving abruptness.

"Would you say," he demanded, "that there had been a definite improvement in the novel within the last fifty years or merely a change? Are novels better to-day or merely different? Is there anyone now writing who could 'put out the eye,' so to speak, of Dickens or Thackeray? What do you think?"

Eunice felt relieved. Here at least was something definite to talk about. "Now, don't be afraid," she told herself, "tell him what you think." She said, stammering a little:

"I think of course one must read the old writers, it's a part of everyone's education; but having read them, I'd much rather read the work of living authors now. For pleasure, I mean. I mean, if I were to go away for a holiday, I'd rather take one of your books with me than a book of Dickory or Thackens. I mean," she said, hurriedly correcting herself and blushing, "I mean Thick—"

"Quite, quite," he interrupted, his face perfectly grave. "I sometimes think myself that I'm as good as Thackens. About Dickory, I'm not so sure. I'm not so sure. There are moments when I think Dickory is the best writer in the world, with the exception, perhaps, of Zolac, or, if you like, Tolstoievsky. But then, of course, Tolstoievsky is—"

Here the waiter intervened, having been sent for earlier.

"I asked for Chateau Lafite 1924," said the Great Man, in gentle reproof, "and you brought me '29." The waiter apologized and removed the bottle. "My enthusiasm for the things of the present," he told Eunice, "does not extend itself to claret. 1929 was a very good year, but—Yes, Constance?" And he turned back to Mrs. Breed.

Eunice sat sipping her wine, the blushes returning again and again to her cheek at the memory of her silly slip of the tongue. When her glass was empty, the Admiral turned to her.

"Here, here," he said, filling her glass again, "you're not doing your share. You mustn't let me do all the work. How are you getting on?"

"Very nicely, thanks," said Eunice, "and I like this wine very much."

"Ah," he said, nodding, "that's good, that's good. We're having a tremendous argument, the gentleman at the end of the table and myself, about aircraft in war. He'd like to abolish the Navy. Excuse me, my dear, I must have at him again." And she listened for a while to a highly technical discussion on the ability or inability of battleships to defend themselves from air attack. Presently the Great Man was addressing her again. He resembled, she thought, a lighthouse, whose dignified revolving beam illumines, every so often, each object within its range, only to leave it in darkness again.

"To what do you attribute," he asked, "this sudden vogue for the past? Novelists, biographers, dramatists, they are all taking their little tin shovels down to that vast shore. Personally, I think history should be difficult. It should be sweated for, with plenty of midnight oil. What do you think?"

"I really haven't thought about it very much," said Eunice, and she tried to think of the name of the writer whose historical essays she had so greatly enjoyed, but her memory stubbornly refused to perform the simple, necessary act of producing it for her. It didn't matter, luckily, for the Great Man then proceeded to express his own views without asking her any alarming questions. He then turned abruptly back to Mrs. Breed.

"No, Constance, a few minutes ago you made a perfectly unjustifiable attack on my mendacity. I never told them the truth about it, never. Do you imagine I've no conscience? I could see with half an eye that the legs were faked, or at least three of them were, but they'd paid two hundred pounds for it, and naturally I'm all in favour of letting them get what pleasure they can out of it."

Eunice sat sipping her wine. She wished she could catch Corry's eye, and then was glad she could not. He was doubtless imagining that she was enjoying every minute of the evening. Before long the Great Man made one of his sudden pounces in her direction, this time to say:

"On the whole then, you approve of this selling of famous men of history at two a penny? I hadn't, somehow, expected it of you." The waiter bent over him. "Yes, a cigar, please. And a double brandy. Constance, you'll join me in a brandy? No? What a pity. Will you, Miss Eunice Maud Raikes?"

"I've never drunk brandy in my life," said Eunice, "but I'd like to try some now."

"Excellent. We'll pledge each other's health. In a few minutes I shall rise to propose the health of the King. After that I shall make a short speech. And after that you shall justify, if you can, your attitude towards these hucksters of history, these barrow-pushers and street hawkers of whom we were speaking."

"I'm afraid I don't know very much about it," said Eunice, in whose mind, at moments of stress, nothing but the simple truth presented itself.

"Neither do they, so you're in a very strong position. Yes, Constance, we said Tuesday. Yes, yes, I'm quite sure. Very well, I'll write it down." He took his engagement book out of his pocket, and glancing at it out of the tail of her eye, Eunice saw that it was scored and blackened with small entries. He wrote, and spoke the words aloud as he wrote them: "Tuesday, at 3.45. Go with Constance to Kippler's to choose a dachshund."

When, later, he got up to propose the health of the King, Eunice drank it in brandy. He then made a speech which she thought witty, agreeable, and adroit. Two other speeches followed, one by a young dramatist, the other by the elderly founder of the Club. Then everyone was free to leave his seat, and at once the Great Man was surrounded. Eunice, after vainly lingering with the idea of saying a polite good night, presently slipped away and went in search of Corry. The fumes of hock and brandy were slowly mounting to her head, but not sufficiently to inconvenience her. Instead she felt a sort of sublime complacence stealing over her, a sweet indifference, a careless acceptance of all things, even of her own shortcomings. What was there to have made such a fuss about? What on earth did it all matter? She

caught sight of Corry and moved serenely in his direction, hardly
noticing the many obstacles in her way. Voices, colours, lights all
blared and blinded and deafened. Although cannoned this way and
that, her expression of bland complacence never altered. Corry saw
her and came forward to meet her.

"Hello," he said. "Had a good time?"

"Lovely," she replied, smiling past him.

"I didn't have a bad time. I liked my little Jap, she was quite
human. The other wasn't so good. How did you get on with old
What's-his-name?"

"Beautifully."

"Want to go home now, darling, or would you like to stay for a bit?"

"Home," she said.

"Well, I don't suppose there's a chance of your seeing the Great
Man again. There's a mob around him. Run along then and get your
coat while I get a taxi."

Still with that bland, sweetly indifferent look on her face, she
proffered her ticket and received her coat. When Corry put her into
the taxi, she leaned her head heavily against him and he put an arm
about her.

"So glad you enjoyed it, old girl. It was worth it, wasn't it? I mean,
if you hadn't sat where you did it might have been a bit dull for you.
Well, tell me what you talked about, you and he. I'll bet you had a lot
to say to each other."

"A lot," she said. Though her outward demeanour was still calm,
her thoughts were stirring. Bright, humorous fancies came to her,
fancies that her tongue itched to express.

"Go on, darling, tell me what you talked about," said Corry.

"We began with turtle soup," she said. "He made a quite absurd
remark about it being the soup you always find on the menu wherever
two or three hundred are gathered together in one place, and I laughed
and said: 'I expect the turtle's rather like me. It takes an occasion
like this to get it out of its shell.' Quite silly, you know, but it amused
him, and it started things off. After that . . . let me see . . . we
talked about all the novelists there were writing novels to-day, and he
asked me how far I thought they'd reach if they were all put end to
end. So I said: 'Why not tale to tale?' Just nonsense, you know, but it
seemed to amuse him. I forget what we talked about after that. Oh,
yes, he wanted to know how many books I'd written, and when I told

him only two he said I ought to be ashamed, but that as I was still young he'd take a lenient view and discharge me with a caution. I said I was surprised at that, as I'd always understood he was noted for his long sentences."

"That was a trifle daring, wasn't it?" asked Corry.

"Not a bit. He loved it."

"Didn't he talk at all to whoever was on his other side?"

"Oh, yes, now and again. That was Mrs. Breed, Constance Breed. She's one of the older novelists."

"Well, go on," said Corry.

"It's hard to remember. He asked me to tell him how I explained the present vogue for the past. Everyone's writing about the past, you know, and history's become quite popular. I said I thought novelists turned to the past because they found the present too fluid for them. I said: 'When about half the world's in liquidation—' "

"I'm not sure that was so good," said Corry.

"Well," she agreed, "perhaps not. But you know how it is, one talks nonsense just to make things go. He called me Eunice Maud Raikes all the evening. I suppose because it seemed friendlier than Miss Raikes. And he said that on the whole I ought to consider myself in a very strong position. Coming from a man like that, such a remark is most encouraging, I think."

"I should say it was," said Corry.

"Well, then we talked about all sorts of things. About cooking and gardening—his knowledge is quite extraordinary—and about old furniture, and even, finally, about dogs. He wants to buy a dachs-hund." Her brandy-induced vainglory was already beginning to wane, her bedtime inventiveness, which, thanks to the alcohol, had come earlier than usual, was flagging. Shame was beginning to make itself felt, though not, as yet, at all strongly. She nestled still more comfortably against Corry's side.

"Some time I'll tell him," she said to herself, "but not yet." And then, a little condescendingly, and in the manner of one who speaks from the heights of Olympus, she murmured drowsily:

"And now, darling, tell me about the little Jap."

A Chance to Talk Informally

HILDA COLE ESPY

This is fun! You will be zipped through a little dinner at home planned by a young professor and his wife to promote his career. You will enjoy dining with the Coxes and Mr. Jessup, who finds that women can keep a secret,—and there are more fireworks than on the Fourth of July!

SALLY COX stood at the foot of the stairs and listened. Yes, they were all in the bathroom. Paul was shaving; the two-year-old twins, Beatrice and Molly, were in the tub and seven-year-old Jasper was washing some of the top soil off them. There was enough confusion to cover a telephone conversation. Still Sally took no chances. She picked up the telephone, backed into a hall closet full of coats and rubbers and closed the door.

"Hello, Mother," she said. "I'm afraid the baby's coming tonight and you'd better stand by to come over later in the evening. I don't want Paul to know about it because we're having a very crucial dinner party. Now wait a minute, darling. You know what a slowpoke I am. With the twins it was eight hours before I had to think of leaving for the hospital. Here's the point: Tonight is Paul's big chance to quit being a college professor. You see, this big international public relations firm got wind of those reader reactions he's been making on his own. Well, Tuesday they called him into New York to talk with them about some surveys they are making in Latin America and last night the head of the firm, Mr. Jessup, asked to come out here and talk informally with Paul and me. So you see how vital it is. Poor Paul's nervous enough about entertaining the man with no cook or maid without knowing that I've picked this peachy time to start having the baby! Otherwise everything's under control. The Winters have gone to Chicago and they said I could put the twins to sleep in their guest room so they won't be right on top of us. Don't worry now, just keep your fingers crossed for my pains to hold off until I've wined and dined Mr. Jessup and Paul cinches the job. See you later! I've got to take a look at the roast."

Sally stepped out into the hall again, a tall woman in a concealing mandarin coat. Her smooth black hair was drawn back into a neat bun that looked well with her slightly Chinese costume. She hoped that Mr. I. V. Jessup, who was due to arrive in half an hour, would never guess how hectic a floor-waxing, silver-polishing, rug-beating day the Cox family had put behind them.

"Mother-r-r-r!" Jasper shouted from the top of the stairs. "Beatrice and Molly are all dry now."

"Put their pants and socks and shoes on," she called, "and I'll be right up to finish them."

SALLY, escorting the freshly pinafored twins downstairs, found Paul nervously setting out cocktail glasses on a tray.

"Lord," he muttered, "I hate this sort of thing! I never was any good at selling myself and I never will be."

"Don't be silly!" Sally spoke heartily. "If you are nervous, just don't show it. Be breezy and dynamic . . ."

"Yeah," said Paul hollowly.

"Stop it!" she said. "Now you two." She bent and put an arm around Beatrice and Molly, proud of their shining hair and bright impatient faces. "You two. When you've said how-do-you-do to Mr. Jessup, Jasper is going to take you over and put you to bed at Aunty Margaret's. And you're going to be very good and quiet for Mummy, aren't you?" She looked into Molly's impish black eyes. Molly smiled and writhed.

"And Jasper—" He was standing by Paul looking very important in his best suit. "You remember not to talk too much or act hammy. And go straight over to Aunt Margaret's after dinner."

"Okay. What are you all excited about?" he demanded in his most superior tone.

"I'm not all excited," Sally denied. She cast an anxious look at Paul, nervously clinking ice. "What makes you think I'm excited?"

"Why, nobody's excited," said Paul through his teeth. "It'll just be a wonder if we don't all wind up in strait jackets."

"Oh-oh," said Jasper from the window. "Here he comes."

"Okay." Sally started for the front door. "Come on, Paul, and don't forget to act natural."

They stood on the threshold watching Mr. Jessup stride up the walk and desperately smiling their welcome.

"How do you do?" Sally extended her hand.

Mr. Jessup was tall and brindle-haired with a quick appraising face and a reserved smile.

Sally ushered him into the living-room where he took a whirling look around and boomed, "Well, well, well," at the children. She held her breath until it became clear that Jasper was going to get the twins out of the front door and over to Margaret's without a crying scene. Then she made herself sit down and smile at Mr. Jessup. Paul, the coward, was stalling an uncommonly long time over the drinks.

"It's really very flattering of you to come all this way to see us," she said.

Mr. JESSUP's smile was very tight. His eyes weren't going to warm up in a hurry, either. Well, Sally thought, you didn't get to be a Big Man without the knack of intimidation.

"You've gathered we're pretty interested in your husband," he said.

He was going to be frank. Sally took her cue.

"I've rather hoped so," she said.

"I never hire a man on the basis of an office interview."

"Really?" Sally wondered how on earth a person could survive socially without dear old "Really."

Paul passed a cocktail to Mr. Jessup and filled Sally's glass with grapefruit juice, looking rather stifled.

"Frankly there are two points about which I am doubtful. Two points."

Sally, trying to ignore a pain, cocked her head.

"It would be interesting to know what they are," she said, wishing that Paul would not sit so stiffly—that he would lean back, cross his legs, flick cigarette ashes and act dynamic.

Mr. Jessup shook his finger at her. It might have been a playful gesture had anyone else made it. But Sally almost flinched.

"I'll tell you what I'm looking for," he said, "at the end of the evening. And I'll tell you whether or not I found it."

Paul took his handkerchief out and wiped his forehead.

Jasper returned, striding across the room and picking up his ginger ale with all the airs of a grown-up at a cocktail party. He held the glass carelessly in his right hand and jammed his left hand into his pocket. He gave Mr. Jessup an appraising look which was every bit as good as the look Mr. Jessup gave him. On the whole, Sally thought, it was a pity Jasper wasn't looking for the job.

"Well, young man," barked Mr. Jessup. "How do you like school?"

"Huh!" Jasper said rudely. "I wish I had a nickel for every time I've answered that one."

"Jasper!" Sally protested.

Mr. Jessup reached in his pocket, jingled some change and handed Jasper a nickel. Paul did his best to laugh merrily at this neat touché.

"Jasper," Sally said quickly. "Will you please come out to the kitchen and give me a hand?"

When the door had swung to behind them, Sally glared at Jasper.

"You're not to say another word, Jasper Cox," she commanded in a shaking voice. "You can't open your mouth without being hammy so you just keep it shut."

She interrupted a squawk of protest by grabbing his arm and shaking it. Jasper looked so astonished that she was ashamed of herself.

"Here." Sally wearily handed him a box of matches. "Light the candles on the dining-room table."

She glanced at her wrist watch. Well, that was one thing to be thankful for. The pains weren't speeding up. Another good thing was that the baby-sitter next door with the twins hadn't barged in to ask any foolish questions.

As THEY sat around the dining-room table, dipping their spoons into wobbling pink madrilene, Sally wished that she hadn't chosen such a jittery first course. The madrilene and Paul looked equally tremulous. She gave him a look which said, "Now! Now's your chance. Talk about yourself." But Paul reached nervously for his glass of water. It was Mr. Jessup who spoke.

"Well, young man," he eyed Jasper. "I suppose you want to be a pilot when you grow up."

He studied him carefully as if hoping to discover some redeeming trait.

Jasper glanced at him, tightened his mouth and reached for a piece of bread.

"Jasper!" said Sally.

"You told me not to talk."

"Really, Jasper." She blushed. "When you're spoken to—"

Jasper sighed gustily.

"No," he said, speaking as importantly as Raymond Gram Swing, "I do not want to be a pilot."

"What then?" Mr. Jessup pursued coldly. "What do you want to be?"

"Do you think I'm good-looking?" Jasper countered.

"Good Lord!" Paul croaked.

"Why, yes," allowed Mr. Jessup.

"If I stay good-looking, I'm going to be an actor," Jasper said. "Like my father."

Paul's mouth fell open. Sally gasped. Mr. Jessup gave Paul a hawk-like look which said, "Ah! You didn't tell us about that part of your background, Mr. Cox."

"That's what he used to be and that's what he wants to be," said Jasper.

Paul cleared his throat.

"Kids have a reputation for telling the truth, for absolute frankness," he said. "And so when they tell a fancy whopper everybody believes them and laughs at their red-faced parents. I'll never forget the time Jasper told a bunch of strangers at a New York tea party that I was a tightrope walker, will you, Sally?"

"I never shall," Sally said grimly.

But Mr. Jessup wasn't listening. Mr. Jessup was interested in something else; something that was going on outside the windows.

"The neighbors," he said, "are doing the strangest things."

Jasper jumped up from the table and looked out the window.

"Oh-oh!" he said feelingly.

"What?" Sally cried.

"Why, they're throwing things out of the window," said Mr. Jessup.

"It isn't the neighbors!" Jasper shouted cheerfully. "It's Molly and Beatrice."

"Excuse me," Sally choked, pushing back her chair.

HER HANDS flew to her face as she stopped short on the lawn under Margaret's guest-room window. Combs and brushes of the bureau set lay among shattered Currier and Ives prints and a broken china candlestick. As she stood tragically gazing at the debris, a cosmetic jar bounced on the grass and a chaise-longue pillow followed.

She flew to the front door and found Jane, the baby-sitter, sprawled angularly on the steps, pushing back her hair and reading a novel.

"For heaven's sakes, Jane!" Sally exploded. "Where have you been? Why aren't you where you can keep an eye on Beatrice and Molly?"

"What's happened?" Jane came to slowly, not even bothering to stand up. "I thought they were asleep."

Sally tightened her mouth and dashed upstairs. Beatrice and Molly had taken off their nightgowns. They had smeared themselves and the wallpaper with lipstick from the ransacked dressing table.

"See what Bea-tiss di'?" asked Molly proudly.

"I see." Grimly Sally swooped and took a twin under each arm. Downstairs she met Paul and Jasper and Jane—and Mr. Jessup—coming in loaded with the objects which Beatrice and Molly had gleefully tossed out the window.

Seeing her, Paul's tormented face smoothed out. He gave her a sweet smile. It startled her. He took the twins from her and handed one to Mr. Jessup.

"Just carry her over and dump her into the bathtub," he commanded.

WITH Molly in his arms Mr. Jessup wore a new helpless look. Sally might have dwelt on it with some pleasure as she watched him walk gingerly toward the house, except for a world-shaking pain which enveloped her as she stood dazedly on Margaret's front steps. It was a new business-like pain and she burst into tears. Jane stood beside her and kept babbling on about how sorry she was that it had happened, that she had been sure they were sound asleep. But Sally scarcely heard her. She thought, it was carrying them down that did it. I should have had more sense.

Paul was hailing her from their own front door.

"Come on over and let's go on with dinner." He sounded sweet and cheerful. Bless his heart, he knew that all was lost with Mr. Jessup, but he didn't care any more. He was worried about her and he wanted to help. "The twins are all washed off and in bed, and I stuck the roast in the oven again."

As Sally returned to her dining-room it dawned on her that something was odd about Mr. Jessup. She focused on him more carefully and discovered that he was wearing Paul's bathrobe and that his hair was wet.

"What happened to Mr. Jessup?" she asked as she dully drew her chair back to sit down.

Mr. Jessup looked sheepish. Paul grinned.

"Mr. Jessup got a little excited trying to make the twins sit down in the bathtub," he spoke cheerfully. "He turned on the shower by mistake."

Mr. Jessup wiped his brow. Some of that dampness was undeniably perspiration.

Sally let a pain come and go as she studied Paul in puzzlement. Paul had changed. He was really dynamic as he carved the roast. He gave Mr. Jessup a reassuring smile which had an almost fatherly quality.

"You know," he stuck a fork into a potato, "I was just thinking about that South American problem you mentioned the other day—"

"You were just *thinking*—" Mr. Jessup barked incredulously.

Sally laughed. It was the fact that another pain came in the middle of the laugh which drew Paul's and Mr. Jessup's attention to her. Her laugh sounded awful as it ran down.

"What is it?" Paul asked. "What's the matter?"

Sally bit her lip. "All right," she said. "I thought maybe I could stall until after dinner but I guess maybe I can't. You'd better call the doctor, Paul."

"Well, well, well," he said. "How long has this been going on?"

"It started before supper," Sally confessed shakily, dropping her role of the Brave Little Woman like a hot potato. "I thought it wouldn't amount to much for a while but now—there it goes again."

"Are you going to have the baby now, Mother?" Jasper shouted. "Are you going to have the baby now?"

Mr. Jessup had jumped up from the table and was pacing the floor. As Paul headed for the telephone Mr. Jessup seized a napkin and began to flap it at Sally.

"There, there," he shouted.

"Take it easy, Mr. Jessup," Paul called from the hallway. "It's all perfectly natural and normal and there's nothing to be concerned about."

But Mr. Jessup continued to flap the napkin at her in a flustered way, eying her as if she were a bomb which might explode at any moment.

"The doctor's on his way to the hospital," Paul reported on his return. "I think we'd better get started too. Mother's line is busy but you'll keep on trying her, won't you, Mr. Jessup? Marshfield 3207—"

"Marshfield 3207—3207—" Mr. Jessup looked around wildly, found a paper and penciled the number, wheeling nervously toward the window.

"Just tell her to come on over and stay with the kids, Mr. Jessup." Paul was helping Sally up. "Meantime will you keep an eye on them? I'll call you from the hospital."

As Paul started the car Sally put her hand on his arm. "Oh, Paul," she said, "I'm so sorry I wrecked things for you."

"How could you help it? The only thing is I hate to leave the kids with that jibbering idiot!"

They backed down the drive but were apprehended by Mr. Jessup, who came tearing across the front lawn waving his arms and shouting.

"Good Lord!" Paul exploded.

"Roll down the window!" bellowed Mr. Jessup. "Roll down the window! This is confidential!"

Paul rolled down the window and Mr. Jessup whispered hoarsely.

"Oh holy jumping elephants!" said Paul. "Okay—thanks—I'll call you."

And they shot out of the drive.

Sally studied Paul's averted face.

"What was it, Paul?" she asked quietly.

"Oh." He removed his hand from the steering wheel long enough to wave it disgustedly. "Tempest in a teapot."

"Paul." Sally used a voice which she used very seldom but which invariably got results. "You may just as well tell me what's gone wrong."

"Your mother," Paul said, "just fell down a few stairs and twisted her ankle. She can't walk on it so she can't come."

JAMES LORING COX was born at ten-thirty P.M. Sally could hardly keep her eyes open after that. When she next awakened the sun was high and Paul was sitting by the bed holding her hand. She smiled at him sweetly and then her head jerked up.

"Paul! What are you doing here?"

"What?"

"Who's looking after the twins and Jasper?"

He pressed her hand and kissed her forehead.

"They're fine," he said. "You should have seen the breakfast they tucked away this morning. Scrambled eggs and . . ."

"Paul!" Sally said. "Don't be evasive . . ."

A nurse opened the door and peeked in.

"Excuse me, Mrs. Cox, but there's someone on the wire who wants to know where you keep the twins' panties. A Mr. Jessup, I believe he said . . ."

Sally closed her eyes. Then she weakly transmitted the information.

"Well, that's fine, Paul," she said. "Altogether I guess I cinched the job for you, didn't I?"

"Sure you have," he grinned. "That's just what you have done."

"Will you kindly tell me how?"

"I'm dying to. Remember those two points that worried Jessup? Well, he told me what they were this morning when we were doing the dishes. First he was afraid that a college professor used to a quiet and studious atmosphere couldn't function in the midst of the excitement and confusion of his high-powered firm. Well, it was Jessup who cracked under the confusion last evening—not I. His second doubt was whether you were the type of woman who could keep things confidential. The way you kept quiet about the baby coming dispelled his doubts there. But that wasn't what really sold him . . ."

"No?"

"No." Paul shook his head and grinned reminiscently. "He didn't really break down until this morning. He finally warmed up when he saw the way the kids went for his scrambled eggs. That's what really got him."

The Romantic Trousers

ROBERT FONTAINE

The Junior Dance required long pants, even if it meant borrowing Father's dress suit. There were hazards, of course, for this French-Canadian youngster—particularly Father.

MISS CORNWALL, who spoke to me of geometry every day in my second year at high school, was as beautiful as a star.

I sat at my desk, my legs curled around each other, my pen dipping aimlessly in and out of the inkwell, watching, enraptured, as she wrote on the blackboard.

She wrote only of the hypotenuse, perhaps, but to me it was a love message.

It seemed to me that there were no eyes so blue in the world, nor hair so golden. She moved to and from the blackboard, I thought, as one dances on the stage of a theater. When she spoke it was the sound of my father's violin.

Well, how old was I—twelve, thirteen, fourteen? . . . I was perhaps not the best judge in the world.

Still, I know that the scent of her perfume, the shape of her body, the ringing of the small bells of her laughter, were in my head like a song that goes around all night in a dream.

My love for Miss Cornwall was utterly pure, mainly, it may be, because I was not very inventive. All I asked was to be where she was, to hear her, to see her, to smell her fragrance.

I longed to tell her of my gallant love, to assure her that it would not be long before I was grown-up and ready for a brilliant marriage. She had but to be patient awhile. The fact that Miss Cornwall was some fifteen years my senior scarcely occurred to me. Had I not been taught by some poet in first-form English that love knows no such barriers?

Yes, I wanted to pour forth my love as if it were a brutal bird beating against my heart. But each time I was near her, even to hand her the blackboard compass, I trembled and became as red as a beet-root. My knees knocked in my knickerbockers like my beloved's ruler rapping on the desk, and when I spoke, the sound was like that of the chalk in her compass squeaking along the blackboard.

So, for days I had my love in poems scratched on foolscap, appropriately. When they were done, I tore them up nervously and felt only a little better.

There came, eventually, a bright day when the Junior Dance was announced. It was rumored that Miss Cornwall would be among those attending this elegant Lower School function.

I was, of course, wild with hope. To dance with her! To speak to her! To hold her in my arms!

Eh, well, what if she *was* several inches taller? I could dance with my head high and my shoulders straight. If she bent her head a little, we would be even.

In bed at night I fashioned in my mind the lines I would speak to her. They would be great, burning, singing lines, so sincere, so lovely, so impassioned she would almost faint in my arms with the strength of my adoration. After that, I had no plans.

Then, one morning when I arose, I realized I still wore short pants. In the delirium of loving I had forgotten how foolish I would look dancing with the most beautiful woman in the world while she wore a black lace evening gown and I wore gray-checked short pants.

I am as stupid as an owl, I thought. It is plain as *bon jour* that such a thing cannot be! Am I to say to her: "I adore you, my beloved. You are as beautiful as the twilight with the first stars in your violet-blue eyes. Please do not notice the short pants"?

That day I begged my mother for a new suit with long pants.

"Why?" she asked.

"Why? But, *Maman,* I am now a man."

"No, *bibi,* you are not a man. You are still too small for long pants."

I sighed and could not eat my dinner.

"Long pants," Papa said, "are fine if you have the length for them. Ah, what is the difference, eh? It is the boy, not the pants."

"It is the pants," I muttered sadly.

"Your uncle Felix," *Maman* observed wistfully, "did not have long pants until he was nineteen."

"That," I said unkindly, "is perhaps what is wrong with him."

187

I spoke no more of the long pants. I went to school and came home like a man who has been condemned to death and who has gotten used to the idea.

The night of the dance came at the end of the week. *Maman* had gone next door to chat with Aunt Felice about stretching curtains. Papa had gone to the Château to play for dinner, and I was alone.

I walked about the house, wishing the walls would close in and crush me as they did in the cinema serials.

I opened and closed doors loudly, muttering oaths bilingually.

By chance I opened the door of my father's closet and, just as I was ready to slam it shut with angry *patatras,* I observed, hanging there, his beautiful black suit that he wore for special conducting events.

I felt the strong, hard cloth and recalled vividly how handsome he had looked wearing this suit when he conducted. He had, in fact, had the suit ten years or more and he spoke to everyone with pride about the garment, mentioning always the need of having such a fine suit for great events. Next to *Maman* and me, I think he loved the suit best.

I knew all this, but it was late and I was angry and frustrated. So I pulled the trousers down and quickly put them on. Glancing at myself in the full-length mirror, I saw that I had already grown taller and was now almost a fit companion for the most beautiful woman in the world.

I found a dress shirt and put it on. It was too large and bulged, but that did not matter. It was a man's shirt, and that was all I cared about.

The tie took me a half-hour to get in place and even at the end one side was larger than the other, like an abnormal butterfly. Even this did not bother me.

The coat was too large, of course, but I discovered that when I threw out my chest and stretched my arms the coat was almost a fit.

ONE remembers when one is older a night here and a night there in the rose garden of youth. One remembers each detail as one might recall each curled petal of a rose.

Such was the night I danced on pink clouds with Miss Cornwall in my father's full-dress suit.

I spoke in her coral ear of how I loved her and she did not laugh or call me a foolish boy. She acted as if I were her equal.

She thanked me graciously for the punch. She spoke to me of her life and told me I was very handsome in my new suit and that my geometry was excellent.

She was a woman and knew, I imagine, what was in my heart, and she did nothing to make it either shabby or painful. She left it there as it was and allowed me to keep my dignity.

One word, one gesture, making me a foolish schoolboy would have broken my heart. She knew it, this wonderful dabbler in angles and curves and lacy nothings woven in Euclid's imagination. She knew it and she did not say the word or make the gesture.

Even when I begged her to permit me to escort her home she said merely that it was such a pity she had already made a previous engagement, and she sounded sincere.

Ah, well . . . I would take her home, anyway, in my young and foolish heart.

It was only after I had summoned up courage enough to kiss her hand and say good night that I realized Papa would soon be home and I must rush to replace the suit.

As a matter of fact, he might even be home already, I thought, and I prayed that he linger, as he often did, to taste the chef's breast of guinea hen.

Dizzy, happy, a man with his head brushing the stars, I skipped joyfully over yard and lawn, my long coattails flying in the breeze like a victor's banner.

It was raised too soon, that banner. They flew too proudly, those coattails. Those stars were not so close as they appeared.

I tripped awkwardly over a small wire enclosing the beginning of a lawn and I went sprawling, seeing only, as I fell to my face, a small sign reading: PLEASE KEEP OFF. It was, of course, too late for such a warning. My hands were already cut and my face and shirt covered with dirt.

"Name of many blue pigs!" I muttered. "Regard me, O Lord!"

But the dirt and the cuts were not the worst.

I felt, blowing behind me, a cool wind, and reaching with fear around the back of my trousers, I found that there the Lord had punished me by placing a large rip.

I sat down on the sidewalk and felt like crying.

"So is the world," I mumbled. "In each apple a worm. Everywhere pain and worms and holes in the pants of one's father."

At last I rose and limped hastily home. Arriving at the house, I did not dare go in. I kept walking around in circles, hoping that some rebellious angel would pass a miracle and restore my seat to normalcy.

But there was no miracle. The angels were in no mood to go over the Lord's head.

In a short time I was so tired I could walk no longer.

I went into the house slowly and walked down the hall like one asleep.

In the parlor, my mother and father stood side by side, regarding me.

"Dear Lord," I said to myself, "enough is enough. Please make it so they are not too angry and hurt. A man in love is selfish and does not think of others. This I know now, dear Lord, thanks to You. Amen."

I stood before them in silence, and they were silent, too.

I knew how I appeared: my father's great and wonderful suit torn and dirty, my face covered with mud and scratches, my tie stained with grass.

To my astonishment, Papa smiled gently.

"Ah, so! The dance was too vigorous, eh?"

I could barely believe my red ears.

"*Comment?*" I asked suspiciously.

"In my time," my father went on with too much joviality, "we did not dance so hard we tore our clothes. Of course, at that time it was mostly waltzes, which are easier on the fabric."

"Come," *Maman* said kindly, "you had better wash yourself and change your clothes. Then you may have some coffee and shortbreads. You must be tired."

With love and wonder I looked at them, and it seemed as if my heart would not remain long inside me.

"I am a fool," I said loudly. "I am a schoolboy who wishes to become a man suddenly."

"No," *Maman* contradicted. "It is not so."

"*Ah, mais non!*" Papa agreed. "You are becoming a man and we do not wish it in our hearts. We have so much love for you that we wish, without hardly knowing it, to keep you forever a small boy with hair that does not comb and stockings which fall down. It is we who are stupid!"

Claudia in Hollywood

ROSE FRANKEN

Claudia is as real as apple pie and is a constant delight. Claudia thought Hollywood was a second Wonderland and almost outdid the role of Alice. But where else could something very pink and very purple lead to a $15,000 contract? Yes, she was fooled by Hollywood, but watch her fool Hollywood in turn.

THE HOUSE SEEMED to be saying good-bye to them as they drove away, down the road. David knew how she felt. "Do you want to go back?" he asked her.

She said, quite jauntily, "Not for worlds." But she didn't mean it. It was all she could do to keep from crying. The way the dogs acted had brought a lump to her throat. They'd known something was in the air, and had eyed the suitcases with distrust. The cat had seemed to feel something, too. He'd run around the house twice as if on important business, and then had scurried up a tree. "Bobby didn't mind so much, though," Claudia mused aloud, and of course it didn't mean anything at all to the baby.

Mrs. Cootz was standing at her gate as they passed, looking like all farmers' wives rolled into one. She waved, and Claudia waved back, feeling sorry for going off on a vacation when Mrs. Cootz had to stay home and keep on working. And then Claudia saw little Joey run to his mother's side, and she felt only envy for Mrs. Cootz, because nothing was going to change in her life.

At the station David shook Fritz's hand. "Look out for the young pigs," he said. "And better keep the brooder going in the chicken house for another week or so."

"Fritz, never mind the pigs and chickens, watch out for the children," Claudia begged.

"I take care of everything," Fritz promised. He looked capable and strong and homely. Claudia remembered making teeth out of orange peel when she was a little girl, and sticking them in her mouth. Fritz looked like that when he smiled.

"I love Fritz," Claudia said, when they were on the train. David said that he did too. They agreed, for heaven only knew how many times, that Fritz was perfect.

It was silly to have taken a drawing room. "A drawing room for a hundred miles," she scoffed, but liked it.

"Why not?" demanded David. "This is our second honeymoon."

"Couldn't it be a little more illicit than a honeymoon?"

"Go as far as you like," he said.

The drawing room made Claudia hungry. She had only to look at a train, and she wanted a sandwich. She still had a choked-up feeling from saying good-bye to Bertha and the children, and from the missing of her mother's figure in the doorway—but just the same she couldn't get her mind off a sandwich. "Go on," said David, "ring for the porter."

"If you insist," she murmured.

The porter was very black, and gave the impression of having come a long way. But he had only come from Boston. The train had only started at Boston. Claudia was affronted. "And then it turns around at New York and just goes back?" It spoiled things a little. And the sandwich was disappointing, as it was made with neither lettuce nor mustard, and the butter was almost invisible. "What kind of meals are on the plane?" she wondered.

"Everything tastes of cardboard," David told her brutally. But she smiled. "I shall like that," she said.

David frowned. "You're not illicit," he sulked. "You're just a glutton."

The plane trip was nothing. Once you were up in the air you might as well have been on the ground. Claudia had to remind herself that she was flying. She wrote postals to Bobby and Bertha and Fritz, and in a burst of whimsey sent additional ones to the baby and Shakespeare and the dogs. She gloated over the small packages of chewing gum that you got for nothing. When the supper was served, she thought it was darling. "But I could do without the fruit salad," she admitted. "Would you like my coffee, David?"

"There's a little thing beside you if you need it," he mentioned.

"Don't be silly," she said coldly. She felt as if she had flown all her life. After the first couple of landings, she didn't even bother to fasten the safety strap, but when David found out about it, he threatened to wring her neck.

The night was long. She asked the steward to tell her when they were over the Mississippi. "Why do you want to know?" David asked her curiously.

"I remember it from school," she told him sentimentally. It was strange to be flying over the Mississippi. It didn't seem real. Hardly anything seemed real. "Supper in New York, and breakfast in Los Angeles." With a little cheating on both ends, it was practically true.

Los Angeles turned out to be a quite remarkable place. Claudia couldn't get over the vegetables—spinach a penny a bunch, and avocados two for a nickel. To say nothing of three dozen grapefruit for a quarter, and my Lord, the oranges— "Such irony to have to go to a hotel," she mourned, fascinated by the beautiful markets. "I'm sure I could keep house for the two of us for about five dollars a week."

They were invited out to the Ferrises on the first evening. Stanley Ferris was an architect, like David, and he lived with his wife in a nice big roomy house, off the lower residential section of Wilshire Boulevard.

"Where," Claudia asked, "does Los Angeles end, and Hollywood begin?"

Mr. Ferris said that it was hard to tell, because Hollywood was more a state of mind than anything else. And Mrs. Ferris, who was approaching middle age in a happy, leisurely sort of fashion, said she was sure she didn't know. "Would you believe," she queried with a note of pride, "that I've never set foot in one of their motion-picture studios?"

Claudia found it almost impossible to believe, but said that she supposed it was like New Yorkers not ever having been to the Statue of Liberty, and Londoners never visiting the Tower of London. It appeared, however, that Mrs. Ferris knew both of these points of interest intimately, and she seemed a little surprised that Claudia had never been to either one. Claudia forebore to mention that she had never been to England, which explained the omission of the Tower, but she did say with the same pride that had tinged Mrs. Ferris's admission that, although she'd always lived in New York up to the time they'd bought the farm, wild horses couldn't drag her to the Statue. "Or to any Points of Interest," she was about to add, when Mrs. Ferris announced, with enthusiasm, "Stanley and I hope to be coming East for a round of sight-seeing this winter." Claudia was ashamed to say it after that, so she just said, "Isn't that lovely," and thought gloomily that she and David would have to entertain them in return for tonight's dinner.

Before the evening was over, Mr. and Mrs. Ferris had laid a great deal more groundwork for reciprocity than a single dinner. Mrs. Ferris not only placed herself and her car at Claudia's disposal, but they invited the young Naughtons to a concert the following Friday evening, and Mr. Ferris, who had once been quite handsome, topped the invitation by saying, "We'll drop in at the Cocoanut Grove later and watch the dancing."

"Oh, that will be lovely," Claudia murmured again, but as soon as they were alone, driving back to the hotel, she grumbled to David, "I didn't come three thousand miles to hear a concert, or watch other people dance. Let's send the Ferrises a dozen roses for tonight's dinner, and call it square."

David said he knew what she meant—which was one of the nice things about David, as he might very well have argued that Mr. Ferris was the salt of the earth. "The only thing I'm afraid of," he said, "is that you're not going to have a very good time, if we don't make contacts."

Make contacts. It meant calling up all the people whose telephone numbers Julia and Roger Killian had written down for them. "I'm Claudia Naughton, Julia's sister-in-law—" or—"This is David Naughton, Roger Killian's partner—" Claudia winced. "Don't let's. It sounds like recommendations from an employment agency."

David said he'd have only done it for her sake, and was she sure she wouldn't get homesick being by herself most of the day?

"That's silly," she said. She wouldn't have told him for anything that she was already so homesick that she could hardly see straight. Every child she looked at sharpened the pain in her breast. She was having a manicure in the hotel beauty salon the morning after the Ferris dinner, when a Filipino chauffeur brought in a little girl exactly Bobby's size, and left her in one of the booths.

"What's that baby doing in here?" Claudia asked the manicurist.

The manicurist glanced up. "Permanent," she said in an offhand way, and lifted Claudia's wrist. "Soak, please."

Claudia soaked. "I have a little boy back East, just about that age," she offered, with her insides feeling mashed.

The manicurist's eyebrow pencil climbed up her forehead. "So what?" the gesture unmistakably implied. She swished the file over Claudia's nails. "Vermilion polish?"

"Oh no—colorless."

The manicurist looked more than ever bored. She dried Claudia's fingers languidly, gazing off into space as she did so. She herself wore vermilion, hanging like bright drops of blood at the end of each long pale finger. She had a remarkable hair-do, also—fully a hundred tiny curls twisted up like corkscrews on top of her head. "Unscrew and comb when ready for use," Claudia made silent comment. The manicurist gave her an inferiority complex. She longed to be home in her simple little Connecticut farmhouse where children were children, and bathrooms were bathrooms. "Oh dear," she thought unhappily, "we've only been here for a day and a half, how can I stand it for three weeks?"

However, she wasn't going to spoil the whole trip by letting David see how she felt, so she pretended to be very gay as she started off to meet him for luncheon at the Brown Derby. Mrs. Ferris had said, "You must lunch at the Brown Derby at least once—I understand all the Movie Stars go there—"

David had specified one o'clock sharp, and had underscored the sharp, as he said Claudia was always late. But he was late himself, and Claudia had to stand in line waiting for a table, which she hated. It was a funny thing that everybody in line looked as if they came from Iowa, but everybody that was already seated looked as if they came from Hollywood.

A girl came in with blue glasses, no hat, and a sloppy long coat over plaid slacks. Immediately, the head waiter rushed up to her and piloted her off to an empty table. A few minutes later, a pretty young man came in, wearing a pink sweater, and the head waiter whisked him off to the same table. A sight-seer standing next to Claudia hissed to her friend, "It's Betty Astwick and Jimmy Toole!"

At that moment David arrived. The sight-seer stared at him, and nudged her friend. She thought David was a movie actor, too. But then the whole thing was spoiled because David said hello to Claudia, and squeezed her hand and said how was she, and why in hell did they have to stand in line like this?

Claudia said, "No tables—" And David immediately got independent and said, "To hell with them, we'll eat somewhere else—"

The waiter must have had ears and eyes in the back of his head, because he instantly rushed over to them waving his arms and crying, "Monsieur, right away! Monsieur, I have a table right away!"

"We were first," expostulated the sight-seeing lady, but the head waiter didn't hear her, and, still waving his arms, led the way down the aisle to a table marked "Reserved." He whisked off the sign, and bowed them in.

"My hero," Claudia said to David.

"To hell with them," said David, for good measure, and gave her his most beautiful smile.

"I love you better than Jimmy Toole," she said. David was pleased, but when Claudia pointed out the pretty boy in the pink sweater, he dipped his spoon in a glass of water, and let her have it. He did it so swiftly and expertly, that nobody knew anything had happened, except her eye. They might have been home, instead of eating in the most famous restaurant in Hollywood.

The menu was huge and Claudia loved it, but in the end, after going through all the fish and meat, she decided on a chef's salad, and iced tea. She threw back her heavy coat. "For heaven's sake," she said, "what's the matter with the weather here?"

"California," said David briefly, who was also hot.

"I've got only winter things," she deplored. "David, have we a little extra cash?"

"No, why?"

"I'm sorry to break the news to you, but I do need clothes."

"That's different—go ahead," said David generously.

"How much can we afford?"

"Oh, a couple of hundred."

"You're mad. Half of that is twice too much."

Thanks to Mrs. Ferris, she had learned that there was only one place to shop—though Mrs. Ferris said she always went elsewhere. But Mrs. Ferris' elsewhere turned out to be in the most downtown part of Los Angeles, so David dropped Claudia off beneath a very imposing porte-cochere not far from their hotel. "It's worth going in, if only to look around," Mrs. Ferris had said. It seemed rather empty —probably because it was so large and the carpets were so thick that you didn't make any noise when you walked. Claudia liked to make a reasonable amount of noise when she walked around a store and certainly if she had been able to do so, somebody might have paid a little attention to her.

After several futile attempts to get waited on, she accosted a distinguished-looking elderly saleslady with white hair, bobbed like a boy's, and big pearl earrings. "Where are the dresses, please?" Claudia asked.

The saleslady said, off the top of her lungs, "You mean gowns, Modom? I'll send the hostess to you—"

Claudia watched her drift off, with a feeling of helplessness. Her pumps felt full of feet, and she wished that she had one of the Giant Malted Milks, for which Hollywood seemed to be famous. The pictures of them were breath-taking—a glass as big as a flower vase, filled with four scoops of ice cream, all for a dime. "I'd like to know how they do it," she thought, and was about to leave the shop and head for the nearest soda fountain, when the hostess appeared. She was slight, and vivacious, like a kindergarten teacher, and smiled with many white teeth rushing to the front of her mouth. "Can I help you?" she cried, investing the "can" with a great deal of voltage.

Out of sheer waywardness Claudia said with her lip thrust out like Bobby's, "I'm looking for the dress department."

"Yes indeedie!— Our gown salon is on the second floor; I'll have someone take you there."

"I can go by myself," said Claudia, but a little errand girl appeared from nowhere and the hostess said, "Show Modom to the gowns."

"Come this way," said the little girl, and Claudia followed. At this point Claudia began to have a very strange feeling. It might have been the heat, or it might have been nerves. "I've been all through this experience," she thought. But as she had never set foot in Hollywood before, she knew of course that the feeling was ridiculous. Still, the little errand girl seemed familiar, and she, Claudia, reminded herself of somebody, but she couldn't imagine who. Then suddenly it came to her. She reminded herself of Alice, and the little errand girl was the rabbit, and Hollywood, without any stretch of whimsey, was getting curiouser and curiouser.

"I'll leave you here," said the little errand girl, in her small high voice, and trotted off down the corridor.

Claudia stood where she was, looking about a vast rotunda of suavest walnut. Occasionally, from behind a sliding panel, a gown, cellophane-swathed, emerged like a discarnate soul, to sweep across the floor toward a prospective buyer. It was comparatively simple to distinguish the customers from the saleswomen on account of the mink coats. She wondered if not wearing a mink coat made her invisible, for nobody payed any more attention to her up here than on the floor below. She was about to leave in a huff, when the minkiest of the coats turned around, and Claudia caught sight of a small dark face framed in the soft folds of a voluminous collar. Claudia frowned. She didn't know anybody in Hollywood, except the Ferrises, and yet she could have sworn she knew that face, with its enormous eyes and rich red lips. She knew the voice, too, throaty and tempestuous and full of ups and downs. Beritza! But of course! Beritza had made two pictures in the past year, and everyone in New York had said, "Beritza's finished. She'll never get back to the Metropolitan, she'll never give a concert again." Even the newspapers had printed words to that effect. Now Claudia's warm heart overcame whatever shyness she might have felt. She walked over to Beritza and held out her hand, and said, "How-do-you-do, Madame Beritza. I'm Claudia Naughton."

Beritza drew back and stiffened.

"Julia's sister-in-law," Claudia hastened to explain. "You stopped by on your way to Boston one day with her and fell in love with our farm, and almost bought it, don't you remember? And then, at the last minute, we decided we just couldn't let it go."

Now, indeed, Beritza remembered. Claudia felt herself clasped in a fragrant embrace. "But, darling, of course!" Beritza cried on a crescendo of delight. "My house in Connecticut will I ever forget it! My dear, this is thrilling to see you, this is really thrilling— Tony!" she broke off imperiously.

A round-faced, portly little man moved into evidence.

"Tony, this is my dear friend, Claudia."

Tony had not good teeth, Claudia noticed at once, and the hand that he extended was utterly limp. "My dear," he said. And that was all he said.

Beritza stamped her small foot in its short-vamped slipper. "Tony!" she prodded him impatiently. "You remember my house in Connecticut, my lovely house, with the great trees, and the cows and the chickens and the sheep and the pigs—"

Tony nodded. "The farm," he summed up wearily.

"Of course, the farm. And this is Claudia! Her husband is the architect who— Is he here with you?" she interrupted herself to ask.

"Oh, yes," said Claudia. "The architects' convention."

"See, I told you!" Beritza was triumphant, as if the convention proved the validity of David's profession. "And you must both come to my party tonight. Mustn't they, Tony?"

"They certainly must," said Tony—which was a very bad sentence for anybody even without a lisp.

"But, oh my dear," Beritza swept on, "wait till you see the dreadful way I live out here. I give you my word I have no room for anything but a canary bird—" She sighed deeply. "Fancy, Tony, my giving up thousands and thousands of acres—"

"Only a hundred and ten," Claudia corrected, a little confused at so glorified a version of their simple saltbox house with its old barns and rolling meadows.

"I have to go!" cried Beritza, changing the subject. "I'm frightfully late! Are you coming, Claudia, I'll drop you?"

"No, I want to buy a dress," said Claudia; she was certainly going to need something to wear to Beritza's party.

"A dress!" Beritza clapped her hands. "Hogate will take care of you, I couldn't live without Hogate, she's marvelous! Where is Hogey, somebody get Hogey!"

"Miss Hogate!" "Miss Hogate!" "Miss Hogate!" Three little errand girls raised their voices like a hospital call board, and scurried off in different directions.

After a moment or so, Miss Hogate appeared, dashing across the floor as if she were coming toward them on skates.

"Hogey!" Beritza adjured her. "Take good care of Mrs. Naughton who is my good friend! And be sure to show her the pink net—"

Miss Hogate had no bosoms, a thin, sallow face, and a determined character. She eyed Claudia up and down, and said with finality, "The pink net won't do at all."

Tony yawned. "Of course it won't," he agreed.

"You loved the dress," Beritza accused him indignantly. "Hogey, get it!"

But Hogey didn't have to get it. It was already there, as if by magic, held aloft by one of the little errand girls. Hogey took it from her. She held it out to Claudia.

"Seven ninety-five," she announced briefly.

Claudia could scarcely believe her ears. Seven ninety-five! Ordinarily she wouldn't have looked twice at the dress, because she didn't like pink and she didn't like net. But seven ninety-five! True, she'd bought little summer dresses at three ninety-five in New York, and there was a certain shop on Twenty-third Street where even Julia occasionally picked up a costume just for the lark of it. "How do you like my newest Paris creation?" she would ask with an absolutely serious face, and actually, Claudia could never tell the difference. "I had the hems gone over by hand," Julia would then confide, "and I changed the belt."

All this went through Claudia's head as she stared at the pink net dress. Mechanically, she reached for the hem. But there wasn't any hem—it was just net, three layers of net. She looked for the cheap telltale finishing of the short puffed sleeves, but they were protected by a concealing fold of muslin. "There's practically no workmanship on the thing," she summed up with an experienced glance. "Nor much material either." Still, she wondered how they could possibly make any profit, selling a dress at seven ninety-five in a shop with such thick carpets and beautiful paneling. But nothing surprised her about Hollywood at this point. The outdoor markets looked like sumptuous bazaars and yet they could afford to sell spinach at a penny a bunch, and give you four blobs of ice cream in a ten-cent malted milk.

Tentatively, she touched the single ornament on the gown, a purple flower, embellished with trailing velvet streamers. Pink and purple. It was a pretty terrible combination. Misgiving assailed her. David wouldn't like it. Gaudy clothes weren't her type, and there was no sense in buying something simply because it was good value. She let the net fall from her fingers. "It's a frightful bargain," she sighed, "and I hate to pass it up, but I don't like the color or the material."

She was immediately aware that her words had an electrifying effect upon the group. A passing saleswoman stopped dead in her tracks. Claudia felt uncomfortable. Had she said something she shouldn't have said? Why was Tony looking at her with his jaw gaping? "What I mean is," she amended apologetically, "I think it's foolish to buy something simply because it's cheap."

Tony was the first to speak. He closed his mouth, and suggested hoarsely, "Why don't you try it on anyway?"

"But you said it wouldn't do for me," she reminded him reproachfully.

"I didn't mean it," he said in a voice like a croak. "I didn't know—"

Beritza patted his shoulder. "All right, Tony. The next time when Beritza introduces you to somebody, you can rest assured it's all right — Darling!" She turned to Claudia. "I must absolutely dash, I'm late for my hairdresser. And you're perfectly right, if you don't like this dress, Hogey will show you something else— See you this evening!— Hogey give Mrs. Naughton my address— Come along, Tony!"

"Until tonight," Tony breathed, and lifted Claudia's fingers to his lips.

"My goodness," thought Claudia, staring after him in bewilderment, "he was positively reverent." Reverent. That was the word. Miss Hogate, and all the little errand girls, and even the saleswoman who had stopped dead in her tracks, and hadn't yet started to move on, looked reverent.

Suddenly Miss Hogate came to life again. "See if a south dressing room is empty!" she commanded. "And call downstairs!"

In less time than it takes to tell, Claudia found herself in a sunny, mirror-lined room surrounded by a bevy of Claudias in faded panties, and a runner. "Oh dear," she said ruefully, and quite dishonestly, "Look at my stocking, it must have just happened!"

Miss Hogate tossed it off with a laugh. "Honestly, isn't it the limit?" she commiserated. "The more you pay for stockings, the worse they wear. That's beautiful underwear," she added with an envious sigh.

"Who, mine?" asked Claudia, surprised.

"I love the French handmade stuff," Miss Hogate continued, slipping the pink net dress off the hanger. "I bet those came right from Paris."

Claudia looked down at herself. Julia, who had always spent a fortune on undergarments, had simplified life after her operation, and had stopped wearing panties for some reason or other, so Claudia had inherited a whole stack of them. "They probably did," she agreed vaguely.

"It's too bad Mr. Anton isn't here." Miss Hogate held the dress in readiness for Claudia to duck into. "He'd adore this on you."

"Who's Mr. Anton?" Claudia demanded from a smother of pink net.

"Why Tony Anton—he was just here with Madame Beritza. One second, Mrs. Naughton, the hook's caught in your hair— I thought you knew him—"

"Ouch!— I never saw him before. What does he do?"

Miss Hogate seemed baffled. "Well, he's—he's just about one of the most important people in Hollywood. There now, it's free. Lift your arms—so—"

"But what does he do?" Claudia persisted, emerging for air. "Write, act, play the violin?"

"Oh, he doesn't *do* anything," Miss Hogate explained. "He just goes with people."

"Oh," said Claudia.

"My dear!" exclaimed Miss Hogate, forgetting all about Mr. Anton. "This is too beautiful for words!" She stood back, clasping her hands. "Perfect, not a bit of alteration! It's stunning! I *love* it!"

Claudia regarded her reflection. Yes, the dress was amazingly becoming, in spite of the atrocious color combination. She looked thin as a rail, but at the same time, she had little round places just where she should have had them. "It is rather nice," she admitted, grudgingly. "I think I'll take it."

At once the room became full of people. The boyish old lady with the pearl earrings suddenly appeared from downstairs, carrying a mass of tiny hats. The saleswoman who had stopped dead, produced a brace of satin girdles. A young man burst in with a tower of toppling shoe boxes. Miss Hogate skated out and then skated right back in again, carrying a short fur wrap, which she arranged across Claudia's shoulders. It looked like rabbit skin. "I don't like it at all with the pink," Claudia stated firmly. "One cheapens the other." Besides, she had a very nice lamé cape of Julia's with her, and also some good brocaded evening sandals which she had never worn because she had bought them at a sale, and they pinched. "They can just go ahead and pinch," she assured herself grimly, and waved the shoe boxes away. "No slippers, but I need stockings," she announced.

It was as if she had waved a wand. "*Stockings! Somebody go downstairs and bring up stockings! Mrs. Naughton wants stockings!*"

Claudia raised her hand. "No don't bother, please—I'll stop at the stocking counter and get them myself." She glanced at her watch. "I'll take the dress with me—"

A little sound of horrified protest flooded the air. Miss Hogate stepped forward. "Oh no, Mrs. Naughton, don't think of it, we'll send it!"

"It's so late, though. Can I depend on a delivery tonight?"

"Of course. You're at the Embassy, aren't you?"

Claudia nodded, wondering how she'd guessed. David had insisted on stopping at the best hotel, and besides he got a professional discount, on account of the convention.

As Miss Hogate buttoned up Claudia's last year's brown jersey, the boyish old lady approached stealthily from behind, and dropped a fluff of chiffon over Claudia's right eye. Claudia laughed outright. She looked as silly as anything. "Heavens, take it off!" she cried.

"Madame doesn't like evening hats," the boyish old lady interpreted regretfully.

"Madame certainly doesn't," Claudia assured her.

She stopped at the stocking counter on the way out. She didn't stop long. "Two fifty a pair, what a nerve!" she muttered, as she marched from the store.

It was already dark, and the boulevard looked like Coney Island with all its signs and posters. She gazed entranced upon a whirling windmill that was nothing more than a baker shop, lit up. A flower vendor approached and offered sweet peas at five cents a bunch, and violets at ten. "A bunch of each," said Claudia, feeling like a millionaire.

"Scented or unscented?" asked the vendor.

"Why—scented of course," she replied, intrigued.

She had to wait while the vendor sprayed the blooms with perfume. She accepted them in a daze. "I'm dreaming," she thought. Suddenly she shivered. It was cold. The wind crept bleakly through her bones. What had happened to summer? She drew her winter coat about her. "Hollywood's crazy," she decided, in a kind of panic, and quickened her steps toward the comparative sanity of her hotel bedroom.

DAVID WAS THERE before her, running the water for a bath. He kissed her, and out of a clear sky he said, "Look, Claudia. Tell me the truth. Are you homesick, or are you having a good time here?"

David was uncanny. He was always like that, knowing things without her telling him. She said decisively, "I'm having a beautiful time, and I haven't thought of the baby or Bobby all afternoon."

"Oh," he said.

She remembered afterwards that he'd acted a little strange, but at the moment she didn't think anything about it. "I made a contact," she continued portentously. "And tonight, we go to our first Hollywood party!"

"You smell to high heaven," he informed her bluntly. "Whose party?"

"I do not. I never smell!"

"Not that kind of a smell," he qualified more kindly.

"Oh," said Claudia. "The violets!" She put them in water, and then banished them outside the window, telling him about Beritza as she did so.

"That jackass?" David expostulated.

"Darling, please. We have to be nice to her."

"Why?"

"Firstly, she's a friend of Julia's. Secondly, she wanted to buy our house. Thirdly, she implied that she was practically down and out, and I'm not going to high-hat her. And last, but not least, I bought a dress, and I want to wear it—you'll die when you hear how much."

"How much?"

"Seven ninety-five. I told you before, you can live for nothing out here."

"You sound like you're in love with the place." There was a gloomy note in his voice, but like a fool she didn't notice it. She gave him back his words. "This is our second honeymoon," she said.

The dress arrived as he got out of the bathtub. He stood in the doorway, with a turkish towel around his loins, while she lifted it out from its folds of tissue paper. His nose went up.

"You don't like it."

"Why pink? Why purple?"

"Why not?"

"It's a little cheap-looking."

"I shouldn't have told you what it cost. You're prejudiced by New York prices. But Tony's a native, and he thinks it's stunning."

"Tony who?"

"Tony Anton. His teeth aren't good, but he's very nice."

"How'd he happen to see you in it? What's his business?"

"He didn't see me in it, he was just there. With Beritza. That's what he does. He goes with people."

"I don't like him," said David firmly. "And I don't like the dress, either."

He held it against his hairy chest, and his bare feet stuck out from beneath the trailing net folds. "It looks like hell," he maintained stubbornly. "Yip off the flower, and it mightn't be so bad."

"Believe it or not, the flower's nice when the dress is on me," said Claudia. "And besides it matches the purple in my brocade slippers— Look."

David conceded that he liked the slippers, and when she was dressed, he conceded also, in reluctant admiration, that she looked like a million dollars. "It's better on than off," he said.

"With a good figure," Claudia modestly pointed out, "you can wear any old rag and get away with it."

"That's so," said David. He dropped his hat and coat and put his arms around her. "For two cents," he said huskily, "I'd stay right here, and let the party go to blazes."

"Me too," said Claudia. "But let's don't."

The cab sped up the boulevard through Beverly Hills and then onward toward the sea. It swung into a parkway, and then it swung into a smaller parkway, with gravel splattering up against the wheels. It stopped. Claudia peered out of the window. "This must be a mistake," she said to David. "This is a mansion of some kind."

"This ain't no mistake, lady," the driver announced with authority. "This is the address you give me."

"Oh," Claudia said faintly.

They walked up marble steps. A butler opened the door as they rang the bell. Then a maid in a gray satin uniform whisked Claudia away into a room padded with white velvet. The maid withdrew Claudia's cape and hung it on a rack. In a daze Claudia walked out into the hall, where David was waiting for her. "I thought you said she was down and out," he greeted her bitterly.

Before he had a chance to say anything else, Tony skipped up to them, crying, "Oh, there you are!" and pulled her into a tremendous room, seething with faces—unreal faces off a screen, with no dimension. "Wait for David," she begged.

"I don't know any David," he said. He dragged her from one to another. "The lovely Mrs. Naughton, wife of the famous architect, the architect who did Beritza's home in the East you know—thousands of acres. . . ."

"How do you do—How do you do—How do you do—"

Now everybody was introducing her, and somebody introduced her to David.

"No," said David, "we haven't met—" He grabbed her by the shoulder, and pushed her out into the hall again. "Let's get out of this," he panted. "It's a lunatic asylum and that dame thinks she owns our house!"

"Yes, I know, but it doesn't matter." Claudia quieted him. "Just let her think so—" She broke off to stare at him. He had a dab of lipstick across his face. "Where'd you get that!" she demanded.

A vision in white flew out at him. "Darling! I've been looking everywhere for you!" She hauled him away by main force, which was the last that Claudia saw of him.

Tony crept up, and put his arm around her. A light flashed. "Thank you!" The photographer moved away. Tony laughed gleefully. "Come outside for a drink," he urged. He led her into a glass-walled enclosure with a lily pond and hundreds of yellow canaries in blue wicker cages. Claudia set her lips grimly. "Poor Beritza. No room for anything but a canary bird."

She kept looking around for David. After a time, she forgot about him; everything became a blur. As soon as she put a drink down, she found another one in her hand. She wanted water but no one would give it to her. Somebody kissed her. She wanted to slap his face but he wasn't very steady on his feet, and she was afraid that she might knock him over. Beritza rushed over to her. She cried, "My lamb!" and called her "Eleanor." "This is my friend, Eleanor, Mr. Belchnick!"

"Don't mind Beritza," Tony counseled. "She never remembers . . ." He hiccoughed. Claudia hadn't known that people really hiccoughed outside of books. "What time is it?" she implored.

"Half past ten," said a melancholy voice.

It wasn't Tony's voice. Tony was gone. Mr. Belchnick stood in his place. He had black curly hair, without charm, and a mole on his face. He looked at Claudia, and blinked twice very fast. Then he wiggled his nose. He was well over forty—much too old to have bad habits, Claudia thought. "I asked Beritza to meet you," he said. (He asked Beritza to meet me?) Claudia smiled politely. He blinked once more, very gravely, and twisted his whole nose around his face in lieu of a wiggle. "Yes," he repeated, in a voice heavy with a one-time accent. "I wanted to talk to you."

"Oh," said Claudia, enlightened.

"I was talking to your husband, but he got away from me," he went on.

"You mean he was dragged away from you."

He ignored the distinction. "I hear he did a good job of Beritza's house in the East."

"He didn't build Beritza's house in the East," Claudia tersely contradicted.

Belchnick's face fell. "Tony said he did. Tony said he's a great architect."

"He is a great architect. He's the greatest architect that ever lived."

"All right then. That's all I want. Tell him he should come to see me at the studio tomorrow morning." He blinked twice more in rapid succession.

Claudia blinked. "But what on earth do you want to see him about? He doesn't like to build ordinary houses, I can tell you that."

"I don't want a house. I've got a house. I've got three houses. I want him for my new picture, 'Up With the Sun.'"

"Who are you?" Claudia asked.

"I'm Belchnick," repeated the man with considerable dignity. He took a box of pills out of his pocket, selected two of them, and thrust them down his throat. "High blood pressure," he explained modestly. "Listen, young lady, you get your husband to my office and you won't be sorry. He won't be sorry either. That's what we need in the movie business. Great architects to design great sets."

Claudia held dizzily to a chair. She didn't know what it was all about, but she thought it was wonderful. David was a genius—she was sure of it—but no one had ever made a fuss over him in New York. "I'll see what I can do," she promised unsteadily. "I'll go and find him right away."

"Thanks," said Mr. Belchnick.

Her knees felt weak with excitement. Tony waylaid her halfway across the room. "Why aren't you dancing?"

"I'll take care of that," said a smooth voice, and Claudia found herself clasped against the stiff shirt of the screen's greatest lover. She tried to pull away, because she had to find David, but he laughed, and held on to her, and there was a sharp scream of tearing material as his foot caught in the delicate net of her skirt. "Oh, sorry. How awkward of me—"

Tony gasped. "My God," he cried out tragically. He lifted the net, dragging on the floor like the broken plumage of some lovely bird, and said again, this time in a stricken whisper, "My God—"

Claudia didn't feel any too pleased to see seven ninety-five go out of the window so to speak, but after all, it was an accident. She examined the damage. "It can be mended," she dismissed it lightly. She felt sorry for the screen's greatest lover, who looked very crestfallen, and she felt that Tony was taking on about it because it was his nature to make tragedies of trifles. She gathered up the flounces, and smiled. "Don't think any more of it, please. I'll have it tacked, and it will hardly show."

A soft ripple of comment followed her across the floor. She reached the dressing room. The maid greeted her with a little moan. "Oh, Madame—what a pity—such a lovely gown."

She opened a white velvet-tufted mushroom standing on mirrored legs, and lo, it was a sewing box, so complete as to make Claudia suspect that ripped gowns were rather usual occurrences at a Hollywood party. The maid chose a perfectly matching spool of silk, and threaded a needle. While she was kneeling at Claudia's side, repairing the damage, Betty Astwick came in to powder her nose. She looked quite different without her dark glasses, but she wasn't anywhere near as beautiful as she was supposed to be, for her hair was quite stringy and she almost had a pimple. "I'm mad about that handsome husband of yours—and that's tough luck about your dress," she said in one breath. "Believe me . . . " She paused, mouth like a fish, replenishing her lipstick, "Believe me, I wouldn't be so good-natured if that had happened to a dress I'd just paid eight hundred dollars for."

Claudia smiled. She was about to retort, "Well, the moral of that is, never pay more than seven ninety-five for a dress," when something vaguely coincidental in the two amounts gave her pause for thought. "What did you say?" she asked.

Betty laughed. "Of course Tony loves to blab prices, but it's no secret what you paid for it because every last one of us wanted to buy the damn thing when it came in, it's so damned chic, only, my God, times are too hard to plunk out more than five hundred for a dress you only wear half a dozen times a season—"

When the room stopped swimming, Miss Astwick was gone, and the maid was saying, "You'd better sit down, Miss, you look sort of sick all at once."

"I am sick," Claudia gasped. There was thunder in her ears, and a dull swollen pounding of her veins against her temples. The maid pushed a chair beneath her, and thrust a cut-glass bottle under her nose. Claudia didn't know what it was, so she gulped at it. It almost killed her, but it cleared her head, and miraculously, stiffened the bones in her legs, so that she could stand up and totter toward the door. "I want to go home," she said hoarsely. "Please call a taxi. . . ."

The maid didn't seem in the least surprised or alarmed. "Madame

Beritza's chauffeur will take you," she said. She put a competent arm around Claudia's waist. "Lean on me," she said, "and I'll lead you out through the terrace. There's plenty can't drink," she added consolingly.

Claudia made no attempt to disillusion her. "My husband—Mr. Naughton—" she couldn't seem to find enough breath to form a sentence. "Get word to him—"

"I'll attend to everything very quietly, Miss," the maid assured her. "And Boyce will see that you get home safe."

Boyce was competent too. He escorted her through the hotel lobby, and into the elevator. "Sure you're all right now, Miss?"

"I'll never be all right again," Claudia thanked him in a shaky voice, "but I'll manage to get upstairs if that's what you mean."

"Some black coffee," he advised her in a friendly undertone.

She had forgotten to ask for the key, but luckily the door to the room was open. She burst in. David was sitting at the telephone. "Never mind it, Operator, I'll put the call through later," he said hastily. He hung up the receiver, and turned to her. "You didn't have to follow me, I came home to phone Roger, I was going back for you — What's the matter, you're white as a sheet?"

She dug her nails into her palms. There was nothing to be gained by beating about the bush. "David," she said, "if you want to divorce me, I deserve it. You can even have the children. I'm not fit to take care of them, I'm not fit to be let loose without a keeper. . . ."

David rose, and advanced slowly in her direction, until his hands reached out and encircled her arms like bands of iron. She could feel her control slip away.

"Oh dear, I don't know how to break it to you," she wailed. "I'd kill myself if it would help, at least you wouldn't have any more expense with me than the funeral, I wouldn't even want a funeral, just a plain pine box and no flowers—"

"Stop babbling. What's happened!"

She wrung her hands. "If you're yelling before you even know about it, you'll simply burst a blood vessel when I tell you!"

"Claudia, you can tell me anything, I promise to understand—"

"Very well. Here goes." Her voice sounded high and toneless, like somebody else's voice. "Could you understand anyone paying eight hundred dollars for something very pink and very purple?"

"What do you mean?"

She tried again. "David, look at me," she besought him desperately.

"I'm wearing a new barn, I'm wearing a year of the best kindergarten with hot lunches for Bobby, I'm wearing all the pure-bred pigs and sheep you're so crazy to get, with maybe a horse thrown in—"

"Well," said David, "it's all very becoming, I must say. Especially the hot lunches."

"Oh, David, you're making it so hard for me! Listen. In plain language, I misunderstood the salesgirl. This dress didn't cost seven ninety-five, it cost seven hundred and ninety-five! Now do you get the point?"

For a long moment, in which she could feel every hair in her head turn gray, she saw significance percolate into his brain like coffee, slow to come to a boil. He didn't say anything, he just stood there looking at her. And then all at once he began to laugh, and he laughed until the tears poured down his cheeks. He laughed until he had to hold his stomach, and when he tried to talk, his voice went up in his head in squeaks. "Hollywood high-hatted by an expert!" he managed to bring out at last. "It's marvelous!"

"You sound like Tony," she adjured him coldly. "And if it contributes to your merriment, I might as well tell you that somebody put his foot through the hem and I can't even send it back—"

"I don't want to send it back," David gasped. "I want to keep it as a memento!" He got a stitch in his side, and in agony, tottered to a chair, where he just sat, making horrid sounds as if he were going to die. She regarded him with sudden apprehension, wondering if people ever really did die laughing. Her instinct told her to jerk him out of it. But he was too old to slap his hands, and she hesitated to slap his face, feeling that under the particular circumstances, it might add injury to insult. Therefore, not knowing what else to do, she summoned her most casual manner, and started to tell him about Mr. Belchnick. Unfortunately, the mention of Mr. Belchnick started him all over again. He fell off the chair and looked up at her with his head practically rolling on the floor. "That's not a name," he moaned; "that's something to apologize for. . . ."

"Nevertheless he wants to see you at his office in the morning. I think he wants to offer you a job."

David climbed back on the chair, and wiped away his tears. "He offered it to me already," he said, weak with exhaustion. "Fifteen thousand dollars to design the sets for his new picture."

"Fifteen thousand dollars!" Claudia's voice went off into a bleat.

"Why that's a fortune! He must be crazy, he's never even seen any of your work!"

"He doesn't have to," said David. "If an architect can afford to dress his wife in eight-hundred-dollar clothes, 'Why that's the man for me,' says Mr. Belchnick—"

"But you *can't* afford it!"

"That's where you're wrong. I can't afford not to, from this point on."

Claudia's eyes almost popped out of her head. "You mean I have to go on dressing in expensive clothes?"

"Too late to stop now."

"That means a mink coat—"

"Two of them. One long, one short."

Her thoughts swam in a vast confusion. "Pinch me," she implored him. He pinched her. She jumped, and said, "Ouch!"

"That's for buying the damn dress to begin with," he scowled at her.

Her anger soared. "You're a snake in the grass!" she accused him hotly. "First you pretend it's funny, and you're not going to even scold me, and then you pinch me! I don't know where I'm at with you!"

"I don't know where I'm at with you either!" He was shouting now, in a most unpleasant way. There was no rhyme or reason to it. She couldn't imagine how they'd gotten into such a state. Then the telephone bell rang, exactly like a cue in a play.

"I'll take it," said Claudia mechanically.

It was Stanley Ferris. He said, "Hello, Mrs. Naughton, I hope I didn't wake you."

"Oh, no," she assured him in a voice dripping syrup for David's benefit, "I was far from asleep."

"Good." Mr. Ferris sounded normal, and kindly. "How about dropping in at the Cocoanut Grove to watch the dancing?"

"What's he want?" asked David.

Claudia mouthed it to him. He nodded violently. "By all means. I've got to talk to him," he said.

It was the last thing she expected. David knew perfectly well how she felt about Mrs. Ferris, and besides she would have liked to go to bed. But evidently he had forgotten that there was such a place as bed. She turned back to the telephone, crucified. "We'd adore to go," she said.

"That's fine," said Mr. Ferris, who didn't recognize irony when he heard it. "As long as you're flying back tomorrow evening, you might as well see something of the place. We'll pick you up in fifteen minutes."

Slowly, Claudia hung up the receiver. Flying back tomorrow when they'd planned to stay a month? When they'd just been planning to stay forever? Her heart stood still. There was something wrong. Of course there was something wrong—David leaving the party to telephone—David acting strangely before they'd even gone to the party—and now Mr. Ferris saying that they were leaving tomorrow. She forgot the dress, she forgot everything except the fear that clutched her throat. "David, the children!"

"The children are fine; what are you talking about?"

Her lips moved stiffly. "I don't believe it. Something's happened at home and you haven't told me!"

"Did I ever lie to you?"

"Yes, because Mr. Ferris just said we were flying back tomorrow. Why should we fly back tomorrow if everything's all right?"

He looked sheepish, and dug into his pocket, withdrawing a telegram. "Here. Stop getting excited over nothing."

The message shook in her hands, the words danced, then steadied. "PLANS FOR RADIO BUILDING ACCEPTED. WOULD URGE RETURN IMMEDIATELY AFTER CONVENTION. CONGRATULATIONS. ROGER."

"Over nothing!" she echoed. "Have you lost your mind, 'Over nothing'?— When did this come?"

"This afternoon."

"Why didn't you tell me!"

"I tried to, but. . ."

"But what?"

"Well, this is our first vacation together and you were just beginning to enjoy yourself. How could I spoil it for you?"

"Spoil it for me— Oh, David, you fool! You fool!"

"You mean you want to go?" he demanded incredulously.

"Does a duck want to swim?"

"But what about Belchnick? What about the mink coat?"

"Must I have one?" she whimpered. "I've always liked tweed. Only what about the pink dress," she remembered in a panic. "How will we pay for it?"

"The pink dress was cheap at twice the price!" He was shouting again, and his grip on her wrists hurt a great deal more than the pinch, only it wasn't the sort of pain one minded, or the sort of yelling one minded. She knew exactly where she was at with him, and he seemed to know exactly where he was at with her, which was one of the wonderful things that happened every now and again, in marriage.

They were still in each other's arms when Mr. Ferris' car was announced. "Let him wait," said David.

Mrs. Ferris seemed rather pleased that it had grown so late. "Stanley doesn't have to get down to the office until eleven tomorrow," she planned happily. "This is the very best time to see the night life of Hollywood. I understand it only begins after midnight."

To her great chagrin, however, the Cocoanut Grove was practically empty when they arrived. There wasn't a movie star in sight, and the few tables that were occupied, held the very same sort of people who had been standing in line at the Brown Derby. "Oh it's just too bad, I'm so disappointed!" she deplored. "It would have been so nice for you to have gotten a peep at the real Hollywood. I can't understand why it's so quiet just when we want it to be gay!"

"Perhaps somebody's giving a big party," David suggested, with an affable smile, "and they've all been invited to it."

"I shouldn't be surprised if that's just exactly the case," Mrs. Ferris agreed at once. "I wonder what goes on at those Hollywood parties?"

"It's a different world," said Claudia dreamily.

"A state of mind," Mr. Ferris neatly topped it. "I always say Hollywood is a state of mind."

"Yes," said Mrs. Ferris. "That's what Stanley always says." She patted Claudia's hand. "You're looking very pretty this evening, my dear, pink is so becoming to you, that's a very charming little frock!"

Claudia pulled herself back into the world that was, into the world that held David, and all that he stood for. And then she caught the dangerous, wicked twinkle in his eye. She gathered her courage in both hands. "Oh," she said casually, "it's just a little rag I picked up for seven ninety-five."

Mrs. Ferris felt the net between her finger tips. "My dear," she said, "that's really dirt cheap. Such lovely quality, and quite a pretty flower." She broke a roll, and sighed. "You can find such wonderful bargains with a slim young figure."

Claudia smiled. Her hand reached back toward Mrs. Ferris' in a gesture of the warmest and purest affection. "You must promise to come and see us in the East," she said, and meant it from the bottom of her heart.

To Springvale for Christmas

Her children arise up and call her blessed.

ZONA GALE

*The story of a mother who has the warm spirit of
Christmas in her heart—an inspiring story of giving and receiving, a story that enriches the lives of
giver, receiver, and, we think, the reader, too.*

WHEN PRESIDENT Arthur Tilton of Briarcliff Col-
lege, who usually used a two-cent stamp, said, "Get me Chicago,
please," his secretary was impressed, looked for vast educational problems to be in the making, and heard instead:

"Ed? Well, Ed, you and Rick and Grace and I are going out to
Springvale for Christmas. . . . Yes, well, I've got a family too, you
recall. But Mother was seventy last fall and— Do you realize that it's
eleven years since we've all spent Christmas with her? Grace has been
every year. She's going this year. And so are we! And take her the
best Christmas she ever had, too. Ed, Mother was *seventy* last fall—"

At dinner, he asked his wife what would be a suitable gift, a very
special gift, for a woman of seventy. And she said: "Oh, your mother.
Well, dear, I should think the material for a good wool dress would be
right. I'll select it for you, if you like—" He said that he would see,
and he did not reopen the subject.

In town on December twenty-fourth he timed his arrival to allow
him an hour in a shop. There he bought a silver-gray silk of a fineness
and a lightness which pleased him and at a price which made him
comfortably guilty. And at the shop, Ed, who was Edward McKillop
Tilton, head of a law firm, picked him up.

"Where's your present?" Arthur demanded.

Edward drew a case from his pocket and showed him a tiny gold
wrist-watch of decent manufacture and explained: "I expect you'll
think I'm a fool, but you know that Mother has told time for fifty

years by the kitchen clock, or else the shield of the black-marble parlor angel who never goes—you get the idea?—and so I bought her this."

At the station was Grace, and the boy who bore her bag bore also a parcel of great dimensions.

"Mother already has a feather bed," Arthur reminded her.

"They won't let you take an automobile into the coach," Edward warned her.

"It's a rug for the parlor," Grace told them. "You know it *is* a parlor—one of the very few left in the Mississippi valley. And Mother has had that ingrain down since before we left home—"

Grace's eyes were misted. Why would women always do that? This was no occasion for sentiment. This was a merry Christmas.

"Very nice. And Ricky'd better look sharp," said Edward dryly.

Ricky never did look sharp. About trains he was conspicuously ignorant. He had no occupation. Some said that he "wrote," but no one had even seen anything that he had written. He lived in town—no one knew how—never accepted a cent from his brothers and was beloved of every one, most of all of his mother.

"Ricky won't bring anything, of course," they said.

But when the train had pulled out without him, observedly, a porter came staggering through the cars carrying two great suitcases and following a perturbed man of forty-something who said, "Oh, here you are!" as if it were they who were missing, and squeezed himself and his suitcases among brothers and sister and rug. "I had only a minute to spare," he said regretfully. "If I'd had two, I could have snatched some flowers. I flung 'em my card and told 'em to send 'em."

"Why are you taking so many lugs?" they wanted to know.

Ricky focused on the suitcases. "Just necessities," he said. "Just the presents. I didn't have room to get in anything else."

"Presents! What?"

"Well," said Ricky, "I'm taking books. I know Mother doesn't care much for books, but the bookstore's the only place I can get trusted."

They turned over his books: Fiction, travel, biography, a new illustrated edition of the Bible—they were willing to admire his selection. And Grace said confusedly but appreciatively: "You know, the parlor bookcase has never had a thing in it excepting a green curtain *over* it!"

And they were all borne forward, well pleased.

Springvale has eight hundred inhabitants. As they drove through the principal street at six o'clock on that evening of December twenty-fourth, all that they expected to see abroad was the pop-corn wagon and a cat or two. Instead they counted seven automobiles and estimated thirty souls, and no one paid the slightest attention to them as strangers. Springvale was becoming metropolitan. There was a new church on one corner and a store-building bore the sign "Public Library." Even the little hotel had a rubber-plant in the window and a strip of cretonne overhead.

The three men believed themselves to be a surprise. But, mindful of the panic to be occasioned by four appetites precipitated into a Springvale ménage, Grace had told. Therefore the parlor was lighted and heated, there was in the air of the passage an odor of brown gravy which, no butler's pantry ever having inhibited, seemed a permanent savory. By the happiest chance, Mrs. Tilton had not heard their arrival nor—the parlor angel being in her customary eclipse and the kitchen grandfather's clock wrong—had she begun to look for them. They slipped in, they followed Grace down the hall, they entered upon her in her gray gingham apron worn over her best blue serge, and they saw her first in profile, frosting a lemon pie. With some assistance from her, they all took her in their arms at once.

"Aren't you surprised?" cried Edward in amazement.

"I haven't got over being surprised," she said placidly, "since I first heard you were coming!"

She gazed at them tenderly, with flour on her chin, and then she said: "There's something you won't like. We're going to have the Christmas dinner tonight."

Their clamor that they would entirely like that did not change her look.

"Our church couldn't pay the minister this winter," she said, "on account of the new church building. So the minister and his wife are boarding around with the congregation. Tomorrow's their day to come here for a week. It's a hard life and I didn't have the heart to change 'em."

Her family covered their regret as best they could and entered upon her little feast. At the head of her table, with her four "children" about her, and Father's armchair left vacant, they perceived that she was not quite the figure they had been thinking her. In this interval they had grown to think of her as a pathetic figure. Not because their father had died, not because she insisted on Springvale as a residence, not because of her eyes. Just pathetic. Mothers of grown children, they might have given themselves the suggestion, were always pathetic. But here was Mother, a definite person with poise and with ideas, who might be proud of her offspring, but who, in her heart, never forgot that they *were* her offspring and that she was the parent stock.

"I wouldn't eat two pieces of that pie," she said to President Tilton; "it's pretty rich." And he answered humbly: "Very well, Mother." And she took with composure Ricky's light chant:

> "Now, you must remember, wherever you are,
> That you are the jam, but your mother's the jar."

"Certainly, my children," she said. "And I'm about to tell you when you may have your Christmas presents. Not tonight. Christmas eve is no proper time for presents. It's stealing a day outright. And you miss the fun of looking forward all night long. The only proper time for the presents is after breakfast on Christmas morning, *after* the dishes are washed. The minister and his wife may get here any time from nine on. That means we've got to get to bed early!"

President Arthur Tilton lay in his bed looking at the muslin curtain on which the street-lamp threw the shadow of a bare elm which he remembered. He thought:

"She's a pioneer spirit. She's the kind who used to go ahead anyway, even if they had missed the emigrant party, and who used to cross the plains alone. She's the backbone of the world. I wish I could megaphone that to the students at Briarcliff who think their mothers 'try to boss' them!"

"Don't leave your windows open too far," he heard from the hall. "The wind's changed."

In the light of a snowy morning the home parlor showed the cluttered commonplace of a room whose furniture and ornaments were not believed to be beautiful and most of them known not to be useful. Yet when—after the dishes were washed—these five came to the leather chair which bore the gifts, the moment was intensely satisfactory. This in spite of the sense of haste with which the parcels were attacked—lest the minister and his wife arrive in their midst.

"That's one reason," Mrs. Tilton said, "why I want to leave part of my Christmas for you until I take you to the train tonight. Do you care?"

"I'll leave a present I know about until then too," said Ricky. "May I?"

"Come on now, though," said President Arthur Tilton. "I want to see Mother get her dolls."

It was well that they were not of an age to look for exclamations of delight from Mother. To every gift her reaction was one of startled rebuke.

"Grace! How could you? All that money! Oh, it's beautiful! But the old one would have done me all my life. . . . Why, Edward! You extravagant boy! I never had a watch in all my life. You ought not to have gone to all that expense. Arthur Tilton! A silk dress! What a firm piece of goods! I don't know what to say to you—you're all too good to me!"

At Ricky's books she stared and said: "My dear boy, you've been very reckless. Here are more books than I can ever read—now. Why, that's almost more than they've got to start the new library with. And you spent all that money on me!"

It dampened their complacence, but they understood her concealed delight and they forgave her an honest regret at their modest prodigality. For, when they opened her gifts for them, they felt the same reluctance to take the hours and hours of patient knitting for which these stood.

"Hush, and hurry," was her comment, "or the minister'll get us!"

The minister and his wife, however, were late. The second side of the turkey was ready and the mince pie hot when, toward noon, they came to the door—a faint little woman and a thin man with beautiful, exhausted eyes. They were both in some light glow of excitement and disregarded Mrs. Tilton's efforts to take their coats.

"No," said the minister's wife. "No. We do beg your pardon. But we find we have to go into the country this morning."

"It is absolutely necessary to us that we go into the country," said the minister earnestly. "This morning," he added impressively.

"Into the country! You're going to be here for dinner."

They were firm. They had to go into the country. They shook hands almost tenderly with these four guests. "We just heard about you in the post office," they said. "Merry Christmas—oh, Merry Christmas! We'll be back about dark."

They left their two shabby suitcases on the hall floor and went away.

"All the clothes they've got between them would hardly fill these up," said Mrs. Tilton mournfully. "Why on earth do you suppose they'd turn their back on a dinner that smells so good and go off into the country at noon on Christmas Day? They wouldn't do that for another invitation. Likely somebody's sick," she ended, her puzzled look denying her tone of finality.

"Well, thank the Lord for the call to the country," said Ricky shamelessly. "It saved our day."

They had their Christmas dinner, they had their afternoon—safe and happy and uninterrupted. Five commonplace-looking folk in a commonplace-looking house, but the eye of love knew that this was not all. In the wide sea of their routine they had found and taken for their own this island day, unforgettable.

"I thought it was going to be a gay day," said Ricky at its close, "but it hasn't. It's been heavenly! Mother, shall we give them the rest of their presents now, you and I?"

"Not yet," she told them. "Ricky, I want to whisper to you."

She looked so guilty that they all laughed at her. Ricky was laughing when he came back from that brief privacy. He was still laughing mysteriously when his mother turned from a telephone call.

"What do you think!" she cried. "That was the woman that brought me my turkey. She knew the minister and his wife were to be with me today. She wants to know why they've been eating a lunch in a cutter out that way. Do you suppose—"

They all looked at one another doubtfully, then in abrupt conviction. "They went because they wanted us to have the day to ourselves!"

"Arthur," said Mrs. Tilton with immense determination, "let me whisper to you, too." And from that moment's privacy he also returned smiling, but a bit ruefully.

"Mother ought to be the president of a university," he said.

"Mother ought to be the head of a law firm," said Edward.

"Mother ought to write a book about herself," said Ricky.

"Mother's mother," said Grace, "and that's enough. But you're all so mysterious, except me."

"Grace," said Mrs. Tilton, "you remind me that I want to whisper to you."

Their train left in the late afternoon. Through the white streets they walked to the station, the somber little woman, the buoyant, capable daughter, the three big sons. She drew them to seclusion down by the baggage room and gave them four envelopes.

"Here's the rest of my Christmas for you," she said. "I'd rather you'd open it on the train. Now, Ricky, what's yours?"

She was firm to their protests. The train was whistling when Ricky owned up that the rest of his Christmas present for Mother was a brand new daughter, to be acquired as soon as his new book was off the press. "We're going to marry on the advance royalty," he said importantly, "and live on—" The rest was lost in the roar of the express.

"Edward!" shouted Mrs. Tilton. "Come here. I want to whisper—"

She was obliged to shout it, whatever it was. But Edward heard, and nodded, and kissed her. There was time for her to slip something in Ricky's pocket and for the other good-bys, and then the train drew out. From the platform they saw her brave, calm face against the background of the little town. A mother of "grown children" pathetic? She seemed to them at that moment the one supremely triumphant figure in life.

They opened their envelopes soberly and sat soberly over the contents. The note, scribbled to Grace, explained: Mother wanted to divide up now what she had had for them in her will. She would keep one house and live on the rent from the other one, and "here's all the rest." They laughed at her postscript:

"Don't argue. I ought to give the most—I'm the mother."

"And look at her," said Edward solemnly. "As soon as she heard about Ricky, there at the station, she whispered to me that she wanted to send Ricky's sweetheart the watch I'd just given her. Took it off her wrist then and there."

"That must be what she slipped in my pocket," said Ricky.

It was.

"She asked me," he said, "if I minded if she gave those books to the new Springvale public library."

"She asked me," said Grace, "if I cared if she gave the new rug to the new church that can't pay its minister."

President Arthur Tilton shouted with laughter.

"When we heard where the minister and his wife ate their Christmas dinner," he said, "she whispered to ask me whether she might give the silk dress to her when they get back tonight."

All this they knew by the time the train reached the crossing where they could look back on Springvale. On the slope of the hill lay the little cemetery, and Ricky said:

"And she told me that if my flowers got there before dark, she'd take them up to the cemetery for Christmas for Father. By night she won't have even a flower left to tell her we've been there."

"Not even the second side of the turkey," said Grace, "and yet I think—"

"So do I," her brothers said.

Mothers Smell Like Lilacs

VALERIA WINKLER GRIFFITH

A new baby helps two stepbrothers establish a firm friendship and unites the family. A warm story straight from the heart.

AFTER FATHER took Doctor Winters upstairs, Tom and Porky Snyder and I just sort of sat in the living room, not doing much of anything. Tom kept smacking his fist into his new pitcher's mitt and muttering fiercely, just like the pitcher did in that game we went to see over at Torberry Park last week. Porky lay on his fat stomach and looked at the stuffed fish on the wall, and I read my new Superman comic book. It was the new one I bought at the drugstore the last time we went into town, but it didn't seem to be very good. Not as good as they are most of the time. Superman's okay, though. I'm all for him. Tom, he's all for the Red Knight.

I shoved my book off the davenport and went and looked up the stairs. "It sure takes a heck of a long time to have a baby, doesn't it?" I said.

Tom smacked his glove real hard. "Plenty," he said. "Plenty." Just like he knew all about it, and it kind of made me mad, because it was my mother that was having the baby, not his.

I went back and sat on the davenport and looked at the little pink china clock on the whatnot. It still didn't seem right to me to see it there. Before Mom married Mr. Rawlins we lived in an apartment in town, and Mom kept the little clock right in the middle of the shelf over the fireplace, with a pot of viney stuff on one side and Dad's picture on the other. Mom told me that Dad gave her the little clock before I was even born. Dad's name was Peter, too, like mine. Mom used to tell me a lot about him when we were living back in the apartment.

When we came out here to the farm after Mom married Mr. Rawlins, he wanted me to call him "Dad," like Tom did. I said well that was all right for Tom, but I guess a guy couldn't have but only one Dad, so Mom said why didn't I call Mr. Rawlins "Father," so I did.

Before we came Mom said it would be nice for me to have a brother and someone to play with, but it wasn't as much fun as she thought it was going to be. Tom's older than I am and bigger. When we did the chores, he wore his boots with a knife on the side and pulled down hay for the horses and brought up the cows. Father had me take care of the chickens and gather the eggs.

It got awful quiet in the room. Porky was sleeping, still on his stomach, and Tom was looking out the window. I jumped off the davenport and stuck out my arms and zoomed across the room. "Look at me," I said to Tom, "look at me. I'm a T-38!"

Tom looked at me and made a face like he was going to be sick to his stomach. "P-38, stupid, P-38. My gosh, you're the dumbest little kid I ever knew."

I guess we woke Porky. He sat up and rubbed his eyes and said: "Jiminy, are you two fellows fighting again? Anybody'd think you was enemies instead of brothers."

"We're not real brothers," Tom answered, awful loud, "just half."

"Well, anyway," Porky said, "you sure do fight a lot. Jiminy, a guy gets tired of listening to you."

"You can always go home, can't you?" Tom said, and I said, "Sure, you can always go home." And Porky got up and looked in the candy dish to see if there was any more gumdrops and there wasn't and he went home.

Father came running down the stairs on his toes, and it looked real funny because he's so big. He stood in the doorway and his hair was mussed up and he had a white shirt on like he was going to church, and it was mussed up, too. He looked pretty sore. "What are you two boys doing in here? I thought I told you to play down at the grove this afternoon. And here you are yelling around in the living room and acting like a couple of hoodlums and poor Polly upstairs nearly—" And then he looked at me and stopped.

VALERIA WINKLER GRIFFITH

I felt sort of lonesome all at once. "I want to see my mother," I said, and I started for the stairs.

Father stopped me and turned me around and pushed the hair out of my eyes. "Listen," he said, "you fellows go on out and play, like a couple of good scouts."

"What about that baby?" Tom said. "Did it get here yet?"

"No," Father said, "but it won't be much longer, thank God." And then a door opened upstairs, and he went tearing up. Tom and I hung around the hall a few minutes, and then we went to the pantry and got some crackers and put sugar and butter on them and went outdoors and sat on the ground in back of the house.

It was awful hot and the sun came right smack down on us and Tom said he bet we'd get sunburned and I said I bet we'd blister and all our skin'd peel off.

"Doc Winters sure has been here a long time," I said.

"Yeah," Tom said, "he must be planning on staying for supper."

Pretty soon I said: "I'm going to teach the baby how to play marbles. He can use my best shooter."

"I'm going to show him my secret place to find wild strawberries and how to set gopher traps," Tom said.

"I'm going to show him how to set gopher traps, too," I said.

"You can't, stupid," Tom said, "because you don't know how, and besides you haven't got any."

Father had got three gopher traps for Tom this spring, and Tom caught a gopher and took the paws to the courthouse and got ten cents. That was the day Father got Tom the boots with a knife on the side and said I didn't need any because my shoes were still good. When we got home, I told Mom I bet if Dad was alive he'd buy me some boots with a knife on the side, and Mom kissed me and said I must never never talk like that.

The sun was hotter than anything. "Who wants any old gopher traps?" I said to Tom. "I bet the baby wouldn't even look at them. Anyway, I'm going to be the one to take him around the farm and show him the cows and things."

"Oh, no, you're not," Tom said. "It's my dad's farm, and all the cows and horses and pigs on it belong to him, so I'll be the one to show it to the baby."

"Yeah," I said, "but it's my mother that's having the baby."

"Mothers!" Tom said. "Pooh!"

223

I wanted to say something back, but Mom said I mustn't ever. She told me Tom's mother went away from the farm when Tom was little and never came back. Mom said she was going to be Tom's mother now, and I said that wasn't what Tom thought, and she said well we'd just wait a while and see.

Tom's pitcher's mitt was lying on the ground. I slid my hand into it and thumped it in the middle the way Tom did, and he said, "My gosh, you little runt, what're you doing?" and I said I was just trying on his glove, and he said, "For gosh sakes, take it right off before you ruin it."

"How'd you like to play a little catch?" I said, and Tom said, "Who'd I play with?" and I said, "Me."

"Ha, ha," Tom said. "You couldn't hang onto a ball if it fell right in your hands."

Then the door banged behind us and we jumped and it was Father and he was grinning all over. "Well, boys," he said, "you don't have to wait any longer. The baby's here."

Father pushed us inside and through the hall. "Now you both can go and see it, but you must be very quiet."

We all of us tiptoed up the stairs.

The door into Mom's room was open, and I could see her smiling at me. She'd been in bed all day. She hadn't gotten up in the morning at all. It sure seemed funny to see Mom in bed in the daytime. She had on an awful pretty nightgown with ribbons, but her hair was just all spread out over the pillow and her face looked sort of wet and hot.

"Gee," I said, "you don't look right. You look sort of sick or something."

She put her arm around me and looked up at Father and laughed. "That's strange," she said, "because I feel just fine." She put her hand on my face, and it felt real cool. "You don't look so well yourself."

"I guess I'm pretty nearly baked," I told her. "Tom and I've been sitting in the back yard, and the sun came right smack down on us."

"I suppose it would have been entirely out of the question for you to have moved into the shade," Mom said. "Did you boys have your lunch?"

"Gumdrops and crackers and pickles," I said.

She looked up at Father and said, "Oh, George!"

He mussed up his hair and said, "So help me, Polly, I forgot all about it."

Mom said: "I can see it's not going to do for me to stay up here long. I'll have to get downstairs and take charge of things."

"Now, Polly," Father said and started fussing around with Mom's pillow, "remember what Doc said. You just lie right back and rest. The boys and I will just get along fine. Won't we, fellows?"

"My gosh," I said, "I forgot the baby. Where's the baby?"

And then I saw Tom across the room, looking down into the basket that Mom had painted white and put pink ruffles all over. Tom looked funny. His mouth was open and his eyes sort of bugged out like they did the time we found the rattlesnake down to the creek.

I went over to the basket. "My gosh," I said to Tom, "is that the baby?"

Tom punched me in the side with his elbow. "Be still," he whispered. "Don't let them hear you."

So I didn't say anything more. I just looked. There was a sort of wiggly red thing in the basket. Its eyes were squinted up. Its skin was wrinkly like an old apple. All of a sudden it began to make funny sounds, and I moved back fast.

Father made a sort of hissing noise at us and pointed toward the door. I looked at Mom. Her eyes were closed, and I followed Tom out, quiet as anything.

Father closed the door behind us and stood there rubbing his hands together and grinning and looking sort of silly. "Well, boys," he said, "what do you think of your new sister?"

"Sister!" I said, and I pretty near lost my balance and fell down the stairs.

"Golly," Tom said, "a girl!"

Then we heard a car, and Father looked out the window and yelled, "Hey, Doc," and ran down the stairs.

Tom and I just stood in the hall looking at each other. "Close your mouth before a fly gets in," I said to Tom.

He shut it up quick and didn't get mad like he 'most always does when I tell him that. "A girl," he said. "Well, what do you know!"

"Tom," I said, "it looked kind of funny, didn't it?"

"Yeah," Tom said, "it sure did."

"Do you suppose it's all right?" I said. "I mean it's so red and shrimpy looking and so awful little."

"I guess it's a terrible shock to Dad," Tom said. "He's been counting on getting that baby for such a long time."

"Mom must feel awful," I said.

Tom blinked his eyes real fast, the way he does when he's made up his mind and is going to do something. "Listen, Peter," he said—I was surprised, because Tom practically never called me Peter, just "runt" or "peanut" or something like that—"we've got to pretend that we think everything's okay, see? That we think it's a swell baby and all that. Maybe it'll make them feel better."

"I'll go in and tell Mom I think it's pretty," I said.

"Gosh, no," Tom said. "She'd know you were just trying to kid her. My gosh, she's seen it for herself, hasn't she? No, just say you're glad we got the baby and you're sure it'll turn out all right. I'll go down and tell Dad that, too." Tom started down the stairs and then he came back. "Wait a minute," he said. "Why don't you go down and talk to Dad about the baby? I think he'd be sort of pleased. I'll go see your mother."

"Gee," I said, "Mom would like that a lot."

I went down the stairs real slow, saying over and over what Tom had told me, and then I bumped into Father in the lower hall and it knocked the words right out of my head.

Father put his hand on my shoulder. "Well, young man, I guess you're not the baby of this family any longer," he said.

I hadn't thought of that. "Gee," I said, "I guess I'm not. It's a nice baby," I said. I still couldn't remember the words Tom told me.

Father got to grinning again. "She's a little beauty, isn't she?"

I looked up quick to see if he was kidding, but I guess he wasn't. And then I thought of something else. "Say," I said, "I bet you'll have the baby take care of the chickens and gather the eggs, because she's a girl and that's sort of girl's work." Father was looking at me kind of surprised. "I mean when she gets bigger," I said.

Father made a coughing sound in his throat. "Peter," he said, "come on into the living room. I think it's time we had a talk. Man to man."

I sat on the little stool and shoved out my feet the way I always did, because then Father might notice how big the hole was getting in my sneaker.

"You know, Peter," Father said, "you've been here quite a while and have learned a lot about the farm. I think it's about time we gave you some chores that'd be more useful than caring for the chickens."

"Golly," I said, "you mean drive the team, maybe?"

"Well, no," Father said, "not exactly. Not right away, anyhow."

"Maybe setting gopher traps," I said.

"Now, that's an idea," Father said. "Tom and I are going over to the east meadow in the morning with a bunch of traps. You come along, and I'll show you how it's done." And then Father looked right down at my sneaker, and I wiggled my toe in the hole. "It looks like you were due for new shoes."

"Boots?" I said real quick.

"Oh, of course, boots," Father said.

"With a knife on the side?" I said.

"Certainly," Father said. "A very special kind. Two blades and a corkscrew."

"Golly," I said. I felt all dizzy inside, like I was going to be sick to my stomach. "Gee," I said, "thanks a lot."

"Don't mention it, fellow," Father said, and he put his arm around my shoulders and we went into the kitchen and he cut me a slice of bread and put honey on it.

"Thanks, Father," I said, and then I ate the bread and was real careful not to let the honey drip on the linoleum. "You know," I said, "if it's all right with you, I think I'll call you 'Dad' like Tom does. If we called you different names, it might get the baby mixed up."

"That's a swell idea, son," he said, and he got out his handkerchief and blew his nose, and I bet if Mother knew he had a cold she'd make him use those awful nose drops, but I wouldn't tell on him. Not for anything.

I WENT out into the yard then, and pretty soon Tom came out and he was smiling and had a shiny look in his eyes like it was Christmas or something.

"How was Mom?" I said.

"Swell," Tom said. "Just swell."

"Did you tell her about the baby?"

"I guess I did," Tom said. "I don't remember very well. I went up to the bed and gosh, she just put her arms around me and kissed me. She smelled awful good. Like flowers. Lilacs, I guess."

"Yes," I said, "that's the way mothers smell."

"I guess I like the smell of lilacs better than anything," Tom said.

"You know," he said, "maybe when the baby grows up a little and gets some hair she won't be so bad."

"She's going to take care of the chickens," I said.

"Girls are always falling into things and getting hurt," Tom said. "We'll have to take care of her."

"We'll take turns," I said. "In the spring we can take her to the woods and pick violets."

"I won't pick violets," Tom said. "I'll just watch her."

"I'll just watch her, too," I said.

Tom picked up his pitcher's mitt and put it on and started smacking it in the middle. "How about playing a little catch?" he said.

I turned around to see who he was talking to, but there wasn't anybody else there. "Do you mean me?" I said, and Tom said sure, and we went down behind the barn and played.

Tom says I can catch a fast ball better than any little kid he ever saw, and I bet you anything that someday Tom's going to be a pitcher on a big ball team and maybe even play at Torberry Park.

The Failure

KATHARINE HAVILAND-TAYLOR

The outstanding motion pictures, "One Man's Journey" and "A Man to Remember," were adapted from this success story of a lovable country doctor.

A GOOD MANY THINGS had combined, Doctor Eli Watt sometimes thought, to hold him back; but at more drear moments he felt that God had designed him to be a country plug in doctors and now, of course, it was too late to do anything about it. He was pushing sixty, and nights of driving, at first behind old Jenny and then in his car, had made him look eighty, and a tired eighty at that.

Folks generally, Doctor Eli realized, wanted young doctors with well-pressed clothes and polished nails, and at the start of things he'd hoped to be that kind; and here he was in Pleasantville, just where he had started.

228

He'd been weak, he knew. At twenty-eight he had had a chance to be the assistant to a surgeon who'd reached the top, and he'd been ready to go, when he realized that if he did go no one would care whether little Abner Peters drank milk and that no one would look after Mamie Henise's babies as they came on—sometimes two a year.

He remembered turning down that offer and remembered the surgeon's prophecies.

"Do you mean to tell me, Watt," the surgeon had said, "that you're going to bury yourself in that one-horse town for the sake of a charity practice?"

The then-young Watt flushed. "It's hard to explain," he answered thickly.

"I'd think so, Watt," said the surgeon, and he smiled a little but without mirth; then suddenly he was irritable. "Look here," he went on sharply, "I'm going to tell you what you'll come to if you stick there. I've noticed your capabilities; a good many of us have. You can be a great doctor if you turn your back on a fringe of human weaklings who are better dead, anyway. If you don't turn your back on them you'll be an overworked, underpaid hack."

Young Watt had nothing to say, and he went back to Pleasantville in a thoughtful and hardening mood.

He guessed rather certainly that he ought to leave. He guessed less surely, that someone would turn up to look after Mamie Henise and little Abner Peters and the rest of them. He even began, that night, to look around his office to see what was worth the trouble of packing, and his dreams of the future began to form as he opened the drawers of his desk to turn over the clutter. The top drawer held English walnuts which had been delivered as part payment on opening a boil. The second drawer held a more varied assortment; there were rolls of bandage. He picked one up, to find it stained with oil, and then he remembered how old Andrew Arnold had driven in to say, "My girl, she burned herself with spillin' an oil lamp. *How much fer comin' out?*" Old Andrew was tight as the bark on a tree.

"How much'll you pay?" asked young Watt.

"Fifty cents and not one cent more," Andrew stated and, words out, his jaw clamped like a trap.

"All right," said young Watt, "I'll be with you in a minute," and he had gone to save a life, for fifty cents.

Also in that second drawer was a moire silk bookmark, cross-stitched, rather unevenly, with the statement that the Lord would provide. Little Aggie O'Brien had made that for Doctor Watt after he had gone out to the O'Brien farm one night, to find diphtheria, and small Aggie fighting a fast-closing throat.

Mrs. O'Brien held the lamp steadily while he used his knife. Once he had seen tears coursing down her brown lined cheeks, yet she had smiled. "I'm cryin' because I was that scared afore you come," she said.

It was nights of such pattern that, even then, were making him look old, and that gave him a series of pictures in which black surrounded the yellow square of a farmhouse door that silhouetted the someone waiting for "Doc."

He'd never get on, he knew, if he stayed.

In the bottom drawer he found admidst more clutter some lamb's wool that made him think of Mrs. Armhime, who had needed rest and had no chance for it, and had needed an operation that she wouldn't have.

"Not even you, Doc, could get me through that; I ain't right for it," she stated; "and there's my kids, you know—five of 'em. If you can keep me above ground till next year, when Molly's fourteen, why, then she can do for 'em."

They thought he was God, to measure their time, to grant requests to live till the kids could manage. And somehow he had kept Mrs. Armhime and a lot of women of Mrs. Armhime's group alive until something in extremely pliant young fabric was able to churn and bake.

Young Doctor Watt closed the lowest drawer of his desk. And as he closed it he knew he could not leave. He mopped his brow. "God," he said, "I've got to miss it. I know I'm weak, but I just can't go, and I hope You'll see Your way to forgive me!"

And he knew, slumping in the chair by his desk, that he must plug along to be a failure.

Two years after that his sister's husband died, and she and her boy came to live with him; and, as Lucy's boy grew, Doctor Eli transferred his own dreams to the youngster.

He took young Jimmy with him often when he made country calls. The boy wanted to be a doctor.

"We'll manage Vienna for you," Doctor Eli would say.

"Yes."

"A year, anyway."

"Yes."

"It's not that their technique is better, but the hospitals offer you every chance to study cases. Now I knew a fellow—he was in my class and he wasn't very smart, but now he's at the top. You see, he went to Vienna."

The tales were long and they were interrupted only by the opening of humble doors through which the doctor disappeared with his bag.

A long bag, young Jimmy learned soon, meant a delivery. He didn't think he'd fool with obstetrics; they took too much time. But his uncle, who then seemed very old to Jimmy, seemed to like them. He'd reappear, after absences that sometimes stretched for hours, gray with fatigue, but smiling. He would almost always say, "She's doing fine; a nice boy"—or "girl"—but when things went wrong, it knocked him.

As Jimmy grew he didn't see the point. "The thing to do," he decided at sixteen, "is to manage a practice, but not let it manage you."

At seventeen he knew his uncle for a country doctor who would never "expand," and at twenty-two he was telling his uncle how the big fellows did it.

Thus the years, and now Doctor Eli Watt sat in his office, which had grown as shabby as he from years of overwork and little in money to do with. He was tired, and the whole day had been patterned to bring facts home. That morning he had taken Rebecca Kyle to the hospital of the big town, some twenty miles away, where his nephew was practicing.

Big modern hospitals nowadays made Doctor Watt feel apologetic; everyone in them knew so well what they were doing. The modern appliances that he didn't half understand made him feel humble. He always tiptoed down the corridors, and when the floor head called him by name, before he'd known it he'd said, "Thank you." That was the way of it.

Jimmy was to operate on Rebecca, three days later. She was to have intravenous glucose preparatory to operation; a new dodge. Old Doc Watt had wandered to the ward after Rebecca was settled and for a little time he sat by her bed. She seemed to want him to stay around a while.

"Doc," she began hesitantly.

"Yes, Becky?" he said gently. She was one of his babies.

"Doc, if I shouldn't get well of this, you look after Tilly, won't you? She takes the cold that easy."

"Why, you know I would," he answered. Then something in the look she gave him made his throat feel tight.

"I knowed you would," she stated, "but I just had to ask like that. It makes me feel better to have you say what I know."

"I'm going home now to give her a little bottle of sugar pills," said Doctor Watt.

Becky smiled. "That'll tickle her," she said happily. She lay thinking of her child, but it seemed right to have old Doctor Watt near as she did this.

"You haven't a thing to worry about," said Doctor Watt. "You know my nephew is operating."

"I know."

"None better, Becky."

"I know," she answered dutifully.

"He's a wonderful surgeon."

"Sure; I know, Doc."

He had to leave then, but before he quitted the hospital he searched out his nephew. Jimmy had been operating, and he appeared in his white, the sterile mouth gauze dropped under his chin.

"What have you been doing?" asked Doctor Watt hungrily.

"Simple appendectomy."

"I see. I brought in Becky Kyle."

"Did you?" A nurse stood waiting with Jimmy's overall. Another stood by with hand lotion. In a corner someone was cleaning instruments.

"She feels a little nervous," said Doctor Watt.

"Scheduled for Thursday, isn't she?" asked Jimmy.

"Yes, Thursday at ten; and, Jim, she'd feel easier if she could talk to you first."

"Oh, good heavens!"

"Well, maybe you can't make the time for it," said Doctor Watt apologetically.

" 'Fraid I couldn't. I have a full week. Coming to the Medical Association meeting?"

"Well, if I can get it in," Doctor Watt answered. "Hilda Archer's baby has pneumonia and I have to be around considerably. I guess you remember Hilda? She was Hilda Jones and she lived in that big house on Elm Street."

Jim did not remember Hilda.

He was cleaned up now, and Doctor Watt inspected his suit with interest. You could see it was a real expensive suit.

"Finished for the day?" he asked.

"No. I have a duodenal ulcer at two; nice case."

"Wish I could stay and see it," said Doctor Watt, "but I got to be getting on."

He turned then to the door, but another thought came to him. Rather uncertainly he retraced his steps.

"How's Miss Cynthia?" asked Doctor Watt. She was, to Doctor Watt, "Jim's girl."

"Quite as usual. She always asks about you, by the bye, Uncle Eli."

"A nice girl," said Doctor Eli heartily; "fine folks she has back of her, but she's not uppish about it."

Jim didn't seem to like this for some reason. "Socially quite suave," he murmured.

"What?" asked Doctor Watt.

Jim led his uncle from the operating room, a white, beautifully manicured hand upon his uncle's shabby coat sleeve. "I meant," he explained patiently, "that she has those gifts I'd expect in a wife."

"Is it fixed?" asked Dr. Watt. He had paused in the corridor.

"Seems so," Jim answered, smiling. The old chap was amusing and —rather pathetic. Suggesting that he, Jim, go in to see this Becky— was it Kyle? No wonder his uncle was worn out and done.

"Well, I'm real glad," said Doctor Watt; he stood nodding, smiling. "That never came my way," he added, "but now I'm kind of getting it through you, the way I do other things."

He thought of a packet of letters in his desk that were postmarked Vienna.

"I guess," he murmured, "that you never will know what you've done for me. Your life holds everything I used to dream, a long while back, might be in mine. And now, to cap it all, you're going to be spliced to Miss Cynthia Morgan; a genteel, lovely young lady if ever there was one!"

"Utterly," Jim agreed. He looked at his watch. "I'm no end sorry," he said, "but I'll have to get along. I'm lunching with Babcock."

"Babcock?" asked Doctor Watt incredulously. "Not *the* Babcock?"
"Who else? He's here for a clinic."

Babcock himself, Doctor Watt reflected, and Jim lunching with him and saying it like that; as if it didn't matter. He'd look around pretty carefully leaving the hospital, Doctor Watt decided, and maybe he'd just get a little peek at him. It would be something to remember.

He asked, voice hushed, what Babcock looked like, and Jim answered, bored, "Oh, like a lot of other people—"

Doctor Watt hesitated, then he spoke. "Jim," he said, "if you don't think Doctor Babcock would think it was kinda pushing of me, you tell him his writings have meant a lot to an old country doctor. It's a little thing, but it might please him."

Without hearing, Jim nodded.

That done, Doctor Watt tuned up his car to turn toward home. On the way he stopped at a flower shop, where he selected a cineraria of violently purple bloom that stood in a pot wrapped in pink pleated paper.

This he had sent to Miss Cynthia Morgan, and on his card he wrote, "A little engagement present for a very lovely young lady." And he went home warmed by the thought of her pleasure.

But at home his elation dwindled. He kept thinking of the hospital, the hurry there, the way Jim had looked, his lunching there with— the great Babcock. It wasn't that he didn't want Jim to have all he had, but it made his own life seem lean.

He had only yawning doors to remember, with simple country people waiting in them for him.

Nothing glorious.

And going to town now seemed to do him up pretty badly. He was getting old.

His telephone tinkled; wearily he answered. He heard, "Doc, you're to come to Greiner's place. Baby has the fits."

He rose slowly to pack a bag. Maybe on the way home he could look in to see Hiram Askins. He guessed one more call wouldn't kill him and Hiram was eased up considerably by describing his pains.

There was a little package on his desk he saw for the first time. He unwrapped it; it held a somewhat worn billfold in which was a note that read: "Dear Doc, This belonged to Henry, and I thought maybe, since I can't pay you no money, it would be something." And it was signed "Mrs. Henry Burger."

"Well, that was nice!" he thought. Suddenly he had to sit down in his desk chair again. He sat holding the purse, looking at it, but seeing the hospital, the bustle there. What was making him feel so old and useless and done?

It was mighty nice of Mrs. Burger. Jim would laugh, Doctor Watt knew, if he saw the billfold. But maybe God knew there were some ways of failing that weren't so bad as others. Of course he was a failure.

Babcock; Jim lunching with him.

His eyes were smarting; what the deuce was the matter with him? "I guess," he thought, "Babcock was the man I wanted to meet more than any other."

He rose then, with the recollection that Baby had the fits. He hurried, leaving, troubled by having kept anyone waiting.

Jim certainly had worn a fine suit, he thought, riding. Jim had lunched with Babcock. He'd try to get in to see Becky again on the chance that Jim wouldn't have time for a visit with her. Jim wouldn't exactly understand, but there were real reasons that she should be heartened and pulled through. She came of a weak stock.

There ahead was the house he was to visit. The door was opened and someone framed by door jambs was awaiting him.

The someone turned to call a triumphant, "Doc's comin', Mom!"

He parked his car and picked up his bag, to move up the path to the door.

"Well now," he said, stepping into the house, "we won't worry! Everything's going to be all right." And a woman began to cry, the way they would when he came and things seemed a little better to them.

Hot water and plenty of it—he guessed the city fellows would try some kind of rays he'd never heard of—and in a few moments the baby was quiet.

He sat, waiting to be sure everything was all right.

The man shambled in. "I can't pay you anything now, Doc," he said.

"That'll be all right, Lem," the doctor answered.

The woman raised her eyes from her baby's face. "When you come," she said, "it was like God stepped into our house."

"I'm only an old hack," he stated, a little bitterly; then he smiled and his voice softened. "But God and the country doctor," he added, "they're both there when they're needed."

235

When he left, a little girl followed him to his car, clinging to a fold of his coat. The woman stood in the doorway, holding the baby; she waved. The man said a gruff "Thanks, Doc," without looking away from his child.

Doctor Watt drove off and toward Hiram Askins' mortgaged farm.

That night was bad; there was a first baby and a man who grew afraid of death as the shadows absorbed all the world he knew. He had a few hours' sleep, to rise to another stretch of work. Doctor Watt reflected, as he ate his breakfast, that if Jim had time maybe he would tell him someday about what Babcock said while they ate together. He'd get out Jim's Vienna letters some night. He hadn't read them for a long time.

Then activities began; house filled with the usual calls and some that were unusual. At noon he gave sugar pills to the younger set and he looked at a pet cat with a sore paw. He took pins for payment, thinking of Jim, and of how Jim would laugh—a trifle scornfully.

After his midday dinner he had a little time and he decided he'd get out Jim's letters from Vienna, and for quite a stretch of minutes he had quite a chance to look hungrily at words that were the bloom of his dreams. He became so absorbed that it was difficult to adjust quickly to the present, as he had to do when a long, smart car drew up at the curb.

Miss Cynthia Morgan was in it. He scanned his vest, to brush it ineffectually. His shirt was dirty, too, he realized.

Mrs. Gaunt, his housekeeper, admitted Cynthia, and it was Mrs. Gaunt who flung open the office door, with a harsh "Someone fer to see you, Doc."

Then Cynthia came across the room to him, both white hands outstretched.

"Maybe," said Doctor Watt, after their greeting, "you'd rather sit in the parlor; maybe that would be more suitable for you? Your dress is so fine."

She shook her head, and to his dismay he saw that she was trying not to cry; she said, in a stifled voice, "I love it—here!"

"Well, then we'll sit here," he said, and she took the chair at the side of his desk that faced the light. It was old-fashioned, he felt, but he could learn a lot about how he could help a patient, from the shifting play of expressions. Of course the big men used blood tests and all that, and of course he was behind the times. Miss Cynthia Morgan drew a deep breath as he settled. "I never can tell you," she said, "what the lovely flowers meant to me!"

She was a beautiful young lady, he decided; all the look of race was there, and more—kindness.

"Well, I just thought they'd please you," he admitted. He laughed. "You know," he added, "I drove home thinking of your surprise at getting them, and it made me very happy."

She said unsteadily, "You're a darling person!" and then she was crying.

He leaned forward to take her hand. "Why, my dear child," he said, "what's troubling you?"

Then he waited. It seemed she couldn't stop crying; but at length she managed to say, "I can't—I can't marry Jim—"

Doctor Watt's face changed. It was a considerable blow. He liked her so much; he'd never liked any other young lady half so well; and, too, he wanted the best for Jim.

"Well, if you can't, you can't, you know," he murmured.

She rubbed her eyes briskly, but tears still darkened her long lashes, to mat them to points.

"I want to explain," she said.

"You take your time," said Doctor Watt.

And yet again he waited. At length she began.

"He doesn't understand what is important," she stated.

Doctor Watt's heavy eyebrows drew close; he wanted to understand, but he couldn't.

"I mean," she went on, "everything *you* have he's missed!"

"I?" asked the old doctor. He looked around. "Why, I don't know," he confided slowly, "just what I do have!"

"You wouldn't know," she agreed. "You don't think of yourself. Don't you see? He's thick and cruel."

"Jim?"

"Yes."

"No, I don't," he answered a little stiffly. Then he realized he must do all he could to fix it because of Jim.

"Miss Cynthia," he said, "you know what Jim needs is someone like you. His mother died when he was eighteen, and while I did the best I could, I guess I wasn't much hand at raising even a one-child family. Of course, I had a lot to do always—with calls and so on—"

"He had every chance, being near you, to have what he lacks," she asserted, and her voice was a trifle strident.

"He's a great success, Miss Cynthia."

"You think so?"

"Why, my dear child, I know so."

"I don't see it."

Again his brows drew close; he couldn't get it, her point of view. Why, Jim was going to reach the top of the ladder. He tried to explain this, and still she was not convinced.

Then she saw the letters and she knew the writing on the envelopes. Without apology she picked one up. "You were rereading them?" she asked, words again a little blurred.

"Well, yes, I was," he said.

"How often does he come to see you?"

"Oh, ever and again."

"Exactly what does that mean, Doctor Watt?"

"Well, I mean once in two or three months. He's a busy man, Miss Cynthia."

She said nothing; her small, sweet chin was hard; her eyes, too, were hard.

Doctor Watt realized that he wasn't reaching her. He leaned forward again, hands on his knees, elbows out. "He's a big man," he stated. "Why, he lunched with Babcock the other day."

"You're a big man," she said. "You could stay here all your days without anyone ever hearing of you, and you'd be a big man."

He laughed. It seemed really funny to him; to hear anyone calling him a big man.

There was no convincing her, or changing her, Doctor Watt found as the call drew out. She felt that Jim had failed, somehow, and he couldn't make her see that Jim was a coming man and even now a big man.

She rose when a clock-stroke made her know she'd been an hour in the old office. Doctor Watt rose, too. She neared him; he felt her hands on his shoulders and he looked down into her deep blue eyes.

"I wish," she said, "that there were some measure for people like you! Some measure that would tell you what you have done and of your success. But it is the people who are never heard of who do the most in the world, and the hard ones travel up—up—up!"

Then, to his great surprise, she kissed him. No one had kissed him for years.

She went off then, and he sat looking at the chair in which she'd sat. Poor Jim. And what a lovely lady she was, despite very strange ideas. He must go to town to see Jim soon. Maybe he could manage that on the morrow. He must do all he could for Jim. The bell of his telephone tinkled.

But it was not until Friday that he went to town, and he went then because Jim sent for him. Becky Kyle's case, seeming very simple, had taken a wrong turning, from no more, it seemed, than her waning interest in life.

Jim met his uncle in the corridor outside the ward. Jim looked older and tired. He was taking it hard, Doctor Watt saw.

"I don't know what's the matter with her," said Jim, "but she'll die, if something can't be done. I don't want to lose a case that's so simple. It's absurd."

"I'll talk to her," said Doctor Watt.

"Do you mind if I come with you?" asked Jim; he seemed changed, different.

"Certainly not," said Doctor Watt.

He entered the ward; Jim followed him. He sat down by Becky's side and Jim stood at the foot of her bed. The screen was near; the one that meant the ward must be isolated from death and the troubles of the dying.

"Well, Becky," said Doctor Watt.

She opened her eyes a second, but they closed again.

"It's looking mighty nice out our way," said the doctor next. "The lilacs by your house are coming out."

Again she opened her eyes; this time she kept them open a little longer.

Doctor Watt talked on; of home and all she knew; of those dear and familiar things that had been dimmed by pain.

When his voice dropped away she whispered a question; it was, "How's my baby?"

The doctor spoke out loudly; he said, "Crying for you, Becky;" then he rose.

"I think," he said, when with his distinguished nephew in the corridor, "that your patient has turned the corner. I can tell you she's going to get well."

It was the next week that Jim asked his uncle to go with him to the County Medical Association dinner. Doctor Eli Watt was surprised and deeply pleased.

"That is nice! And mighty kind of you," he said, "and of course I'll come; that is, if Mary Smith's baby appears when it should."

Jim smiled affectionately, and not with seared enjoyment as at those who will follow wrong roads. "You'll have to come," he said; "there's a reason."

But Doctor Eli Watt was late that night, the baby having delayed its arrival. He reached town tired; it had been a long, hard confinement and his arms still ached and his knees felt shaky.

He made his way to the rooms slowly, thinking that perhaps he could still eat a course or two of the dinner that he knew would be mighty fine. He hadn't had a chance to eat anything since morning.

To his surprise he found that the dinner had not yet begun and that the group seemed to be waiting. And when he appeared the big fellows kept coming up, greeting him, it seemed, especially, and more than one of them said, "Very honored to be here, Doctor Watt."

Then he found his place; it was at the head of the table. He settled timidly after he had asked the man on his right whether there had not been some mistake. The man, a stranger, said, smiling, that he thought not, and the dinner began.

Doctor Watt ate heartily. "I'm pitching in pretty hard," he explained to this man on his right, "but I haven't eaten since morning. Some of my people have been real sick and they certainly keep you going—"

The man was studying him closely, he realized, and this made Doctor Watt speak. "My name's Watt," he said, "I'm a country doctor. I know you're a stranger, and what might your name be?"

"Babcock," said the stranger.

Doctor Watt blinked. And suddenly his nephew rose to speak; Doctor Eli Watt began to shake, and cold sweat trickled from his brow. His nephew was telling about how he, an old country plug in doctors, had saved Becky Kyle's life, and it sounded very well. Too well; of course, it was true, but it wasn't psychiatry; it was sense.

And someone else rose to tell of what he—Eli Watt—had done in a country town.

The dinner was for him; he had to lay down his fork, his hand was shaking too disastrously.

And then all around the table men were pounding with feet and clapping and calling, "Watt! Watt!"

He rose; he saw them through a blur, he began to speak, a tear slipped down his cheek.

"Gentlemen," he said, "I'm sorry about this, acting this way, but nothing like this has ever happened to me before, and you see, I know what I am, a failure, and when you get to knowing that—a thing like this can hurt, because—I can't explain. And as for Becky Kyle, gentlemen, I don't know anything about the mind, so you mustn't give me any credit. I couldn't keep up, there was too much to do. I can only use sense. But to be here, and know you have room for me, a very humble man beside you all—" he had to pause. "That's something," he ended, "that I'll never forget, and it'll help to go on till the end at taking care of my folks—"

Then he sat down; and he had to wipe his eyes.

Doctor Babcock turned to him. "I wish," he said, "you'd come down to look at a patient of mine that I haven't the wisdom to get inside. You have—"

Doctor Babcock talked on; asking his opinion. Other men turned to him. He sat, forgetting hunger and the need to eat; smiling, for the most part silent; very tremulous.

Once and again he thought, "Why, this can't be true!" and once he whispered it.

At eleven he started back to his village and his folks. He was still dizzy.

Passing the Morgan house, he saw from a light that someone was still up, and temptation won him and he stopped his car. If the person who was up was Miss Cynthia, he wanted to tell her of this; this great thing that had happened to him.

It was she who was up and she opened the door to him.

"Miss Cynthia," he said, "I guess stopping so late must seem queer to you, but I want to tell you about my evening. You'll never believe it, but Jim gave a dinner for me and he had the cream of the profession there. And they made speeches."

She said, warmly, "Darling!" She put her hands on his shoulders; she raised her face, she kissed him.

"Nothing they said was true, I must admit," he said, "but it's a thing I'll never forget. I'll keep it around in my heart, the way I keep Jim's letters from Vienna in my desk. I just can't tell you the nice things they said, and I sat at the head of the table with Babcock, *the* Babcock, on my right. . . . Yes, sir, and they had ten courses."

"Jim did it?" she asked.

He drew a deep breath and nodded. "And, funny thing," he said, "at the start and before I knew that dinner was for me, I was awful tired, and now I feel as if I could lick a hyena single-handed. And another funny thing, I have a case out there—back in the hills—and I was discouraged about her, but now I know I can pull her through. But I mustn't be keeping you up."

She patted his hand, held between hers. "I told you you were wonderful," she said.

"I?" he asked.

She was smiling.

"Wonderful," she repeated. She went on, "And you can tell Jim I've changed my mind; tell him that I've decided that I have to be related to you. And tell him, too, that tonight made me feel he is going to reach the top some day and be a worthy successor of his uncle."

He sat in his office an hour later, smiling mistily. They had all greeted him as an equal, a man of importance. Well, maybe he had done some things. He wondered whether God remembered the day when he had turned his back to getting on, because his sick folks needed him.

"I couldn't do anything else," he murmured, "and I guess maybe God understands better'n I do. And now I have that dinner."

The telephone tinkled. He answered it. "Doc," he heard, "you're to come up to Seefey's place; the missus is bad."

He realized the ten miles ahead of him as he started his car, but the thought of them and a night call didn't tire him as usual. He was feeling young again, he realized, and he could go, with any luck, for a good many years longer. And suddenly he wanted those years as he had in his young days; years for work; years in which he could give to those who had need of all he could give. . . . He looked up; the stars were bright and they seemed close.

"A little more time," he said, as his patients, who must live, seemed to speak to him, "and then whatever You want." And he added, seeing a long table, faces turning his way, his distinguished nephew speaking of his work, which seemed, after all, to count, "And *thank* You!"

The house lay ahead; the door was open—he knew by the square of yellow printed against the night.

And someone, seeing the headlights of his car, turned to call, "It's all right! Doc he' a comin'!"

Ocean Air

IAN HAY

It takes ocean air to free Mr. Finch from his in-hibitions and to get him to set his cap for Miss Greig. This humorous and very appealing story of mistaken identity gives us the famous Ian Hay at his best.

AN OCEAN VOYAGE affects you in one of two ways: either you are gloriously stimulated or profoundly depressed. More-over, salt air plays tricks with character itself. It gets into a man's blood for the time being, and sometimes makes him do things which surprise him.

Jacob Finch was bitterly disappointed in his first experience of the deep. He had pictured himself revelling in the luxury of a great ocean-going hotel, making pleasant acquaintances and taking a prominent part in the social activities of the ship. In short, he had dreamed the dreams that a thoroughly shy and thoroughly undistinguished in-dividual generally does dream at the prospect of escaping from the society of people who have known him and disregarded him all his life, into a world where nobody knows him at all and where he fondly imagines he will have his handicap revised.

Having recently come into money—a comfortable income from a comfortable aunt lately departed this life at Chislehurst,—Jacob had decided to see the world. Being a young man of secret yearnings and little initiative, he had begun with Monte Carlo, where for three days he persevered in a dismal exercise which he described to himself as "entering into the life of the place." That is to say, he loafed forlornly round the Casino, looking over the shoulders of people gambling at the tables, or sat forlornly in a restaurant watching the backs of people eating and drinking. Of course when he returned home he would be able to tell his relatives in Little Tushingham how he had run over to Monte and had a flutter at the tables. But—*il faut souffrir pour être viveur.*

One day he noticed in the hotel lounge a bulletin which announced that a White Star liner from New York, bound on a spring cruise to various attractive Mediterranean ports, would call at Monaco on the morrow to take up intending passengers. Jacob realized at once that in Monte Carlo he was in his wrong setting. His rugged island nature was plainly unsuited to the pursuit of enervating and effeminate pleasures ashore; his home was obviously upon the rolling deep. So straightway he paid his hotel bill and transferred his person, effects, and lonely soul to an excellent cabin in the great ship *Empiric,* where he was excessively unwell for twenty-four hours. On the whole these were the happiest hours that he was destined to enjoy for some days to come; for when he recovered and endeavoured to "enter into the life of the ship," he did so with as little appreciable effect upon the other participants therein as before. He strolled about the smoking-room, watching gentlemen playing poker. He tramped round the promenade deck, timidly eyeing the rows of passengers tucked into deck chairs, and vainly trying to summon sufficient courage to wake one of them up and start a conversation. He lingered wistfully in the vicinity of the athletes who played shuffle-board and deck-quoits. He sat in the corner of the lounge after dinner and watched the dancing couples, whistling defiantly through his teeth to show himself that he was enjoying the music. At mealtimes he shared a table with four other passengers. Unfortunately they were all English, and strangers to one another as well; so conversation was limited to requests for the mustard.

Jacob had applied for and received a numbered and reserved chair in the long line that ran from end to end of the starboard side of the promenade deck. He had built high hopes on this. To sit wedged between two fellow-creatures for hours at a time and for days on end without occasionally exchanging some sort of greeting or observation is a human impossibility, even under the Union Jack. As a matter of fact Jacob had secretly hoped to find himself between two Americans, because experience had taught him that Americans are an intrepid and adventurous race, and will frequently risk addressing a remark to a stranger where an Englishman would insist upon waiting either for a formal introduction or a shipwreck.

Here again he was unfortunate. On the left of his chair came a gap in the line, caused by the intervention of the smoking-room doorway. Still, there was a chair upon his right. It was empty, and it remained empty for two whole days. But after that an event occurred which changed the whole face of the world.

Jacob had completed his usual solitary morning constitutional, and was making for his moorings, carrying a rug and two magazines, when he observed that the chair next to his was occupied. In fact, at that very moment the deck-steward, with the solicitous tenderness of his race, was tucking a passenger into it—a girl. Somewhat fluttered, Jacob halted at a convenient distance, and examined her covertly. She repaid examination. She possessed large, dewy, grey eyes, a rather pert little nose, and a clear, delicate skin. But what Jacob chiefly noticed at first glance was her smile, which struck him as the most beautiful thing that God had ever created. The smile in question was directed at the deck-steward, in recognition of his ministrations; but some of it flowed past him and was intercepted by Jacob Finch. Simultaneously something which felt like a miniature torpedo struck Jacob fairly and squarely in the chest, and exploded. His heart, not unnaturally, ceased to beat: then, suddenly, it began to bump tumultuously. Jacob's head reeled: the blood sang in his ears. Dazed and trembling, he groped his way mechanically into his chair, and arranged the rug clumsily over his knees. Apparently unconscious of his presence, the vision beside him opened a book, found the place, and began composedly to read.

But pretty girls are seldom as unconscious as they look. Jacob's neighbour was fully aware that a healthy young male of presentable but slightly melancholic appearance had sat down beside her. Had she been stone blind she must have known, for she could hardly have failed to hear the beating of his heart. It was a still, sunny morning, and the great ship, heading south, slipped peacefully through the blue waters of the Mediterranean. The scene was set for comfortable chatting and pleasant confidences. The deck was almost deserted, and their nearest neighbour was an elderly gentleman fast asleep.

Presently Jacob's little companion laid down her book for a moment, in order to adjust her steamer-rug. Straightway the volume slid from her lap onto the deck. Jacob dived for it, and returned it, dumbly. The girl thanked him with a smile, resumed her reading—at least, she continued to keep her eyes upon its pages,—and silence reigned again.

Here was an opportunity; but seize it Jacob could not. Shyness is a potent and paralyzing thing. He sat rigid. The girl presented her left shoulder to him, and turned over another page.

Twenty minutes passed, and Jacob's tongue was still fast bound in misery and iron. Turning hither and thither in his extreme discomfort, he cast a side-long glance upon the volume on his neighbour's lap. It was a new novel which half the ship was reading, called "Faint Heart." The cruel appropriateness of the title cut his dumb soul like a whiplash.

"Go on!" he exhorted himself. "You're fellow-passengers, aren't you? Say something! You miserable brute! Say *anything!* Tell her it's a fine day! Ask her if she's a good sailor! Oh, you wretched, cowardly funk! Make her smile again! Say something funny! Do something! Do *anything!* Pah!"

It was no use. Speak he could not, without some friendly lead.

Presently his companion finished a chapter, laid down her book, opened a little bag, and produced a cigarette. Then she made further search in the bag, presumably for matches; but without success. She gave a little sigh of annoyance, and restored the cigarette to its case.

It was now or never. Jacob, his fingers in his waistcoat-pocket and his heart in his mouth, nerved himself for the supreme effort of his life.

He swallowed his heart, cleared his throat in a distressing manner, and said huskily:

"May I offer you a light?"

"Oh, please!" replied the girl. "It was stupid of me to leave my matches in the cabin." Her voice was fresh and clear. A student of intonation might have hazarded a guess that she was a native of London, but to Jacob Finch she sounded like the soloist of the Heavenly Choir. He handed her his match-case without a word. It did not occur to him to take out a match and light it for her. He knew nothing of such niceties of overture.

The girl lit her cigarette, and returned the match-case.

"Thank you so much," she said. "I hope my smoking doesn't upset you. You are a good sailor, I suppose?"

"Yes, very good," replied Jacob. "At least," he added more cautiously,

"I hope I shall be. This is my first long sea trip, and I only came on board at Monaco."

"Monaco? Oh? Did you come from Monte?"

"Yes. I—I—had a run over from Town for a week, to have a flutter."

"Had you any luck?"

"I was just all square." This was literal truth, for Jacob had not adventured a penny piece at the tables, being quite ignorant of the necessary procedure and much too shy to seek advice on the matter.

"We came on board at Marseilles," said the girl. "I didn't enjoy the first few days much, even on this nice big boat. This is the first time I have been on deck."

"I was wondering where you were," said Jacob, with a temerity that surprised himself.

"Why? Did you—?"

"I mean, I was wondering who was going to sit in that chair," explained Jacob. "Are you a large party?"

"I am with an aunt of mine. She is down below—and likely to stay there, poor thing!"

"Is she still si—unwell?"

"Dreadfully. It was sweet of her to come at all, considering what a bad sailor she is. But I was dying to take the trip, and she always spoils me. I love being spoiled." Again the smile flashed out. "Don't you?"

"That's right," said Jacob—and felt thoroughly exasperated with himself. It was his habit, being a man of unambitious vocabulary, to say "That's right" whenever he could think of nothing more original to say. It was plain that his companion had just given him the chance to say something very gallant indeed. But the fence was too formidable for him.

At this moment the ship's bell somewhere forward chimed twice, and a well-nourished youth in tight blue uniform and brass buttons, emerging from the doorway beside him, proceeded to shatter the gossamer of romance by means of an ear-splitting rendering of "The Roast Beef of Old England" upon the key-bugle.

DURING the next few days Jacob Finch, having tumbled headlong in love, sank down, down into the lower depths, until he touched bottom. There he stayed. He had never been in love before. That is to say, he had never lost his heart to any girl, though he had been timidly in love with love itself ever since his sixteenth birthday. Consequently he suffered with all the severity incident upon a first experience. A lover is popularly supposed to pass his time alternately in the heights and in the depths, in correspondence with the mood of his lady. But this is not true. It is all a matter of disposition. Your sensitive lover—the unfortunate person who cannot get along without systematic encouragement—resides almost permanently in the abyss. He is morbidly sensitive about intruding where he is not wanted: and once a humble-minded individual gets that idea into his head, he is in for a fairly agonizing time of it. The only man who ever ought to become a lover is your thick-skinned fellow with a good conceit of himself. He is in his element all the time: he is convinced that he is being a glorious and continuous success, and as often as not wearies his beloved into capitulation from sheer despair of making him understand that he is not indispensable.

But Jacob Finch was not of that mettle. As already stated, having dived into the ocean of love, he went straight to the bottom and stayed there. His knowledge of women was of the slightest, and his faith in his own powers of attraction slighter still. He cherished a theory that in order to inspire a woman's affection a man must be gallant, handsome, and above all notable in some way—a success, in short. The fact that there is more than one feminine instinct to which a man can appeal was unrevealed to him. He did not know that some women like mothering failures. So his longing soul clave to the dust—or rather, to the well-scrubbed deck-planking which supported the pretty feet of Miss Myra Greig. (That was her name, he discovered, by consulting the table-plan on the saloon staircase.)

Attractive girls on board ship are not easily monopolized, especially by diffident suitors. The greater part of Jacob's time now was spent in dumbly enduring the spectacle of Miss Greig being taken for walks, Miss Greig being instructed in deck games, Miss Greig dancing the fox-trot with a variety of more or less expert and eligible gentlemen. True, she was his companion and neighbour for a quite appreciable period every day, for she was an insatiable reader and spent long hours in her deck-chair. But Jacob reflected despondently, even as they reclined with elbows touching, that she was there by accident and not from choice.

Still, he persevered, in his own painstaking way. He studied Miss Greig's character, endeavouring to define her taste in men, in order that he might instantly model himself upon her ideal. He thought of interesting topics and entertaining anecdotes, and noted the same down upon his shirt-cuff, that he might never cease to be entertaining. He lay awake half the night envisioning his lady under various circumstances, and rehearsing exactly what he would do in the somewhat unlikely event of her falling overboard. In fine, by brooding and dreaming where he ought to have been pursuing a more active policy, Jacob worked himself into a state which may account for his subsequent surprising behaviour.

On the third afternoon after their first meeting Miss Greig, who had been immersed for half-an-hour in the closing chapters of "Faint Heart," closed the book with a little sigh of rapture, and sat up. The faithful shadow beside her quivered responsively.

"Well, that's over!" she remarked regretfully. "I wish I could write!" She turned to Jacob. "I'm afraid I've been very unsociable: but I've been in a trance for the last half-hour." She shivered delicately. "It's quite cold, isn't it?"

"Would you like to walk round the deck?" inquired Jacob eagerly.

"I should love it. Hold my book for me, will you?"

Jacob extracted his divinity from her chair, much as a connoisseur might extract a porcelain shepherdess from a packing-case, and they set out for their walk. Not that Jacob had any particular realization that he was walking: he had a vague feeling that he was swimming. He was immediately in conversational difficulties, as usual, and began furtively to work his left shirt-cuff out of his sleeve.

They reached the rail which marked the sternmost limit of the promenade deck, and surveyed the receding vista of the Bay of Naples, which they had left an hour before. Above the city towered a mountain, from the summit of which now and then emerged a puff of smoke, suggestive of a comfortable gentleman smoking a cigar in his club.

"I suppose that is Mount Aetna?" said the girl.

"Yes," replied Jacob tactfully. "Vesuvius, rather." He referred stealthily to his shirt-cuff. "It is four thousand and twenty feet—"

"How wonderful it must be," said Miss Greig, a trifle hastily, "to know things like history and geography! Do you remember how clever you were about Corsica when we touched there—Napoleon, and all that? I suppose you have travelled a great deal?"

"Well, of course one covers a certain amount of ground," replied Jacob, trembling with pleasure. "One knocks about, and so on." Then he added tentatively:

"Have you seen much of the world?"

"No, I am quite a little stay-at-home. I have spent most of my life in Devonshire. We have a place there. Of course it isn't in the least grand, but it has been in the family a good long time now."

"I take it," said Jacob with a gulp, "yours is what is called a county family."

"I suppose so," said the girl carelessly. "At least, if a tumbledown old Jacobean house with a stone terrace, and a flock of deer on the lawn below, and a few acres of land, and some funny old tenants are the qualification, we are."

Jacob's heart sank. Already the adamantine bars of the English caste system were lowering themselves between him and his crazy dream. Suddenly the girl looked up at him with an adorably confidential little air.

"Do you know," she remarked, "I have been wondering lately what you are."

"What I am?" Jacob's heart quickened again. She had actually been thinking about him.

"Yes—your profession. Now don't tell me: it's such fun guessing!"

"What do I look like?" asked Jacob, endeavouring to get his shoulders back without attracting notice.

"Well—are you in business of any kind?"

"No."

"I am glad: I think commerce is so dull. Let me see, now—what else could you be? A lawyer—an engineer—an architect—an artist? No? Well—"

"What would you like me to be?" asked Jacob. It was an audacious flight for him, but Miss Greig did not seem to mind.

"I know what I should like to be myself, above all things in the world," she replied.

"What?"

"An author." She laid a caressing hand upon the cover of "Faint Heart," which Jacob was carrying.

"I would give anything in this world," she said, "simply to be the man who wrote that book!"

Jacob Finch gazed down into her small, eager, flushed face. Her lips were parted; her eyes shone. Something seemed to snap inside his head, and an unknown and omnipotent force from outside took possession of him.

"I'm afraid you can't be him," he said gravely. "But—"

"But what?" asked the girl, her attention caught by the tone of his voice.

"You can meet him, if you like."

"What do you mean?"

Without a tremor Jacob Finch turned back the cover of "Faint Heart," and pointed to the author's name upon the title-page.

"My *nom de plume!*" he announced.

Miss Greig clasped her hands, and gazed up at him breathlessly.

"*You?* You are really Julius Mablethorpe?" She almost whispered the question.

Jacob Finch nodded defiantly.

NEWS travels fast on board ship. Within twelve hours it was known to every saloon passenger that the rather colourless young man, who wore a made-up tie at dinner and spent his time mooning about after that rather saucy little piece with the big eyes, was no less a personage than the famous Julius Mablethorpe, the author of nineteen Best Sellers and a household word (or byword, according to your standard of literary taste) throughout the English-speaking world.

The consequences were immediate and numerous, and entirely beyond anything that Jacob Finch—or indeed most people—could have anticipated. We can divide these into the consequences affecting his relations with the world in general, and those affecting his relations with Myra Greig.

The first naturally was that Jacob became a ship's topic of the first rank.

"Curious how hard some of these celebrities are to spot," said the passengers to one another. "One would never have singled out this chap. But when you come to look at him, you can see—you can *see!* There's something there—something that we haven't got. Look at his forehead, the way it bulges! Look at his ears, the way they stick out! Look at his chin, the way it goes in! Watch his eyes! They seem to see nothing, but I bet you they're taking in everything! You and I will be in his next book, as likely as not. We must be careful how we behave—eh?"

Next, lifelong admirers closed round Jacob Finch and discussed with him at length the works of Julius Mablethorpe—to the extreme discomfort of the former, whose acquaintance with the writings of the latter was of the slightest. But even when detected in palpable unfamiliarity with his own handiwork, his disciples counted the fact to him for righteousness.

"Most interesting, these geniuses!" they said. "This one really seems quite fed up at being asked about his own stuff. Can't even remember which book of his a character belongs to. Queer, reserved, dreamy, unpractical creatures—what? Barrie's another of 'em."

Then they would ask Jacob Finch for the favour of Julius Mablethorpe's autograph—which was granted, they noted, with characteristic diffidence—and retire below to record the whole episode in their diaries.

Secondly, the effect upon Jacob's relations with Miss Greig. For perhaps six days he lived his dream—oblivious of everything save the consciousness that this matchless creature found him above all men desirable. He did not think; he did not reflect; he simply accepted the inconceivable bliss which had descended upon him.

Then, suddenly, he came to himself. The sun was blotted out; a pall of black despair spread over heaven; and he realized exactly what he had done. Previous to this he had had a chance—how good or bad he did not know; but a chance—to win Myra Greig for his own. Now that chance was gone forever. Plainly he could not marry Miss Greig without telling her that he was an impostor; and equally plainly if he told her he was an impostor she would not marry him. He worshipped her with all his body and soul—and by one single act of madness he had cut himself apart from her forever. No wonder the autograph-seekers found their lion a little *distrait*.

It was evening, and he sat upon the edge of his bed smoking a cigarette. He had an appointment with Miss Greig on the boat deck —such appointments could be had for the mere asking now—at ten minutes to nine, to look at the moon, which was at the full. He closed his burning eyes and reflected for the hundredth time.

"If I carry on till the end of the trip, and then slip off the ship quietly, and disappear forever—that will be the end of the whole business, in a manner of speaking. Of course it will mean that I can never see her again. She will think that I have let her down. She will think me a cad—!"

He choked, and genuine tears forced their way beneath his eyelids.

"—And if I go upstairs and make a clean breast of it now, that only means that she will give me the chuck on her own account straight off, and never speak to me again! Oh, dear!" He dropped his face into his hands, and writhed in the tangled web which he had so artlessly woven for himself.

Still, taking him all in all, Jacob was a man, and a gentleman. He sat up, and looked at his watch. The hour of the rendezvous had come. He dipped his face into cold water and scrubbed it with a rough towel—and there are less practical ways of achieving moral regeneration,—after which, having brushed his hair and rearranged his tie he surveyed himself resolutely in the mirror.

"I will!" he said aloud. "I will! It's the only decent thing to do. I'll do it now!"

Miss GREIG was reclining in a lounge chair in the moonlight, on the boat deck, and welcomed him with a little air of demure proprietorship which at once thrilled and tortured him.

"I have a message for you," she announced importantly.

"A message?" Jacob started. "Who sent it?"

"The Passengers' Entertainment Committee. There is to be a Concert in the Saloon tomorrow night, and they want you to take the chair."

"*Me?*" exclaimed Jacob in a voice of horror.

Miss Greig smiled indulgently.

"Yes—you! Celebrities mustn't be too modest, you know. If you *will* be Julius Mablethorpe, you must expect to have to do things like that. You have brought it on yourself," she concluded, with perfect truth.

"But isn't there anybody else?"

"No. You are easily the greatest celebrity on this ship. You will do it, won't you?" Miss Greig raised her eyes appealingly.

Jacob resolutely avoided them.

"I can't," he said miserably.

"Not even to please me?"

Jacob writhed. "Tell her now!" commanded a stern voice within him. "Go on! The longer you look at it the less you will like it." He drew a deep, shuddering breath.

"I would do anything in the world to please you," he began, leaning closer to the girl and speaking in a low, choking voice; "but—but— well, there is something I must tell you first. There is a reason—"

"A woman doesn't want to listen to reason," retorted Miss Greig petulantly.

"But this reason—"

"Never mind reasons." She gave him a quick glance. "I'm not really thinking about the Concert, or the silly old other passengers. I'm asking you to do this just to please me, and for nothing else. There! Won't you? I shall be so proud of you. Please?" Miss Greig laid an impulsive hand upon Jacob's sleeve.

Without doubt, argument between the sexes under the moon on a semi-tropical sea should be prohibited, or at least supervised, by the State. The consequences were automatic. Next moment Jacob had taken possession of the hand, and was kissing it passionately.

"I love you!" he said; "I love you! I would do anything for you. I don't care what happens now. I've said it—there! And I'm glad, any- way!"

This was not what Jacob had intended to say, nor anything like it; but Miss Greig showed no disposition to be critical. Neither did she withdraw her hand. Indeed, Jacob was conscious, to the very marrow of his soul, of a soft, responsive pressure. He gazed down upon her: her long lashes were drooping.

"Look up!" he said, in a voice entirely unfamiliar to him.

The girl obeyed; and Jacob, inexperienced though he was, realized at a glance that fate had put something into his keeping that night which would never entirely pass out of it again or ever be given to another.

"Do you know," said Myra ten minutes later, "you rather frighten me!"

"Do I?" replied Jacob in genuine astonishment. "Why?"

"Well, all my life I have dreamed that when I came to be loved by somebody, it wouldn't be anybody famous, or clever, or strong; but just somebody who was nobody in particular, if you know what I mean—some man who was rather lonely and helpless and wanted taking care of." She gave a shy laugh. "That was what first made me feel"—she leaned her head comfortably against his arm—"feel this way about you. I really thought you were lonely and helpless. Wasn't it cheek of me? Do you mind, dear?"

"No," said Jacob unsteadily, "I don't mind. I'm glad. At least—I would have been."

"If you hadn't been what you are?"

"That's right," said Jacob, with a heart of lead.

The girl rose to her feet.

"Let me go now," she said. "No, don't kiss me—yet. Tomorrow I shall have to speak to you about something. May I tell them that you will take the chair at the Concert?"

"Whatever you say," assented Jacob mechanically. "Good-night, my dear!"

"Bless you!" said the girl. She threw him a last smile over her shoulder, and disappeared down the stairway.

Left alone, Jacob stood gazing over the moonlit sea—silent, motionless, not without a certain dignity. Finally he clasped his hands over his heart, and closed his eyes.

"O God," he murmured, "please let her go on smiling at me like that for a little while longer. Then I will tell her. I promise! But not just yet—please!"

THE PURSER, a stout gentleman of paternal appearance and enormous acquaintance, tapped discreetly upon the sitting-room door of Suite Number Seventeen, on B Deck, and entered.

Sprawling in an armchair, with his feet on the table and a litter of proof-sheets upon the floor all round him, sat a large man with greying hair, in his shirt-sleeves, angrily puffing an unclean pipe and stabbing at a proof-sheet with a fountain pen.

He looked up.

"Go away!" he said. "Remove yourself! Go and purse somewhere else!"

But the Purser merely grinned, helped himself to a cigar unbidden, and sat down upon the sofa.

"So they've punctured your blessed old incognito after all," he remarked.

The large man looked up from his proof-sheet and glared.

"What do you mean? I don't understand your filthy vernacular, I only speak English."

"Then why don't you write it, old son?" asked the Purser gently. But Julius Mablethorpe was not to be drawn. He wanted this alarming allusion to his incognito explained.

"Don't play the pantaloon," he urged, "but tell me."

"I have told you. Your disguise appears to have been penetrated."

"What makes you think so?"

"Well, there is a notice up on the board outside my office to say that you are to take the chair at the Concert tonight. I presume the announcement has been made with your knowledge and consent. Between ourselves, I shouldn't wonder if you had offered to do it. I have always suspected this incognito business of yours of being an advertising stunt."

But these gross insults, which in most cases would by this time have precipitated a most enjoyable wrestling-match between two short-winded but light-hearted sexagenarians, failed of their usual effect. Julius Mablethorpe (entered on the passenger list as Lemuel K. Baggs) rose from his seat, scattered his impedimenta upon the floor of the cabin, and gazed earnestly down upon his old friend.

"You're speaking the truth, I suppose?"

" 'I always tries to utter lies, and every time I fails,' " quoted the Purser.

"Either some one has found out that I am on board," said Mablethorpe slowly; "and has put my name up as a sort of challenge to me to come forth and make a holy show of myself, or else—well, it has happened before, and may happen again."

"What?"

"I wonder! What a rum coincidence if it *has,* with me actually on the same ship. *The Long Arm,* eh? Not a bad title for a short story! Now—"

"Abandon these senile and mercenary maunderings," urged the Purser, "and say what you're driving at."

Mablethorpe told him.

"Go and find out who he is, like a good chap," he said when he had finished.

"I will," replied the Purser grimly, and left the cabin.

In twenty minutes he returned.

"You're right, old fellow," he announced. "You are being impersonated."

Mablethorpe nodded.

"Somebody with mutton-chop whiskers and a cummerbund, I suppose?" he said gloomily.

"More or less."

"I knew it! Well?"

"Apparently he revealed his identity—that is to say, your identity—two or three days ago, and has been the big noise on this old packet ever since. I suppose I ought to have heard about it sooner, but I have been busy in the office with manifests and things ever since we left Algiers. Anyhow, your understudy has been having a wonderful time —surrounded by adoring females, telling them where he gets his inspirations from, and writing autographs. What are you going to do about it? Shall I ask the Old Man to put him in clink?"

"Not at all. Why should I deprive a fellow-creature of his innocent pleasures? But I should like to meet the gentleman. When is this perishing Concert of his to take place?"

"Tonight, at nine."

"Bring him in here before dinner, will you?"

Two HOURS later Jacob Finch, gloriously arrayed for his evening's official labours, was ushered, not altogether at his ease, by the Purser into Suite Number Seventeen. There he beheld a large man with twinkling blue eyes and a preternaturally solemn expression, sitting behind a table.

"Purser," announced the large man in a voice of thunder, "you can get out!"

"Yes, sir," replied the Purser respectfully, and departed.

"Sit down, please," said the man to Jacob, indicating the sofa. "Drink this."

He rose and placed a glass of whiskey-and-soda within reach of his guest, and resumed his magisterial pose behind the table.

"Now," he said, "you will naturally desire to know who I am, and why I have invited you to this *tête-à-tête*. I will tell you. I write novels, of a distressing but popular character. I have been for the last four months in the United States, collecting material for another. I am now rounding off my trip by circumnavigating the Mediterranean. I have been occupied during the past fortnight in revising the proofs of a new book which has to be delivered to my publishers next week. In order to secure complete privacy and freedom from interruption, I have remained almost entirely in my cabin, and I am entered on the passenger list under an assumed name. You will find it given there as

Lemuel K. Baggs. I made it up myself: I think it is rather good. My real name, in point of fact, is Julius Mablethorpe. . . . Here's another drink for you. Now, old man, tell me why you did it."

Mr. Mablethorpe resumed his seat, leaned back, lit a cigar, smiled benevolently, and waited. He had to wait some time, for his visitor found himself for the moment incapable of speech. He sat huddled upon the sofa, gaping like a stranded fish.

"Take your time," advised Mablethorpe. "In fact, you may as well listen to me for a bit longer."

He exhaled a long cloud of cigar smoke, and proceeded:

"A man impersonates another man for one of three reasons. Firstly, to gain some fraudulent advantage—make money out of the game, in fact. I may say at once that I acquit you of any such intention."

"That's right, sir," murmured Jacob faintly.

"Secondly, in obedience to a curious but not altogether unnatural craving—the craving for fame, distinction, notoriety—anything, in fact, which will lift a man out of the ruck of his fellow-creatures and make him conspicuous for a moment. Men have been found willing to die for such a moment. I suppose you have never written to the police pleading guilty to a murder, have you?"

"No, sir."

"Ah! Well, I assure you lots of people do. It is a fact that after a murder of any importance has been committed, the difficulty of the authorities is not so much to find the guilty man, and hang him, as to avoid hanging some perfectly respectable citizen who insists that he did the deed and none other. It may seem strange that people should come and make bogus confessions; but they do, by the dozen. Why? Well, if there is one thing that galls a certain type of utterly undistinguished individual, it is the consciousness that the world at large has never heard of him, and never will. So he makes up his little mind to achieve immortality somehow—even if he has to invoke the assistance of Madame Tussaud. Of course that is an extreme way of putting it. Probably most of these self-confessed desperadoes do not expect to be convicted: after all, there is no evidence against them. What they really hope for is a couple of days in the public eye and a few really gratifying press-notices. After they are acquitted—that is, kicked out—they return home branded as celebrities, and live happily ever after. But you say you have never been taken that way?"

"No, sir."

"Good! Forgive me for talking so much, but I don't often encounter such an indulgent audience. Of course there is a milder variation of the disease. Did you, for instance, ever write to a Patent Medicine Company, informing them that you were once a nervous wreck, but that since consuming three bottles of their specific you are now fit to hang from the chandelier by your heels?"

"No, sir."

"Well, I assure you thousands of people do it. There is an impression that patent medicine testimonials are paid for by the proprietors. Stuff and nonsense! They simply pour in unsolicited, from people who probably never touched the stuff, but hope that their ungrammatical letter, accompanied by an unrecognizable portrait, will be published in the advertisement columns of the press. You see, Madame Tussaud's again—from a less ambitious angle! It's a queer world. But you say you have never done any of these things?"

"No, sir."

"Then that brings us to the third alternative. There is only one other reason why a man should endeavour to assume a personality which for some reason he regards as more desirable than his own, and that is to enable him to create an impression in some particular quarter. Of course it must be a temporary impression, because naturally he's bound to be found out if he goes on too long. Still he does it—and I rather think *you* have done it, my friend!"

Julius Mablethorpe abandoned his judgment seat, crossed to the sofa, sat heavily down upon it, and laid a gentle hand on Jacob Finch's shoulder.

"Now tell me all about her," he said.

And to this eccentric but tender father confessor, Jacob recounted the whole pitiful story of Faint Heart and his Fair Lady.

"I DON'T know what you must think of me, sir," he remarked miserably, when he had finished.

"There are two kinds of sin," announced Mablethorpe—"human and inhuman. The first kind can always be forgiven—and that's where you come in. If you had robbed an orphanage, or written a psycho-analytical novel, it would have been different."

"But I deliberately took your name, sir, and—"

"Don't you worry about that. It's not the first time it's happened. Why, a couple of years ago a friend of mine telegraphed to me from a Swiss hotel, to say that there was a fellow staying there who said he was me! Was he to have him arrested? I wired back and asked what the gentleman looked like, and how he was behaving himself. My friend replied: 'A most presentable person. He has a large stock of your novels with him, and is giving them away.' I sent a final wire: 'Encourage him to continue.'"

"It was very generous of you," said Jacob.

"Not at all: it was good business."

"But it was generous to let him off."

"Oh, one has to make allowances, you know. There is something about the air of foreign hotels, and indeed ocean liners, which gives a curious twist to the moral fibre for the time being. It makes people extraordinarily elastic in their conception of who and what they really are. They are separated for the moment from those who are in a position to contradict them, so they hurriedly avail themselves of the opportunity—the opportunity of a lifetime to many of them—to allow the ineradicable human craving for telling lies about one's self full play. That's all, I think. Go along and have dinner."

Jacob rose unsteadily to his feet.

"You—you forgive me, sir?" he asked humbly.

"Lord bless you, yes! I forgive you. But I'm going to make two conditions."

"Anything, sir! Anything!"

"In the first place, you must make a clean breast of it to the young lady. You need not tell her I am on board; in fact, I would rather you didn't tell anybody that. But tell her that you are not me."

"I will, sir; I will, indeed! I was going to, in any case. I have been so miserable about it. I will tell her tonight, and leave the ship at Alexandria. What was the other condition, sir?"

Mablethorpe's eyes twinkled.

"I am a retiring individual," he said. "You must take the chair for me at the Concert."

Jacob Finch's knees turned to water.

"But, sir—" he stammered.

"They are fair terms, I think," said Mablethorpe: "I have forgiven you, and granted you full permission to continue your impersonation of me until you leave the ship. You owe me something for that. Take the chair you shall!"

"I—I—have to make a speech. What shall I say?"

"I will write something out for you. Look in here after dinner for it. And see you deliver it nicely, because I am coming to listen to you. Now run off. By the way, will you forgive a personal suggestion?"

"Certainly, sir—anything!"

"As you are going to give an imitation of me, would you mind dressing the part a bit? For instance, I usually tie my evening ties myself, instead of wearing the extremely neat and symmetrical arrangement favoured by you. I can give you one when you come in for the speech—and tie it for you if necessary. *Au revoir!* I'm glad to feel that we understand one another."

"That's right—I mean, God bless you, sir!"

"I was so proud of you tonight," said Myra softly. "You speak as well as you write."

Once more they were sharing the boat deck with the moon. The Concert had been a great success: thanks to a moving appeal from the Chair a more than usually satisfactory sum had been collected for the Seamen's Orphanage. They reclined in their deck-chairs side by side, sharing a rug, with fingers intertwined.

Myra's testimonial evoked no direct response, but it gave Jacob what he had been groping for—a cue. He disengaged his cold fingers from those of his beloved, and rose to his feet.

"I am leaving the ship tomorrow," he said abruptly.

Myra caught her breath, and gazed up at him with suddenly dilated eyes.

"You are going to—*what?*" she asked.

"I am going to leave this ship tomorrow," repeated Jacob.

"But why? I—I—I hope you haven't had bad news, or anything."

"No. But I must leave."

"Tired of me already?" The girl laughed a little unsteadily, and avoided his gaze.

"For God's sake, don't joke about it."

Myra heard the agony in his voice, and looked up again quickly. Then she saw his face in the moonlight. Swiftly she extended a slim arm and drew him gently down.

"Will you tell me about it?" she asked.

He dropped into his seat again.

"Yes—I will. That is why we are here now. Don't look at me, please; just turn your head away and listen. I have something to say to you.

I am not Julius Mablethorpe at all. My name is Jacob Finch, and nothing else. Until six months ago I was a bank clerk in a little country town in Norfolk. Then an aunt died and left me some money. I've never been anywhere or seen anything in all my life, so I thought I would take a trip abroad. I went to Monte Carlo. I hated it. I came on this boat. I hated that, too. And then—then I saw you. I thought you were the most beautiful thing God ever made—especially your smile. When I got to know you, and you told me about yourself—your country place in Devonshire—the old family you belonged to—and—and the flocks of deer—and the terrace, and everything—I felt so miserable I didn't know what to do, you were so far above me. You see what I mean? I had no appearance, no accomplishments; nothing to impress a girl at all. I simply had to do something, to—to—get you to like me, even if it was only for a week. Then suddenly the chance—the temptation—came, when you said you admired people who could write, especially Julius Mablethorpe. It was all over in a flash. I was mad, I think. But it was my one chance to win your respect, and I seized it! . . .

"I never meant to tell you I loved you, though. I was trying that night to make a clean breast of everything. Instead, I—well, it just happened: Fate was too strong for me. And when you said that you— *you*—cared for me—well, I simply couldn't give you up right away. I had to have my happiness, if only for a few days of my life. So I have been acting a lie to you for more than a week. . . .

"Well, it's all over now: I have confessed. It's a relief, really, though it ends everything for me. Now you know why I leave the ship tomorrow. We shall not meet again, of course; our stations in life are so different: so I hope that, not having to see me, you will manage to forget this slight I have put upon you. I hope, too, you won't reproach me more than you can help. My punishment is about all I can bear already. You see, I am losing you. That's enough: don't add any words to it, if you don't mind. . . . That's all, I think. No, there's this. I am going to have a pretty bad time when I go away from you, but there's just one thing will keep me up. Do you know what that is? Remembrance! I have had my hour! I have been a liar, and an impostor, and a cad, and I have borrowed—stolen—something I had no right to; and I'm going to be punished for it. But I have had my hour! Nothing can ever take that away from me. Please say to me, if you will, that you won't grudge me that. Then I will take my leave and go below. I will be off the ship tomorrow before you come on deck." His voice grew husky. "Will you please say—what I asked?"

Their two heads were very close together now. The girl, with face still averted, lay motionless in her chair.

"Please say it," he whispered—"that you don't grudge me—that! Will you?"

Slowly she turned her face to him; and he saw her eyes were full of tears.

"My dear," she said, with a laugh that was mainly a sob, "I can't tell you how happy you've made me!"

"Happy! Why? How?"

Myra took his hand.

"Why? How? Don't you see, ever since you said you were the Mablethorpe man, I have felt that things were all wrong. I was so proud about it—but I was wretched underneath. You were too high up in the world for me, my dear. The fact is, I"—Jacob opened his mouth to offer an obvious protest—"I know! You are going to remind me about my county family, and my house in Devonshire, and the flock of deer (or was it covey?), and the terrace, and the tenants! Well, forget them, will you? They're a castle in the air of mine. In fact, I got them out of one of Mablethorpe's books! I live with my aunt in Highgate, and I work in an office in the city. I had influenza badly, and the Boss was very good about it, and sent me on this trip to pick up again. That's what I am, really. That's why I told you the other day that I was frightened of you. I was speaking the truth that time, all right. Besides, there is another thing that made me wretched. There was nothing I felt I could really *do* for you. You mustn't think a woman always wants to be a wife to a man: sometimes she wants to be his mother. That's what I wanted to be to you—you poor, sensitive, solitary thing! And for more than a week you have been cheating me out of that hope, you bad boy! But it's all right now. We are ourselves again, thank goodness!—just our two plain, ordinary little selves—and we love one another, and tomorrow Auntie and I are going straight back home with you when you land. You're my own Jacob: by the way, I'm going to call you Jack; and I'm your own—oh, there's one thing more! My name isn't Myra Greig at all: it's Molly Grigg. Call me Molly, will you?"

Jacob complied at once, with immense solemnity.

"You're quite sure you don't like Molly less than Myra, do you?" inquired Miss Grigg, with a slight inflexion of anxiety.

"I prefer her," replied Jacob. "She is more in my own class—on my level."

But Molly shook her head.

"You're worlds above me still," she said. "Look at the little speech you made at the Concert tonight! It was beautiful. So long as you can make up things like that, there's no need for you to pretend to be Julius Mablethorpe, or anybody else."

"Oh, that was just a flash-in-the-pan," replied Jacob modestly.

But Molly shook her head again.

"I don't agree with you. I agree with that big man with the grey hair who got up and seconded the vote of thanks to the Chair. He said that your speech would always linger in his memory as the most perfectly conceived and most happily phrased thing of its kind he'd ever listened to. What was his name, by the way?"

"Baggs, I think."

"Well, Baggs is a good judge. Anyhow, he knows how to read character. I like Baggs."

"So do I," said Jacob, with feeling.

"I like Mablethorpe, too. Of course he's only a name to us; but—well, I feel somehow that I have Mablethorpe to thank for you!"

"That's right," said Jacob.

But I am not so sure. Julius Mablethorpe and "Faint Heart" between them may have given Jacob his preposterous impulse, but I doubt if he would have obeyed it on land. The responsibility, in my opinion, rests with ocean air.

Meet Corliss Archer

F. HUGH HERBERT

Corliss Archer, aged fifteen and one half, is prac-
tically America's girl friend on stage, screen and
radio. Herein, the dog Moronica litters up the place
with puppies and Corliss writes her mother an ode
before returning to normalcy and the heckling of
one Dexter.

CORLISS ARCHER, aged fifteen and one half, was
losing an argument with her father (a somewhat rare occurrence) but
she was still in there pitching. Across the dining-room table she looked
at him soulfully with large, reproachful, melting brown eyes.

"Maternity," said Corliss profoundly, "is a beautiful and terrific
thing, and it shouldn't happen in the garage."

"Rubbish," said Mr. Archer amiably. "That's what the garage is for."

"But, Daddy," said Corliss, "Moronica *hates* the garage, and I've
already made a nest for her on the back porch where she knows and
loves every *smell*." Her voice sank to a seductive murmur. "You want
to make everything as cozy and easy as possible for our darling
Moronica, don't you?" she pleaded.

"No," said Mr. Archer firmly. "A thousand times no. Our back
porch has been used for every function from bridge teas to clambakes,
but I will *not* permit that fool dog to be confined there." He lit a cigar
and glanced across the dining-room table at his wife. "Don't you agree
with me, Janet?"

"Of course, dear," said Mrs. Archer, smiling. "And I told Corliss
not to argue about it, but *she* said that—"

"Mum, don't you dare tell him," Corliss interrupted, laughing.

"Go ahead, Janet," Mr. Archer urged. "She said *what?*"

"*She* said," Mrs. Archer declared, over Corliss' frantic protests,
"that you were a sentimental male and a complete pushover for any
emotional pleas and that she'd win you over to her side in five
minutes because you were always putty in her hands."

"A gross and vicious libel," Mr. Archer announced, "which I trust I have now scotched once and for all."

He looked into the smiling face of his pretty daughter and tweaked her ear affectionately. He was the first to recognize that there was more than a grain of truth in Corliss' boast.

Corliss moved her chair a little closer to her father's and patted his sleeve with a small, deeply tanned, daintily manicured hand.

"I also said that you were an angel and that I adored you," she murmured, batting her eyes demurely.

"A likely story," said Mr. Archer with a somewhat smug and satisfied smile.

Moronica, whose destiny had been under discussion, came waddling into the dining room. She was a large, fat, amiable Springer spaniel whose name derived from the fact that she was held by the Archers to be definitely moronic in mentality, and also from her habit of sitting with one huge, untidy ear draped over one eye in the well-known manner of Veronica Lake's hair-do.

Corliss instantly slid off her chair and, sitting on the floor, flung her arms around the dog lovingly.

"Moronica, darling," she crooned, "I did my best for you, honestly, you hideous, horrible beast—but I'm afraid you'll have to have your old puppies in the garage after all."

She remained on the floor rocking back and forth with the dog in her arms, while, in tones of the most cloying affection, she continued to murmur loving insults into her ear.

Mr. Archer also got up and, stooping down, fondled the dog for a few moments.

"Filthy old flea bag," he murmured. "Take her out and lock her up, Corliss."

"Yes, darling," said Mrs. Archer, "and do it right away—because you've got a lot of homework to do, and you're *not* going to the movies until you've done it."

"Golly," said Corliss, glancing at the clock, "I had no idea it was so late."

She got up off the floor and stretched herself slowly and gracefully, a form of calisthenics to which she was much addicted.

Louise, the Archers' maid, was clearing away the dishes. Louise was a privileged and outspoken character who had been with the Archers for twenty-two years.

"When you've quite finished admiring your reflection in that mirror, Corliss," said Louise bluntly, "I'll thank you to come and help me with the dishes."

Corliss flushed slightly. Louise was always noticing things that she wasn't supposed to notice.

"Okay, darling," said Corliss. "Don't be crabby now."

She snapped her fingers and whistled to Moronica who lay inert upon the carpet thumping her abridged stump of tail.

"Come *on*, you imbecile dog, you," Corliss urged.

"When are the puppies due, anyway?" Mr. Archer inquired.

"Oh, not for two or three days, Harry," said Mrs. Archer. "At least, that's what the vet said—but of course Corliss doesn't think he knows what he's talking about."

"Mum," said Corliss eagerly, "when the puppies *do* come, may we send a cable to Lenny?"

Lenny was Corliss' brother, now a lieutenant in the Army Air Corps, stationed in North Africa. Lenny was twenty, and, prior to the war, Corliss had frequently and passionately gone on record to the effect that Lenny was a severe pain in the neck. Since Pearl Harbor, however, when Lenny promptly went into the Army, Corliss had made a remarkable discovery. She had found out (a discovery which sometimes actually embarrassed her in the light of her previous sentiments) that you could love a brother almost as much as you loved your parents.

"Oh, Daddy, let's *do* send him a cable," Corliss insisted.

"Cables are quite expensive, Corliss," Mr. Archer reminded her.

"I know, Daddy, but please let's. I'll pay for it out of my allowance if you like. Lenny simply *adores* Moronica, and he'd be so thrilled. I bet he'd simply bomb the daylights out of Berlin or some place, just in her honor."

Mrs. Archer gave the traditional answer, hallowed by generations of mothers.

"We'll see, dear," she murmured.

Corliss walked over to her father, put slim arms around him, and strained him to her childishly.

"Angel," she cooed, *"make* her say yes."

Mr. Archer, who felt himself weakening, shoved her away, chuckling.

"Save that smooch," he advised, "for that unhappy youth next door. It doesn't cut any ice with me."

He brushed the soft dark hair out of her face and rubbed his knuckles against her smooth, cool young cheek. He knew that he lied in his teeth. It cut a lot of ice. Corliss could generally smooch him out of almost anything.

"Corliss," said Mrs. Archer firmly, "take Moronica out into the garage and then do what you're supposed to do." She got up from the table and walked to the door. "I'm going up to write to Lenny," she announced.

THE Archers' back porch (ruled out for Moronica's *accouchement*) was a large, cluttered, comfortably shabby room which had literally grown with the years. Originally just a deck with an awning, it had acquired, in the passage of time, a solid roof, four walls, a huge fireplace, innumerable closets, window seats and lockers, and, above all, a distinct personality.

The Archers loved the porch as much as they loved Moronica and spoke of it in not dissimilar terms. "A shambles of a room," was Mr. Archer's favorite description, but he always headed for the porch in preference to any other room in the house. "I *must* do something about that *ghastly* porch" was a phrase frequently heard on the lips of Mrs. Archer, but it was an empty phrase because she never did anything about it except live there, nor did she ever seriously intend to do anything about it.

In the course of its evolution the porch had seen service as a nursery (first for Lenny and then for Corliss); as a playroom when the children grew older; as a sewing room for Mrs. Archer; as a workshop while Lenny was going through high school; as auxiliary storeroom for Louise's preserves and for the second best china; as an office for Mr. Archer (he still had an old rolltop desk there which always stuck); and as the general repository for Corliss' many and varied "collections," ranging all the way from species of seaweed and shells through dolls of all nations, and china dogs, to an extensive gallery of Petty and Varga girls, clipped from *Esquire*, which now adorned practically all the available wall space.

Here in a comfortable armchair (long since demoted from the living room because of its shabbiness) Mr. Archer was now reading his evening paper while Corliss, her various chores accomplished, pecked away dutifully at her portable typewriter in the throes of her homework.

After a few minutes the clicking of the typewriter ceased and Corliss looked at her father speculatively.

"Daddy," she sighed, "put down your paper a sec—no, don't just wink at me over the top—put it right *down*."

Mr. Archer, a tractable parent, complied amiably.

"Well, what is it?" he inquired.

"Would you like to help me with my English Lit?" said Corliss eagerly, her manner that of one conferring a tremendous boon.

"In a word, no," said Mr. Archer, reaching for his paper again.

"Oh, come on, Daddy, be a sport," Corliss pleaded. "I have to write an essay, and I want it to be a wow, and if *you* help me, I know it'll simply *slay* 'em." She blew him an airy kiss. "I mean, you're so frightfully clever," she added.

"Subtle as a sledge hammer," Mr. Archer chuckled. "Ask your mother." He glanced around the room. "Where is she, anyway—still upstairs?"

"Uh-huh," said Corliss. "Did you want her for something, Daddy? Shall I go and get her?"

Mr. Archer blew out clouds of contented blue cigar smoke.

"No, it's not important," he said. "I just like to have her around so I can look at her. Attractive person, your mother. Very soothing to the eye."

Corliss wrinkled her nose at her father, smiling. She always found his fondness for saying nice things about her mother one of his most endearing traits.

"She's beautiful, Daddy," said Corliss gently. "And she's a darling, and that's why I want you to help me with this essay, because it's about *her*."

"In that case," said Mr. Archer, "I'll be happy to pitch in and help."

"Oh, that's swell," Corliss gloated. "I'll read you what I've got, so far, shall I?" She cleared her throat daintily. " 'My Mother,' " she intoned, " 'A Character Sketch by Corliss Archer.' "

There was a long pause during which Mr. Archer grunted approvingly.

"Well, go on," he suggested.

269

"Well," said Corliss, "that's as far as I've got."

"It's a magnificent opening," Mr. Archer chuckled. "A little master-piece in its way."

"Daddy, *please* don't be funny," said Corliss hastily, anxious to nip in the bud her father's well-known tendency to be facetious. "*Help* me. How can I begin?"

"Begin by describing her character," said Mr. Archer.

"Okay," said Corliss, her fingers poised over the keyboard. "What'll I say?"

"Are you writing this essay or am I?" Mr. Archer inquired.

"Well, *I* am, of course, Daddy—but you've known Mother so much longer than I have. How would *you* describe her?"

"That depends," said Mr. Archer, "on whether she'd recently muffed a little slam in no trumps, vulnerable, redoubled at a tenth of a cent."

"Yes, Daddy," Corliss sighed wearily, "that's *very* funny—but now please help me."

She took a bobby pin out of her hair and chewed it thoughtfully.

"You see, Daddy," she mused, "I want to say how perfectly super she is and all that, but I *don't* want to be mushy."

Mr. Archer nodded in sage endorsement of this resolution.

"How'd this be?" asked Corliss. "I scribbled it down in pencil, but I haven't typed it yet." She searched frantically among her papers. "Oh, yes. Here we are: 'Most children at some time or another are heartily ashamed of their parents for various reasons, but I am proud to say that my mother, at least, has never embarrassed me.' Do you like that, Daddy?"

"Very striking," said Mr. Archer, "but I don't know whether I like that 'at least.' Does that mean you've ever been heartily ashamed of me?"

"Why, of *course*, Daddy. *Oodles* of times," his daughter informed him blandly.

"Name one," Mr. Archer challenged her.

"I suppose," said Corliss, "you've forgotten the time you fell fast asleep during the music recital at school? I was so mortified I wanted to shrivel up and die."

"That was at least five years ago, baby," said Mr. Archer apologetically.

"But I still blush when I think of it," Corliss avowed. "You were sitting right next to my home-room teacher, too, and you snored."

"Rubbish!" said Mr. Archer airily. "I may have breathed heavily—but I *never* snore."

"You do, too," Corliss smiled. "Mother says so."

"And your mother's never caused you a blush, huh?"

"Nope," said Corliss, "never. I think she's perfect. I really do. I think she's super, don't you?"

Mr. Archer got up and walked over to close the door.

"Can you keep a secret?" he inquired in a hoarse whisper.

Corliss nodded eagerly.

"Promise not to tell your mother?" he insisted.

"Cross my heart," Corliss assured him.

Mr. Archer leaned over Corliss' chair and in the manner of a conspirator whispered into her ear.

"I think she's super, too," he said.

"Oh, Daddy, you're sweet," said Corliss. "All right, now, how'll we go on?"

Mr. Archer went back to his chair and settled himself comfortably.

"Well now, let's see," he murmured. "You could say how—you could enlarge upon her—you could describe how she—you could—good Lord, child, there's a million things you could say. Don't just sit there and grin at me."

"Daddy, were you very good in English Lit when you went to school?" Corliss inquired disingenuously.

"Certainly. I was terrific," said Mr. Archer. "Why?"

"Because you're not very helpful now," Corliss told him bluntly.

"Now you've wounded me to the quick," said Mr. Archer, "and I shall retire behind my newspaper, where I desire to remain *incommunicado*."

Mr. Archer, an attorney, enjoyed the use of such phrases, and Corliss, tolerantly, considered it a fairly harmless indulgence. She chewed on her bobby pin thoughtfully.

"Oh, *you*," she sighed. "Maybe I could choose the other theme. We have a choice of two."

"What's the other theme?" Mr. Archer asked.

"I started that one, too," said Corliss. "Where is it? Oh, yes, here we are." She rattled some papers noisily until she could see that she had Mr. Archer's attention. " 'My Father,' " she affected to read, " 'A Character Sketch by Corliss Archer.' "

"A splendid alternative," said Mr. Archer. "Then you can get

Mother to help you with that and leave me in peace to enjoy my paper."

"But, Daddy," Corliss' voice was all honey, "wouldn't you like to hear how I started the one about you?"

"Go ahead," said Mr. Archer, putting aside his newspaper.

Corliss held the paper in front of her, but across the top of the sheet she watched Mr. Archer covertly.

" 'My father is a remarkable man in many ways,' " she pretended to read glibly, " 'but unfortunately he has a warped sense of humor, which is often very trying to members of his family, who love him in spite of it.' " She lowered the sheet of paper and looked at him poker-faced.

"Pray continue," said Mr. Archer gravely.

"I'm kidding, Daddy," Corliss giggled. "I haven't written a word. I think you're super, too—but I decided to write about Mum. You know, ladies first and all that."

"Then *write* something," Mr. Archer counseled, "and when you've got something on paper, I'll be glad to read it and make constructive suggestions."

"Okay, Daddy," said Corliss happily. "I just had a wonderful idea, anyway."

She turned back to her typewriter and for several minutes the back porch hummed with industry. Then the noise of typing ceased and was succeeded by a metallic crunching as Corliss sought inspiration by chewing on her bobby pin.

"Daddy," said Corliss, "what rhymes with tenderness?"

"Huh?" said Mr. Archer. "Are you writing a poem or an essay?"

"I'm writing my theme," said Corliss, "only I want mine to be different from everybody else's, so I'm going to make it poetry. What rhymes with tenderness?"

"Blenderness," said Mr. Archer promptly.

"What?"

"Blenderness," Mr. Archer repeated gravely. "B-l-e-n-"

"There's no such word, Daddy."

"Make it a name, then," suggested Mr. Archer, grinning. "My mother is Mrs. Blenderness, and she is full of tenderness. Not only rhymes beautifully, but it scans, too."

"Yes, Daddy," Corliss sighed, her worst fears realized. "That's *excruciatingly* funny. But I'm really serious. Mother's so *swell*, and I want to write something simply *beautiful* about her."

Somewhat reluctantly Mr. Archer put down his paper again and gave the matter serious consideration.

"Well, let's see," he mumbled. "Tenderness, huh? Let's go through the alphabet—benderness, cenderness, denderness, genderness, henderness—couldn't you think of some easier word?" he asked a little testily.

"Well," Corliss conceded, "I could say 'love,' I guess, but I'd have to switch the whole line around."

"Be a darn sight easier to rhyme with, I can tell you that," Mr. Archer declared. "Dove, above, shove, glove—the possibilities are endless." ·

Corliss was staring raptly into space.

"Shh, don't interrupt me, Daddy," she implored. Suddenly she snapped her fingers. "I've got it," she announced. "I'm changing tenderness to solicitude."

She typed for a few moments and then surveyed the efforts of her composition with an almost breathless pride.

"Here's how it begins, Daddy," she announced. " 'When I think of my mother's eternal solicitude, my heart brims all over with tum-da-dum gratitude.' "

"*What* kind of gratitude?" Mr. Archer inquired.

"Oh, I just said tum-da-dum temporarily, to make it scan," said Corliss. "I need a word there that *sounds* like tum-da-dum. An adjective. Can you think of one, Daddy?"

"Words that sound like tum-da-dum don't grow on trees," said Mr. Archer judiciously. "Let's see now—tum-da-dum. Battleship? No. Tum-da-dum. Gasoline?"

"An *adjective*, Daddy," Corliss reminded him patiently.

"Ah yes, an adjective. Tum-da-dum." He smiled happily. "I've got it—infinite."

"Oh, that's swell," said Corliss. "Thanks, Daddy. That's wonderful."

"Delighted to've been of service," Mr. Archer murmured graciously. "Please feel free to call upon me at any time."

He lit a fresh cigar and picked up his paper.

"On the other hand," he added, "if you interrupt me again within the next ten minutes, I'm liable to swat you one."

"Don't worry, angel," Corliss purred soothingly, glancing up from her typing, "I'm hitting on all six now."

She paused to read what she had already written, and her voice became almost husky with awe.

"Golly," she said, "this poem's honestly going to be out of another world. I bet I'm a poet or something. I think when I've finished this one about Mother I'll write one about you, Daddy."

"You think I rate a poem, too?" Mr. Archer chuckled, highly gratified.

"Absolutely," said Corliss warmly. "Honestly, Daddy, if the gods had picked any other parents for me but you two, I'd've simply *refused* to be born."

"Oh, get along with you," said Mr. Archer. "I'll bet that's what you say to *all* your parents."

Louise came onto the porch to put away some things.

"Corliss," she announced, "your mother wants to see you upstairs right away."

"Okay, thanks," said Corliss.

She ripped her poem out of the typewriter and put it away carefully in the drawer of a bureau.

"Don't breathe a word about this, Daddy," she said. "I don't want Mum to see it until it's all finished. I want to surprise her."

She ran into the hall and looked up the stairs where Mrs. Archer was standing.

"What is it, Mum? Anything wrong?" Corliss inquired cheerfully, noting her mother's stern face as she ran up the stairs.

"There is indeed, Corliss," said Mrs. Archer. "I've just been inspecting your bedroom."

She opened the door of Corliss' room and pushed her daughter gently inside.

"Oh, golly," said Corliss, "it *is* in a bit of a mess, isn't it?"

"Oh, Corliss," Mrs. Archer sighed, "it's an absolute disgrace—just look at your things—flung every which way. And after all the things I've told you!"

"Well, Mum," said Corliss faintly aggrieved, "you just happened to choose a bad day, that's all. I was going to tidy all my things tomorrow."

In a grim, methodical manner Mrs. Archer opened closet doors, and pulled out drawers.

"You're going to tidy everything tonight, my child," she said. "Right *now*. And you're going to press your slacks and your tan skirt, too."

"But, Mum," Corliss wailed, "I haven't finished my homework yet."

"That's too bad," said Mrs. Archer. "And look at your mending—you haven't touched it! You're going to do that, too. *Now*."

"But, Mum," Corliss yelped, "that'll take simply hours."

"Yes, I'm sure it will," Mrs. Archer replied unfeelingly. "In fact, it had *better*."

"But, golly," said Corliss, "I can't possibly do it tonight. I mean, Mildred'll be along any moment for us to go to the movies."

Mrs. Archer shook her head.

"No movies for you tonight," she announced. "You'll have to tell Mildred that you can't go."

Not for the first time in her life, Corliss wished devoutly that her mother were as easy to handle as her father. Although she had very little hope that the device might succeed, Corliss swiftly added an effective tremolo to her voice.

"Mum," she said reproachfully, "you can't *do* that to me. You *wouldn't!* I swear that tomorrow I'll—"

Mrs. Archer cut her short.

"Corliss," she said, "I don't wish to hear another word. You'll do all the things you've neglected, right now. And then you'll finish your homework—and by then it'll be way past your bedtime."

"But, Mother," Corliss protested in anguished tones, "what'll Mildred *think*? I mean, golly, she knows I'm much too old to be punished."

Mrs. Archer was unable entirely to suppress a smile.

"Oh, no, you're not, darling," she said gently. "And it's your own fault. You've got to be taught somehow."

The front doorbell was ringing and Corliss clutched her mother's arm imploringly.

"Oh, golly," she babbled, "that's probably Mildred now. Mum, do I *have* to tell why I can't go? I mean, you don't insist on *humiliating* me in addition to punishing me, do you?"

Mrs. Archer kissed the tip of her daughter's nose.

"No," she said. "You can tell Mildred anything you like—but you're not going to any movie."

A plan whereby she might save face with her girl friend had already formulated in Corliss' active and resourceful mind.

"Okay, Mum," she said hurriedly, "then do me just one favor, would you, please?"

Mrs. Archer stepped out into the hall.

"What, for instance?" she inquired curiously.

"Just tell Mildred I'm up here in my room. Tell her to come up here and don't tell her *anything* else."

"All right, dear," Mrs. Archer agreed.

She went down the stairs into the hall where Louise was just admitting Mildred Ames.

Mildred was an attractive girl only a month older than Corliss and, ever since they had gone to kindergarten together, her inseparable companion.

"Hello, Louise. Evening, Mrs. Archer," Mildred greeted them gaily. "Is Corliss ready?"

Mrs. Archer glanced dubiously up the stairs.

"Well," she said slowly, mindful of her promise, "I'm not sure. I don't think she *is,* quite. She's in her room. Why don't you go on up?"

Mildred shook her head sadly.

"That girl," she announced, "is always late for everything. I'll dash up and tell her to make it snappy."

As familiar with the Archers' home as she was with her own, Mildred tore up the stairs three steps at a time and entered Corliss' bedroom without the formality of a knock.

She was somewhat surprised to find the room in darkness and to see Corliss stretched out on her bed.

"Jeepers," said Mildred, "what's the matter with *you?*"

"Oh, my dear," said Corliss in a weak, quavering voice, "I'm so sorry, but I have a *splitting* headache."

Mildred snapped on the light and walked slowly over toward the bed.

"Gosh, that's too bad," she said. "When did it come on?"

"It hit me all of a sudden," Corliss whispered.

"Golly, it must've done," Mildred declared. "You never said a word over the phone—and that wasn't over an hour ago."

She looked at her friend sympathetically and tried to feel her forehead, but Corliss gently waved her away.

"There's nothing more ghastly than an agonizing headache," she complained sadly.

"Have you taken anything for it?" Mildred inquired.

"Oh, my dear," said Corliss, "I know this headache of mine. *Nothing* helps it."

"When *I* have a headache," Mildred informed her, "my mother makes cold compresses for it with eau de cologne. Why don't you ask your mother to—"

Corliss sat up quickly and put her fingers to her lips.

"Shh—quiet!" she enjoined fiercely. "I don't want Mum to know I don't feel well."

"Why not?" Mildred inquired, faintly puzzled by this show of reticence.

"Because I hate to worry her," said Corliss virtuously. "You know how mothers are."

She lay prone again and closed her eyes as if in exquisite pain.

"Then I guess you won't feel like coming to the movies," said Mildred. "Gee, that's too bad, Corliss. It's a swell bill, too—Gary Cooper *and* Spencer Tracy."

"I'll prob'ly be feeling okay tomorrow," said Corliss hastily. "We'll go then."

"You're crazy," said Mildred calmly. "I haven't got a headache. *I'm* going tonight."

Corliss raised herself up on one elbow and looked reproachfully at her friend.

"And leave me here to suffer alone?" she yelped. "What's wrong with going tomorrow instead?"

"Those pictures won't be there tomorrow," Mildred announced, "and I wouldn't miss them for the world."

"Okay," said Corliss bitterly, "okay. You wouldn't care if a person died. A fine friend *you* are! Believe me, if *you* were sick in bed, *I* wouldn't go without *you*."

Mildred tinkled with faintly derisive laughter.

"Obviously not," she said, "because you happen to be broke and *I've* got the money to take us."

"Okay," Corliss sighed. "You win. Go ahead."

Mildred glanced at her wrist watch and decided that she had a few minutes to spare in which to visit with the invalid. She perched herself companionably on the side of the bed.

"Finish your homework yet?" she inquired.

"No."

"Which theme did you choose, Corliss? I did a pip on my mother."

"Oh, did you?" said Corliss coldly.

"Sure," said Mildred, scratching a shapely knee thoughtfully, "it's a cinch to write essays on your mother because mothers are so swell."

"Uh-huh," said Corliss, brooding.

Mildred developed her theme enthusiastically.

"I mean, they really are wonderful, don't you think so?" she gushed. "I mean, where would a person be without one?"

Corliss winced visibly. Mildred patted her arm in affectionate sympathy.

"What did you say in *your* essay, Corliss?" she inquired.

"I haven't quite made up my mind yet *what* to say," Corliss declared ominously.

"You mean you haven't even started?"

"Oh, I started all right," said Corliss, "but I think I started off wrong. In fact, I'm sure I did."

Mildred consulted her wrist watch again. It was a fairly recent present, and Corliss was of the opinion that Mildred consulted it far too often and far too ostentatiously.

"You're going to be late for the movies," said Corliss frigidly.

"Yes, I think I'll scram," said Mildred, rising. "I always hate to come in in the middle of Gary Cooper."

She leaned over the bed and kissed Corliss good-bye.

"So long, dear," she murmured. "I do hope you feel better."

Corliss waited a couple of minutes until she heard the front door slam and then, heaving a sigh of relief, she grimly surveyed the tasks assigned to her in her room.

These occupied her for slightly over an hour, during which time she brooded darkly over the perfidy of friends and the tyranny of mothers.

Having darned and put away the last pair of bobby socks, Corliss went downstairs and strolled onto the porch. Her mother and father glanced up from their game of gin rummy.

"Finished, dear?" Mrs. Archer inquired amiably.

Corliss looked at her mother coldly.

"Yes, Mother," she announced in a polite, martyred tone. "I've done every last thing I was told to do."

"I'm glad to hear it," said Mrs. Archer brightly and went on with her game.

Corliss gave vent to a deep, audible sigh and started rummaging among the magazines scattered on the couch.

"Daddy, have you seen the new *Esquire* lying around?" she inquired.

"It's on top of the radio," Mr. Archer grunted.

"Corliss," said Mrs. Archer, "before you settle down on the couch with that magazine, you've got your homework to finish."

"But, Mum—can't I just glance through it for a sec?" Corliss pleaded.

Mrs. Archer was absorbed in her cards and her answer was practically an automatic reflex action.

"When you have finished your homework—if there's still time."

"Honestly," Corliss complained tragically, " a person might as well be living in a jute mill."

"Yes, dear, I know," Mrs. Archer laughed. "You're terribly abused."

"Well, look, Mother," said Corliss, "may I at least go out and see if Moronica's all right?"

"You're not to waste time playing with that fool dog now," her mother promptly decreed. "You're to finish your homework and no more excuses."

Corliss sighed hopelessly. She retrieved her homework from the drawer in which she had secreted it and went back to her typewriter, scowling darkly. Then, in a determined manner, she inserted it into the roller and for several moments typed rapidly. Mrs. Archer glanced back over her shoulder with an approving smile.

"How quickly you're typing, dear," she said. "You're getting good speed."

Corliss met her mother's gaze, unsmilingly.

"I'm just exing things out," she said coldly.

"Want any further help on your theme for English Lit?" Mr. Archer volunteered.

"I don't think so, Daddy," Corliss answered significantly. "I have to make a lot of *drastic* changes first."

She squinted at her paper dubiously for a moment and then typed a few sentences.

"Daddy," said Corliss, "should cold-blooded have a hyphen?"

"I believe so," said Mr. Archer casually.

Corliss typed a little more and then paused for another interruption.

"Daddy," she inquired, "are there two r's in tyranny?"

"No, only one," said Mr. Archer.

He put down his cards and looked at his daughter quizzically.

"Did you say tyranny?" he inquired.

Corliss nodded soberly.

"Could it be," Mr. Archer chuckled, "that you are still working on the same theme?"

"Yes," said Corliss icily, "but from a different viewpoint."

She ripped the poem out of the typewriter, inserted a fresh sheet and started typing anew.

Absorbed in her composition, Corliss scarcely heard the familiar crunching footsteps on the gravel in the backyard which heralded the approach of a visitor.

This visitor, who came barging onto the porch unbidden, was Dexter Franklin who lived next door. It was not without sound reason that Mr. Archer had previously referred to Dexter as an unhappy youth. Dexter was a gangling, amiable boy just short of seventeen whose years of adolescence were being sorely complicated by the fact that he adored Corliss with all his large and extremely vulnerable heart —a circumstance of which Corliss was pleasantly aware and of which she took full advantage. She adored Dexter too, but, being of the feminine gender, was far more shrewd and reticent about her emotions. It was Corliss' pleasure, particularly during the last few years, to harass, bewilder and humiliate the adoring Dexter whenever she deemed such a course advisable—which was pretty often.

Dexter's voice had recently changed, and he spoke now habitually in a rasping, cheerful croak.

"Hi, everybody," said Dexter by way of greeting.

Corliss, without interrupting her typing, replied with an observation that was not inept.

"You look like something out of *Tobacco Road*," she observed, and was gratified to note that Dexter blushed and that Mr. Archer suppressed a chuckle.

Dexter's attire consisted of a soiled, frayed garment designed as a shirt, but now doing business as a jacket, its original four buttons reduced to one; his trousers, which it was somewhat inconceivable to believe had once been white ducks, were upheld precariously by a sorry piece of rope; and his unusually large feet were covered by a pair of sneakers in a deplorable state of disintegration. His extremely soiled hands and the moisture which glistened on his face suggested that he had probably been engaged in strenuous manual labor.

"Mrs. Archer," said Dexter, "Mother sent me over to find out if you and Mr. Archer would like to go over and knock off a few rubbers of bridge."

Mr. Archer, a bridge addict, rose promptly to his feet.

"Sounds reasonable, Janet," he urged hopefully. "Let's go over and take 'em to the cleaners."

"All right, dear," said Mrs. Archer amenably.

She paused by Corliss' desk.

"Darling," she said gently, "when you've finished your homework, turn down the lights and go to bed."

"I'll be finished very soon," said Corliss. "Can't I stay up a little while?"

"Gee whiz, it's Friday, Mrs. Archer," Dexter hastily interposed. "There's no school tomorrow. Let her stay up till—"

"You keep out of this, Dexter," Mrs. Archer interrupted, laughing.

In moments of domestic crisis Dexter almost invariably went to bat for Corliss, often cheerfully assuming blame for crimes of which he was quite innocent, if thereby he could save Corliss from just retribution.

Dexter flung himself noisily and untidily onto a couch, his legs draped over the back.

"Holy cow," said Dexter, "I don't think people should be *too* strict with people."

"Oh, come on, Janet," said Mr. Archer tolerantly. "Give the kid a break."

"Well, all right," Mrs. Archer conceded. "You can stay up until eleven, Corliss."

Ignoring her mother, from whom this handsome concession had been obtained, Corliss looked at her father and accorded him a dazzling smile of gratitude.

"Thank you, thank you, Daddy," she purred. "You're a *lamb*."

Mr. Archer held open the screen door for his wife, and, behind her back, winked at his daughter.

"Think nothing of it, Corliss," he said. "I'm opposed to tyranny in any form."

"Which is more than *some* people are," said Corliss darkly. She caught her father's eye again and beamed at him fondly. "Here, Daddy," she cooed, throwing him a kiss daintily. "Catch."

"Is it all right with you if I share this kiss with your mother?" he inquired, grinning.

Corliss did not even look up from her typing.

"It's out of my hands now," she replied indifferently.

"I'm afraid I'm not very popular with Corliss at the moment," Mrs. Archer laughed. "Come on, Harry, let's go."

The screen door slammed behind them. Dexter, still horizontal on the couch, moved one of his feet to permit a better view of Corliss.

"Why are you scowling like that?" he inquired. "Are you mad at me again?"

"No," said Corliss, still typing, "not at you."

"Gee whiz, that's a change," said Dexter, cheered by this information. "Who're you mad at?"

"Mother," said Corliss.

Dexter pulled himself up to a sitting posture.

"Is that why you didn't kiss her good-night?" he asked.

"Yes," said Corliss. "I don't believe in being a hypocrite."

"I don't think that's right," said Dexter. "I always kiss *my* mother good-night, even when I think she's been acting like a heel."

Corliss was not impressed by this evidence of Dexter's magnanimity.

"That just goes to show you haven't any character whatsoever," she declared.

She ripped the sheet of paper out of the typewriter and read over what she had written carefully.

"I finished that old theme," said Corliss finally. "Would you like to hear what I wrote, Dexter?"

"Not particularly," said Dexter honestly. "But you're obviously itching to read it, so go ahead."

"'My Mother, A Character Sketch by Corliss Archer,'" Corliss read. "'Cold-blooded intolerance and lack of understanding on the part of parents causes more unhappiness in the world than all the drinking, gambling and other things you could think of.'"

"Holy cow," said Dexter. "You can't—"

"Shut up," Corliss enjoined crisply, "and don't interrupt. New paragraph. 'My mother, who has many fine qualities, is addicted to this vice.'" She glanced at Dexter, not without pride, to observe the effect of this blistering indictment.

"Holy cow," said Dexter, "that's a terrible thing to say. You can't accuse your mother of a vice. I don't believe you wrote it. You're making it up."

Corliss handed him the sheet of paper.

"Read it yourself," she suggested.

Dexter read the theme, his lips moving as he mouthed the words.

"Hey," said Dexter, "vice isn't spelled with an 's.'"

"It isn't?" said Corliss skeptically.

"No, Corliss. With an 's' it means a thing you hold things down with—you know, a thing that grips and you can't escape from."

"That's all right," said Corliss, "let it stand. That fits my mother, too."

"Do you realize," said Dexter, "that these themes are going to be read out in English Lit?"

"I'm well aware of that fact," said Corliss with dignity.

"Holy cow," said Dexter, "you want everyone at school to think your mother has vices?"

"Oh, give it to me," said Corliss, snatching the paper away from him. "Trouble with you is you don't know a good theme when you see one."

"Well," said Dexter, "if you want *my* opinion, *I* think your theme *stinks.*"

"I'll thank you," said Corliss frigidly, "to keep your silly opinions to yourself."

She marched across the porch to the kitchen.

"I'm going to fix some warm milk for Moronica," she announced over her shoulder.

Dexter, who had been promised one of Moronica's puppies, followed Corliss into the kitchen to help.

"Don't forget now," he insisted, "I get the biggest male."

"You'll get whatever I give you," said Corliss, busy over the stove. "Moronica's my dog and her puppies are mine, too."

"Okay, okay," said Dexter soothingly, "but don't try to palm off a runt on me—or worse yet, a female."

"Just for that crack," Corliss bristled, "I may decide not to give you a puppy at all."

She poured the warm milk into a bowl and walked to the door.

"All right, Dexter, you can at least make yourself useful," she snapped. "Bring the flashlight."

With Dexter at her heels, she shoved open the back door and, carefully carrying the bowl of milk, walked down the driveway to the garage.

There was no sign of Moronica in the dusty, cluttered garage.

"That's funny," said Corliss after whistling a couple of times. "The idiot dog's usually waiting at the door wagging her silly tail. I wonder—"

Dexter suddenly gripped her by the arm.

"Shut up," he whispered fiercely. "Listen."

In the rear of the garage from Moronica's dog-house, which she usually spurned, came a series of faint, unmistakable whimperings.

"Oh, golly," Corliss squealed excitedly. "I bet she's had her puppies. I've said all along they were due today."

Frantic with haste, she wedged herself past the Archer sedan and struggled toward the rear of the garage.

"Oh, Dexter, quick! Bring the flashlight," she cried.

Cautiously the beam of the flashlight probed the dark interior of the dog-house.

"Oh, golly," said Corliss deeply awed, "she *has* had them. Oh, Dexter, look. Aren't they *sweet?*"

Moronica gave a short, strange, warning bark.

"Moronica, baby," Corliss crooned, "don't be scared, darling. We won't hurt them. Oh, Dexter, look—aren't they simply adorable?"

She squatted down by the dog-house and cautiously and tenderly patted Moronica's flanks.

"Hey," said Dexter, "how many are there? Why've you turned off the flashlight?"

"Because it's too bright for their poor little eyes, dopey," said Corliss.

"Holy cow," said Dexter, "their eyes aren't even open yet. Don't you even know that? The light won't hurt 'em, Corliss. Honestly. I want to see how many there are."

He took the flashlight from Corliss and, shoving her out of the way, attempted to take a preliminary census. Corliss' voice was hushed with wonder and awe.

"Oh, look at that little one with the black spot!" she whispered.

"Shut up, will you?" Dexter rasped. "Now I've lost count. One—two—three—four—five—six."

"She's sort of lying on top of another one," said Corliss. "That makes seven."

Dexter appeared to be on the verge of crawling into the dog-house. "I think she might be crushing that little one," he said. "I better—" Corliss yanked him away peremptorily.

"Don't touch them," she ordered. "It's very bad for them. Then they smell of humans and the mother eats 'em."

"Oh, don't be a drip," said Dexter.

He reached into the dog-house and picked up a puppy.

"Dexter Franklin," Corliss ordered in shrill, imperative tones, "put that puppy down at once!"

"Well, wait a sec," Dexter protested. "I just want to see if it's a male."

"Never mind now," Corliss stormed. "This is no time to bother about sex. Put it down."

Dexter deemed it prudent to obey.

Enchanted, the two youngsters kneeled by the entrance to the dog-house.

"Gee whiz," said Dexter, "they look like guinea pigs, don't they?"

"For heaven's sake," said Corliss, "haven't you any tact, Dexter? That's a fine thing to say when a mother can hear."

"You're crazy," said Dexter. "You act as if Moronica could really understand."

"She's a mother," said Corliss comprehensively, "and she understands everything."

She watched Moronica and her puppies and there was a strange little lump in her throat.

"Oh, Dexter, look," she sighed. "Look how she's washing that little one's ears! Oh, isn't it the most beautiful and touching thing you ever saw?"

"Washing a puppy's ears isn't very touching, I don't think," Dexter averred. "It's just natural."

He gazed into the dog-house, trying to determine which of the puppies was the largest and huskiest. Presently he became conscious of the fact that Corliss was sniffing a little.

"You gotta cold?" he inquired solicitously.

"No," said Corliss in a strange little choked voice.

She turned her head away. Puzzled, Dexter switched the flashlight right into her face. He was distressed to notice that her eyes were full of tears.

"Gee whiz, Corliss," said Dexter. "Are you crying?"

"Uh-huh," Corliss sobbed, "a little."

"What for?"

Corliss sniffed noisily and wiped her eyes with the sleeve of her sweater.

"The way she licks them is so beautiful," she said.

"Are you crying because she licks their ears, for goodness' sakes?" Dexter inquired, somewhat baffled by this essentially feminine reaction.

Corliss shook her head.

"There's no use explaining, Dexter," she said. "You'd never understand because you're not a woman and a mother."

"Well, nor are you," said Dexter. "You're only a little over fifteen."

"Nevertheless," said Corliss, "I still know how women and mothers feel." She choked a little again. "It's *beautiful*."

Tact was never one of Dexter's outstanding characteristics.

"Oh, yeah," he said derisively. "What was that you just wrote: 'My mother, who has many fine qualities, or something, is addicted to this vice'?"

The harsh reminder now brought on a real flood of tears.

"Oh, Dexter," Corliss sobbed, "why did you have to bring it up? I feel like a swine."

"That's just how you *oughta* feel," said Dexter uncompromisingly.

"Mum was quite right to keep me from the movie," said Corliss between sobs. "My room was like nothing human."

She scrambled to her feet and did some rapid thinking.

"You go and tell the others about the puppies, Dexter," she said. "I'm going to dash back to the house. I've got something to do."

She raced down the driveway, tore onto the porch and, in a determined fashion, sat herself down in front of her typewriter.

She was still pecking away dutifully when, about half an hour later, her parents returned.

"Hello, baby," said Mr. Archer. "How come you were able to tear yourself away from the puppies? We just saw them."

"I hadn't quite finished my theme," said Corliss.

"They're *so* sweet, darling," said Mrs. Archer. She stood by Corliss' chair and ran gentle fingers through the soft, silky hair. "You can run along out, dear," she said understandingly. "Your homework can wait, under these special circumstances."

"Oh, no, Mum, it can't," said Corliss. "I've just *got* to finish it."

From the garden came Dexter's raucous voice.

"Hey, Mr. Archer," he yelled, "do you suppose I could borrow your meat scales?"

"What the devil for?" said Mr. Archer, peering out into the garden.

Dexter appeared briefly and breathlessly on the steps of the porch.

"I want to weigh the puppies and see which is the heaviest," said Dexter. "If you want healthy puppies, you've gotta keep statistics on 'em."

"Daddy," Corliss implored, "*please* go out there and see that he doesn't *touch* the puppies."

"All right, Corliss," said Mr. Archer amiably.

The assignment was not distasteful to him. He rather wanted to have another look at the puppies himself.

Mrs. Archer settled herself comfortably on the couch and took out her knitting. She was a little puzzled by Corliss' sudden devotion to industry. Normally, she mused, it would have taken dynamite to pry the child away from the puppies.

Presently Corliss took her theme out of the typewriter and walked over to the couch.

"I've finished, Mother," she said gently.

"That's good, dear," said Mrs. Archer, absorbed in her knitting. "Read it to me."

For several moments her needles clicked comfortably.

"Mum," said Corliss in a very small voice, "would you mind taking that knitting off your lap for a sec?"

"Why, dear?" Mrs. Archer asked, looking up smiling.

Corliss was very pale and her lip was trembling childishly.

"Because I'd like to sit there," said Corliss almost shyly. "If you don't mind."

Puzzled, Mrs. Archer put her knitting aside quickly and pulled Corliss onto her lap. Corliss buried her face in her mother's neck and sobbed openly.

"Why, darling," said Mrs. Archer, "what's the matter?"

She held comforting arms around her daughter until the sobs died down into tearful sniffs. Silently, Mrs. Archer offered Corliss a handkerchief.

"There now—comfy?" she inquired.

"Uh-huh," Corliss sighed contentedly.

"I was beginning to be afraid you were getting too big to sit on my lap," said Mrs. Archer.

Corliss blew her nose vigorously.

"Oh, Mum—I'm such a little swine," she said. "I feel simply awful."

"You're a little dope," Mrs. Archer smiled.

"I let you go out this evening," said Corliss, her voice dripping with self-reproach, "without kissing you good-night."

"I know," Mrs. Archer nodded. "You were simply furious with me."

"Mum, do you think I'm horrible?" Corliss inquired anxiously.

Mrs. Archer deftly fixed a bobby pin in Corliss' hair.

"You're very untidy," she said lightly. "But outside of that, I rather like you."

Corliss rubbed a soft, cool cheek against her mother's chin.

"Oh, Mum, you're so nice," she said. "I adore you."

"That's good," Mrs. Archer laughed. "You loathed me cordially when I stopped you from going to the movies with Mildred."

Corliss was now sufficiently composed to discuss the matter less emotionally.

"You know what made me change my mind, Mum?" she asked.

"What?" said Mrs. Archer.

"Moronica and her puppies," said Corliss. "Oh, Mum, she's so wonderful with them." She heaved a deep but not unhappy sigh. "I think all mothers are simply super and I don't know how they stand their horrible children. I really don't."

"Oh, sometimes the children aren't so awful," Mrs. Archer laughed. "Some of them have their points."

"Mum, here's my theme," said Corliss. "Will you read it?"

"You read it to me," Mrs. Archer suggested.

"Okay," said Corliss. "Only I won't stand up like we do in Public Speaking on account of I'm much too comfy on your lap." She wriggled for a few moments, frowning at the paper. "It's called 'My Mother, An Ode by Corliss Archer,'" she announced, "and this is the ode:

"*When I think of my mother's eternal solicitude*
My heart brims all over with infinite gratitude.

And when I reflect on the depths of her love
I yearn for a chance my devotion to prove.
Of justice and fairness she's always the soul
And maternal perfection is ever her goal.
She's an angel, a darling, and her maiden name was Cooper
Which happens to be perfect because it rhymes with super.' ''

Having finished, she looked into her mother's face eagerly.
"Darling," Mrs. Archer smiled, "that's very sweet."
Corliss hugged her mother happily.
"Not nearly sweet enough," she whispered, "for you."
Frantic, skidding footsteps on the gravel in the garden once more advertised the approach of Dexter.
"Hey, Corliss," he screamed, "you know what? There are five males and two females. Isn't that terrific?"
Corliss scrambled off her mother's lap.
"Dexter Franklin," she yelled as she dashed off the porch, "if you touch those puppies again, I'll *brain* you!"
With a gentle, contented smile, Mrs. Archer picked up her knitting again. Corliss was back to normalcy.

Mr. Chips Meets a Star

JAMES HILTON

When the old British schoolmaster, Mr. Chips, mistakes a handsome young movie star for one of his boys, both he and the star have a glimpse of a world strange to them.

"COMING OUT of the Royal Hotel the other day, who should I espy but Randolph Renny . . ." wrote Miss Lydia Jones ambiguously, ungrammatically, but in substance correctly. For it really was Randolph Renny himself, and by identifying him she made the scoop of a lifetime. A pretty long lifetime, too, for she had been doing an unpaid-for social gossip column for the Brookfield *Gazette* for over thirty years. Prim and spinsterish, she knew the exact difference (if any) between a pianoforte solo "tastefully rendered" and one "brilliantly performed"; and three times a year, at the Brookfield School end-of-term concert, she sat in the front row, notebook and pencil in hand, fully aware of herself as Brookfield's critical and social arbiter.

She had occupied this position so long that only one person could clearly remember her as an eager, ambitious girl, hopeful about her first and never-published novel; and that person was Chips. She had been a friend of his wife's, which was something he could never forget. As she grew primmer and more spinsterish with the years, he sometimes meditated on the strange chemistry of the sexes that so often enabled a man to ripen with age where a woman must only wither; and when she withered out of her fifties into her sixties and Brookfield began to laugh at her and the *Gazette* to print fewer and fewer of her contributions, then Chips' attitude became even more gentle and benevolent. Poor old thing—she meant no harm, and she loved her work. He would always stop for a chat if he met her in the village, and he only smiled when, from time to time, she referred to him as "the doyan (sic) of the Brookfield staff."

Indeed, it was Chips who had given her the scoop about Randolph Renny—a scoop which many a bright young man from Fleet Street would have paid good money for. But Chips chose to give it to Miss Lydia Jones, of the Brookfield *Gazette,* and Miss Jones, faced with something far outside her customary world of whist drives and village concerts, could only deal with it in the way she dealt with most things . . . that is to say, ambiguously, ungrammatically, but in substance correctly.

THIS IS HOW it had all happened. One August evening Chips had been returning by train from London to Brookfield.

The school was on summer vacation, and though he had long since retired from active teaching work (he was over eighty), he still experienced, during vacations, a sense of being on holiday himself. Traveling back after an enjoyable week end with friends, he had been somewhat startled by the invasion of his compartment at the last moment by a youngish, almost excessively handsome, and certainly excessively well-dressed fellow who slumped down into a corner seat breathlessly, mopped his forehead with a silk handkerchief, and absurdly overtipped a porter who threw in after him some items of very rich and strange luggage.

Now it was Chips' boast that he never forgot the faces of his old boys, that somehow their growing up into manhood made no difference to his powers of recognition. That was mainly true; but as he grew older he was apt to err in the other direction, to recognize too often, to accost a stranger by name and receive the bewildered reply that there must be some mistake, the stranger had never been to Brookfield School, had never even heard of Brookfield, and so on. And on such occasions, a little sad and perhaps also a little bothered, Chips would mumble an apology and wonder why it was that his memory could see so much more clearly than his eyes.

And now, in the train, memory tempted him again—this time with the vision of a good-looking twelve-year-old who had almost established a record for the minimum amount of Latin learnable during a year in Chips' classical form. So he leaned forward after a few moments and said to the still breathless intruder: "Well—umph—Renny . . . how are you?"

The young man looked up with a rather scared expression. "I beg you, sir, not to give me away . . ."

"Give you away . . . umph . . ." Some joke, obviously—Renny had always been one for jokes. "What is it you have been up to this time—umph?"

"I'm trying to get away from the crowd—I thought I'd actually succeeded. . . . I chose this compartment because—if you'll pardon me for saying it—I noticed you were reading the paper through double spectacles—so I guessed—I hoped—"

"I may be—umph—a little shortsighted, Renny—but I assure you —umph—I never forget a Brookfield face. . . ."

"Brookfield? Why, that's where I'm going to. What sort of a place is it?"

CHIPS looked astonished. Surely this was carrying a joke too far. "Much the same—umph—as when you were there fifteen years ago, my boy."

Then the young man looked astonished. "I? . . . But—but I've never been there before in my life—this is my first visit to England, even . . . I don't understand."

Neither did Chips understand, though he certainly—now that the other had suggested it—detected an accent from across the sea. He said: "But—your name—it's Charles Renny . . . isn't it?"

"Renny, yes, but not Charles . . . Randolph—that's my name—Randolph Renny. I thought you recognized me."

"I thought so too. I apologize."

"Well, I hope you won't give me away now that I've told you."

"Give you away? I—umph—I don't know what you're driving at."

"My being Randolph Renny—that's what I mean. I'm traveling incognito."

"Mr. Renny, I still don't understand."

"You mean you don't recognize my name?"

"I fear not. . . . My own name—since you have been good enough to introduce yourself—is Chipping."

"Well, Mr. Chipping . . . you've never heard of me! You must be the only person on this train who hasn't seen some of my pictures."

"Pictures? You are an artist?"

"I should hope so. . . . Oh, I see—you mean a painter? . . . No, not that sort of artist. I'm in the movies. Don't you ever go to the cinema?"

Chips paused; then he answered, contemplatively: "I went on one occasion only—umph—and that was ten years ago. I am given to understand—umph—that there have been certain improvements since then . . . but the—umph—poster advertising outside has never—umph—tempted me to discover how far that is true."

Renny laughed. "So that's why you've never heard my name? Wouldn't I like to show you round Hollywood! . . . I suppose you're not interested in acting?"

"Indeed, yes. In my young days I was a great admirer of Henry Irving and Forbes Robertson and—umph—Sarah Bernhardt—and the immortal Duse—"

"I guess none of them ever got three thousand fan letters a week—as I do."

"*Fan* letters?"

"Letters from admirers—total strangers—all over the world—who write to me."

Chips was bewildered. "You mean—umph—you have to read three thousand letters a week?"

"Well, I don't read 'em. But my secretary counts 'em."

"Dear me—umph—how extraordinary. . . ." And after a little pause for thought, Chips added: "You know, Mr. Renny, I feel—

umph—somewhat in the mood of the late Lord Balfour when he was taken to see the sights of New York. He was shown the—umph—I think it is called the Riston Building—and when—umph—the boast was made to him that it was completely fireproof, all he could reply was—'What a pity!'"

"Good! I'll remember that one. Tell me something about this place Brookfield."

"It's just a small English village. A pleasant place, I have always thought."

"You know it well?"

"Yes, I think I can say I do. But why—if I may ask—are you going there?"

"Darned if I know myself. Matter of fact, it's my publicity man's idea, not mine. Fellow named McElvie—smart man. . . . You see, Mr. Chipping, your English public—bless their hearts!—has fussed over me so much during the last few weeks that I'm all in—gets on your nerves after a time—signing autographs and being mobbed everywhere. . . . So I said to McElvie, 'I'm going to take a real rest cure, get away to some little place and hide myself, travel incognito . . . just some little place in the country—must be lots of places like that in England?' . . . And then McElvie suddenly had one of his bright ideas. You see, I was born in Brooklyn, so he looks it up and finds there isn't a Brooklyn in England, but there's a Brookfield. Sort of sentimental association . . . you see?"

"I see," answered Chips, without seeing at all. He could not really understand why a man born in Brooklyn should have a sentimental desire to visit Brookfield; he could not understand why letters should be counted instead of read; he could not understand why a man who wished to avoid publicity should travel around with the kind of luggage that would rivet the attention of every fellow traveler and railway porter. These things were mysteries. But he said, with a final attempt to discover what manner of man this Randolph Renny might be: "In my young days we used—umph—to classify actors into two kinds— tragedians and comedians. Which kind are you, Mr. Renny?"

"Oh, a hero, you know—romantic hero. Fact is . . . I guess it sounds stupid, but I can't help it. . . . I've sometimes been labeled the world's greatest lover."

Chips raised his eyebrows.

293

THUS they talked till the train arrived at Brookfield, by which time Chips had grown rather to like the elegant strange young man who seemed to have acquired the most fantastic renown by means of the most fantastic behavior. For Chips, listening to Renny's descriptions of Hollywood life, could not liken it to anything he had ever experienced or read about. For instance, Renny had a son, and in Hollywood, so he said; the boy was taken to and from school every day in a limousine accompanied by an armed bodyguard—the reason being that Renny had received threatening letters from kidnapers. "To tell you the truth, Mr. Chipping, I almost thought of sending him to a school in England. D'you know of any school?"

"Umph," replied Chips, thinking the matter over—or rather, not needing to think the matter over. "There is a school at Brookfield."

"A good school?"

"Well, I have—umph—some reason—to believe so."

"You were educated there yourself?"

Chips answered, with a slow chuckle: "That—umph—is a matter of opinion. But I rather imagine I have picked up a little knowledge there during—umph—the past half century or so. . . ."

By such exchanges of question and answer Chips and Hollywood's ace film star came to know each other and each to marvel at the strange world that the other inhabited. It was on Chips' advice that Renny tore some of the labels off his luggage and wrapped up his Fifth Avenue hatbox in brown paper and did a few other simple things to frustrate the publicity he was apparently fleeing from. And at the Royal Hotel (still taking Chips' advice) he registered as plain Mr. Read, of London.

A FEW days later he rang up Chips on the telephone, said he was feeling a little bored, and suggested a further meeting. Chips asked him to tea at his rooms opposite the school, and afterward showed him over the school buildings. Renny was horrified at the primitiveness of the school bathrooms, and was still more horrified when Chips told him they had just been modernized. But he was pleased and relieved when Chips told him that there had not been a single case of kidnaping at Brookfield for the past three hundred years.

"Before that—umph—I cannot definitely say," added Chips. "There were very disturbed times—we had a headmaster hanged during the sixteenth century for preaching the wrong kind of sermon—yes—umph—we have had disturbed times, Mr. Renny."

"You talk about them, sir, as if they were only yesterday."

"So they were," replied Chips, "in the history of England. And Brookfield is a part of that."

"And you're a part of Brookfield."

"I should like to think so," answered Chips, pouring himself tea.

The two men met again, several times. One afternoon they lazed in deck chairs on the deserted school playing fields; another day Chips took Renny to the local parish church, showed him the points of historic interest in it, and introduced him to the verger and the vicar as a visiting American. Renny seemed surprised that neither recognized him, and uttered a word of warning afterward: "You know, Mr. Chipping, you're taking a big chance showing me round like that."

"No," replied Chips; "I think not. There are—umph—quite a number of people in England who—umph—have never heard of you, Mr. Renny. The vicar here, for instance, is much more familiar with the personalities of Rome during the age of Diocletian—he has written several books on the subject . . . while our verger is so passionately devoted to the cultivation of roses that—umph—I doubt if he ever goes to the cinema at all. . . . So I think you may feel quite safe in Brookfield—nobody will annoy or molest you."

But after another few days had passed and there had been other meetings, a dark suspicion began to enter Chips' mind. Renny looked much better for his rest cure; idle days in sunshine and fresh air had soothed the tired nerves of an idol whose pedestal too often revealed him as merely a target. All the same, there was this dark suspicion—a suspicion that suggested itself most markedly whenever the two men walked about the streets of Brookfield. Just this—that though Renny was doubtless sincere in wanting to get away from crowds of autograph-hunting admirers, he did not altogether relish the ease with which in Brookfield he was doing so. There were moments when, perhaps, the success of his incognito peeved him.

It would have been truly awful if a mob of girls had torn the clothes off his back (they had done this several times in America), but when they didn't, then . . . well, there were moments when Renny's attitude might almost have been diagnosed as: Why the hell don't they try to, anyway . . . ?

All of which came to a head in the sudden appearance of McElvie on the scene. This wiry little Scots-American arrived in Brookfield like a human tornado, expressed himself delighted with the improvements in Renny's health, demanded to meet the old gentleman with whom he had been spending so much time, wrung Chips' hand effusively, and opined (gazing across the road at the school buildings) that it certainly looked "a swell joint."

"And see," he added, taking Renny and Chips by the arm and drawing them affectionately together. "I've got a swell idea, too. . . . I'll work up a lot of phooey in the papers about your disappearance . . . 'Where is Randolph Renny?'—'Has anybody seen him?'—'He's hiding somewhere—where is it?'—you know the sort of thing . . . and then, when all the excitement's just boiling over, we'll discover you here . . . spending a vacation with the old professor. . . ."

"I'm not a professor. . . ." protested Chips, feebly.

"Aw, it's the same thing . . . and you knew Irving, too . . . and Forbes Robertson . . . Sarah Bernhardt . . . the immortal Dewser . . ."

"I didn't know them," protested Chips still feebly. "I only saw them act."

"Aw, what does that matter . . . after all, you saw 'em and you're old enough to have known the whole bunch of 'em . . . they gave you tips about acting—and you took in what they said—and now you pass it all on to Renny here. . . . Oh, boy, what an idea—handing on the great tradition—Randolph Renny vacations secretly with Dewser's oldest friend—you were roommates, maybe, you and Dewser—"

"Hardly," answered Chips. "It was before the days of coeducation. . . ."

"Oh, a woman?" replied McElvie, seizing the point with an alertness Chips could not but recognize and admire. "I beg your pardon, Mr. Chipping—no offense meant, I'm sure. . . . But you got the idea, haven't you?—why, it's stupendous—it's unique—I don't believe it's ever been thought of before. Oh, boy, it'll be the greatest scoop in the history of movie publicity! . . ."

WHICH was why, that same evening, Chips gave Miss Lydia Jones the news that Randolph Renny was staying in Brookfield at the Royal Hotel. He decided that if there were to be a scoop at all (whatever a scoop was), Brookfield, as represented by the Brookfield *Gazette* and by its social reporter, should have it. And thus it came about that Miss Jones began her column of gossip ambiguously, ungrammatically, yet in substance correctly with the words: "Coming out of the Royal Hotel the other day, who should I espy but Randolph Renny . . ."

It only remains to add that the following term Renny's son began his career at Brookfield School, and, during a preliminary interview with Chips, remarked: "Of course you know who my father is, don't you, sir?"

"I do, my boy," Chips answered. "But—umph—you need have no fear—on *that* account. We all know—but at Brookfield—umph—we do not care. . . ."

Female

DARRELL HUFF

The best laid plans behind the wedding present from the other woman almost worked. An ingenious story that you can't put down.

RUTH LET the heavy package slide through her hands onto the unscratched top of the new maple table in front of the living-room window. Her warm gray eyes glowed as they looked carefully away from the writing on the brown paper. Like a child she loved surprises, and like a child she made them last as long as she could.

As she patted her blonde hair back to its usual neatness, she listened to the growl of the parcel-post truck as it moved on down the street, and speculated delightedly about the tall box.

"It must be a belated wedding present for George and me," she told herself, and her lips moved soundlessly as she checked off the names of relatives and friends. "Aunt Martha, Aunt Jennie, Aunt Erma. Joe and Bob, and the Burtons in Tuscaloosa. The boys in George's office. George's family and his brother in Boston, and Corinne Putnam. . . . Oh!"

Corinne Putnam, the girl George grew up with, the girl everyone had expected him to marry. Corinne Putnam, who was George's age, not ten years younger, like Ruth. Corinne, the sophisticate, who had been everywhere and seen everything, while Ruth had grown up in a small town and worked in the city barely a year before George saw her, proposed in a week, and married her in a month. Corinne, with her famous collection of Early-American porcelain. Haughty Corinne, who hated Ruth, and whose present no doubt would be something distinguished and memorable—and somehow humiliating to the girl who had dared to take her man.

Ruth turned the package around. Yes, there it was. From Corinne Putnam, in Boston.

Ruth thought she had forgotten the scene that had occurred the day before the wedding, but now she found it still alive and burning in the back of her mind, where it had lain these past five weeks. She was back in the high-ceilinged drawing room of George's family's house in Boston. It was the only house she ever had been in that had anything called a drawing room, and that fact had awed her almost as much as knowing that the giant breakfront had been in the family a hundred and forty years and was worth more than the whole house she had grown up in.

She was sitting in the drawing room, and it was the day before the wedding, which couldn't take place in Ruth's family home because she had neither family nor home. Corinne Putnam was there, and so were other people, friends of George's family; but Ruth hardly saw anyone else through the haze Corinne put before her eyes.

Corinne was asking Ruth questions. Intimate little questions, designed to draw her out to disadvantage. They were ingenious, calculated to show Ruth up as an outlander, without family or background, without culture or tradition. And this in a room musty with the traditions of an uninterrupted century of the things called family and breeding.

"What is it like to go to public school in a little Western town?" Corinne asked. "What in the world did you do then, darling? And did your father really run a hatchery? How quaint! . . . I do think you're so clever to make your own clothes. Did you make that little dress you have on?"

Things like that. Nothing, of course, anyone could possibly take offense at.

In the Iowa town in which Ruth had grown up, if someone deviled you beyond endurance, you struck back with whatever blunt words you had. So Ruth stood up, and lashed out at Corinne; she hadn't seen George walk into the room a moment before, or perhaps she would not have said the things she did. It had been a miserable scene, and George hadn't understood it. He had been ashamed of Ruth's outburst, had put it down to some incomprehensible form of feminine jealousy; and she had resolved that he never would see anything like it again.

THE GARAGE DOOR banged and brought Ruth back to the present. "I must have been in a sort of trance," she thought. "I didn't hear George drive in. He'll be here in a few seconds, and he'll want to open the package right away, of course, and I'll have to say something appropriate. I won't know what to say and he'll think it's jealousy and he'll be angry—" Ruth seized the package and with uncharacteristic swiftness hustled it into the linen closet in the hallway.

Then George was in the room, kissing her as he always did, and patting her, and she was responding as she always did. And all the while part of her mind was saying: "Tomorrow I'll open it and see what it is and think what I can say when I show it to George tomorrow night. If I have time to think, everything will be all right."

George was looking around the living room. "Any mail?" he asked. "Did the present come yet, the one Corinne said she was sending? I'll bet it'll be something terrific out of that precious porcelain collection of hers."

"Corinne's present?" Ruth said flatly. Then: "When did Corinne say she was sending a present? I haven't heard anything from her since the wedding."

"I had a note from her at the office the other day," George said. "Didn't I tell you?"

"You didn't say a word about it!" Ruth said sharply. "You didn't tell me she was writing you at the office."

AFTER GEORGE had left the next morning and Ruth was wiping the blue breakfast dishes, she wondered if it had been the way she'd said those words that had started the quarrel. It hadn't been much of a quarrel, she assured herself, but it had been the first time she had talked to George that way and the first time he ever had flashed back at her. And he had said: "Get hold of yourself, Ruth. You're imagining things. You're simply jealous of Corinne, and there's no sense in it. Anyway, if there's anything I hate it's a jealous, narrow-minded woman."

In the end he had apologized, although what he'd been apologizing for hadn't been quite clear to either of them. And she had cried and he had kissed her and that had been the end of it and neither of them would ever mention it again and they'd never quarrel any more, not even if they lived to celebrate a golden wedding.

But still, it had been their first quarrel. "I guess we're a real married couple now," she thought with bitter humor.

All the pleasure with which she first had looked at the box was gone now as she took it from its place in the linen closet and carried it into the living room. It clinked dully as she put it on the table.

She stripped off the heavy brown paper and found a wooden box about a foot square and two feet high. With a can opener and a table knife she worried off the lid. Inside there was excelsior. Bits of it littered the shiny maple table and spilled onto the blue twist rug as Ruth unpacked the box. Then her quick fingers stopped. Under the excelsior there was nothing.

Except that at the bottom of the box was a heap of broken porcelain.

Ruth spread the wrapping paper on the table and, lifting the box with both hands, poured out dozens of pieces of porcelain. Heedless of sharp edges, she searched among the pieces for some clue to what they had been.

Ah, here was a piece with a part of a picture on it—the head of Napoleon. There was his thin, sharp nose, and that was the hat he so often is shown in. And here was a curved piece, like the handle of a cup, but much larger.

It must have been some sort of vase or pitcher, Ruth concluded. As George had guessed, some rare piece from Corinne's collection of porcelain.

George! What would he say when he learned that Corinne's valuable—if useless—present was in fragments? Would he believe it had been broken in the mail, Ruth wondered fearfully, or would he suspect her of having carelessly dropped it and then of being afraid to confess?

Or worse. Ruth felt that she could see his mind, primed by last night's quarrel, proceeding logically to a false conclusion. Things are not often broken in the mail, he'd reason. None of the other presents had been damaged, so why this one? Then he'd remember Ruth's outburst before the wedding, her anger of last night, and think she had smashed the thing in a jealous rage. At best, he never could be quite sure she hadn't.

Hide it or throw it away, was Ruth's first panicky thought. But that would never do. One day Corinne would come to call, and the thing would have to be on display.

There was only one thing to do, and Ruth faced it grimly. She moved the pile of porcelain pieces to the kitchen table. She cleaned up the spilled excelsior. She ran down the street to the grocery store and bought three little tubes of china cement. She sat down at the table and began to search for pieces that could be fitted together. Yes, it could be done.

When dinnertime approached—and a poorly prepared dinner it would be—Ruth hid the box and the wrapping paper and the porcelain in the closet. After nearly a day's work the task seemed more hopeful. By slow, patient search Ruth had been able to find almost all the pieces with fragments of the picture of Napoleon. Painfully pieced together, these formed a curved surface that Ruth estimated took her one fourth of the way around one part of the porcelain pitcher or vase.

The second day she assembled thick pieces into a heavy square that seemed to be the base. Several small, curved pieces became another handle, a duplicate of the unbroken one. Clearly the thing was a large vase.

And then there were days of discouragement. With no clues to guide her, with no method of procedure except trial and error, Ruth sometimes spent an hour or more without finding a single pair of fragments that would fit together.

She was growing snappish now. Her back hurt and her eyes ached. When her tiredness showed in her disposition in the evening, George pointed out unsympathetically that it really couldn't be too terribly arduous to keep up a five-room house with no children, and why didn't she take a nap in the afternoon?

There was nothing she could say to this, of course, and it made her furious. Sometimes it made her say things she quickly wished she hadn't.

EACH MORNING she returned to her grim puzzle, hunting and everlastingly hunting for pieces that fitted. She hardly realized it for a while, but even on the worst days she made some progress. On the eleventh day, though her eyes were red-rimmed and her fingertips were a mass of tiny lacerations, she suddenly spoke aloud in joy at the discovery that the vase had taken full shape and only a handful of broken bits remained. She was so relieved that when the parcel-post man came with a package of books for George she smiled to herself at the absurd thought that it would be only fair to ask the man to come in and help her finish the task he had brought upon her.

She was more cheerful that night, and her husband remarked on the change.

"I've just had a blue spell, I guess, George," she told him. "I think I'll be all right now."

Two days later Ruth coated the last tiny fragment lightly with the quick-drying china cement and pressed it into place. Her pleasure at the approaching end of her task was tempered by chagrin that a few pieces were missing. How could she have been so careless as to lose any, she wondered, and then she thought, "It must have been when I first opened the box, before I knew what I would have to do."

She experimented a little and found that patching plaster would fill the crevices where pieces were missing. She looked at her finished job from halfway across the room, then went closer, and finally picked up the mended vase, handling it with infinite care, and examined it minutely.

She saw, as though seeing them for the first time, the date 1833 on the underside of the base, the stripes that ran around the curved portions, the still colorful painting of Napoleon watching what Hitler was never to see—the burning of Moscow.

It had been a long time since the vase was new; anyone looking at it would accept as natural the cracks and generally aged appearance; she had done a wonderful job.

Now she carefully placed the vase on the living-room table, neatly in the center of its maple top. There was dust on the shiny surface and she wiped it away, thinking that from this day on she would have time to be a housewife again. She arranged the wrapping paper beside the vase and placed the wooden box on it. Everything must look as though the package had been delivered only an hour before.

Ruth rehearsed a little speech for George. "I must say: 'What a lovely old vase'; I must say: 'How dear of Corinne to send it!' I must say: 'I'll bet it's more than a hundred years old, one of her treasures!' "

But when George came home, he kissed her, as usual, and patted her, as usual, and then he saw the vase before she had time to say anything.

"What's that?" George said. "Oh, it's the present from Corinne, of course. And it's just the kind of monstrosity she'd pick, isn't it?"

He walked to the table and swung the vase carelessly into the air with one hand. "Far as I'm concerned," he said, "we can shove it right back into its box and leave it there. We can always trot it out if Corinne threatens a visit." He lowered the heavy vase into its box. It went only part way in. "Why, look at this, darling," George said.

Ruth went nearer and looked. She could see that the vase was fully half an inch wider than the box.

"That's funny," George said, frowning a little. "Nobody could possibly get this vase into the box without smashing it to pieces first."

Mothers

WALLACE IRWIN

Scuttle was a braggart. Was he boasting when he said that his mother was beautiful? "It's just the way her face looks," he said. Has this child made a discovery that most of us fail to gain in a lifetime? This story is unforgettable.

Last summer Perry Weeks of Dartmouth was a counselor at a boys' camp. Boys, he told me, aren't naturally good sportsmen. They're too candid to pretend they like to come in second best, and the ones who don't brag a little aren't much good. Like all simple things boys are hard to understand. This was an illustration:

At Bradford's Camp last summer, he said, there were two boys who bossed Tent Seven—athletic rivals and pretty good friends at that. One they called Strawberry—his hair, you know—and they called the other one Scuttle because the family name was Cole. As for me, said Perry, I got off with the name of Houdini—no matter why. It was a high compliment, and I tried to live up to it.

Strawberry and Scuttle, those boys in Tent Seven, they were the right sort. Every other word "Gee" and "What's the idee-a?"—you know. Crack swimmers, both of 'em—made me hustle sometimes. Scuttle had the edge on Strawberry in the hundred yards. They groused a lot about it behind the scenes. Kid stuff. They were as different as frogs from firecrackers. Scuttle was a noisy, black-eyed little devil, talkative and sort of affectionate. Strawberry was quiet; you had to bully him into writing home. Scuttle knocked off a letter to his mother about once a day.

One night Scuttle comes to me, looking pretty down. "Houdini," he said, "I guess I made Strawberry sore. Gee. He's dumb to be sore."

I was used to the kids telling me a little of everything, so I asked, "Why's he sore?"

"We got to talking about mothers."

"That shouldn't start a war," I said.

"But Strawberry got sore. I didn't say a thing about *his* mother, and he couldn't say much. He said she wasn't all wet, but she wasn't anything to advertise. And he said, 'You think everything you've got's beautiful. Your crawl-stroke and your mother and everything.'"

I gave Scuttle a lecture on being high-hat. Boys shouldn't be high-hat. Boasting makes enemies, gets you nowhere. I talked very fine, but it was the way Scuttle looked at me— I knew he hadn't said it all. There was something I couldn't fool with, like religious conviction.

"Is she really very beautiful?" I asked.

"Yes, sir." You could watch his eyes and be convinced.

"In what way?"

"Houdini, I guess you know when a woman's beautiful. It's just the way her face looks." This was no description, and Leonardo da Vinci couldn't give a better one. This boy knew his mother was beautiful, and he couldn't tell why. If he'd been a little older—seventeen, say—he'd let it go at that. But he tried to explain—just vague. Bright gray eyes and hair sort of silky. Such a nice mouth people stopped to look at her. And, gee. She knew how to put her clothes on.

A lot of stuff like that. Funny too. It gave me a sort of picture of something very lovely. And young kids are good judges of beauty, only they seldom admit it.

Well, I patched up the affair between Scuttle and Strawberry. And I got sorry for Strawberry, wanted to do something to help him out. I pretended to jump on him for not writing home oftener, but that was my excuse to ask if his mother wasn't pretty too. "She's all right, I guess." That was as much as I could get out of him, and I could see how sensitive he was. Scuttle had the prize mother and Scuttle was trimming him right along in the hundred yards.

I tried to be sore at Scuttle; but when I saw him at night in the Main House, pegging away with his red fountain pen, just talking to his mother with ink on paper, I knew that what he'd said amounted to more than kid show-off.

Well, the season was over after a while. On the last day of camp we always have a shindig with speeches and ice cream and a presentation of medals. This pleases the parents when they come to take the boys home. Scuttle, the night before the big racket, was proud as a peacock—he'd won the gold medal for swimming, his beautiful mother would be there to see it pinned on. Strawberry was booked for a second prize. Poor Strawberry. Second in swimming, second in mothers. More trouble for Tent Seven, I guessed.

The ceremony was set for noon, and the droves of parents motored in. Kissing and reunions all over the lot. I was busy, but my eye was out for Scuttle's mother. Somebody in the crowd said, "Mrs. Cole," and finally I spotted her, talking to Dr. Sedley. He was turning himself inside out. And no wonder. "They're coming right up from Tent Seven," he said.

I could see why Scuttle worshipped that woman. She was ravingly angelic to the eye. All violet—eyes, hair, gown—that's how she looked. Slim and young and used to being gazed at. Glorious!

I saw the two boys coming up the trail. Scuttle was running, eager as a pup. Strawberry was hanging back. I just had to see what Scuttle would do when he could meet his idol face to face.

But he didn't do anything. Simply nothing. It was darned hard to understand, the way he walked up to her, scarcely noticed her, walked on again. Then I saw him jump into the crowd like a little wild dog, let out a whoop and grab a shortish, fattish lady around the neck. "Mother, I got the gold medal," he yelled, "and I want you to sit on the front seat."

Her clothes were a sort of washed-out gray, like her eyes. She had a tired face, rather made-up. Her hair was bleached, but she had a nice mouth, just as Scuttle had told me.

When Strawberry saw the perfect woman in violet he said, "Hello, Mother." I suppose she kissed him. She was mainly worried about his necktie, and what sort of effect she was making.

Scuttle and the homely one were walking arm in arm. They hadn't an ounce of good looks between them, but they were tremendously beautiful, as I saw them. It proved what he had said about his mother —it's just the way her face looks.

Then Came the Legions

MacKINLAY KANTOR

We might find it odd that ne'er-do-well Cap could command the respect of the men he drilled. We will find it stranger still to learn who Cap really was. Here is Mr. Kantor's tale of a great American, a beautifully written page out of our country's history.

THE GUARDS were drilling, but Cap had not gone up the crooked street to watch them.

In the first place, he had seen a great many soldiers drilled, before this. In the second place, a substantial farmer had just entered the leather-store, and Cap surmised that he had come to buy that double-harness which Orvil had been trying to sell him since the autumn before.

Cap was quite aware that he was incapable of managing this sale or any other sale. If he tried, and bungled the job, he would be subjected to the wrath and sarcasm of Orvil and Simpson. Cap planned to stay out of their way until the harness sale was consummated.

The Guards were at drill. . . . Along brick façades sounded their trampling. The young officer who shepherded them seemed almost fearful of the boyish rabble who trooped behind.

From his seat on the empty barrel in a walled nook beside his brothers' store, Cap squinted into the late afternoon sunshine. The approaching column was awkward enough. They didn't keep their lines dressed or their files closed. All the boys talked in the ranks; they waved their guns and hooted pleasantries to citizens who lined the sidewalk.

At Crary's grocery-store, Ephraim Crary and Lawyer Hollingsworth stood in the open doorway. "There comes the company," announced Crary.

The lawyer played with the snuff under his lip. "Look at Cap, over there on that barrel. Been drinking again."

"Anyway," said the grocer more charitably, "whether he's been drinking or not, he's playing hooky from the store, certain. I don't see how Orvil and Simpson put up with him."

"I don't see *how*, but I certainly see *why*." Hollingsworth felt the quid of snuff bite into his tongue. "It's because their old man in Covington pays the bills. He really set the boys up in that business, Crary. And when Cap got down-and-out, his old father had him and his wife and children all shipped up here to live off the family. I hear his folks pay him seventy dollars a month. Seventy dollars a month more'n he's worth!"

Crary said, against the hubbub of the approaching Guards: "I hear he had quite a record in the regular army."

"Record for drinking!" snapped the lawyer. "That was what cooked his goose for him."

The militia reached the half-turn in front of the store, parading directly toward the curbstone. His face scarlet, the young lieutenant ran backward ahead of them, waving his sword. He opened his mouth; he tried to howl a command, but no words came. Steadily, gleefully, the column mounted the curbstone.

"Stop, fellows—hang it—*stop!*"

Snickers exploded along the ranks. But even so, the Guards did not falter. At least they had been taught to march in a straight line, and march in a straight line they would, for all the vagaries of their village street.

With a muffled thud the foremost squad halted with its noses against the window of Crary's store. The Guards marked time. They counted, in humorous chorus: "*One*, two; *one*, two; *one*—"

The boy officer slammed his sword into its scabbard. He stood with eyes blazing, fists clenched.

"Think you're smart, don't you? Well, I'll lick you for this, one at a time! Just because I didn't know the proper—"

Lawyer Hollingsworth recovered from his laughter enough to thrust his face past the door-jamb. "Harry, why'n't you ask Cap to help you?"

The youth's eye followed his indication: that squat figure on the upended barrel by the leather-store.

"I guess I will," he said decisively. "Cap ought to know, anyway. —Column—*halt*," he told his army, and crossed the street.

Cap climbed down from his perch.

The lieutenant prayed: "Cap, will you help me out?"

Whisky breathed in a faint perfume. "Certainly, Harry," said Cap. "What seems to be the trouble?" His voice was calm, level; and again the young militiaman felt a queer respect rising in his mind—the respect which was so aborted when applied to a ne'er-do-well like Cap.

"You see, the street bends a little. It isn't a right-angular turn. I couldn't wheel 'em completely to the right or left—"

The bearded face moved in a nod of understanding.

"Take this sword," offered Harry. "I want to see how you'd do it. Like—when you were in the army." And then he held his tongue; every person in town knew the story of this man's disgrace.

Cap accepted the sword and buckled the sword-belt over his shabby coat. He walked out into the street.

"Fall out!" he ordered. And then: "The company will form, in column, ten paces in front of me."

They got into line, still snickering. This was odd, being ordered about by such a man as Cap. But there was something—

"The order for a half-turn is 'Left oblique,' or 'Right oblique.' It is followed by a command of execution. The company will observe the officer."

He pivoted, drew Harry's sword, and held it to his shoulder. "Forward," he chanted. "*Ha!*" His left foot lifted. He paced steadily away from them. "*Left oblique*"—his voice seemed more crusty and alert than ever they had heard it—"*Ha!*"

He returned to the staring militia.

"You see how it goes. Now we'll try it back up the street."

He strode to the rear of the column, eyes fixed on nothingness.

"*Company—right-shoulder—Ha!*" And they did that as their young officer had learned it from his Primary Manual.

"*Company—right about—Ha!*"

Now their eyes were staring into his blue ones, where little pink flames of whisky still danced. . . . They marched. It was a right oblique, this time, and they followed him very well.

Harry came up, full of admiration.

"You're a trump, Cap," he said.

"Glad to be of service, Harry."

The officer accepted the sword-belt as the older man relinquished it, but he seemed unwilling to buckle it on.

"Cap," he said, "it's hard lines, drilling, when you don't know how. Our own captain is—Cap, I wish they'd elected you captain of the Guards. Anyway, will you come to drill tonight and help me some more with the company?"

A small boy in a ragged shirt scampered forward to grasp Cap's hand.

"Hello, Buck," Cap greeted him. But he kept looking at the youthful lieutenant.

Buck chirped: "Pa, Ma says she's tired, and wants to have supper early. Says for you to hustle up."

"Very well, sonny." The bearded man was glad, even after this military triumph, that he didn't have to go back and face his brothers, Simpson and Orvil.

He told the officer: "You can count on me. I'll be glad to help in any way I can. You see, I was trained at the expense of the National Government. And in this emergency which faces—"

"You'll be a lot of help!" The young militiaman raced away to take charge of his hungry squads.

Trudging behind Buck as they climbed steep steps toward their little brick house on the north hill, Cap played with the idea. He imagined himself fashioning the Jo Daviess Guards into a veritable Old Guard. Yes, he should write to the War Department. It was human decency for him to do so. And he need not mention Fort Humboldt, the whisky-barrel, and the resigned commission.

He began to build a letter in his mind: *"I have the honor to tender my services . . . In view of my present age and length of service, I feel myself competent to command a regiment, if the President in his judgment should see fit to intrust one to me . . . I am, very respectfully, your obedient servant, U. S. Grant."*

from Mrs. Appleyard's Year

LOUISE ANDREWS KENT

Delightful Mrs. Appleyard, who spends her summers in Vermont and her winters in Boston, comes alive with the first sentence and keeps on going after the last page. Visit the Appleyards with us for a happy New Year and discover that even late Christmas shopping can be fun.

JANUARY: *Happy New Year*

FAULTS Mrs. Appleyard certainly has. As she looks them over on the first day of the New Year they seem to her like the 'other articles too numerous to mention,' always mysteriously listed in auctioneers' advertisements. Since she has had most of her defects for over half a century, she is well acquainted with them. Some of them, indeed, have become enjoyable simply because she has had them so long. For instance: if she did not impulsively bring home a large Chinese cabinet (because it was such a bargain) instead of the lacquer finger bowls she started out to buy, her family would be deprived of the pleasure of observing: 'Now, isn't that exactly *like* mother.' If she had not followed up this triumph of serendipity—which means, in case anyone wants to know, the art of finding something when you are looking for something else—by acquiring a Chinese ancestor in a blue robe (well, somebody's ancestor anyway) to hang above the cabinet, Sally would have had no cause to remark: 'This cabinet was a bargain that I always knew was going to cost us money!'

Expressions like this give a great deal of innocent pleasure to their makers. So do the comments on Mr. Appleyard's fondness for looking up things in the dictionary during meals. Were the children allowed to bring their books to the table? Yet both parents set them a pernicious example. Mr. Appleyard is if anything a little worse of the two. His pet digestive literature is the encyclopaedia with occasional digressions into *Who's Who*. As a comment on this habit, Hugh gave his father for Christmas the working drawings for the Appleyard Food and Book Trough.

The table looks like any other. There is even the centre piece (cemented down) displaying the usual Christmas bowl of fruit. The specifications call for three well-dried tangerines, one persimmon (soft), four apples (with wrinkle remover), one bunch of grapes (partly eaten), and two ossified pomegranates. This still life—or *naturemorte,* as the French call it for some reason—stands on a circular piece of wood cut away from the rest of the table. The crack is veiled by a square of rare old brocade. Hugh says his mother can easily pick this up some day when she is buying some artichokes—or something.

Underneath the table is an ingenious mechanism by which Mr. Appleyard can step on a pedal and raise the centre piece eighteen inches, revealing a revolving bookcase containing the *Encyclopaedia Britannica, Webster's Dictionary,* unabridged, the *Social Register,* the *Appleyard Genealogy, Bartlett's Familiar Quotations, Who's Who,* and *The Corpse in the Chartreuse Bathtub*—or whatever Mr. Appleyard is reading to take his mind off whatever else he is reading.

Without waiting for the Book Trough, the Appleyard children have already equipped the table with a disrespectful piece of apparatus. There is a ledge underneath, once a useful resting place for breadcrusts and raisins, carefully picked out of cookies by Sally. It has also been tried and found wanting as a repository for creamed codfish and spinach. What it now contains is simply a pencil and a small notebook.

It is the custom for the irreverent young Appleyards to listen politely to their parents' well-worn anecdotes and then pull out the notebook and remark: 'Ah! Number 83B!' or, 'Let me see—when was this last told? What, not since 1939? It hardly seems possible.' Or on rare occasions: 'Quick, Hugh—the notebook! A new one! We must give it a number. Shall we put it under "Moral Tales" or "Incidents of Travel in Early Days"?'

When their neighbor, Mrs. Tremaine—who believes in respect for parents whether they deserve it or not, because, as she very reasonably says, if they had to deserve it who would get any?—reproached Cicely for this flippant attitude, Cicely opened her soft hazel-green eyes, with that stare like an innocent kitten's, and said: 'But, Mrs. Tremaine, you don't understand. We're *proud* of Mother and Daddy. We don't believe there's another couple in the *world* that has three hundred and fifty-eight stories, all different. We think it's *remarkable!*'

It was Cicely, the minx, who invented the phrase 'to pink-sugar' anyone.

This interesting addition to the Appleyard family dictionary, which occupies two pages of the under-table notebook, arose in this way. Anecdote number 83 under 'Moral Tales' deals with the time Mrs. Appleyard, then a not very innocent child of three, mashed up a quantity of strawberry juice and powdered sugar, concealed the delectable mess in a large mussel shell in the stove of the doll's house kitchen—and then forgot about it. It was not very attractive when it was found six weeks later. That is all there is to the story, but in Mrs. Appleyard's hands it used to occupy some time in the telling and the point about the stupidity of hoarding was of course subtly indicated.

The Appleyards like to grasp strawberries by the hulls and mash them into sugar. It is Mrs. Appleyard's contention that a strawberry not worth eating this way is not worth eating in any form. So in June, when the first Marshfield berries come into the Boston market, and later in Appleyard Centre, the episode of the pink sugar comes naturally to mind. One season, when the Appleyard Centre berries were like rather small filets mignons, Mrs. Appleyard told it three times. She was asked to tell it. It was not until the third time that she realized that her fiendishly innocent-looking offspring were trying to see how many times she *would* tell it. That is why, when she is asked to tell a story, she uses Cicely's phrase suspiciously: 'Are you pink-sugaring me?'

Even the sight of a strawberry now makes her feel as self-conscious as a hippopotamus on cellophane. She admits that repetitiousness is a fault and she tries to get over it, although after a study of the situation she has come to the conclusion that it is difficult to have all conversation brand-new and that one factor in any friendship is the ability to listen to it as if it were.

She intends to improve on both points this year. She also plans to glance occasionally at her engagement book instead of keeping the entries in it a secret from herself. She hopes she will keep her desk looking less like the town dump in a heavy fog. She means to do better about the relation between buttons and Mr. Appleyard's lingerie. When people ask her how she is, she will try to bite her tongue before she tells them. If inquiries about her children are added, she will strive earnestly to conceal the fact that they are extraordinary. She thinks even the proudest mother ought to be able to tell about four children in four paragraphs. She admits that after twenty-seven years she might learn that Mr. Appleyard's blood pressure goes up when the roast beef is served on a small, cold platter instead of on a large, hot one. She doesn't blame him a bit.

She could, of course, go on counting over the rosary of her faults, but she has decided it is too depressing; so she has taken a little time to dwell upon her virtues, too. If she doesn't, who will? Compared to the achievements of Joan of Arc they may seem slight, but then Mrs. Appleyard is only a housewife. She knows she is because she read it in the Overbrook Town Report.

As such she has certain virtues.

She has never piped whipped cream around the edge of a grapefruit.

She does not call wineglasses 'stem-ware.'

She uses the brakes on her car instead of the horn.

When she remembers an engagement at all, she gets there on time.

She speaks little of her servant problem.

She balances her own checkbook, no matter how long it takes.

She likes the same people she liked when she was twelve years old. And some she never saw until last week. In fact she likes people. She likes hummingbirds, too.

She never makes a fourth at bridge to help anyone out. She found out long ago that she was no help.

She enjoys praise, but she knows that most praise implies surprise, so if she gets any she is grateful but calm.

She realizes that at about her age women generally begin to think about either their souls or their figures and that it is too late to do much about them. Therefore she never mentions reducing while she is eating cream of mushroom soup, sweetbreads sous cloche, candied sweet potatoes, and chocolate marron parfait. Thoughts on this subject she keeps for her interviews with the bathroom scales.

She chuckles over the remarks that her friends make about each other and forgets them.

Really, as she thinks it over, she feels almost unbearably virtuous. Perhaps her own best contribution to a pleasant New Year for everyone would be for her to indulge in her vices a little more. So that is her Resolution.

DECEMBER: I. *Cards of Cheer*

Mr. and Mrs. Appleyard belong to different schools of thought on the subject of Christmas cards. Mr. Appleyard likes to save them for one vast orgy of opening on Christmas Day. His wife likes to open them as they come, choosing the handsomest and the funniest to put on the living-room mantelpiece, leaving the others lying around in piles wherever she happened to be when she was opening them. Mr. Appleyard slits envelopes neatly along the top and writes changes of addresses in the book that records Mrs. Appleyard's twenty-year struggle not to forget anyone. The battle has not been simplified by her habit of tearing envelopes open impetuously and hurling them into the wastebasket without paying any attention to the back flap.

Mrs. Appleyard gave up her career to marry Mr. Appleyard. It was that of a librarian. She often wonders why the libraries have not put up a statue to Mr. Appleyard . . .

For dealing with the card situation, the following compromise has been worked out and without calling in the Supreme Court. Mr. Appleyard opens neatly all the cards that come to his office. It is he who looks over the list and says: 'The Nelsons sent us one. You still have time to get one in the mail.' It is Mrs. Appleyard who, moaning low, repairs the error. In order to conduct such bookkeeping operations the cards obviously have to be opened before Christmas, so Mrs. Appleyard has her wild way with those that come to the house and Mr. Appleyard roots patiently among the various piles, seeing some cards eleven times and others not at all. Mrs. Appleyard, however, undertakes not to throw any away until she has collected them all in one box and given that box into Mr. Appleyard's hands with a sworn affidavit that *these are all.*

Mr. Appleyard was particularly touched, when the cards were finally shucked and harvested this year, to see how people, many of whom the Appleyards have never even met, remembered them. There were, for instance, the gentlemen who cleaned rugs. They had been only musical, mouthfilling names to the Appleyards. Mrs. Appleyard had always thought of them as living their strenuous Armenian lives in an atmosphere of gasoline and camphor, sucking up dirt with enormous vacuum cleaners, playing hoses like fat pythons, swishing rugs up and down in vats of the purest and most ethereal soapsuds, peering through miscroscopes in search of moth eggs, trapping the moths themselves with smiles, sweet cream, and honey, weaving little palm leaves in spots used too frequently as ash trays by members of the best families so often mentioned in the rugmen's advertising. How often, on reading the reminder that it was time for her rugs to be cleaned, has Mrs. Appleyard's heart swelled with pride to think that her rugs would associate with the rugs of the most exclusive families; that they might even share the same soapsuds! She has always felt that it was very democratic of the rug people to give her ancient and weary floor coverings this social set forward.

And how more than kind and condescending it was of them to sit right down in all that bustle and send the Appleyards a card showing a blazing fireplace, stockings, Scottie dogs, candles, and not a rug in sight. (All at the cleaners' probably!)

It was genial of the lobsterman to remember them—and with that handsome picture of a camel! Mr. Appleyard said he had never seen lobsters transported by camels, but he would like to. Natural history is reticent on this point, but he thinks perhaps camels may keep one compartment especially for lobsters. He also said, somewhat ungratefully, that with lobster prices what they are, he would have preferred a claw to a camel.

Mrs. Appleyard suggested, in a tone of false meekness, that the Appleyards had not sent the lobsterman any card and had she better, etc., etc., . . . ? Mr. Appleyard did not show any enthusiasm. He seems to suspect a selfish motive in these greetings.

Mrs. Appleyard says that at Christmas-time he should stifle such unworthy sentiments. She feels sure that, when the garageman sent that spirited picture of a stage-coach, he had no recollection of having changed one very flat tire, supplying two quarts of Never-Ready No-Vap and a set of mudhooks (of which Mrs. Appleyard has since lost three). She knows the butcher can't be uneasy about his bill because he sent not only a succulent turkey, but also a gaily illuminated bit of parchment hoping they were pleased with his services. The Appleyards take this opportunity to assure him that they are and also that they will be in the market for a tip of the sirloin, weighing about seven and a half pounds, cut from a nice heavy steer, just as soon as they get through the turkey-soup stage.

In the midst of this era of good feeling—when even the hardware-man saluted Mrs. Appleyard with such a magnificently painted bunch of mistletoe that she feels shy about trying to exchange that splendid barometer for a sanitary garbage receiver—there is one crumpled rose leaf. Right in the heart of the Christmas mail, without so much as a sprig of holly on it, was a card from the library remarking in the tersest way that the books she borrowed in November were now liable to a fine of fifty-six cents.

In her first moment of irritation, she decided not to let them put up that statue of Mr. Appleyard, or even a bronze tablet. However, we have not written of this disturber of filing systems to any purpose if we have given the impression that she has much leisure for harboring grudges. After a brief spasm of planning to get even with them by becoming a librarian, after all, she put the card on the mantelpiece among the other gems of the season.

'Ah, well,' quoth Mrs. Appleyard, hunting for her pocketbook, 'into each life some rain must fall.' (Unquoth.)

II. *Shopping Late*

Mrs. Appleyard knows perfectly well that she ought to shop early for Christmas. She knows that it is only common sense to buy presents early, choose them according to their usefulness, wrap them up at her convenience, mail them shortly after July Fourth, and be sure of waking brisk and active on Christmas morning with a clear conscience and unruffled temper. Yet somehow unless she joins in the last-minute bustle and jostle, unless she buys at least one present that is fascinating, frivolous, and beyond her means, for her it just isn't Christmas.

A few years ago there was started a Society for the Suppression of Useless Giving. It did its work so well that it vanished, leaving—according to Mrs. Appleyard—a sensible but dull world behind it. She likes to think of the days when a young bride's first act on going to housekeeping was to gild three broom handles, cover the lid of a butter box with green velvet, edge it with yellow fringe, and thus create what the furniture trade now chastely calls an 'occasional table.' You could paint bulrushes on a mirror, too, or pond lilies. Strange and wonderful things could be done with milkweed. There were magazines that told you how, in case your natural ingenuity failed.

In those days presents had to be useless to be acceptable. Of course there was no objection to finding some use for them—if you could—

but in the Bric-à-Brac Era a useful present implied that you couldn't buy the thing for yourself, and that was a deadly insult. Somehow it has ceased to be one. The possibility of affronting her friends and relations was not Mrs. Appleyard's worry this year as she hurried past one red and silver and green window after another.

'Darling Clarabelle says dolls are babyish—I'll have to give the one I got for her to someone else . . . that comes of shopping early. Now, what shall I get for the br . . . the dear little thing? Perhaps she needs a cigarette case—she's seven . . . Horace? Horace wants neckties—he said so. But he says the ones he got last year were lousy. Christmas dogs he called them. It would serve him right if I bought him that one with the petunias on it . . . I wonder if Bertha Tremaine means to give me anything this year. She had a meaning look in her eye the third time she told me how much she was doing for the Greeks. Well, I can keep it—a folding card-table always comes in handy. I can lend it to the church . . .'

In spite of such ripples in her stream of consciousness, Mrs. Appleyard took time to be glad that she does not need to ruin her eyesight at midnight by embroidering pallid violets on a whisk broom holder, or making a glove case by punching holes in linen and then filling them up again with spider webs.

She is glad that anything is acceptable—from lipsticks to lingerie, fur coats to frying pans, caviar to collar buttons. She likes to think of Serena Brown, the president of the Overbrook Hill Garden Club, whose husband gave her a cord of manure for Christmas. Serena rejoiced in its fragrance, thinking of it later as transformed into lilies and roses. Practically Adam had said it with flowers. He apologized for not wrapping his present up in tissue paper and red ribbon, but Serena refused to see anything unromantic in it. Anyway, he had thoughtfully decorated it with a sprig of mistletoe.

He realized that a present without either an air of mystery or a touch of decoration lacks that dash of sentiment that, even in a practical age, we still demand. American enterprise has tied ribbon around refrigerators, wrapped tire chains in holly-papered boxes, swathed toothbrushes in gold cellophane, but for some reason no one has taken up the idea of fertilizer trimmed with mistletoe. It is a pity, for there is something substantial and sensible about such a gift. Mrs. Appleyard heard of one man who took his wife's car to the filling station Christmas morning and had some of the free air put in the tires. He is unmarried just at present. Mrs. Appleyard has his address—in case anyone wants it . . .

She plunged into a revolving door. They get going faster and faster at Christmas-time. Someone dove into it with her. Luckily the newcomer was thin. She and Mrs. Appleyard filled the compartment solid so they were able to slow the door down, thus saving the life of a little old lady carrying a small pair of skis, and giving a lot of innocent pleasure to those who saw Mrs. Appleyard emerge on the other side. She makes a business of slowing down doors at Christmastime. She is not a Girl Scout, but that is no reason for not acting as a brake for a revolving door if that is your talent.

'Smug people with their presents all in cold storage miss half the fun,' she thought as she adjusted her hat and waded into the scuffle.

The shop was a dazzle of light and color, pleasantly warm and stuffy after the raw chill outside. The air was full of exciting smells. She fought her way past the perfume counter burying her nose in her collar. Farther on, new blankets, new sheets, new bolts of silk all gave off their clean scent. The luggage section was so agreeably pungent that she paid twice as much as she had planned for Hugh's new kit-bag. Near-by, in the fur department, salesmen trod silently across plush carpets through an atmosphere rich with moth flakes and refinement. Even on Christmas Eve fur salesmen do not forget their dignity. The most condescending of them all, a kind of bishop among furriers, condescended sufficiently to say that the coat she and Sally had looked at the other day was now reduced in price. It was nice of him to mention such a sordid subject, Mrs. Appleyard thought, for it evidently gave him pain, and she could see that he hated to part with the coat. However, she bought it. She had meant to, the moment she had seen Sally's eyelashes flutter over it.

She had resisted the camera for Stan when she went up the escalator. It was a wonderful camera. It would do everything except paste the pictures in a book. She bought it as she came down. Stan would get it by New Year's, she explained to herself guiltily, and plunged down to a floor where the smells were especially stimulating. In the space of a few hundred feet Mrs. Appleyard's nose detected popcorn, warm fir balsam, *narcisse noire*, hot dogs with mustard relish, Frenchfried scallops, phonograph records, and salt-water taffy. Radios blatted cheerfully, drowning the sound of tired, shuffling feet and the murmur of weary voices. People talk to themselves a good deal on Christ-

mas Eve and sometimes to Mrs. Appleyard. She learns interesting
things about their home life and has acquired an impression, of course
on insufficient evidence, that there is a lot of happiness and kindness blowing about the world that does not get into official statistics.

Still everyone is not in a happy mood.

'Where did I put it? Oh, where did I put it?' inquired a distracted
lady whose gray hair hung in strings under her ancient velvet hat.
She seemed to be addressing her remarks to an electric washer which
went on whirling suds about with heartless indifference. Another
scanned a tattered slip of paper and murmured hopelessly, 'Chafing
dish Aunt Abigail Howard socks size eleven or was that Chester Grace
hates peach panties.'

A small mother lugged a baby almost as big as herself. He was sound
asleep and his white boots dangled limply from his pink leggings.
She kept right on talking to him. He was called Toots or sometimes
Donald after his grandfather . . . Others were not asleep—far from
it. The toy department echoed with their wails. Yells too. Also
chuckles of pure joy. Who has seen Christmas whose ankles have not
been endangered by a kiddy car shaped like an airplane? Who has
not stood spellbound while the electric train clicks merrily out of
the tunnel? Who has not had Mickey Mouse balloons exploded in
her face? Not Mrs. Appleyard certainly.

She looked a little disapprovingly at the grandmothers. She could
tell them by their expressions of foolish fondness for what seemed to
be very average children. Mrs. Appleyard's grandchildren—if they
had existed—would have been infinitely superior and at home in bed.

Aside from this she approved of everything. She liked the woman,
rigid-looking when seen from behind, who turned out to have a smile
on her face, a wreath of pine and red berries over her arm, a weary
paper bag with a large toy lamb breaking through it under the other,
and a spare hand to give to a tear-stained urchin who had lost his
mother. The gap between him and his mother was not large and it
was quickly bridged. The small boy received a good shaking and felt
better at once . . . There was a big man with a walrus moustache
who stood helplessly at the stocking counter trying to decide between
sunset glow and rose beige. Mrs. Appleyard was swept past him without finding which he chose. She had taken a great liking to him. She
even liked the pushing.

Christmas pushing is good-natured. People who would scowl at having their elbows joggled on other days submit to having their feet stepped on with urbanity. Mrs. Appleyard saw a pink-faced old gentleman's square-topped hat knocked off by a refractory pair of ski poles. His arms were full of many-angled packages, but he put them all down, picked up his hat, and, turning to the owner of the ski-poles, who was also carrying a bird-cage, a lamp-shade, and a small tin pail that Mrs. Appleyard instantly diagnosed as goldfish, smiled and wished him a Merry Christmas. So don't blame her for believing in miracles . . .

She had a private one of her own. All the children but Stan had come home for Christmas. He was too far away. The others were waiting for her now with the car on Park Street. She hurried toward it because she was later than she had said. The big box with the coat in it and the clumsy bundle that was the kit-bag took some manoeuvring through the crowd. She managed them both, however, and did not even drop any of the smaller packages, not even the waistcoat buttons for Mr. Appleyard; but when she arrived, panting slightly and with her hat over one eye, there was no car there—at least, no dusty car that might be either green or gray according to whether you were an optimist or not. The street was filled solid with cars that had been polished for Christmas. It was a handsome sight, and the State House looked very well, too, with its Christmas lights, but Mrs. Appleyard's feet hurt too much by this time for her to be really appreciative of the sights of her fair city. Even the lighted Christmas Tree on the Common began to look tawdry instead of gay.

'I thought beauty was in the eye of the beholder, but I believe it's really in the feet,' Mrs. Appleyard murmured to herself.

Just then she saw the car. It came round the corner of Tremont Street just as the light changed, with a fine free swing that made Mrs. Appleyard think, 'Cicely's driving!'

So she was. All roads are alike to Cicely. Tom was still clutching the door handle as they whizzed up to the curb. Mrs. Appleyard threw him a glance of sympathy. She assumed that it would be welcome. Cicely, like her father, was a very skilful driver.

Tom got out, saying, 'Sit in front, I'll get in back. I'll put the packages in the trunk—it's not quite full yet.'

Somehow the car was fuller than it should have been—not with bundles. Mr. Appleyard and Hugh and Sally were sitting on the back seat with packages around their feet, mysterious last-minute packages

—but that was hardly enough to account for the fact that they all looked like cats who had just eaten a cageful of canaries with perhaps a few love birds thrown in. Sally's face, the most impish of the lot, had no business to be so high up in the air. She was sitting on someone and that someone was—here Mrs. Appleyard began to hunt for her handkerchief—yes; it was Stan's face that emerged from behind Sally: Stan, who was supposed to be in Texas painting a mural in a post office. Mrs. Appleyard had spoken crossly about the Government only that morning and about Texas. At this moment everyone from the President down suddenly seemed worthy of a halo. And Texas—what a wonderful state it must be that had sent Stan, brown, red-cheeked, with his sunburned hair falling down over his forehead, his blue eyes crinkled in the smile that was only Stan's—home for Christmas.

'Take mine,' said Mr. Appleyard, 'it's clean.'

'What,' thought Mrs. Appleyard happily, 'does a woman do whose husband doesn't carry a clean handkerchief for emergencies? How wonderful men are! Kleenex is absolutely no good at a time like this.'

'It was a miracle,' Stan was saying. 'I had just twenty minutes to catch the plane . . .'

Yes, it was a miracle. Mrs. Appleyard is sure of that.

Love's Price; or the $2.20 Heart

GRAEME AND SARAH LORIMER

If you are in your teens and want to learn how to catch your man, take a lesson from teen-aged Maudie. Mirthful is the word for this comical episode in which Maudie deflates a man's ego. Learn why she evaluates his worth at $2.20! Post teenagers will laugh, too!

IT WAS REALLY LUCKY, sort of, that Cooper Eves flickered out, because getting Sylvia married in a big way made things so hectic around home there wasn't any time or place for me to have any love life of my own. Practically every day for weeks before Sylvia's wedding our house was full of little elderly ladies with this-year hats pinned to their pompadours and feathers around their necks, who would look at Sylvia's trousseau night-gowns and squeeze Mother's hand and say, "To think that you have a child old enough to get married! My dear, you're too young!"

I got to looking at Mother in an entirely different light. You don't usually think of your mother as being too young for things, especially a perfectly natural thing like having your daughter get married.

It did make a change in Father and Mother, though. You would see them gazing at each other over the roast beef as if they were remembering things about each other which they had both practically forgotten; and it seemed like I was always hearing Father calling Mother "little girl" right in front of people who I was afraid might think he was warped or something.

It was a relief to have a little sentiment around our house, though, considering we were about to have a wedding, for Sylvia and Jerry spent practically all the time opening wedding presents, and writing them down with about as much romance as two tax collectors, and every time they did sit down it was usually on a crate, and instead of talking about the long beautiful years ahead, they would worry over people which said their invitation to the wedding hadn't come; and usually it was some one that we had crossed off the list and so of course their invitation hadn't come,—only you couldn't tell them that. Really, I thought, your last days for being a girl seemed to have more problems than most people's whole married life.

The most surprising thing about the whole wedding and the weeks before it was how kind Sylvia was to me. She used to always act like I was a kind of a strain on her most of the time, but I suppose she began to realize that I was about to practically drop out of her life and all my faults began to seem rather endearing. I used to go in and sit on her bed and talk for hours without her once telling me I was probably sitting on her hat or stepping on her mules, and we would kiss each other good night, which we would both have died of shock if we had done it a year ago.

But love mellows people, I realized, and besides I was getting more mature myself. Mother was already talking about giving me Sylvia's pass-down fur coat on account of her getting a new one in her trousseau.

"Not that I will ever love another coat as well," Sylvia said sadly, laying it on Mother's bed with a gesture of renunciation, the day we went over her things. "Think of all the lovely things I did in it!"

"Never mind," I said comfortingly, dumping the camphor out of its pocket. "I can go right on taking it to football games and out in people's roadsters on cold nights, like you did. I'd wear it to the automobile races with Davy right now if it wasn't June. I might even get engaged in it, if it holds up."

"Is that a promise?" Jerry said, standing in Mother's doorway, where we noticed him for the first time. Fiancés are always underfoot.

"Not really," I said. "I'd have to wait till next winter."

"For heaven's sake," Sylvia said. "Have you any one in mind?"

"Of course she has," Jerry said. "Any time Maudie hasn't some man in mind, she's sick. Or he's a pretty terrible scrunch."

"Or engaged," I said coldly. Jerry has a habit of being right in a perfectly horrid way. "Do you want me to hang this on the line, Sylvia? If we leave it here, Mother will smother in her sleep."

"Seriously, I mean," Jerry went on, "June is a great month for romance, Maudie. Just look at us."

"Well, suggest some one," I said. "I'm devoting myself to you and Sylvia this month."

"Take the shoes too, Maudie," Sylvia said, pouring more camphor out of them. "These velvet ones are strong enough to walk."

"Then why don't we let them," I said, staggering through the doorway with the coat and six dresses and two suits.

"Here," Jerry said, trying to take the bottom thing in that helpful way men have. "A broken neck never helped any girl's sex appeal. Anyway, I want to see you make good on that promise, Maudie. Will it be Davy? There's a worthy lad."

"Well, I'm going to the races with Davy," I said, kicking open the back stairs. "Did you ever notice how often you don't want to give things to the people who deserve them the most? They sort of remind you of an unpaid bill, or a person you forgot to send flowers to, when they had their appendix out or something. That thing is the mop. Nora always leaves it there, in case she might need it."

"She won't ever need it again," Jerry said. "I just stepped on it. Open the door, will you? Everything's slipping."

There were nine new wedding presents in the kitchen. Silas was hammering the end off one box with smashing sounds that made the cups jump.

"It's plates," Jerry said, as we backed out the door. "Whenever you hit something an awful wallop, it turns out to be plates."

"And that present all tied up in burlap and stuffed with tissue paper, which Sylvia and I opened like it was eggs, might have been solid rock," I said, hanging the coat on the line. "It was an antique coffin stool, very quaint and convenient. You can set other things on it besides coffins."

"Good Lord!" Jerry said. "Who sent it?"

"It said Mr. Charles Lee," I said.

"That's too bad," Jerry said. "He's one of the ushers. I was just going to mention him to you as the ideal easy catch, only now I suppose you'll be prejudiced."

"Not specially," I said. "It won't be my coffin. But who wants an easy catch? I like my men hard to get."

"Well, what about Ted Felton?" Jerry said. "He took quite a shine to you that time you tried to make a match between him and Sylvia."

"No," I said firmly, "he might try to sell me something. I don't believe in life insurance." That had been a very disillusioning experience for me, when it turned out that Ted Felton's interest in Sylvia was all for the interior motive of getting close to Father.

"Why not?" Jerry said, tying shoes on the line.

I sat down on the back steps to think. "Well," I said, "I figure that a person with my kind of personality isn't worth anything when they're dead. Haven't you anybody more inspiring than Ted? Somebody I could really enjoy suffering for?"

"Sure," Jerry said, in a rather scornful voice, "there's MacKean Andrews, my best man, but you couldn't get him, so don't try. You're too young to develop an inferiority complex."

"No fear," I said just as scornfully. "Why couldn't I get him?"

"Because older and more worldly women than you have tried for ten years," Jerry said, "without success."

"Oh, is that all?" I said. "I thought maybe he was married or studying to be a monk or something."

"Maudie," Sylvia called out of the nursery window, in a wild voice, "I've lost those cards I was going to write in the book. What was on them, can you remember?"

"There was two hot-milk pitchers," I said, my mind being very clear, "and four more carving sets, which you can't return three of them, because they got monograms on them. And then there was that picture of the Tower of London from Uncle Eustace which Silas broke, and Mrs. Jeffries' coffee table."

"Ah," Jerry said, "who sent that?"

"Mrs. Jeffries, dumb-bell," Sylvia said, starting to close the window. "I wish you'd come up and help unpack this last batch, Jerry. It's more plates, worse luck, and we still haven't any glasses or finger bowls."

Jerry went immediately, with that look on his face that all men get when they start thinking about their life work. I sat on the back steps after he left, feeling rather sad, for some reason. Why is it that when you see people in love and all worn out with getting married and looking like a wreck over buying furniture and kitchen things with not enough money, you usually envy them? I began to wonder if there was something about it all that I didn't understand.

A truck stopped on the drive just then and a man came up the back path with three packages.

"This Mason's?" he said, dumping them down in a casual way so that something inside me said, "Plates."

"Yes," I said. "Are you married?"

The man shoved his cap back and laughed. "Whatsa matter, girlie?" he said. "Some guy walk out on you?"

"No," I said. "I just wondered if you were married. I'm just interested in marriage, that's all."

"So was I—oncet," he said, taking his pencil from back of his ear. "Now I gotta wife and two kids and it's gimme, gimme, gimme, all the time, till I tell you the truth, girlie, I'm wore out. I gotta have this here signed for."

"What did you get married for?" I said, while I wrote my name in his book. He set the packages at the back door where the next person out would step on them.

"I'm asking you, sister," he said. "You know how it is when you've went together for three years. That top one is glass, you wanta tell every one."

"I know," I said; "I heard it."

"Well, s'long," he said, sticking the pencil back of his ear again. "Hope your sweetie turns up." He ran down the path and jumped on the truck as it came around the bend.

I sat there feeling very depressed. I wondered if Sylvia would say gimme, gimme, gimme, after she was married to Jerry. The door opened and Nora fell over the boxes, and a few minutes later Silas began opening them in the kitchen, with loud crashes and splitting sounds.

I went on sitting on the back steps, where I was practically falling asleep in the sun, when the back gate opened again and another man came up the path. He had on gray flannel trousers and a blue coat and a lot of gray in his hair, which probably came from some secret sorrow rather than just being old, on account of he didn't look a bit feeble or anything. I guess he was about thirty.

I still had on my sneakers and yellow socks and the shorts Davy and I had been playing tennis in, and of course I realized I looked terrible, but I didn't care. It is sort of restful to sit back thinking your thoughts without having some one rushing you off to a bath or something, which people are usually doing to me nowadays. I look terrible a lot of the time, but it is usually because I am thinking, not because I forgot to wash.

"I wonder if you can tell me, sonny—" the man said, and then stopped as I sat up. "I beg your pardon. I thought you were a boy."

"If I was a boy," I said, "I wouldn't be the kind that wore yellow socks. I'm a girl."

"So I see," the man said in a polite voice, with a smile that wasn't in the least polite. "And a very pretty one, I should say."

"When you say it that way," I said, gazing up at him with a cold expression, "I feel like a horse."

"Well," he said, laughing, "open your mouth and I'll tell you your age."

"If I opened my mouth," I said, getting up and smoothing down my shorts with dignity, "you'd probably jump down my throat. Did you want something when you came in here, or are you just out for a walk?"

"Now don't be nasty till you have the facts," the man said. "I rang the front doorbell but nobody let me in."

"Silas is making such a racket that nobody ever hears the bell," I said, feeling a little apologetic. "And Sylvia is having a tea in the library."

"So I came around to find some one to help me. You see," he went on, giving me a first-magnitude smile, "I'm looking for a charming lady named Miss Maudie Mason. Does she live here?"

I gazed at him. "I'm Maudie Mason," I said, "and you're not looking

for me, because I never saw you before. If you want Sylvia, I'll get
her. Who are you?"

He put his hands behind him and smiled up at me. Offhand, he
looked to me like Yale and a penthouse and a few trips to Europe.
You know, there are people that seem to be immune to even the depression, just like some people never get the mumps.

"My name is MacKean Andrews," he said, bowing, "and I am
looking for Miss Maudie Mason, because I've just arrived in town to
be the best man at a wedding where she's to be the maid of honor,
and I feel that she and I could be friends, after the things Jerry has
told me about her."

Well, I could just imagine the things Jerry had probably told him,
as one old college friend to another. Remembering what Jerry had
told me about MacKean Andrews, I thought about what I had been
saying to him with great satisfaction. Right then I was sure I couldn't
have done better. I might have gone coy on him just at the wrong
moment, and anybody knows that the way to get a popular man is to
be hard to get yourself, even to the point of being rude to them.

"Oh, I've heard lots about you too," I said naïvely, realizing here
was a God-given chance to work a swell line I'd read somewhere. "I
almost didn't want to meet you. I was afraid."

"Afraid," MacKean said, sort of puzzled, but pleased. "Why?"

"Afraid I'd be bored." It's all over now, I thought, congratulating
myself much too soon, as it turned out. "Are you staying with us?"
I added without interest, opening the kitchen door.

"No," he said, "I'm over at the club, holding Jerry's hand. Besides,
you seem to have a houseful already. I looked in the front window
and the woods were full of pretty women."

"I'm glad to meet you," I said. "I've always wanted to know one of
these men that goes around looking in people's windows. Those were
the bridesmaids. They come over every afternoon about this time to
look at the new wedding presents. Come on in this way. I'll let you
in through the dining room."

MacKean was looking at me with an amused expression. I didn't
kind of like it—it made me feel like a dog which has been doing a
trick.

"Really," he said, "you are a rather terrible child. I suppose it's this
younger generation I've been hearing about."

Everybody flocked out to meet him at the library door and I slid

327

out to sit on the landing. There is a sort of an opening there which you can look into the library from, without people thinking to look at you, and I could watch MacKean and every so often hear what he was saying. He smiled and talked and everybody was terribly, terribly glad to see him, but all the time he wasn't talking, he had that amused expression on his face, as though he didn't believe anybody could show him anything he hadn't already seen.

The more I watched him, the more I began to realize that there is a difference between popular boys and popular older men. Popular boys are very aloof and haughty on the surface, but they melt quicker than most, inside—sort of like one of those chocolate bars you bite into and it turns out to be ice cream—but popular older men aren't like that. They're charming and friendly and helpful on the outside, but the more I looked at McKean, the more I was sure that beneath that velvety surface there beat a heart of granite.

I remember the time Uncle Eustace shot some wild ducks somewhere and we ate them for dinner, and every time you took a big exotic mouthful, your teeth bit a bullet, which just about tore out your nervous system. I began to realize that if you could get so much pain out of a dead duck, you might have a nervous breakdown over a person like MacKean, if you happened to make a mistake about him. I wondered if my idea on the back porch would work, because whereas the way to get a popular man is to be hard to get yourself, if he doesn't want to get you, you can go and turn into a public problem and still he won't care. You can crush a person like Davy under your heel and have him oozing sweetness, but I suspected that with a person like MacKean, I would have to take an ax.

"Bit off more than you can chew this time, didn't you, kid?" I heard a voice behind me, and of course there was Jerry, underfoot as usual, coming downstairs. "Or are you already engaged?"

"Neither," I said. "I'm looking him over."

"Well," said Jerry, "how does he look? Come on in and I'll introduce you."

"You don't have to," I told him without excitement. "He picked me up in the back yard."

"Really?" Jerry said: "Well, don't bank on it, Maudie. Funnier things than that have happened to that guy. Did you see Sylvia?"

"Listen," I said, rising to my feet and languidly pulling out Jerry's tie, "I'll bet you on him. If I get him, will you give me two dollars and twenty cents?"

"Anything," Jerry said, slapping me in a very disrespectful sort of place, "anything."

The minute he had gone, I dashed down to the telephone room and called up Davy.

"Listen, Davy," I said, "come over in about ten minutes."

"Hey, what do you think I am," Davy's voice said, very irritated, "the village taxi? Anyway, I saw you all morning. Doncha know I can't give you all my time?"

"So that was a gift," I said coldly. "Thank you for nothing. I need a whole lot of help, and will you help me or will I call up Chi or Bob or Bill or—"

"Heck," Davy said, "what kind of a five-alarm fire is this?"

"I'll tell you next time I see you, next month sometime," I said, making banging sounds with the telephone which sounded like me hanging up the receiver.

"Maudie!" Davy howled. "Wait a minute! I'll check in, in ten minutes."

I smiled to myself—a maternal smile. "When you get here," I said, "I want you to yell under my window. Then when I don't answer—"

"Hey, what is this, what is this?" Davy said, very mad. "What do you mean, when you don't answer?"

"Then you are to go and yell under Sylvia's window," I went on calmly, "and when I don't answer, you're to open our front door and yell in the hall."

"What am I, babe," Davy said, "the town crier? I suppose then I turn around and pull you out of somebody's derby. Listen, is this a game?"

"No," I said, "it's a drama and you're the menace." And I quietly hung up, knowing that in his soul Davy always thinks of himself as a menace, ever since he got that Panama hat to crown his dark beauty with.

I dashed upstairs and peeled off my socks and shorts and got out a blue dress I have with a ruffle down the front. Then I fluffed my hair out in the back and tied a ribbon around my head, very naïve. I had just about finished when I heard Davy roar under my window. I peeped out at him, and would you believe it, for the first time I was struck with the fact that Davy is getting very handsome in a rather lean and hungry-looking way. It gave me quite a shock.

Davy didn't see me and in a minute he ran and yelled "Maudie!" under Sylvia's window. I went down to the landing and looked through the opening into the library, where people were, some of them looking out the window to see who was calling, while others were looking around to see where I was, and practically everybody was remembering having seen me somewhere around that day. If I'd been there, I couldn't have caused more excitement.

Pretty soon Davy came banging into the hall and yelled "Maudie!" in a loud, angry voice. I saw every one jump and laugh and MacKean walked over to the door and said, "Quite a larynx, son," in a voice that made Davy go white under the eyes with rage.

Then Sylvia said, "What do you want, Davy?" and so did Ting and Helen Tyson and Carroll Emery; and Davy kept saying, "I'm looking for Maudie," because naturally he didn't know what he wanted because I hadn't told him. The madder Davy got, the handsomer he got, I noticed, very pleased, and finally, just as MacKean said, "You have to have a warrant to search the house, you know," I rushed down the stairs like a breath of spring practically into Davy's clenched fists and we spun out the door, without a look or a word at MacKean, who began to look rather fascinated out of the corner of my eye.

"Listen, biscuit," Davy said, as I steered him down the drive, "I wouldn't make such a mutt of myself for any woman alive if there wasn't a reason. Is there?"

"Of course there is," I said. "Jerry has bet me anything I want that I can't snare MacKean Andrews—he was the man talking to you in the doorway."

"Terrible beazle," Davy said sourly. "Who would want him?"

"Nobody," I said, not very truthfully. "It isn't wanting him that matters; it's getting him."

"Well, just get him then," Davy said, "and give him to me. Listen, be your age, Maudie. You can swing a bat in any league around here and knock one over the fence, but you won't get to first base with an old guy like that. He's been around."

"So have I," I reminded him. "Don't you worry about me, darling. Just be a sweet and do what I tell you, and if I win we can make Jerry buy us the tickets for the auto races."

"Okay," Davy said, brightening. "Okay."

Sylvia was having a buffet supper that night and of course I was there in my blue dress and hair ribbon, passing sandwiches and pouring out iced tea. The ushers had all come and there was about ten other men and all the bridesmaids and some girls that were having babies, and their husbands, and Sylvia and Jerry and me and MacKean. He was getting a roll from the bread tray on the piano when I came down and, of course, he stopped me with his mind full of the ideas I had put there.

"Hello, hello!" he said. "I began to wonder whether we'd see you again."

"Why?" I asked. "We just went to the movies, that was all." I gave him an innocent smile.

"That was a very passionate young man," he said, "and what a voice! He wanted Maudie; there was no question about that."

"Of course he wanted me," I said. "It isn't that way with every one, but Davy and I—we feel that way about each other. You know how it is." I looked at him pleadingly, and noticed how the gray in his hair made little white lines over his ears in the lamplight. His eyes looked very soft and sort of human.

"Maudie," he said, linking his arm through mine and strolling with me into the hall, "you make me feel my age. I'd almost forgotten people ever got that way about each other. Now that you mention it, I believe I did myself once, about fifteen years ago. It was up in the Adirondacks in a canoe, with a great big moon sailing over our heads and somebody playing music across the lake."

I shook my head scornfully. "That's not the way I feel," I said. "That's just being mushy. Why, I can love Davy in a traffic jam after it's rained on my hat. You don't understand at all." And I shook his arm out of mine and ran out onto the porch, where I bumped into some one so hard I banged my head on their jaw. It was Davy.

"Maudie," he said passionately, "I just happened to hear what you just said to that guy—gosh, Maudie—"

"Listen," I said, very provoked, "where is your ticket?"

"Don't be funny, biscuit," Davy said. "I heard you tell that guy you could love me in a traffic jam."

"Well, this isn't a traffic jam," I said. "And what is the matter with the human race, anyway? People are getting a perfect epidemic of looking in other people's windows."

"If you mean me, I wasn't looking in your window," Davy said haughtily. "I just brought Ting over here for supper, on my way over to Pauline's. I'm stepping her to-night for a change." He gave me a triumphant look and I smiled sweetly.

"Have a good time," I said, "and tell Pauly I do hope she's a lot better."

Davy looked suspicious. "Whatsa matter with her?" he said.

"Nothing serious," I said, "just hives. G'by."

"Maudie," Sylvia called from inside, "what time did Miss Edgar say they would have those hats done? Helen's gone and cut her hair, the dummy, and I'll bet hers will have to be done over."

"Gosh, I'm sorry, Sylvia," Helen was saying futilely. "I never thought."

"She didn't say," I said, "but I can call her up and find out. She still has to-morrow. She could finish it on Saturday if she had to. The wedding isn't until twelve."

Chairs were piled up against the door to the telephone room, so I went into Father's study, wondering how I was ever going to get along without a helpful younger sister like me when I got married.

"What are you doing in here, all by yourself?" I heard a voice say, and there was MacKean again, big as life.

"I'm worrying," I said. "That was Davy on the porch. He heard what I was saying to you, just as if I didn't have enough trouble already."

"I've been talking to Jerry about you," MacKean said, sitting down on the sofa. "He tells me you have quite a genius for breaking hearts. I suppose Davy is only one of many."

"He's the only one that counts," I said. "Except perhaps yours. It's worth money to me, if I only had time to do something about it."

"This is very interesting," MacKean said, in a tone of voice that convinced me that Jerry, who had no morals, had told him about the bet. "I didn't know my heart was worth anything to any one."

"It's worth two dollars and twenty cents to me," I said. "The twenty cents is a tax."

MacKean began to laugh. "Maudie," he said, "this is marvelous. I've never heard such an accurate appraisal. Won't you explain?"

"There isn't anything to explain," I said, sitting down at the other end of the sofa. "Jerry told me a whole lot about your past and how women always long to possess you—"

332

"Good Lord!"

"And he bet me I couldn't get you, that's all."

"Well," said MacKean, "but what about the two dollars and twenty cents?"

"Oh, that was if I got you," I said. "Davy and I want to go to the automobile races and that would pay for our tickets."

"I see," he said. "You bet Jerry that you can catch me so that you can take Davy to the races. Very involved."

"Too involved," I said. "It isn't worth it."

"Who isn't?" MacKean said. "Jerry or Davy or me?"

"The races," I said. "Davy and I can always play tennis. The races would be swell though." I felt wistful.

"So you haven't tried to get me at all?" MacKean said. "What a disappointment! Weren't you even tempted, just on general principles?"

"I have no general principles," I said. "Yes, I was tempted, of course."

"Ah," said MacKean, "I feel better. Won't you tell me what it was about me that tempted you?"

"The two dollars and twenty cents," I said. "Do you mind if I telephone about Helen's hat? She went and cut off her hair."

Miss Edgar was very wild and excited over the telephone, but finally she said it could be arranged, as they always do. When I finished, MacKean was still there, chuckling.

"I want to ask you a great many things," he said, as I got up. "Don't go."

"I'm supposed to be passing sandwiches," I said. "Mother told me I was to be helpful."

"You are," MacKean said, "you're helping me. I'm feeling sort of let down on this business of the bet. Apparently I don't measure up to some of these hearts that lack a cash basis. What is my chief fault?"

"Well," I said, "you can't help it, of course, but you are sort of old and disillusioned, compared to Davy. And, anyway, I don't break hearts consciously. They just break."

"How do you know I'm so old?" he said. "The gray hair?"

"Oh, no," I said, "Chi has gray in his hair and he's only nineteen. The reason I think you must be old is because you talk to me as if I was so very young."

"Gosh," MacKean said, "do I?"

"Yes," I said. "And then you called me pretty the minute you saw me. I had on those yellow pants and my sleeves rolled up and my hair was mussed and my face was all sunburned. The boys I know only call a girl pretty if she really is, not because they think she would like to think she is, when she knows darn well she isn't."

MacKean smoothed the back of his hair while shaking his head.

"I've made a hideous first impression, I can see," he said. "You frighten me, Maudie. Can't I do anything to square things? There are a few good apples on this old tree really. Give me another chance." He looked up at me with a smile that would raise most people's blood pressure.

I walked over to the window and looked out. Carroll Emery and Ting and Ted Felton and Otis Boyer were out there, mostly laughing. I looked back at MacKean.

"I wish I had that two-twenty," I said. "We none of us ever have any money the end of June. Davy spent all his fixing the car, so we could go, only we didn't know about the tickets. There's one thing you could do—" I stopped and he said:

"Check. What is it?"

"Could you just go through the motions of having a broken heart— just enough to convince Jerry? Or are you the kind that will go and tell him?"

MacKean put his head back on the sofa and laughed.

"A complete double-cross," he said. "Certainly I won't tell him. My only kick is that I have to put on this act all by myself. You haven't really lifted a finger, you know."

"I know," I said, "but the real reason is because I'm so busy managing Davy that I don't get a chance to think much about any one else." (That was to lull him into feeling perfectly safe with me.)

"Of course," MacKean started to say, but just that minute Connie Duveyn and Jerry and those two Sellers boys that I can never tell apart came bursting in the door. Jerry gave me a teasing look, which I returned, and Connie said:

"Sorry to break in on this cozy party, but we're calling the roll for one last fling for the bride and groom. Who wants to go to Willow Grove?"

"I do," I said. "There's one horse on the merry-go-round there that knows me."

"If Maudie wants to go, so do I," MacKean said, getting up. Carroll looked in the window and waved.

"Sylvia's calling you from upstairs, Jerry," she said. "She says something about plates. Who's going to Willow Grove?"

"Everybody," said one of the Sellers. "We've just broken up this combination to get a little action."

"How will we divide up?" Connie said, looking dreamily at Mac-Kean, but it didn't work.

"In another minute I'm going to do the most outrageous thing," Carroll said, framed in the window curtains. "I'm going to rush the best man. I have a weakness for young men with gray hair." Carroll has sort of knock-down-and-drag-out tactics.

"My hair is turning gray from worry," the other Sellers boy said, helping Ting, who had just come in with Helen, into her coat. "Can I be your weakness, Carroll?"

"You couldn't pay me to ride with MacKean," Helen said loudly. "He's a wild driver."

MacKean just laughed and said, "Helen, you flatter the car. At any rate, I can take three, one with me and two in the rumble. Who besides Maudie wants to go?" He winked at me and I winked back to assure him I understood it was all in fun.

Well, if looks could have burned, I would have been a crisp, but of course every one acted very noncommittal. Sylvia and Jerry came down from the wedding-present room and we all went out to the cars parked in the drive.

"Maudie!" Sylvia said. "Bread-and-butter plates at last! From Mrs. Felton, the divine soul."

In the end, Ting and Charlie Lee went in our rumble. I didn't know it was Charlie Lee until MacKean told me, as there were four ushers I didn't know and he was one of them.

"I hope I get a chance to speak to him later on," I said, as MacKean got in beside me.

"Why?" he said. "Any special attraction?"

"Yes," I said. "He sent Sylvia a coffin stool. If a person must think of the future, I should think they would choose something with a happy thought connected with it. I could think up quite a few presents for a bride that would suggest a radiant future."

"So could I," MacKean said with a quizzical smile, and of course we were both thinking of a kiddie coop. People always are when there is a bride around.

We drove very fast until we came to the York Road, where there were a great many other cars with mussed, contented-looking people in them, just out for a ride and not going anywhere. There was a little wind shaking the leaves and the sky was very pale and peaceful, making you feel peaceful just to look at it. People were rocking on their front porches and sprinklers were whirling around in everybody's front lawn, and every so often a light would go on somewhere. I would have been perfectly happy to go riding on through the whole summer, but before I knew it, there was the sky suddenly decorated with chains and wheels of lights, with music beating out from somewhere, and people climbing out of cars in the parking field.

First we went to the merry-go-round, and I found my horse, while MacKean stood beside me, looking amused. There is a wonderful airy feeling to the merry-go-round, I think. Everybody was getting on things and getting off them, but I just rode solemnly up and down because I love merry-go-rounds. Then we went to a place where you ride around in little cars, bumping into each other and laughing. Helen tried to get MacKean to ride with her, and so did Carroll, and so did Connie, and even Sylvia tried, but MacKean said, "Wherever Maudie goes, I go too," looking very calm at everybody.

Jerry helped me in and said, "What is all this, siren?" in my ear, but I just gave him a cold look. Then we went over to a high-slide—a terribly scary-looking slide.

"I won't go down," I said, as we crowded past people to the platform where you get a little piece of carpet to sit on. "It looks perfectly awful." For some reason I always get slide fright; maybe I was dropped when I was a baby.

"Don't be silly, Maudie," Sylvia said, sitting down at the top of the slide, "it's lots of fun—just like flying. Don't you start till I get half-way down, Jerry. You might run over me."

"I'll start you, little girl," Otis said, trying to shove me after Sylvia. "Just keep in the straight and narrow path, that's all."

Everybody laughed and laughed, and Helen and Ted began to argue about who was next, and in the end Charlie pushed Helen and she screamed all the way down.

"Come on, Maudie," Charlie said; "be a sport."

"It's only a slide, dumb-bell," Carroll said.

"I can't help it," I said, very apologetic. "I'll watch you all. I know it's only a slide, but it just looks like sliding down the side of City Hall from here."

MacKean got a piece of carpet and sat down on it. He smiled up at me.

"Coming with me?" he said, and before I could decide, he lifted me down in front of him and put one arm around me. I don't weigh much, and I lost what weight I have just from fright, as we practically fell into space.

"Want to do it again?" MacKean said, as we stopped sliding.

"No," I said, "but I'll have to go back up to the top a minute." I looked up at him.

"What for?" he said, not beginning to get up.

"I left my stomach up there," I said.

MacKean suddenly hugged me with the arm that was still around me.

"Maudie," he said, "you're priceless."

"It seems wrong," I said, "when you are only worth two dollars and twenty cents."

We climbed out onto the floor and I saw some hot dogs across the road which I hurried over to, on account of I love hot dogs just pleasantly raw, the way they have them at Willow Grove. I heard Sylvia say, "MacKean!" and then "Don't do it. She's only a kid. It isn't fair," and I smiled to myself. Anybody that wants to put anything over on me has to get up yesterday.

"I don't want any mustard," I said to the hot-dog man, "just the dog."

"O.K.," he said; "wanna kennel?"

I looked at him a little aloof, thinking he was being funny, but just then I heard MacKean say behind me, "He means a roll," and I said, "Yes," in a disinterested manner. MacKean put his arm through mine as we walked away.

There was something different about MacKean, I began to notice. He kept looking at me with that soft, human look and trying to hold my hand as well as my arm, only each time he tried he would turn out to be just holding the hot dog.

"Maudie," he said, after a while, "you aren't giving me a chance to act my part."

"You don't have to now," I said. "Jerry went on with Sylvia and the rest. We can just be ourselves."

"Why, yes, that's so," he said and his voice sounded sort of disappointed. We walked along in silence while I daintily munched my

dog and MacKean ate sticky popcorn with one hand and steered me
over to a bench near where the band was playing with the other.

"Sit down," he said, "and be nice to me. Aren't you the least bit
interested in me as a person, you little gold digger?"

I sat up very straight. "I'm not a gold digger," I said. "I can pay
you back for that hot dog out of my allowance. Of course, I'm interested in you as a person. Human nature always interests me."

"Don't hedge," he said. "You think of me as a ticket to the automobile races, and nothing else, don't you?"

"Two tickets," I said.

MacKean clenched his fists over his head. "Girl, have you no soul?"
he said. "Or are you riding me? Have some respect for my gray hairs,
please."

I ran my finger over the gray above his right ear. "I like them," I
said.

The rest of the evening we rode on the scenics and I tried very
hard to seem nonchalant, although really I thought I would collapse
when Otis told about four people being killed on a scenic somewhere
out West last week. I shuddered all the way home.

Helen jumped into MacKean's car when we got ready to come
home and was very cute about refusing to move. Charlie and I sat in
the rumble and sang all the way. He knows a swell song that begins:

> "Oh, the President went to Princeton
> And the Governor went to Yale
> And the Cabinet came from Notre Dame,
> But the Senators go to jail."

All the next day presents came and people called up, and Mother
rushed around talking to caterers and florists, and Father and Silas
carried things and opened things. Sylvia looked very pale and excited
and I was really the only calm person in the family, my idea being that
people wouldn't have gotten married for the last two thousand years
if it wasn't a perfectly normal thing to do.

I have never been so sort of uplifted, though, as I was on Sylvia's
wedding day. There was a kind of holy excitement about it all, with
Mother and Father and Sylvia and me being very sweet and tender
with each other, and everybody asking everybody else what time it
was every few minutes in a casual tone of voice, as though they were
just interested in having good, accurate clocks around, that was all.

Sylvia began to dress at eleven o'clock, and every simple thing she put on was brand new, even her shirt. She had twelve garters on one leg which people had given her to wear for good luck—that is, good luck for them, which meant getting a man, of course; and while she was waving her hair, I sewed them all together, thinking how ghastly it would be if they fell off going down the aisle.

"Don't stick me, Maudie," Sylvia said. "I'm scared to death I'll burn my ear."

"I won't," I said. "Do you feel awful queer, Sylvia?"

"All hollow," Sylvia said. "I'll bet I won't have any voice when I have to say 'I will.' "

"Never mind," I said; "I'll say it for you, if you give out."

"Sylvia, dear," Mother said, coming in with Sylvia's veil held up high, and the end of it over her other arm, "Miss Edgar is here to fix your veil. Maudie, you'd better get dressed."

My dress was a dream—all yellow and slithery, with long full sleeves and a high nunlike neck, and a wide hat tipped over my right eye, with a lot of brim standing up in the back. I was just admiring myself when in came Ting and Helen and Carroll, looking better than I would have believed possible in darling yellow creations and armloads of snapdragons and larkspur and yellow roses. Helen's hat was a little cock-eyed in the back, where Miss Edgar took the piece out, but I didn't tell her so—I was feeling too mellow.

"Maudie, you look cute," Carroll said. "Doesn't she look cute, Ting?"

Ting smiled at me. I still love Ting very much.

"A great girl," she said. "Your father wants us all downstairs. Oh, Sylvia!"

Sylvia came floating in, all veil and satin train and starry eyes. Her bouquet simply dripped lilies of the valley, and she looked like such a complete bride that I could hardly believe it was Sylvia.

"Come on, girls," she said. "It is ten of twelve and any minute I might weaken."

Mother smiled in at us from the hall, looking really marvelous in one of those mother-of-the-bride costumes that I never thought I would live to see her wear.

"Pull your hat down in the front, Carroll," she said. "Girls, you look lovely."

The organ was playing when we got to the church and the ushers were rushing up and down the aisle with people while we lined up in the vestibule. The church seemed to be full of people that I never saw before, so that I began to wonder if this was the right church.

"For goodness' sake, let's keep together," Connie whispered to everybody. "Last night Helen and Carroll looked as though they were going to a fire."

We must have looked very artistic coming down the aisle, for every one smiled mistily at us and at each other, and made little shaking motions with their heads. I saw Davy halfway down, and he gave me a very intense look. He might have been thinking of me in a bridal way, but I guess it was just the tickets. By the chancel steps Jerry and MacKean were standing, looking very handsome and dominant.

Oh, it was all so wonderful! When Sylvia said, "I, Sylvia, take thee, Jerome," with the sun shining through the window on her veil, I made a resolution I would never do another bad thing as long as I lived. I felt so holy I nearly suffocated.

I didn't think much about MacKean until we got outside and every one began getting into cars. MacKean steered me across the drive to where his car was parked.

"You ride with me, lady," he said. "I'll take care of your frills."

"I'll get in," I said, "and then you give me my flowers. Everything about me can muss awful easy."

For the second time I climbed in, and we started off in the direction that most of the cars weren't going.

"To-morrow," MacKean began, "I'm going away. Ever since I met you—"

"Day before yesterday," I added helpfully.

"Day before yesterday," he said. "I've been doing you a favor, haven't I?"

"I'll let you know," I said, "when and if I collect from Jerry."

"You'll collect all right," he said. "I was talking to Jerry last night at the club. The point is this: Do I or don't I get anything out of this?" He gave me that soft, human look.

"Yes," I said, "you get the knowledge of a deed well done."

He laughed. "Horrible thought," he said. "I feel like a public monument."

"That's where I got that," I confessed. "Under General Grant."

"Good heavens!" he said. "Do I suggest him at all?"

"He's a statue," I said, "and you look real. Are you?"

Instead of answering, he stopped the car suddenly and put his arm around me.

"Don't try to stop me," he said. "I'm going to kiss you."

"Is it necessary?" I said coldly, sitting up very stiff.

"It isn't because it's necessary," he said; "it's because I want to. What would you say if I told you that I really have fallen for you, in deadly earnest and without misgivings?"

"It wouldn't surprise me a bit," I said, leaning back casually, with my life in my hands. "Practically all men say that to me some time or other."

"Good Lord," MacKean said, sinking back in his corner of the seat. "Maudie, my girl, you must have a soul of iron."

"Not of iron," I said, giving him my most charming smile, "just stainless steel."

Jerry sent me the money for the tickets from Manchester, where he and Sylvia went on their honeymoon, and Davy and I had a marvy time at the races. We screamed so loud I was hoarse for six days. It wasn't till Jerry got back that I got a chance to really gloat over him, and it was much more fun because I had a letter from MacKean to show him.

"I still don't see how you did it," Jerry said, as we sat at Sunday breakfast, waiting for other people to wake up. "That bird is absolutely immune, I tell you."

"Well," I said, "he really did it himself. I just got him to go through the motions for fun and pretty soon he meant it. You know how it is. Like when you pretend the dark is full of ghosts, and pretty soon you really are scared. I figured it was the only way to get a person who was too blasé to start from natural causes."

"Maudie," Jerry said, pouring out his coffee, "did you ever hear of the James-Lange theory?"

"No," I said, "who's he?"

"Never mind," Jerry said. "Do you know, two great psychologists devoted their entire lives to discovering that truth that you've spouted so nonchalantly?"

"How dumb," I said, buttering my muffin. "Why didn't they just ask some girl?"

They Called Her Mousie

GRACE SARTWELL MASON

She must have been "Mousie." She even lacked the courage to ask for a new typewriter. Well, then, how could a mouse of a girl such as this tame a raging lion with macaroons? Or did she?

WHEN MOUSIE lifted her gaze from the typewriter and saw that in a few minutes she would have to take the wire basket of letters to Mr. Erickson she began to tremble. Dread caused her thin ribs to stick together; she drew delicate breaths with a tiny bit of her lungs and made herself even smaller than usual.

In fact, she became almost invisible behind her machine, which was not difficult, for it was built on the lines of Grant's Tomb and was known to the outer office as Big Brute. It was because of this redoubtable machine, indeed, that Mousie had come by her name.

The unwritten rule of the outer office assigned Big Brute to the latest hired. But though girls and men had come and gone, Mousie still remained stuck with the meanest old rattletrap that ever reduced a conscientious girl to tears. By some hocus-pocus the three other girls in the outer office had managed to get and keep for themselves able-bodied if not new-minted typewriters, while on Janey Carlton's desk Big Brute sulked, decrepit and evil, month after month because Janey simply could not get up courage to complain to Mr. Erickson.

Thus she had come to be called Mousie. She did not like the name any better than she liked Big Brute, but she put up with them both because—she knew it sadly—she was a coward.

"Trouble with you, Mouse, you got no guts." The other girls in the outer office—great husky blondes and redheads—would remind her from time to time. "Listen, what you want to do is to breeze up to old Erick and tell him you gotta have a new machine. Look, do it like this . . ." And they would get themselves in stitches, as they said, giving imitations of themselves mowing down Mr. Erickson.

They got a lot of fun out of Mousie and her typewriter. They did

342

not know real terror when they saw it, but they did know that watching Mousie's eyes growing bigger and bigger, her little three-cornered face growing whiter and whiter and her hands fluttering in a panic they could not in the least understand, was almost as good as the movies.

She never contradicted them when they said she was lacking in courage, for it was the truth. There was almost nothing she was not afraid of. Starting at the top of the list with brother-in-law Bill, she was afraid of an enormous number of things—snakes and policemen, thunder and dark hallways, the subway and germs and violence of any kind, hostesses in tea rooms, Mr. Erickson and the elevator starter, loud voices and the thought of cruelty.

Of course, more than anything else she was afraid of losing her job, which would put her completely at the mercy of Bill and Lilian, who had loud, scornful, decided voices and a habit of borrowing all her spare dimes. In an unguarded moment she had told them about Big Brute, and they, too, nagged her persistently to take the matter up with Mr. Erickson.

"You gotta have guts in this world," Bill would say, helping himself to the lion's share of bacon. "You can't be a rabbit, see? The way I'd do it, I'd walk right in and I'd say . . ."

Mousie knew he was right, she knew they were all right, but she simply could not bring herself to ask Mr. Erickson to give her another typewriter. At last she had bought herself a little book entitled: "Your Powers: How to Develop Them," and every night before she went to sleep she firmly informed the world—in a whisper—that she was not afraid. Not of anything. That she was getting to be a stronger character every day. That very soon, now, she would walk right up to Mr. Erickson and demand another typewriter.

She knew exactly what she would say to him. In fact, she had memorized the words: "Excuse me, Mr. Erickson, but if you don't mind, I would like another typewriter. I try very hard to get along with the one I have, but you can't do good work when half of the letters get tangled together and the other half stick down. I don't ask for a *new* typewriter, Mr. Erickson, but one that's just a *little* newer, please."

She worked on this speech, polishing it and revising it of a morning in the subway, but so far she had not succeeded in getting it off. Once she had actually stopped at Mr. Erickson's elbow, and clinging with a cold hand to the corner of his desk, had said faintly: "Excuse me, Mr. Erickson, but if you don't mind—" And then he had raised his irritable eyes to hers and her bones had turned to jelly. She had not been able to go on.

But today somehow she knew she could not put off speaking to Mr. Erickson any longer. For one thing, Big Brute was getting worse. He was wearing her out with his meanness. But aside from that, she suspected that if she did not speak to Mr. Erickson today she never would.

She sat for a moment staring at Big Brute. Somehow, he had become mixed up with Lilian who was bossy and Bill who despised her; and the lumpy divan on which she slept at night; and the never having any privacy; and the one boy who had ever come to see her, whom Bill had haw-hawed right out of existence; and her own secret scorn of herself. If she didn't get rid of Big Brute she would never get rid of the weakness that made all these things possible.

The clock struck twelve-thirty, and she jumped. Her legs barely carried her down the hall to Mr. Erickson's door.

When she opened the door she saw that Mr. Erickson appeared to be doing nothing, gloomily. She opened her mouth, while her heart gave a desperate flop, like a fish on the dock.

"Excuse me, Mr. Erickson, but if you don't mind, I—"

Mr. Erickson at once became busy. He raised a large impatient hand and seized the telephone. "Get me Mr. Wainwright." He lifted to hers an eye as cordial as a cold boiled potato and inquired: "Huh? What say?"

She tried again. "Excuse me, Mr. Erickson, but—"

"Oh, murder!" she thought. "I said that before."

And Mr. Erickson suddenly leaned to the telephone, while a happy grin warmed his face. "That you, Sam? How 'bout biting a bean with me? Yeah, same place, be there right away. G'by."

He sprang up, seized his hat, waved an impatient hand at her, muttered, "S'm'other time," and pranced out.

Mousie leaned against the wall, her eyes shut, her face as white as milk. "Murder!" she breathed. "I fell down again."

Her failure this time left her more hopeless, more scornful of herself. On the way to lunch not even the golden warmth of autumn, nor the sound of a ribald calliope in front of Jimpson's Wild Animal

Show around the corner, had the power to revive her. Shrinking under the eye of the traffic policeman who every day for almost a year had saved her life at twelve-thirty—she got the jitters in traffic—she crossed Forty-second Street and was shot through the revolving doors of a tea shop.

She said: "Pea soup, caramel sundae and macaroons, please."

She felt a certain wan satisfaction as she thus went the limit. After all, she thought, to be extravagant like that was something, wasn't it? She ate neatly, sitting on her stool at the long counter, taking care not to jog the elbows at right and left of her and thanking the black-browed lordly boy when he gave her a glass of water. He made her feel of no consequence, but she knew a trick to combat that. She had learned a way by which when she was alone in a crowd she could forget to feel humble or scared. She could think about a room of her own.

Bending her head over the caramel sundae and allowing small delicious spoonfuls of it to melt in her mouth, she thought about a time when she would have a room of her own somewhere far away from Bill and Lilian. It would be a small room, of course, but that did not matter. With her imagination she chose its furniture.

One of the best characteristics of this dream was that when she gave herself up to it, it could make her forget everything around her. Now, wrapped comfortingly in her dream, she ate the last spoonful of caramel sundae and began on the macaroons. She was not aware that outside the windows something had all at once begun to agitate the passers-by. The first sound that penetrated her bemused state was a woman's scream.

With a start she turned her head toward the sound, and then saw that all the customers in the place were standing in arrested attitudes craning their necks and staring toward the revolving doors.

Caught as in a little cage of glass, a plump lady stood within the revolving doors. She seemed to be suffering from some sort of seizure. She was making little leaps into the air, without progressing either forward or backward, and all the time she kept up a horrified screaming.

Mousie shrank on her stool in distress. She could not bear violence of any kind, and the plump lady's sounds were really quite unbridled.

The crowd was increasing outside the revolving doors. Inside the tea room a bright young hostess sailed down the room. "What's all this screaming about?" she demanded. "Madam, either go out or come in, will you, please?" She laid a firm hand on the revolving doors.

Then instantly the bright young hostess herself began to scream. And well she might, for as the plump lady propelled herself out onto the sidewalk, the doors revolved and something swept into the tea shop past the hostess' knees—something that sent her plunging through the doors into the outer air. In short, a lion.

With a mere handful of puny words it is impossible to describe the effect the appearance of this outrageous customer had upon the clientele of the tea shop. Just for a fraction of a second there was a stunned silence, an incredulous silence. Everyone in the place—customers, waitresses, white-coated boys behind the soda counter, pretty girls behind the cake counter—stood or sat gaping, frozen.

And the lion, too, stood still, slightly sprawling as the revolving doors had deposited him, unfeigned astonishment on his countenance. Then he lowered his head slightly—and at this movement everyone came alive. Everyone screamed or squealed or grunted, and then climbed upon, or burrowed under, something.

It was really amazing how acrobatic everyone became. Even the girl in the cashier's cage, who of all persons there surely was the safest, climbed up on the little ledge inside her cage and draped herself half fainting over the glass. Two ladies buying pecans at the candy counter got up on a radiator. A man with half a doughnut in his mouth shot across the soda counter on his stomach as if he were sliding for third base.

Mousie sat perfectly quiet on her stool. She knew that just in a minute or two she would die of fright. Terror like an agonizing cold ran through her veins, paralyzing her. It choked the breath out of her lungs and detached her limbs from her body.

Unlike the others, she was completely unable to climb up on anything. She could only sit there staring, staring at the lion.

As for the beast, he at first appeared to feel pretty much the same way. Sprawling and unkinglike he stood there, expressing nothing save an embarrassed astonishment. Then, as if he knew something more was expected of him, he lifted his head, shot his lower jaw forward and roared. A tentative roar, mild as roars go, but filling the room with the most heart-shaking sound in all the world. Then it died away in a rumble deep in the beast's throat. He took a step forward.

"This," thought Mousie, "is the end." She wanted to shut her eyes but she could not. She became dimly aware that one of the boys behind the soda counter was tugging at her arm, imploring her to climb up on the counter, but she could not move. Far off sounded the voices screaming suggestions. "Telephone the police . . . The fire alarm . . . Hit him with a chair . . . No, a marble-topped table . . . Blind him with pepper . . ."

One of the pecan ladies screamed from her radiator: "Boy! Boy, get a red-hot poker!"

And the lion raised his head. His sepia-brown and tawny-red mane fell back; his golden eyes opened and closed slowly; his black-leather-lined nostrils freckled with pink sniffed the air. As if above the de-testable smell of human beings he caught an odor that pleased him, the lion slowly put his great head on one side. A foolish, affecting gesture.

The voices that had been momentarily awed to quiet by the beast's uplifted head now broke out again, and a girl who had climbed the shelves behind the candy counter threw down an armful of empty boxes. The lion started nervously and waved the gray-beige tuft on the end of his tail. Everyone screamed at Mousie: "Look out! Get up on the counter. Quick!"

Mousie was aware that it was very strange indeed, sitting there unable to move, with everything far off and blurred except that great head moving toward her. She scarcely heard the voices screaming be-hind her. But the soft padding of the lion's paws she heard distinctly. And it was odd how sharply she saw each hair of the beast's head.

Almost dreamily she was aware how beautiful he was; how the great mane blended from sepia to pumpkin to tawny-red; how softly fawn-colored was his flowing body; how deep and darkly golden were the slanting eyes.

On each sleek foreleg he wore a modish half-ruff of fur. Insanely enough, this affectation caused in Mousie a desire to laugh aloud. But the laugh was confined to her interior, for she could not move her diaphragm. It seemed hours since she had last breathed; indeed, she felt certain she would never breathe again, for now the lion stopped, slowly stretched out his neck, slowly raised his eyes to her hand—and slowly licked his lips.

He had a tongue as innocently pink as the tongue of a puppy or a kitten. Bound in an icy spell, Mousie watched that tongue. It licked the cream-white and black-leather of his upper lip, and then, ridiculously, it remained sticking out a bit while almost imperceptibly the beast moved forward, flowed forward.

WITHIN a mere few inches of her he stopped, wrinkled his nose as if he did not like the smell of her, hesitated, and then, as if desire overcame his prejudices, he suddenly thrust forward his head. A low groan of horror sighed through the room, and all except a very tiny bit of Mousie died of terror. But the furry chin stopped at her knee, the broad pink tongue came out again; it found her hand, licked it.

The room was deadly quiet, filled with a horrified expectancy. Mousie sat frozen, motionless except for her eyes, which stared down at her hand. She saw then that crushed in this paralyzed hand she held the remains of a macaroon.

As if the sight of that familiar sweet unlocked a little the frozen valves of her heart, she drew a shallow breath, she became aware of warmth stealing into her icy fingers from the warm broad tongue lapping across them. Slowly, finger by finger, she uncurled her fist; she turned her hand slowly palm upward.

The great furry head pressed closer to her knee, the pink tongue wrapped itself around the macaroon. And then it licked her palm; from her thin wrist to the tips of her fingers it traveled; it found a crumb of sweet between two fingers and it curled in there gently.

Moving her left hand cautiously, she reached behind her and found the last macaroon on her plate. The furry throat swallowed against her knees. The beast looked up, up until his golden eyes met hers.

And then a strange thing happened to Mousie. Under the terror that paralyzed her, all her senses seemed to sharpen, to become like the unblurred senses of primitive man. She could see and smell and feel. Staring down at the beast, she saw that over each slanting eye was a sort of small question mark of dark-brown velvet. Between the short ears there were three deep furrows of anxiety. There was a dark scar across the fawn-colored nose.

"Are you afraid, too?" thought Mousie.

And deep in the golden eyes she read the answer: "Yes."

It was then that the black-browed boy behind the soda counter got into action. He plucked at Mousie's elbow. "Get up on the counter, quick!" he said hoarsely. "For I'm goin' to give 'im this—right in the schnozzle!"

Mousie with an effort moved her head around. The boy was standing by the big nickel urn. He was drawing out of it boiling water into a copper container. Mousie saw the steam floating up from it. Her stomach contracted. She felt in her own body the pain of the boiling water.

"No!" screamed Mousie suddenly. "Don't you dare to throw that water, you great big coward, you! Don't you know boiling water will *hurt* this poor lion?"

She slid down from her stool and put her body between the lion and the embattled boy. She could feel the beast pressing close to her knee. His chin of soft white fur nuzzled the palm of her hand, asking for something. Her left hand went out of its own volition, her finger tips touched the short sepia-brown fur behind an ear.

A thrill of deep delight ran up her arm; it enlivened her whole being as if tingling life ran between her and the beast. She scratched gently, and the lion put his head on one side, smug and pleased. Mousie suddenly laughed aloud.

For an extremely odd thing had happened to her. She was no longer afraid. It was as if she had dropped through the very bottom of deadly terror and had come out into a place where there was not and never had been any fear.

"Don't be afraid," she murmured. The lion lifted his golden eyes. They exchanged a profound look. Mousie touched the deep scar that plowed the fawn-colored nose. "Poor lamb, have they hurt you?"

Screechings and general hubbub broke out again in the room, and the lion quivered; the beige-gray tuft at the end of his tail began to swish back and forth.

"Stop it!" she called to the horrified onlookers. "Stop screaming and stand still, you silly fools."

She twined her hand firmly in the pumpkin-colored mane and spoke to the lion in the scolding, indulgent tone of a mother. "And as for you, what are you doing here, anyway?"

The lion shook his head sorrowfully from side to side. He did not know.

"Well, then," said Mousie, "you'll have to behave yourself. There, there, don't tremble. I won't let anyone hurt you. Just remember what I told you—there's nothing to be afraid of, really."

The lion lifted one eyebrow, as if he said: "Oh, yeah?" and then suddenly began to tremble more violently than ever. For the revolving door was spinning. It spilled into the room first the traffic policeman who so many times had scornfully waved Mousie across the street, and at his heels two reporters who were passing on their way to their office.

"Hi, there, what's all this about?" the traffic man was yelling.

But when he saw what it was all about, he paled. He pointed a wicked gun. "Jump to one side, sister," he whispered hoarsely.

"Jump yourself! The very idea!" said Mousie. "Shooting a poor defenseless lion. Can't you see this lion is scared to death? If you hurt him, I shall certainly report you."

One of the two reporters behind the candy counter called: "Is he your lion, miss? What's your name and address?"

"Mind your own business!" said Mousie stoutly.

At that instant the lion made a mournful sound and his haunches sank, the beautiful head went down, the frown of worry deepened between the golden eyes. A chunky man in a dirty sweater to which straw was sticking charged in, barking: "Hey, you Cæsar! Down, down, you old so-and-so!"

Behind him men were backing up to the emergency door a weather-beaten dirty cage that said: "Jimpson's Wild Animal Show." At sight of it the lion roared, but there was no heart in it. In fact, it was a roar slightly of relief. But the chunky man flourished a club.

"You're not going to hit him, are you?" cried Mousie.

The chunky man stared at Mousie. "Gawd!" he muttered. No one noticed a third reporter with a cameraman behind him sidling through the revolving door. There was a flare of light, a puff of sound, a roar from the lion—and then pandemonium.

When things had cleared up a bit, there was Mousie alone in the center of the room, and there was Cæsar in his cage. In the farther-most corner of it he drooped. His golden eyes looked out at the crowd, resigned and noble; his pink tongue licked from one whisker an invisible crumb of something sweet and lost. Anyone could see he was just an old lion, tired and bored.

The reporters paid no attention to him, for on all sides they were hearing a fabulous tale of a girl who had tamed a raging lion with macaroons, keeping him from tearing a dozen people limb from limb. They swarmed toward Mousie, shouting questions, clicking cameras.

Mousie flinched before the flare of a flashlight. She was plainly scared. "Oh, please, please, let me go! Please! I shall be late at the office."

Finally, such was her distress, they let her pass, and she fled. She arrived at the office ten minutes late, and Mr. Stone murmured sarcastically: "Any time, any time, Mousie."

With shaking hands, she took the cover off Big Brute. Eight letters in her notebook. Big Brute shied and jibbed and got his insides in a tangle. "Murder!" sighed Mousie in a panic.

The girl at the next desk grinned. "Whyn't you tell Mr. Erickson you've gotta have a new machine, Mousie?"

"I'm going to."

"Sure, go on, do it now, girlie."

Mousie put some finished letters into her wire basket and went down the hall to Mr. Erickson's office. Moistening dry lips, she put the letters on Mr. Erickson's desk and drew a long breath. "Excuse me, Mr. Erickson, but if you don't mind, I—I would like—like a new—"

Mr. Erickson lifted his head wearily from a cross-word puzzle. He spoke without punctuation as he always did when very cross: "Oh for cripes' sake a man's got no peace in this office always something now you go along out and let me have one minute to think in cripes!"

Mousie crept rapidly out. Despair was in her face. "I can't do it. There's no use trying. I'm just a coward."

She felt so sick and shaky that she had to go to the washroom to compose herself. It seemed to her this was the end. She would never amount to anything; she would never be anything all her life. Just Mousie. Just a coward.

Dispiritedly she brushed at the front of her skirt. Then she stooped to stare at it. Just above her right knee clung at bit of tawny fur. She touched it softly. She sniffed. There was no doubt about it—she smelled of lion.

In the mirror over the washbasin she caught sight of her own face, bewildered, questioning. What was the matter with her? Why did she ache inside with something she had no words for?

"OH, DEAR, am I going to cry?" thought Mousie. But no tears came; instead, a harsh, dry wind seemed twisting her heartstrings. And suddenly she knew what was the matter—she was mad clear through. Angry with something she could never put into words—the rebellion, the regret, the comicalness of everything. She ran to the door. She was out in the hall; she was wrenching open the door of Mr. Erickson's office; she was glaring at him across his desk.

"Mr. Erickson, I've got to have a new typewriter! I'm the only one in this office who would put up with that old typewriter, and I won't do it any longer. Not even if you discharge me, Mr. Erickson. And my raise—where is it? I've been here a year, and you told me there'd be a raise at the end of the year, and there isn't any, and I'll have to keep on living with my sister and sleeping on the divan, and I won't do—it—any—longer, Mr. Erickson." She banged a fist on the desk between each word.

Mr. Erickson's eyes bulged out. "Jumping Pete, what is this?" he muttered.

"Do you know what they call me, Mr. Erickson? They call me Mousie, and I hate it—I won't stand it any longer—I can't—"

Her voice broke. Terror swept her. What was she doing? Ruined, she was. She stared at Mr. Erickson.

She saw a bald-headed, middle-aged man with the scars of life plain upon him. Astonished, she met his eyes.

"Mr. Erickson, have you got a headache?" she faltered.

"No, I haven't got a headache, but I'm tired and discouraged," he said, before he knew what he was saying. "The cement business knocked to blazes, my digestion can't stand clams any more, and Sam's moving out to the Coast. What a heck of a day!"

"Oh! I'm sorry!" She looked at him compassionately. Strange. As if a door had opened, she was back again in that place where there was no fear. She wanted to take Mr. Erickson in there with her, it was such a pleasant place. "Look, Mr. Erickson, there isn't anything to be scared of, honest."

Mr. Erickson lifted a grizzled eyebrow; he stared at her, and then suddenly he grinned. "Well, by heck, you're the first person's given me a good word today. Maybe you're right. Anyhow, you tell Mr. Stone to give you another typewriter. Jumping Pete, you tell him to give you a brand-new one."

"And shall I speak to him too about the raise, Mr. Erickson?"

"Oh, I suppose you might as well. A little more won't sink us, I guess, Mousie. Er, I forgot you don't like that name."

Mousie smiled fleetingly. "I don't mind it—now. Thank you, Mr. Erickson."

Then she scuttled quickly to the door, for the ridiculous thought had occurred to her that if she stayed there another minute she would be scratching Mr. Erickson gently behind the ears.

Guinea Pig

RUTH McKENNEY

Ruth, at summer camp, went through six easy lessons in lifesaving, but as the rescued—not the rescuer. This hilarious story is such delightful light summer reading that a hammock should be strapped to it.

I WAS NEARLY DROWNED, in my youth, by a Red Cross Lifesaving Examiner, and I once suffered, in the noble cause of saving human life from a watery grave, a black eye which was a perfect daisy and embarrassed me for days. Looking back on my agonies, I feel that none of my sacrifices, especially the black eye, were in the least worth while. Indeed, to be brutally frank about it, I feel that the whole modern school of scientific lifesaving is a lot of hogwash.

Of course, I've had rather bad luck with lifesavers, right from the beginning. Long before I ever had any dealings with professional lifesavers my sister nearly drowned me, quite by mistake. My father once took us to a northern Michigan fishing camp, where we found the life very dull. He used to go trolling for bass on our little lake all day long, and at night come home to our lodge, dead-beat and minus any bass. In the meantime Eileen and I, who were nine and ten at the time, used to take an old rowboat out to a shallow section of the lake and, sitting in the hot sun, feed worms to an unexciting variety of small, undernourished fish called gillies. We hated the whole business.

Father, however, loved to fish, even if he didn't catch a single fish in three weeks, which on this trip he didn't. One night, however, he carried his enthusiasm beyond a decent pitch. He decided to go bass fishing after dark, and rather than leave us alone in the lodge and up

353

to God knows what, he ordered us to take our boat and row along after him.

Eileen and I were very bored rowing around in the dark, and finally, in desperation, we began to stand up and rock the boat, which resulted, at last, in my falling into the lake with a mighty splash.

When I came up, choking and mad as anything, Eileen saw me struggling, and, as she always says with a catch in her voice, she only meant to help me. Good intentions, however, are of little importance in a situation like that. For she grabbed an oar out of the lock, and with an uncertain gesture hit me square on the chin.

I went down with a howl of pain. Eileen, who could not see much in the darkness, was now really frightened. The cold water revived me after the blow and I came to the surface, considerably weakened but still able to swim over to the boat. Whereupon Eileen, in a noble attempt to give me the oar to grab, raised it once again, and socked me square on top of the head. I went down again, this time without a murmur, and my last thought was a vague wonder that my own sister should want to murder me with a rowboat oar.

As for Eileen, she heard the dull impact of the oar on my head and saw the shadowy figure of her sister disappear. So she jumped in the lake, screeching furiously, and began to flail around in the water, howling for help and looking for me. At this point I came to the surface and swam over to the boat, with the intention of killing Eileen.

Father, rowing hard, arrived just in time to pull us both out of the water and prevent me from attacking Eileen with the rowboat anchor. The worst part about the whole thing, as far as I was concerned, was that Eileen was considered a heroine and Father told everybody in the lake community that she had saved my life. The postmaster put her name in for a medal.

After what I suffered from amateur lifesaving, I should have known enough to avoid even the merest contact with the professional variety of water mercy. I learned too late that being socked with an oar is as nothing compared to what the Red Cross can think up.

From the very beginning of that awful lifesaving course I took the last season I went to a girls' camp, I was a marked woman. The rest of the embryo lifesavers were little, slender maidens, but I am a peasant type, and I was monstrously big for my fourteen years. I approximated, in poundage anyway, the theoretical adult we energetic young lifesavers were scheduled to rescue, and so I was, for the teacher's purpose, the perfect guinea pig.

The first few days of the course were unpleasant for me, but not terribly dangerous. The elementary lifesaving hold, in case you haven't seen some hapless victim being rescued by our brave beach guardians, is a snakelike arrangement for supporting the drowning citizen with one hand while you paddle him in to shore with the other. You are supposed to wrap your arm around his neck and shoulders, and keep his head well above water by resting it on your collarbone.

This is all very well in theory, of course, but the trick that none of Miss Folgil's little pupils could master was keeping the victim's nose and mouth above the waterline. Time and again I was held in a viselike grip by one of the earnest students with my whole face an inch or two under the billowing waves.

"No, no, Betsy," Miss Folgil would scream through her megaphone, as I felt the water rush into my lungs. "No, no, you must keep the head a little higher." At this point I would begin to kick and struggle, and generally the pupil would have to let go while I came up for air. Miss Folgil was always very stern with me.

"Ruth," she would shriek from her boat, "I insist! You must allow Betsy to tow you all the way in. We come to Struggling in Lesson Six."

This was but the mere beginning, however. A few lessons later we came to the section of the course where we learned how to undress under water in forty seconds. Perhaps I should say we came to the point where the *rest* of the pupils learned how to get rid of shoes and such while holding their breath. I never did.

There was quite a little ceremony connected with this part of the course. Miss Folgil, and some lucky creature named as timekeeper and armed with a stopwatch, rowed the prospective victim out to deep water. The pupil, dressed in high, laced tennis shoes, long stockings, heavy bloomers, and a middy blouse, then stood poised at the end of the boat. When the timekeeper yelled "Go!" the future boon to mankind dived into the water and, while holding her breath under the surface, unlaced her shoes and stripped down to her bathing suit. Miss Folgil never explained what connection, if any, this curious rite had with saving human lives.

I had no middy of my own, so I borrowed one of my sister's. My sister was a slender little thing and I was, as I said, robust, which puts it politely. Eileen had some trouble wedging me into that middy, and once in it I looked like stuffed sausage. It never occurred to me how hard it was going to be to get that middy off, especially when it was wet and slippery.

As we rowed out for my ordeal by undressing, Miss Folgil was snappish and bored.

"Hurry up," she said, looking irritated. "Let's get this over with quick. I don't think you're ready to pass this test, anyway."

I was good and mad when I jumped off the boat, and determined to Make Good and show that old Miss Folgil, whom I was beginning to dislike thoroughly. As soon as I was under water, I got my shoes off, and I had no trouble with the bloomers or stockings. I was just beginning to run out of breath when I held up my arms and started to pull off the middy.

Now, the middy, in the event you don't understand the principle of this girl-child garment, is made with a small head opening, long sleeves, and no front opening. You pull it on and off over your head. You do if you are lucky, that is. I got the middy just past my neck so that my face was covered with heavy linen cloth, when it stuck.

I pulled frantically and my lungs started to burst. Finally I thought the hell with the test, the hell with saving other people's lives, anyway. I came to the surface, a curious sight, my head enfolded in a water-soaked middy blouse. I made a brief sound, a desperate glub-glub, a call for help. My arms were stuck in the middy and I couldn't swim. I went down. I breathed in large quantities of water and linen cloth.

I came up again, making final frantic appeals. Four feet away sat a professional lifesaver, paying absolutely no attention to somebody drowning right under her nose. I went down again, struggling with last panic-stricken feverishness, fighting water and a middy blouse for my life. At this point the timekeeper pointed out to Miss Folgil that I had been under water for eighty-five seconds, which was quite a time for anybody. Miss Folgil was very annoyed, as she hated to get her bathing suit wet, but, a thoughtful teacher, she picked up her megaphone, shouted to the rest of the class on the beach to watch, and dived in after me.

If I say so myself, I gave her quite a time rescuing me. I presented a new and different problem, and probably am written up in textbooks now under the heading "What to Do When the Victim Is Entangled in a Tight Middy Blouse." Miss Folgil finally towed my still-breathing body over to the boat, reached for her bowie knife, which she carried on a ring with her whistle, and cut Eileen's middy straight up the front. Then she towed me with Hold No. 2 right in to the shore and delivered me up to the class for artificial respiration. I will never forgive the Red Cross for that terrible trip through the water, when I might have been hoisted into the boat and rowed in except for Miss Folgil's overdeveloped sense of drama and pedagogy.

I tried to quit the lifesaving class after that, but the head councilor at the camp said I must keep on, to show that I was the kind of a girl who always finished what she planned to do. Otherwise, she assured me, I would be a weak character and never amount to anything when I grew up.

So I stayed for Lesson 6: "Struggling." After that I didn't care if I never amounted to anything when I grew up. In fact, I hoped I wouldn't. It would serve everybody right, especially Miss Folgil. I came a little late to the class session that day and missed the discussion of theory, always held on the beach before the actual practice in the lake. That was just my hard luck. I was always a child of misfortune. I wonder that I survived my youth at all.

"We were waiting for you, Ruth," Miss Folgil chirped cheerily to me as I arrived, sullen and downcast, at the little group of earnest students sitting on the sand.

"What for?" I said warily. I was determined not to be a guinea pig any more. The last wave had washed over my helpless face.

"You swim out," Miss Folgil went on, ignoring my bad temper, "until you are in deep water—about twelve feet will do. Then you begin to flail around and shout for help. One of the students will swim out to you."

All of this sounded familiar and terrible. I had been doing that for days, and getting water in my nose for my pains.

"But when the student arrives," Miss Folgil went on, "you must not allow her to simply tow you away. You must struggle, just as hard as you can. You must try to clutch her by the head, you must try to twine your legs about her, and otherwise hamper her in trying to save you."

Now, *this* sounded something like. I was foolishly fired by the attractive thought of getting back at some of the fiends who had been ducking me in the name of science for the past two weeks. Unfortunately, I hadn't studied Chapter 9, entitled "How to Break Holds the Drowning Swimmer Uses." Worse, I hadn't heard Miss Folgil's lecture on "Be Firm with the Panic-Stricken Swimmer—Better a Few Bruises Than a Watery Grave." This last was Miss Folgil's own opinion, of course.

So I swam out to my doom, happy as a lark. Maybelle Anne Pettijohn, a tall, lean girl who ordinarily wore horn-rimmed spectacles, was Miss Folgil's choice to rescue Exhibit A, the panic-stricken swimmer.

I laughed when I saw her coming. I thought I could clean up on Maybelle Anne easily enough, but alas, I hadn't counted on Maybelle Anne's methodical approach to life. She had read Chapter 9 in our textbook, and she had listened carefully to Miss Folgil's inspiring words. Besides, Maybelle Anne was just naturally the kind of girl who ran around doing people dirty for their own good. "This may hurt your feelings," she used to say mournfully, "but I feel I have to tell you . . ."

When Maybelle Anne got near me, I enthusiastically lunged for her neck and hung on with both hands while getting her around her waist with my legs. Maybelle Anne thereupon dug her fingernails into my hands with ferocious force, and I let go and swam away, hurt and surprised. This was distinctly not playing fair.

"What's the idea?" I called out.

"It says to do that in the book," Maybelle Anne replied, treading water.

"Well, you lay off that stuff," I said, angered, book or no book. Maybelle Anne was a Girl Scout, too, and I was shocked to think she'd go around using her fingernails in a fair fight.

"Come on, struggle," Maybelle Anne said, getting winded from treading water. I swam over, pretty reluctant and much more wary. Believe it or not, this time Maybelle Anne, who was two medals from being a Beaver or whatever it is Girl Scouts with a lot of medals get to be, bit me.

In addition to biting me, Maybelle Anne swung her arm around my neck, with the intention of towing me in to shore. But I still had plenty of fight left and I had never been so mad in my life. I got Maybelle Anne under water two or three times, and I almost thought I had her when suddenly, to my earnest surprise, she hauled off and hit me as hard as she could, right in the eye. Then she towed me in, triumphant as anything.

Maybelle Anne afterward claimed it was all in the book, and she wouldn't even apologize for my black eye. Eileen and I fixed her, though. We put a little garter snake in her bed and scared the daylights out of her. Maybelle Anne was easy to scare anyway, and really a very disagreeable girl. I used to hope that she would come to a bad end, which, from my point of view, at least, she did. Maybelle Anne grew up to be a Regional Red Cross Lifesaving Examiner.

I'll bet she just loves her work.

Qwerty and the Bird Man

ALICE MEANS REEVE

Typing on a little balcony in the shadow of jasmine blossoms, with a companionable cat in her lap, Ann sets the stage for a gay romance with a red-headed ornithologist who could scale a balcony with the ease of a cat, but couldn't outsmart this one, namely QWERTYUIOP!

THE NEW APARTMENT seemed too wonderful to be true. Even late that first afternoon Ann Mallory had her fingers crossed as she lay under the gnarled old jasmine vine on the balcony, watching Qwertyuiop lick the butter off her paws. Her grandfather had always said, "If you move a cat to a new home, rub its paws with butter. Then, by the time the cat has sat down and licked the butter off, it will feel so much at home it won't even think of running away."

"It seems to be working," Ann thought. And then she just lay there on the chaise longue with the fragrant yellow jasmine blossoms dropping around her. Behind her the sun setting over the Golden Gate was a priceless sight but after spending the whole day getting settled she was too relaxed and comfortable even to turn her head.

It seemed as if this old mansion made over into apartments and perched on the wooded side of Garber Hill was the loveliest place she had ever lived. And Qwerty liked it too. Already Qwerty had discovered that the huge old jasmine vine with its three-inch trunk made a marvelous stairway to this second-story balcony, and between paw-washings she'd run up and down a dozen times, chasing her tail and birds and butterflies.

The jasmine vine climbed on up the side of the building above Ann's balcony and she thought dreamily what a temptation it could be for the Barefoot Burglar, who'd been tantalizing the local police for so many weeks.

Peace flowed around her and the humming-birds whirred among the jasmine. Ann's eyes closed and she was drifting into that delicious half-sleep when suddenly she heard a wild shaking in the jasmine vine. Her eyes flared open. Qwertyuiop stopped washing her paws and looked up expectantly.

A man's tousled red head appeared above the balcony railing as he came up hand over hand on the jasmine vine. His movements were catlike and for a moment he didn't see that there was anyone on the balcony.

Then simultaneously Ann leaped to her feet, cried, "Oh! The Barefoot Burglar!" and Qwertyuiop leaped toward a bird that was hopping up the vine above the man's flaming red head.

The man gave a snort of disgust, stepped over the railing to the balcony and said crossly, "What'd you have to go yelling that way for? Now it's got away!"

When Ann saw that the man had shoes on and obviously wasn't the Barefoot Burglar, she said, "I don't know what it was that got away—unless it was your temper—but I wish you'd stay off my balcony!"

"Your balcony!" said the man. "You don't mean that you and that —that feline have moved in here?"

"This morning," declared Ann. "I take it you aren't the reception committee?"

"Lord, no!" he muttered.

Qwertyuiop had returned and after sitting on her haunches and watching the man for a few seconds she walked over and began rubbing against his legs and looking up into his face and purring.

360

"Hey," yelled the man, making a pass at Qwerty with his foot, "get away! I'm an ornithologist and I hate cats!"

Ann grabbed up the purring cat and stood glaring at the man.

"You're a very rude disagreeable unpleasant person!" she said. "And the sooner you get off my balcony the better."

The man gave her a startled look, as if he wasn't used to being spoken to this way, and then he turned and began climbing on up the jasmine vine.

"Where are you going?" Ann called sharply.

"Home," shouted the ornithologist, throwing one long leg over the sill of a window above. "I live here."

"And I was told," said Ann, "that the tenants in this building were of the highest class!"

"They were," said the man, "until they began letting cats in!"

Ann, with Qwertyuiop in her arms, stalked into her apartment. She was still furious as she bustled around getting dinner.

In the living-room Qwerty sprang up on the mantelpiece and began weaving daintily in and out among the bric-a-brac.

"Now you be careful!" Ann said.

QWERTY sat down in front of Horace Pring's picture, smelled every inch of it and then calmly lifted one silvery paw and scratched a long jagged gash right down across Horace's handsome face.

Ann cried, "Why, you—you little vixen!" and leaped for Qwertyuiop, but Qwertyuiop was quicker and jumped down and streaked under the davenport.

Ann said, "You've never acted like this before! What's got into you, Qwerty? It must be the bad influence upstairs. I feel like scratching things myself."

And then she went back and finished getting dinner and while she was eating it, thought about Horace and wondered if she really would marry him. He'd asked her so many times, but his last letter had been practically an ultimatum. He'd said his company was sending him through Berkeley on his way north. His itinerary was all made up and three weeks from tonight his train would stop at the Berkeley station for five minutes. They might as well get this settled once and for all —if she loved him and wanted to marry him, she'd be at the station to see him. If not, it was all off.

Ann couldn't help laughing—this was so typical of Horace's idea of a man with a maid. Though that was all right with her, except that she hadn't quite made up her mind whether she'd be at the station or not.

The next morning, thrilled anew with her apartment, Ann left Qwerty chasing jasmine blossoms while she walked up to the campus to see if they had any typing for her. Ann was such a good typist she wouldn't have had any trouble getting a job, but she liked much better to take typing home and do it when she felt like it.

When she got to the office on the campus, the woman in charge said, "I was just going to phone you, Miss Mallory. I have a book manuscript of Professor Thomas Pepper's. He said he wanted a perfect job, and you're the one person to do it."

Ann took the manuscript and went on home; and before she went up to her apartment she got her mail and examined the names of the other mailboxes to see who her neighbors were. And then suddenly she began to laugh.

She went upstairs and Qwerty met her at the door to the balcony. Pretty soon, after lunch, she moved her typewriter out there and spent the afternoon copying Professor Pepper's book.

SHE was having a lovely time working under the jasmine blossoms, with Qwertyuiop curled companionably on her table, when there was a sudden noise from the apartment above, like a chair being overturned, and then the red head of the bird man appeared in the window above and he yelled, "I'm a reasonable man but too much is enough! Do you have to type *all* day long?"

Ann looked up at him demurely. "It just happens," she said, "that I earn my living typing and the only reason I'm doing so much right now is that this is your book, and Miss Carruthers said you were in a hurry for it. Any other complaints?"

"Oh," he stammered, "I—I didn't know. Then you must be Miss Mallory who does such good typing, so they *say*."

Ann bent her head over the typewriter and snickered to herself.

"Yes, I'm Ann Mallory and my typing is good when people aren't bellowing out of windows at me all the time. Well, good-by, Dr. Pepper, I'll let you know if there're any of these hen-tracks of yours that I can't make out."

Qwertyuiop rose, stretched and looked up and said, "Meow," to the professor. The professor's angry red face and flaming topknot disappeared in silence and Ann went on with her typing. Qwertyuiop went high-tailing down the jasmine vine, as if she'd just thought of something important.

Ann went on typing then and chuckling to herself, and there was peace for a while in the warm flower-scented afternoon. She was typing something about the mating dance of the black-chinned hummingbirds and it was so interesting and so well written that she didn't notice when Qwertyuiop came up the jasmine vine and went on up and into the apartment above through the open window.

But a moment later there was a sound from above, something like a cross between a buzz-saw and the yelp of an infuriated coyote. Ann jumped and looked up and there was Thomas Pepper hanging out his window holding a lizard-like little newt by its tail. Qwertyuiop sat on the window sill rubbing against him as if they were the best of friends.

Ann said nervously, "If you drop that thing on me I'll scream!"

Thomas Pepper looked at her with disgust and with one simple twist of the wrist flipped the squirming creature out into the treetops beyond the balcony.

"Your charming cat brought that up and laid it right on my desk," he said scathingly.

Ann laughed. "That's a compliment. Qwerty never brings presents to anyone she doesn't like. I guess there must be *something* good about you."

"I am not at all interested in your cat's opinion of me," Professor Pepper replied. He added stiffly, "And besides, I can't have that cat sneaking in here this way, because one of these days my fiancée is coming up from the South and she hates cats."

Ann said indignantly, "Qwertyuiop, come down here. You ought to know better than to stay where you're not liked."

"Qwertyuiop!" said Thomas Pepper. "Silliest name I ever heard!"

"She's a typewriter cat," Ann explained. "When she was just a kitten she walked along the top row of letters on my typewriter—the row that says q w e r t y u i o p , and so I named her that."

Something almost like a smile rippled across Thomas Pepper's face and then was gone. "Typewriter cat or not," he said, giving Qwertyuiop a light slap on her gray rear and sending her down the vine, "keep her away from my apartment or I'll make a rug out of her!"

Qwertyuiop jumped lightly into Ann's outstretched arms. Ann said to Thomas Pepper, "You're a gentle creature, aren't you!" and went in and slammed the door and busied herself around the apartment. She'd thought this place was too good to be true. Yesterday she'd wanted to stay here forever, but now, with this red-headed jumping-jack upstairs, she wasn't so sure. Maybe marrying Horace was the answer. He would certainly never shout at her or beat her.

Ann wondered if Thomas Pepper was ever lonely, as she was? Probably so self-sufficient that he didn't even know what loneliness was. And then suddenly she remembered he had mentioned his fiancée. And Ann knew at once she'd be a creature she thoroughly disliked.

Somehow a vague sense of disappointment deepened in Ann. She kept having the sneaking notion that if she did marry Horace, she might be doing it just to keep from being lonely.

Ann had hoped when she moved here that she might meet some congenial young people. Well, Thomas Pepper was young and she supposed he might be called good-looking, if you liked tall lean men with carroty hair, but he certainly wasn't congenial. Well, pooh to Thomas Pepper! And right then and there, she decided practically definitely that she would go to the station to meet Horace.

THE days drifted by for Ann and Qwerty. They ate out on their balcony and there always seemed to be yellow jasmine blossoms caught in Ann's dark hair. She finished typing Thomas Pepper's book manuscript and took it up to him.

"It's the best typing I've ever had done," he admitted grudgingly.

"I didn't know birds could be so interesting," Ann said. "It must seem grand to have your book finished."

"But it isn't finished," he told her. "There's one chapter lacking. There's more material I have to have and I've just about given up getting it."

He sounded so gloomy that Ann started to say something sympathetic, when suddenly Qwerty ran up the vine and hopped from the window sill to the floor of Thomas Pepper's monastic living-room. She laid a small dead gopher at the feet of Thomas Pepper, looked up at him and said, "Meow," and then began to rub against his legs and purr.

Ann began to laugh and Thomas Pepper began to scowl. "This has got to stop!" he bellowed. "If you can't keep your cat out of my apartment, I'll—I'll—"

"You could keep your window shut," Ann interrupted.

"And smother?" he demanded.

Ann sighed and picked up Qwerty.

"I'll try to restrain Qwertyuiop," she said and went out and shut the door behind her. She thought she heard Thomas Pepper say, "But, Miss Mallory—" in an apologetic sort of voice but she kept right on going.

Things went from bad to worse after that. Ann and Thomas Pepper seemed to meet oftener than ever and several times they seemed on the verge of being friends, and then some ridiculous thing would happen; Qwerty would bring one of her absurd gifts—a lizard or a little field mouse—or some of Qwerty's friends would serenade her from the balcony, and Thomas Pepper's red hair would flame and he would roar like a wild creature. And then the next day he would come down very apologetically with a handful of letters and ask Ann to type them for him. And then Qwerty would do something and it would begin all over again. And once Thomas Pepper roared at Ann, "If you didn't have that confounded cat—!" and she, furious, had roared back, "And if you didn't have that confounded temper—!"

And that was the way things stood that lovely bright sunset, when Ann hung over her balcony windowbox picking a bunch of white violets to wear when she went down to the train to meet Horace Pring that night. She'd finally made up her mind to marry Horace, and was trying to hum happily to herself—when a voice spoke suddenly from the walk below her balcony:

"I beg your pardon, but is this where Professor Pepper lives?"

ANN saw a tailored young woman with a bright efficient face. With her was a large older woman built on pouter pigeon lines.

Ann looked down on these two self-sufficient females and suddenly she felt terribly sorry for Thomas Pepper.

She smiled down demurely and said on a slightly malicious impulse, "Oh, you mean Tommy Pepper! Why, he lives right above me. I suppose you'll have to go around to the front door. Of course Tommy usually climbs right up the jasmine vine to my balcony and goes up to his apartment that way, but I don't suppose you're dressed for climbing." She laughed merrily. And the two faces below her looked as if they had been chipped out of ice.

"Just go around to the front door," Ann said. "Shall I run up and tell Tommy you're coming?"

The younger woman with the efficient face said very coldly, "My fiancé is expecting us, thank you," and then they disappeared from Ann's vision.

"So that's his fiancée!" Ann said to herself. "I knew I wouldn't like her!"

Ann and Qwertyuiop had their supper out on the balcony as usual. Voices from above had such a carrying quality that she couldn't help hearing them.

The mother-in-law voice bayed: "You and Zelda certainly won't live here after you're married, Thomas?"

"Why, yes, I think so," Thomas replied. "You see, just at the top of this hill is a reservoir, which attracts a great many birds. I get material here."

"From what I've seen of the tenants," Zelda said, "I couldn't bear living here!"

On the balcony below, Ann, hearing this, thought: "Why, you little—" And then she laughed.

"A man has to live where his work is," said Thomas Pepper. "Birds are my living."

Suddenly down on the balcony Ann cried, "Tommy, Tommy, come to the window, there's a marvelous bird down here!"

Thomas Pepper's red head appeared at the open window above. "Where is it?" he demanded, reaching inside for his binoculars.

"It was on that branch just over the table," Ann said, grabbing up Qwerty.

Tommy Pepper climbed over the window sill and came down the jasmine vine like a creeping panther.

Ann said softly, "It had the most beautiful purple topknot ringed around with jade green and gold and—"

Tommy gave her an odd look.

Qwertyuiop said, "Meow, meow," and jumping out of Ann's arms, leaped on a low branch of the vine.

Ann said, "Oh! It flew away! And it was such a gorgeous thing too!"

Tommy Pepper said, talking like a ventriloquist, without moving his lips, "I'd like to skin that cat of yours!"

Ann was conscious of Zelda and her mother hanging out the window above.

She said, "Well, never mind, Tommy, there are other birds." She patted his arm comfortingly.

Just then there was a snort from above. Tommy Pepper looked up into the hostile eyes of his fiancée and his prospective mother-in-law and he turned a beet-red. Then he swung around and climbed up the vine, and a minute later Ann heard the mother-in-law voice saying, "I don't believe there was a bird at all! Whoever heard of a purple top-knot ringed around with jade green and gold! I think that creature down there is a designing little—"

"Not at all," Thomas Pepper said. "The bird she saw was undoubtedly a Qwertipus Fantasticus, which is a very rare bird indeed."

Ann gave a sudden snicker and ducked into the apartment. Qwertipus Fantasticus! So he knew all the time there hadn't been a bird!

She was just about to go out the door when she heard a shrill scream from the apartment above. She ran out on her balcony just in time to see Qwerty streaking down the jasmine vine from the window above, like a silver zipper.

Two shrill feminine voices were shrieking:

"It was a lizard!"

"Or a snake!"

Tommy Pepper saw Ann and bellowed, "The next time I get hold of that cat I'm going to kill it! I've had all I can stand!"

"You've had all you can stand!" Ann said. "What about Qwerty and me?" Down the street she heard the streetcar coming that would take her to meet Horace. Before she ran to get it she called, "There's a bird down here, Tommy—for you."

And with that she put the tip of her tongue between her teeth and made a very derisive sound in the direction of Thomas Pepper, ornithologist. And then she ran from the apartment and down the street.

HALF an hour later she arrived just as the train was whistling into the station. In another minute now she'd be looking up into Horace's eyes. She and Horace would be married. She reached a big pillar and stood leaning against it, catching her breath. She was hidden from the people getting off the train but she could see them.

Suddenly under a big arc light she saw Horace step down from the train and stand looking up and down the platform in a puzzled sort of way. As if it were absolutely unthinkable that she might not be there. She didn't run forward to meet him right away. From looking puzzled, he began to look annoyed. He strode up and down. He looked to Ann like an utter stranger. Why, he was someone she didn't know at all. He—he didn't even look like a man who would like cats. He and Qwertyuiop had never met. And she remembered suddenly how Qwerty had scratched his picture, not in sudden feline anger but after a great deal of sniffing and deliberation.

And then Ann remembered suddenly again how from the very start Qwertyuiop had shown such a strong liking for Tommy Pepper. And no amount of harsh words and abuse could shake her liking apparently.

Ann knew suddenly that she didn't love Horace. She could not, she would not, marry him. Stepping farther beyond the pillar into greater safety from Horace's possible glance, she heard the train whistle. Horace looked up and down the platform angrily once more, and then he shrugged his shoulders and jumped on the train.

Ann turned slowly and walked toward the street. And then she suddenly remembered Tommy Pepper's parting words, that the next time he got hold of Qwertyuiop he was going to kill her. And she'd gone off in such a hurry that she'd forgotten to lock Qwerty inside. She stepped hurriedly off the curb and there was a sudden jangled blurring of honking horns and shooting stars with long comet-like tails, and then the street, it seemed to Ann, gave a mighty lurch and banged against her head.

At the hospital they were soon telling her how lucky she was. Her arm had suffered only a contusion, instead of the break that had at first seemed certain. But she must remain quiet for a while.

Late the next afternoon Ann, feeling very weak and tottery, let herself into her apartment and went at once to the balcony. There was no sign of Qwerty.

She climbed the stairs to Tommy Pepper's apartment, her knees shaking, and knocked at the door.

Tommy Pepper threw it open. His eyes flared in surprise and he said, "You're white as a sheet! What's happened?"

Ann's voice trembled from weakness and shock. "Qwertyuiop's gone!" she gasped. "If you've done anything to her, I—"

And then she looked beyond Tommy Pepper's shoulder and there lay Qwertyuiop, sound asleep on the cushioned window seat. And on the floor below were saucers of cream and salmon.

For a minute Ann thought she was going to cry. But just then Qwerty opened a green eye and saw her. She rose, stretched and then sped, like a silver arrow, straight into Ann's outstretched arms. Ann buried her face in Qwerty's warm gray fur.

"Come over here and sit down," Tommy said gruffly, leading Ann to the window seat. Qwerty was purring like a dynamo.

"Just ten minutes ago," Tommy Pepper said, "I finished that last chapter in my book. And I owe it all to your cat. You know those gifts Qwerty was always bringing me?"

Ann nodded and held her breath.

"Well," he continued, "she finally caught on to the idea that birds were what I was after. And this morning she found me a Sonoran red-winged blackbird. I've always maintained that it was possible to find one this far north. And the proof of that was the one thing I needed to finish my book. So when I saw Qwerty fixating on a bird on a branch and found it was a Sonoran—Well, now you can type the last chapter. But where were you last night? I waited all night to hear you come in."

"I was in the hospital," Ann said.

"In the hospital!"

"Yes. I went down to the station to tell a man I'd marry him, and on the way back I ran into a car and they took me to the emergency hospital and kept me under observation until just a little while ago when they decided I was all right."

Something happened to Tommy Pepper's face.

"Ann," he said and neither of them seemed to realize that this was the first time he'd ever called her that, "Ann, I won't let you marry that other man!"

Ann looked up into Tommy Pepper's face and it didn't seem like the face of a stranger at all, and she said, "Why?"

"Because since that first day when I barged onto your balcony and found you with jasmine blossoms in your hair, I haven't been able to think of anything else."

"Not even Zelda?"

"Zelda and I came to the parting of the ways last night. Now, about this man you said you were going to marry—?"

"Oh," said Ann, "you mean Horace! I couldn't marry him. Qwerty hates him!"

Tommy said, "Oh, I see." And then his eyes began to glow. "Hey," he said, "Qwerty's crazy about me!"

"I know," said Ann softly; "that was the point I was trying to get over."

"Hey!" said Tommy Pepper again, folding Ann and Qwertyuiop into his arms. "Who said fur and feathers don't mix!"

Grandma and the Sea Gull

LOUISE DICKINSON RICH

It was total war between Grandma and her neighbor, Mrs. Wilcox. But in this case the worst of enemies turned out to be the best of friends.

MY GRANDMOTHER had an enemy named Mrs. Wilcox. Grandma and Mrs. Wilcox moved, as brides, into next-door houses on the sleepy elm-roofed Main Street of the tiny town in which they were to live out their lives. I don't know what started the war—that was long before my day—and I don't think that by the time I came along, over thirty years later, they remembered themselves what started it. But it was still being bitterly waged.

Make no mistake. This was no polite sparring match. This was War Between Ladies, which is total war. Nothing in town escaped repercussion. The three-hundred-year-old church, which had lived through the Revolution, the Civil War and the Spanish War, almost went down when Grandma and Mrs. Wilcox fought the Battle of the Ladies' Aid. Grandma won that engagement but it was a hollow victory. Mrs. Wilcox, since she couldn't be president, resigned from the Aid in a huff, and what's the fun of running a thing if you can't force your mortal enemy to eat crow? Mrs. Wilcox won the Battle of the Public Library, getting her niece Gertrude appointed librarian instead of my Aunt Phyllis. The day Gertrude took over was the day Grandma stopped reading library books—"filthy germ things" they'd become overnight—and started buying her own. The Battle of the High School was a draw. The principal got a better job and left before Mrs. Wilcox succeeded in having him ousted or Grandma in having him given life tenure of office.

In addition to these major engagements there was constant sallying and sniping back of the main line of fire. When as children we visited my grandmother, part of the fun was making faces at Mrs. Wilcox's impossible grandchildren—nearly as impossible as we were, I now see—and stealing grapes off the Wilcox side of the fence between the gardens. We chased the Wilcox hens too and put percussion caps, saved from July 4, on the rails of the trolley line right in front of the Wilcox house, in the pleasant hope that when the trolley went by, the explosion—actually a negligible affair—would scare Mrs. Wilcox into fits. One banner day we put a snake into the Wilcox rain barrel. My grandmother made token protests but we sensed tacit sympathy, so different from what lay back of my mother's no's, and went merrily on with our career of brattishness. If any child of mine—but that's another story.

Don't think for a minute that this was a one-sided campaign. Mrs. Wilcox had grandchildren too, remember; more and tougher and smarter grandchildren than my grandmother had. Grandma didn't get off scot free. She had skunks introduced into her cellar. On Halloween all loose forgotten objects, such as garden furniture, miraculously flew to the ridgepole of the barn, whence they had to be lowered by strong men hired at exorbitant day rates. Never a windy washday went by but what the clothesline mysteriously broke, so that the sheets wollopsed around in the dirt and had to be done over. Some of these occurrences may have been acts of God but the Wilcox grandchildren always got the credit. I don't know how Grandma could have borne her troubles if it hadn't been for the household page of her daily Boston newspaper.

THIS household page was a wonderful institution. Besides the usual cooking hints and cleaning advice it had a department composed of letters from readers to each other. The idea was that if you had a problem—or even only some steam to blow off—you wrote a letter to the paper, signing some fancy name like Arbutus. That was Grandma's pen name. Then some of the other ladies who had had the same problem wrote back and told you what they had done about it, signing themselves One Who Knows or Xanthippe or whatever. Very often, the problem disposed of, you kept on for years writing to each other through the column of the paper, telling each other about your children and your canning and your new dining-room suite. That's what happened to Grandma. She and a woman called Sea Gull corresponded for a quarter of a century and Grandma told Sea Gull things that she never breathed to another soul—things like the time she hoped that she was going to have another baby but didn't, and the time my Uncle Steve got you-know-what in his hair in school and how humiliated she was, although she got rid of them before anyone in town guessed. Sea Gull was Grandma's true bosom friend.

WHEN I was about sixteen Mrs. Wilcox died. In a small town, no matter how much you have hated your next-door neighbor, it is only common decency to run over and see what practical service you can do the bereaved. Grandma, neat in a percale apron to show that she meant what she said about being put to work, crossed the two lawns to the Wilcox house, where the Wilcox daughters set her to cleaning the already immaculate front parlor for the funeral. And there on the parlor table in the place of honor was a huge scrapbook; and in the scrapbook, pasted neatly in parallel columns, were her letters to Sea Gull over the years and Sea Gull's letters to her. Grandma's worst enemy had been her best friend.

That was the only time I remember seeing my grandmother cry. I didn't know then exactly what she was crying about but I do now. She was crying for all the wasted years which could never be salvaged. Then I was impressed only by the tears and they made me remember that day. Now I know that something happened that day worthier of remembrance than a woman's tears. That was the day when I first began to suspect what I now believe with all my heart; and if ever I have to stop believing it, I want to stop living. It is this:

People may seem to be perfectly impossible. They may seem to be mean and small and sly. But if you will take ten paces to the left and look again with the light falling at a different angle, very likely you will see that they are generous and warm and kind. It all depends. It all depends on the point from which you're seeing them.

The Fishing Fool

MARY ROBERTS RINEHART

It was the hairdresser who steered Peggy into safe waters with the fishing fool. The story is told with freshness and conviction in Mrs. Rinehart's inimitable style.

I WAS GIVING one of the waitresses a permanent wave the night it happened. It was about one o'clock in the morning and I had just finished wrapping her, Minnie being the sort of girl who wants fifty curls for five dollars, and she didn't get down from the hotel dining room until almost eleven.

Right away when she came in I saw something had happened.

"They've had a quarrel or something, Ethel," she said. "He's eating at his own table tonight, and he looks fit to be tied."

"Maybe he's got some sense at last," I said bitterly. "He only had ten days, and for seven of them he's been firing golf balls into the Gulf of Mexico instead of fishing."

"That's love, I guess," said Minnie.

"That's poppycock," I said sharply. "Now he's lost Joe, the best fish guide on the island. He hasn't even a boat. And the tarpon are in."

I was pretty sore. For years, ever since he used to come from college on Easter vacation, Win McKnight and Joe had kept up the reputation of the island for tarpon against all the other resorts around. Almost always he got the first fish, and almost always the biggest. He'd had five gold-button fish in the last five years, which means that each weighed over a hundred pounds, and all of us felt that the season hadn't really commenced until he got there. Now he had only ten days' leave before he went into the army, and for an entire week, instead of being out in the Pass for the big fellows, he had been trailing a girl around the golf course. And making a fool of himself doing it.

I shoved Minnie over the basin for the shampoo to shut her up, but she came up still talking.

373

"It's funny, isn't it, Ethel," she said. "That she won't fish, I mean."

"Maybe her mother was scared by a fish before she was born."

Minnie giggled but I was still sore. The hotel stands on a slope, and my shop is in the basement at the rear. From my windows I can see the guide dock, and I knew that every boat on the island was in the Pass that night, ready to fish the slack tide at two A.M. Even Joe was there. But not Mack. Win McKnight was always Mack to us. No, not Mack. He was upstairs in bed. Not sleeping. I didn't think he was asleep. But letting us down when we needed the business, and that because he'd fallen for a girl who probably thought one went after tarpon with a worm for bait, and just didn't give a damn anyhow.

Not that Mack meant anything to me personally. At forty-five and a hundred and sixty pounds a woman quits fooling herself. But I'd always liked him. He'd stick his head in my door on his way down to the guide dock and grin at me.

"How's the beauty business, Ethel?"

"Rotten. What's the use? You men never look at anything but fish."

As I say, I liked him, which made it worse. When I had appendicitis it had been Mack—and Joe—who wrapped me in a blanket, carried me to the boat and got me to the hospital on the mainland before the abscess ruptured. He paid my bills, too. After that he could have used me for tarpon bait if he'd wanted to, and when I heard he was going into the army from the National Guard I took the newspaper down to Joe, and we both looked pretty sick.

"He's a good guy," Joe said. "Best man with a fish I ever saw."

Only tarpon are fish on the island. The other little fellows have names.

Naturally then there was considerable excitement when we learned he was coming. His wire said: "Have ten days before showing army how to fight. Wake Joe from his winter sleep. Also notify fish."

It meant a lot, because the season had been late; late and cold, with now and then a tarpon rolling but none taken. You see, Mack was a sort of legend by that time. And when he did arrive about half the hotel met him on the dock. I myself was there. We let out a cheer when we saw him, and he grinned and waved. But the cheer sort of died away when we saw that he wasn't alone. There was a girl behind him, and the way he helped her off the boat showed me right away how things stood.

"Well, here we are, Miss Jeffries," he said. "Welcome to Corella Island."

She looked around her, at us and at the island; at the cocoanut palms and the orange trees and the blooming hibiscus and the long stretches of white sandy beach. It is beautiful, if I do say it. But I thought she looked rather queer.

"It's lovely," she said. "But it *does* smell fishy, doesn't it?"

"Sure it does," he said happily. "And how!"

I caught Joe's eye as the bellboys were taking off their stuff. Mack had his usual leather rod-case and tackle-box, but the Jeffries girl had a bag of golf clubs. Joe looked at them, and I could tell pretty well how he felt. You see, we get two sorts of guests, the fishing crowd and the golf crowd, and the split between them would make the Grand Canyon look like a drainage ditch. He took the tackle after Mack had shaken hands with him.

"Good tide tonight, Mack," he said. "Slack water at half-past ten."

But Mack looked undecided.

"I'll let you know, Joe. I've had a long trip."

Right then and there I knew it was all over. So did Joe. And if you'll believe me, it was. They had met on the train, the Jeffries girl and Mack, and I gathered that the only time he'd taken his eyes off her since was when he was asleep.

She was worth looking at, at that. I see all sorts of girls in my business, but Peggy Jeffries was about tops; one of those natural blondes who don't need a sunshine rinse, and so slim that I went off bread and potatoes that very night at dinner.

By that time, of course, everybody knew something was wrong. Usually when Mack arrives he is in fishing clothes as soon as he can unpack them, and in the Pass as soon as he can get there. But that evening he put on white flannels and a snappy sports coat, and if you'll believe me he and the Jeffries girl played backgammon until bedtime. I don't think he knew what he was playing. I slipped up the stairs once to put a quarter in one of the slot machines and Slim, the bartender, came to the door and winked at me.

"What will you bet she lands him?" he said. "He isn't even jumping to throw the hook."

"Maybe he's tired."

"Maybe I don't know a bottle of Scotch when I see it."

The worst news came the next morning. When Bill, the golf pro, came to lunch in the staff dining room he said he had bought a set of clubs and was taking lessons, with the girl looking on.

"How is he?" I asked, my heart sinking.

"Terrible," he said. "I left the caddies in bathing trunks, hunting for the six new balls he drove into the water."

Well, that's the way it was, day after day. Joe sitting in his boat waiting, with nothing to do; nobody catching any fish, and Mack on the links, with his face grim and the girl insisting on making a golfer of him if it killed him.

I saw him myself one morning when I was taking a walk before I started work. He was twisted up like a pretzel, and he was in a bad temper, too. The girl was standing by, watching him anxiously.

"Look, Mack," she said. He was Mack to her by that time, of course, and she was Peggy. "You don't have to kill it. It isn't Hitler. It's just a plain little white ball, waiting to be smacked."

"I'll smack it all right," he said furiously.

He hauled off and hit at it, and it should have gone three hundred yards. It only rolled about thirty feet however, and he looked as if he couldn't believe it. Then he turned and gave her a funny sort of smile.

"Look," he said. "I can do a few things. I can ride a horse. I can play tennis. I can shoot a gun. I can even fish. Then why the eternal hell can't I hit that ball?"

"You'll get it, Mack. It only needs practise."

She teed her ball and sent it clear down the fairway to the edge of the green. She waited until it stopped rolling, and then looked at him. Not patronizing. Not even proud of the shot. She really was a nice girl, only she didn't understand a man like Mack. Or that any man hates to have a girl make him look like a fool.

"Of course I've played for years," she said apologetically.

But he didn't reply. He stood looking off at the ball. Then he dropped his club.

"Oh God!" he said, and left her standing there.

I had a bit of hope then, but the next day she had him back. The plain truth was that, as Slim said, the poor lug was so in love with her that he couldn't keep away from her. And she hadn't the faintest idea what she was doing to him. She looked frightfully happy. She never noticed that he was avoiding the other guests. But she simply refused to get in a boat, and he wouldn't go without her.

Everybody on the island was watching, of course. The water was warming up, and here were the tarpon coming in—or showing up. Because there is an endless argument about them among the guides, one side believing they are in the Pass all year, but only showing in the spring; the other insisting that they spend the cold weather somewhere out in the Gulf, watching the thermometer until it's well toward seventy before they move. And here was our last hope playing the infatuated fool: golf and a swim in the morning, a sunbath in the afternoon, bridge or backgammon at night. And the Pass full of boats from everywhere around, waiting to take our record away from us.

I saw Joe alone at the guide dock one afternoon. All the rest were gone, and he was fishing for pinfish with a speck of shrimp and a hook about the size of my little fingernail. As I watched him he got one about five inches long. He put it carefully in the fish well. Then he looked at me.

"Can that girl swim, Ethel?" he inquired.

"Like a duck," I said. "Why?"

He drew a long breath. "I was thinking of taking her somewhere and drowning her."

He caught another pinfish and looked at it with anguish. "Look. That's bait if I ever saw it. I'm loaded with bait. Them fish is going to strike any day."

"Maybe I can work on her," I told him. "I don't think she really understands, Joe."

"You work on her and see where it gets you!"

I had a try, at that. She came down that afternoon for a manicure, and I told her she had good hands for fishing, strong enough even for tarpon. She just smiled.

"It's funny," she said. "So many people here want me to fish. It's silly, isn't it? I can't see why any man thinks it's sport to pull some helpless little thing out of the water and gasp itself to death."

"There's nothing little or helpless about a tarpon, Miss Jeffries."

"They kill them, don't they?"

"Only the first one, or something extra special. They let the others go."

I tried to tell her about it. How when the tarpon really come in and you see them, you never forget it; how they come up and roll, and it's your guess whether they weigh fifty pounds or a hundred and fifty. How when you strike one you think you're going out of the boat after it, and how it leaps into the air and shakes its head, and the chances are two to one that it will throw the hook and depart for parts unknown.

But I saw it was no use. She just wasn't interested. However she gave me a dollar tip, which is unusual, and I had Slim in the bar change it into quarters and took them to the slot machine. I got a lemon every time, and Slim grinned at me from the door of the bar.

"Why don't you break the glass?" he said. "That's the only way you'll get anything out of it."

I went in to the bar and got a coke. Slim's an old friend of mine.

"I wish you'd tell me something, Slim," I said. "What sort of a fellow lets a girl make a doormat of him with welcome on it?"

"Every fellow, once in a lifetime. Why don't you let that machine alone?"

"I'm trying to get my train fare back home."

"You might try saving it, just for a change," he said. "I suppose Mack's the doormat?"

"He is."

"Give him time. It took a stiff Scotch to get him to that backgammon board last night. And the girl's all right. Just needs experience. You watch. He'll break her neck some day and she'll like it."

"I'd like it myself," I said.

The truth was we were all pretty much on edge by that time. The fishing crowd was talking about going North, which meant closing the hotel. So every one was grumpy, including the guides, and one day someone put an anonymous sign on the bulletin board.

"When will Mack break the hoodoo?"

He tore it down when he saw it, but the next morning things began to happen.

The tarpon showed up. All at once word came that the Pass was full of them, and I knew what that meant. The hotel simply seethed that day. At the guide dock the bait man was doing a big business in pinfish, crabs and dried mullet. The tackle stand was selling reels and fresh lines, and about noon I met Joe, loaded down with lunch boxes, on the way to his boat. I don't know when I've been so excited.

"Bring me back a big one, Joe," I said.

He stopped and looked at me.

"What sort?" he inquired. "Angel wings or conch?"

"Are you being funny?"

"Funny!" he snarled. "The fish are in. The place is full of them. So we're going to lunch somewhere on a beach and then gather shells. I've been in this business thirty years. I've guided for Mack for five. I got him the only diamond-button fish on this island since Wilson was President. So I'm going shelling."

He dropped one of the lunch boxes and deliberately put his foot on it.

"Maybe them hard-boiled eggshells won't be so good when she gets them," he said.

I wanted to howl my head off.

I watched them start that day, and if ever a man had a hangdog look Mack had. But she still hadn't an idea what she was doing. She saw me at my window and waved, but to save my soul I couldn't wave back. I went up and put a quarter in the slot machine, just to work off steam. I got two dollars out, but like a fool I played them back for the jackpot and lost them all.

Mind you, I don't think Mack let go without a struggle. He had even coaxed her to troll a line on the way across the bay to the shell beach. According to Joe she got a sea trout, and a big one. But she wouldn't look at it. She made Joe put it back in the water, which hurt since trout were scarce and it would have made Joe and some of the other guides a supper.

So I think nobody was surprised when Joe quit that night. You have to get the way a guide's mind works. He's there to get fish. It's his job and he's proud of it. The first man to bring in a tarpon has it all over the rest. Then too the first tarpon is news. It gets in the papers, and naturally all the resorts try to get it.

So Joe quit. He waited until all the other boats had gone out to fish the night tide, and he quit right outside my window after I had put out the light and was going up to bed. I suppose he thought I had gone. The first thing I heard was his voice.

"Sorry to bother you, Mack," he said. "I thought I'd better tell you. I'm through."

"What the hell are you talking about?" That was Mack, and madder than a wet hen. But Joe was beyond caring.

"I'm a fisherman," said Joe stolidly. "I'm no shell-gatherer, and I can think of better things to do just now than picnicking among the fiddler crabs on a beach. Besides Mr. Renwick's here, and he needs a guide. So I'm quitting."

Well, of course, that just isn't done. A guide takes you for better or worse. But Joe had made up his mind.

"I know when I'm licked," he went on stubbornly. "You haven't been in the Pass since you came, and I've yet to hear of a fish being caught on the golf course. Or in the hotel either. Mind you," he went on, "it's your business. If the young lady doesn't like to fish that's all right with me. Only it happens fishing's my business, and I don't aim to spend the rest of the time just wearing out the seat of my pants."

"Damn it, you're being paid for it," said Mack, savagely.

"Not for wearing out my pants, Mack. I'll bring your tackle up, and you can leave a check at the desk. I'm through."

There is no use arguing with Joe when he is in that mood, and Mack knew it. I heard Joe go up the stairs to the lobby, evidently to tell Mr. Renwick, but Mack didn't move. He stood still for a minute. Then he lit a cigarette and started down the beach. I guessed the Jeffries girl wouldn't see him again that night, and I was right. I met her on the way up, looking pretty as a picture and rather breathless, and she asked where he was.

"He was going to play backgammon," she said. "I wonder where he is?"

"The last time I saw him," I said, "he was starting for a walk up the beach."

"A walk? But he said—"

"I don't think he feels like playing games," I said coldly. "You see, he's lost his guide, and I guess it's upset him."

She looked bewildered.

"Why should that upset him?" she inquired. "He hasn't fished anyhow."

"That seems to be the trouble," I told her, and left her standing there.

Well, as I say, she didn't see him again that night. I undressed for bed, and as I was raising the window I saw her limping back to the hotel alone. She stopped once to empty sand out of her slippers, and I had a good look at her face. I thought she had been crying.

Then of course the first fish was caught. At one o'clock in the morning I heard a boat horn tooting, and Joe brought old Mr. Renwick in, with the first fish of the year. It weighed only sixty pounds, but it was a tarpon and it was news. Joe didn't look any too happy; but Amy, the telephone operator, phoned the news to the New York papers the next morning, and wires for reservations began to come in from all over the country.

I didn't sleep much that night. Mack had only three days of his leave left, and that brat of a girl had spoiled them for him.

He didn't play golf the next morning. I was in the staff dining room when he came down to breakfast, and as the door into the main dining room was open I could see and hear him as he stopped at her table. She gave him a bright smile.

"It's a perfect day," she said. "If we can get off before the rest—"

"Sorry, my dear," he said. "You'd better get somebody who knows how to play golf and likes it. I don't."

She looked stunned.

"Of course," she said, "if that's the way you feel—"

"That's the way I feel," he told her, pleasantly. "You see, I'll never make a golfer, and I know it. So I'm going fishing, for a change."

"But I thought—hasn't Joe resigned or something?"

He smiled at that, but it was slightly twisted.

"I wouldn't say that he's particularly resigned. He's quit. That's all."

"Then how can you fish, Mack?"

"I'll tell you, if you're interested," he said. "I'm going to dig out some fiddler crabs from the beach, and I'm going to try for sheepshead off the old dock by the golf course. The kids have been getting some there."

She didn't get it. Not even that about the children. And of course she didn't know that to a tarpon fisherman going after sheepshead is as if a tennis champion took up tiddledewinks. She even hoped he would have good luck, although I could see she was puzzled and hurt. Then Minnie came to my table to arrange for a permanent that night, and I missed the rest of it.

Well, as I said at the beginning, I gave Minnie her permanent that night. Dinner had been late, for when the fish are in, meals are served if and when people come for them. Minnie was full of talk. She told me about Mack eating alone that night, and so on.

"He must be feeling terrible," she said. "No boat and no guide."

But I didn't want to talk about him. I was seeing the Pass at night, as I'd seen it now and then when some guide had an evening off: the boats with their white lights like drifting stars, the splash of the fish when they rolled, the blood-chilling snort of a porpoise when he came up to blow close at hand, and the dim outline of the palms. And Mack out of it, sulking alone some place. Not even with the Jeffries girl. I felt uneasy somehow. But there is no shutting Minnie up.

"Slim says he put forty dollars in the fifty-cent machine after dinner and lost it all," she said. "Ouch, you hurt, Ethel."

"That's right."

"What's right?"

"I hurt," I said.

She looked at me, and I pulled myself together. "Somebody's going to get that jackpot soon," I said. "Maybe I'll get my fare North after all."

I got her wrapped and under the machine. Then I borrowed fifty cents from her and went upstairs. But there was no sign of Mack, and after I'd lost the money I went back to Minnie. It was almost one o'clock by that time, and I was dead on my feet. Minnie was peevish.

"What's the idea of leaving me alone?" she said. "What if the place caught on fire?"

I didn't answer, for I had just seen a funny thing. I'd seen Mack sneaking down the back stairs, and unless I was seeing things he had his heavy tarpon rod with him. It just didn't make sense. What is more, I realized all at once that a storm was coming up. It's like that down there. One minute it's clear and calm, with the stars as big as saucers. Then the palms begin to rattle, there is a warning shower or two of rain, all at once it's blowing hard, and there is enough thunder and lightning to make one want to crawl under a bed.

I got Minnie shampooed and under the drier. Then I stepped outside. It didn't look too good. The palms had stopped rattling and begun to swish, and there wasn't a star in sight. Far away too I could hear the boats coming back. The Pass is no place to be in a storm.

When I went back the Jeffries girl was in the hall. She hadn't much on under her bathrobe, and she looked young and sort of helpless, if you know what I mean.

"I wonder if you've seen Mr. McKnight?" she said breathlessly. "I've tried to get him on his room telephone. I wanted to tell him something, but he doesn't answer."

I felt sorry for her. She looked like a kid, and she looked worried. Minnie was watching us both, but of course she couldn't hear anything with the drier roaring in her ears.

"The last time I saw him," I said, "he was going up the beach with a tarpon rod in his hand. Don't ask me why. I couldn't tell you."

She seemed relieved.

"Are there tarpon around the island?" she asked.

"Not unless they've got legs to walk here."

All at once she began to cry. She didn't have a handkerchief, so I got her a towel.

"I've been such a fool, Ethel," she said, wiping her eyes. "Why didn't he tell me? I'd have understood. I thought—I thought he just liked playing around."

"Playing your game," I said coldly.

She looked at me.

"I'd have thought more of him if he had played his own," she said.

I remember that now. It didn't register then, because at that moment I heard a boat engine starting up. That was queer, because there wasn't a boat left on the island. Then I remembered the old speed-boat tied up at the dock off the golf course, and I knew.

That fishing fool had got the engine going and was on his way to the Pass, storm and all, to fish the two o'clock tide alone.

You've got to know what that means. It takes two people to manage a tarpon. One is the person who has it on the line. He has a man-size job from the start. He's got a fighting devil to try to hold, unless he wants to throw away a hundred and fifty dollars' worth of tackle. And you can't tell what the fish will do. It may come up under and knock a plank or two out of the boat. I've heard of that happening. It may even jump into the boat, in which case it's ten to one somebody is knocked overboard, or gets a broken leg. So the minute a fish is on, the guide starts the engine and keeps moving. Not fast. Just enough to keep the big boy out of mischief.

So now Mack was on his way alone to the Pass in that leaking wreck of a boat. Not only that. The other boats were coming back, which meant that he would be alone in the Pass in a gale of wind; and the Pass in a stiff blow looks like the North Atlantic in a hurricane.

And I knew him. He would get a fish, storm and all.

I guess I was pretty excited.

"Do you hear that boat?" I said. "That's your young man going out to commit suicide. That's what it amounts to. Just hope I can get a boat and a guide there in time. That boat's fast, when it goes at all."

She didn't cry any more. I'll say that for her. She just stiffened.

"I'm going with you," she said.

"You're staying right here," I told her. "I won't answer for what Joe will do if he sees you."

I clean forgot about Minnie. I grabbed a raincoat and headed for the dock. Joe had just come in. He was helping Mr. Renwick out from under the canvas, but when he saw my face he let him go.

"Anything wrong, Ethel?"

"You and your sickly pride!" I yelled, over the wind. "Mack's on his way to the Pass in the old speedboat."

"The old jackass," said Joe.

I jumped in and he cast off. But just then the Jeffries girl landed beside me. However, Joe didn't throw her out. There wasn't time. He merely gave her a look of hatred and pushed off.

Well, of course we couldn't catch Mack. He had too good a start for that. But we went all-out to the Pass, and Joe saw him in a flash of lightning before I did. There was a big sea on, waves coming in from the open Gulf so that I could hardly stay in the boat. As for the thing Mack was in, it was riding as if it was half full of water. Joe headed straight for it, and I didn't like his face. He looked scared. He was muttering to himself too, and if I hadn't known him I would have said he was praying.

Then suddenly something leaped out of the water not far from us, and we heard Mack's voice above the wind.

"Keep back, you fool," he shouted. "I'm all right. It's a big one."

He was standing up, trying to hold that excuse for a boat into the sea with one hand and gripping his rod with the other. And he was laughing. I'll never forget that. He hadn't really laughed since he hit the island. Joe had edged up as close as he dared, but when I urged him to go nearer he shook his head.

"If I make him lose that fish he'll kill me," he said.

"He's crazy. You're all crazy!" I yelled. Joe shook his head.

"He'll play it until it's tired," he said. "Then I'll pick him up."

I knew it wasn't any use. They were both fishing fools, and it's against the rules to touch another man's tackle when he has a fish on. All this time the Jeffries girl hadn't spoken a word. I thought she was scared dumb. But I just didn't know her.

Because the next flash of lightning showed no boat and no Mack, and while I was screaming my head off she was taking off her shoes. Joe caught her just in time.

"Stay where you are," he said. "I suppose you can't run a boat?"

She didn't answer. She merely went forward in her stocking feet and took the wheel.

"Don't go over until you see him," she said, as quietly as if we weren't alone in the Pass in the middle of the night and a storm on. "Get your searchlight, I'll manage the boat all right."

Well, even Joe says she handled the boat as if she had been born in one. But at first it looked pretty hopeless. It's all right in the Pass when it's smooth and the head of a big loggerhead turtle looks like that of a man swimming; but in that rough water there wasn't a sign of Mack where the boat went down, and even Joe looked hopeless. It was the girl who found him.

She was dead white, but still quiet. Using her head too, for she said:

"What way would that fish go? Toward the Gulf?"

"What the hell does that matter?"

"He might still be holding on to it."

Well, I know it sounds crazy, but that is the way we found him. She took a big circle toward the Gulf, and we picked him up just inside the bar. He was pretty well winded. Joe got him aboard, and if you'll believe it, he still had his rod in his hand. What's more, the fish was still on!

I just went up to the girl and kissed her. Then I shoved her away from the wheel and took it myself. When Mack looked around he saw me there and grinned.

"Good work, Ethel," he said. "Never knew you could handle a boat."

"I can do a lot of things," I told him.

He didn't even hear me. He was sneezing and dripping salt water all over the place, but he had only one thing in mind. He sat down in the swivel chair, put the butt of his rod into the rest, took a breath or two and began to pump the fish in. He looked happier than I had seen him since he came.

"Golly," he said. "I feel like myself again, Joe. How much would you say that cockle-shell will set me back?"

I had a chance then to speak to the girl. Mack hadn't seen her at all.

"Listen," I said. "I'm sorry about taking that wheel. But you've done

385

enough to him, you and your golf. Better not let him know you saved his life."

She got it that time all right. When at last the fish came in and Joe leaned over the side of the boat with the release hook, Mack saw her for the first time. He looked stunned.

"What on earth are you doing here?" he asked.

And I'll give that girl credit. If she was acting, it was well. I didn't think she was, however. She was the complete female then, all scared and shaky.

"I was frightened, Mack," she said, in a small voice. "I made them bring me."

"It's no night for you to be out," he told her, all male and disapproving. "What have you got on, anyhow? Get a coat or something. You'll take cold."

I knew then it was all right. He had stopped being a doormat, and from the way she smiled I knew she liked it.

Joe was holding the fish.

"Big boy, Mack," he said. "Looks like a diamond-button to me."

Mack looked down. In the light from the mast the fish was lying on its side. It must have been seven feet long—at least it looked it. Mack stared at it and grinned.

"He gave me a good fight," he said. "Let him go, Joe. I owe him something."

I think Joe's heart almost broke at that. He didn't even measure the fish. He took out the release hook and stood back, and maybe the water on his face was sea-water and maybe not. We all watched as the fish began to move a little, his tail first, then the big smooth muscles of his sides. Even then he stayed awhile, getting his breath, and the girl reached down and touched his silver body with her hand just before he moved off.

"Good-bye," she said.

It gets you, you know. I was darned near crying myself, what with excitement and everything. A game fish and a game man—but what am I rambling about anyhow? If you've never seen it you wouldn't know.

All this time, remember, we'd been rolling about like nobody's business. I felt queasy myself, and I'm a good sailor. It was after we'd started for home that the Jeffries girl spoke.

"Does the Pass ever get much rougher than that?" she asked.

386

"Not unless there's a hurricane," said Joe.

She laughed. It was a shaky laugh, but it was real enough.

"Then I guess I can fish after all," she said. "I haven't been seasick at all."

I think that was the first time Mack had looked at her with any real expression since Joe had quit.

"What's this about getting seasick?" he said.

"I used to. Dreadfully, I have to stick to rivers and things. That's the reason I couldn't fish. Not with you anyhow, Mack. I was ashamed to let you know."

If ever I've seen a man with a load off his mind it was Mack just then. He clean forgot that Joe and I were there. He leaned over and put his hand under her chin, so she had to look at him.

"Listen, my darling," he said. "Did you really think that a man would care less for you because you upchucked your last meal? What do you think love is?"

I guess he told her. I know I turned my back after that, but from the way he helped her out of the boat when we got back I gathered it was all right. But he stopped me and held out his hand.

"Thanks a lot, Ethel," he said. "If you hadn't been in the boat I guess I would be fighting the sharks about now. Joe too."

"Don't be a fool," I said sharply. "I don't know a thing about—"

And then the girl pinched me. It was a hard pinch. I think I have said she had good strong hands.

"Wasn't she wonderful?" she said. "She heard you start out, too, Mack. If it hadn't been for her—"

Yes, she had learned her lesson all right. Unless Win McKnight reads this he will always think I saved his life. Maybe I did, at that.

Minnie was still under the drier when I got back. She was sound asleep, but she roused when I went in.

"Where have you been?" she said fretfully. "I've read this whole magazine."

I turned the clock so she couldn't see it.

"Well, you're good and dry," I told her, and took the pins out. That was one set that lasted, if I do say it. She still talks about it. But I got her off at last. She paid me in half dollars and quarters out of her tips, and I locked it away in the cash drawer and started up to bed.

The hotel was quiet. The night clerk was asleep behind the desk and the bar was dark and deserted. The storm was over, too. All I could hear was the dripping of the trees. But there was a light on over the slot machines, and tired as I was I went down again and got a half dollar of Minnie's money. I had a feeling that it might be my lucky night.

It was. I pulled the lever, and in a minute there was silver money all over the place. I'd broken the jackpot.

In Sickness and in Health

ISABEL SCOTT RORICK

Poor Mr. Cugat! He was so ill he had to stay home. He couldn't do a thing—except blow a fuse, lose the cat, sell his best winter coat, and make a wreck of Mrs. Cugat. Many housewives will agree it's a trial to have their husbands home all day!

LITTLE MRS. CUGAT turned in her bed and blinked lazily at the quiet alarm clock on the table beside her. Half-past eight. Slices of yellow morning sun came through the Venetian blind; coffee flavored the air; a remote hum, off in another part of the house, droned up and down, singing of well-ordered, early vacuum-cleaning. She stretched placidly, reached for a cigarette, and jerked upright. There in the other bed was Mr. Cugat—still there, hunched all up under his covers at eight-thirty.

"Hey!" she cried, swinging her feet out. "Look at the time!" Mr. Cugat did not move, but his eyes opened slowly—clouded and apathetic.

"I know," he said with effort, and closed them again.

Alarm washed over her, and she regarded him wide-eyed while she groped for her slippers and got into her bathrobe. "You aren't going to the office?" she asked uncertainly.

"No," he replied, eyes still closed. "I'm sick."

She bent to feel his head—it was hot. Mr. Cugat hunched deeper into the covers. Hurriedly closing the window, she pattered into the

388

dressing-room and then distractedly out again and into the hall, where she rang urgently for the maid. Mr. Cugat was *never* sick—even the commonest seizures and distempers passed him by; his sinus, duodenum, gall bladder, and appendix were imperturbable; Poisonous Wastes took splendid care of themselves. It seemed appalling that, judging by the look of him, everything had given way at once.

"Anna!" she called, leaning over the stair rail, "Mr. Cugat isn't feeling well this morning—will you bring up some hot coffee right away!" She hurried back. Mr. Cugat had roused himself and was sitting on the side of his bed, staring at his feet. As she came in, however, he rose and tottered across to the bathroom. "I'll come down to the dining-room," he said, and disappeared.

"He says he'll come down, Anna," she shouted, hurrying back to the banister.

The vacuum-wielder appeared below and tilted up an anxious countenance. "The dining-room's being cleaned," she said, wide-eyed.

"Oh. Well, you'll have to bring breakfast upstairs, then."

"We only got that one big tray, you know. Can I get everything on it?"

"No—you'll have to set up a card table in the dressing-room."

"It's Friday." Dark significance clothed this last.

"I know, Anna, but you'll have to *put off* the cleaning until later. Don't you understand? Mr. Cugat may be dangerously ill!"

"Saints!" said the face and vanished.

Mrs. Cugat returned from the hall and stuck her head in the bathroom door. Mr. Cugat was gargling.

"Shall I call Doctor Buell?" she asked anxiously.

"Maybe you'd better," he said, spitting without vigor and turning to examine the contents of the medicine cabinet blankly.

She dashed some water on her face in the guest-room bathroom and flew to the phone, colliding in the hall with the approaching card table. The laundress, damp and foreign and obviously wrested from her own pursuits to be hurled into the breach, labored in the table's wake with an abundant tray. Compassionate eyes were bent on Mr. Cugat, who drifted out of the bathroom just then and went to sit miserably on the edge of the window seat in everybody's way. He looked self-conscious and unwanted. Having left word for the doctor, Mrs. Cugat hastened back to his side, love and concern welling up within her. When she reached it, however, she was smitten with unexpected shyness. Mr. Cugat, ill, was a complete stranger. She felt his head again timidly.

Breakfast took some time. It was a cereal morning. Mr. Cugat, toying listlessly with his, said it would be all right with him if they had just boiled eggs always, but never to mind this morning, he wasn't very hungry for anything. Nevertheless, it seemed advisable to start all over and try him with an egg. She shouted down the stair-well again, "Anna! Mr. Cugat thinks he might like a nice egg—" and resignedly, the vacuum died away. By the time the egg arrived, however, Mr. Cugat had retired once more behind the bathroom door.

Mrs. Cugat got dressed anxiously, as best she could without her comb, her powder, or her girdle, which were closeted with Mr. Cugat, and hastened down to rearrange her day. Her hair appointment would have to be canceled; she must get somebody to take her place at the Red Cross Rummage Sale; she must call her mother and tell her *not* to bring Cousin Melba from Cincinnati to tea. She was cold with apprehension, and between phone calls kept running to the living-room windows to see if she could see Doctor Buell. Suffocating pictures of life alone presented themselves. Mr. Cugat's last words—weak but brave. Mr. Cugat in his coffin, with his cutaway on, tucked down into the white satin like candy in a fancy box. Mr. Cugat's pallbearers coming back to the house, the way Tommy Spencer's did, for one last sad drink. Her throat ached.

Mr. Cugat put an end to this by coming downstairs. He had put on a pair of gray flannel trousers over his pyjamas and an old sweater used for duck-hunting; around his neck was his best white silk monogrammed evening scarf, and over all his oldest bathrobe. He shuffled over to the coffee table and sat tentatively down on its edge without saying anything. His hair stuck up and he looked wistful.

"Do you think you ought to be downstairs?" she asked anxiously.

"I don't know, they're doing something to my bed," he said.

While she was looking into this the doctor came.

Mr. Cugat had a cold. Nothing serious, but he'd better stay home for a day or so and take care of himself. Plenty of rest—stay out of drafts—lots of liquids—two pink tablets alternating with one tan tablet every hour—and gargle with salt water. Mr. Cugat, consoled and interested, sat back in his big chair reviewing his symptoms. Vivacious with relief, Mrs. Cugat saw the doctor to the door and sped upstairs to finish dressing. There was just time to get her hair appointment after all. On her way home she would stop and pick up a detective story and some movie magazines for him. What fun having him home! Darling Mr. Cugat, suddenly vulnerable and inadequate, with his hair sticking up—the Weaker Vessel. Goodness, how she loved him! She could hardly wait to get back downstairs to see if she could do anything to make him more comfortable before she left.

"What about lunch?" Anna caught her at the garage door. "We planned peanut salad, you know. Will He eat it?"

Of a certainty He would not. "Ask him what he thinks he'd like, Anna, what sounds *good* to him. I'll be back at one o'clock."

Laden with two books, three magazines, a pot of tulips, and some white grapes, she came eagerly back up the walk at one to meet Belda, the laundress, resplendent in mufti, emerging from the front door.

"Em goink by da 'A' on 'P'," she beamed in explanation.

"The 'A and P'?" said Mrs. Cugat. "What for?"

"Eh nice stek."

"Why doesn't Anna go?"

"Shiss bissy."

"Oh—What else did Mr. Cugat order for lunch?"

"Franch frice—"

"Ah, yes, of course—"

"Vechtible soup—"

"Oh."

"Shoclit keck—home med. Pore seeck men"—her voice crooned—"hees hongreh!"

Mrs. Cugat steadied herself. "And what about the ironing?" she queried.

"Ha! Becawss da fuce—*iss* no ionink!"

"Fuse? What fuse?"

"Da men fuce. Mist Cugat feexis lemps togedda—Zick! da men fuce blos. Now iss no lides—no hut ion. Iss med, da ledy in nomba fife—shess eh cot poddy effta launch now iss no lides in heh house nedda!"

"You mean it blew out hers *too*?"

"Anna sess so."

Mr. Cugat was discovered in the basement dispiritedly screwing and unscrewing things—apparently at random. He looked downhearted and was persuaded back upstairs again. In the library she came upon the chain-arrangement of lamps that had been designed to bring light to him over in an obscure corner by the woodbox (out of drafts). His chair was there, and two dismantled shotguns with their cleaning equipment and a highball and the white velvet chaise-longue cover from the guest room.

"Did anyone call an electrician?" she asked starting to pull things out from where they were and sticking them back where they belonged.

Mr. Cugat lifted absorbed eyes from his new *Film Fun*. "Yes," he said, "but all the electricians are striking today, Anna says. I told her," he added helplessly, "that she'd better get some candles."

Lunch, after all, was disappointing. It was funny, he said, but nothing had any taste. Might as well be eating straw! Surreptitiously Mrs. Cugat, to the best of her capacity, ate for two while Anna was out of the room, but she was obliged to feed most of Mr. Cugat's chocolate cake to Lillian, the cat.

After lunch she went upstairs and got out her knitting. Now they could settle down for the afternoon, cozy and domestic, in front of the fire. She would see that he took his medicine and didn't get bored. Perhaps he'd let her read aloud. Maybe he'd feel like backgammon. How nice—on a cold, dark day like this! When she got back to the library, however, after some delay at the phone (the lights of the people in No. 4 were all *out!* Were the Cugats'?), she found the room empty, the windows open, and the curtains whipping and streaming. Mr. Cugat, at the mercy of the elements and clutching his bathrobe, was out on the balcony, hanging over the rail.

"It's funny about that cat," he replied, in answer to her squeaks of protest. "She disappeared like *that!*"

"The cat! Don't tell me you let Lillian out!"

"Only for a minute. She ought to get more exercise—she's getting fat," he explained reasonably.

"But darling, we *never* let her out alone! She acts like a perfect idiot. Streaks across the street in front of cars and eats garbage and gets up in trees and doesn't know how to get down. Oh, dear! There's not a sign of her. Anybody'd think, with a valuable animal like Lillian, you'd be a little careful. What had I better do, I wonder."

It seemed sensible that Mrs. Cugat go right out and hunt for Lillian. Mr. Cugat, looking sheepish, came in from the balcony, took a double dose of pills, wrapped his knees tenderly in the white velvet chaise-longue coverlet, and settled down by the fire with one of the guns and a can of oil. He looked meek and apologetic and offered to call a man he knew at the City Hall.

It took endurance to hunt Lillian. Chilled and anxious, Mrs. Cugat wandered up one block and down another, through alleys and across strange gardens calling, "Here, Lilli, Lilli—come, kitty!" in a persistent and weary falsetto. Curious faces peered at her from back windows and interested children vouchsafed conflicting information. However, as generally happened, just when she was ready to give up, she heard the familiar mew above her—far above her. Lillian was on a telephone pole this time—clinging galvanically with all four feet and looking fearfully down over her shoulder.

"Somebody's cat," said a small boy conversationally at Mrs. Cugat's side, "and he can't get down."

"It's my cat," said Mrs. Cugat hopelessly, peering up and shading her eyes with her hand.

"Don't he know what to do next?" inquired the tot interestedly.

"I guess not," she said. "Here, Lilli, Lilli—back *up*, you fool, and come down without looking!"

"If I was up there, I'd know what to do," the boy said. Mrs. Cugat glanced at him. He looked as agile as a little spider.

"You couldn't climb up there and bring the kitty down, could you?" she ventured doubtfully. "I'd give you a quarter if you would."

"Sure. Oh, boy! Give me a boost."

Mrs. Cugat lifted him carefully up to the first rung and he started in sturdily to climb. The rungs were far apart, and she watched his small rubbers and blue-legginged legs with increasing anxiety. He was a littler boy than she'd realized.

"Are you all right?" she called foolishly when he was about three-quarters of the way up.

"Sure," he grunted without stopping. "This is fun."

Reassured, she bent her neck to ease it and then looked again. He had Lillian by the tail. "Oh, be careful!" she called. "Don't hurt her or she'll scratch you."

A shriek tore the air. Mrs. Cugat swung around. Reeling across the street came a blonde woman in lavender slacks. "Hang on, Eddie!" she screamed. "Mother's coming." Eddie, up until this moment the personification of coolness and aplomb, let go Lillian's tail, peered over his own shoulder, and turned pale green. Then he let out a bellow. Doors popped open all along the street and people streamed out.

They called out the fire department in the end, and with it came the press. Eddie and Lillian aloft on their pole and again on the ground posed for the early editions. Mrs. Cugat gave her name and address—to everybody. Eddie's mother threatened suit. Eddie demanded his quarter. The crowd muttered menacingly. Mrs. Cugat, wondering what it felt like to be lynched, emptied her purse of three dollars and sixty cents. Then Eddie wanted to know if the lady'd let him keep the kitty. The crowd said, "Aw—how cute!" and looked challenging. Clutching Lillian, Mrs. Cugat turned and fled up an alley.

When she reached home, however, she found the front door open and no one in sight but an unreliable-looking man cleaning his nails in the front hall.

"Did you want something?" she asked doubtfully, dumping Lillian, who threw up Mr. Cugat's chocolate cake and crawled off under a radiator.

"Harry Hirsch. I buy old clothes," he explained briefly. "The boss is getting me some."

Anna and Belda and Mr. Cugat were in the storeroom looking for that striped suit Mr. Cugat used to have. All the sealed moth bags had been unsealed, but they hadn't found it yet.

"I gave it to the Clothing Center, darling, two years ago. Hadn't you better get back to the library? There's no heat in here."

Mr. Cugat had become diverted by his old navy uniform, which he hadn't seen in years. He was trying the coat on and throwing his shoulders back in front of the mirror. Moth balls rolled about on the floor. Anna and Belda were still with admiration. Harry Hirsch, presumably lonely, wandered in and joined them. When he got a good look at the storeroom, his eyes glistened, and he picked up one of Mr. Cugat's best winter overcoats and began going over it like a squirrel with a nut.

"A small size and plenty wore," he said with relish. "I'll give you a dollar and a half for it; there's no call for this kind of thing."

Mr. Cugat, still in uniform, was coaxed back to the library and both a tan tablet and a pink tablet were administered—he couldn't remember which he'd had last. Harry Hirsch was coaxed to the front door by Mr. Cugat's winter overcoat and a checked golf suit thrown in at two dollars the lot. (No call, at all, for checks.) She had a feeling that now that he knew about the storeroom she would see more of him.

She cleaned up Lillian's chocolate cake and got back to the library, to find Mr. Cugat up on the bookcase ladder shifting things around on the top shelf and lighting the upper gloom with safety matches.

"What are you looking for?" she asked, regarding him thoughtfully.

"My Law School books. What's been done with them?"

Law School books? She didn't think she'd ever seen them. As a matter of fact, she didn't believe she ever knew he'd ever been to Law School. Maybe they were at his mother's. They must be. Unconvinced, he remained disconsolately atop the ladder. She handed another tan pill up to him.

"God," he mused, marveling and rummaging around again with renewed interest, "doesn't anybody ever think to clean up here? It's positively filthy! Look—" A little cloud of dust rose to his righteous puff, but she wasn't looking. Her eyes were closed.

Then a bell pealed sharply. "There's the doorbell," he said, alert and clambering down. "Is somebody going to answer it?"

"I don't know why not; they always have," she said shortly, without opening her eyes.

"Oh—well—I was only wondering—" Limping a little, he went over and took another tan pill, let himself carefully down in his chair, and put his head back with a sigh. "Funny," he said pensively, "I'm weak as a kitten."

Anna appeared in the door. "Mr. Cartwright and Mr. Sturm are here to see Mr. Cugat," she announced. "Mr. Cartwright's brought some things from the office for Mr. Cugat to sign, if he's able."

"Mr. Cartwright! Good old Cory?" Mr. Cugat's face lit up with the touching eagerness and incredulous gratitude of a man who has spent the past ten years of his life on an island retreat of nuns. "Tell 'em to come in here, Anna," he said, removing the chaise-longue coverlet with a walloping kick. "And better bring some White Rock." Mrs. Cugat had opened her eyes again and was busily lighting candles.

"Well, well! How's the invalid?"—"Well, Georgie! What's all this about?"—"So they finally got you down, did they?" In came the Messrs. Cartwright and Sturm, looking fit, well combed, and ruddy. Mrs. Cugat's heart smote her. Mr. Cugat in his scarf and navy tunic and bathrobe, with his hair sticking up, seemed frail and touching. *Was* frail and touching.

"Do stay awhile and talk to him," she urged, hovering with little pats and a rush of renewed tenderness. "It will do him good."

Poor darling, she thought contritely, hurrying up the stairs for lipstick—Were those pills strong enough? They gave one very little confidence, somehow. Perhaps she'd better have Doctor Buell drop in again tonight to check up. There was that weakness—She left word for the doctor and then, suddenly weary, decided just to stay upstairs and take a bath.

Floating in pine oil and sipping a glass of hot milk, she grew relaxed and sentimental. Pathetic evidences of Mr. Cugat were all over the bathroom. His yesterday's shirt hung limply on a hook; his keys and wallet and watch huddled, abandoned, on the dressing-table; his shoes, with a look of discard, were unexpectedly under the washstand. Tears smarted behind her eyes as she looked at them.

There was a knock at the door. Anna's voice muted to a rasp came through. "Mr. Cugat's asked the gentlemen to dinner!" She scrambled for her bathrobe and upset the milk. The voice deepened significantly. "We're having them veal birds, you know."

"What else, Anna?" she chattered, mopping at the milk.

"Squash."

Veal birds and squash. Cory Cartwright was one of those men who broil things over charcoal and make their own salad dressing. Howie Sturm's wife said her chef used to work at the Colony.

"Is Belda still here?" she hissed, sticking her head out.

"Just going."

"Stop her and send her to the 'A and P' for another steak and some lettuce and tomatoes and a quart of drugstore ice cream. You'll have to try Baked Alaska again, I'm afraid."

Dinner was very late and the Baked Alaska much as usual—leaky. After four Old-Fashioneds, though, nothing matters. Nothing, anyway, but bed. Her throbbing head propped up by the chin and her eyes glazed, she listened through a meandering eternity to the wealth of detail embellishing what Cory Cartwright told the head waiter at the Ambassador about wild turkey—and about grouse (ruffed grouse) —and about woodcock—and about terrapin. "Of *course* you were right, Cory!" she heard her own voice saying, far away. Mr. Cugat told Howie Sturm about the same old time at Reisenweber's with Connie Bennett; Anna, out beyond, banged dishes and rattled silver in a vicious tune.

But the door bell finally rang. Anna, on her way to answer it, without her apron and apparently not caring who knew it, tossed an eloquent look. Was it the doctor at last? It was. Nothing goes on forever; if one could only remember that. The Messrs. Sturm and Cartwright, taking a good deal of time over it, tactfully and jocosely withdrew. She waved them good-bye at the front door and sent her love to Mrs. Sturm. Then she went back to the library. Mr. Cugat, uninterrupted by the stethoscope, was telling Doctor Buell about Reisenweber's and Connie Bennett. Doctor Buell, also undeterred, produced a little silver funnel and peered into each of Mr. Cugat's ears.

"Well," he said, folding everything up, "you're a pretty good nurse, young lady!"

"I am?"

"Yes, I believe he'll be well enough to go back to the office tomorrow. Now, if I might have just half a glass of water—"

"Hell, doc," said Mr. Cugat robustly, "I don't need any more medicine!"

"No," said Doctor Buell gently, "but I think we'll just fix a little something for Mrs. Cugat."

Mother Has Gone to the Mountains

RUTH BURR SANBORN

When Ready couldn't convince her husband Terrin to go to the mountains, she went into action. Where and what the mountains are is for you to discover. How she finally persuades him to join her is for you to enjoy.

"BUT WE'RE GOING to the mountains," said Ready stubbornly. It was not like Ready to be stubborn. "It's our anniversary. You promised, Terrin."

"I didn't know then that this MacNinery business was coming up."

"Something always comes up," said Ready. "It's five years since we planned to go to the mountains. That was the year we built the house."

"Don't you like the house?" said Terrin.

"Yes," said Ready. He expected her to say she loved the house. She did not say it. The house was white-pillared and gracious. It was too big. The guest wing had the view. It was the right background for the architect, Terrin Clune. He had given it to Ready for her tenth anniversary. He had also given her the mortgage. She said, "The next year the children had the mumps."

"I didn't know the Watchett child had mumps when I asked them here."

"No," agreed Ready. "He just looked like any bloated plutocrat."

"You don't blame the children for having mumps, do you?" Terrin spoke with controlled exasperation. It was his self-control that infuriated Ready. They were too civilized to shout at each other.

"No," she said. "And I don't blame Tink for having his teeth straightened the next summer; and I don't blame Becky for going to the Dreamer camp the summer after, so she could get clubby with the Heathfield children before they built Heathfield; and I don't blame Terry for going round the world with young Wimpincott and young Wimpincott's tutor the summer before the Wimpincotts built Wimpincott-by-the-Sea. I don't even blame Aldous MacNinery for marrying a chorus girl half his age and building her a playhouse."

"Then what's it all about?" said Terrin.

"I want to go to the mountains," said Ready stubbornly.

It was a symbol for all the things they had ever promised themselves. It meant being alone with Terrin, the way she never was alone with him any more. It meant belonging to each other. Sometimes she thought it would have been easier if she had not loved Terrin so much. Ready loved Terrin completely. She loved even the bad things: the tension that governed his unconquerable thinness, the tempestuous darkness of his eyes and the tempestuous mouth. She loved him in his black moods, when he clung to her, wordless and rebellious, in the night; most then, because she could give him most. But sometimes she saw him abstractly, as she saw him now. She saw the things that mattered so much because they did not matter. She saw the white lock in his hair. Once Terrin had kept the lock short, brushed his hair to cover it. Now he made it show. It was striking with the white nick in his eyebrow. It gave him distinction. Terrin Clune needed distinction. The white lock was a symbol too.

"I love you, Terrin," she said soberly. As if it needed saying.

"Of course," said Terrin, "I love you too." Very offhand, as if it didn't need saying at all. "Don't be childish, Rebecca."

"I'm thirty-three," said Ready. She was amazed, because she was thirty-three.

She was eighteen the night she ran away from her wedding with Paul Parrington Linwood, III, to marry Terrin Clune. They stood on the minister's doorstep with Terrin's hand on the bell. "You're sure?" he said. "You're ready?" . . . "Ready for anything," she said. People thought Terrin called her Ready because of her hair. It was not spelled like that. Terrin did not often call her "Rebecca."

"Things happen," Terrin said. "You can't help things happening."

"Things happen to everybody. But the mountains are still there. Life," said Ready sagely, "is what you make it." She stopped, appalled at what they had made of their life. They had made so much of it.

The first years had been hard. Terrin had finished architectural school and got a job. It was not a very good job. They wanted four children, and they had four children in spite of the depression. The children were grand. Terry was moody and talented like his father. Becky was going to be beautiful. Tink was their problem child, shy and untouchable, and Ready loved him most. Bubbles was a sweet lump. But children have diseases and accidents and crooked teeth and camps and clothes and temperaments and emotions. Children complicate things.

When Terrin got the award for the Burgan Memorial, they had success. They had too much success too quickly. Success is harder to cope with than insecurity. Terrin had to have contacts. They had to join things. He had to entertain clients. They built the house. There arose immediately the servant problem. People said the way Jeams handed a roast on a silver platter was an inspiration. He was inspired by ten thousand rehearsals with Ready. There were other problems. The telephone problem and the doorbell problem. They had two cars and there was a car problem.

Ready gave a May breakfast every spring and a garden party every fall, because she had a garden. She was president of the garden club, and vice-president of the Book Chat, and secretary of the civic association; when Terrin built the library, she was chairman of the decorating committee and went to bed every night with an icecap on her head. That was when the looks problem arose. She had a standing appointment at the hairdresser's.

Terrin put a copper panel on the stair landing. Ready had nightmares in which she galloped past the panel in a gingham playsuit, with her long white legs twinkling, and her long red hair on her shoulders. But at dinnertime she paced down sedately, with her hair high on her head and her eyes on the toes of her green slippers to keep from tripping on her train. Her eyes came up slowly under the spread wings of her brows, and they were green like her shoes; the green lights in them were picked up by the emeralds in her ears. So, in ten minutes, she would go down to meet the MacNinerys. The MacNinerys were dining. The dinner would be perfect.

"Terrin!" She took an impulsive step toward him, lifted her hands in a gesture oddly supplicating. "Let's go to the mountains anyhow."

If he had moved to meet her, if he had taken her in his arms and held her close, steadying her, it might have been different. If he had caught her to him roughly, needing and demanding her, if he had crushed the breath half out of her, and shaken her, and tousled her costly hair, and maybe torn her dress, it would have been different surely. But Terrin put his hands lightly on her shoulders, so he should not disarrange her gown. He tipped up her head with one finger, so he should not muss her curls. He kissed her swiftly.

"I don't dare to let this MacNinery thing pass," he said. "MacNinery will go the limit on price. His little chorus girl is expensive. He'll do anything to keep her."

"Will he?" said Ready slowly.

"If we send Terry to the Chadwick School, we can't afford the mountains."

"Can't we?" said Ready.

"You understand, don't you?"

"Yes," said Ready gravely. "I understand. Too well. I'm going to the mountains."

The alarm rang at seven the next morning. That meant it was time for Ready to get Terrin up. He was lying on his back with his arms flung over his head. Terrin looked young and malleable when he was asleep, as if he might have been anything: a miner or a magician. It struck Ready that in repose the lines in his face were all down lines: the wayward mouth and the tilted shadows at the corners of his eyes. If she kept on looking at him she would stroke his hair. She rolled over.

The next time Ready woke, Melody was thumping at the door,

and Terrin was shouting, "It's eight o'clock. I've got an appointment with MacNinery at nine." Ready did not move.

Terrin came over and looked at her. She could feel him looking. She could feel him bending down and listening to her breath. "Are you sick?" asked Terrin.

"No," said Ready. "I've gone to the mountains."

"What are you talking about?"

"The mountains," said Ready gently.

"Do we have to go all over that again?"

"No," said Ready. "It's settled. I've gone."

"You haven't either gone," said Terrin crossly. "You're here."

"It's my spirit that's gone," Ready explained. She added painstakingly: "It won't cost anything. Spirits can travel free." She wondered abruptly if they could.

"How long are you going to keep this up?" Terrin demanded.

"I shall be gone a month," Ready decided. She opened her top eye and regarded him. She looked like a green-eyed minx with a ribald eyebrow; Terrin used to tell her so. She said: "It would be nice if you could run up for a week end."

"Week end!" said Terrin. He went into the bathroom, and there was a sound of too much water being drawn too fast. He came back again to the bed. "I can't find a shirt," he said.

"That's too bad," said Ready.

"Aren't you going to do anything about it?" said Terrin. "Can't you as much as find a shirt for me? Are you going to lie there and let me go off to meet MacNinery with no shirt?"

Ready closed her eye. She looked like a minx with her eye closed.

"If you want to, I don't see how I can stop you," she said gently. "You couldn't wire me to come home from the mountains to find your shirt. It would be quicker to find your shirt yourself. It would be quicker to ask Melody to find your shirt. It would be cheaper to go out and buy a shirt. Do be reasonable, Terrin."

"Reasonable!" said Terrin.

He found a shirt. And put it on. And went out.

When Ready woke next time, it was eleven, and Melody was standing at the foot of the bed. Melody had nursed Terry and Becky and Tink and Bubbles; she had cooked and cleaned and laundered, and taken walks in the country and brought home mysterious chickens. She weighed two hundred and fifty and would not wear uniforms.

Ready did her best with sprigged calico and big white aprons. The effect was picturesque.

Melody stood with her arms akimbo. "Is yo' got a mis'ry?" she inquired.

"No," said Ready. "I've gone to the mountains."

"Yo' bettah come back," said Melody uncompromisingly. "Mist' Clune he done ain' et no breffust, on'y fo' cupsa bilin' coffee, an' de cah won' sta't, an' he can' fin' no key to yo' cah, an' he done rid off a-cussin' in a taxi. Mas' Terry he tooken he papa's cah to pieces to fin' out why ain' it go, an' laid de pieces outen de drive, an' de milk truck done run ober one; an' Mis' Becky she done cut up mah bes'es' red sprig to mak herse'f a gypsy skirt; an' Mas' Tink he gotten de toofache; an' Mis' Bubbles she gotten a rose tho'n a inch long in her bottom. De cook done say will yo' please kin'ly tell her what's fo' lunchum an' also fo' dinner, an' is dey guests; an' Jeams he say iffen dat cook once mo' swing de swing do' in he face an' mak him bus' a cup he ain' nebber buttle in dis house no mo'. Miz Pendergas' say will yo' come fo' lunchum an' make plans fo' de hospittle benefits, an Miz Ramsbuckle say will yo' come fo' tea an' de civic directs meetin', an Mis' Cobb say what 'bout de festervul? An' Mist' Clune say tell yo' de MacNinerys be heah fo' de week end."

"Is that so?" said Ready.

"An' I say what yo' gwine do 'bout it?"

"Nothing," said Ready placidly. "I can't, because I'm in the mountains." She explained about the mountains. "Send the children in. I want to say good-by. Tell cook she'll have to plan the meals while I'm away. Tell her she can find out about guests from Mr. Clune. Tell Jeams not to leave till I get back. Tell Mrs. Pendergast and Mrs. Ramsbuckle and Miss Cobb that I've gone to the mountains and you don't know when I'll be back. And give my love to Mr. Clune and tell him I hope he'll have a nice week end with the MacNinerys." She stretched luxuriously. "I'll have my breakfast on a tray."

A white rim appeared around Melody's eyeballs.

"In de baid?" she asked.

"Yes," said Ready. She tried to remember when she last breakfasted in bed. It must have been when Bubbles was born. She had not slept till eleven since she was engaged to Paul Parrington Linwood, III. She said: "I'll have broiled grapefruit and buttered toast and coffee."

"Yo' wants yo' grapefruit *hot*?" said Melody.

402

"Very hot," said Ready. "With a cherry in the middle."

"Is yo' done gone crazy?" said Melody.

"I've gone sane," said Ready. "I'm going to do all the things I haven't had time to do for fifteen years." She called Melody from the door. "Two cherries," she said. "Brandied."

Ready was finishing her breakfast when the children came. It always impressed Ready to see what a lot of nice children she had. The boys looked like her, with wild red hair and fair skins, and their father's impetuous body. The girls were dark, with a deceptive air of saintliness. Becky sat demurely on the bench before the dressing table; she had enormous eyes under heart-shattering lashes, and her hair was bound in a little red halo. Bubbles stood by the pillow, finishing the toast and dropping crumbs in the bed.

"I have to stand," she explained importantly, "because of a certain reason."

Terry prowled with his hands in his pockets. "It was a little wire," he said, "with a crook in the end. The truck went off with it in their tire."

"Probably they had a blowout," said Becky helpfully, "and the truck turned over. You better call the garage before father comes home and sees his car all over the back yard."

"I don't need the garage," said Terry. "I just need a wire."

"My big tooth aches," said Tink.

"Jeams can take you to the dentist's in mother's car."

"I took my car to the mountains," said Ready.

They did not even regard her. "You can go on the bus," said Becky, "and I'll go with you. It isn't safe for a young child to go on the bus alone."

"I'm not a young child."

"You're two years younger than I am."

"I wouldn't be alone. There'd be the bus driver. You can go, but you can't look in my mouth."

"I don't want to look in your old mouth."

"How can a young child have an old mouth?"

"It's all full of old wires anyhow."

"I shall keep my mouth shut," said Tink. "Terry will want my wires for the car."

Ready raised her voice to make herself heard. "I sent for you," she said, "to tell you that I've gone to the mountains."

It was easy explaining to the children about the mountains. The young are adaptable. They have imaginations. Anything is possible to the young.

"It's a game," cried Bubbles delightedly.

"It's a game," said Ready. "But it's a real game. It has rules."

"What rules?"

"It's just the same as if I were really gone," Ready explained carefully. "You can't see me, nor hear me, nor ask me things. Neither can anyone else. When people want me, you just say: 'Mother has gone to the mountains.'" She added conscientiously: "You must be good, and do everything father tells you."

"If we do," said Bubbles, "we'll be busy."

"I'm the oldest daughter," said Becky, complacently. "I'll be the official hostess." Ready wiped her mouth elaborately. "Can I order the meals?"

"Cook will order the meals," said Ready. She had visions of lobster and whipped-cream pie.

"Can I give a party?" asked Becky. "Kind of a gypsy party?"

"You'll have to ask your father."

"But if he doesn't care, you won't care?"

"I don't know," Ready reminded her, "because I won't be here."

A smile of ineffable sweetness overspread Becky's round bright face. "I see," she said gently.

"What if we have something important to say?" Tink asked gruffly.

"You can write," said Ready. "And I'll write to you. If it's something that can't wait"—her voice stumbled and went on—"then you can telephone. But remember it's a toll call, and a toll call costs money."

The gleam in Terry's eye told Ready that he had thought of a wire for the car. She resolutely did not imagine what wire. "I guess we'd better say good-by," he suggested.

They kissed her—Terry with dignity, and Becky with a whiff of Ready's best perfume, and Bubbles with toast and butter. "Have a good time," they said. Tink did not kiss her. He gave her a rough, adoring shove, and stalked out without looking back. It disturbed Ready because she was more sentimental over the parting than the children.

After the children went, Ready moved. "I am not quite satisfied," she told Melody, "with the accommodations. It is cramped and noisy.

I want a large single room, with bath; a western exposure, with a far view, and a balcony with an awning."

"Is yo' talkin' 'bout the bes'es' room to de front o' de gues' wing?" Melody inquired.

"You have such a room?" said Ready brightly. "Show it to me, please."

"Is yo' heah or ain' yo' heah?" muttered Melody. "Ah don' hol' wif ghostes."

Ready had a lovely day. The room was done in old gold and cream with a faintly rosy ceiling; it looked peaceful and deliciously empty. Ready took a deep warm tub with her best bath salts, and put on a raspberry-meringue negligee that Terrin had never liked, and lay on the balcony and kicked off her mules. She set a box of chocolates beside her and opened a best seller nine months old. Ready had always wanted to sit right down in the middle of a day and read a book.

Dusk was faintly gathering when Ready finished. The western sky was rosy and golden like her room, and the distance was the aching blue of desire. Ready could not see the mountains, but her mind stood at horizon's rim. The trees turned from green to black against the sky. Trees were lovely at night. Lights came on in the town below her, shaping houses that Terrin had designed. The jut of the guest wing spread her own house before her, and the wideness of the lawn. By leaning over the rail she could see the back yard. The outside lights were on at the garage. In their yellow circle, Terry was sweating over his father's car. Terry, she thought with pride, had perseverance. The rest of the house was oddly still. There were no lights in the dining room. Terrin was dining out. There was a crash from the kitchen. The swing door. Ready sprang up before she remembered it was no affair of hers. She sat down and lifted the telephone.

"Room service," she said.

"What yo' wan' now?" demanded Melody tartly.

"Dinner," said Ready. "Lots of dinner."

It was late before Terrin came home. Ready's mind followed him through the house. It was longer than she expected before she heard his footsteps in the hall. He knocked peremptorily at the door.

"Don't be a fool, Rebecca," he said, and rattled the knob. Ready did not answer. He said more quietly: "Ready."

Ready padded across the rug in her bare feet. She put her hand on the key. She did not turn it. You can't turn back time, and people, with a key. She laid her palms flat against the door. "Ready," Terrin said again. And suddenly she pressed her whole body tight against that door, until she could feel the boards in her bones, until it seemed as if Terrin must hear her heart knocking on wood. She could feel him there, with the door between them. Her flesh quaked with her need for him. There had been doors between them so long.

Ready stayed at the door till Terrin went. When her knees stopped shaking, she took up the telephone. "Mr. Clune," she said, and heard the buzzer ringing. "Hello, darling."

"Look here," said Terrin. "I called and called, and you didn't answer."

"I didn't get any call," said Ready. "You must have had the wrong connection. I just wanted to tell you I got here all right. It's so quiet and restful. I have a lovely room, with a balcony that looks toward the mountains."

"Will you talk sense for a minute?" said Terrin.

"Three minutes," said Ready. "The children are all right, aren't they? Give them my love. I hope you had a good day."

"Ready," said Terrin, "the MacNinerys are coming for the week end."

"That's nice," said Ready. "Then you won't be lonesome. Better give them the mauve room. It's Mrs. MacNinery's type. Not so deep as purple. Be sure to show her the garden by moonlight. That bench beside the pool."

"You didn't do this because of last night, did you?" said Terrin.

"Silly!" said Ready lightly. "I didn't mind your kissing Mrs. Mac-Ninery."

"You must understand—" began Terrin ponderously.

"Of course I understand," said Ready. "I've understood that for years. The three minutes are up. Good night, Terrin."

She lay in the cream-and-gold bed and watched a spot of moon on the rosy ceiling. It was a very large bed for one.

Ready didn't mind Terrin's kissing Bette MacNinery. There had been a time when she minded. That first time, in the back yard at Dover Street, had been fire and pestilence. It didn't mean anything— that time. There had been a time when she was not so sure. Mrs. Burgan was so dazzling that it was beyond nature not to be dazzled. It was one of the ironic crooks of life that after the Burgan Memorial brought Terrin success, he had too much success to spare time for Mrs. Burgan. Ready knew quite clearly now that Terrin's charm was part of his career. Women bent their heads over plans, and lifted their heads, and waited. Terrin would have been churlish not to kiss them. Terrin was never churlish. It was part of his gift that he could fire imagination, and then give imagination form in lovely line. Someday, she recognized, it would take another form. Not with Bette Mac-Ninery. She was too obvious, too blatantly starry-eyed. Ready could see Terrin kissing her beside the pool, lightly and expertly, with just the right hint of promise. She did not mind that. What she minded was his kiss for her: swift and adequate, without passion. A kiss for a client. And a kiss for a wife. Nicely adapted to each.

It was late when Ready slept. To her annoyance she woke at seven the next morning. That was Tuesday.

Ready spent three days doing all the things she never had time for. She wrote her duty letters, and her friendly letters, letters to old school friends with whom she had lost touch. On an impulse she wrote a letter to Paul Parrington Linwood, III, and hoped he had lived happily ever after. She read the novels she had discussed at dinner tables all winter on the strength of the reviews. One of them was about a woman who died and didn't have time to go to heaven. She dipped into The World Week After Next and All The Modern Verse That's Fit To Print. She found them rather heavy. She tried the petitpoint embroidery she had started years ago. She had forgotten how the pattern went, and she got knots in the thread. She threw it over the railing, and it fell into a ravine between the mountains. Afterward she saw Bubbles sewing at it. It was a child's pastime. She wrote long letters to the children, full of cautions and instructions. She tore them up and wrote gay little notes beginning: "I am having a fine time in the mountains."

Ready lay on her stomach to brown her back, with her chin poked between the bars of the iron rail. Lying like that, she could see her world spread before her. She could even hear Melody's rich disapproving accents. Bubbles' sweet pipe: "Mother has gone to the mountains. She is very sorry, but she can't be on any committees, because you can't be on committees in the mountains." The children amused and frightened her. They were so young and wise.

She had, lying there, a panoramic, an almost cosmic, view, so that she saw the whole in its completeness: details that she had never noticed when she was near, and the littleness of things that seemed important. The chrysanthemums were dry, and Tink was standing straight, and Terrin came in late every night. She had a strange sense of disembodiment, as if she had died, like the woman in the book, and yet remained earthbound. Once she saw Tink lead a half a dozen ragged youngsters across the lawn. Tink had never liked people; he skulked at dancing school and refused to cut birthday cakes. "It's all right," he was saying, "mother has gone to the mountains."

The next day Becky gave a party. She wore the gypsy skirt and Ready's lace blouse. The refreshments were strawberry shortcake with whipped cream and chocolate sauce, and cigarettes. There was a great deal of coughing. Ready wondered how many would be sick. They were all sick. Ready wanted to go down. She did not go. Ready was rather sorry for God that night. It must be hard to watch the world and not reach down a hand and straighten it. It must take a lot of courage to be God. It was very late when Terrin came home.

Ready tried to think what else it was that she had wanted so much to do. She wanted to work in the garden. But you couldn't be seen in your own garden when you were in the mountains. A walk in the woods, she decided. She drove until she found woods, and resolutely she walked. The woods were empty except for the trees, and they crackled underfoot. Ready had never walked in the woods alone; Terrin used to go with her. She walked faster and faster; then she ran.

She was not surprised when she heard the shot. The bullet pinged in a tree above her head.

A man came up with a gun and a white face. "Lady," he said, "you shouldn't ought to bring that hair out here. I thought you was a red bird."

"I thought I was a dead bird," Ready said. She laughed, but it was not funny. A fine thing the papers would have made of it: "Rebecca Clune, wife of the distinguished architect, Terrin Clune, was found shot to death this morning in the woods a few miles from her home. Mrs. Clune, who had been missing for several days, was reported by the family and servants to have gone to the mountains. Mr. Clune—whose latest commission is said to be a playhouse for Bette Mac-Ninery, night-club bride of Aldous MacNinery, the financier—declined to make a statement. The inquest—"

Ready drove into the city. There were a lot of people in the city. She went to a movie called My Heart Is Not Here. She thought it much overestimated. Afterward she went to a French restaurant she had always meant to try; Terrin did not like French restaurants. She had ordered her dinner before she realized that ladies did not go there unattended. The man at the next table stared and stared. Ready left hastily.

When she got home there was a round robin from the children, and a wire from Terrin:

"Return at once. The MacNinerys are coming for the week end."

No "please." No "love." No anything. Ready knew the taste of failure. She called the telephone company and wired downstairs:

"Sorry. Am not ready to return."

She got into bed and cried. Ready had not cried for years. There had not been time.

The next morning the garage burned. There was the explosion, and then there were the flames, and Melody's voice.

"Call the fire department!" Ready shouted. *"Look out for the children."*

Then she was running, and her legs would not run; they melted under her, and she dragged herself to the railing and looked over. There were red flags in the sky, and a red fire truck in the drive. Terry was helping with the hose. Bubbles was dancing up and down. Becky was very efficiently herding everyone aside. Tink, with half a dozen boys in vaguely Indian costume, was hiding in the shrubbery. They were safe. She could see them all. She counted out loud: "One, two, three, four; one, two, three, four."

Nothing Ready had ever done was so hard as staying still. She wanted to gather up the children, and touch them, and feel them, and hold on to them. With every beating inch of her she wanted to *be there*. "One, two, three, four," she counted. And did not go. There was a strength that held her, some innate honesty more powerful than her body. The children had played fair with her. She must play fair with them. She shook the iron rail. "One, two, three, four," she shouted.

Half an hour later the garage was a smoldering heap of embers, with hot pieces of metal sticking out, and the rail round the balcony was bent.

It was Tink who called Ready. "I blew up the garage," he said directly.

"Is that so?" said Ready. "How?"

"I and my gang," said Tink, "were storming the fort, and we shot some flaming arrows, and one went in some waste, and some gasoline blew up, and the garage burned down."

"I see," said Ready.

"I suppose," said Tink diffidently, "that your car would have burned up, too, if it hadn't been in the mountains."

Ready had a hysterical impulse to laugh. She did not laugh. "That was lucky, wasn't it?"

"Yes," said Tink. "Terry says ask you if he can have the pieces— you know, the pieces that would be left if the car wasn't in the mountains."

"Tell him yes," said Ready.

"Listen, mum," said Tink urgently, "you won't blame the fellers, will you? It was my idea. They elected me captain."

"Did they? That was nice." She knew he was crying.

"You're all right, mum," he said thickly, and hung up.

It was because the other call came immediately afterward that it happened the way it did. Ready lifted the receiver and said, "Hello, Terrin. How did you know?"

"This is Paul Linwood," a voice said.

"Who?" said Ready.

"Paul Linwood." She did not answer, and he said: "You were engaged to me once."

"Oh, yes," said Ready absurdly. "I remember."

"You wrote me a note the other day."

"Did I?" said Ready.

"I'm in town," he went on, "and I thought you might have lunch with me or something."

"I might," said Ready.

"The Regency at one-thirty," he said. He had gone before Ready remembered she was in the mountains.

After all, Ready thought, *why not?* In the mountains she would have lunched with people. She could not rebuild the garage by sitting there and shaking. She looked in the mirror. She had never looked so terrible. One does not wish to look terrible when she lunches with the man she did not marry.

Ready took a bus to the city. She bought a tight black skirt seventeen inches from the floor, and a tight black jacket embroidered with snow-flakes. She bought a slightly larger snowflake called a hat, and a small wisp of cloud; she went to the hairdresser's and had her hair done in that new way that rolls up with curls on top of the hat. At one-thirty she stood in the Regency lounge looking like a million dollars.

Paul had changed. She saw that as he came toward her. It was not that he was older, though he showed that too; something had gone out of him that was arrogant and sure. She noticed with a sense of shock that in a weary man's face he had a boy's unformed chin. Terrin had a way of tipping his chin up when things went wrong, so that you could see the under part. "Steam shovel," she used to tease him.

"Hello, Paul," she said.

He held her hand too anxiously, too long. His palm was moist. "You're looking well," he said.

"Thanks," said Ready. She felt ostentatious, too obviously dressed. Paul did not look well. It was not that he was shabby. But he had an uncomfortable air of wearing his best, of making a good impression.

"Let's go out for lunch," he said. "Somewhere quieter."

"Let's," said Ready too quickly. She guessed that he could not afford the Regency. He would have to account, perhaps, for spending so much. It made a furtive thing of it at once.

"Any choice?" he asked her.

"One of those little French places," she said. And knew that she had chosen so because they would not be likely to meet Terrin.

It was a very little one that Paul chose, but it was quiet. Almost too quiet. A clandestine gloom lurked in the corners, and the candles threw crooked shadows on his face and drew a gargoyle's lines about his mouth. He ordered with a conscious lavishness.

"Tell me about yourself," he said when the waiter had gone.

"I have four children," said Ready briskly. "All superlative. How many have you?"

"One," said Paul. "That's enough." And to her startled look: "He's all we can afford."

"We couldn't afford any when we had them," said Ready touchily.

"I guess you can afford anything now."

"Anything but the mountains," said Ready lightly. She meant it for a joke. She meant to explain.

Paul did not take it so. It broke something inside him. Some decent personal reserve. Paul began to talk.

Ready let him talk at first because she thought it would do him good. Afterward she could not stop him. He could not stop himself.

He talked without restraint or shame or pride. He said things no man should say.

"The old man lost his money. I was only trained for spending. I married Phoebe Wilderness. I thought she was rich. She thought I was rich. We found out the truth a month later. It's been trouble, trouble, trouble, ever since."

He described with horrible particularity the details of his private troubles. Things he ought never to have remembered. The lunch came and went, and the hours.

"I must go," Ready said. She had said it before. This time she stood up.

"Stay for dinner," he begged her.

"I can't possibly," she said. "We're having guests. Some clients of Terrin's. The MacNinerys." It sounded definite and urgent.

Paul drove her home. She could not refuse when she had no car. He walked with her to the house.

Crossing the terrace, she could look through the French windows into the dining room. Inside Terrin was dining with the MacNinerys. The backs of his ears were red. Bette was waving her lashes. The tablecloth was slightly crooked. The flowers were too lavish and not very well arranged. Orchids for the table. Really. And pink candles. They were using the Sèvres plates and the wrong finger bowls.

Jeams was handing the dessert. Something was wrong with Jeams. He was the color of spring lush. Becky sat in Ready's place. She wore black lace and emeralds.

Paul did not see the details. Paul saw a beautiful room and a richly set table, the color note from the Della Robbia plaque; he saw the flagged terrace and the tall white pillars and the garden and the moon in the pool.

His voice was bitter and mocking. "You were wise," he said. "You picked the winner."

Ready was angry. "I picked the man I loved," she said hotly. "I never loved you, Paul. You never loved me, either. You never loved anybody."

Even as she spoke, she knew his tragic truth, and with the knowledge anger went out of her. Paul had no capacity for loving.

The moon shone across the terrace and she saw his empty eyes. He groped for her, his hands fumbling, forever frustrated.

"Couldn't you love the boy?" she said, with pity. "You could still save him."

She kissed him lightly, comfortingly, because it was not in him to love anyone the way she loved Terrin.

Over Paul's shoulder she saw Terrin opening the terrace windows.

IT WAS sooner than she expected when she heard Terrin's footsteps in the hall. He was running. He pounded on the door.

"Open it," he said, "or I'll break it down." She saw the panels bulging.

The lock snapped, the door banged open, and the knob knocked a hole in the plaster. Terrin plunged in on the tide of his own violence. He checked himself and shouted: "The garage blew up."

It was so exactly what she had not expected him to say that Ready laughed. Laughter illuminated her words. "Tink's gang," she said. "They chose him leader. Tink just never liked the people we tried to have him know."

"Becky," said Terrin, "has had a permanent."

"Becky needs more responsibility," said Ready.

It was strange how clear everything was, seen from afar, and how simple; as simple as love, and loving.

"That dinner," said Terrin furiously, "I told cook the kind of dinner you ordered for the MacNinerys. Ready, it was the *same dinner*. The same, I tell you."

"That's the trouble with well-trained servants," said Ready thoughtfully. "You teach them to jump through hoops, and if there is no hoop they'll jump through the hole in a doughnut."

"We didn't have doughnuts," said Terrin. "We had stuffed tomatoes. Cook swung the door in Jeams' face, and he dropped a tomato on his pants. We had to wait while Jeams changed his pants. The tomatoes were lukewarm. The lettuce was lukewarm. We had lukewarm strawberry tarts with lukewarm cream. Terry had taken the refrigerator to pieces."

"Terry," said Ready with a flash of insight, "will never be an architect. He ought not to go to the Chadwick School. He ought to go to Tech." Bubbles should be in public school next year. She must tell Terrin when there was time. There wasn't time now.

"You kissed him," he was shouting.

"I was sorry for him," said Ready.

"So am I," said Terrin. "He has no technique." He took Ready by the shoulders and shook her. The pins flew out of her hair, and the curls fell down from the brim of the snowflake hat. Terrin threw the snowflake on the floor. He threw the wisp of cloud after it. He buried his hands in Ready's hair and pulled back her head and kissed her. The tight little jacket ripped, and he kissed her bare shoulder through the hole. He kissed her till she was dizzy, and her knees bent under her. He held her up by her arms. "That," said Terrin, "is how it should be done." And kissed her again. Harder.

"Where are the MacNinerys?" said Ready, when she could speak.

"Gone," said Terrin.

"Gone," said Ready. "Where have they gone?"

"I don't know," said Terrin. "I don't care. I told them I had a more important job than theirs."

"Have you?" said Ready. "What sort of job is it?"

"A big job," said Terrin with deliberation, "restoring a castle in Spain. It's a lifework, but I'm going to start right away."

He kissed her once more. Not with violence, this time. Slowly, deeply, and fully. He held her close against him, and she felt the same flame kindled in both their bodies. In its light everything was clear.

"Life," said Terrin, "is what you make it." Bless his heart, he believed he thought of that. "When will you be ready?"

"*I'm* ready for anything," she said. "What's next?"

"I thought you knew," said Terrin. "We're going to the mountains."

He picked her up and they started for the mountains.

The Face Is Familiar, But—

MAX SHULMAN

*What's in a name? Everything—as you will see
when Henry tries to find out the name of his new
date. His hilarious trials and disappointments make
this a sparkling story of the younger generation.*

You NEVER CAN TELL. Citizens, you never can tell.
Take the weekend of May 18. From all indications it was going to be
a dilly, a dreamboat. Saturday night was the fraternity formal, and
Sunday night Petey Burch was taking me to the Dr. Askit quiz broadcast. Every prospect pleased.

At 7:30 Saturday night I got into my rented tux and picked up my
rented car. At 8:30 I called for my date and was told that she had
come down with the measles at 7:30. So I shrugged my rented shoulders, got into the rented car, and went to the dance alone.

I had taken my place in the stag line when Petey Burch rushed up to
me, his seventeen-year-old face flushed with excitement. He waved a
letter at me. "I got it! I got it!" he cried. "Here's a letter from my
parents saying I can join the Navy."

"That's swell, Petey," I said. "I got some news, too. My date got
the measles."

"That's too bad," he said sympathetically. Then he suddenly got
more excited than ever and hollered: "No! No, that's perfect. Listen,
Henry. There's a bus leaving here tonight that will get me to Min-
neapolis in the morning. I can be at the Navy recruiting station as
soon as it opens."

"But what about the dance? What about your date?"

"The Navy," said Petey snapping to attention, "needs men *now*.
Every minute counts. How can I think of staying at a dance when
there's a war to be won? I've got to get out of here, Henry. I owe it to
the boys Over There."

"What are you going to tell your date?"

"That's where you come in, Henry. You take my girl; I go catch

415

the bus. I won't tell her anything. I'll just disappear and you explain it to her later."

"Won't she mind?"

"I suppose she will. But this is the first date I've ever had with her. It doesn't matter. I'll probably never see her again." He set his jaw. "God knows when I'll be coming back from Over There."

"I understand," I said simply.

"Thanks, old man," he said simply.

We shook hands.

"By the way," I said, "what about those two tickets you've got for the Dr. Askit broadcast tomorrow night?"

"They're yours," he said, handing them to me.

"Thanks, old man," I said simply.

"Here comes my date now," Petey said, pointing at the powder-room door. I took one look at her and knew what a patriot he must be to run out on a smooth operator like that. She was strictly on the side of angels.

"Where'd you find her?" I drooled.

"Just met her the other night. She's new around here. Now I'll introduce you and you dance with her while I make my getaway."

"Solid," I agreed.

SHE walked over to us, making pink-taffeta noises. The timing was perfect. The orchestra was tuning up for the first number just as she reached us.

"Hi," said Petey. "I want you to meet a friend of mine. Henry Ladd, this is—"

At that instant the orchestra started to play and I didn't catch her name. And no wonder. The orchestra was led by a trumpeter who had a delusion that good trumpeting and loud trumpeting are the same thing. Between him and Harry James, he figured, were only a few hundred decibels of volume. Every time he played he narrowed the gap.

"Excuse me," shouted Petey, and left.

"Dance?" I yelled.

"What?" she screamed.

I made dancing motions and she nodded. We moved out on the floor. I tried to tell her while we were dancing that I hadn't caught her name, but it was impossible. The trumpeter, feeling himself gaining on Harry James, was pursuing his advantage hard. And the kind of dancing we were doing, I was too far away from her to talk. She was a smooth dancer, all right. At last there came a short trumpet break, and I made a determined stab at it.

"I don't like to seem dull," I said to the girl, "but when Petey introduced us, I didn't catch your—"

But the trumpeter was back on the job, stronger than ever after his little rest. The rest of the song made the *Anvil Chorus* sound like a lullaby. I gave up then, and we just danced. Any girl that could dance like that I had to know her name.

Came the intermission and I tried again. "I know this is going to sound silly, but when we were intro—"

"I wonder where Petey is," she interrupted. "He's been gone an awfully long time."

"Oh, not so long really. Well, as I was saying, it makes me feel foolish to ask, but I didn't—"

"It has, too, been a long time. I think that's an awfully funny way for a boy to act when he takes a girl out for the first time. Where do you suppose he is?"

"Oh, I don't know. Probably just—oh, well, I suppose I might as well tell you now." So I told her.

She bit her lip. "Henry," she quavered, "will you please take me home?"

"Home? It's so early."

"Please, Henry."

Seventeen years of experience had taught me not to argue with a woman whose eyes are full of tears. I went and got my Driv-Ur-Self limousine, packed her into it, and started off.

"I—live—at—2123—Fremont—Avenue," she wailed.

"There, there," I cooed. "Try to look at it his way. The Navy needs men *now*. The longer he stayed around the dance tonight, the longer the war would last. Believe me, if my parents would sign a letter for me, I'd be Over There plenty quick, believe me."

"You mean," she wept, "that you would run off and stand up a girl at a formal affair?"

"Well," I said, "maybe not that. I mean I would hardly run out on a girl like you." I took her hand. "A girl so beautiful and lovely and pretty."

She smiled through tears. "You're sweet, Henry."

"Oh, pshaw," I pshawed. "Say, I've got a couple of tickets to the Dr. Askit quiz broadcast tomorrow night. How about it?"

"Oh, Henry, I'd love to. Only I don't know if Daddy will let me. He wants me to stay in and study tomorrow night. But I'll see what I can do. You call me."

"All right," I said, "but first there's something you have to tell me." I turned to her. "Now, please don't think that I'm a jerk, but it wasn't my fault. When Petey introduced us, I didn't—"

At this point I ran into the rear end of a bus. There followed a period of unpleasantness with the bus driver, during which I got a pithy lecture on traffic regulations. I don't know what he had to be sore about. His bus wasn't even nicked. The radiator grille of my car, on the other hand, was a total loss.

And when I got back in the car, there was more grief. The sudden stop had thrown the girl against the windshield head first, and her hat, a little straw number with birds, bees, flowers, and a patch of real grass, was now a heap of rubble. She howled all the way home.

"I'm afraid this evening hasn't been much fun," I said truly as I walked her to her door.

"I'm sorry, Henry," she sniffled. "I'm sorry all this had to happen to you. You've been so nice to me."

"Oh, it's nothing any young American wouldn't have done," I said.

"You've been very sweet," she repeated. "I hope we'll get to be very good friends."

"Oh, we will. We certainly will."

She was putting her key in the lock.

"Just one more thing," I said. "Before you go in, I have to know—"

"Of course," she said. "I asked you to call and didn't give you my number. It's Kenwood 6817."

"No," I said, "it's not that. I mean yes, I wanted that, too. But there's another thing."

"Certainly, Henry," she whispered and kissed me quickly. Then the door was closed behind her.

"Nuts," I mumbled, got into the car, returned it to the Driv-Ur-Self service, where I left a month's allowance to pay for the broken grille, and went back to the fraternity house.

A few of the guys were sitting in the living room. "Hi, Henry," called one. "How'd you come out with that smooth operator? Petey sure picked the right night to run off and join the Navy, eh?"

"Oh, she was fine," I answered. "Say, do any of you fellows know her name?"

"No, you lucky dog. She's all yours. Petey just met her this week and you're the only one he introduced her to. No competition. You lucky dog."

"Yeah, sure," I said. "Lucky dog." And I went upstairs to bed.

It was a troubled night, but I had a headful of pains when I got up in the morning. After all, the problem wasn't so difficult. Finding out a girl's name should be no task for a college sophomore, a cross-word-puzzle expert, and the senior-class poet (1942) of the Salmon P. Chase High School, Blue Earth, Minnesota.

First I picked up the phone and dialed the operator. "Hello," I said, "I'd like to find out the name of the people who live at 2123 Fremont Avenue. The number is Kenwood 6817."

"I'm sorry," replied the operator, "we are not allowed to give out that information."

"But this is an emergency."

"I'm sorry. We're not allowed to give out that information."

I hung up. Then I tried plain No. 2. I dialed Kenwood 6817. A gruff male voice answered, "Hello."

"Hello," I said. "Who is this?"

"Who is *this?*" he said.

"This is Henry Ladd. Who is this?"

"Who did you wish to speak to?"

Clearly, I was getting nowhere. I hung up.

Then I went and knocked on the door of Ed Beasley's room. Ed was a new pledge of the fraternity, and he was part of my third plan. He opened the door. "Enter, master," he said in the manner required of new pledges.

"Varlet," I said, "I have a task for you. Take yon telephone book and look through it until you find the name of the people who have telephone number, Kenwood 6817."

"But, master—" protested Ed.

"I have spoken," I said sharply and walked off briskly, rubbing my palms.

In ten minutes Ed was in my room with Roger Goodhue, the president of the fraternity. "Henry," said Roger, "you are acquainted with the university policy regarding the hazing of pledges."

"Hazing?"

"You know very well that hazing was outlawed this year by the Dean of Student Affairs. And yet you go right ahead and haze poor Ed. Do you think more of your own amusement than the good of the fraternity? Do you know that if Ed had gone to the Dean instead of me we would have had our charter taken away? I am going to insist on an apology right here and now."

Ed got his apology and walked off briskly, rubbing his palms.

"We'll have no more of that," said Roger, and he left, too.

I took the phone book myself and spent four blinding hours looking for Kenwood 6817. Then I remembered that Petey had said the girl was new around here. The phone book was six months old; obviously her number would not be listed until a new edition was out.

The only course left to me was to try calling the number again in the hope that she would answer the phone herself. This time I was lucky. It was her voice.

"Hello," I cried, "who is this?"

"Why, it's Henry Ladd," she said. "Daddy said you called before. Why didn't you ask to talk to me?"

"We were cut off," I said.

"About tonight: I can go to the broadcast with you. I told Daddy we were going to the library to study. So be sure you tell the same story when you get here. I better hang up now. I hear Daddy coming downstairs. See you at eight. 'Bye."

"Good-bye," I said.

And good-bye to some lovely ideas. But I was far from licked. When I drove up to her house at eight in a car I had borrowed from a fraternity brother (I wisely decided not to try the Driv-Ur-Self people again), I still had a few aces up my sleeve. It was now a matter of pride with me. I thought of the day I had recited the senior-class poem and I said to myself, "By George, a man who could do that can find out a simple girl's name, by George." And I wasn't going to be stupid about it either. I wasn't going to just ask her. After all this trouble, I was going to be sly about it. Sly, see?

I walked up to the porch, looking carefully for some marker with the family name on it. There was nothing. Even on the mailbox there was no name.

But in the mailbox was a letter! Quickly I scooped it out of the box, just in time to be confronted by a large, hostile man framed in a suddenly open doorway.

"And what, pray, are you doing in our mailbox?" he asked with dangerous calmness.

"I'm Henry Ladd," I squeaked. "I'm here to call on your daughter. I just saw the mail in the box and thought I'd bring it in to you." I gave him a greenish smile.

"So you're Henry Ladd. The one who hung up on me this afternoon." He placed a very firm hand on my shoulder. "Come inside, please, young man," he said.

The girl was sitting in the living room. "Do you know this fellow?" asked her father.

"Of course, Daddy. That's Henry Ladd, the boy who is going to take me over to the library to study tonight. Henry, this is my father."

"How do you do, Mr. Zzzzzm," I mumbled.

"What?" she said.

"Well, we better run along," I said, taking the girl's hand.

"Just a moment, young man. I'd like to ask you a few things," said her father.

"Can't wait," I chirped. "Every minute counts. Stitch in time saves nine. Starve a cold and stuff a fever. Spare the rod and spoil the child." Meanwhile I was pulling the girl closer and closer to the door. "A penny saved is a penny earned," I said and got her out on the porch.

"It's such a nice night," I cried. "Let's run to the car." I had her in the car and the car in low and picking up speed fast before she could say a word.

"Henry, you've been acting awfully strange tonight," she said with perfect justification. "I think I want to go home."

"Oh, no, no, no. Not that. I'm just excited about our first real date, that's all."

"Sometimes you're so strange, and then sometimes you're so sweet. I can't figure you out."

"I'm a complex type," I admitted. And then I went to work. "How do you spell your name?" I asked.

"Just the way it sounds. What did you think?"

"Oh, I thought so. I just was wondering." I rang up a "No Sale" and started again. "Names are my hobby," I confessed. "Just before I came to get you tonight I was looking through a dictionary of names. Do you know, for instance, that Dorothy means 'gift of god'?"

"No. Really?"

"Yes. And Beatrice means 'making happy,' and Gertrude means 'spear maiden.'"

"Wonderful. Do you know any more?"

"Thousands," I said. "Abigail means 'my father's joy,' Margaret means 'a pearl,' Phyllis means 'a green bough,' and Beulah means 'she who is to be married.'" My eyes narrowed craftily; I was about to spring the trap. "Do you know what your name means?"

"Sure," she said. "It doesn't mean anything. I looked it up once, and it just said that it was from the Hebrew and didn't mean anything."

We were in front of the broadcasting studio. "Curses," I cursed and parked the car.

We went inside and were given tickets to hold. In a moment Dr. Askit took the stage and the broadcast began. "Everyone who came in here tonight was given a ticket," said Dr. Askit. "Each ticket has a number. I will now draw numbers out of this fishbowl here and call them off. If your number is called, please come up on the stage and be a contestant." He reached into the fishbowl. "The first number is 174. Will the person holding 174 please come up here?"

"That's you," said the girl excitedly.

I thought fast. If I went up on the stage, I had a chance to win $64. Not a very good chance, because I'm not very bright about these things. But if I gave the girl my ticket and had her go up, Dr. Askit would make her give him her name and I would know what it was and all this nonsense would be over. It was the answer to my problem.

"You go," I told her. "Take my ticket and go."

"But, Henry—"

"Go ahead." I pushed her out in the aisle.

"And here comes a charming young lady," said Dr. Askit. He helped her to the microphone. "A very lucky young lady, I might add. Miss, do you know what you are?"

"What?"

"You are the ten thousandth contestant that has appeared on the Dr. Askit quiz program. And do you know what I am going to do in honor of this occasion?"

"What?"

"I am going to pay you *ten* times as much as I ordinarily pay contestants. Instead of a $64 maximum, you have a chance to win $640!"

"I may have to pay $640 to learn this girl's name," I thought, and waves of blackness passed before my eyes.

"Now," said Dr. Askit, "what would you like to talk about? Here is a list of subjects."

Without hesitation she said: "Number Six. The meaning of names of girls."

I tore two handfuls of upholstery from my seat.

"The first one is Dorothy," said Dr. Askit.

"Gift of god," replied the girl.

"Right! You now have $10. Would you like to try for $20? All right? The next one is Beatrice."

Two real tears ran down my cheeks. The woman sitting next to me moved over one seat.

"Making happy," said the girl.

"Absolutely correct!" crowed Dr. Askit. "Now would you care to try for $40?"

"You'll be sorry!" sang someone.

"Like heck she will," I hollered.

"I'll try," she said.

"Gertrude," said Dr. Askit.

"Forty dollars," I mourned silently. A sports coat. A good rod and reel. A new radiator grille for a Driv-Ur-Self car.

"Spear maiden," said the girl.

"Wonderful! There's no stopping this young lady tonight. How about the $80 question? Yes? All right. Abigail. Think now. This is a toughie."

"Oh, that's easy. My father's joy."

"Easy, she said. Easy. Go ahead," I wept, as I pommeled the arm of my seat, "rub it in. Easy!"

"You certainly know your names," said Dr. Askit admiringly. "What do you say to the $160 question? All right? Margaret."

"A pearl."

The usher came over to my seat and asked if anything was wrong. I shook my head mutely. "Are you sure?" he said. I nodded. He left, but kept looking at me.

"In all my years in radio," said Dr. Askit, "I have never known such a contestant. The next question, my dear, is for $320. Will you try?"

"Shoot," she said gaily.

"Phyllis."

"A green bough."

"Right! Correct! Absolutely correct!"

Two ushers were beside me now. "I seen them epileptics before," one whispered to the other. "We better get him out of here."

"Go away," I croaked, flecking everyone near me with light foam.

"Now," said Dr. Askit, "will you take the big chance? The $640 question?"

She gulped and nodded.

"For $640—Beulah."

"She who is to be married," she said.

The ushers were tugging at my sleeves.

"And the lady wins $640! Congratulations! And now, may I ask you your name?"

"Come quietly, Bud," said the ushers to me. "Please don't make us use no force."

"Great balls of fire, don't make me go now!" I cried. "Not now! I paid $640 to hear this."

"My name," she said, "is Mary Brown."

"You were sweet," she said to me as we drove home, "to let me go up there tonight instead of you."

"Think nothing of it, Mary Brown," I said bitterly.

She threw back her head and laughed. "You're so funny, Henry. I think I like you more than any boy I've ever met."

"Well, that's something to be thankful for, Mary Brown," I replied.

She laughed some more. Then she leaned over and kissed my cheek. "Oh, Henry, you're marvelous."

So Mary Brown kissed me and thought I was marvelous. Well, that was just dandy.

"Marvelous," she repeated and kissed me again.

"Thank you, Mary Brown," I said.

No use being bitter about it. After all, $640 wasn't all the money in the world. Not quite, anyhow. I had Mary Brown, now. Maybe I could learn to love her after a while. She looked easy enough to love. Maybe someday we would get married. Maybe there would even be a dowry. A large dowry. About $640.

I felt a little better. But just a little.

I parked in front of her house. "I'll never forget this evening as long as I live," she said as we walked to the porch.

"Nor I, Mary Brown," I said truthfully.

She giggled. She put her key in the front door. "Would you like to come in, Henry—dear?"

"No thanks, Mary Brown. I have a feeling your father doesn't care for me." Then it dawned on me. "Look!" I cried. "Your father. You told him you were at the library tonight. What if he was listening to the radio tonight and heard you on the Dr. Askit program?"

"Oh, don't worry. People's voices sound different over the radio."

"But the name! You gave your name!"

She looked at me curiously. "Are you kiddin'? You know very well I didn't give my right name. . . . HENRY! WHY ARE YOU BEATING YOUR HEAD AGAINST THE WALL?"

We Visit Mr. H. G. Wells

CORNELIA OTIS SKINNER
and EMILY KIMBROUGH

Cornelia may have had a feather in her hat when she played tennis with H. G. Wells, but it wasn't because she had scored. And Emily, after her host unwound her at luncheon, mislaid her dignity. You'll roar at this story of the Nineteen Twenties.

WE ALL ARRAYED ourselves in our best. Emily and I had notions that Sunday at an English country house called for sport clothes. But the only ones we had were the baby blue outfit of mine and Emily's Shakespearean tweed, and after a visit to Fortnum and Mason we'd begun to have our doubts about them. Accordingly, we fixed ourselves up in our crepe marocains. Emily's was dark blue and mine, I'm afraid, was black. Emily's hat was a smart little milan straw while mine, I'm further afraid, was that red Irene Bordoni gem with the cock feather swooshing down across my chin. We both wore high heels and I added the further exotic touch of some earrings I had purchased in a Brompton Road antique shop. They were dark tortoise-shell, carved like Egyptian urns, and I thought them beauti-

425

ful. I even thought myself rather beautiful when I wore them, but I wasn't. Thin and hollow-cheeked, my face, which was already too long, with these dangling appendages took on the proportions of a primitive Greek horse.

It was a beautiful day and the drive through the smiling countryside was heavenly. Our chauffeur, who was inclined to be loquacious, got so enthusistic pointing out passing sights of interest he missed a few important turnings, and after a bit we found ourselves quite lost amid the winding avenues of a vast estate. We drove past miles of moor and woodland, through forests cleared of all underbrush where giant trees that might have shaded the Plantagenets rose from a tidy green carpet of moss, fern and ancient lawn. Herds of fallow deer grazed in the open fields or rested in the cool bracken, and just to make the setting complete, some stately peacocks crossed our path. We stopped a man on a bicycle who told us it was Lord Somebody's Park. Emily said it wasn't at all like McCullough Park back in Muncie which in lieu of herds of deer boasted one moth-eaten Rocky Mountain elk. It was all very lovely only, as Mother pointed out, it was already one o'clock, the hour we'd been asked for lunch, and we were still miles from Dunmow. When finally we turned in at Mr. Wells' gate it was almost two-thirty. We were all decidedly embarrassed, and Emily and I were not only embarrassed but suddenly horribly awed. Emily said it had just come over her all of a heap that she was about to meet Mr. H. G. Wells and she hadn't planned what she'd say to him.

"I can't meet Mr. Wells!" she cried. "Not till I've thought, anyway," and she slid down onto the floor of the car as it came to a stop and saying, "I'll just stay out of sight until I can collect myself," she went into a curious crouching position like a praying mantis. At that moment the door behind her was flung open and she bulged out rear first into Mr. Wells himself, so the formality of a conventional introduction was side-stepped. Mother tried to ease the situation with one of her charming streams of incoherencies to the effect that this was her daughter's friend Emily Kimbrough and she guessed she must be looking for something she'd dropped and the chauffeur had lost the way and we were so mortified to be so late.

She needn't have bothered, as Mr. Wells didn't appear to be in the least surprised. I guess he thought all Americans were crazy, anyway. He was shorter than I'd anticipated, but broad-shouldered and very stocky. The most surprising thing about him was his voice. From the looks of that burly neck one expected it to be a roar; instead, it came out in a sort of high-pitched tone which occasionally broke as if it were changing. He was cheery and full of welcome and the Lord knows replete with teeming vitality. One was instantly aware of it; not nervous restlessness, but bursting energy inadequately harnessed and rarin' to go.

He herded us into the house explaining that they'd finished lunch. Mother tried again to say that we'd gotten lost but he wouldn't let her. Talking a steady stream, he bustled us into the dining-room, set plates before us, went to the sideboard to cut some beef, found it already cut, waved to a young man who had drifted in, a gesture which seemed to imply that he was to put the beef on our plates, pulled out a chair beside Emily, hurtled himself into it and said:

"Now, young lady, tell me all about what you do. What do you like? Do you read? What sort of things? Are you educated? How old are you? What part of America do you come from? Marvelous place, America. Ever been to Hollywood? The coming intellectual and artistic center of the world. Greatest commercial center now. Do you like roast beef?"

He didn't give her time to answer all his questions but she did manage to talk to him. She had had a job in a Buffalo book shop for a few months and that background gave her the courage to discuss with him books, publishers and authors. Mr. Wells talked with her as if she had been a contemporary and she played up wonderfully well. She knew all about the latest editions of the "Outline" and her tactful references to that went far to make up for her awkward preliminary and somewhat backward encounter with its distinguished author. The rest of us ate and listened avidly. Occasionally he'd turn the mill-race of his conversation in our direction but it was aimed for the most part at Emily. In his enthusiasm he'd lean so close to her face she'd have to hold her fork with the roast beef on it well off to one side until he'd made his point. I never heard more brilliant summings up, opinions and epithets and we wish we'd written it all down that night after we got back to London, because we've forgotten his exact words. What we do remember, apart from the tumbling exuberance of it, was his generosity toward other writers. He would quote with admiration a phrase from one author, an idea from another; he would speak almost with awe of the scope of this novelist, the sense of color of that one.

He couldn't say enough, I remember, about James Harvey Robinson's "Mind in the Making."

From time to time he'd break off to ask if we were all getting enough to eat. During one of these intervals Mother cooed, "Your son makes a very good butler, Mr. Wells." The young man who had been waved toward the roast beef had in some way been identified as a son.

"Yes," said Mr. Wells. "He gets butler and butler every day," and he squealed happily over his wit. This made me feel better and Mother laughed tactfully, but Father, who was always embarrassed by puns unless they were of his own making, hastened to cover up such a lapse in a great man by enquiring:

"Are you a Cambridge man like your son?"

Mr. Wells screeched more happily than ever. "Lord, no, man! At his age I was a draper's assistant! But I'm going to send him to Hollywood. He'll make money there."

We got through lunch quickly. Emily had really outdone herself and although she had again proved her superiority to me, I was bursting with pride for her. It was obvious she was somewhat giddy about herself. Luncheon finished, she rose feeling, she later said, like the Comtesse de Noailles or some such glamorous intellectual. Mr. Wells pulled out her chair from which she turned with a willowy swoop and a brilliant smile for our host, intending to sweep on away from the table. There was a crash and a sort of whizzing sound, and instead of sweeping on away from the table she stood stock still, looking less like the Comtesse de Noailles than Lot's wife.

"Good God!" Mr. Wells said. "What have you done?" Emily said she didn't know but it felt as if she'd been caught in some sort of trap, at which Mr. Wells said, "Ah yes, the electric table-bell." It was the sort that is attached from the floor to the table-edge by a cord. In that willowy swoop of hers she had in some way hooked her toe in a loop and snapped the bell off its mooring with such violence the released wire had whipped itself in coils about her leg from ankle to knee, like an Elizabethan cross-garter, which, being still attached to the floor, held her immovable. Mr. Wells, equal to every occasion, was equal even to the sort Emily conjures up. For a moment he looked at her in astonishment, then pulled his glasses from his pocket and fitted them carefully on his nose. After which he got down on his hands and knees, lifted the tablecloth, crawled under and set to work unwinding. Mother stood by making little mooing noises of distress, Father looked

428

on with amused compassion, while I smothered my face in a portière to keep Mr. Wells from hearing my maniacal yells of rapture.

He got her unwound, crawled out from under the table and straight over to Mother, rose and escorted her with dignity into the library, where Mrs. Wells, whom we then met for the first time, was entertaining the more punctual guests. We were more or less introduced to people. That is, Mr. Wells would lead us up to someone and without bothering about introducing anybody would start talking, or rather, continue talking. There was another American present, Mrs. Sanger. . . . He then led us over to a very distinguished looking gentleman with a shock of white hair and said in his falsetto rush of words, "This is the greatest educationalist in all England. Do you know what an educationalist is?" And that was the nearest approach we got to an introduction to him. We never did learn his name, although we felt pretty sure it wasn't Bertrand Russell. There were also present two young men, obviously Cambridge buddies of Wells, Jr. (or do they call it Minor in England?). They were very pink cheeked and healthy and they answered to a couple of those appalling British nicknames like Bubble and Squeak. Only now that I remember, I believe people addressed them as Bungy and Poodles. They were later joined by a third young man whom Mr. Wells with happy laughter over his own humor called "Face." We wondered why. There was nothing out of the ordinary about that portion of the young man's anatomy, but Face he was called, and the other young men chortled heartily and said it was a jolly good name for him, too.

We had no sooner got comfortably seated than one of those summer showers began its deluge outside. That was Mr. Wells' cue for jumping to his feet and announcing, "Now we'll all go out and play the Wells game!" Emily and I were sunk with horror. Was it for this we'd rigged ourselves up in our best city finery? Mrs. Wells, seeing our expressions and realizing that Americans are made of less waterproof stuff than Britons, tactfully suggested to her husband that it was raining, dear. To which he cheerfully replied that that being the case we could play on the indoor court. Our despair deepened. Emily remembered all too clearly her deck-tennis débâcle and as for me, the mere thought of any game more active than Twenty Questions made me sick at my stomach. Besides, how could we hope to move with any agility in those high heels and tight fitting crepe dresses? We murmured that much as we were dying to play, we weren't dressed for it. But that didn't in the least deter Mr. Wells, who squealed happily that Mrs. Wells had an extensive collection of old tennis shoes for just such emergencies . . . bushel baskets of them . . . weren't always mates, ha-ha! . . . but just right to play in. Then he opened a French window onto a terrace and darting through it, told us to come along. The quick deluge had turned into a slow drizzle, an inconvenience we'd more or less learned to disregard. We followed along, Mother and Father, Emily and I, Mrs. Sanger and the Great Educationalist. Bungy, Poodles and Face bore the bushel baskets of tennis shoes as if they had been the pick of a bumper crop of prize clingstones. We went down through the garden and past several enchanting little thatched huts. "Recreation huts during the War!" Mr. Wells called out as we passed. "Furbished them up a bit and set them here. Don't know now and didn't then what for."

We reached a barnlike structure, the inside of which was fixed up with nets, racquets and other evidences of activity. This was obviously Mr. Wells' *Rumpus Room*. He pottered about, tossing tennis shoes around, tightening a thin and quite high little net and getting out a large rubber ball. Thinking that perhaps the young men could take our place we suggested that as there were already so many people, maybe it would be better if we just sat and watched. But Mr. Wells wouldn't hear of it. One of the special beauties of the Wells Game, he said, was that it could be played by any number at a time, and would we please hurry and get into our shoes? With sinking hearts we kicked off our pumps. I recall now with a sick shudder that I had a hole in my stocking through which my large toe was peering. Catching sight of it, I concealed it as best I could by standing on it with the other foot.

Mournfully Emily and I pawed over the piles of tennis shoes, trying to find a pair that would fit. With all due modesty I may say that we both happen to have unusually small feet. All the shoes were men's sizes. Mrs. Wells hadn't bothered to collect any women's. Eventually we each managed to find some which didn't drop off every time a foot was lifted, although Emily's were so big for her she was apt to step with one heel on the toe of the other, a movement which, in order to regain her balance, precipitated her into a series of little running steps.

Emily took off her dark blue milan and in her trim navy dress she didn't look too odd. Maybe her appearance benefited by comparison with mine. I had arranged my hair, which was long, in such a way that if I took off my hat, it fell down. Under these circumstances I was forced to keep on the red Irene Bordoni number with the drooping cock feather. This being the case, there seemed to be no necessity for taking off those Egyptian urn earrings. The immense white tennis shoes set it all off something lovely.

Mother, who wasn't going to play, had settled herself on a bench along the wall where, amid a good deal of mental and physical discomfort, she could look on. Father, who was told he had to play, meekly took off his shoes and paddled about among the bushel baskets looking for some footgear to his fancy. Mother watched him nervously, as was her wont; and then she began a series of those little cooing sounds which we knew indicated extreme agitation. We couldn't discover what was the cause of it until we happened to look down at Father's feet. My distinguished parent for years had had a theatre valet named William Venus. He was long and cadaverous and resembled anything but his voluptuous namesake. Moreover, he was completely color-blind. For untold reasons he had been in the habit of darning Father's socks, using what the wardrobe mistress could spare him in the way of thread, most of which matched the varicolored costumes of the rest of the troupe. Venus, even if color-blind, was handy with a needle and his darning lasted a lifetime. Father had become so used to wearing socks that had been repaired in vivid hues, he never gave them a thought. And there he was, pattering about in a particularly lurid pair that had been darned in vermilion, green, royal purple and blush pink. At this point in the proceedings the Americans were, sartorially, anything but ahead.

After we'd all gotten more or less fitted out, Mr. Wells explained the game, and he did so with the earnestness of a school boy enlightening the rules of cricket to a team of novices. It had to do with a number of people being on each team (five in this case) and swatting the ball with the flat of the hand from one to another until the person nearest the high little net smacked it over the top, after which it went down that team in similar fashion and back over the net. It was somewhat akin to the game in "Mr. Britling." There were any number of rules and side-issues, but he talked so fast we considered ourselves geniuses to catch the main idea, and we let the side-issues go. One point we did gather, however, and that was the rule that one person must never under any circumstances hit the ball twice in the same play. That was a most heinous foul and counted a score for the opposing team.

Father, Mrs. Sanger and Emily were on one side, Mr. Wells, the Great Educationalist and I on the other. The remaining places were filled in by the visiting Brownies whose true names we never knew.

Off we started, amid a good deal of activity, the brunt of which was borne by the Brownies and Mr. Wells—the latter dashing wildly about, batting the ball either over that high-flown net or at various ones of us on his side, shouting "Hit it! Hit it!" with an intensity that might lead one to believe the honor of Oxford and Cambridge was hanging in the balance. We all tried manfully. The Great Educationalist played the way one would imagine a great educationalist would, which was to avoid with dignity as much participation as possible. Mrs. Sanger wasn't so bad, and I don't believe she was so good either, but at least she was moderately inconspicuous. The remainder of us were awful. Emily might have done better if she hadn't gotten constantly tripped up by herself in those tennis shoes. Father behaved a good deal in the manner of Marcelline, the famous Hippodrome clown whose chief activity was to rush about making all sorts of attempts to be helpful just too late to accomplish anything. He went through a lot of energetic motions when he himself was lamming at the ball and when someone on the other side was hitting it, he kept up the same pantomime. It was all very effective but he seldom achieved a direct wallop. As for me, I never once connected up with the wretched object. I would aim my hand at it and swing with all my might, but the only thing I ever succeeded in hitting was my own shoulder.

Mother, watching from the sidelines in acute chagrin, kept up her cooing noises and a little running fire of apology for us, interspersed with a few agonized exhortations:

"Gracious, Mr. Wells! I'm afraid our girls aren't quite . . . Otis, dear love, couldn't you just hit something? . . . You see, Mr. Wells, they're not just used to . . . BABY!!!" (Even the cock feather and the long black earrings didn't deter her from calling me that and it added to my humiliation.) "Do try!" God knows we were all trying.

My day had been a decided failure up to then and I made up my mind I must do something to prove my worth. When confronted by the seemingly impossible, I am prone to summon up imaginary situations of patriotic heroism. The Americans by now were behind not only sartorially; they were giving every evidence that ours was a rapidly disintegrating nation. I felt something must be done to vindicate us and done quickly. The ball was coming my way and Mr. Wells was whooping at me to hit it on over the net. I summoned up all my strength and whispering fiercely to myself, "I'm doing this for Uncle Sam and the Spirit of '76," hauled back my arm like a pitcher in a Big League game, closed my eyes and swung with might and main. This time I hit it and it went straight into the face of the Great Educationalist, who was on my own side and no further from me than a couple of feet. It was the only time during the course of the day his face changed expression, but being a man of great self-discipline he didn't say anything. Mr. Wells, however, did. He jumped up and down and shouted, "It's a foul! It's a foul!" and instead of berating me he turned upon my victim. "You did it! You touched the ball twice!" The Great Educationalist, with a calm logic which under the circumstances seemed almost Socratic, pointed out the fact that one of the touches had been in the pardonable act of self-defense, but to Mr. Wells, that was only a weak excuse. I was too horrified at what I'd done even to apologize. After going over his face with his fingers and making certain his features were still there, the eminent worthy changed places with the Brownie who was the person furthest away from me, and the game continued, but not for long. Every stroke that followed seemed a dull anticlimax. Finally, blessedly, Mr. Wells called a halt to the happy contest. We never did catch the gist of his method of score-keeping. Perhaps he intended it that way, for to everyone's astonishment, despite my act of assault and battery, he announced that our side had won, and nobody questioned him.

My Mother Breaks Her Pearls

MARION STURGES-JONES

*A gay and amusing tale of Mother's innocence.
Mr. Duprez, the famous jeweler, may have served
the Prince of Wales and the Aga Khan; but you
can be sure he will never forget Mother or her
pearls the day they broke.*

By THE YEAR 1918 my mother had, off and on,
been companion to half the elderly ladies who lived on trust funds in
Philadelphia's brownstone front section. Many of them had been
pretty grim old parties, and there had been a fair share of crashing
bores among the lot. When Mother came up against a domineering
character, like Aunt March in *Little Women*, for instance, she usually
took to her heels and ran, having the good sense to know that nature
had not endowed her with either the ability or the inclination to deal
with such a specimen. She was not, as a matter of fact, particularly
well-suited to be a paid companion at all, having none of the success-
ful companion's capacity for reducing her own personality to insignifi-
cance. No matter whom Mother was serving, she remained completely
and absolutely herself. Occasionally, of course, this British assurance
of hers—this inability even to recognize the fact that her position
demanded humility—caused rage in the breast of an employer, and
Mother was fired. More often, however, she left a job of her own
volition and was loudly mourned. Her appearance and address were
so pleasing that she invariably landed any position she sought, which
was a good thing because she was not inclined to remain in any one
situation for long. In relation to her old ladies, Mother behaved somewhat like an artist friend of ours toward a model who fell in love
with him and haunted his studio. The artist was happily married and
not interested in the girl's advances, but he was too kind to rebuff
her rudely. "We are fond of you, Olga," he told her one day, "and
we are glad when you come to see us. But don't stay *long*." Practically
all of Mother's old ladies fell in love with her, and she loved a good

many of them, but she was happiest when she didn't stay long. It grew distinctly tiresome hearing about the same grandchildren and the same ailments day after day, and a new job at least varied the assortment.

Mrs. Effingham, who lived at the Clinton Hotel around the corner from us, was a jolly old soul with whom Mother hit it off from the first. A life of social propriety was behind Mrs. Effingham; she now had (as Stella Gibbons once put it), "everything in the world a woman could want, including a husband who was dead." Mother's fidelity to her ideal, in the face of all practical obstacles, amazed and delighted Mrs. Effingham, and she made no secret of the fact that her new companion found great favor in her eyes. This inevitably worried her relatives—a worry they might have spared themselves, however, since Mother never had the faintest thought of wangling a legacy out of any of her old ladies. She liked Mrs. Effingham; she regaled her with stories of the theater, encouraged her to buy unsuitable hats, and was genuinely concerned over her rheumatism.

This rheumatism of Mrs. Effingham's eventually did Mother a good turn, because it grew so troublesome that Mrs. Effingham decided to try the treatments of a New York doctor who was popular at the time. Mother hadn't been to New York for two or three years, and when Mrs. Effingham told her that she was to go along, and that they would stay at the Hotel Plaza for a week, Mother's excitement knew no bounds.

She was in the middle of telling me the good news that evening when a cloud came over her face.

"I hadn't thought about clothes!" she gasped. "What on earth will I wear? The only thing I own that is good enough for the Plaza is my silk faille suit and I can't wear that every day for a week—!"

"There's my blue Georgette—!" I said, and ran to the closet to appraise our joint wardrobe.

"Oh, I can't take the blue, darling!" Mother protested. "It's your very best dress and it does look so sweet on you!"

"Looks sweet on you, too," I said firmly.

Mother and I were very much the same size and were able to wear each other's clothes. The blue Georgette—which reached to the ankles and was banded at the neck and wrists with squirrel fur—had been my extravagance of the spring and we both admired it beyond words. There was no question but that it had to go to the Plaza; the only question was whether there was anything *else* that was fit to go. There was, indeed, little. Putting all our possessions together did not produce even one wardrobe decent enough for such a trip, and since we were both buying Liberty Bonds with every spare dollar, the outlook was not encouraging.

"Of course I've got my pearls," said Mother thoughtfully. "A black dress to wear with the pearls would really fix me up."

"Um? Oh yes, the pearls," I said.

I had given Mother a string of pearls the previous Christmas, a good string costing $3.98 at John Wanamaker's, and she had been talking ever since about getting just the right black frock with which to wear it. Since she loved pearls (I thought to myself) and since she said that nothing made her feel more elegant, maybe we could manage a new black dress.

"Let's go around to Mr. Solomon's and see if he has anything in stock that would do you," I said.

Mr. Solomon ran a shop on South 12th Street where theatrical people bought and sold their clothes, and Mother and I had been his customers for years. Gorgeous dresses could often be had for a song— dresses that were far too gorgeous for *our* needs. Mr. Solomon, however, was a friendly little man who always made us feel so welcome that I was frequently lured into making my needs fit the dresses. This resulted in my appearance now and then in clothes that surprised even myself. The *femme fatale,* for instance, has never been my type, but whenever there was a Quartermaster Corps dance I appeared in a Gaby Deslys sort of gown which startled all the benevolent old Colonels into a fear of dancing with me in front of their wives.

"I'll take the pearls along," said Mother, rooting in the top drawer of the chest, "so there won't be any mistake."

"Soooo?" said Mr. Solomon when we had told him our problem. "How would you like a dress with a history? A dress that is the exact duplicate of one worn by Pauline Frederick? This dress was made for her understudy who is a nice girl but has no luck. Miss Frederick was never sick, so her understudy finally lost heart and took a job entertaining the A.E.F. with Elsie Janis. She sells me the dress— and here it is!"

It was indeed a creation, and I exclaimed in delight. But Mother shook her head. "I'm afraid not," she said. "Too many sequins. I want to wear my *pearls.*"

"Pearls are very refined," Mr. Solomon agreed from the depths of a showcase. "Could you use purple?"

"Just black," said Mother. "Just a simple black dress."

The miracle was that Mr. Solomon eventually produced a black dress that seemed made for a string of (good) pearls. It was a mixture of *crêpe de chine* and chiffon; it had a long, graceful overskirt, a cowl neckline, and bell sleeves that were banded with a fur that looked *very* much like sable. The effect was one of quiet elegance, suggesting the Hotel Plaza at tea-time, and I knew that to Mother it spelled instant success for her trip.

Mr. Solomon caught the undercurrent of excitement with which we surveyed the dress, and he entered into the spirit of the purchase.

"For you," he said, "for you and the pearls that dress is only nine dollars!"

We carried it home with us that evening and hung it up on the chandelier where we could see it sway dimly as we went to sleep. Miss Kenworthy admired it extravagantly the next day, Miss Hinckley came over from Spruce Street to exclaim over its beauty, and the second night I came home from the office to find Mother down on the third floor landing, exhibiting the dress to four or five of the Professor's tenants.

"I got it to wear with my pearls," said Mother simply, and everyone cried, "How lovely!"

Two evenings later I pressed the dress myself, and we put lots of tissue-paper around it in the suitcase so it wouldn't crush. Then, since Mother was a little nervous about missing the ten o'clock train next day, I went downstairs to the telephone and ordered the taxi that was to take her and Mrs. Effingham to the station.

I kissed Mother an emotional good-by the next morning before I left for the office.

"Have a wonderful time, darling," I said, "and don't bother to write! Send me a line, of course, telling me that you've arrived safely, but I won't look for a real letter."

Partings always make Mother tearful and she was weeping into her handkerchief by then.

"Take good care of yourself, darling," she sobbed. "And don't *you* bother to write, either. Go out every evening and enjoy yourself!"

These altruistic admonitions were a pure matter of form on both our parts, since Mother and I are inveterate letter-writers and are never parted for any length of time without the most voluminous exchange of correspondence. I knew darn well that Mother would write to me several times during her week in New York, and that I would write to her as often—and if either of us failed there would be frantic worry and indignation, followed by an exchange of telegrams.

For the next few days I had ecstatic little notes from Mother.

"Hotel wonderful beyond words—pure linen sheets on the beds!! and fresh ones every day!! I wore my black with the pearls this evening. Mrs. Effingham loved it and ordered Sauterne for dinner, we both felt so gay! She said what *would* her Chestnut Hill relatives think if they saw us! We had two glasses each and felt a little tipsy all evening!"

"Mrs. Effingham taking treatment today so I walked in the theater district, looking at billboards. Dear Grant Stewart was here in a Barrie play but it closed for the summer last week. Saw Mr. and Mrs. Lou Tellegen coming into the Plaza today!! Miss Farrar looked simply ravishing in a large hat with two ostrich plumes, a magnificent furpiece over her Georgette dress, and slippers with huge buckles. She was languishing on Mr. Tellegen's arm and I must say I didn't blame her as he was *very* romantic looking!"

"Mrs. Effingham a darling but I find she *likes sight-seeing*. Thank fortune her poor rheumatism prevents museums!! She takes another treatment tomorrow so I can look up dear Tyrone Power, who is playing Brutus in *Julius Caesar.*"

A second note written the same day, however, added a bit of minor bad news. "I broke my pearls today, darling," she mourned. "My black dress needs them so badly that I must see if I can get them restrung immediately."

On the fifth day of her absence I received a postal from Mother. "Don't worry about my pearls, Toots," she said. "I got them restrung, but had a most curious experience! Will tell you all about it when I see you."

It was only after Mother was safely back in Philadelphia and had told me all her adventures three times over that I pieced together the real story of the pearls. Their restringing was, in fact, so definitely the high spot of her trip that I must unfold the tale from beginning to end.

The pearls broke in the lobby of the Plaza when Mother and Mrs. Effingham were coming through from dinner one evening.

"Oh dear! My pearls!" Mother cried, and gave a little shriek. There was a momentary sensation; several guests paused in their passage, but a gallant Navy officer came to the rescue and began gathering up the pearls from the Aubusson carpet at Mother's feet. In less than a moment the captain of bellboys appeared, sweeping the Commander firmly aside.

"I beg your pardon, sir," he said, "but I shall take charge of this until the chief detective gets here. Everyone will please step aside so that we can describe an arc around the lady and see that no pearls are overlooked."

"Oh, thank you!" said Mother. She and Mrs. Effingham had had champagne for dinner that evening and her cheeks were a little flushed. She thought it delightful of the hotel to be so assiduous in serving her, and she fluttered around murmuring her appreciation until the last pearl had been retrieved.

"Shall I seal these in an envelope and put them in the hotel safe until you can have them restrung, madam?" asked the chief detective.

"I think that's a splendid idea!" said Mother, and waited happily at the desk for a receipt.

Mrs. Effingham was feeling more fit that evening, so she and Mother went to see Billie Burke in a revival of *A Marriage of Convenience*. Mother was sure that this was *the* play to see because her favorite critic, Arthur Hornblow, had recommended it in his monthly article for *Theatre Magazine*.

The next day Mrs. Effingham went again to her doctor, and Mother was free to roam the city as she chose. She walked down Fifth Avenue, looking at the lovely things in the shop windows. Outside an elegant jeweler's she paused to glance covertly at a beautiful woman who had stopped to see the display of pearls—this, she recognized, was Miss Mary Boland, wearing a dark blue satin-and-chiffon dress, with snowy white spats. Mother lingered as long as Miss Boland did, for the pleasure of watching her, and, when Miss Boland had strolled on, it suddenly struck her that fate had carried her to *just* the place for the restringing of her pearls.

She went in. A tall gentleman in tails greeted her.

"Could I get my pearls restrung in the next day or two?" Mother inquired. "I'm here from Philadelphia and I would like them done immediately if it is possible."

The gentleman was excessively civil. "I'll find out," he said. "Does madam have the pearls with her?"

"No," said Mother with regret. "I left them in the safe at the Plaza."

Nodding sympathetically, the gentleman picked up a golden telephone and held a polite conversation with another part of the building. "Our Mr. De Witt could call at the Plaza this afternoon and get them, if madam is not otherwise engaged," he said. "We would like madam to accompany Mr. De Witt and the pearls here, so that she can witness the restringing."

Mother was a little dizzy from so much attention. How perfectly delightful everyone had been about her pearls! She had a moment of wondering why New York was considered a callous city. Never in her life had she been treated so considerately!

"I'd *love* to watch the restringing!" she said gratefully. "My pearls are my very dearest possession and I really would hate to part with them."

"Precisely," said the tall gentleman. "Shall we say three o'clock?" and he wrote Mother's name and suite number on a slip of paper.

Mother had the pearls, still sealed in their envelope, in her bag when Mr. De Witt appeared. He was a handsome man in his sixties who looked like a United States Senator, and Mother felt herself being envied as she walked through the lobby with him. It was quite thrilling, too, to return to the jeweler's in the private limousine provided, and Mother was glad she had her silk faille suit to wear. Miss Boland's appearance that morning in white spats had inspired her to get a pair for herself, so she felt quite dressy enough for the occasion.

When they arrived at the jeweler's, Mr. De Witt conducted Mother past all the counters of diamonds, emeralds and rubies; past the sterling silver and the exquisite crystalware, until they came to a group of handsomely-furnished rooms at the far end. Mother was ushered into one of these, where she was seated at a table, and a cloth of heavy black velvet was put before her.

"Our Mr. Duprez does the stringing, madam, and will be with us in a moment," said Mr. De Witt. "I remain present, if you don't mind."

"Of course not," said Mother. "It is too kind of you!"

Mr. Duprez, a sharp-featured little Frenchman with fancy mustaches, bowed his way into the room. Sitting down, he placed a tray of implements on the table, smoothed out the velvet, and reached for the Hotel Plaza's envelope. They all watched as he opened it with thin, careful fingers and let the pearls roll out. He was about to put on a pair of spectacles when he suddenly stiffened. His hand trembled;

he hesitated, and then he adjusted the glasses hastily over his ears. He took a slow, steady look at the pearls and then he breathed suddenly with a sharp, hissing sound.

"Madam has been robbed!" he cried. "The police must be summoned! These are not pearls!"

Mother blinked. "Oh, I'm sure I haven't been robbed!" she said. "Everyone at the Plaza was so nice—I—I couldn't think such a thing of them!" She leaned over and stared at the beads that were lying spilled on the velvet. "No," she said, and heaved a sigh of relief. "Those are my pearls all right—I remember the clasp quite well. You see, it is a *fleur de lis* design in gold and diamonds—not *real* diamonds of course, dear Toots couldn't afford such a thing—but it's a charming clasp, don't you think?"

Mother turned to Mr. Duprez, and from him to Mr. De Witt. Both gentlemen seemed to be on the verge of some sort of fit. Mr. De Witt was scarlet of face and looked ready to have a stroke, while the little Frenchman had turned gray-white and was grasping the arm of his chair to steady himself. His mouth opened, but no sound came.

"Is something the matter?" Mother asked in alarm.

Mr. De Witt was the first to recover the power of speech. "Madam," he said, "you are sitting in a private room of the world's most exalted dealer in gems. On that very chair you occupy the Aga Khan has sat while new designs were drawn for his priceless emeralds. The Prince of Wales has brought family jewels to this very room, to discuss resetting. All this, you understand, is in the day's work for us. In spite of this, we are not too proud to restring the pearls of any American citizen. But, madam, we do not restring beads that have cost ninety-eight cents!"

Mother drew herself up. "I think you are being very rude," she said coldly. "This is a *good* string of pearls—not *real* pearls, of course, I never said they were real!—but they are certainly not the ninety-eight cent variety. My daughter gave them to me for Christmas and while I never inquired the price—something I dare say you couldn't understand—I know that they are good pearls. If you don't care to restring them, you are at liberty to decline, but I must say I think your manner is far from courteous."

By the time Mother had finished speaking, Mr. De Witt had pulled himself together and had risen to his feet.

"Madam is right," he said, looking like a United States Senator once more. "The error was ours! I apologize for forgetting myself as I did—it was just that, in all the thirty years I've been with the firm —but never mind that! The error was ours, and we will not make madam suffer for it! Duprez, you will restring madam's—er—madam's *pearls* at once—"

"Oh thank you!" said Mother, all smiles again.

"And there will be no charge!" Mr. De Witt added.

His expression was one of pain, but it was of pain nobly borne.

Letter to the Dean

GLADYS TABER

It's strange how little information there is to offer when you fill out that college application for your daughter. Yet, when you look back, you realize there certainly were moments . . . trials . . . pains . . . happiness . . .

STATE UNIVERSITY
MONONGAHELA
OFFICE OF THE DEAN OF WOMEN

MRS. KENNETH MARCH,
RIVERSIDE.

My dear Mrs. March: Your daughter's credentials are now complete and we hope that she will be with us at State University next year.

The office of the Dean of Women exists for the purpose of serving the women students; all that concerns the life of the campus is our responsibility. Our function is to offer assistance and advice in the difficult process of adjusting to a new environment which the new student faces.

Therefore we are asking your co-operation in order that we may assist your daughter in making a satisfactory and happy beginning. We should like you to write us frankly and freely and objectively about your daughter, telling us fully about her health, ambitions, temperament and tastes. Though the letter will of course be strictly confidential, it will be of great help to us in supervising your daughter's welfare.

Cordially yours,
ELIZABETH WINTHROP,
Dean of Women

EW:k

My dear Miss Winthrop: I have your letter asking me to write you about my daughter, frankly, freely and objectively.

My daughter Mary is sixteen. Her birthday is December 24.

I didn't want to have a baby. I wasn't the kind of girl you read about who has one eye on the wedding ring and the other on a kiddie pen. I liked to stop on the street and admire fat little bundles done up in pink or blue and smelling of milk and talcum and damp diapers. But then I wanted to walk on, swinging my skates over my shoulder, or swishing off clover heads with my tennis racket. I wanted to drive fast in the roadster with the top down, and dance late, and canoe down the big river at night under a tender moon. Something in me was always trying to escape, to be more free, to be just my own self, alone. Separate.

I was frightened. Something dark and formless reached around me and smothered me. I could never get away again. My throat was full of fear. I walked the floor and cried and bit my lips until blood and rouge were mixed. Yes, I beat my hands together and cried. And then, of course, I felt sick and dizzy from crying, and I was sure that was because I was going to have a baby.

But I didn't dare tell anybody how it was with me. Maybe it wasn't so bad to be a coward if nobody found it out. So I told Kenneth casually, and he said it was just marvelous and weren't we going to be happy. How would I like to celebrate with chop suey? I've never been able to eat chop suey since. And afterward Kenneth bought me some long-stemmed roses, and I thought, *Flowers for the funeral, the death of my youth.*

We were very gay and smart about it, and then Kenneth sneaked away to his desk, and I could see him getting out his insurance policies and making figures on yellow scratch paper, and I knew he was afraid too. Babies cost money. And he was just getting started, and we just about got by on his salary.

Nine months is a long time. Getting up in the night to chew dry soda crackers or drink hot milk, trying not to feel so ill. Being clumsy and wearing sloppy clothes. Aching feet and cold hands. A knife nicking away in your back. Fatigue like a heel pressed in your temples. Oh, yes, a fine thing for a girl who wasn't ready, who still wanted to run—to fly.

Snow came early that year. It was the long winter. Snow was falling on the twenty-third of December. It was dusk and I had been in the house all day. My lungs were tight with heated furnace air. So I bundled up and crept slowly around the block, feeling snow on my dry mouth, bracing my body against the throbbing kicking of that other life. Lights were on, Christmas trees shone through the windows, and at the Gregorys' they were dancing. I could see Kathleen Gregory, light and slim and smooth, doing an intricate step with Phil; she wasn't so good as I had been, but of course the Kenneth Marches regretted. Kenneth was doing some extra work, worrying about the hospital expenses.

I heard the music and laughter, and I looked hungrily at the lights, and wondered if another Christmas would find me fixing a tree, or whether Kenneth would be carrying a wreath to the cemetery. It would be funny if I should die and Kenneth would have to start all over again. Just as I had learned to make coconut-cream pie too.

The snow fell deep and heavy, but my cheeks were hot. Thoughts pounded in my head, almost too fast to sort out; the way they do sometimes: It must be strange to be dead and not know whether it is snowing or daffodils are out. That would be a terrible thing, not to know what season it was. I wished I had a mother, who would talk to me, and rock me in warm strong arms, and stand between me and my fear. If I died, would Kenneth marry the Williams girl? She would be pretty glad if I died; she was wild about Ken; I knew it.

Then my baby would be brought up by a stepmother. I stopped and wiped snow crystals from my lashes. My teeth were chattering. That minute I thought about it as my baby—when I thought about a stepmother. "No, please, God, please, please," I said, "please don't have another woman take care of my baby. It's not fair—it's not fair to do that."

Suppose, I thought then, that the baby wasn't all right? There was George MacIntyre, who lived on Peach Street. When I was a little girl, he was there, sitting on the front porch in an old rocking chair. All day long he sat and rocked and grinned, and he rocked so hard the chair almost stood on end. They said he was forty years old, and he wore the clothes of a fourteen-year-old boy. Sometimes his mother came out and stopped the rocking chair, and then he would cry like a baby until she went away and let him rock again. Suppose my child was like that? Forgetting that I was dead and under the ground, with

Ken laying wreaths on my grave, I went through a lifetime of waiting on a child who rocked all day long and grinned and had to be fed with a spoon.

I was crying to myself, so I missed the snow-deep curb, and I fell down, and as I fell a sword sliced right through me. I couldn't get up for a minute, and then I stumbled somehow to the door of the house, and Kenneth was just going in.

"What in the world are you out in this blizzard for?" he said sharply; and I said, "Call the doctor, Kenneth; tell him to hurry."

But it was a whole day later when the doctor said, "You've got a fine beautiful baby girl, a Christmas present."

I came out of the tangled jungle of pain and death and looked vaguely at what they held up for me to see. It was wrinkled and small and the color of a cinnamon drop, and a small sound came from it.

"You mean that's mine?" I whispered.

"I think she looks like you," said the nurse. "Look at the beautiful shape of her head, and see all that dark hair."

Kenneth was standing there, and his face looked odd. He was crying.

I said, "What in the world has upset you?"

"I'm all right," he said gruffly, and turned his back. After a while he came over and looked down. "I always wanted it to be a girl," he said shyly.

The nurse took her away, and Kenneth and the doctor went out.

I could see that outside it was still snowing. All that time it had been snowing. And I was still alive and I had a baby in the nursery. A whole, perfect baby. My child, my daughter Mary.

My daughter's health is excellent.

It was funny, when I had rejected the idea of a baby, that I would hardly let her out of my sight after we were home again. Kenneth and I agreed that we wouldn't spoil her, no matter what. We had a book to raise her by, and when she cried, Kenneth got out the book and read aloud to me what the book said. Then we would decide that she was simply crying to be picked up.

"Just ignore her," Ken would say.

"She's sick of lying there," I would say. So finally I would pick her up and just rock her a little bit—not enough to spoil her for good.

At night I always got to thinking perhaps she had too little cover on. "Ken, do you think she has enough blankets?"

"Now, don't begin that again. We've got to get some rest. She's all right."

I would hold out my hand, feeling the air. And listen to hear her breathe. I always argued half an hour, and then got up and went in to put on a blanket and feel her little face.

But it was no good, because then I'd get afraid she was too hot, and if she got overheated she might catch cold and it might go into one of those respiratory diseases it told about in the book. By then it was usually around one, and I'd get up again and go in and take off a blanket. And feel her little curled fist.

"Good Lord," Ken said, "you'll kill her, covering and uncovering her all night, the way you do."

But in some ways it was only a minute before she was trotting off to kindergarten in her blue bunny suit, her white overshoes on her little feet and her face framed in fur. She had grave dark eyes and coppery ringlets and a funny little nubbin of a nose and a firm mouth.

By the time she was in third grade she was asking for a baby brother or sister from Santa Claus, but by that time it was clear there couldn't be another baby. Santa Claus was nice about bringing rabbits and guinea pigs and kittens, though.

Kenneth insisted that I go with him on that business trip to Florida to inspect the bank investment. We had a maid by then, and we got a practical nurse, and Mary was eight. We were going to be away only three weeks, he said, and he didn't think a vacation would do me any harm. We could dance and swim and have a time, he said.

Kenneth caught a blue marlin and I got sand fleas and we ate a lot and swam. We could racket around day and night, just the way I always used to like. I had a trunkful of new smooth clothes and a new haircut, and we learned to hum the new tunes—off key.

Ken said, "You look like twenty." He said, "Isn't this swell? I'm taking the rooms for another week."

I walked up and down the sun-bright streets, looking at the children. Once I saw a little girl in a blue dress with that coppery shade of hair, and I walked quickly away. Then I bought a baby alligator, a revolting thing, to send back to Mary. Every time I felt bad, I bought her something. I had three suitcases full of what I bought.

When the phone call came, it was like something happening that I knew about. People must feel that way who live at the edge of a volcano, when the lava finally does erupt. Or when a building collapses. You see the first swaying and the fault line of the concrete, and then the whole thing crashes, and you were waiting for it.

The nurse said, "We don't want to alarm you, Mrs. March, but the doctor feels you'd better come home. It may be pneumonia."

Ken was out on an all-day fishing trip. I didn't wait. I caught the plane, and then the train.

I sat in the local day coach, and counted telephone poles. When I couldn't focus on them any longer, I counted cows and horses. There was an Italian woman in the next seat with three dirty little children.

She fed them bananas and oranges and chocolate; the smell of orange peel was strong. She had three, all healthy, probably raised on a diet of spaghetti and garlic and red wine. "Please, God, she's all I have. Please, God, please, please listen to me."

When I got to the house, I couldn't open the door. But the maid had seen the taxi, and she opened it so fast I fell in. I ran up the stairs without a word to her, and I got in Mary's room. I was on the floor by the bed.

Mary opened her eyes and a little smile came on her lips. "I knew you would come back," she whispered.

The doctor said, "Every child has to have a little sickness—measles, mumps, and so on. It wasn't your fault she got a bug; you can't keep her in cotton wool all her life. Brace up now; Mary's fine. Too bad you haven't got six children."

"If I had six, I'd be dead," I said.

He said, "I want you to let her run around with those little Irish kids in the alley; they're healthy as pigs. You wrap her up too much. She's a healthy child, but she needs toughening."

So Mary tore around like a hoodlum for the next five years.

My daughter's ambition is to be a great actress.

Maybe she has some talent. At first she used to make up little plays. "Mamma, I'm the little Lord Jesus; you be the wise men and wisshop me. . . . Mamma, I'm an Indian chief, and I'm going to want your fox fur to trim my leggings. . . . Mamma, I'm going to be Joseph in

447

the Christmas pageant at Sunday school. Where can I get a beard?"

Then, when the new dancing teacher came, Mary was going to be a dancer. She practiced hours before the mirror, and walked with a peculiar swinging gait that annoyed Ken a lot. He said it looked as if she might get unhinged any minute.

But after we went to the big football game, she wanted to be a football player. "Oh, Mamma, why wasn't I a boy? I'd rather play left end than anything in the world. Boys have all the opportunities. It's dumb being a girl. I'd rather play end than be quarterback."

Maybe she could at least play in the band. So she borrowed a trombone from somewhere. She practiced a lot.

Kenneth said, "Mary, does that instrument have any soft pedal? Couldn't you kind of quiet it down some?"

"No," she said, "when you play a trombone, you have to give, Papa."

"A trombone sounds all right to me in a bunch of things," Ken said, "but all by itself it's kind of melancholy. Maybe if you could play it on the key, it would be more cheerful."

"There; you see, that's all the encouragement I get from my family." She was getting deep in the misunderstood stage.

Kenneth got her the riding tickets to take her mind off the trombone now and then. But then she wanted to run a livery stable. She wanted him to build over the sun room for a horse stall. She said the house was big enough. We had moved to a big brick place at the edge of town. There was a garden and a bird bath and a game room. But there wasn't a stable. We had the horse question pretty hard, but just as Kenneth got to wondering if we could put a horse in the garage and keep the sedan in the laundry, the famous poet came to lecture.

Poetry broke out like measles. Mary shut herself away and wrote poetry. Some of it was printed in the school magazine, and Mary got to be editor that way. "Your daughter has a real gift for writing," all the teachers told me. "You must do all you can for her artistic future."

Kenneth said he couldn't understand some of the poems. They were kind of abstract. He said, "I hope she's not going to take after my Aunt Emily. She was a poet, and she went crazy." He said, "She used to run around town carving things on the trees." He said, "Poetry isn't a thing to get involved with. Didn't you tell me Emily Dickinson used to lower a basket from her window for her meals? How would you like it if Mary got to lowering a basket from the bedroom window for her supper? You better get her out with boys and girls more. Besides, if she's going to be a poet, she better begin hunting up million-aires to support her."

I said, "You can't thwart her. All the books on child adjustment say it's bad to thwart them."

"Mamma, do you think I could be a poet?" She was intense.

That was the only thing certain about her. She was fiercely ardent about whatever it was she was doing. That intensity was almost frightening. She never could take things as they came along. She was never easy. Now she was all dark grave eyes and sensitive mouth, and her hair was like a mist in her neck, and there was always a book in her hand.

I said, "Don't worry about it, Mary. If you're supposed to be a poet, you will be."

"But, Mamma, my life is a third over, and I've got to hurry! I'm al-most fifteen! Look at Thomas Chatterton. He was a great poet and al-ready dead at seventeen. Look at Keats! Look at Shelley and Byron!"

I said weakly, "Well, Wordsworth lived quite a while, didn't he?"

"Oh, Wordsworth," she said, turning up her nose.

Since the senior play she wants to be an actress.

My daughter's temperament and tastes are—

Well, what are they? What is she like, really, underneath? Do I know her at all? Mothers can be lonely. I know Mary wears her stock-ings through at the heel and tears her slips at the shoulder. I know she won't eat cauliflower and is crazy about ripe olives. I've been right in the house with her for sixteen years, and now she is as remote as polar ice. She withdraws into some world of her own right while she is buttering her mashed potato at supper. She leads a secret life; she is a person. Now and then she looks down at me from some mountain-top and waves. I see awareness in her eyes. Then it is gone.

There was the party. Mary didn't want to go. But I got her a new dress and an evening jacket. Kenneth and I worried and worried over how to get a boy to ask her; you can't just hire an escort. Kenneth thought he could take her, and Mary just burst into tears.

"I'd be disgraced for life," she said. "Do you want to disgrace me for life?"

Finally I had a brilliant idea. I gave a dinner party for the whole class, with the idea that they could go on and dance at the party afterward, in a clump. There were twenty of them. We had three extra maids. The boys all stayed in the study, throwing pennies, and the girls giggled in the living room until dinner. Two of the boys got to wrestling and broke my best Lalique vase. Mary had as much life as a soap carving. She just stood by the fire. Corinne Walker went boldly in with the boys and picked out the best-looking one, Wade Harmon, and got him to dancing with her in the hall. Mary just didn't make an effort.

What does a mother do when she is afraid her daughter will be socially unacceptable? Wring her hands and say, "Be charming. Make the boys like you"? You can teach Latin and history and trombone playing, but you can't teach sex appeal. It's there or it isn't. What had I done that I shouldn't have? Maybe she'd been a tomboy too long— but that was for her health. Her health was fine.

She looked shy and serious, and Corinne was laughing and kittening with Wade Harmon. I was lighting candles, and my hands felt spatters of hot wax. I called them in, and they fell on the dinner like wolves. The dining room looked like a wreck after they charged out. They began to pair off, then, to go on to the party at the club.

Mary stood by the stairway with her hand tight on the bannister; she smiled a fixed smile. "Good-by, Perry; see you later. . . . Sure, Billy; good-by; see you later . . . Glad you liked it, Corinne." When there were only two more left, Mary gave me one look. I smiled brightly. Mary stiffened then and said, "Guess I'll mush on with you."

"Oh sure, c'mon; we'll be late."

The door slammed. I rushed to the phone and called Ken out of a board meeting for the new school. "Come home," I said; "I have got to go on to the dance. I can't stand it."

"Hey, I'm working."

"You come home quick," I said.

"Oh, all right," he said helplessly. "Just hold everything."

I got into a black dress. This was a dance I wasn't going to miss, but I didn't care whether I got on the floor or not. I brushed my hair and got some make-up and walked up and down waiting for Kenneth.

"What's the matter?" he called as he came in. Then, as he saw the house, he whistled. "You had the marines?" he asked.

By the time he got his tux on, it was late. We got to the club about ten. We came up on the porch, and I said, "Let's look in first, Ken." My hands were cold.

The floor was crowded. The girls and boys looked young and gay; the girls wore shining frocks, and flowers over their ears in the style. The dance music made a pattern of lovely rhythms. Corinne and Wade were at the punch bowl, and she was lifting her face as she drank the pink stuff. It was an old trick; I used to do it; the light falls just right on lashes and cheeks, and it makes a male feel protective, especially if you get the right softness on your mouth.

Mary was sitting beside an artificial palm with two other girls. Every time a boy walked that way, she bent her head and looked at the floor as if something important were there. Her mouth was carved in a smile and her eyes, when she did look up, were like the eyes of a wounded wild bird.

"Well, let's go on in," said Kenneth.

"Oh, no, we can't. I guess we can't go in."

"Are you crazy? You got me out of an important meeting and into these damned clothes, and now you want to go home."

"Oh, Kenneth, Mary will never forgive us if she knows we came."

"Then what's the idea coming at all?"

"I thought if she were having a grand rush—But the way it looks— Mary's so proud."

"Why can't we go in and take her home, if she's not having a good time? I'll get her."

"No, Ken, it's like the law of the jungle. We can't help her. I guess maybe," I said slowly—"maybe you've got to run with the pack, and learn it somehow."

We went on home. I sat up in the living room holding a book and listening. It was a cool moonlit night, an April night. Trees were misting with buds, and the sky was heavy with young stars. Dance music came in over the radio, sweet and dreamy, and then hot and rackety with swing. Kenneth sat up a while, and then went on to bed.

I kept going to the window and looking down the moonlit street. I got out my basket and mended her slips where the straps were pulled out. I emptied all the ash trays and straightened the sofa pillows. I looked out.

She came down the street alone, walking with her head up. Her face was frozen in that smile. She walked fast, almost running, but when she got to the front walk, she slowed and came creeping softly to the door.

I had my head over the book again as she came in. I said lightly, "Oh, hello, Mary."

"Hello, Mamma." She spoke carefully. "Thank you for the dinner. It was very nice." Her face had that shut secret look.

"Did you . . . have a good time at the dance?"

"Oh, yes, I had a good time."

If I could have comforted her, eased the hurt! Or let her know I understood!

"Good night, Mamma."

She hurried upstairs and closed her door. Shutting out the alien world.

I turned out the lights and went up too. I could hear, through her shut door, the long, strangling sobs. But I couldn't help her.

Two weeks later she came home from school with Wade Harmon, and when I was passing by the living room I saw her lifting a cup of hot chocolate for him. She looked up at him with a soft little smile. The afternoon light fell on her long amber lashes and on the curve of her cheek. Wade was looking protective.

At supper, she said, "I'm going with Wade to the next dance. I'm going to change the way I do my hair," she added.

Kenneth's jaw fell open, and I said very quickly, "What dress will you wear?"

I stepped on what I thought was his foot under the table, but it was the buzzer, and the maid flew in.

"More coffee," I said.

"The pot's full, Ma'am," she answered.

Mary said dreamily, "I'll wear the green. Green is Wade's favorite color."

Kenneth burst out, "How did he happen to ask you? Why, only two weeks ago—Ouch!" he finished, glaring at me. It was the foot that time.

Mary gave him a feminine and disarming smile. "Oh," she said gently, "I just happened to drop a note to one of the girls, and he happened to find it and read it. So he wanted to know why I thought he was handsomer than Clark Gable."

"Now, Mary, you don't mean to say you think that pimple-faced—"

"Corinne was telling him he was kind of like Leslie Howard," Mary continued pleasantly. "He doesn't admire Leslie Howard, because he wears glasses."

That was in May. On December twenty-fourth, her birthday, Mary came in while I was buttering the breakfast toast. She had an apricot breakfast coat on and her hair drawn back from her forehead. She was slim and softly rounded, and the childish look was gone from her dark eyes, but somehow her nose still looked childish to me. Her mouth was intense; I knew that intense tight look. But I couldn't think what it was.

I said happily, "Such a beautiful day for your birthday. I thought we might do the Christmas last-minutes this morning. I forgot Aunt Caroline, and she's so fussy."

Mary nibbled an edge of toast. "I promised Wade I'd go out with him," she said. "A bunch of us are going someplace. Wassail, Mamma. Send Aunt Car a magazine subscription; it's so easy."

I said, "Mary, your father feels you ought to go out with different boys. You've been out every night this vacation with Wade."

Her face got hard as an icicle. She said harshly, "Why can't you let me alone ever?"

"Why, Mary," I said, "I only meant—"

But she was gone. I started after her, and then noticed that she had managed to eat two pieces of toast and drink her orange juice and milk and get away with three slices of bacon, just in that delicate way. Her stomach was all right. She'd been up too late, nights. It made her edgy.

I heard Wade's auto horn, and I thought I should ask if he had a heater in the car and chains on. But I didn't. It made the children so mad to be questioned. They were always trying to be free. Suddenly I remembered that was the way I had felt before Mary was born. I had wings, too, once. Sixteen years ago.

So when Mary whisked past me in her squirrel jacket, I called, "Have a good time, darling!"

She checked her mad speed, and said, "I may bring Wade for dinner. Could you have duckling? He loves it."

It began to snow at noon. "Going to be a blizzard," said the butcher, as I ordered the duckling. I had so many errands that I had to go downtown after lunch. The streets were deep with snow and the street trucks already were frantically swallowing it up. Christmas lights shone; holly and mistletoe on the sidewalks made mounds of white. Everybody staggered against the drifts with arms thick with packages for the forgotten relatives. My hands were so cold in the ermine mittens that I went into the drugstore to warm up.

"Terrible storm. I'd hate to be out in it," said the druggist. "Hasn't been such a snow for sixteen years. I remember the date because my nephew got stalled in the country that day. Him and his wife wound up the windows and turned the motor on to keep warm. They both died of monoxide gas. Road shovelers found them dead. I don't know why folks will shut the windows like that."

I said, "Give me some aspirin. I'm aching all over."

"You got to watch for flu," he said. "This is flu weather."

I went out, and it was dusk; the snow was a dusk all of its own, thick and silent, falling and falling from a close thick sky. It was cold too.

A horse was down in the street and the driver cursing as he struggled to get it up. Ice formed around the soft deep lips, ringed the nostrils. I began to run; the world always seems out of key when a horse is down.

When I got home, Mary wasn't there. She ought to have been back long ago, wrapping her things for the tree. I could smell the duckling, a brown smell, as if it should be out of the oven. Ken was listening to the radio report of the weather.

"Hey, where's Mary?" he asked. "Say, this is a real old-time blizzard; the trains aren't running. What do you know?"

I said, "Mary and Wade went out right after breakfast."

"Where?"

"She didn't say."

"They'll be along. But she ought to be here."

The phone rang. I ran to answer it. It was Mrs. Harmon, and her voice was thin and taut over the wire: "Where's Wade?"

Well, I didn't know. She was nearly frantic, she said; Wade was supposed to be home by two-thirty to take the Christmas basket to the orphans' home, and he knew the orphans had their things Christmas Eve.

I tried to quiet her down, and she hung up at last. The maid came in and said dinner was practically ruined, so I said we would have to eat. I ran upstairs to wash my face and hands. There was nothing to worry about. But Mary always came in on time; she was good that way. And the weather was frightful, and then, too, it was Christmas Eve.

All the families in our crowd were having their family suppers; the children conceded Christmas Eve to their parents, and Easter Sunday. So there wouldn't be a last-minute dance at the club or anything.

No harm calling the club, to be sure. I called on the upstairs phone. Nobody was at the club except the staff, getting ready for a banquet.

As I went past Mary's room, I stopped to close her window. Snow was deep on the sill; the curtains dragged in it, and I stopped to wipe it with a bath towel. Then I saw that the draft had blown open Mary's little blue diary that was on her desk. There was the date, "December twenty-fourth," and under it in black ink a single line: "I'm glad we decided not to wait. I love him too much."

I sat down on the bed, pressing my knees together. I had a strange feeling that the night and the snow and the whirling wind were right in the room with me. Something was ringing in my head; I tried to push the sound away. Then I realized it was the phone. I got up and answered it, and it was Mrs. Harmon. "I've phoned all over town!" she said wildly; "absolutely everywhere I could think of! I even called the ice-cream parlors. They just aren't—they just aren't anywhere!"

My hands were shaking. I said, "We are sure to hear pretty soon."

"I don't see why you let your daughter go off without telling you," said Mrs. Harmon; and I said sharply, "I assumed she was all right with your son."

Kenneth called, "Now don't start arguing, you mothers!"

I got him upstairs and showed him the diary, and his face got suddenly white. "You don't think—you don't think they—No, of course not. Come and eat something hot, and they'll be along."

"But where are they?" He didn't answer. We sat and choked down a little duckling.

Of course they could have driven over the state line. If that was what they meant. Mary was just sixteen. She was so intense about everything.

About nine-thirty we couldn't stand it, just waiting. Kenneth got the car and we drove out. Kenneth wanted to get the police, but then he said we better wait a little longer; publicity was a mess. The lights were glowing all over town, and the snow was lessening a little. No taxis were running, the streetcars were off the tracks. But the carolers came down the street singing, "God rest you merry, gentlemen, let nothing you dismay."

Kenneth took the main road from town, but ran head-on into a snowdrift. When he backed out again, he said, "I'm going to call the traffic men. You know, they might be stuck somewhere."

"Oh, Kenneth, would they shut the car and leave the motor running?" That was a new terror.

Kenneth said, "Don't think about it."

The snowplows were out, the men said, and they were opening up the roads as fast as possible. Now the snow was letting up, they'd have everything clear before dawn.

Before dawn!

We went home again and had hot coffee. Then Kenneth said he was going back uptown and try to ride out with the road men. He'd phone me. He kissed me and said, "Keep your chin up, lady."

I walked up and down in the empty house. I thought of everything, and it all happened in my heart. The minister saying, "Do you take this man—" and Mary, her face fresh and cold with snow, saying trustingly, "I do." A cheap hotel or a heated tourist cabin near Bayside. Or the closed car and snow drifting on the running board, and Mary and Wade holding hands. Or maybe they hadn't meant marriage. Maybe they didn't mean that. You could annul a marriage, but you couldn't annul memory.

I began again. The way she looked at him, with a kind of soft wonder. The way he put on her coat, as if his hands loved to touch the fabric that warmed her young slim body. The way they laughed at secret jokes.

I must have failed. I had pushed her into this boy-and-girl game myself. Trying to adjust her socially. Then I'd been so blind. I could have forbidden him to come, taken her away, talked to her—Oh, no, I couldn't. Mothers were helpless. All those old foolish things that parents tried never really protected their children.

"Please, God!" I said, "please, please, not Mary. Not yet."

The house was deathly cold, and finally I turned the thermostat up. I roused the fire in the fireplace. I put on an old chenille robe. I knew death must come cold like that in the reluctant bones.

Dawn made a faint smear in the gray sky. Then the whole pure snowy world took on a faint light of its own. I pushed the curtains aside and stared out, my eyes hot and the lids tight.

A milk truck labored down the street. It stopped before our house. Mary and Wade got out and waved to the driver and ran up the steps. I couldn't move. I stood like stone as they burst in.

Mary said, "Why, Mamma, what are you doing up at this hour? Were you worried?"

"Worried," I said. "Oh, Mary!"

"We're starved. Can we eat something?" She was flinging off her things. "Wait till I tell you! Oh, Mamma, it was so exciting!"

"Exciting," I said faintly.

She said, "When we went out in the country the other day to pick the Christmas tree, the man had some darling beagle puppies, and I fell smack in love with the littlest one, and Wade said he'd buy it for me when it was bigger. But I wanted him so much, Wade said that he'd give him to me for Christmas, and we went out yesterday to get him. And what do you think? It stormed so that we were stuck fast! . . . Weren't we, Wade?"

"I'll say we were," he laughed. "The old bus like to sunk down to China."

"Go up and wash; you're pig-dirty," Mary said to him. "I'll scramble some eggs in a minute."

"Not till you've told me what happened."

"Well, we found a farmhouse," she said. "And it was the very place where the puppies were! The wires were all down, so we just had to leave the car forever! And we played backgammon all night. And this morning we had breakfast there, and Wade bought my present."

She unrolled the scarf, and there was a small shivering puppy about the size of a pint milk bottle. Mary said, "Isn't he perfect? And the marvelous thing is, it snowed so hard we couldn't tell where we were stalled, and here the first house we came to was the one where the beagles were! Isn't it amazing the way things work out!"

"Yes," I said, "it's amazing. Mary, your father's out hunting you."

"We met him. He'll be along, soon as he gets the car going," she said.

"Mary, I thought—I was so afraid—and I'm sure Mrs. Harmon thought—you and Wade—had run away to—had eloped."

Her mouth fell open. "My goodness, Mamma!" she said. "What ever would put such an idea in your head? Wade said his mother would have a fit, but I said you would figure out that we couldn't phone on account of the storm, but we could look out for ourselves O.K."

"Well," I said, "it looked—different from this end."

Mary yelled up the stairs, "Wade, phone your mother! She thinks we ran away to get married!"

The puppy began to whimper, and Mary put it up to her neck. She kissed it. She said, "You ought to know I wouldn't trick you, Mamma. Besides, when we get married, we want to have a real wedding. You get some presents then."

She smiled at me over the wobbling puppy head. "You wouldn't really worry, would you, Mamma?" she asked. "Look, wouldn't it be a good idea to raise beagles?"

Miss Elizabeth Winthrop,
Dean of Women,
State University,
Monongahela.

My dear Miss Winthrop: I have your letter asking me to write you about my daughter, frankly, freely and objectively.

My daughter Mary is sixteen. Her birthday is December 24. Her health is excellent. My daughter's ambition is to be a great actress. Her temperament and tastes are those of the average sixteen-year-old girl.

I feel sure she will adjust satisfactorily to the university, and will not be a trouble. She has never given me cause to worry.

Sincerely,
MARY MARCH,
(MRS. KENNETH MARCH.)

Little Gentleman

BOOTH TARKINGTON

The tar fight made history. Some say Penrod started it. Others blamed the barber, and still others, the fly on the barber's nose. At any rate, why should the taunt of "Little Gentleman" incur anyone's wrath?

THE MIDSUMMER SUN was stinging hot outside the little barber-shop next to the corner drug store and Penrod, undergoing a toilette preliminary to his very slowly approaching twelfth birthday, was adhesive enough to retain upon his face much hair as it fell from the shears. There is a mystery here: the tonsorial processes are not unagreeable to manhood; in truth, they are soothing; but the hairs detached from a boy's head get into his eyes, his ears, his nose, his mouth, and down his neck, and he does everywhere itch excruciatingly. Wherefore he blinks, winks, weeps, twitches, condenses his countenance, and squirms; and perchance the barber's scissors clip more than intended—belike an outlying flange of ear.

"Um-muh-ow!" said Penrod, this thing having happened.

"D' I touch y' up a little?" inquired the barber, smiling falsely.

"Ooh-uh!" The boy in the chair offered inarticulate protest, as the wound was rubbed with alum.

"*That* don't hurt!" said the barber. "You *will* get it, though, if you don't sit stiller," he continued, nipping in the bud any attempt on the part of his patient to think that he already had "it."

"Pfuff!" said Penrod, meaning no disrespect, but endeavoring to dislodge a temporary mustache from his lip.

"You ought to see how still that little Georgie Bassett sits," the barber went on, reprovingly. "I hear everybody says he's the best boy in town."

"Pfuff! Phirr!" There was a touch of intentional contempt in this.

"I haven't heard nobody around the neighborhood makin' no such remarks," added the barber, "about nobody of the name of Penrod Schofield."

"Well," said Penrod, clearing his mouth after a struggle, "who wants 'em to? Ouch!"

"I hear they call Georgie Bassett the 'little gentleman,'" ventured the barber, provocatively, meeting with instant success.

"They better not call *me* that," returned Penrod truculently. "I'd like to hear anybody try. Just once, that's all! I bet they'd never try it ag— *Ouch!*"

"Why? What'd you do to 'em?"

"It's all right what I'd *do!* I bet they wouldn't want to call me that again long as they lived!"

"What'd you do if it was a little girl? You wouldn't hit her, would you?"

"Well, I'd—Ouch!"

"You wouldn't hit a little girl, would you?" the barber persisted, gathering into his powerful fingers a mop of hair from the top of Penrod's head and pulling that suffering head into an unnatural posi-

459

tion. "Doesn't the Bible say it ain't never right to hit the weak sex?"

"Ow! *Say*, look *out!*"

"So you'd go and punch a pore, weak, little girl, would you?" said the barber, reprovingly.

"Well, who said I'd hit her?" demanded the chivalrous Penrod. "I bet I'd *fix* her though, all right. She'd see!"

"You wouldn't call her names, would you?"

"No, I wouldn't! What hurt is it to call anybody names?"

"Is that *so!*" exclaimed the barber. "Then you was intending what I heard you hollering at Fisher's grocery delivery wagon driver fer a favor, the other day when I was goin' by your house, was you? I reckon I better tell him, because he says to me after*werds* if he ever lays eyes on you when you ain't in your own yard, he's goin' to do a whole lot o' things you ain't goin' to like! Yessir, that's what he says to *me!*"

"He better catch me first, I guess, before he talks so much."

"Well," resumed the barber, "that ain't sayin' what you'd do if a young lady ever walked up and called you a little gentleman. *I* want to hear what you'd do to her. I guess I know, though—come to think of it."

"What?" demanded Penrod.

"You'd sick that pore ole dog of yours on her cat if she had one, I expect," guessed the barber derisively.

"No, I would not!"

"Well, what *would* you do?"

"I'd do enough. Don't worry about that!"

"Well, suppose it was a boy, then: what'd you do if a boy came up to you and says, 'Hello, little gentleman'?"

"He'd be lucky," said Penrod, with a sinister frown, "if he got home alive."

"Suppose it was a boy twice your size?"

"Just let him try," said Penrod ominously. "You just let him try. He'd never see daylight again; that's all!"

The barber dug ten active fingers into the helpless scalp before him and did his best to displace it, while the anguished Penrod, becoming instantly a seething crucible of emotion, misdirected his natural resentment into maddened brooding upon what he would do to a boy "twice his size" who should dare to call him "little gentleman." The barber shook him as his father had never shaken him; the barber buffeted him, rocked him frantically to and fro; the barber seemed to be trying to wring his neck; and Penrod saw himself in staggering zigzag pictures, destroying large, screaming, fragmentary boys who had insulted him.

The torture stopped suddenly; and clenched, weeping eyes began to see again, while the barber applied cooling lotions which made Penrod smell like a housemaid's ideal.

"Now what," asked the barber, combing the reeking locks gently, "what would it make you so mad fer, to have somebody call you a little gentleman? It's a kind of compliment, as it were, you might say. What would you want to hit anybody fer *that* fer?"

To the mind of Penrod, this question was without meaning or reasonableness. It was within neither his power nor his desire to analyze the process by which the phrase had become offensive to him, and was now rapidly assuming the proportions of an outrage. He knew only that his gorge rose at the thought of it.

"You just let 'em try it!" he said threateningly, as he slid down from the chair. And as he went out of the door, after further conversation on the same subject, he called back those warning words once more: "Just let 'em try it! Just once—that's all *I* ask 'em to. They'll find out what they *get!*"

The barber chuckled. Then a fly lit on the barber's nose and he slapped at it, and the slap missed the fly but did not miss the nose. The barber was irritated. At this moment his birdlike eye gleamed a gleam as it fell upon customers approaching: the prettiest little girl in the world, leading by the hand her baby brother, Mitchy-Mitch, coming to have Mitchy-Mitch's hair clipped, against the heat.

It was a hot day and idle, with little to feed the mind—and the barber was a mischievous man with an irritated nose. He did his worst.

Meanwhile, the brooding Penrod pursued his homeward way; no great distance, but long enough for several one-sided conflicts with malign insulters made of thin air. "You better *not* call me that!" he muttered. "You just try it, and you'll get what other people got when *they* tried it. You better not ack fresh with *me!* Oh, you *will*, will you?" He delivered a vicious kick full upon the shins of an iron fence-post, which suffered little, though Penrod instantly regretted his indiscretion. "Oof!" he grunted, hopping; and went on after bestowing a look of awful hostility upon the fence-post. "I guess you'll know better next time," he said, in parting, to this antagonist. "You just let me catch you around here again and I'll—" His voice sank to inarticulate but ominous murmurings. He was in a dangerous mood.

Nearing home, however, his belligerent spirit was diverted to happier interests by the discovery that some workmen had left a caldron of tar in the cross-street, close by his father's stable. He tested it, but found it inedible. Also, as a substitute for professional chewing-gum it was unsatisfactory, being insufficiently boiled down and too thin, though of a pleasant, lukewarm temperature. But it had an excess of one quality—it was sticky. It was the stickiest tar Penrod had ever used for any purposes whatsoever, and nothing upon which he wiped his hands served to rid them of it; neither his polka-dotted shirt waist nor his knickerbockers; neither the fence, nor even Duke, who came unthinkingly wagging out to greet him, and retired wiser.

Nevertheless, tar is tar. Much can be done with it, no matter what its condition; so Penrod lingered by the caldron, though from a neighboring yard could be heard the voices of comrades, including that of Sam Williams. On the ground about the caldron were scattered chips and sticks and bits of wood to the number of a great multitude. Penrod mixed quantities of this refuse into the tar, and interested himself in seeing how much of it he could keep moving in slow swirls upon the ebon surface.

Other surprises were arranged for the absent workmen. The caldron was almost full, and the surface of the tar near the rim. Penrod endeavored to ascertain how many pebbles and brickbats, dropped in, would cause an overflow. Laboring heartily to this end, he had almost accomplished it, when he received the suggestion for an experiment on a much larger scale. Embedded at the corner of a grass-plot across the street was a whitewashed stone, the size of a small watermelon and serving no purpose whatever save the questionable one of decoration. It was easily pried up with a stick; though getting it to the caldron tested the full strength of the ardent laborer. Instructed to perform such a task, he would have sincerely maintained its impossibility; but now, as it was unbidden, and promised rather destructive results, he set about it with unconquerable energy, feeling certain that he would be rewarded with a mighty splash. Perspiring, grunting vehemently, his back aching and all muscles strained, he progressed in short stages until the big stone lay at the base of the caldron. He rested a moment, panting, then lifted the stone, and was bending his shoulders for the heave that would lift it over the rim, when a sweet, taunting voice, close behind him, startled him cruelly.

"How do you do, *little gentleman!*"

Penrod squawked, dropped the stone, and shouted, "Shut up, you dern fool!" purely from instinct, even before his about-face made him aware who had so spitefully addressed him.

It was Marjorie Jones. Always dainty, and prettily dressed, she was in speckless and starchy white today, and a refreshing picture she made, with the new-shorn and powerfully scented Mitchy-Mitch clinging to her hand. They had stolen up behind the toilet, and now stood laughing together in sweet merriment. Since the passing of Penrod's Rupe Collins period he had experienced some severe qualms at the recollection of his last meeting with Marjorie and his Apache behavior; in truth, his heart instantly became as wax at sight of her, and he would have offered her fair speech; but, alas! in Marjorie's wonderful eyes there shone a consciousness of new powers of his undoing, and she denied him opportunity.

"*Oh, oh!*" she cried, mocking his pained outcry. "What a way for a *little gentleman* to talk! Little gentlemen don't say wicked—"

"Marjorie!" Penrod, enraged and dismayed, felt himself stung beyond all endurance. Insult from her was bitterer to endure than from any other. "Don't you call me that again!"

"Why not, *little gentleman?*"

He stamped his foot. "You better stop!"

Marjorie sent into his furious face her lovely, spiteful laughter.

"Little gentleman, little gentleman, little gentleman!" she said deliberately. "How's the little gentleman this afternoon? Hello, little gentleman!"

Penrod, quite beside himself, danced eccentrically. "Dry up!" he howled. "Dry up, dry up, dry up, dry *up!*"

Mitchy-Mitch shouted with delight and applied a finger to the side of the caldron—a finger immediately snatched away and wiped upon a handkerchief by his fastidious sister.

" 'Ittle gellamun!" said Mitchy-Mitch.

"You better look out!" Penrod whirled upon this small offender with grim satisfaction. Here was at least something male that could without dishonor be held responsible. "You say that again, and I'll give you the worst—"

"You will *not!*" snapped Marjorie, instantly vitriolic. "He'll say just whatever he wants to, and he'll say it just as *much* as he wants to. Say it again, Mitchy-Mitch!"

" 'Ittle gellamun!" said Mitchy-Mitch promptly.

"*Ow-yah!*" Penrod's tone-production was becoming affected by his mental condition. "You say that again, and I'll—"

"Go on, Mitchy-Mitch," cried Marjorie. "He can't do a thing. He don't *dare!* Say it some more, Mitchy-Mitch—say it a whole lot!"

Mitchy-Mitch, his small, fat face shining with confidence in his immunity, complied.

" 'Ittle gellamun!" he squeaked malevolently. " 'Ittle gellamun! 'Ittle gellamun! 'Ittle gellamun!"

The desperate Penrod bent over the whitewashed rock, lifted it, and then—outdoing Porthos, John Ridd, and Ursus in one miraculous burst of strength—heaved it into the air.

Marjorie screamed.

But it was too late. The big stone descended into the precise midst of the caldron and Penrod got his mighty splash. It was far, far beyond his expectations.

Spontaneously there were grand and awful effects—volcanic spectacles of nightmare and eruption. A black sheet of eccentric shape rose out of the caldron and descended upon the three children, who had no time to evade it.

After it fell, Mitchy-Mitch, who stood nearest the caldron, was the thickest, though there was enough for all. Br'er Rabbit would have fled from any of them.

When Marjorie and Mitchy-Mitch got their breath, they used it vocally; and seldom have more penetrating sounds issued from human throats. Coincidentally, Marjorie, quite berserk, laid hands upon the largest stick within reach and fell upon Penrod with blind fury. He had the presence of mind to flee, and they went round and round the caldron, while Mitchy-Mitch feebly endeavored to follow—his appearance, in this pursuit, being pathetically like that of a bug fished out of an ink-well, alive but discouraged.

Attracted by the riot, Samuel Williams made his appearance, vaulting a fence, and was immediately followed by Maurice Levy and Georgie Bassett. They stared incredulously at the extraordinary spectacle before them.

"Little GEN-TIL-MUN!" shrieked Marjorie, with a wild stroke that landed full upon Penrod's tarry cap.

"*Oooch!*" bleated Penrod.

"It's Penrod!" shouted Sam Williams, recognizing him by the voice. For an instant he had been in some doubt.

"Penrod Schofield!" exclaimed Georgie Bassett. "What does this mean?" That was Georgie's style, and had helped to win him his title.

Marjorie leaned, panting, upon her stick. "I cu-called-uh-him-oh!" she sobbed—"I called him a lul-little-oh-gentleman! And oh-lul-look! —oh! lul-look at my du-dress! Lul-look at Mu-Mitchy—oh—!"

Unexpectedly, she smote again—with results—and then, seizing the indistinguishable hand of Mitchy-Mitch, she ran wailing homeward down the street.

" 'Little gentleman'?" said Georgie Bassett, with some evidences of disturbed complacency. "Why that's what they call *me!*"

"Yes, and you *are* one, too!" shouted the maddened Penrod. "But you better not let anybody call *me* that! I've stood enough around here for one day, and you can't run over *me,* Georgie Bassett. Just you put that in your gizzard and smoke it!"

"Anybody has a perfect right," said Georgie, with dignity, "to call a person a little gentleman. There's lots of names nobody ought to call, but this one's a *nice*—"

"You better look out!"

Unavenged bruises were distributed all over Penrod, both upon his body and upon his spirit. Driven by subtle forces, he had dipped his hands in catastrophe and disaster: it was not for a Georgie Bassett to beard him. Penrod was about to run amuck.

"I haven't called you a little gentleman, yet," said Georgie. "I only said it. Anybody's got a right to *say* it."

"Not around *me!* You just try it again and—"

"I shall say it," returned Georgie, "all I please. Anybody in this town has a right to *say* 'little gentleman'—"

Bellowing insanely, Penrod plunged his right hand into the caldron, rushed upon Georgie and made awful work of his hair and features.

Alas, it was but the beginning! Sam Williams and Maurice Levy screamed with delight, and, simultaneously infected, danced about the struggling pair, shouting frantically:

"Little gentleman! Little gentleman! Sick him, Georgie! Sick him, little gentleman! Little gentleman! Little gentleman!"

The infuriated outlaw turned upon them with blows and more tar, which gave Georgie Bassett his opportunity and later seriously impaired the purity of his fame. Feeling himself hopelessly tarred, he dipped both hands repeatedly into the caldron and applied his gatherings to Penrod. It was bringing coals to Newcastle, but it helped to assuage the just wrath of Georgie.

The four boys gave a fine imitation of the Laocoön group complicated by an extra figure—frantic splutterings and chokings, strange cries and stranger words issued from this tangle; hands dipped lavishly into the inexhaustible reservoir of tar, with more and more picturesque results. The caldron had been elevated upon bricks and was not perfectly balanced; and under a heavy impact of the struggling group it lurched and went partly over, pouring forth a Stygian tide which formed a deep pool in the gutter.

It was the fate of Master Roderick Bitts, that exclusive and immaculate person, to make his appearance upon the chaotic scene at this juncture. All in the cool of a white "sailor suit," he turned aside from the path of duty—which led straight to the house of a maiden aunt—and paused to hop with joy upon the sidewalk. A repeated epithet continuously half panted, half squawked, somewhere in the nest of gladiators, caught his ear, and he took it up excitedly, not knowing why.

"Little gentleman!" shouted Roderick, jumping up and down in childish glee. "Little gentleman! Little gentleman! Lit—"

A frightful figure tore itself free from the group, encircled this innocent bystander with a black arm, and hurled him headlong. Full length and flat on his face went Roderick into the Stygian pool. The frightful figure was Penrod. Instantly, the pack flung themselves upon him again, and, carrying them with him, he went over upon Roderick, who from that instant was as active a belligerent as any there.

Thus began the Great Tar Fight, the origin of which proved, afterward, so difficult for parents to trace, owing to the opposing accounts of the combatants. Marjorie said Penrod began it; Penrod said Mitchy-Mitch began it; Sam Williams said Georgie Bassett began it; Georgie and Maurice Levy said Penrod began it; Roderick Bitts, who had not recognized his first assailant, said Sam Williams began it.

Nobody thought of accusing the barber. But the barber did not begin it; it was the fly on the barber's nose that began it—though, of course, something else began the fly. Somehow, we never manage to hang the real offender.

The end came only with the arrival of Penrod's mother, who had been having a painful conversation by telephone with Mrs. Jones, the mother of Marjorie, and came forth to seek an errant son. It is a mystery how she was able to pick out her own, for by the time she got there his voice was too hoarse to be recognizable.

Mr. Schofield's version of things was that Penrod was insane. "He's a stark, raving lunatic!" declared the father, descending to the library from a before-dinner interview with the outlaw, that evening. "I'd send him to military school, but I don't believe they'd take him. Do you know *why* he says all that awfulness happened?"

"When Margaret and I were trying to scrub him," responded Mrs. Schofield wearily, "he said 'everybody' had been calling him names."

" 'Names!' " snorted her husband. " 'Little gentleman!' *That's* the vile epithet they called him! And because of it he wrecks the peace of six homes!"

"Sh! Yes; he told us about it," said Mrs. Schofield, moaning. "He told us several hundred times, I should guess, though I didn't count. He's got it fixed in his head, and we couldn't get it out. All we could do was to put him in the closet. He'd have gone out again after those boys if we hadn't. I don't know *what* to make of him!"

"He's a mystery to *me!*" said her husband. "And he refuses to explain why he objects to being called 'little gentleman.' Says he'd do the same thing—and worse—if anybody dared to call him that again. He said if the President of the United States called him that he'd try to whip him. How long did you have him locked up in the closet?"

"Sh!" said Mrs. Schofield warningly. "About two hours; but I don't think it softened his spirit at all, because when I took him to the barber's to get his hair clipped again, on account of the tar in it Sammy Williams and Maurice Levy were there for the same reason, and they just *whispered* 'little gentleman,' so low you could hardly hear them —and Penrod began fighting with them right before me, and it was really all the barber and I could do to drag him away from them. The barber was very kind about it, but Penrod—"

"I tell you he's a lunatic!" Mr. Schofield would have said the same thing of a Frenchman infuriated by the epithet "camel." The philosophy of insult needs expounding.

"Sh!" said Mrs. Schofield. "It does seem a kind of frenzy."

"Why on earth should any sane person mind being called—"

"Sh!" said Mrs. Schofield. "It's beyond *me!*"

"What are you *sh*-ing me for?" demanded Mr. Schofield explosively.

"*Sh!*" said Mrs. Schofield. "It's Mr. Kinosling, the new rector of St. Joseph's."

"Where?"

"*Sh!* On the front porch with Margaret; he's going to stay for dinner. I do hope—"

"Bachelor, isn't he?"

"Yes."

"*Our* old minister was speaking of him the other day," said Mr. Schofield, "and he didn't seem so terribly impressed."

"*Sh!* Yes; about thirty, and of course *so* superior to most of Margaret's friends—boys home from college. She thinks she likes young Robert Williams, I know—but he laughs so much! Of course there isn't any comparison. Mr. Kinosling talks so intellectually; it's a good thing for Margaret to hear that kind of thing, for a change—and, of course, he's very spiritual. He seems very much interested in her." She paused to muse. "I think Margaret likes him; he's so different, too. It's the third time he's dropped in this week, and I—"

"Well," said Mr. Schofield grimly, "if you and Margaret want him to come again, you'd better not let him see Penrod."

"But he's asked to see him; he seems interested in meeting all the family. And Penrod nearly always behaves fairly well at table." She paused, and then put to her husband a question referring to his interview with Penrod upstairs. "Did you—did you—do it?"

"No," he answered gloomily. "No, I didn't, but—" He was interrupted by a violent crash of china and metal in the kitchen, a shriek from Della, and the outrageous voice of Penrod. The well-informed Della, ill-inspired to set up for a wit, had ventured to address the scion of the house roguishly as "little gentleman," and Penrod, by means of the rapid elevation of his right foot, had removed from her supporting hands a laden tray. Both parents started for the kitchen, Mr. Schofield completing his interrupted sentence on the way.

"But I will, now!"

The rite thus promised was hastily but accurately performed in that apartment most distant from the front porch; and, twenty minutes later, Penrod descended to dinner. The Rev. Mr. Kinosling had asked for the pleasure of meeting him, and it had been decided that the only course possible was to cover up the scandal for the present, and to offer an undisturbed and smiling family surface to the gaze of the visitor.

Scorched but not bowed, the smoldering Penrod was led forward for the social formulae simultaneously with the somewhat bleak departure of Robert Williams, who took his guitar with him, this time, and went in forlorn unconsciousness of the powerful forces already set in secret motion to be his allies.

The punishment just undergone had but made the haughty and unyielding soul of Penrod more stalwart in revolt; he was unconquered. Every time the one intolerable insult had been offered him, his resentment had become the hotter, his vengeance the more instant and furious. And, still burning with outrage, but upheld by the conviction of right, he was determined to continue to the last drop of his blood the defense of his honor, whenever it should be assailed, no matter how mighty or august the powers that attacked it. In all ways, he was a very sore boy.

During the brief ceremony of presentation, his usually inscrutable countenance wore an expression interpreted by his father as one of insane obstinacy, while Mrs. Schofield found it an incentive to inward prayer. The fine graciousness of Mr. Kinosling, however, was unimpaired by the glare of virulent suspicion given him by this little brother: Mr. Kinosling mistook it for a natural curiosity concerning one who might possibly become, in time, a member of the family. He patted Penrod upon the head, which was, for many reasons, in no condition to be patted with any pleasure to the patter. Penrod felt himself in the presence of a new enemy.

"How do you do, my little lad," said Mr. Kinosling. "I trust we shall become fast friends."

To the ear of his little lad, it seemed he said, "A trost we shall bickhome fawst frainds." Mr. Kinosling's pronunciation was, in fact, slightly precious; and the little lad, simply mistaking it for some cryptic form of mockery of himself, assumed a manner and expression which argued so ill for the proposed friendship that Mrs. Schofield hastily interposed the suggestion of dinner, and the small procession went in to the dining-room.

"It has been a delicious day," said Mr. Kinosling, presently; "warm but balmy." With a benevolent smile he addressed Penrod, who sat opposite him. "I suppose, little gentleman, you have been indulging in the usual outdoor sports of vacation?"

Penrod laid down his fork and glared, open-mouthed at Mr. Kinosling.

"You'll have another slice of breast of the chicken?" Mr. Schofield inquired, loudly and quickly.

"A lovely day!" exclaimed Margaret, with equal promptitude and emphasis. "Lovely, oh, lovely! Lovely!"

"Beautiful, beautiful, beautiful!" said Mrs. Schofield, and after a glance at Penrod which confirmed her impression that he intended to say something, she continued, "Yes, beautiful, beautiful, beautiful, beautiful, beautiful, beautiful!"

Penrod closed his mouth and sank back in his chair—and his relatives took breath.

Mr. Kinosling looked pleased. This responsive family, with its ready enthusiasm, made the kind of audience he liked. He passed a delicate white hand gracefully over his tall, pale forehead, and smiled indulgently.

"Youth relaxes in summer," he said. "Boyhood is the age of relaxation; one is playful, light, free, unfettered. One runs and leaps and enjoys one's self with one's companions. It is good for the little lads to play with their friends; they jostle, push, and wrestle, and simulate little, happy struggles with one another in harmless conflict. The young muscles are toughening. It is good. Boyish chivalry develops, enlarges, expands. The young learn quickly, intuitively, spontaneously. They perceive the obligations of *noblesse oblige*. They begin to comprehend the necessity of caste and its requirements. They learn what birth means—ah,—that is, they learn what it means to be well born. They learn courtesy in their games; they learn politeness, consideration for one another in their pastimes, amusements, lighter occupations. I make it my pleasure to join them often, for I sympathize with them in all their wholesome joys as well as in their little bothers and perplexities. I understand them, you see; and let me tell you it is no easy matter to understand the little lads and lassies." He sent to each listener his beaming glance, and, permitting it to come to rest upon Penrod, inquired:

"And what do you say to that, little gentleman?"

Mr. Schofield uttered a stentorian cough. "More? You'd better have some more chicken! More! Do!"

"More chicken!" urged Margaret simultaneously. "Do please! Please! More! Do! More!"

"Beautiful, beautiful," began Mrs. Schofield. "Beautiful, beautiful, beautiful, beautiful—"

It is not known in what light Mr. Kinosling viewed the expression of Penrod's face. Perhaps he mistook it for awe; perhaps he received no impression at all of its extraordinary quality. He was a rather self-engrossed young man, just then engaged in a double occupation, for he not only talked, but supplied from his own consciousness a critical though favorable auditor as well, which of course kept him quite busy. Besides, it is oftener than is suspected the case that extremely peculiar expressions upon the countenances of boys are entirely overlooked, and suggest nothing to the minds of people staring straight at them. Certainly Penrod's expression—which, to the perception of his family, was perfectly horrible—caused not the faintest perturbation in the breast of Mr. Kinosling.

Mr. Kinosling waived the chicken, and continued to talk. "Yes, I think I may claim to understand boys," he said, smiling thoughtfully. "One has been a boy one's self. Ah, it is not all playtime! I hope our young scholar here does not overwork himself at his Latin, at his classics, as I did, so that at the age of eight years I was compelled to wear glasses. He must be careful not to strain the little eyes at his scholar's tasks, not to let the little shoulders grow round over his scholar's desk. Youth is golden; we should keep it golden, bright, glistening. Youth should frolic, should be sprightly; it should play its cricket, its tennis, its handball. It should run and leap; it should laugh, should ring madrigals and glees, carol with the lark, ring out in chanties, folk songs, ballads, roundelays—"

He talked on. At any instant Mr. Schofield held himself ready to cough vehemently and shout, "More chicken," to drown out Penrod in case the fatal words again fell from those eloquent lips; and Mrs. Schofield and Margaret kept themselves prepared at all times to assist him. So passed a threatening meal, which Mrs. Schofield hurried, by every means with decency, to its conclusion. She felt that somehow they would all be safer out in the dark of the front porch, and led the way thither as soon as possible.

"No cigar, I thank you." Mr. Kinosling, establishing himself in a wicker chair beside Margaret, waved away her father's proffer. "I do not smoke. I have never tasted tobacco in any form." Mrs. Schofield was confirmed in her opinion that this would be an ideal son-in-law. Mr. Schofield was not so sure.

"No," said Mr. Kinosling. "No tobacco for me. No cigar, no pipe, no cigarette, no cheroot. For me, a book—a volume of poems, perhaps.

471

Verses, rhymes, lines metrical and cadenced—those are my dissipation. Tennyson by preference: 'Maud,' or 'Idylls of the King'—poetry of the sound Victorian days; there is none later. Or Longfellow will rest me in a tired hour. Yes; for me, a book, a volume in the hand, held lightly between the fingers."

Mr. Kinosling looked pleasantly at his fingers as he spoke, waving his hand in a curving gesture which brought it into the light of a window faintly illumined from the interior of the house. Then he passed those graceful fingers over his hair, and turned toward Penrod, who was perched upon the railing in a dark corner.

"The evening is touched with a slight coolness," said Mr. Kinosling. "Perhaps I may request the little gentleman—"

"B'gr-r-*ruff!*" coughed Mr. Schofield. "You'd better change your mind about a cigar."

"No, I thank you. I was about to request the lit—"

"*Do* try one," Margaret urged. "I'm sure papa's are nice ones. Do try—"

"No, I thank you. I remarked a slight coolness in the air, and my hat is in the hallway. I was about to request—"

"I'll get it for you," said Penrod suddenly.

"If you will be so good," said Mr. Kinosling. "It is a black bowler hat, little gentleman, and placed upon a table in the hall."

"I know where it is." Penrod entered the door, and a feeling of relief, mutually experienced, carried from one to another of his three relatives their interchanged congratulations that he had recovered his sanity.

" 'The day is done, and the darkness,' " began Mr. Kinosling—and recited that poem entire. He followed it with "The Children's Hour," and after a pause, at the close, to allow his listeners time for a little reflection upon his rendition, he passed his hand over his head, and called, in the direction of the doorway:

"I believe I will take my hat now, little gentleman."

"Here it is," said Penrod, unexpectedly climbing over the porch railing, in the other direction. His mother and father and Margaret had supposed him to be standing in the hallway out of deference, and because he thought it tactful not to interrupt the recitations. All of them remembered, later, that this supposed thoughtfulness on his part struck them as unnatural.

"Very good, little gentleman!" said Mr. Kinosling, and being some-

472

what chilled, placed the hat firmly upon his head, pulling it down as far as it would go. It had a pleasant warmth, which he noticed at once. The next instant, he noticed something else, a peculiar sensation of the scalp—a sensation which he was quite unable to define. He lifted his hand to take the hat off, and entered upon a strange experience: his hat seemed to have decided to remain where it was.

"Do you like Tennyson as much as Longfellow, Mr. Kinosling?" inquired Margaret.

"I—ah—I cannot say," he returned absently. "I—ah—each has his own—ugh! flavor and savor, each his—ah—ah—"

Struck by a strangeness in his tone, she peered at him curiously through the dusk. His outlines were indistinct, but she made out that his arms were uplifted in a singular gesture. He seemed to be wrenching at his head.

"Is—is anything the matter?" she asked anxiously. "Mr. Kinosling, are you ill?"

"Not at—ugh!—all," he replied in the same odd tone. "I—ah—I believe—*ugh!*"

He dropped his hands from his hat, and rose. His manner was slightly agitated. "I fear I may have taken a trifling—ah—cold. I should—ah—perhaps be—ah—better at home. I will—ah—say good night."

At the steps, he instinctively lifted his hand to remove his hat, but did not do so, and, saying "Good night," again in a frigid voice, departed with visible stiffness from that house, to return no more.

"Well, of all—!" cried Mrs. Schofield, astounded. "What was the matter? He just went—like that!" She made a flurried gesture. "In heaven's name, Margaret, what *did* you say to him?"

"I!" exclaimed Margaret indignantly. "Nothing! He just *went!*"

"Why, he didn't even take off his hat when he said good night!" said Mrs. Schofield.

Margaret, who had crossed to the doorway, caught the ghost of a whisper behind her, where stood Penrod.

"You bet he didn't!"

He knew not that he was overheard.

A frightful suspicion flashed through Margaret's mind—a suspicion that Mr. Kinosling's hat would have to be either boiled off or shaved off. With growing horror she recalled Penrod's long absence when he went to bring the hat.

"Penrod," she cried, "let me see your hands!"

She had toiled at those hands herself late that afternoon, nearly scalding her own, but at last achieving a lily purity.

"Let me see your hands!"

She seized them.

Again they were tarred!

My Heart Is Like a Singing Bird

DOROTHY THOMAS

"My heart is like a singing bird

. . . .

Because my love is come to me."

Word of mouth publicity has won a growing audience for Dorothy Thomas' love stories. We take particular pleasure in presenting this one.

LOUISE WOKE TO BIRD SONG and to happiness. The bird song mingled rightly, assuringly, with the experimental crowing of young roosters, the bawling of calves, and her brothers' whistling, and was like that of the seven June mornings she had wakened to and waited through, only better, more joyous, and the happiness—there were words for the happiness, a woman's words. Louise had found them in a book of poems, had learned them by heart and said them over and over, sung them, rather, on the half-mile walk to the little country school she taught, the mornings of the last long week of May, and meadow larks had answered from field and fence: "Louise, Louise, Bill's coming. It's true! It's true!" It was for this morning, now come, the poem had been learned and saved. It was for just such a morning in a woman's life it had been sung in the first place, Louise was sure. It began:

My heart is like a singing bird

and ended:

DOROTHY THOMAS

Because the birthday of my life
Is come, my love is come to me.

Beside her pillow, half under the edge of it—she would put up a sleep-limp hand in a moment to it—was the blue cardboard box that held Bill's letters, his eighteen letters. They were brief, matter-of-fact, one-page letters. They began, every one of them, "Dear Louise," and ended, "So long, Bill." Every one was written on a Sunday in answer to hers of the Sunday before. The last one, the one she meant to read in a moment, though she knew it word for word, that had to do with the business of getting ready for final exams, a stock-judging contest and the modest records of tennis triumphs, closed with "Be home the second week in June. I'll be over. So long, Bill." That was all in reality, in plain fact, but there was a world of which the world of plain fact was only the beginning; a world that came into its own with the second week in June; with cherry time, haying time and Bill's homecoming.

Only the morning before, out in the side yard to see whether the cherries were really going to be ripe enough for Sunday pies, she had stood, the sun warm on her hair, watching the orphaned black lamb that the boys had brought to the house yard to bottle-feed, leaping and whirling, and had run to him and caught him up and said to him: "You think this is June? It's nice, all right, but you wait, you wait! This is nothing to what it's to be—nothing, nothing!" And she was sure in her heart that for Bill, too, the world waited, promised in every leaf shadow across a professor's desk in classrooms where he sat and listened. He had wanted, she believed, for some good reason of his own, to wait; to save their world whole, without one word said, outright, for it, until school was done for him; until he could come home to her. That was Bill, and she loved him.

She had meant to read the last letter again before she got up, but she heard her mother's step on the stair and slid the box farther under her pillow. It was from shyness only that she hid it. Her folks liked Bill, she knew; liked him and his folks. There was pride for her in her being Bill's girl in her brothers' teasing, and a kindly satisfaction in the way her father would hand her one of Bill's letters, having come in the mail while she was at school. Several mornings that spring, she had slept late and been hurried getting ready, and so forgotten to put the blue box away, only to think of it after she was well on her way or at school, and to smile, safe in knowing that her mother would put it away for her in the left-hand top dresser drawer, where its place was.

"Well," her mother said fondly, " 'bout time you got up, isn't it, sleepyhead? Your father says he's going to call you when he calls the boys, after this. He says you've had vacation enough. What we got a girl for, anyhow?"

"I wondered how long I was going to be babied," Louise said. "It has been good not to have to get up early."

"I guess he babies you because it looks like we might not have you around much longer," her mother said, and sat down on the bed beside her.

"What?" Louise asked, startled. Never before had her mother spoken so openly about the time they all expected to see come; when Bill would take her away from them. Now her mother laughed and gave her a little spank. "Well, that's the way the land lies, isn't it? You look like you did when you were little; open those brown eyes so wide, all innocence! You get your quiet ways from father's folks. They were all like that. I suppose you'd have us think a boy like Bill would go with a girl all summer, write her all winter, and neither of you have anything serious in mind? What you blushing for?"

"We didn't go together all summer," Louise said. "He didn't ask to go with me until August and—"

"Well, he certainly didn't let any grass grow under his feet, once he started coming here. He was over about every night, seemed to me."

"No, mamma; just nine nights and two Sunday afternoons," Louise said.

"Well, he's a good boy, and your father and I are both glad to see you choosing a boy from a family we know, close neighbors, like the Atwells. The only thing is, I hope they fix it for Bill to farm their place and that they don't settle him way off somewhere, like the other boys. Mrs. Atwell said, the other Sunday, Jack and Mamie hadn't been home but twice since Christmas. Papa says—"

"Mamma," Louise cried, "please! It scares me to have you and Papa talking it over like that. You don't understand—"

"Now, dear, your father's not hasty. What do you suppose Frank Atwell wants to talk to him about, if not about where Bill's to be, to settle and farm?"

"Mr. Atwell?" Louise exclaimed, and sat up in bed and grasped her mother's wrist with both hands. "Mamma, has Mr. Atwell been over here? Is—is Bill really home? Did he come over with him? Mamma, what's happened?"

"Nothing yet. He just called and asked if Papa was here, and I told him he hadn't got to the field yet, and he said I was not to call him in; that he'd be over directly; that he wanted to see him."

"He didn't say what about? He didn't say anything about Bill—he didn't say he was home?"

"No, he didn't, but he's home all right."

"Did he call?"

"No, but he's home; he's not up yet. His mother was calling his Aunt Mina. She said he got home last night; drove home with a friend from school."

"Late?"

"I guess so. I expect he got in too late to call you, and sat up late, visiting with his folks."

Louise leaned back against the pillow and clasped her hands behind her head, lost in the wonder of Bill's being home for sure, asleep still in his old room upstairs in his father's house, not quite two miles away.

"I'll get up," Louise said, and made her words honest with one quick movement.

"I guess you better, missie," her mother said. "Bill'll come, if you don't look out, and catch you not up yet, and he'll think he'll have to get his own breakfasts." Her mother left, turning in the doorway to smile fondly on her daughter as she stood stretching lazily in the bright sun from the east window.

It was possible, of course, that Bill might come early. Thinking on that, Louise put on her blue-and-white gingham with the fluted organdy collar that had taken so long a time in the ironing. It was a plain dress but for the collar; plain enough so that her brothers would not be likely to say "H'm, what you all dolled up for, sis? Somebody coming?" but pretty, quite pretty. Gravely, in her eagerness to look her loveliest and yet not look too "fixed up," she brushed her hair to careless waviness before the dresser mirror and tied a narrow blue ribbon around her head.

It did frighten her, trouble her, to have her mother speak out so about Bill and about the future. It was one thing to treasure in her heart, in quiet happiness, every word Bill had ever said, every word he had written, and to dream of his coming, and quite another to have her mother speaking of him and of her, much as she might speak of Ruth and Art, her married sister and her husband. Love itself did not belong to the world of everyday reality, and by rights should not, until Bill had come home; until he had come over to see her and had told her he loved her—told her in words. She must ask her mother not to talk so.

There was only her mother in the kitchen when she came down, and she was busy with the breakfast dishes. "Oh, Mamma," Louise said, "why didn't you leave them for me? I'll finish them."

"No, there's no sense in Bill coming and finding you with your hands in the dishwater in a hot kitchen. It's going to be a warm day, don't you think? Your father's not gone to the field. When I went out and told him Atwell was coming over, he said he'd wait. There's coffee, though I guess it's pretty strong by now, and there's pancake batter on the warming oven in the crock. The boys got away with all the strawberries you stemmed last night, but there's more in the basket here. I mean to get at them, soon as I get the dishes done, and, if I can, get them put up before dinner. Help yourself."

Louise helped herself to the strawberries, idly dipping berries by their stems into a little mound of sugar in her saucer, sipping her coffee between berries.

"Was that our ring I heard while I was dressing?" she asked, trying to make her voice sound casual and not too eager.

"Yes, it was. It was Ruth. She called and said she'd be over. She's made the baby rompers. What do you think of that! Made him a good pink pair and two pair to creep in, out of the backs of Art's old work shirts. Won't he be cute? She's coming over, she said, this morning, just as soon as she can put up a lunch for Art and get her work done up. My, I don't see how she drives, with that baby. He's so wiggly now, and grabby. But she straps him in with that harness outfit Art fixed, and drives right along."

"She didn't say anything about—anybody?"

"Yes. She did. She said she heard he was home. She said Mrs. Atwell was calling her other sister, over that way, when she was trying to get the line to call us. She said she said he drove home with a friend of his, a school friend, and his sister."

"His sister?"

"Yes, this friend's sister."

"Did she say— Are they staying to visit over at Atwells', or are they going on?"

"She didn't say, and I didn't ask. Now, Louise, you dust in the front room and dining room, and keep cool. You look awfully nice. Friends are as likely to have sisters as not. You—"

"Of course," Louise said. "Bill has lots of friends. He plays tennis with girls, Home Ecs. girls. Did Ruth say anything else?"

"Not that I remember. . . . Oh, yes, she said Bill's mother said he was changed."

"Changed? How?"

"She didn't say. A boy's bound to change some, in a school year. It would be funny if he didn't. . . . What's wrong with you, Louise? You're not getting nerves, are you? You seem so—so kind of jumpy this morning. You've worked too hard, that's what. Your father said he wished he hadn't let you teach this year, not with so many enrolled in this district, and those Bowler boys in school. Don't you ever worry about any old boy's sister! If Bill was the kind to have his head turned, he'd have had it turned months ago, and wouldn't have been like he's been, written like he has, steady."

"I'm not worried, Mamma," Louise said, "and, Mamma, I wish you wouldn't talk about it."

"Well, dear, I'm not talking about it. You know neither your father or I are any hand to talk about things like that, and you know we've all respected how you feel about it, all of us. You girls are as different as you can be. Why, Ruth talked everything over with me, right from the start, right from the time Art began coming here, and here Papa and I don't even know how long you and Bill have been engaged. I can understand it, because you're just like my father's people. It's all right. You have to do things your own way, and I understand. But here, when we've tiptoed around a whole year, nearly, about this, surely there's no harm in speaking of it, now Bill's home. You don't look like you feel well, Louise. If you don't feel like it, don't dust. I'll do it."

"I feel fine," Louise said, and got the dust mop and dustcloth from their place on the basement landing and went into the dining room.

"Better set the plants up on the dining table," her mother called after her. "You know what the baby did last time. Ruth was scared eating that dirt would make him awfully sick, but I told her I thought it'd not hurt him a bit, and it didn't. You know I think he really likes the plants, the color; he's so noticing. Is that someone coming? Is it Frank Atwell or Ruth?"

"It's Mr. Atwell," Louise said, and drew back from the now-bare windows to watch the Atwell car, empty of Atwells except for the grey-haired head of the house, come up the slope from the highway, pass the twin cottonwoods by the house-yard gate and turn toward the stables.

"See," her mother said, coming into the dining room, with the pancake griddle which she was washing in her hand, to see for herself, "a man busy as Frank Atwell doesn't come over the middle of the morning to talk about the weather. And I bet you've got a better notion of what he's come over to talk to your father about, young lady, than your father or I have. I bet Bill's drawn up and sent you the plans of his house. Be sure of one thing, dear. No, two! Be sure, while it's still on paper, that you're to have good big closets, and enough of them, and that there's east sun in the kitchen and low enough windows. A man'll stick the windows up under the ceiling where you'll get no earthly good of them, every time, if you don't watch him."

"Please, Mamma!" Louise whispered, raising both hands in a hushing gesture.

"There they are, sitting out there by the barn door," her mother said. "Your father's got him a stick to whittle. Isn't that like him?"

Louise, dusting the living room, and too far from the kitchen for her mother to talk to her, felt a little easier. She wished Bill would come soon; come before her sister Ruth came with her newly rompered baby. It would be fine if he would come almost at once—just as soon as she had finished dusting the piano—come to the front door instead of to the kitchen door; come and meet her, with the two of them alone in the shady, vine-covered front porch. Now that his coming was so near, she was afraid, with a heart-pressing, happy fear.

How would he greet her? What would his first words be? Would he be wearing the blue-checked shirt she liked best? Maybe he'd have on his white linen suit. His mother had told her, a couple of Sundays ago, while the two families stood visiting after church, that Bill had bought himself a new white linen suit. Ruth had told her mother that his mother said he had changed. "School changes a boy," her mother had said, with seeming satisfaction. She had not thought about Bill changing. He had not changed in his letters. If he changed while she stayed the same, would he be changed toward her?

Dusting the piano, she could see her reflection in the shining wood. Would he find her fair? How her breath had caught when her mother told her he had driven home from school with a friend and his sister! Was she one of the girls he played tennis with, she wondered. Why was it, now, now that he was home again, learning that a girl was there—a sister of a friend—could make her feel faint with anxiety? Why now, when the school-year long she had only to reread Bill's letters, to remember their parting, to feel secure? In parting, he had kissed her and said, "We'll write; and I'll see you Christmas, Louise." But he had not come home Christmas. His family had been quarantined with chicken pox. His eldest brother's children had got it while with their grandparents and he had Christmased with an aunt and uncle in a town nearer the university, and had a very dull time. It was wrong of her, and silly, too, to think of other girls now. This was the day of Bill's coming. He was home. The birds her mother was shooing with the broom from their cherry trees might be singing in the Atwell trees any minute now.

Louise whisked the dustcloth from one end of the keyboard to the other, and standing, her head thrown back, played a chord that said, for all the house to hear:

The birthday of my life is come!

Her mother came around to the front porch and stopped to shoo some pigeons from the back of the porch swing.

"I declare," she said to her daughter, through the open window, "I don't know what your father keeps them for. He likes the sound of them, he says. Go on and play something, dear. I hope you keep up your music. I've not said anything to your father about it yet, but I don't see why you can't have the piano. It was bought for you girls, and you know Ruth'll never do anything more with her music. She never did care much about it, anyway. And I know how proud Bill is you can play as well as you can. We could put Papa's roll-top desk where the piano is. He's always wanted it back in the living room. Goodness knows why. . . . Here's Ruth now!"

Louise's mother leaned the broom against a porch pillar and went to the yard gate to meet her elder daughter and take her one and only grandchild to her heart.

"Well, did he go to sleep?" she cried. "Did he go to sleep strapped in this mean old harness? Louise, come see, come see him in rompers.

Fix a place for him, won't you? There! Grandma's boy can go right back to sleep again. Fix the lounge in the living room for him. Fold up that scratchy old shawl; it'd be too hot for him. Fetch that quilt from the foot of my bed, Louise, that blue-and-white one. It's folded on the foot of my bed."

Louise ran for the quilt and Ruth put down the basket of garden stuff she had brought. "Maybe you've got more radishes and onions than you can use, Mamma," she said, "but Art pulled these and we can't begin to use them all, so I brought them over."

"That's nice," her mother said. "There! Grandma'll take off his little shoes. We've got them, Ruth, but I've not been up to the garden in three or four days. I've told the boys to weed up there, and I hope they have. 'Deed we can use them. I've just been snowed under with work. I thought I'd have more time, with Louise home and free to help, but I declare— Isn't he sweet in that pink! And hasn't he grown though?"

"Grown! I should say he has," his mother agreed happily. "And, Mamma, he's trying to walk! Art's folks were over Sunday and had Art's grandmother along, and she took on so about how fast he creeps. Art and his dad were coaxing baby to walk and Art had a good hold of him, of course, and you know what his grandma said to me? She said, 'Girl, you let that boy walk at his age and you'll have him so bowlegged you won't be able to get pants on him!'"

"Nonsense!" her mother laughed. "You walked at nine months, or was it Jim? And there's no bowlegs in this family. Come on out in the kitchen. I've those strawberries I'd like to get put up before time to get dinner, if I can. Louise, you don't need to help. It's too warm out there."

"I'll help," Louise said.

"What's the matter, Louise," asked her sister; "don't you feel well?"

"I feel fine," Louise replied.

"She got a little run down," her mother said, "that last month of school. It's no wonder; those Bowler kids in school, and one of them to get through the eight-grade examinations. Well, she did it all right. All three of her eight-graders passed with good grades. How she ever drilled that boy up to pass the spelling examination, I can't see."

"Don't I know!" exclaimed Ruth, turning to have her mother tie her apron for her. "But I think one year of teaching is enough. It was enough for me. Wasn't that the Atwell car I saw out by the barn?

No need to ask if it's Bill. If it was, he'd be up here at the house."

"It's his father," her mother said, "and Louise is feathering up and shushing me all over the place for saying I bet he's come over to talk about where Bill's to live. They'll build; they'll just about have to. I don't know where they'd expect them to live, if they don't."

"Oh, say," Ruth interrupted, "did you hear about Agnes Marshall?"

"No," her mother answered; "what's happened to Agnes? I didn't know she'd got home. I was talking to her mother last Sunday and she said they didn't expect her for another week yet. Her school lets out later than Bill's does."

"Well, she's got home. She's married!"

"Why, the idea! I thought her folks were going to give her a church wedding. Were they married down there at school?"

"She didn't marry Bryan; she married somebody else!"

"She didn't! Well!"

"No, she married somebody she met down there at school. Her folks didn't know a thing about it, not until she wired yesterday."

"Well, I declare! Louise, what do you think of that? How'd Bryan take it?"

"I don't know. Art's mother talked with Agnes' mother last night and then she called me. Her folks hadn't known a thing; Bryan's either. Art's mother said to me, 'That's all right. Bryan can do better, and not have to go out of the neighborhood!' She'll say what she thinks, you know. I never did think they were suited, really, did you, Mamma?"

"They looked nice together," Louise said.

"Well, that's how it is; one here and another there," their mother said. "I'm glad Bill wasn't taking but the two-year Ag course and that he'd had one year out of the way before he started going with you, Louise. It's not a good idea to be so long apart, and so far."

"Yes," Ruth agreed. "I'm glad Art was never away. Except, it would have been nice to have had some letters from him. You know, Mamma, I've not had one single letter from Art?"

"Bill's mother said this morning, when she called her sister, that both the boys, Bill and this school friend, she didn't call him by name, were still asleep, but that the girl was up and out picking some daisies to put on the breakfast table. Town girl, I guess. She said Bill's driven half the way himself; he and the boy took turns, and they talked late, last night."

"Well, that's nice," her mother said. "Did she say— Louise, go in and have a look at the baby, will you? There's an old fly in there, I noticed when we put him down, bothering around. Here, take the swatter and see if you can get him."

Louise knew well that her mother wanted to get her out of the way, so that she could ask Ruth if Mrs. Atwell had said anything else about these friends of Bill's; about this girl who got up early to pick daisies for the breakfast table. The fly vanquished and the voices still low and guarded in the kitchen, she sat down in the chair by the lounge and fanned the baby gently with a folded newspaper.

The baby slept with his hands up either side of his head, his fists limply curled. His knees were tanned and dimpled. Louise bent and laid her lips lightly against one of them. Dear boy! Ruth was so happy, so settled, so right in her life, with her one year of teaching, her Art, her determination to make Art's people see she was a good manager, her sewing and canning, and her fine baby. There they were, her mother and sister, out in the kitchen now, plotting and planning just such a life, just such a secure happiness for her, with Bill.

Agnes Marshall? Why, she was to have married Bryan Haywood toward the end of June! She and Bryan had gone together the last two summers while Agnes was home from school. True, they had more than one quarrel the summer before, and it was said they had "quit for good," but Agnes and Bryan had written, while Agnes was away—that she knew. And they had been engaged; Agnes had Bryan's ring. "Not a good idea to be so long apart, and so far," her mother had said. What had she done! What had she done, to stake her whole happiness on those short and impersonal letters? Bill had been in school, like Agnes; been where he had met hundreds of pretty, attractive girls. He had written her about them; had said, "I played doubles this afternoon with a couple of Home Ecs. and Ed Fischer."

A couple of Home Ecs.! This sister of Bill's friend was likely one of them. Well, why didn't she stay in the house and help Mrs. Atwell get breakfast then, if she knew so much about cooking? Maybe there was a course in flower arrangement. Likely there was. Likely this girl was one Bill knew very well. Maybe, oh, maybe she was Bill's girl down at school! He'd never mentioned any girl, by name. Maybe he had brought this girl home, so his folks could meet her and see how pretty and how clever she was, with all she had learned in cooking and sewing classes. Maybe he had brought her home to show her the

DOROTHY THOMAS

place, to let her pick out a spot where she would like a house. Maybe
it was with her he had drawn the plans for a house, with plenty of
closets and low enough windows in the kitchen.

How could Bill do this to her? How could he write to her the winter
through, every other Sunday, as he had written; how could he look
at her as he had looked down at her in saying good-by, and other times,
too; how could he kiss her, in parting, as though she were the most
precious thing in life, and not love, not—? But maybe she was the
one in the wrong. What did she know about men and about love
anyway? Maybe men did look at girls like that, did kiss them like that,
and mean nothing at all. Other men, maybe, but not Bill, surely,
surely! His letters; they were not love letters. What was there real in
them, to build on? Only to a foolish, heart-willed girl could they mean
anything. What was true then? The world of facts—"cold facts" her
father always called them—was true, and not that other world of the
heart's making.

He was home. He had been home over twelve hours now, and he
had not called, had not come over. Breakfast was not a meal to be
lingered over. And he was lingering, with the girl and the daisies she
had picked.

Was he staying away because he didn't know what to say to her,
because he was astonished to come home and find how things stood for
him? Likely his folks talked them over, just as hers did. What would
he think of her? He would think she was a dishonest simpleton, that's
what he would think. He would not know that she had said nothing,
but had only kept still and let them think what they would. Likely
Bill didn't love her. He had only written to her; written good friendly
letters and remembered her kindly. Now, now his people and hers
and all their neighbors would think he had treated her as Agnes
Marshall had treated Bryan Haywood, and blame him and pity her.
Bryan would be all right. He would go back to Art's younger sister,
Fran. He had had a hard enough time making up his mind between
Fran and Agnes. He would be all right, better off, surely. Fran would
make a better farm wife than Agnes. But for her, Louise, there would
be no consolation, no comfort. Let her heart ache! It deserved to ache,
it had been so stupid. She would not let them go on thinking she
and Bill were sweethearts. She would go out in the kitchen, no matter
how hard it was now, and tell her mother and sister how it really

485

was, and then, then she would go right out to the barn, where her father and Mr. Atwell were talking, and tell them.

She got up, pushing her hair back, and the baby wakened, looked up at her with his round blue eyes and sleepily held up his arms to be taken. The feel of him, the utterly confiding way he nestled to her and drooped his warm head on her shoulder, gave her courage. She walked with him into the kitchen, where his mother and grandmother were still busy with the strawberries, still talking.

"Well," her mother cried, "did grandma's boy have a dood seep? Did him? Bless his heart! Grandma will fix him something. Grandma will fix him some nice strawberries."

"Oh, Mamma, do you think you should?" Ruth asked anxiously. "He's never eaten strawberries!"

"I'll crush them good. Crush them and put a little cream on them, and some sugar. They won't hurt him at all. He's nearly a year old. Grandma wouldn't do anything to hurt her boy, now, would she?" She leaned toward the baby and chortled lovingly.

"Well, I don't know," Ruth said. "Mamma, I feel so responsible! If I took him over here and gave him something to eat that made him sick, Art's mother and grandmother would never forgive me. Honestly, Mamma, I think they think I don't know how to take care of a baby! They make such a fuss when they see him. They're afraid I let him sit in the sun too long, they're afraid—"

"Well, he's our first grandchild just as much as he's theirs, and they don't care an iota more for him than we do, so there! If you think it might hurt him, I won't give it to him, Ruth, but I'm sure it wouldn't."

"I'm sure it wouldn't either, he's so well," Ruth said. "Go ahead, mamma, but just a little."

"Mamma," Louise said, "listen, I want to—I've got to tell you something!"

"There goes Mr. Atwell now, and here's Papa coming to the house," Louise's mother said, and with a dish of berries in her hand, she went to the screen door to open it for him. "Well," she said brightly, "having rather early morning callers, aren't you?"

"Nope, just one," he said. "Well, hello! How are you, scalawag! Come over to see your old granddad, did you? Well, well! Come to granddad! Golly, Ruth, just heft this boy! And good and hard too! No sissy, are you, scalawag? Want to go up? Want grandpa to toss you up?"

"Now, Papa," his wife said anxiously, "be careful how you toss him up. He's only a baby, even if he is in rompers; you might make him bite his tongue. If you hurt that child, Art's folks— Papa, what was Atwell over here about?"

"Nothing. Nothing much. Up d'go! Up d'go! Whee! See, he likes it! Knows his granddad wouldn't drop him, don't he? Hear him laugh?"

"Yes," his wife said, "he sounds just like Jim did when he was a baby, doesn't he? Did you hear me? What was Atwell over here about?"

"I told you, nothing much. He just wanted to know what I thought about Bill building on that rise there on our cornfield between our places."

"On our cornfield?"

"Yes, that's what he wanted to know about. He don't want the whole field, Mamma, he just wants two acres, there by the road. There's that row of cottonwoods there, along the road, and it really makes a better place for a house than any they got on their land, unless they built right up by their house, and he thinks the places would be better a little farther apart. He aims Bill to pretty well take over their place, I guess. Both the other boys have settled quite a piece off. He'd like Bill there, near, but not right on the doorstep. He thinks Bill wouldn't like that."

"But," his wife asked, "what about Bill? Why didn't he come over to see you about it himself, if that's the place he'd like to build? It's all right with me, Papa. I always did think that would be a good place for a house. But why—"

"Well, now, hold your horses, Mamma! He just wanted to look into this before he said anything to Bill about it. He said the boy wasn't up yet, when he came over. He said he wanted to know what I'd think about it too. He knew the boy'd want to build, all right. He's been counting on that. He said he remembered Bill saying, last fall, he thought that would be a good site for a house. What do you think about it, sister?" He had put the baby down and now he came and put an arm about his younger daughter and patted her shoulder. "I guess they, Bill or any of them, wouldn't put up a house without being pretty sure you liked the site. After all, you're the one's to live in it. What do you say about that place?"

"Papa, did Mr. Atwell say anything about me?" Louise asked.

"No, honey, not 'specially, but—"

"Did he mention me; did he say anything at all about me?"

"No, that's not his way, Louise, but that's understood. He'd leave it for Bill to talk to you about it. You know that."

"Of course," Louise's mother said with—Louise felt—not quite enough conviction in her voice. "Louise, he'll be over soon as those people are gone, you know that. A person can't jump up and run off and leave company, especially after they've brought him home. You're just nervous. I know—"

"Oh, Mamma, look!" Ruth cried. "Oh, Mamma, how many do you suppose he's eaten?"

The baby stood, braced against a chair, helping himself with both hands to unstemmed strawberries. The berries were all over his cheeks and some in his hair. His grandmother caught him up and thrust a searching forefinger into his mouth. "Spit it out, dear; 'pit it out for grandma!"

"Stems and all!" wailed Ruth. "Mamma, how many do you suppose he got down? Will they hurt him? Do you think they'll hurt him? Oh, darling, why did you eat them?"

His grandmother was able to extract only one berry stem from the baby's mouth. His grandfather took him, howling and kicking, and talked him into going up again. "Up? Want to go up?" he cried. "That's it, don't cry. Few old berries won't hurt you. What do all these women think you are, a sissy? At-a-boy—up he goes!"

"Papa, don't! You'll upset his stomach. Those berries!" Ruth cried.

"Well, if they come up, all the better. But they won't hurt him. Say, last time he was over here he pulled a pot off the plant shelf and ate fistfuls of dirt before you caught him, and it didn't hurt him a lick." He set the baby down again, heading him toward his mother. "Sister, how about it? I asked you what do you think of that knoll for a house site? Won't be a big place, I guess, but I think it'll be pretty nice. Atwell says Bill's had a course in building down at school. He mention that to you, sister?"

"Yes," Louise said, "he did. He made good grades in it, too, and the teacher—he's a real architect—picked a barn Bill planned, to put up to show them all. But, Papa, you mustn't think—"

"My goodness," her mother wailed, "Ruth, I thought you were looking after this baby! Here, lamb, let grandma get them. Here, 'pit it out. Stems! Both hands full—his mouth full of stems! Ruth, why'd you set that pan down on that chair? Well, he couldn't have swallowed many before I got him. Louise, take him, won't you? Hold him. Don't let him down."

Louise took the baby; now he squirmed in her arms and kicked to be let down for further ventures. "Papa," she began again. "Please! It's all a mistake. Bill's not going to build a house for me!"

"Now, Mamma, what'd I tell you?" her father asked sternly. "I told you Louise was getting run down, worn out. We shouldn't ever have let her teach; she's not husky like you, Ruth. She's not herself, talking like that."

"I know just how you feel," Ruth consoled. "Mamma, do you remember what a goose I was? I felt just like you do, Louise. The morning of the day I married Art, with all the folks downstairs, I think it was hearing his grandmother down there talking about the things Art would and wouldn't eat. I told Mamma I was scared to pieces, that I didn't want to get married, that I was afraid I didn't love Art! Think of that! It's because you've not seen him for so long. I know just how you feel. The minute he walks in the door, you'll see how—"

"There! That's our ring!" her mother cried triumphantly. "That'll be Bill now. I bet anything. Louise, you answer it, dear."

"All right," Louise said. "I will." She handed the still-squirming baby to her sister but her mother cried, "No, you answer it, Papa. Look at her! Child, you're white! You're in no shape to answer the phone and talk with Bill. What would he think? Go on, Papa. Now, you just get hold of yourself, dear." She was pushing her husband toward the door that led to the dining room and the telephone.

They all, even the baby, feeling the tenseness, quieted and listened. Louise's mother put an arm about her and whispered, "Now, you just brace up."

"Hello," her father shouted in his telephone voice. "Well, hello, Bill, how are you? . . . Your dad? He just left. Must be home, 'bout now. . . . Sure, thought he oughta be— Well, we'll be glad to see you. Good-by."

"There!" Louise's mother said, again. "Now run upstairs, dear, and put on your blue linen. That's not too dressed up and it looks so nice. And put a little color on."

"Papa," Louise asked gravely, "what did he say? Is he coming over here?"

"Sure, he's coming over here."

"Did he say he was?"

"Of course he said so," her sister said, trotting the baby. "Go on and get dressed, Louise. Can I help you any?"

"Papa, did he say he was coming over here?"

"Louise, what's got into you?" her father asked. "Give me a chance to get my breath and I'll tell you every word he said."

"Well, go ahead," his wife impatiently urged. "How many times must she ask you?"

"I asked him how he was. He said he was all right. Then he asked if his dad was over here, and I said he had been, and that he oughta be home by now. He said there he was, driving in right now, and I said we'd be glad to see him. There! Now I'm goin' on out to the field. I've wasted the whole morning. Might bring him on out to the field, Louise, if you get around to it."

"He didn't say he was coming over here, papa?"

"No, not in so many words, but why else would he want the car?"

"Did he say he wanted the car?"

Her father stood looking at her, shaking his head. "Mamma," he said, "I think you better put this girl to bed. She's not herself. Louise, I'd have sworn you had the best head in the family; that you had more good sense than any child we got, but I don't know what's got into you. What's the matter, anyway?"

"There's nothing the matter, except she's a little nervous, with Bill coming home when he's been away so long. Go on, papa. And, Louise, run change your dress, dear, do! It's not but two miles; he'll be over here. Go on!"

"And I'll change the baby's rompers," Ruth said. "I should have put the blue ones on him first and saved the pink until Bill came, but I don't suppose he'll be noticing the baby much. . . . Look, darling, grandpa's waving you good-by. Wave to grandpa! Want your clean rompers on?"

Louise went upstairs to her room. She took the blue dress from its hanger in the closet, and looking on the perfection of its smoothness, and remembering the good half hour she had spent ironing its pleats, tears came to her eyes and a tiredness came into her knees.

She sat down on the bed. He had not said he was coming over, but he was, likely; he had not even asked to speak to her. He would be there in a minute, and she would go down to meet him; and somehow, when they were alone, she would tell him how, through just keeping still, she had let her folks come to believe, and had let them go on believing, that, that—how could she ever say it? But she would, she must.

What would he think, in his astonishment, in his embarrassment? He would understand, though. Why should she doubt him in that? He would say, "That's all right, Louise. People get notions. We can still be good friends, can't we? Don't you worry about it." And then, maybe then, he would tell her about this girl, this girl at his house, and she would tell him she was glad for him, and wish him happiness.

She went to the dresser and picked up the brush and brushed the hair back from her face and adjusted the blue ribbon around her hair.

A car! There it was, coming up the lane, dappled with leaf shadow and sun from the cottonwoods, and Bill was in it. He had come. She must go down to him. Her heart beat hard. "My heart is like a singing bird!" the words came to her mind. Well, it was true, still, still! Even though she had been a fool, even though all she had dreamed and hoped for was not to be, still her heart was like a singing bird, because Bill had come; because, after a near-year of waiting, she should see him, she should hear him saying, "How are you, Louise?"

There was no time to put on the blue linen dress. She heard the car door close while she was on the stair. There he was, coming up the front walk, hurrying. Scarcely knowing what she did, her hand went out to the screen door, then she was on the porch, and then on the walk, going to meet him, for she had seen his face even while she was on the stairs, seen his face lifted to see her coming down, coming to meet him, and in it was the answer to every promise her heart had ever known. Bill was home.

With Helen and Warren

MABEL HERBERT URNER

And now, by popular request, two happy adventures of the famous Helen and Warren.

A NATIVE HAWAIIAN FEAST

A NATIVE Hawaiian feast!

The only one scheduled during their stay. And all the tickets sold!

"Trailed way out here for nothing!" Warren's cane prodded the grass.

"Dear, if we wait—When everyone's seated there may be room!"

"Hang around all night on a chance? Now we'll beat it back to Honolulu for dinner."

"But to be in Hawaii and not go to a native feast?" pleaded Helen. "Oh, there must be some way—"

"Now you don't cook up any scheme to crash this party!"

"It isn't a private party—just a club. And anyone can buy a ticket."

"Not when they're sold out!" he grunted. "Hello, at least we can buy a drink. Over there on the veranda."

On the long latticed "lanai", an impromptu bar. Well patronized by the crowd waiting for the feast hall to open.

"What'll you have—sherry?" motioning her to a rustic bench.

Helen waiting in the soft tropic dusk. The lawn strung with Chinese lanterns. Golden glows among the palms.

Watching the mixed crowd. Many prosperous natives. The men of fine physique. Lovely girls with dark hair and eyes, the older women rather stout.

All so friendly. Smiling as they passed—welcoming smiles for a stranger.

Through the swinging door, tantalizing glimpses of the hall. Long low tables spread with green leaves. Surely room for two more places—

Her reckless impulse! Why not? Quick, before Warren could stop her!

Over to the ticket booth. Here the reservations checked off.

"Good evening," greeted the club-badged member. "The name, please?"

"Mr. and Mrs. Warren Curtis," straining to sound confident.

His pencil running down the list. Then a puzzled:

"I don't see your name here. You're sure the tickets were reserved?"

"Why, we—we asked the hotel to reserve them," flushing.

That was true! They HAD asked—and been told all the reservations sold!

"Oh, I'm sorry if there's any mistake. We're sailing Saturday," wistfully.

"Your only chance for a native dinner? Then we'll have to fix you up," he smiled. "Two tickets we've kept for an emergency."

"Oh, thank you, thank you!" elatedly, fumbling in her purse.

The price printed on the tickets. Only two dollars each!

Back to the bench just as Warren came up, a glass in each hand.

Not tell him now. After his sherry, perhaps in a less critical mood! Always grim disapproval of her fabrications—even when only implied.

And the tickets gladly given. The Hawaiian hospitality to visitors from the "Mainland."

She would try to repay—by enthusiastic letters and postcards home!

"Can't nurse that drink all night, Kitten. Got to take back these glasses."

Just returned when the doors opened. Eight o'clock! The crowd filing in. A gala crowd—many evening gowns and white dinner coats.

"Jove, look in there! Real thing, all right. Well, come on, way past my feeding time. We'll eat in Honolulu."

"You wouldn't prefer this native feast?" demurely handing him the tickets.

"Great guns, what've you been up to?" his incredulous scowl. "How in blazes'd you wangle these?"

"I bought them! You needn't glare as though I stole them!"

"What yarn did you spring?" sternly. "See here, you didn't say we'd reserved 'em?"

"I—I may have implied it," laughing guiltily. "But dear, he wanted us to have them. They really do everything for visitors. Now don't scold!"

"Well, blamed awkward to turn 'em back," he shrugged. "May as well use 'em."

Inside the garlanded hall, an attendant taking their tickets. Leading them to the table nearest a bowered platform.

"And you landed ringside seats!" Warren's relenting grin.

Six long tables seating about thirty each. No cloths. The scrubbed boards spread with large green leaves.

No knives or forks. Only fingers used at native dinners!

At each place, a koa wood plate. And a paper saucer with four tiny mounds.

"This red stuff's salt!" Warren tasting it. "But stumped on the rest."

"That's the red salt of Kauai," explained the elderly man beside Helen. "And the others ground seaweed—three kinds. All used as condiments."

An old resident. His kindly explanations about the feast. These "luaus" given yearly by this club. To keep up the old Hawaiian customs.

Now great baskets of flower leis being distributed. One of the long garlands slipped over the head of each guest.

"Dear, mine's jasmine—oh, so fragrant! And I think yours is hibiscus."

"Feel darn self-conscious with posies around my neck," he grinned.

Next native waitresses with trays. Leaving at each place a small earthen bowl of grayish paste.

"This must be the 'poi'," Warren digging into his. "Read enough about it."

"Yes, pounded taro root," verified their neighbor. "Just use one finger."

Explaining the one, two, and three-finger poi! According to consistency. This the one-finger kind—thickest and best.

"Tastes like library paste," Warren licked his poi-crusted finger.

"I disliked it, too, when I first came to the Islands. But it grows on you."

The next course delicious! Red salmon "massaged" under water and cooked with tomatoes and pungent herbs.

Followed by another fish course. Leaf-wrapped octopus tentacles!

"Tender as bicycle tires!" grimaced Warren. "Got to wash this down."

No wine served. Just fruit drinks in calabashes—scalloped cocoanut shells. Cocoanut milk, fresh pineapple and papaya juice.

All the tables animated now. The laughing, tanned faces. To Helen, like a play—with the exotic setting and food.

"Dear, they keep eating the poi with everything! Like bread."

"Well, I can't go that goo," he muttered. "I'll take a repeat on the baked bananas. Get your two bucks worth, all right—seconds on everything."

"I love this red salt! If the shops have it I'll buy some to take home."

"Hello, here comes the floor show!"

Native dancers in green grass skirts, gardenia leis and bracelets. Even gardenia anklets on their bare feet. To the ukelele rhythm, their slow graceful hula.

"Aren't they lovely?" murmured Helen. "Watch their hands!"

As they left the platform, the main course being served. Roast pork. From small pigs wrapped in leaves and roasted whole on stones underground.

Really delicious! But hard to manipulate without knife or fork. Warren copying the native technique—gravy sopped up with bits of the meat.

"Just one paper napkin!" dismayed Helen. "I've used mine up. And these leaves too stiff."

"Out of luck, Kitten. Not even a tablecloth to wipe your digits on! Here's where the dry cleaners cash in."

"Wait, I've something," taking pink facial tissues from her purse. "Oh—oh, your shirt—"

"Only one spot? Think I'm doing darn well. Ought to come to these feasts in bathing suits. Then to the beach for a moonlight swim!"

"But all the others manage beautifully!" Her shirt-front inventory.

"Well, they've had practice," scooping up a gravied morsel. "Lay off the lecture. Want to enjoy this. A feast, all right."

All through the dinner, native songs and dances. Now a bamboo hula. The girls kneeling, swaying and waving bamboo wands.

"Guess I've done justice to that porker," Warren utilizing a pink tissue. "Must be the finale of this feed."

But still another course! Chicken stewed in cocoanut milk.

"By George, Kitten, the best yet!" denuding a drumstick. "Ought to get the recipe."

"And it has bones," laughingly. "Easier to eat with your fingers. And I love this seaweed salad. If only they'd serve fingerbowls!"

Finally the dessert—fruit paste and macadamia nuts. And all relaxing in friendly conversation.

Warren passing his cigar case to their neighbors. Talking of their trip.

At last a general exit. All drifting off in groups.

Their cordial good-byes, and out into the moonlit night.

A velvety tropic night. Eerie shadows from the tall palms. The fragrance of exotic plants.

"Dear, didn't you love it?" effervesced Helen, taking his arm.

"Yes, that was tops!" His cigar a red ember in the dark. "Best thing we've struck this trip."

"And the way you blew out at me! We'd have missed it—"

"If you hadn't sprung that reservation yarn, eh? Well, not sorry we horned in. Now let's try our luck at nailing a cab."

As they crossed the lawn, meeting the ticket-selling member.

"Did you enjoy the dinner?" his pleasant inquiry.

"Certainly did! Great spread."

"Yes, we loved it!" glowed Helen.

"I'm glad you came. You wouldn't want to leave the Islands without attending a native feast."

"That's why I—Oh, I feel rather guilty!" her confessional urge. "We asked our hotel for reservations but they said you were sold out! So we really didn't—"

"Well, I'd an idea it was something like that," he smiled. "But I wanted you to have this memory of Hawaii."

Then he had known all along! Her flushed, embarrassed thanks. Yet reassured by his friendly warmth.

"And you thought you put one over!" scoffed Warren, swinging her on toward the road. "So sure he fell for your phoney reservations!"

"But dear, he did give me the tickets! You'd have gone off without trying. And they seemed really glad to have us."

"Yes, couldn't have been more cordial. Even gave us ringside seats. But no thanks to your reservation yarn. That whiskered line didn't get our tickets—just Hawaiian hospitality!"

WARREN'S BOOK CLUB TALK

"BUT DEAR, you can't read this! It's all crossed out and written over."

"I can read it, all right." Warren slitting a magazine wrapper.

"And at those dinners they never have a good light."

"Now stop beefing! Shouldn't have told you. Anyway, it's the last talk they'll rope me into!"

Helen skimming the eight-page manuscript. Typed, but so many of his penciled corrections. Almost illegible.

"Dear, this second page is the worst! Miss Martin might've retyped that!"

"She's had enough to do, with Jerry out all week."

Helen still studying the second page. Why couldn't she copy it? All of it!

Not quite four. The dinner at seven-thirty and he wouldn't leave before seven. Even with her any-finger method, she could do eight pages in three hours.

A snowy Saturday afternoon, with Warren home. An ideal time. She'd love copying it.

Out to the hall closet for the portable. Soon settled by the desk lamp. All the lights on. A golden glow against the snow-streaked dusk.

Try not to bother Warren. Never curious, he wouldn't notice what she was typing.

But on the first page a penciled insert with a word she couldn't decipher. Better read it all first, mark the illegible words. Then bother him only once.

An informative talk on "Famous Literary Forgeries." But so wordily written! Long involved sentences, so unlike his usual crisp style.

"Dear, some words here I just can't make out!"

"Eh? See here, you copying that?" glowering up from his magazine. "Now I came home to rest up, not to be hounded about that darned talk."

"Only this once," perching on his chair arm. "I've marked all the words. On the first page, just that one."

A puzzled frown at his own careless scrawl.

"Facsimile," curtly.

"You could hardly make it out yourself. What if you stumble like that tonight?"

"I'd know by the context. Not just one word sprung on me."

"Then why not read it all? Shorten some of these sentences—"

"Nothing doing!" disgustedly. "Not working on that thing now."

Grumpily deciphering the other marked words, ungratefully he elbowed her away.

The first page typed, Helen starting on the second. But here a repeated reference. She'd have to speak of that.

"Dear, just a moment," again by his chair. "This Chatterton forgery —the very same reference on the fourth page. And you don't need it here."

"Then cross it out," indifferently. "Guess it's all pretty punk. But I'll not read it word for word—just so I get the ideas over."

"But I can't understand why it's so wordy. Your letters are so concise. This isn't at all like you!"

"Well, I just dictated some notes to Miss Martin. She put 'em in shape. But go ahead and fix it up if you want."

His secretary's version. No wonder it was so diffuse, so unlike him.

Now feeling free to condense and simplify. Going over each page before typing it.

By ten past six, all copied. Then reading it through. A glow of achievement. How much simpler, clearer! And shorter by almost a page.

Now a real inspiration! Underline the main points in red.

What she did on her talk for the Women's Animal Aid. After the first page, gaining confidence, she had only glanced at the red-penciled lines.

"Still snowing!" Throwing down his magazine, Warren strode to the window.

"Dear, come see what I've done." Eagerly explaining the under-scored lines.

"Red flags, eh?"

"They're like notes. The gist of it—if you don't want to read it all."

"Not a bad idea," lighting his pipe.

"Now you've time. Sit down and go over it. Please! See if I haven't crisped it up. Shorter sentences—much easier to read."

Pretending to straighten around, not watch him as he read. Looking out at the thickening snow and lovely white-etched trees.

"That's all right. Not a bad job." His faint-praise verdict.

"And you'll not start with any trite remarks about 'distinguished guests' and 'a privilege to be here'?"

" 'Privilege' is good!" he snorted. "Well, twenty of seven. My things laid out?"

"No, but it won't take a minute. And I'll put this on your dresser," carefully folding the manuscript.

In the bedroom laying out his dinner coat, black tie, pleated shirt.

"Dear, that suit you have on goes to the cleaner's tomorrow." Telling him before he took it off—easier for him to clear his pockets.

Now back to the library. Putting away the portable. Straightening the desk.

Miss Martin's wordy copy—Throw that away? No, better leave it.

"Where's my muffler?" Warren at the door, settling his dinner coat. "Did I forget that?"

The muffler as always in a flat white box in his dress-shirt drawer. But incredibly helpless about his clothes.

"Oh, this black spot!" examining the heavy white silk. "Ink! And your new muffler. Is there anything you don't get ink on?"

"Not taking a pen tonight. Got any decent pencils?" rummaging the desk. "Short one, for my vest pocket?"

"Here's one. Wait, let me sharpen it."

Dashing out to the pantry. A new automatic sharpener by the sink.

"Yes, you can put on dinner," at Anna's inquiry. "Mr. Curtis's just leaving."

Warren already in the hall, jerking on his overcoat.

"Fine!" thrusting the pencil in his waistcoat pocket.

"Dear, you've everything? Oh, your rubbers!"

"Won't need 'em. I'll taxi."

Now forlornly to her own dinner. A book propped before her. Dinner always their relaxing hour together. A lingering, happy hour.

But now soon back to the library. Curling up in his chair. Feeling less alone.

Racing through the war novel started at the table. Almost three hundred pages. Finished by quarter past ten.

Why must she read so fast? Really a dissipation. Now all tense.

Into the bedroom to turn down the beds. Stepping on something —A quarter.

Dropping it into his handkerchief drawer. The repository for pocket things when he changed suits. Now several letters, a legal envelope, and underneath—

The manuscript!

Forgotten! The things from his pockets tossed on it. Then all swept into the drawer.

What could she do? Too late to get it to him. After ten—and only a short talk. All over by now.

But why, why hadn't he sent for it? Too late when he missed it?

Visioning his embarrassment. Even his nonchalance hardly equal to this. To give such an informative talk—without any notes. And before that critical Book Club.

Had he tried to carry it off extemporaneously? Or frankly admitted his notes forgotten?

Despairingly back to the library. Not snowing now. The park a moonlit Christmas card. But too distraught to watch for him.

Turning from the window. The desk—Suddenly conscious of something missing.

Miss Martin's copy not there! Yet positive she'd left it on the blotter.

Gone—He'd taken it—while she was sharpening that pencil!

Then her copy not forgotten! The original taken instead. His own scribbled inserts—he'd wanted them all along!

But why hadn't he said so? Why imply that she'd improved it? Just to satisfy her? Had she been so insistent?

Now a surge of self-condemnation. Yes, at times she was insistent. Her eagerness to help him just an annoyance?

Something he'd said the other day—"Now just let me work this out alone!" Not so much the words, but the way he said it. As though she was always interfering.

Thinking of the Courtneys, how she corrected and instructed him. And in public! Was she growing to be like Mrs. Courtney?

Warren's key in the door. The next moment breezing in.

Instantly she knew there had been no embarrassment, no stumbling. The talk had gone off well.

A rush of relief for him, then a withdrawing aloofness. But Warren unobservant, as always.

"Dr. Wayne wants me to give the same talk for the Philadelphia Book Club. Told him I couldn't. Didn't have the time."

Reaching into the wastebasket for paper, he tore a strip for a pipe cleaner.

"I'm glad it went off so well," Helen adjusting a lamp shade. "Even if you did disapprove of my editing."

"Disapprove? Why, that was a grand job, Kitten. That red penciling was a real help."

Pretending he had taken it? When he was always so direct—never, never evasive!

"Then it didn't matter that you left my copy here?"

"Here! By George, I thought I'd lost it in the taxi."

But Helen now staring at the strip of paper he was twisting. A typed strip—Miss Martin's typing—from the old copy! Yes, the rest in the basket.

Then there all the time! He hadn't taken it—he'd thrown it away! Darting over to him. Now on the footstool beside his chair.

"Oh dear, I've the smallest, the meanest, the most suspicious mind!" abjectly, her head against his knee.

"Now what? Great Scott, how anybody can follow your mental quirks!"

"Instead of my copy, I was sure you'd taken the old! I didn't know it was in the basket until you tore off that piece for your pipe. And I was just wretched!"

"You cook up more things to anguish over!" stroking her hair. "Now Kitten, keep your copy. I was darned glad I'd read it. Remembered those red-scored points. And if things ease up, I might give that Philadelphia talk, after all!"

"... Unto the Least of These"

Condensed from a radio broadcast

ALEXANDER WOOLLCOTT

> *Today more than ever before, in a world filled with the needy, the hungry and the homeless, can we be inspired by this beautiful dream in which the blessedness of charity is revealed to Miss Vilda.*

I'VE A STORY to tell as a free-will offering to a cause which is close to my heart. A cause important enough for its own sake—in terms of the wounds it will heal, the eyes it will dry, the hearts it will reassure. But also a cause which, as a symbol, is of an importance I have no words to convey.

I think every decent person in this country felt a wave of relief when
news came from Washington that Senator Wagner had introduced
the bill now known as the Wagner-Rogers Bill proposing, for this
year and next, so to raise the German quota that 20,000 youngsters—
the oldest no more than 14—can come into this, a free country. Here's
a small boy adrift because his folks are Catholics. Here's a little girl
whose black crime is that her grandfather was a Jew. Here's a kid
whose dad is in a concentration camp because he had the spunk
to show a little of that independence which you and I take for granted
as our birthright. Twenty thousand kids. Homes here are waiting for
them. The Quakers, those Friends in gray who always stand by in
time of trouble, will see that all creeds and all kinds are represented.
All that is needed is this temporary change in the immigration law.

I assume that bill will pass. I hope it passes unanimously . . . a
fresh reminder that this country is still strong enough to be a refuge
for the oppressed. It's the least we can do for the least of these.

When I heard the bill had been introduced, I found myself wishing
that someone would tell the story of Miss Vilda's Dream. That story
seemed to me meant for this moment. I first came across it in a dog's-
eared old book called *Timothy's Quest*, by the late Kate Douglas
Wiggin.

Timothy was a shabby and stout-hearted foundling—a nine-year-
old ragamuffin who played knight-errant in behalf of a girl called Gay.
Gay needed a protector for she was very beautiful and only four, and
like Timothy himself, she too had been left on the doorstep of the
world.

In a swarming alley in the meanest part of Boston, a blowsy old
wanton had, for a time, been paid by some person or persons unknown
to look after Timothy and Gay, but when she died there was no one
to say who the kids were or where they had come from. So among the
neighbors who laid her out there was talk of shipping them off to an
orphanage. When the anxious Timothy overheard that talk, he and
the lady Gay lit out for parts unknown, the boy pulling her in a
home-made cart. Gay must go to no orphanage. She must have a
home and he was going to find one for her.

It was close to sundown when this lady in distress and her champion,
stained with the dust of the road and now almost tuckered out, paused
before a neat farmhouse with elms standing sentinel beside it, and a

white picket fence 'round about. This, Timothy said, will do, and he knocked at the door.

In that house so spotless, so cheerless, there lived a bitter and lonely old maid—Miss Vilda Cummins. Imagine her feelings when she opened the door and found those two refugees standing expectant on her front stoop. Land o' liberty! "Please," said Timothy, "do you need any babies here, if you please?" Dear me, suzz, what a commotion. The hired man thought it was a good idea. Might make Miss Vilda human. And in the kitchen, Samantha Ann 'lowed as how it was a good idea, too.

But Miss Vilda, rocking furiously, would not listen. What? Take in two dirty little waifs from heaven knew where? They must be crazy! Would she turn the children out then? Well, no, not exactly. Not with night coming on and them so hungry and tired. She was a good Christian woman and she hoped she knew her duty. She'd wash them and feed them and give them a bed for the night. But in the morning she'd send them to an orphanage. That's what Miss Vilda thought when she went to bed. But in the night Miss Vilda had a dream.

She dreamt that on a day of blinding heat it was her doom to climb a mountain. The way was steep and the road was rough and the briars caught at her skirt. A little girl, with a face like Gay's, came running toward her, holding out her hands as if she wanted to be taken up into Miss Vilda's arms. But Miss Vilda pushed her aside. It was all she could do to go on alone. Again the child appeared before her and again she pushed her away and again she went on with the weary climb, her spirit fainting, her strength almost gone. When once more the child reappeared, Miss Vilda was too weak to put her aside and the child crept into her arms.

And then, quite suddenly, Miss Vilda felt no more the heat of the sun. The stones scattered before her step. The briars parted to make a path for her. She lost all sense that she was climbing at all, the way now seemed so easy—so easy. Before she knew it, she had reached the top. And there an angel was waiting and took the child from her. Stooping, the angel dipped a finger in the dust and with it wrote on Miss Vilda's forehead a single word. And the word that the angel wrote was "Inasmuch."

Acknowledgments

The Editor is deeply grateful for the help she has received, in compiling this book, from her assistant editors: George Eaton, Margaret Foster, Jane McHenry, Kay Ropp, Mathilda Schirmer, Audrey Stone, and Betty Stone. For permission to use these stories the editor and publishers wish to thank the following authors and publishers, as well as the agents, Brandt and Brandt, Jacques Chambrun, Inc., Harold Matson, McIntosh and Otis, Inc., Paul R. Reynolds and Son, Virginia Rice, Sydney A. Sanders, A. P. Watt and Son, and Willis Kingsley Wing.

Susan's Dinner Party, by Dorothy Aldis. From *Poor Susan*, published by G. P. Putnam's Sons. Copyright, 1939, 1942, by Dorothy Aldis.

You'll Hear from Hallie Thane, by Barbara Aldrich. Copyright, 1944, by Hearst Magazines, Inc.

Love Me, Love My Sailor, by Faith Baldwin, reprinted by permission of Faith Baldwin. Copyright, 1943, by Faith Baldwin.

The Sobbin' Women, by Stephen Vincent Benét, from *Thirteen O'Clock*, published by Farrar & Rinehart, Inc. Copyright, 1926, by Stephen Vincent Benét.

My Ninety Acres, by Louis Bromfield, from *Pleasant Valley*, by Louis Bromfield. Reprinted by permission of Harper and Brothers.

A Man's Mother, by Gladys Hasty Carroll. Permission to reprint granted by Paul R. Reynolds & Son, 599 Fifth Avenue, New York 17, N. Y.

The Man Who Was Born in Grand Central, by Robert Cenedella, reprinted from Good Housekeeping Magazine.

Big Operator, by Marian B. Cockrell. Permission to reprint granted by Paul R. Reynolds & Son, 599 Fifth Avenue, New York 17, N. Y.

Romeo and Violet, by Whitfield Cook, reprinted by permission, from *Violet* by Whitfield Cook. Copyright, 1941, 1942, by Whitfield Cook.

Father Hires a Cook, by Clarence Day, reprinted from *Life with Father*, by Clarence Day, by permission of Alfred A. Knopf, Inc. Copyright, 1922, by Alfred

A. Knopf, Inc. Copyright, 1933, by Clarence Day.

Woman's Work, by Elizabeth Dunn. Copyright, 1944, by The Curtis Publishing Company. Reprinted by permission of the author.

Didn't I Tell You?, by Paul Ernst. Copyright Paul Ernst, 1945. Reprinted by permission of Willis K. Wing.

Big Frogs and Little Frogs, by Susan Ertz, from *Big Frogs and Little Frogs*, by Susan Ertz. Reprinted by permission of Harper and Brothers.

A Chance To Talk Informally, by Hilda Cole Espy, reprinted from the Woman's Home Companion, published in the October 1944 issue.

The Romantic Trousers, by Robert Fontaine, from *The Happy Time*, by Robert Fontaine. Copyright, 1945, by Robert Fontaine and published by Simon and Schuster, Inc.

Claudia in Hollywood, by Rose Franken, first chapter from *Claudia and David*, by Rose Franken, copyright, 1939, 1940, by Rose Franken Meloney, and reprinted by permission of Farrar & Rinehart, Inc., Publishers.

To Springvale for Christmas, by Zona Gale, reprinted by permission of William Ll. Breese.

Mothers Smell Like Lilacs, by Valeria Winkler Griffith. Copyright Hearst Publications, Inc. 1943. Reprinted by permission of Sydney A. Sanders, as agent for the author.

The Failure, by Katharine Haviland-Taylor. Copyright, 1932, by Katharine

ACKNOWLEDGMENTS

Haviland-Taylor. Reprinted by permission.

OCEAN AIR, by Ian Hay, from *The Lucky Number*, by Ian Hay; Houghton Mifflin and Company, and A. P. Watt and Son.

MEET CORLISS ARCHER, by F. Hugh Herbert. Copyright, 1944, by F. Hugh Herbert. Reprinted by permission of Random House, Inc.

MR. CHIPS MEETS A STAR, by James Hilton, reprinted from Collier's Magazine, by permission of the author.

FEMALE, by Darrell Huff, reprinted from Good Housekeeping Magazine by permission of the author.

MOTHERS, by Wallace Irwin. Copyright, 1930, by The Crowell-Collier Publishing Company.

THEN CAME THE LEGIONS, by MacKinlay Kantor, from *Author's Choice*, by MacKinlay Kantor, copyright, 1944, by MacKinlay Kantor. "Then Came the Legions," copyright, 1934, by The McCall Corporation and reprinted by permission of Coward-McCann, Inc., Publishers.

(From) MRS. APPLEYARD'S YEAR, by Louise Andrews Kent, from *Mrs. Appleyard's Year*, by Louise Andrews Kent, published by Houghton Mifflin Company.

LOVE'S PRICE; OR THE $2.20 HEART, by Graeme and Sarah Lorimer, from *Stag Line*, by Graeme and Sarah Lorimer. Reprinted by permission of Little, Brown & Company.

THEY CALLED HER MOUSIE, by Grace Sartwell Mason. Copyright, 1934, by Hearst Magazines, Inc.

GUINEA PIG, by Ruth McKenney, from *My Sister Eileen*, copyright, 1938, by Ruth McKenney. By permission of Harcourt, Brace and Company, Inc.

QWERTY AND THE BIRD MAN, by Alice Means Reeve, reprinted by permission of the author, and the Woman's Home Companion.

GRANDMA AND THE SEA GULL, by Louise Dickinson Rich, from Woman's Home Companion. Copyright, Louise Dickinson Rich, 1945. Reprinted by permission of Willis K. Wing.

THE FISHING FOOL, by Mary Roberts Rinehart, from *Alibi for Isabel*, copyright, 1941, 1942, 1943, 1944 by Mary Roberts Rinehart, and reprinted by permission of Farrar & Rinehart, Inc., Publishers.

IN SICKNESS AND IN HEALTH, by Isabel Scott Rorick, from *Mr. and Mrs. Cugat*, by Isabel Scott Rorick, reprinted by permission of Houghton, Mifflin Company.

MOTHER HAS GONE TO THE MOUNTAINS, by Ruth Burr Sanborn. Copyright, 1939, by The Curtis Publishing Company.

THE FACE IS FAMILIAR, BUT—, by Max Shulman, reprinted from Good Housekeeping Magazine. Copyright Hearst Magazines, Inc., 1945.

WE VISIT MR. H. G. WELLS, by Cornelia Otis Skinner and Emily Kimbrough, from *Our Hearts Were Young and Gay*, by Cornelia Otis Skinner and Emily Kimbrough. Reprinted by permission of Dodd, Mead & Company, Inc. Copyright, 1942, by Dodd, Mead & Company, Inc.

MY MOTHER BREAKS HER PEARLS, by Marion Sturges-Jones, from *Babes in the Wood*, copyright, 1944, by Marion Wescott. Courtesy of G. P. Putnam's Sons.

LETTER TO THE DEAN, by Gladys Taber. Copyright, 1940, by The Curtis Publishing Company.

LITTLE GENTLEMAN, by Booth Tarkington, from *Penrod, His Complete Story*, by Booth Tarkington. Copyright, 1913, 1941, by Booth Tarkington. Published by Doubleday Doran & Company.

MY HEART IS LIKE A SINGING BIRD, by Dorothy Thomas, reprinted from the Saturday Evening Post. Copyright, 1937, by The Curtis Publishing Company.

WITH HELEN AND WARREN, by Mabel Herbert Urner. Copyright, 1940 and 1944, by Mabel Herbert Urner. Reprinted by permission of the author.

". . . UNTO THE LEAST OF THESE," by Alexander Woollcott. By permission of The Viking Press, Inc., New York.

Subject Index

THE YOUNG AND BREATHLESS

PUPPY LOVE

TWO'S COMPANY

NEEDLES AND PINS

THE MIDDLE YEARS

THE BEST IS YET TO BE

DOROTHY ALDIS
FAITH BALDWIN·
ROBERT CENEDELLA
CLARENCE DAY·
HILDA COLE ESPY
JAMES HILTON·
MAC KINLAY KANTOR
DARRELL HUFF·
GRACE SARTWELL MASON
ALICE MEANS REEVE·
ISABEL SCOTT RORICK
MAX. SHULMAN·
BOOTH TARKINGTON